PROTECTORS OF THE ELEMENTAL MAGIC

BOOKS 1-3

MARNIE CATE

Copyright (C) 2023 Marnie Cate

Layout design and Copyright (C) 2023 by Next Chapter

Published 2023 by Next Chapter

Cover art by Lordan June Pinote

This book is a work of fiction. Names, characters, places, and incidents are the product of the author's imagination or are used fictitiously. Any resemblance to actual events, locales, or persons, living or dead, is purely coincidental.

All rights reserved. No part of this book may be reproduced or transmitted in any form or by any means, electronic or mechanical, including photocopying, recording, or by any information storage and retrieval system, without the author's permission.

REMEMBER

PROTECTORS OF THE ELEMENTAL MAGIC BOOK 1

*In the honor of my Gram whose love and guidance were with me in each page.
And my sweet Lilli, you were not only my furry muse....*

Acknowledgments

Thanks to J.M. Northup for her editorial support. From our collaboration, I learned so much about not only writing but the editorial process.

CHAPTER ONE

Smoke filled the skies, and the heat from the flames of the burning homes and storefronts was unbearable. Main Street was empty. Stores that were not ablaze had been ransacked.

The ice cream shop, once filled with happy customers, looked as if a tornado blew through it. Broken tables, chairs, and meals littered the ground. My eyes fell on a silver name tag surrounded by ash. I cringed when I saw the burnt body of a waitress underneath. Her badge was the only item not blackened or damaged.

I forced myself to keep moving as I searched for anything or anyone familiar. I continued to find only destruction. It was futile. I was alone.

Fighting back my tears, I looked to the sky and cried out, "Gram, I am not strong enough!"

A blinding light surged through me, and I fell to my knees. My world went dark. The next thing I knew, a hand gripped mine and dragged me. Stumbling and confused, I pulled against my captor.

"Stop fighting me," the familiar voice of my grandmother scolded.

Gram stopped long enough for me to confirm it was her.

"Where are you taking me?" I questioned.

"No time for talking."

Once again, we were moving quickly through the tree line. I no longer resisted as my grandmother led through the forest. My home was being destroyed, and I didn't know who to blame or how to stop them.

The dark smoke grew thicker, and my chest burned. I began to cough. I fell to my knees, unable to go on any farther.

"No, get up. We are almost there." Gram ripped a piece of fabric from her dress and wrapped it around my mouth.

When the coughing stopped, she tugged my hand and encouraged me to stand. When I complied and she propelled us onward, our pace was even faster. Just when I thought I would collapse again, Gram stopped in front of a broad oak tree.

She looked around, though I wasn't sure why. There was not a sound in the forest. We were alone.

Suddenly, she ducked into the overgrown plants. Her hand trailed the thick trunk of the tree. When we reached a split in the bark, Gram pushed me forward into the crevice.

"Hide here," she commanded.

I resisted and grabbed onto her. Choking back my tears, I begged, "No, let me go with you."

She hugged me and smoothed my hair. "Mara, my little one, always remember that you are my treasure. You must prepare to be strong for when the darkness appears."

"Don't leave me," I sobbed.

"Hush. You will hide and survive, Mara." She pressed a cold metal object into my hand and kissed my cheek. "This ring will be your guide when I am not here to remind you."

I wanted to ask her where she was going and what I needed to be reminded of, but I never got my chance. With those words, she shoved me into the hiding spot and left. I struggled to hold back my tears. I resisted the urge to follow my grandmother away from the safety of trees and back towards the smoky flames of the burning buildings.

Clutching the ring, I could feel cold energy releasing from the blue stone. The surrounding silver calmly pulsed small, almost indistinguishable bursts of electricity like a heartbeat. The charm slowly chanted, "Go there, go there."

But where? I wondered, closing my eyes, and centering my thoughts on the stone.

I saw the Starten Forest with its deep green and lush trees. The bright full moon shone above a nest. It was like none I had ever seen before. The large nest was made of silver twigs with a lavender glow in the center.

"I know where to go now, Gram," I whispered.

A loud crash sounded, and I heard the cries of a child.

It was my sister, Meg.

She needed me, but I could not see where she was. I fumbled in the darkness, trying to reach her. My heart was racing as I frantically searched for my escape. I banged my shin on something hard and fell to the ground.

As I lay writhing in pain, a small crack of light appeared. Awareness washed over me, and everything began to make sense. I patted the hardwood floor underneath me before I laughed out loud.

I was not in the forest. Reaching up for the switch, I flipped on the overhead light and looked around my closet. I let out a sigh of relief that I was home.

Trembling as the adrenaline of my night terror began to wear off, I quickly exited the closet. The sounds of the busy kitchen below comforted me. I breathed in the sweet cinnamon pancakes and freshly brewed coffee. My home grounded me.

"It was just a dream," I told myself.

Pushing away the unsettling dream, I looked around my bedroom. Unsurprisingly, my little sister's bed was empty. The nine-year-old seemed to have a surplus of energy that, even though I was only seventeen years old, I couldn't keep up some days. Meg was full of ideas and dreams that I had forgotten many years ago.

Sizzling sounds of bacon and the clatter of dishes being laid on the table jolted me into action. In Gram's world, there was no sleeping in. Not wanting to worry her, I quickly dressed.

I glared at the wavy curls that plagued me, and I pulled my long raven hair into a ponytail. *I should just cut it all off.* I shuddered at my thought as I remembered the short haircut I gave myself when I was ten. I vowed to never play with scissors again after that day.

My image in the mirror would not please my grandmother. Gram would be concerned by the dark circles around my eyes, which only enhanced by my pale white skin. I didn't want to tell her the nightmares – that had been gone for so long – had suddenly returned. However, a full night's sleep seemed like a distant dream, and it was starting to show.

Quickly dusting my face with powder and lining my hazel eyes with dark purple, I looked at my reflection again. "Add some dark red lipstick, and you can look like a vampire from those old books Gram loves," I said aloud. With a long sigh, I glossed my lips with cherry lip gloss and then practiced a fake smile.

It was time to join my family.

As I climbed down the ladder of the loft bedroom, I stopped to inspect each rung. The ladder was aged, and each step had a different name carved on it. On the sixth rung, I ran my fingers over the letters. Slowly tracing the letters, I tried to remember her. *How can I barely recall this person – my mother?*

"Today isn't the day to think of the past," I scolded myself. Feeling frustrated for even thinking about her, I finished the descent down into the warmth of the kitchen and my family.

My grandmother's home – my home – was a large spacious house. When you entered it, you immediately felt a warm, inviting feeling. The colors of the house were bright and cheery, but not overwhelming.

A half-wall divided the spacious kitchen, where Gram could usually be found, from the living room. The white walls of the large room contrasted with its comfortable furniture. The variety of bright colors welcomed you to sit and relax. You could sit on either the purple or lime green overstuffed couches. Both would wrap you in a big fluffy embrace as you settled into them. If you wanted to be alone, you could pick one of the overstuffed chairs. Depending on my mood, I could choose to snuggle up on either a yellow, an aqua, or a red one.

The loft bedroom I shared with my sister was nestled above the cozy kitchen and over the sleeping quarters of the house. The high half-wall made my bedroom private, but not closed in.

"I thought you were going to sleep the day away." Gram greeted me with a kiss on the cheek and handed me a plate filled with fresh fruit, fluffy pancakes, and two slices of thick, crispy bacon.

"Good morning, Gram, this looks great." I threw on my fake smile, forcing myself to be cheery.

She gently touched my forearm before returning to the stove to stir the pot of berries she was slowly cooking.

I flopped into the seat by my sister and took a long sip of the tea that had been waiting for me. It was the perfect temperature. For some reason, even the delicious breakfast and giggles of Meg could not break the gloomy mood I was in.

"Can I have your pancakes, Mar?" Meg whispered while eyeing our grandmother. "Gram only made me a tiny stack, and they are sooooo good!"

Meg's big green eyes, surrounded by thick black lashes, pleading were hard to resist. "Just one." I slid it onto her plate and tapped her on the nose with my finger.

"What about the bacon?" Meg asked with a sly smile. "Mar ahhhh..."

Using the nickname she had given me usually was the key to her getting her way with me. Marina Addisyn Stone was the name I was given, and nicknames from childhood friends came and went. Then along came Meg and her inability to pronounce Marina. Her name for me became the name I loved the most – Mara.

"You may be pushing it, kid." I laughed.

Gram quietly chuckled before turning away from the sink to give me a wink — her silent blessing to continue.

Once Meg ate the last bite of her breakfast and helped clear my plate, she gave her standard thumbs-up, confirming the meal was delicious. I couldn't help but laugh at how cute my little sister could be.

"Gram, you didn't eat anything." I placed the cleared dishes in the sink and began to wash them. "You need to keep your strength up to keep up with Meg."

"I know, love." Gram took the plate I was washing and put it back into the sink. "Let these soak."

I looked over at my sister, who had moved to a small game table in the living room. The stuffed animals she had lined up were getting a lecture on the importance of eating breakfast. The smell of cinnamon, vanilla, and lavender filled my nose as Gram drew me into her arms and tightly hugged me.

"Gram, do you think we'll ever see her again? I don't understand how she could just disappear, and no one knows where she went for so long."

Gram's eyes grew dark as they always did when I asked about my mother. She cleaned a dish and handed it to me, nodding at a nearby kitchen towel. This signaled the conversation was over, and there would be no point in pressing further.

I dried and neatly put each item in its place in the cupboards. Dishes in bright shades of red, orange, yellow, green, and blue made a rainbow of color. Not one matched but still seemed to be part of a perfect set to me.

Gram returned to the jam she was making. Her face was washed with a sadness that I had caused. I wished I could take back my question.

I kissed Gram on the cheek and swiped the spoon from her hand. Quickly, I stuck it in my mouth before I lost my stolen treat. "Mmm. You outdid yourself on this batch."

"Really, Mara," Gram scolded.

I grinned sheepishly and put the spoon in the sink. "I'm going to meet Cole. He is going to teach me how to catch trout today."

"Trout, huh?" Gram smirked.

"Yes, he said I would chicken out. Of course, I can't let him be right."

"But you are a scaredy-cat," Meg called.

"I am Mae Veracor's granddaughter. There isn't a weak bone in my body," I teased, tousling Meg's light brown locks. "What does a little princess like you know anyway? The summer has faded your hair so much that We'll have to start calling you Cinderella."

Meg stuck her tongue out at me before falling into a fit of laughter.

Bounding out the door, I carried the satchel filled with the day's necessities. I followed the paved road in front of my house that would eventually lead to the center of town. The lingering terror of my dream haunted me as I traveled. Images of burned homes and burnt bodies flashed before my eyes.

There was no fire. Everyone is safe, I scolded myself.

After less than a mile and having passed several homes, I reached my destination. At the end of a cobblestone walkway, I casually strolled towards the pale-yellow house. When Cole saw me, he dropped the ball he had been bouncing.

"Took you long enough! I have been waiting all morning. I thought you chickened out." Cole grinned.

Cole Oliver Sands always took my breath away when I saw him. His dark brown hair had grown long over the summer, covering his deep blue eyes, which were framed with thick black lashes. With a big breath, he blew the offending hair out of his face and continued to scold me.

"I really thought I might grow old and die waiting for you to show up." Cole feigned a swoon and slumped over the patio railings.

"I'm not late." I handed him the bag I had packed. "You, my dear, are just impatient. I was getting the things you insisted we needed. I still question the necessity of peanut butter and jam sandwiches. Whoever heard of trout swarming for PB&J?" I put my hands on my hips in mock anger and gave him my signature eyebrow lift.

Laughing, he tore one of the sandwiches out of the bag and began to devour it. In three large bites, the sandwich was almost gone, and Cole had forgotten I was late. "Yes, these will do. Gram's is the best cook in the town," he greedily proclaimed.

I couldn't disagree. Gram was known for her delicious food. When I was younger, my grandmother had taught me that mashing ripe berries with lemon juice and brown sugar made the best jam. Each jar was an individual batch she made with love. Even her homemade peanut butter was really unique. She added a pinch of cinnamon and cayenne pepper that tasted amazing with the jam. Adding these flavors with the sweet wheat bread that was made yesterday morning, the sandwich would make it hard for anyone to not be happy.

Cole popped the last bite into his mouth. "Now, with my need for sustenance out of the way, I should thank you properly for your kindness."

In a swift movement, he grabbed my hand and swept me into his arms. His firm grip felt warm and even a bit sticky from the sandwich. But not even that could change the way my heart felt when I was with him. Everything seemed right. He kissed me tenderly and proceeded to nuzzle my neck.

Cole was strong, but not overly muscular. His hug seemed to soften the dark feelings I felt, and the warmth of the affection drowned out the negative emotions that were haunting me. I felt safe in his arms.

As quickly as he had begun, he let go of me. "Tempting to stay here all day, Mara, but if you want to be trained in the way of a trout fisherman, we best get going."

Sighing, I composed myself. I had asked for this adventure. I only hoped I wouldn't regret it.

CHAPTER
TWO

Cole led us past the cottage behind his house, deep into a part of Starten Forest I was not familiar with. The thickness of the trees threw off my internal compass. The woodland began to thin as we started down a path.

Ignoring my apprehensions, I pushed away my fears. Cole knew exactly where we were going. However, my trust wavered the higher we climbed. We were too far from my home.

"You didn't say we were going to climb any mountains today," I complained. "Gram is going to kill you if you get me lost up here."

"She won't. See that path right there?" He motioned towards large stones and overgrown brush. "We are going to follow it down to the river."

I had no doubt there would be snakes and spiders, waiting to attack. If there was a trail to follow, I couldn't see it.

"The path over there looks smooth and safer. Why don't we look for trout up there?" I suggested.

"Gram will kill me if we go up there. If we keep walking, we'll be joining the Drygens for dinner." Cole clutched his heart in mock fright.

I wrinkled my nose at the thought. The wealthiest family in town was also known for being the cruelest. Gram had taught me from a young age that money didn't have a heart and, sometimes, greed could turn a person cold. I looked from the beaten path to the treacherous one, weighing my options. *Death by a snake or being pushed off the mountain by a Drygen*? Neither sounded appealing.

Cole laughed. "Be brave, Mar. We're going down there, even if I have to carry you." He wrapped his arms around my waist as if doing just that. I cried out in protest.

He nuzzled my neck and whispered, "Shh, Mar, look out there."

We were so high up that I could see even the farthest edge of Starten. Nestled within the emerald-green trees, I could see our community. Our homes were little boxes of color.

"Oh," I murmured in surprise.

"Isn't it amazing how s our little town's problems are if you look at it from afar?" he asked softly. "Up here, we can just breathe and forget our worries. When will you ever trust me, Mar?"

"I trust you," I whispered my half-truth.

Cole and I had known each other for so long that he understood my fears. He held me tighter and allowed me to take in the view silently. After our brief moment of contentment, we reluctantly began down the pathway.

I tried to focus on everything around me to prevent my mind from racing. It was easy to do since the trail was so overgrown. I knew it had been forgotten. *Our secret place,* I thought.

In no time, we left the quiet of the mountain for babbling water. The river we walked along was purple with blue froth. The current grew stronger as we continued. I knew if we kept walking, we would eventually reach the rainbow-colored waterfalls that fed into Sparrow Lake.

A flock of gold and silver butterflies appeared. I stopped to watch as they swam against the current. *Here, I could learn to calm my mind,* I realized.

In the quiet of the forest, I recalled Gram's stories of magic. It was as if everything around me had a tale. Watching the butterflies, I remembered the story of *Three Billy Goats Gruff*. The gold and silver powder from butterfly wings had been used to put the troll to sleep, so the bridge could be crossed.

One day, I found a book at Thompson's Used Book and Sauerkraut Store. It contained all the stories Gram had told me at bedtime, but the stories were slightly different. There was not a butterfly sleeping powder that helped the goats, but rather, an older, stronger goat had pushed the troll into the water.

When questioned, Gram patted my hand and said, "My stories are more memorable."

A high-pitched squeak pulled me back to the present. Above us, a fighting trio of green squirrels drew my attention. The rodents' metallic green fur glimmered in the sunlight, and reflections bounced off the water as they flew through the air.

Gram had told us the stories about Starten, and what it had been like before the Drygen Cannery explosion. She'd explained how the water sources had been polluted. Some liked to believe it was magic that changed everything, but the hefty fine paid and admittance of fault, by the cannery proved more feasible.

Gram loved to show us pictures of her mother's world. A time before the change. Everything seemed so odd. The only flying squirrels did was to glide from tree-to-tree. Butterflies flew in the air and avoided water. They did not swim in streams. Instead, trout swam in the river and were caught using poles with a worm on a hook at the end. The thought of that always grossed me out.

"Are we close yet?" I whispered, shaking off the repulsive thought.

Cole nodded and placed one finger on his mouth to remind me not to speak. In the brush ahead, I saw bright, colorful tails, swaying back and forth. Tugging Cole's hand, I pointed. He nodded and grabbed the net gun from his bag.

As we got closer, he motioned for me to stay put and handed me a hand-woven net on a stick. I raised my hands to question this.

"Catch any that get away," he whispered.

Cole picked up a rock from the stream and threw it at the bush. The trout began scrambling out from under it, heading towards him. He launched the massive silver net. It flew through the air before it landed and trapped six adult trout. They snapped their teeth and slammed their black and pink bodies against their captor.

Several small gray baby trout scurried towards the area where I waited. Quickly, I lowered the net and covered them. When several escaped, I rapidly shoved them back under the net with my boot.

The net confused them, and they began circling. "Cole! What do I do now?"

Cole laughed and came towards me. The net over his shoulder held two large trout. Each was over a foot long and no longer moving. The ones selected to live were now scrambling into the underbrush. They were probably going deep into their holes to wait for the danger to go away.

As he walked, Cole threw a trail of crumbs from his sandwich behind him. When he was about ten feet from me, he said, "Lift the net now. The little ones need to go back to their nest to grow."

I lifted the net and watched the grey babies scamper back to their home, stopping along the way to gobble the crumbs Cole had dropped.

"This should be enough to feed us for months," Cole said and handed me the net. The net was at least thirty pounds.

"Shouldn't I have watched you decide which adults to let go and how to...you know?" I asked, uncomfortable with the thought that the trout were living just minutes before.

"You know this is crazy." He grabbed my hand and pulled me close. "You won't ever be without me. There is no need for you to prove you can do this. I promise I will always take care of you."

He leaned in and slowly kissed me. Quickly, the gentle kiss became harder and more demanding. Wanting to be consumed in the feeling, I kissed him back, slowly running my free hand up and down his spine. Cole abruptly pulled away, taking the net from me. I sighed in frustration. *How quickly he can abandon me,* I thought bitterly.

"Come on, Mar. Don't be mad. It's getting late, and Gram will worry." Cole kissed my hand.

Once again, he chose to be practical over being consumed by passion. I couldn't help feeling disappointed. I removed my hand from his grasp.

"Don't be like that." Cole brushed his lips against my cheek as he whispered, "We wouldn't want Gram to think I'm not a gentleman, would we?"

I nodded and wiped the scowl from my face. The way Cole always considered my grandmother's feelings was one of the things that made me love him. However, sometimes, I just wanted to get lost in the moment. For just a second, I could feel all fear and doubt fade away while lost in his embrace.

As we walked back, hand-in-hand, to deliver our catch to Gram, I suddenly felt a lingering sense of dread wash over me. Forever promises never seemed real. The dark feeling did not make sense to me. I had spent the day with the man I loved and trusted. How could I feel forever was possible one minute, wanting to be swept up away, and then allow myself to drown in the nagging sense that anything I loved would be lost the next? *Must I always destroy things before they have a chance to hurt me?*

Later that evening, Gram cooked up the trout with her special peach sauce and served it on a bed of golden rice. The fresh vegetables from the garden were crisp and flavorful. The water, with lemon raspberry ice cubes, was refreshing.

"Mae Veracor, you're the best cook. I should ask you to run away with me, right now," Cole joked between bites and reached for another helping.

Gram swatted him and laughed. "Save some food for the girls."

Light conversation filled the dinner table, and my fears from earlier faded. I felt calm and at ease while I watched my family joking, enjoying the meal. I could not understand why my emotions were always such a roller coaster ride. Perhaps, I just needed to learn to live in the moment and stop worrying about the unknown.

Meg savored each bite. When she thought Cole was not looking, she stole nibbles from his plate and giggled. As much as I wanted to enjoy her playfulness, I still felt tense.

A voice snuck into my head. It softly reminded me not to believe this would last. It never did.

I won't listen, I told myself. Shaking away the doubt, I began clearing the table.

"Who has room for dessert?" Gram asked.

"Two scoops for me, Gram!" Meg shouted.

Dessert was homemade black licorice ice cream. Gram dished up two tiny scoops, added red sprinkles to the top of Meg's treat and handed it to the little girl.

"But...I'm ten years old. I'm old enough for a bigger helping," Meg protested.

"You aren't ten yet. Don't wish away your youth." Gram gently kissed Meg on the head. "Let's save room for later."

I smiled at Gram. We both knew Meg's eyes were larger than her little tummy. I set the bowl Gram had scooped for me onto the table.

"Thank you for everything. I love you so much." I hugged my grandmother tightly. Her silver hair felt soft against my cheek.

"I love you, too, Mara." No matter how my day had gone or how confused my emotions could be, Gram always made me feel better. "I want you to come with me," she whispered.

When I released her, she grabbed my hand and softly patted it. "Cole, can you watch Meg for a bit? I want to steal Mara away."

"I think I can handle this little ball of trouble." Cole stole a bite of her ice cream from my sister's dish and laughed.

"Not fair, Cos," Meg whined, using the nickname she had given him. Gram had said the nickname stuck because Cole was always the cause of any mischief that started.

Meg retaliated by scooping up a considerable amount of his dessert. I smiled as my sister filled the air with her devious giggles.

Cole raised his hands in surrender. "Ok. Ok. You win. You win. Look, Mara is leaving her ice cream. We should eat hers."

"You know he is going to get her more ice cream if we are gone too long," I warned.

"I would expect nothing less from that boy," Gram responded.

CHAPTER
THREE

Gram led me down the hallway, passing the bedrooms, and into the enclosed patio. She rummaged through a white cupboard, moving bottles and bags until she found a small white box. She pulled out a small crystal vial attached to a silver chain from the container. It was filled with a purple liquid that shimmered with green, blue, yellow, and red sparks. Something felt so familiar about this moment.

Holding the vial out to me by the chain, she said, "When you were young, Mara, you knew things about the magic that I had not known until I was much older."

"Magic? I just had a good imagination," I interrupted.

She raised her eyebrows at me.

"Sorry, I'll listen," I apologized.

"By the time you were six years old, you were so comfortable with your gift that I became worried. I had begun to suspect that your mother was using her magic for Cedric Drygen.'

My gift? Is Gram losing her mind? I wondered.

She put the vial into my palm, enclosing my finger around it. She held my hand tightly. "Please forgive me for taking away your memories and the magic you held. I only did what I thought was best."

"What are you talking about?" I asked, staring at the vial in my hand. *My grandmother has definitely lost her mind.* "Magic isn't real, Gram."

"I needed to protect you. Please trust me. Drink this, and you will soon have the answers you seek," Gram pleaded. Her brown eyes glistened with tears which she quickly blinked away.

Her desperation frightened me, but I had no choice – I trusted her. My grandmother was the strongest person I knew. So, I took the top off the vial and inhaled the sweet-smelling liquid. Without another thought, I drank it. The cold fluid turned warm as it slid down my throat.

"It just tastes like blackberrsh..." The room began to spin. I reached out to my Gram, afraid of what was happening.

"You will be fine, love. Sit down and rest." She led me to the wicker love seat, where I closed my eyes and drifted off to sleep.

The sound of a child humming roused me. Blinking to clear my vision, I found myself in my parents' bedroom. Glancing over, I saw a young girl, admiring herself in front of a mirror.

Smiling, she smoothed her lengthy black curls and adjusted the white ribbon in her hair. She shifted the bow on the headband, ensuring it was in the perfect position – off to the left. With her hair in shape, she seemed focused on the lacy edges of her white socks. When they were folded perfectly, and her black shoes were shiny, she spun around. The girl giggled as her lavender dress lifted and showed white ruffles.

Strong feelings overwhelmed me, and I wanted to twirl until the room blurred into colors, and the light took ahold of me. That was when I realized I wasn't watching a stranger. I was spying on a younger version of myself.

A creak sounded, and I whipped around to see the door open. I was faced with my grandmother. She looked so young, and her hair was no longer silver. Instead, she had long, light brown hair that she wore loose. She was beautiful in a long, sage green dress. I had forgotten how vibrant she could be.

I gasped when she walked through me as if I wasn't there. *Of course, you aren't here. This is a memory,* I chastised myself.

Calling out to my younger version, Gram laughed, "Come along, my little dancer. Let's get your shoes on. We don't want you to be late for your guests."

Running towards my grandmother, my young self crowed, "I have already put them on. I even buckled them without help."

"Why, yes you did, Marina." I cringed at her using my full name. The name my mother insisted on using, even though she knew I preferred the nickname Meg gave me. "Aren't you so smart." Gram opened her arms to welcome the child.

"Do you think I look pretty today, Gram?" Young Marina wrapped her arms around Gram's neck and hugged her tightly. I felt a twinge of envy.

"You're always pretty, my love. You're what is most important - beautiful inside and out."

Gram set her down. Then, she held out her hand, and my younger version clasped onto it tightly.

I followed them as they left the bedroom and moved onto the patio. I half-expected to see myself sleeping there, but the chair was empty. Continuing to follow as they walked outside into the backyard, I inhaled the smell of the fresh-cut grass. The familiar scent of wood chips drew my attention to Gramp's workshop, which hummed with sawing and buzzing sounds.

I gasped in surprise as I saw over a dozen chickens and six cows grazing on grass and feed. The animal life had dwindled long ago as everything fell on Gram, and it became too much to maintain. She gave up the responsibility and chose, instead, to keep the vegetation.

Tall trees of a bright green were bursting with colored fruits, and the garden was overfilled with vegetables of all kinds. Gram had a natural way with plants, so much so that she made an arrangement with the local butcher, David Jones. She would keep him stocked with produce in trade for meat.

Young Marina's giggles pulled me back from my thoughts. We had reached the largest tree in the yard. Under the oak, a blue and white flowered picnic cloth had been laid out. In the center, a teapot and a plate of biscuits had been set up. Five small teacups, resting on saucers surrounded them, creating a ceramic rainbow of colors.

Young Marina sat in front of the white cup, and immediately exclaimed, "Raspberry tea biscuits! My favorite. Thank you so much!"

Gram kissed her cheek and said, "Have a nice tea party. I will check on you later."

I wanted to follow my grandmother, hoping she was going to Gramp. I longed for one more glimpse of him. One more silly joke. One more warm hug. However, I knew my wishes were foolish. I was here for the return of my memories, not too long for what was gone.

Turning my attention back to Young Marina, I watched her fill her cup with hot tea. The citrus scent of the Lady Gray tea permeated the air. Gram only made her favorite black tea on special occasions. She once told me that it was the only kind of tea her mother, Genevieve, would drink.

After taking a small sip of her beverage, Young Marina murmured, "Delicious." Humming, she began to fill the other cups, and carefully added several of the tea biscuits along the rim of the saucers.

As Young Marina sat patiently waiting for her guests, a great ball of white light appeared above her. It danced with colors of reds, blues, greens, and yellows that swirled in the center until it exploded into four separate balls. Bouncing directly over Young Marina, the four orbs were a breathtaking sight. The yellow ball held feathery streaks of blue that blew wildly inside. Flickering flames of orange tinged with pink filled the red one. Inside the blue orb were glittery white and aqua waves. The green sphere seemed to sprout little brown leaves and yellow flowers.

Dancing around each other, the balls of light hummed with magical sounds. It was a melody I felt I had heard before. It felt like a song I knew, but I couldn't remember the words.

What a delight it was to see the free spirit within my young self. I wanted to join her as she clapped and danced joyfully. I wanted to feel carefree again. When the music stopped and the balls stilled, I wanted to cry out, "More! More!"

The red ball was the first to catch my eye as it began to grow. Expanding, it changed from a red ball to an orange flame that twisted and turned until it formed into a beautiful young woman. The petite girl was no more than a foot tall. Her long slender frame was covered in a red dress layered with shimmery orange scales. Large catlike eyes shone with golden radiance. Her long hair, a salmon-orange in color with dark red streaks, waved down her back.

"Blaze," I said to myself, as I looked at her. I felt like I knew her.

The blue ball of light bounced up and down, pulling my attention away from Blaze. It went up high into the sky, moving faster and faster. In one swift moment, it suddenly stopped and came crashing down in a rapid descent. As it hit the ground, it splashed into a hundred droplets. As quickly as it had come apart, the water came back together and formed, yet another beautiful girl.

Both girls had round angelic faces and were not much taller than most of my old dolls. However, this time, the lady's catlike eyes were piercing silver. She had straight blue hair with aqua streaks running through it that was tied up into a high ponytail. It was held by a seashell band that matched her glittery aqua dress.

As she twirled the short and frilly frock, the edges turned up, showing white and seafoam green petticoat. Her feet were covered by sparkly sandals of silver with straps that wrapped up around her calves. Spinning around, she laughed while spraying droplets of water flung about.

"Bay," Young Marina called, "would you like some tea?"

Halting her movement, Bay plopped down in front of a blue cup and said, "Of course, and another biscuit."

Sighing, Blaze rolled her eyes and shook her head at Bay's entrance, and then stared at the activity above. The green and yellow balls had begun circling around each other. Weaving up and down, it seemed as though they were competing. I could only assume they were trying to decide who would be next to join the party. Around and around, they went until they collided, both dropping to the ground.

The green sphere looked like it had destroyed itself. Instead of a round and green orb, it was now just a large brown mound of dirt. As I stared in shock, I watched a small green blade poke out from the soil. As it grew long, it began to sprout a yellow bud that grew until it formed a large white flower. It twisted and turned on the stem, taking shape as it rose. Another beautiful girl's face formed in the yellow center of the blossom.

Young Marina laughed. "Daisy! Join us before your tea grows cold."

As her body formed, a dress of white adorned her tiny frame. This garment – covered with white and pink petals – went to just below her knees. Around her waist, she wore a sage green belt, and her bare feet had dark green painted on each of her toenails. Laughing, her deep emerald cat eyes widened as her wavy yellow locks grew out. The shoulder-length hair was messy and wild yet looked perfect on her.

"Thank you," she said, as she kissed my younger version on the cheek before settling beside her cup.

With a burst of speed, the yellow ball swirled all around Young

Marina until it turned into a small blue bird. Zipping by Daisy, the bird nipped the tea biscuit out of her hands just as she was going to take a bite.

Daisy shrieked, "Breeze, stop showing off!"

With a dramatic landing, the blue bird quickly changed, as the others had. She had pure white hair that was streaked with blues, greens, and gold. Her shoulder-length hair was fashioned in a long angled-cut style, where it was longer in the front than the back.

Her deep blue eyes glared at Daisy, and her pink lips turned into a pout. "If Bay had not shown off with her ridiculous splash, I would not have had to fly around to dry off."

Smoothing her long blue dress, the fabric changed color with each run of her hand. When she was finally done fixing herself, the dress was no longer a deep navy blue, but rather, a peacock variety of colors shimmered throughout the fabric. I expected her to grow a fan of feathers, but instead, she settled by a teacup and pouted.

I watched on as they each took turns showing off for Young Marina, who delighted in everything they did. I felt so comfortable. I had an intense longing to join them, though I refrained from doing so.

"Caterpillar. Where are you?" The fun was interrupted by the loud male voice calling for me.

The tea party guests instantly disappeared. Young Marina straightened herself up and turned toward the man. I could see four marble sized balls flying high up in the tree.

Caterpillar was the nickname my father had given me. He would say that as I grew, I would change from a young worm into a powerful butterfly that would be respected and adored. A lump formed in my throat. I had grieved the loss of him for so long that the pain had finally subsided.

"There you are," my father, Elliot Stone, called.

My heart raced. I wasn't ready to see him again. I couldn't lose my father twice. *It's a memory,* I chided myself.

The choice was made for me when my father walked through me. His light blond hair glistened, and his ordinally sun-kissed skin was a deep tan. I stared at his ruggedly handsome face, not sure how to feel.

He had died when I was ten, but I often thought of what life would have been like if he had not.

Another ghost from my past was before me.

"Hi, Daddy," Young Marina said as she ran to greet him. He picked her up and swung her around. "Did you come to join my tea party?"

Looking around at the partially eaten cookies and half-full cups of tea, he said, "It looks like your party was interrupted. Where did all your guests go?"

"They all..." She began to answer his question until a leaf fell from the tree and landed on the back of Young Marina's head. The blade grew a small hand that began tugging on the long strands of her hair.

She continued as if she understood the warning, "They are right here. You know Sally, Susie, and Sandy." She gestured around herself towards imaginary friends.

"Only three guests, but you have four cups?" he questioned.

"Oh, right and...and..." she stammered.

"Samantha," I whispered as I remembered my lie.

As if she had heard me, she quickly responded, "Samantha. You know how shy she is."

"Yes, of course, Samantha. How could I forget her? You must tell me all about your friends," he said. He sat down and took a tea biscuit from Blaze's saucer, popping it into his mouth.

"Marina," I turned to see my grandmother waving from the patio door. "I'm starting to make those cookies you wanted to bake. Are you ready to help me?"

"Yes, Gram," she replied. "Sorry, Daddy, I promised I would help." Standing up and smoothing off her dress, she turned and headed towards the house.

"Wait," he said, pulling the leaf out of her hair and handing it to her. "It looks like you have a hitchhiker."

"Thank you." Young Marina giggled. She took the leaf and then broke into a run.

Watching my father, I could see him inspecting the area. He seemed to be looking for something. From the house, my grandmother stood staring at him with a worried look in her eyes. The odd interaction made me wonder.

Regarding my father for one last time, I said, "I miss you." Then, I walked back to the house without looking back.

I found Gram and Young Marina talking in the kitchen.

"You are right, Marina. We should introduce them to your mother and father. Why don't we plan a special party this weekend?" Gram suggested.

Around her, I could see the four balls of light bouncing up and down in agreement.

"Now, drink this and let me know what you think of the taste." I watched my grandmother hand my young self a crystal vial on a silver chain filled with purple fluid, similar to the one that I drank.

"It's really sweet." She licked her lips and tipped the rest of the vial's contents into her mouth. With a feeling of both sadness and wonder, I watched my younger version consume the liquid. When Young Marina collapsed into Gram's arms, my grandmother gently rocked her.

Her soft words were filled with pain. "This is the only way to protect you. I hope you will, one day, understand why we couldn't tell them."

Tears flowed from my eyes. It explained why I always thought I would lose things I loved. Suddenly, the world spun around me, and the images blurred. I closed my eyes to push back the nausea. As everything slowed, I opened my eyes and found myself in my grandmother's arms, once again.

"I'm sorry, love. I really wish I didn't have to take your memories from you." Gram's eyes shone with tears.

Hugging her tightly, I cried. "I understand, but no more secrets, ok?" I broke away, and our gaze locked onto each other.

"Now that you remember the magic I took from you, it is time for you to decide if you are ready for it. You're right. No more secrets," Gram vowed.

CHAPTER
FOUR

Gram brought me to her bedroom. The space was bright and airy. Lavender, vanilla, and cinnamon faintly scented the air. The walls were bare, except for a large oval mirror. The silver frame had a straw-like design. To me, it looked like it was cradled inside a bird's nest.

Gram pulled out a silver chest from under her king-size mahogany bed. I had seen the chest as a young girl, snooping around. When I found it, I asked about the names engraved on it. She told me it was very special, and that mine would, one day, be on it, too. I begged for her to put my name on it, then and there. She laughed and promised I would learn more when it was time – the right time.

Gram set it before me. "Open the chest, love. It is time you learn who we are and what's inside. This box was given to me by my mother. Each of the women on this chest promised to keep the elemental magic safe from those who would misuse it."

I traced the names with my fingertip. The name *Genevieve* felt warm and tingled as if it was a song. Tracing my grandmother's name, I felt the same warmth along with a rush of peace and tranquility. When I moved to the next one below Gram's, I stopped and stared. *Eliza* was icy and made my heart beat faster.

"Why does her name feel so cold? Does it mean she's dead, Gram?" I whispered.

"Open the chest, and you will have answers to your questions," she promised, unable to hide the sadness in her voice.

When I opened the lid, the chest began to glow with a lavender light so intense that it lit up the room. Deep inside the box, resting on a satin bed, was a ring. Braided silver surrounded the robin egg blue stone. I picked it up and held it.

Looking back into the chest, I saw a dark-haired woman smiling as she placed a ring. It looked like the same piece of jewelry, except for her purple stone. Her image faded.

When the next woman appeared, I gasped as I recognized her. It was my grandmother. She was a teenager with long brown hair pulled into a delicate braid. White flowers were laced throughout the twisted locks. Her soft brown eyes shined as she held a dark blue ring in front of her and said, "I promise to always protect this magic. I vow only to use it to protect and guide, never for self-benefit."

The first woman appeared again. She spoke in a firm voice as she gazed deep into my eyes. "Marina Addisyn Stone, do you promise to protect this magic from those who would misuse it? Will you stand strong, and defend the magic when the time comes?"

Before I could say a word, an image of a young girl appeared. It was undeniably my mother, Eliza. Her dark red hair flowed down her back in loose curls, and her green eyes shone proudly as she swore her oath as a protector while holding a ring with a light pink stone.

It was eerie to watch Eliza transform into a woman. This time, she was holding a black-haired baby. She sang sweetly to her cooing child – me. A burst of light flashed, and suddenly, Eliza held Meg, a bright-eyed baby with blonde curls. My ten-year-old self stood next to them. The way we felt was palpable.

The image turned gray. As it became clear again, I saw Eliza was no longer smiling. Her dark red hair was still long and flowing, but it was now a blackish-red streaked with pure white. Her once green eyes were black.

She wore a restrictive black bodice with fitted black pants that were embossed with a silver snake pattern running up the legs. The skintight clothes hugged her body as she walked slowly, carrying a gold-jeweled goblet. Her black boots had silver spiked heels that clicked on the dark granite floor, announcing her entrance to a man sitting in a large chair.

The man was dressed in a tight black T-shirt and wore black leather pants with the same snake pattern on the legs. The man's raven-colored hair was short and spiked with white tips. He had a long silver scar under his left eye.

The coldness in his black eyes seemed to warm as the woman approached him. He accepted the goblet she offered, and then pulled this dark version of my mother onto his lap, kissing her passionately.

Eliza placed her hand on his cheek and pushed him away. The ring on her finger was no longer pink. Instead, it glowed blood red. As she stroked the black stubble along his jaw, he gazed into the ring and smiled.

"Soon, love," she whispered. "Soon."

The image of my mother faded, and the comforting vision of the first woman returned. She repeated her question, "Marina Addisyn Stone, my great-granddaughter, do you promise to protect this magic from those who would misuse it? Will you stand with us when the time comes?"

Clutching the ring, I shut the chest and hid the woman within it. Hot tears fell down my face as I turned to face my grandmother.

"You knew where my mother was all along? How could you keep the truth from me? How could you keep it from Meg? You know how much we have worried about her."

"It was not safe for you to know." Gram grabbed my hand and held it tightly. "If circumstances had not changed, I'm not sure I would have told you yet. But they are growing stronger. Hiding the truth from you is no longer protecting you. Sit and I will tell you what you need to know."

I held the anger that was welling inside me, took a deep breath, and sat down on the bed. My grandmother had always been there for me. If she held anything from me, it would have only been to protect us. She loved my mother as much as I did, and I could see the hurt in her eyes as she looked at me.

Gram took my hand and patted it in the comforting way she had done when I was a child. Then, she cautiously began her story. "Your grandfather was fifteen years older than me, and after years of marriage, I never thought I would be blessed by the Goddess with a child. When I was twenty-three, I had Eliza. Eliza was a wild child, full of mischief. She never wanted to hear 'no'. If I warned her not to do something, she would run off and give it a try, no matter how risky it was.

"I repeatedly warned her about how dangerous it was to go off alone, especially into the Starten Forest. One day, when she was fourteen, she left the house early in the morning. When she hadn't come home by sunset, I had decided to search for her. I met her in the backyard. Her face was streaked with dirt, and her hair was covered with leaves.

"I could tell she was frightened, so I asked her about it. She claimed nothing was wrong. Eliza said she had just been lying in the grass, watching the clouds in the sky, when she drifted off to sleep. When I pressed her, she grew angry. I knew she wasn't telling me the truth, but forcing the issue would be of no use. My daughter was never the kind of child that would run to me for help.

"After that day, Eliza seemed more cautious and listened to my warnings. She met your father not soon after and, four years later, they were married. After you were born, she seemed so happy." A faint hint of a smile showed in Gram's expression, but it disappeared quickly.

She sighed deeply before resuming her tale. "It was not until your father died that her behavior began to change. There was a darkness inside her. She began to dress provocatively, and she would sneak out of the house after you girls were sound asleep."

As Gram spoke softly, she continued to lightly pat my hand. The circular tapping motion of her palm seemed to erase my anger.

"One night, I followed Eliza. I found your mother with Cedric Drygen at Sparrow Lake. I suspected she had been meeting him, but that night, I confirmed my worst feelings. As they lay on the rocky shore, he convinced her to use the magic for him. He made promises of all the things he would provide for her. Eagerly, she charmed his rings and cast spells as they laughed and drank.

"Rushing home, I cast a spell and bound her pure magic. I couldn't let her use our magic for the Drygens. When Eliza returned that evening, she was enraged and screamed that she knew what I had done. At first, she cursed me, but then she tried to convince me to reverse it. Eliza said breaking the binding would be the best thing for you. Not believing her reasons, I told her she would no longer abuse our family's magic and that I would only consider her request when she was ready to honor the promise she had made to protect it.

"She spat in my face and laughed. Eliza told me my silly promise would be the end of me. Without even packing a bag, she left the house and went straight to Cedric Drygen." My grandmother shook her head sadly. "If she were in her right mind, she would not have left my girls. The darkness inside her had turned her into a hateful person. Someone I no longer recognized.

"Yes, Mara. I knew all along where she went." Gram took a long breath. "I'm sorry I kept that from you."

"You must be wrong!" I said, trying to hold back my rage. "She would never leave us for him."

"Yes, love, she left all of us for him, but more so, to feed the dark magic that was beginning to grow inside her. The Drygen family has always been able to be kept under control because we could limit the magic they had access to. However, your mother was always so strong that I knew my binding was not going to last forever.

"Forgive me for not telling you, until now, but I had to make sure you were safe. I have kept many things from you that I have always felt guilty about. Still, all my decisions have been to, first, keep both of you girls safe and, second, to honor my promise. Now, they have warned me that I will not be able to do this alone. I will need you, child. You will be the one to save the magic and keep it pure," Gram said with hope in her voice. "Look inside the chest again when you're ready to give your answer."

A crash sounded from the living room.

My grandmother scowled. "I should find out what is going on with those two." She patted my hand gently, one last time, and kissed me on the cheek. "I will leave you to decide for yourself. We've more to talk about, but it can wait."

Walking through the white door, she left me alone in her room with the silver chest and a mind full of thoughts.

"I can't do this," I thought painfully. "Eliza is my mother. Why would my own mother leave me...leave Meg...for him? She must be under a spell. She must be..."

I stopped myself from making excuses for her. I knew what my grandmother said was true. I knew my mother was too strong-minded to be forced to do anything she did not want to do.

My mind drifted back to when I was that little girl with the dark braids I had just watched in the chest.

One morning, I awoke to Meg crying. The sun was shining into our room. I sleepily called down to my mother, but there was no answer. Climbing out of bed, I wiped the sleep out of my eyes and looked down the loft ladder. I could not see anyone, but I heard the faint sounds of whispers and laughter.

I carefully crept down the hallway that led to the back patio to investigate. A man's indiscernible words could be heard. I thought the deep voice belonged to my father, and I moved faster. I stopped, suddenly, as I saw my mother. She was kissing a man, but this man was not my daddy.

Frightened, I didn't know what to do. Cautiously, I turned around and silently ran back to my room. I returned to Meg. Picking up my baby sister, I held her close as she cried and carried her down the ladder, careful not to drop her.

Her cries became softer and softer as I sang to her, "Goddess, I ask you to calm this child. Remove her sadness and calm her fears. Protect my baby throughout the years."

When I reached the bottom, I realized my mother was behind me, watching.

"Thank you, darling. I was just coming back with her bottle." She took my baby sister from me and began to feed her.

I hadn't told anyone about what I had seen that night and, until now, I had not remembered it.

Shaking off the memory, I gazed at the blue ring in my hand and slid it onto my finger. Knowing what I needed to do, I opened the box and, as my great-grandmother, grandmother, and mother had all done before me, I made the promise.

"I promise to protect the magic from those who would misuse it for self-benefit," I confidently declared. "I will stand with you when the time comes, even if it means standing against her."

I gently closed the silver chest and placed it under Gram's mahogany bed. Wiping the tears from my eyes, I decided to return to my family.

As I left the room, I caught my reflection in the mirror as I turned to close the door. The reflection told me, "You're strong enough and soon, you will know how strong you can be."

CHAPTER
FIVE

Cole smiled at me as I entered the kitchen. "Gram just took Meg to bed. I just finished cleaning up the bookcase we knocked over." He smiled and patted the seat next to him. "Sit, you look like you have seen a ghost."

I started to tell him, but something inside me silenced my words. How could I explain to him that my grandmother knew where my mother was all along? That I had taken an oath to protect magic? I didn't know where to start.

I filled the tea kettle with water, contemplating my words. "Let's go into the living room and sit by the fire. I'm just cold."

Cole opened his mouth as if to ask a question but promptly changed his mind. Relief filled me. He would give me space and let me tell him on my own terms.

"Why don't I start the fire?" Cole suggested.

"Good idea. Did you want any tea? Gram traded Mrs. Everstone some jam for her blueberry orange spice tea leaves."

"Sure, and a snack," he called back as he left the room.

Shaking my head, I smiled to myself. He seemed to always be hungry.

Fixing two mugs of warm tea with a splash of fresh milk and a bit of honey, I pulled down a crystal cookie jar that was full of tea biscuits. These hard cookies were flavored with blackberries soaked in orange zest. Not only had Gram turned the berries we picked into delicious jams, but she took the time to make my favorite treats.

I popped one in my mouth and picked up the tray I had prepared. The sweet, buttery taste of the biscuit was followed by the bitter citrus. Finally, the complimentary blackberry sweetness filled my senses. I hummed softly in delight.

I joined Cole in the living room. He had turned all the lights low and was adding more wood to the fire. He stopped his task and took the tray from me. When I settled next to him, he covered me with one of the soft throw blankets. We sat in silence, sipping our tea, and nibbling the cookies.

My mind played over, and over, how I would tell him everything I learned. The flames of the fire, dancing in front of us, quieted my thoughts. *Another night to reveal your secrets,* I decided.

After the small plate of cookies was gone, Cole took the teacup from me and set it on the coffee table in front of us. He turned back to me with a serious look in his eyes.

"When I told you, today, that I would be there for you – always – I meant it, Mar." Cole pulled me close to him before he withdrew a delicate silver band from his pocket.

The front of the ring was the infinity symbol. Inside, the band was engraved with two small hearts, linked together, and the words *forever in my heart.*

"In three months, you will be eighteen, and we can get married. I have loved you for as long as I can remember, and I will continue to love you forever."

I stared at the ring, not knowing how to respond. My heart wanted me to throw my arms around him and be lost in the moment forever, but my mind cautioned to let him go. The soft look in his eyes comforted me.

This is Cole. Your rock. He will never hurt you, I reminded myself. *But don't they always leave?* The dark thought washed away my brief belief in forever.

I gently placed my hand on his cheek. "I love you, too, Cole," I sighed. "Don't promise forever. Neither of us can promise tomorrow."

"No, I won't listen to this anymore." Cole's eyes burned with an intensity I had never seen before. "I will love you forever because you are meant to be loved. And I won't leave you, so stop trying to push me away."

He took my hand from his cheek and pulled me into a deep embrace. I held him tightly, not wanting to let go. His lips trailed the curve of my neck. The soft kiss and the warmth of his touch made me melt. His fingers tangled in my hair.

"I'm not pushing you away," I said, unable to find the right words. "I need you to..." Trailing off, I suddenly felt a cold chill in the air and heard the creak of the front door opening.

"Marina, my dear, are you not going to come give me a hug? How I have missed you," purred the voice from behind me.

Turning to face the voice that I had not heard for many years, I glared at the intruder, "Hello, Mother."

Eliza strode over to me and grabbed both of my hands with her icy fingers. "Let me look at you. My, how you have grown." With surprising strength, she pulled me to my feet. "Why, you're a woman now, Marina. I always knew you would be a beauty."

I yanked away from my mother and coldly glared. "To what do we owe this honor, Eliza?"

My heart began to beat faster, and I could feel the anger inside me rising. The sting of finding out why she had left us was still fresh. My emotions were too strong.

Eliza stood back, eyeing me. "That isn't a warm welcome, darling. Now, come to me, and all will be forgiven." She opened her arms to welcome me into a hug.

Stepping back, I kept my frigid stare trained on her. "Why are you here?" I asked, not hiding my fury, "Don't you have your new life with Cedric Drygen? I can't imagine what we could offer you. Are you in need of jam? You can buy this at the market on Main Street." I continued aggressively, "You do remember where that is, right?"

"Don't be ridiculous." She moved towards me. "I came for you. I have missed you so much. It was painful for me to be kept away from you for so long." Her eyes glistened with tears.

The show she was putting on did nothing but harden me even more against her.

"You need to leave!" I shouted. Anger that I had never felt before boiled inside me. "You're not welcome here anymore!"

Eliza's eyes widened in surprise at my reaction. I thought she was going to slap me when her eyes narrowed.

"I shouldn't be surprised to find my daughter turned against me by you."

I turned to see Gram coming down the loft ladder.

"Enough of this nonsense. Pack a bag for you and your sister, Marina. I will explain everything once we are home." Eliza turned back to me with a look of hurt. "I have so much to tell you."

My heart ached. I wanted to fall into my mother's arms and ask her to come home...beg her to love me again.

"You will not be taking these girls anywhere. Mara was right in saying you aren't welcome in this home anymore." Gram stepped forward and blew small flowers into the air. The smell of lavender and cinnamon engulfed the room.

The flowers turned into white smoke tendrils that surrounded my mother. Shock filled her eyes as the small strings bound her arms and began to circle around her neck. Eliza turned from the room, grabbing and pulling at the tendrils attaching to her.

Quickly, opening the front door, she exited and turned to say, "You cannot keep them from me, Mother. They are mine."

Gram held her hand out in front of her, causing a warm wind to blow through the room and slam the door shut.

"No, Eliza," my grandmother corrected. "They are mine."

No one spoke for minutes. When my eyes caught Cole's, I could see the sadness that filled them. He knew how much I had missed my mother. He understood how desperately I wanted everything to go back to the way it was before she disappeared.

Closing my eyes, I breathed in the lavender that scented the air and tried to calm my heart. I could feel gentle patting on my hand. When I looked down, I saw the tendrils of smoke that had chased my mother away. The smoke was warm, and it felt like the soft touch of my grandmother's hand, comforting me. I closed my eyes again and let myself be reassured.

"Cole, go home and pack some of your things. You're staying here for a few days," Gram ordered.

Cole began to protest. "Gram, I don't need protection. I will be..." His voice trailed off as he saw the serious look in my grandmother's eyes.

She walked to the fire and grabbed the iron poker. With wide eyes, Cole watched, waiting for her next move. The white and gray stone of the fireplace shimmered as if millions of little stars were buried in the material.

Gram held the poker high in the air, making tiny circles. Her circles turned into silver chains that began to twist and turn in the air around us. Even when she put the poker down, the tendrils continued to weave themselves into small circles. Abruptly, the rings dove at Cole.

"I said I was going," he cried out.

Cole lifted his hands to stop the attack. Instead of striking him, the silver slowed and wrapped his wrist. Twisting and twisting, it formed the most elegant silver bracelet. Circles entwined, creating an oval shape that resembled an eye.

When the weaving stopped, Gram held Cole's arm and closed her eyes. The ocular-shaped silver turned a glowing red. I thought it would burn him, especially when Gram released her hold on his arm. I expected Cole to cry out in pain, but instead, he curiously stared at his wrist.

Slowly, the red faded, and then the silver disappeared, leaving his wrist covered in a black ink tattoo. On the inside of his wrist, he bore an eye. The pupil was a color I had never seen before – a vibrant blue that almost seemed to change into shades of purple, and then green. It was a peacock feather of colors.

Gram grasped his hand and gently patted it. "Cole, this will protect you, warding off any harm. Go quickly and gather just what you need for a few days."

"Ok, I will be back soon. I will only grab a few of my things." Cole kissed me on the cheek. "We will continue our conversation when I return."

I watched as Cole walked out the same door my mother had left.

"He will return," a whisper on the wind told me.

"Mara, do you remember the prayer I used to say over you each night? Go to Meg and sprinkle this in a circle around her bed while saying that prayer." Gram handed me the purple bag of the herbs she had just used.

"Gram, I remember the prayer, but I can't create magic like you just did." I tried to hand the bag back to her.

"You will do just fine." Gram held my left hand in front of me. The blue ring on my middle finger swirled with magic. "Trust your promise. I have been preparing you for this day all of your life. Now go." She gently swatted me away.

Not feeling confident in my so-called 'gift', I climbed the ladder. When I touched my mother's name, anger built up inside me. I was reminded of why I committed to my promise.

I found Meg tucked in bed and softly snoring. She was deep in sleep. The energy she expended during the day always ensured her night's sleep was deep. Amazingly, not even the chaos from below had woken her.

I pinched a small amount of the herbs from the bag. They grew warm between my fingertips. Slowly, I began sprinkling the purple flowers around Meg's bed. I recited the words I had heard my grandmother say as she tucked us in each night.

"Goddess, I ask for your guidance on this night and ask you to aid in invoking the elements that guide."

"With my hands to the east, I call upon you, Air, and ask you to blow away any harm and to clarify my thoughts." A rush of air sent the herbs I had dropped up into the air about me and swirled my hair.

"With my hand to the south, Fire, I call upon you and ask you to burn away any fear I have and burn away those feelings that harm." Taking more herbs from the pouch from my left hand, I watched as the light purple turned to small, red embers as they fell to the ground and quickly died out.

"With my hand to the west, Water, I call upon you and ask you to wash away my fears and cleanse those who wish to harm." The herbs I dropped from my right hand turned into a droplet of water. When it landed on the floor, I heard a string of chimes.

"With my hands to the north, I call upon you, Earth, and ask you to ground me in goodness and strengthen me." I felt the wood beneath me move. It turned into a grassy field, and I could smell the fresh grass and dirt. The herbs I dropped disappeared into the grass for a moment, but then a small yellow flower began growing from the dark green blades under my feet. I half expected Daisy to appear from the bloom.

"Goddess, my request is complete, and I ask you to keep us safe. Please guide this child as she sleeps and wake her with the light of morning." The herbs I dropped, this time, turned into white tendrils of smoke that emitted a sound – almost like a small child's laughter. The essence danced through the air and swirled around my slumbering sister. A small smile covered Meg's face as she continued to sleep soundly.

"Thank you, Goddess," I whispered, and then I kissed my sister on the cheek. "Sleep sweet, my little Meg, sleep sweet."

Her small eyes barely opened, and she wrapped her arms around my neck before she dozed off again.

Holding my sister in my arms, I felt all the doubt I had been carrying around, off and on, all day fade away. I shifted myself and lay beside her. Before I knew it, I had drifted off, too.

CHAPTER
SIX

I was jolted by a set of sharp nails digging into my forearm. The hot searing pain filled me as I tried to yank away. The harder I pulled, the tighter the grip became.

"How ridiculous you are to think that anyone but me will truly ever love you," the voice of Eliza snarled.

I searched the darkness for her.

"Everything you are and will be is because of me."

Looking around for an escape, all I could see was darkness.

"You can run, but I'll always be able to find you. You are *my* child. You're from *my* blood. Soon, you will forget the ridiculous ideas that have been planted in your head by that woman, and you will see what real power the magic you hold has in store for you."

Tearing myself away from her, I felt a sting of pain in my arm as the skin ripped. Falling to my knees, I tried to find something to stop the warm blood from running down my arm. Blinded by the void, I jammed my shoulder into something sharp. Feeling helpless, I cried out for my grandmother.

Eliza's taunts continued as I tried to move in the opposite direction of the voice. However, she was everywhere, and instead of escaping, I trapped myself. There was nothing but solid walls around me.

"She can't save you now, Marina. Only I can...only I can," my mother hissed coldly. The faceless voice began to shake me violently. "Listen to me, Mara, join me..."

I let out a bloodcurdling screaming, praying someone would save me.

"It's me, Mara; it's me," a soft voice pleaded, "Please, wake up, please."

Light penetrated my consciousness. I looked around, expecting to see my mother. Instead, I saw a rainbow mural on the wall and a small bed covered with, at least, twenty different stuffed animals on top of a pink bedspread. The moon shined in the round window, and I could see the stars shining in the night sky.

Realization washed over me. I must have fallen asleep, but I was safe in my room. Recognizing that it was all a bad dream, I began to take in the damage I had caused.

I was crouched in the corner of the loft bedroom I shared with Meg. I had wedged myself between the nightstand and the wardrobe. My jewelry box and all my vanity items were strewn across the floor. The picture frame that held the photo of my mother and father was shattered. Sticking out of it was a large piece of blood-soaked glass. Blood droplets formed a trail that led to me.

My frightened little sister came into focus. "I'm sorry, Meg. It was just a nightmare. Did I hurt you? Are you ok?" I apologized. Shaking, I held out my arms to her.

Meg's green eyes were wide and filled with concern. "I'm ok, but you're bleeding." She pointed at my arm.

She was right. I had a deep cut that ran from the ring finger of my left hand to my elbow. Conscious and with the adrenaline wearing off, I could feel how severe the injury was.

"Can you bring me a towel from the bathroom, please?" I asked calmly, trying not to frighten my sister more than I already had. "It looks worse than it is. Stupid nightmares. Lucky I didn't fall off the ladder, huh?"

Trying to make light of the situation didn't appear to be working. My little sister still wore a brave face, but I could tell she was trying to hold back her tears.

"It will be ok, Meg. Can you just grab the first towel you see?"

Meg nodded and rushed towards the bathroom we shared. Moments later, she returned with a small, hot pink bath towel.

I held out my arm, and asked, "Can you open it, fold it in half the long way, and place it around my arm?"

My little sister was definitely still a child, but when needed, she could follow directions as well as any adult. She quickly folded it just as I had asked. Then, she gently laid it on over my hand, covering the deepest part of the cut.

I carefully removed my fingers and tightly wrapped my makeshift bandage around my throbbing arm. Putting on my best *don't worry little sister* face, I patted her on the head. "Let's go downstairs and see Gram and Cole. Cole should be back. He is going to stay with us for a few days. I bet they will make us hot chocolate with peppermint marshmallows."

She nodded with a subtle trace of a smile on her face.

My nightmares were nothing new to Meg, but this time I had really scared her. Guilt filled me. I was supposed to protect my litter sister, not hurt her.

I handed Meg the fluffy white robe that was hanging on a peg beside her bed. "Put this on. You don't want to catch a cold."

Narrowing her eyes at me, she retorted, "You can't catch a cold from being cold. Everyone knows that." Begrudgingly, she slipped her arms into the soft robe, covering her satin blue princess gown while mumbling.

"Very true, smarty. How did I get such a wise little sister?" I asked.

Shrugging, she remarked as she began to climb down the ladder, "You're lucky, I guess?"

"Yes, I am."

When I reached the last step, I was met by Gram. "Oh dear, what have you done to yourself?" she asked before lifting the towel to see how badly I'd been injured. Her face flashed with worry. "Come with me."

I followed Gram to the sink and let her clean the wound.

"Is she ok?" Cole asked.

"She will be. Cole, go to the pantry and grab my emergency kit." Turning towards me, she asked, "What cut you?"

"It was just a nightmare, Gram," I tried to reassure her, grimacing as the cold water flushed the laceration. "I knocked a picture off my dresser and broke it. I'm ok. It really doesn't hurt," I lied.

Cole brought Gram the bag. "What can I do to help?" he questioned me.

"You could make Meg some hot chocolate," I suggested.

He shook his head. "I'll stay with you."

"I'm fine. I promise. You know how I am – these nightmares are more painful for those around me than they are for me." I squeezed his hand. "Please. Meg needs you more than I do, right now."

Cole looked at my sister, who was sitting on the ladder still. He went to her without further delay. Kneeling down beside her, he asked, "You want to know something good?"

"Uh-huh," Meg half-heartedly replied.

"At least, she didn't have one of those nightmares where she screamed so loud that Old Lady Callaghan was sure the banshees were coming for her again."

The two shared a laugh at my expense. I couldn't be mad, though. Cole was effectively comforting my little sister.

"Ok, Meg, let's get you something warm to drink. I'm sure Mara's shrieks chilled you to the bone."

"She screamed so loud I thought all the windows would crack," Meg said seriously.

"What are we going to do with your sister?" Cole picked Meg up and swung her around.

Giggling, she grabbed onto his neck. "We should sell her at the next Market Fair."

The two of them fell into a fit of laughter again. They were entertained by all of the suggestions about what they could do with me.

Gram and I left them to make their hot chocolate. We moved to the living room, so she could mend my wound.

"You're very lucky it didn't cut any deeper. Tell me what happened."

Lifting the formerly hot pink towel, which now looked like a red Rorschach test, she, once again, washed the blood from the injury. The blood flow had lessened, and I was finally relaxed enough to tell my grandmother what had happened.

As I retold my dream, Gram listened patiently as she coated my cut with a purplish mixture. She smoothed the cold goo in long strokes, followed by a slow figure-eight pattern. The paste stung, at first, but then warmed. It felt like hundreds of hot pins were being poked into my arm. Thankfully, the pinprick feeling began to subside as I finished my tale.

"Did I do the blessing wrong?" I built up the courage to ask, not really wanting to know the answer. I feared her response. "When I called the elements, I felt all of them come to me. Shouldn't it have protected Meg from harm, even from me?"

"No, love. You say you felt all of the elements come to you? If that is true, then you did everything correctly. The Goddess wouldn't have blessed you in such a way if she didn't feel your open heart."

Taking a cream-colored roll of linen bandages from her bag, she lightly wound the fabric around my forearm. It created a cast-like protection.

"I'm sure that what happened tonight was just a dream. You know that these come more often when you're worried. If you didn't have a nightmare, especially tonight of all nights, I would have been surprised." She stood up and gathered all her supplies, stuffing them back into her bag. "Now, let's finish this up and go check on those two."

In the kitchen, we found clues that hot chocolate had been made. Crumbs indicated cookies had been added for additional comfort. Not wondering whom the cookies were really comforting, I smiled.

Cole and Meg were sitting on the couch, reading a book. I sat down next to Cole and put my head on his shoulder. "Thank you for being here for us tonight."

He kissed the top of my head and said, "Always."

"Let's all go to bed." Gram picked up Meg, who was unsuccessfully fighting sleep.

Her slight frame gave the illusion that she was frail, but my grandmother could outwork most men in town. My little sister seemed like a light cloth in her arms as she lifted her with ease and carried her off to bed.

Stopping, she turned, and spoke, "Cole, you can sleep in the guest room since you have already put your things in there. Mara, there is plenty of room in my bed for the three of us. Don't be too long with your good nights. We can deal with things tomorrow."

Watching Gram carry my little sister away, I felt a wave of sadness wash over me. *I can't keep putting her through this. I need to figure out why my dreams are so real. I need to control them for her sake.* My grandmother had more to deal with than was fair. If Eliza was as persistent as she was in my dream, I feared what she would do.

As though he sensed my internal struggle, Cole held me tightly. "I won't ask what your dream was about, tonight, Mar. I'm just glad you're safe. Do I dare look at the damage in your room?"

"I don't even want to think about that right now. I just want you to hold me and tell me it will be all ok."

"It will be ok," he said with a smirk. "Now, let's get you off to bed before I have to face the wrath of your grandmother. I don't want her to weave any protection spells on you that I won't be able to undo."

Cole led me past the dining room towards the hall to the downstairs bedrooms. As we passed the ladder that led to my room, I looked up. The white half walls on each side of the ladder blocked my view. I could only see a portion of the rainbow mural. I looked away, not wanting to think about the mess I had caused.

Once we reached the door to Gram's bedroom, Cole wrapped his arms around me and gently kissed me. "Love you, Mar."

"I love you, too."

He reluctantly released me from his embrace, kissed me on the cheek, and walked down the rest of the hallway into the guest room. The same room that had once belonged to my parents.

I watched him go for a minute before I closed my eyes. "Goddess, please, protect all those who sleep in this house tonight."

CHAPTER
SEVEN

When I entered the room, Meg and Gram were sleeping. I changed into the long T-shirt that my grandmother had left for me at the end of the bed. It was one of my grandfather's.

Chester Veracor was a tall, handsome man with silver hair. His blue eyes held a mischievous sparkle, especially when he teased Gram. I was only nine years old when he died, but I remembered spending time with him while he worked on his creations.

His work area was behind the house in a wood building that he called a barn. Gramp had told me it was once full of animals that lived on the property. They would roam the forest behind us during the day, looking for food, and then return to the barn for shelter at nightfall. We had a small, covered area that my grandfather had designed to provide them with shelter from the weather.

Gramp's workshop was his pride and joy. He used it to build furniture to sell at the market and for improvements around the house. As he sanded, stained, painted, and polished his wood creations, he would tell me stories about his life had been growing up. Whenever I smell fresh-cut wood, my mind is transported back to the time I spent with him.

Suddenly feeling exhausted, I pushed away my memories. I put my clothes into the hamper in the master bathroom and skipped brushing my teeth or even washing my face. I wanted – no, I needed – to just sleep.

I climbed into the big bed beside my sister, and I nestled into the feather mattress pad. The large mauve comforter was warm, and the sheets were so soft. My grandmother had a gift for making the most comfortable beds. It was like being stuffed between two fluffy clouds.

Taking a deep breath, I inhaled the lavender, cinnamon, and vanilla intermingled with the freshness of the linens. The grandfather clock chimed ten times. It seemed so much later to me.

As I lay, listening to the soft breathing of my grandmother and sister, the moonlight cast a small light on the ceiling and the glitter in the paint sparkled. When I was a little girl, I would stare at the ceiling and count the stars. The soft tick of the clock with the comforting chimes broke into my thoughts reminding me to sleep. Slowly, counting back from one thousand, I deeply inhaled, again, willing myself to just let go and sleep. Nothing was going to be resolved in my mind tonight.

"Nine hundred ninety-nine, nine hundred ninety-eight, nine hundred ninety-seven," I softly counted. Somewhere after six hundred forty, I lost count and faded into a deep, dreamless slumber.

I woke to a small foot kicking my head. Looking out the window, I could see it was still dark outside. I felt like I had just fallen asleep.

Pushing Meg's foot off me, I sat up and settled on the edge of the bed. Of course, my sister continued to sleep. There was no sign of my grandmother, but there was a stack of my clothes on the fabric-covered trunk at the end of the bed.

Looks like I'm being dressed by my grandmother today, I thought with a smile.

I hopped off the bed and instantly regretted it. The wood floor was ice cold and there was a chill in the air. Gathering up my assigned clothing, I entered the bathroom to prepare for the day.

I moved quickly, hoping to warm up, and shed my nightwear. I pulled the white shower curtain open before stepping into the white tiled enclosure. Without thinking, I turned the water on and was blasted with a frigid burst of water.

"Damn it," I hissed.

Jumping back, I held my hand under the stream until it became lukewarm. I, then, dared to slip under the running water again. When I did, I turned the silver knob to the left, trying to make it even hotter.

The hotter the water, the better, I thought.

As I washed my hair, I realized I still had the bandage on. Holding my arm out while trying to rinse the soap out of my hair was impossible. Therefore, I simply gave up.

By the time I was done, the bandage was starting to fall off, so I slowly unwrapped it. There wasn't any pain, just a slight itching. I envisioned finding an oozing gash that would scar terribly. Instead, I found the long cut had already scabbed over.

I gently rubbed the purplish paste and bits of dried blood off my arm. I sat under the hot water spray, just letting it beat on my face. I must have been in the shower for a while because the hot water began to cool.

Grabbing a towel from the hook, I wrapped it around myself and stepped out onto the fuzzy, white bathmat. I stood under the heat lamp, just absorbing the warmth. Thoughts of the day ahead pushed me to hurry up and just get ready. I finished drying off, and then looked through the clothes that Gram chose. Jean shorts, a black V-neck T-shirt, my favorite black bra, and white panties with a rainbow on the back.

"Funny, Gram," I said, holding up the underwear to inspect them.

At least, she didn't buy the days of the week pack she had threatened to get when she found them at the store. I had not seen this purchase. She must have been saving them for a special occasion...the special occasion being the giggles that would erupt from my little sister as the gift was given at the most inconvenient time. Knowing her, she probably intended it for one of my birthday gifts, planning to have it opened in front of my friends.

I finished dressing after toweling off my hair. Grabbing my extra toothbrush from the holder, I put the peppermint toothpaste on the brush and let the foam get to work. Once I looked appropriately rabid, and each tooth felt sparkly fresh, I rinsed my mouth.

Next, I began to work on my hair. Not wanting to spend time trying to dry it, I twisted it into a long braid. I took my bath towel and squeezed out all the extra moisture. Opening the vanity drawer, I pulled out Gram's mauve lipstick and lightly covered my lips. Once again, thoughts of *good enough* filled my head.

I quietly opened the bathroom door, not wanting to wake Meg. She was still sleeping as I left the room and headed towards the kitchen. There was a soft light above the table. Gram was sitting in her light blue housecoat, writing in her lavender journal. In front of her was a steaming cup of coffee.

"Join me. I'm just finishing this." Gram patted the chair next to her and closed her writings.

Sitting down, I looked into her light brown eyes. They were filled with worry. "What do you think she will do now that we sent her away?" I questioned.

Closing her eyes, she replied, "I'm not sure. I really am not sure what she has planned, but we'll be ok."

Not wanting to cause her any more worries, I stood up, kissed her on the top of her head, and replied, "You're right. We'll be fine. Now, I'm going to my room. I want to clean it before Meg wakes up."

I picked up the red mug my grandmother made for herself and took a big gulp of the warm liquid. Gram's coffee consisted of a strong black brew with generous sprinkles of cinnamon and sugar, and an even more generous splash of cream. The sweet concoction made me smile.

"This was for me, right?" I coyly asked, giving her my best *aren't I cute* impersonation. "When I'm done upstairs, we'll talk about your choice in underwear for me."

She took the half-full cup back from me. "You're lucky I love you. It isn't everyone I share my morning coffee with. Now, grab yourself a piece of the apple bread before you head up to your room. Coffee alone does not make a breakfast."

Doing as I was told, I grabbed a big slice from the platter in the middle of the table and, this time, I kissed my Gram on her cheek. Her soft skin felt like silk.

"I love you, too," I called back to her as I headed up the ladder.

CHAPTER
EIGHT

With my apple bread in hand, I, once again, climbed the ladder. I greedily took large bites while I made my ascent. Each portion had caramelized apples, and raisins swirled into it. As I popped the last morsel into my mouth, I stopped to stare at the sixth rung from the top. Running my fingers over the name *Eliza*, I frantically scratched my nails across the engraving. I tried to erase it completely, but my efforts were in vain. My short nails did nothing to the hard wood.

My quick breakfast felt like a rock in my stomach. An urge to scream while destroying everything my mother ever touched overcame me. "Air, I ask your blessing of peace," I pleaded. "Please, blow away the anger I'm carrying."

A small burst of wind twisted around me, and I could hear soft twinkling laughter as it encircled me. The warm breeze lifted my damp braid and then dropped it.

"Bright blessings, Air," I thanked the element.

I began to feel calmer, so I continued my climb. I looked forward to not thinking about Eliza. Hope-filled, I had a way to eliminate the anger and sorrow that consumed me. With the help of Air, I would be stronger, and I could be in control of my emotions.

The burst of Air made one last spin around me before it trailed down the ladder. Surprise filled me that the element had not only responded to me but stayed to make sure I was ok.

I found a bucket of cleaning supplies at the entrance to the loft. Gram must have put it up here for me. Looking at the mess I had made of our room, I was thankful Gram hadn't cleaned it for me. She knew I needed to see for myself what damage I had done.

My section of the room was on the north wall. My bed had not been disturbed by my night terror. The purple bedspread was in place, and the lime green pillows had not been touched. My small, black lamp sat on my white nightstand. Perched up against it, undisturbed, were a little stuffed wolf and a tiny lamb. Gram had given them to me when I was younger, to comfort me when I was scared.

I followed a small trail of blood around my bed to the corner where it pooled. Pulling out a fresh rag, Gram's homemade cleaning solution, and a large paper bag from the bucket of supplies, I set to work. Taking care not to cut myself, I put the broken pieces of glass into the bag before I scrubbed the dark blood off the floor. With it as clean as possible, I sought my next project.

My long dresser was bare since everything had been thrown onto the floor. Most things were still in good condition. They just needed to be wiped off where the blood droplets had dried. As I cleaned each item, I put everything back into the correct place.

Wiping down my black and white polka dot makeup bag, I realized it held more cosmetics than I would ever use. *I always find myself wanting to try new things*, I thought with a gentle shake of my head. *I ought to throw half of this stuff away without bothering to clean them.* Of course, feeling extremely clingy to my things, that's not what I did.

In complete contrast to the bag, my white, porcelain jewelry box was less full. I placed my silver earrings, rainbow bangles, and barrettes back into the container. I replaced the lid and set it on the dresser, where I stared at the box for a moment. I felt like I was seeing it with fresh eyes. I knew the flower's half petals, which decorated the case, had represented the four elements. However, I never really understood how much they were around me.

"Thank you for always being here for me, even when I didn't know you were," I said to the elements. The arch-shaped petals each came to life for the briefest moment and danced in front of me. It was as if they said, "You're welcome."

Out of the corner of my eye, I saw the broken picture frame that injured me. I took the color photo of my parents from it and threw the rest into the garbage bag. I loved this image of my parents.

My mother's hair was pulled high on top of her head with large curls cascading over her shoulders. Always stylish, she had chosen a short, dark green dress, and white thigh-high boots. The four-inch heels matched her height to my father, Elliott Stone.

They were a beautiful couple. While my mother was fair, he looked sun-kissed. The contract was aesthetically pleasing.

My father's blond hair was short and spiked. He stood six feet tall with a slender frame. He wore a matching dark green shirt and a light pair of khakis. His soft green eyes were joy-filled, and a big smile was on his face.

At first look, they seemed so happy, but as I continued to examine the picture, something felt wrong. I could not put my finger on exactly what was disturbing me. Perhaps it was the darkness in Eliza's eyes, which I had never noticed before.

I initially found this picture after my mother left. When I showed it to Gram, she told me it was taken on the day Eliza found out they were expecting me. I was so excited to have the first family photo.

Now, holding it in front of me, I wanted to tear it up and erase her from my memory, forgetting she existed. As I contemplated destroying it, I found myself examining it more carefully. My gut told me I was missing something, so I continued to search for the answer.

After a few minutes, I finally realized my mother was wearing a silver snake ring on her small finger. The ring twisted into the same design embossed on the black clothing she wore in the image the spirits showed me. I could not remember seeing her wear the ring before. I held the picture closer, scrutinizing the intricate design of the snakes.

Thinking back, my mind drifted to my father. I could not remember him wearing any jewelry, except for his wedding band. He never even wore a watch. I recalled asking him why he didn't wear one, especially since Gramps wore his. He had told me the only time he needed to tell was by the beat of our hearts.

Shaking me from my memories, Cole called out from the ladder, "Taking a break already?"

I quickly folded the picture and shoved it in my pocket. I needed to find out more before I shared it with Cole.

"No, I was just finishing up." I quickly got to my feet. "Come look around and tell me what I missed."

Cole picked up several stuffed animals and put them back onto Meg's bed. He added them to her collection, which included a mermaid, variously dressed bears, dragons, and other animals. He finished making up Meg's bed, and then pulled a necklace from under it.

"Is this yours?" he questioned.

I looked at the twine string with various charms attached to it. Taking it back, I replied, "Yes, I have been adding to this since I was twelve."

Eventually, when we had more time, I would share with him how I began adding charms soon after I began to think of him as more than *just the boy I grew up with* – when I first started considering him *mine*. I would tell him how the first charm I added was the screw nut that fell out of his pocket when he constructed the rope swing on the large sycamore tree in our front yard.

I placed the necklace inside the box, set it on my dresser, and then relayed to him everything that had happened the night before. I started with my acceptance of the ring and the promise to protect magic. As I told him my story, he sat on Meg's bed, just listening. When I told him about the blessing, he smiled.

"I know this may sound crazy to you," I said, "but I still feel the elements around me. Just before I finished the climb up the stairs, I was feeling so angry that I thought I was going to explode. I asked the element, Air, to remove my negative thoughts, and I was surrounded by wind."

"I don't think any of this is crazy. I have always known you were special." Cole reached into the pocket of his jeans and held the ring out to me. "I hope you won't be adding this to your jewelry box." Cole kissed my hand before he slipped the promise ring onto my finger.

I started to respond, but he stopped me.

"Before you say anything, let me speak. I spoke to your grandmother this morning about us. She warned me that the tattoo she gave me was not only to protect me from harm, but it would also protect you and your family. If my heart isn't pure and my promises to you are false, I'll feel a pain like no other, she warned." The bright eye in the center of his wrist seemed to change colors as if confirming Gram's promise.

"She then took my hand and called the elements. I felt each one as they surrounded me. I don't know whether she wanted to scare me off or prepare me for our future. The entire time, I just kept thinking about you, so I'm going to ask you this again."

Cole guided me to sit on the bed before he knelt before me. "Mara, I have always loved you. Over the years we have known each other, the love I have felt for you has only grown stronger and deeper with each breath I have taken. I'm offering you this ring as a promise to love you and take care of you until the day I die. I want to spend the rest of my life with you, and only you. No matter what this life holds for us, I want to face it together."

I put my hand over his lips and said, "If you let me speak, I can answer you. You don't need to sell yourself to me. I realized I loved you when I was twelve, and you hung the swing for me in the front yard. I've only loved you more each day. Last night made me realize how I have been holding back out of fear of losing you. I can't keep doing that. I can't push you out of my life and end up making what I feared most come true. I can't be, and will not be, in this world without you."

Cole kissed my hand as he removed it from his lips. "You won't be without me, Mar." Cole joined me on the bed, grinning from ear-to-ear. "I can't believe you finally admitted you love me. You have made me the happiest man in the entire world."

He held me in his arms and pressed his lips to mine. Our soft kisses quickly turned stronger as I pulled him towards me. With Cole, I felt safe, and I was able to ignore the negative voice that kept telling me I didn't deserve his love.

My feeling of contentment was loudly interrupted by a high voice. "Gross! Gram they're up here kissing." Meg called down to my grandmother.

"Don't be like that, Meg. She has finally agreed to marry me." Cole stood up and ran his fingers through his hair.

"It's about time, Cos," Meg quipped, still standing on the ladder. "I thought I was going to be old and gray before she ever stopped being silly."

"*She's* right here." I gave my sister a stern look. "We'll have plenty of time for this discussion later. Did you come up here for a reason, other than being sassy?"

"Well, if you weren't such a crab, I would tell you breakfast is ready." Meg stuck her tongue out at me and quickly scrambled back down the ladder.

"We better tell Gram the good news," Cole said, unable to hide the excitement in his voice.

"Why don't you go ahead and get your breakfast? It won't be long before I follow."

"You haven't changed your mind, have you?" Cole's face paled.

Kissing him on the cheek, I said, "I've never been so sure of an answer. Go on. I'll only be a minute."

What we would face was not going to be easy, but I had to believe we were stronger together than apart. With that knowledge, I called after him, "I love you, Cole."

Watching him descend the ladder, I reached into my pocket to pull out the picture of my parents.

"What else are you hiding from me, Eliza?" I asked, glaring at the image of my mother. Afraid I would find out soon enough, I put the picture into my jewelry box, and then went downstairs for breakfast.

CHAPTER NINE

After making sure everything was back in its place, I found the kitchen had become a controlled chaos. Crates lined the counter, full of glass jars of jam, bags of dried herbs, and tonics. The smell of fresh loaves of bread and scones baking permeated the room.

People from all over would come to buy and trade goods while participating in the entertainment. Meg was old enough to join the other young girls in the traditional lunar dance. She had been practicing for months to make sure she knew all the steps.

"Mara, sit and eat your food before it becomes cold." Gram handed me an omelet overflowing with fresh vegetables, including mushrooms, onions, and peppers. I took a large bite, savoring each cheesy morsel.

Meg eyed my plate, and I playfully growled at her. "Mine. Eat your fruit," I whispered.

Meg scooted away in pretend terror.

"Finish eating girls. We have much to do." Gram took advantage of Meg sitting still to brush her messy hair. "Meg, we'll be busier than normal tomorrow. You'll need to stay with me at our stand until it is time for your performance. No running off where I can't see you," she instructed.

"Will I get to see the other stands?" Meg slouched in her chair.

"I'm sure Mara and Cole will cover us, and we'll take a break. Now, stop pouting and sit up," Gram ordered.

Meg meekly obeyed, and Gram twisted my sister's hair into two long braids. When she weaved flowers into Meg's hair, I was reminded of the image I had seen, last night, of my grandmother as a young girl. Meg was the spitting image of her.

When my grandmother finished her hair, she patted Meg on the head and said, "Now, run along and practice your dance. Later, we'll have you try on your dress to see if we need to make any more adjustments."

Cole joined us in the kitchen. He squeezed my shoulder gently and kissed my cheek.

Gram directed her attention towards my boyfriend. "If you got enough breakfast, can you help me gather some tonics from the pantry?"

Cole stole a piece of the cut fruit from my plate and popped it into his mouth. "Yep. I'm all done. I'm now at your service, fine lady."

My grandmother handed a sheet of paper to Cole. Watching her go over how she wanted the tonics stacked and assigning him additional duties, I could see the love she had for him. Cole brought so much happiness to my family, and he made Gram's eyes brightened as he joked. He was so much more than just my boyfriend.

A twinge of sadness filled me as I thought about Cole's life. It had not been perfect. A few months after his sixteenth birthday, Cole's mother, Sarah, died. Less than a year later, his father, Thomas, remarried a woman he had just met. His new wife, Rosalind, was a selfish, cruel woman.

Gram warned me to stay away from Rosalind. My grandmother told me she had never seen a person wear so many masks of deceit. That the woman was hiding something, but what, we didn't know.

When Rosalind and Thomas married, she insisted Cole give up his room for her son. Instead of arguing, Cole moved to the cottage behind the house. He ended up spending more time at my home than at his own.

Six months ago, when he turned nineteen, his father announced that they were leaving Starten. He said they wanted to be closer to Rosalind's family, who lived thousands of miles away. Leaving the family house in Cole's care, Thomas walked away and had only sent one letter to his son since then.

The click of the last bottle of rosemary hair tonic and lemongrass oil being stacked broke my focus.

"Good. We are ahead of schedule," Gram said. She took a seat next to me. "Cole, let's sit for a while and talk about everything."

Cole joined us with three mugs of piping hot coffee, just the way I liked. Gram took a small sip and nodded her thanks.

"I knew the time would come when we would be talking about this. Marriage isn't something either of you should take lightly," Gram began, "Saying that, I love you both, and I wholeheartedly support your decision. The two of you are meant to be together. Do you have any plans for when this will happen, or will it be a long engagement?"

Cole shook his head. "We haven't discussed details yet. I was —"

Interrupting him, I said, "The day after my birthday."

"Well, you have your answer then. In less than three months, we'll marry," Cole declared with a delighted look of surprise on his face.

"Are you sure you don't want to just get married tomorrow?" Gram teased.

"Now, Mae," Cole started with a deep southern drawl and tipping an imaginary hat at her, "no bride of mine shall be expected to plan a wedding extravaganza as fine as the one we shall have on less than a day's notice. Why the person that suggests such a thing should be tarred and feathered."

I interrupted the remaking of *Gone with the Wind* that I was sure would ensue, and I took both of their hands in mine. "Enough of the wedding talk, we'll have plenty of time to discuss the *small*, simple event. We need to talk about the red elephant in the room that we have been avoiding. What are we going to do about my..." Unable to call her my mother, I started over, "What are we going to do about Eliza?"

No one spoke for what seemed like ages. The ticking of the clock sounded like a bomb waiting to go off.

Tick tock tick tock tick tock

Minutes went by before the silence was filled with a long sigh and Gram's soft voice began, "Since you were a little girl, I have been preparing you for the path you accepted last night. Think back to the stories I told you."

Frustrated, I asked, "I just found out our family is the protectors of magic. How can you think a story about pigs, and other such nonsense, can even begin to prepare me for this? You dropped a bomb in my hand, last night, that I don't know how to handle."

"Tell me the story of the pigs." She patted my hand, and a calming warmth surrounded me.

Her comforting touch brought me back to the little girl I had once been. When I would snuggle into her arms while she told me magical tales.

"Remember, *there were three little pigs that lived with their grandmother,*" she prodded. Continuing where she left off, I closed my eyes and began to retell the story. "*When the little pigs became old enough to live on their own, their grandmother told them five things they would need to make a strong home that would keep out the wolves. 'Gather up these supplies, my little piglets – airy lavender from the east, fiery cinnamon from the south, a water lily from the west, salt of the northern earth, and a blessing to the Goddess by your door.' With the reminder, the piglets set out to build their new homes. Each with a plan.*"

Hesitating, I looked at Gram. When she nodded for me to go on, I took a deep breath and, focusing, I continued, "*The oldest pig laughed at their grandmother's advice and decided his home would be made of sturdy brick. The middle pig went searching for the items his grandmother said he would need, but he gave up after only gathering lavender and salt for the stable wood home he built. However, the youngest pig spent many days gathering all of the supplies that the grandmother had told him were necessary. It had taken him so much time to find everything that he only had time to gather nearby straw to build his home.*

"*As the last piece of hay was added, the small pig joyously danced around his new home in a circle, sweeping a small broom as he sang: 'Goddess, I ask for your guidance on this night and ask you to aid in invoking the elements that guide. I place this lavender from the east, and I call upon you, Air, to blow away my fear and those who wish me harm. I place this cinnamon from the south, and I call upon you, Fire, to burn away all fear I have and burn away those feelings that harm. I place this lily from the west, and I call upon you, Water, and ask you to wash away my fears and cleanse those who wish to harm. I place this salt from the north, and I call upon you, Earth, and ask you to ground me in goodness and strengthen me. Goddess, my request is complete. Thank you for the blessings you have bestowed upon my home.'*"

As I finished the little pig's song, I felt all of the elements dancing around me. The smells and sounds that invaded my senses overwhelmed me. I closed my eyes and took one last breath before I continued, "*When the older pigs visited their brother's home, they snorted. 'Your home will never keep out the wolves. You will become their breakfast before the sun rises.' Laughing, they danced away to their homes.*

"*When night fell, and all three little pigs were tucked into their beds in their new homes, the oldest pig heard wolves howling and banging at the front door of his brick house. The force was so strong that the wood door began to splinter. Afraid, he quickly ran out the back door of his home and straight to his middle brother.*

"*Inside the wooden home, the two brothers huddled together, afraid to sleep. Again, the howling of wolves began banging at the front door. Just as the door fell down, the brother pigs escaped out the back door and ran down the road to their little brother's straw house.*

"*Inside the straw home, the three pigs sat around the kitchen table. The howling began outside the door, and the oldest brother cried out, 'This house will not keep them out, we must leave now.' Realizing that the straw house didn't have another exit, the middle brother began to cry.*"

A soft voice beside me began to speak. "*The little pig said, 'Don't fear brothers, I have made this home in honor of the Air of the east, the Fire of the south, the Water of the west, the Earth of the north, and with a request of the blessing of the Goddess. We'll be safe.' As he spoke these words, the howling of wolves began to softly fade away.*"

In unison, the little voice beside me, and I finished the story, "*And in the end, everything was all right because the little pig listened to his grandmother.*"

Laughing, I pulled my sister into a hug. "How long have you been eavesdropping, Meg?"

Meg pulled away and gave me a stern look. "You can't blame me. You keep calling all of my friends down here. You interrupted our tea party. If you're through telling stories, we can go play again." With that, she turned on her heel and stomped away in a huff.

"I'll leave you both to talk. I want to see what this party is all about." Cole winked at us and followed after my little sister.

I stood up and began to follow her, but a hand clamped on my shoulder. "Let her go back to her friends. I can answer all of your questions."

"No, Mae we can handle this. We'll —" a familiar woman's voice called from behind me.

An intense feeling overwhelmed me. My vision blurred. As everything seemed to spin around me, small voices were talking, but the words spoken made no sense.

Suddenly, the world went black as I collapsed to the ground.

CHAPTER
TEN

"Just give her time to adjust. We've given her a lot to take in," I heard Gram say.

I tried to sit up to see who was talking, but my body was just too weak. Fighting against the exhaustion I felt, I pushed myself up onto my elbows. As I began to give up my efforts, strong hands gripped my shoulders and helped me to sit up the rest of the way.

"Take it easy, you have been through a lot," said the soft voice of my grandmother.

When my eyes focused, they locked with the Air Elemental, they called Breeze, and, instantly, my memories rushed back. I was pummeled with years of contained images and sounds. Like a pitcher being filled with liquid, I absorbed an overwhelming number of memories.

As the barrage of information slowed, I could see everyone around me. I was surrounded by the dolls from my childhood. Bay, with her silly giggles and her plans for adventures. Daisy, who had listened patiently to the secrets and dreams I shared with her. Breeze, the one that always had the answers to my worries and fears. And now, Blaze, who had been my strength and comforted. She had a dragon-like spirit that scared off any *creatures* in the night.

"I don't understand. How can this be? These are just my dolls. What magic are you using, Gram, and why?" I asked, still fighting the clouds of confusion.

"You are correct, Mara. You do have a toy version of each of them. Not soon after Meg was born, you became more vocal about the elements. The more you spoke of the magic around you, the more scared I became. Honestly, I was growing suspicious of your mother and her commitments. To protect you, I made an elixir that would hold your memory of the magic until it was safe."

Gram knelt down next to me. "We agreed it would be best," she said.

Each elemental nodded, confirming her story.

"Why didn't you give me my memory back when she left? Why wait until now? Why wait until it was too late for me to learn anything?" A strong feeling of hopelessness consumed me.

"Mara," Blaze spoke, "you already know everything that you need to. It is inside you, as it always has been. We have been with you the whole time. You just didn't realize that we were here."

I sat silently, embracing my memories. I had no words to tell them how I felt about the secrets that were freed. Small things that I had always felt began to make more sense. An image of my mother, brushing my hair while she asked me questions about the time I spent talking to myself, returned. Even then, I knew I wasn't supposed to tell her, but I didn't know why.

I wanted to scream, to strike out at everything in front of me. Still, no matter how strong the urge to fight which boiled inside me, I was equally consumed with immense sadness and defeat. Tears streamed down my face, and I did the first thing that made sense – I fell sobbing into my grandmother's arms. I needed her above all.

Calmly speaking as she stroked my hair, Gram said, "Let it out, my love."

In the warmth of her arms, I cried. Every bit of emotion I had been holding back for so long came rushing out. Minutes went by before the sobs escaping my body began to slow. I was left with a fantastic sense of understanding. The peace I was feeling was not only from the love of my grandmother but from the elemental magic swirling around me and pulsing through my veins.

Composed, I stood up from the floor and offered my hand to my grandmother. "I know why you did it, Gram. You had no choice. I understand what the promise we both made means."

With a look of relief, she smiled and kissed my cheek. "I hoped you would understand. Now, we need to make plans to fulfill our promise." Gram immediately began to gather bottles and bags. "Cole, can you carry this box to the kitchen?" she asked, and then handed him her supplies.

Turning towards me, my grandmother put her lavender journal into my hands. "I have been writing everything you need to know down since you were a small girl."

Slowly leafing through the book, I could see her wavy handwriting along with small drawings and diagrams. I stopped on a page that said *Memory Potion*. It read:

<u>Memory Potion</u>

- Rainwater collected on the eve of a full moon
- Two cinnamon sticks soaked in vanilla bean oil for at least six days
- Crushed lavender leaves
- Pinch of sea salt
- Combine all ingredients at sunrise and place half into a small vial. Upon consumption of the potion, refill the bottle with the remaining liquid and keep in a safe place.

!! Warning !!
This spell will not erase – only contain – the memories.
Memories can be returned only with the remaining potion if the herb of memory is added.

"This is the spell you used, right? Do you have any more of the potion left?" I questioned.

Bay danced around on the table, spinning her long blue ponytail. "She has the ingredients to make more. Now, get your nose out of the book. You have much to remember."

"Ignore her." Blaze glared at the Water elemental. "She is easily excited." Taking the book from me, she handed it to Gram and said, "Come with us."

"Why not go to your favorite picnic spot? Let's stay close, today," Gram suggested.

Bay spun around excitedly. "I love picnics...and dancing...and tea with cookies...and..."

"Stop, we don't have time for games," interrupted the commanding voice of Breeze. "We'll have time for fun later. Today, we need to help her not only recall but also *understand* all of her memories."

A soft whisper in my ear said, "Don't worry about them. My sisters are just anxious. We missed spending time with you."

Looking at the source of the voice, I saw the calming green eyes of an old friend. "Thank you, Daisy," I whispered back. "I have missed you, too."

In all the confusion, I had completely forgotten about Cole. Looking around, I found him sitting in the living room. I smiled at him, and he winked at me.

"Cole will be fine. I have a list of things for him to do. After all, we still need to finish getting ready for tomorrow's Lunar Festival." Gram handed me a small, white picnic basket.

My grandmother was a superwoman. After calming my meltdown, she was able to whip up a snack in the blink of an eye. *How did she do this without being noticed*? I wondered.

"Just a little treat. Enjoy your time with elementals," she whispered and kissed me on the cheek.

"Thank you." I accepted the basket. "Can we spend some time together when I return?"

"Later. Go enjoy the afternoon," Gram said.

I wanted to tell her I needed more answers...that I had so many questions, but I held back my words. In my heart, I knew she had done the right thing despite the doubt taunting me. An endless battle raged inside me. I had to decide whether to listen to my heart or to let my mind control me.

CHAPTER
ELEVEN

I followed Blaze into the backyard. We took the same path that Young Marina had taken in my memory. Flowers and fruit colored the lush trees along our route. This time, there were no sounds coming from my grandfather's workshop. The silence was deafening.

When we approached the largest green tree, images of tea parties flashed in my mind. My time with the elementals had been filled with laughter and magic. A familiar sensation washed over me as I set the picnic basket down and pulled out the soft yellow blanket. Daisy was quick to help me spread it out.

Bay flopped down, and asked, "What did she pack us to eat? I'm starving from all of the work I've done, today."

Blaze harrumphed at her.

I pulled the treats out one-by-one. I laid out fresh cheeses, a variety of cubed bread, and a container that held deep red slices of tomatoes sprinkled with basil, sea salt, and olive oil. The last items I found inside the basket were a bottle of white grape juice and a small tin that I knew held tea biscuits.

Bay clapped. "She didn't forget what I liked!"

We munched on our food, savoring the flavors, and Breeze began to speak. "When your great-grandmother was a child, the Goddess decided to reward her for her help in saving the magic. My sisters and I were sent to guide the ancestors of Genevieve Silver as they learned how to use the elemental magic. With Mae, we found our time here was an easy job of magical play. By the time your mother was born, we realized, to keep your family safe, we needed to be silent observers. The four of us never appeared to Eliza in our fae form. Instead, we kept our contact to the basic elements that we represent. When she turned fourteen, we knew our reservations had been correct."

"This isn't the time," Blaze scolded. The gold of her eyes grew dark, and the red streaks of her hair began to burn with fire. "We'll have plenty of chances to discuss the path of Eliza, but today, we've got a small amount of time to help Mara connect again."

Blowing a burst of wind to put out the flames Blaze was emitting, Breeze agreed, "No need to become upset. You're right. The story can keep for another day."

Blaze turned to me, staring hard and said, "Now, show us what you have inside you."

"What do you mean?" I asked, not hiding my frustration. "I have nothing, but confusion and jumbled memories inside of me."

Without notice, Blaze threw a ball of fire in front of me onto the picnic cloth. The small ball erupted and began to burn the yellow fabric. I stared at the fire, unsure what to do. In response to my inaction, I felt a small gust of wind blow past me towards the now growing fire. The flames danced and flicked at the wind as if inviting a new friend to the party.

Closing my eyes, I held my hands out and lowered them over the fire. "Wind of Breeze, Fire of Blaze, Water of Bay, and Stone of Daisy, I call upon you to contain these flames." Opening my eyes, I noticed it began to flick at me, but my words had done nothing. The fire grew stronger.

Taking a deep breath, this time, I held out my hands and placed them closer to the fire. "Winds of Air, flames of Fire, drops of Water, and salt of Earth, I command you to come to me."

Plunging my hands into the fiery flames, I felt the red-hot heat lick my fingers, but it wasn't hurting me. Instead, it rushed towards me like hot lava flowing down a mountain. In the palm of my hand, it formed into a ball.

Clasping both hands together, I felt the power of fire rush inside my veins. As the warmth ran through me, I opened my now empty hands. Only small, white tendrils of smoke remained.

No sooner had I recovered from the fire than the earth under me began to shake, and the ground split open. The blanket began to sink into the crevice. Once again, I recited the command.

The earth stopped shaking, but now, there was a ball of mud. It grew larger as it rolled at me. I wrapped my fingers around the cold, soft soil, and shivered as it ran throughout my body like an army of worms.

Feeling a mist on the back of my arms, I turned to face what I expected to be a sphere of water. Instead, I stared at a ten-foot wave that was being swayed by a strong wind. I was not prepared for such a sight and my hesitation cost me the precious moments I needed to stop it.

The swell crashed down on me and pulled me into the center of it. As I was spun and twisted through the watery cage, I could not speak for fear of drowning. Realizing how the other elements had responded, I held out my hands and willed the water to consume me.

After several long seconds, the waves slowed. They gently rocked me down to the ground, cradling me as if I was a small baby. As it set me down, small droplets danced around me, and a warm breeze dried me off.

Holding my hands out again in front of me, I strongly spoke, "Winds of Air, flames of Fire, drops of Water, and salt of Earth, I command you to come to me."

The water and the air around me pressed against my palms before they burst inside me. I gasped at the contrast of ice and warmth that ran through my body. As white smoke emitted from both my hands, I knew I had passed the test.

We spent the rest of the time talking about the lessons they had taught me as a child. My first priority was to always be safe and to use my magic carefully. Though we spoke for a few hours, the conversation still felt rushed. It was as if they were trying to teach me seventeen years of knowledge in one afternoon.

When Daisy settled on my lap with a sad expression on her face, I knew what was coming.

"I won't see you again, will I?" I questioned, hoping I was wrong.

With a soft smile, she answered, "Not for a while, but we are always with you. We'll be in the air you breathe, the water you drink, the warmth of the fire, and the ground beneath you. We've always been here to remind you what you already have inside." She kissed me on the cheek and said, "You know what the next step is, Mara. Follow your heart. The Goddess has blessed you."

"Enough of this sentimentality, Daisy," Blaze chided. "She needs to be strong now."

"And to use her intuition," said Breeze.

"Oh, and to never forget her joy," Bay added.

"More than just *being* strong, she has to know she *is* strong," Daisy said.

"Most importantly," a divine voice whispered, "she needs to remember she is loved."

The elements clasped hands and spun until they formed white streams of smoke. As if saying farewell, they twirled around me one last time.

"I won't forget my promise," I whispered as they faded away.

CHAPTER
TWELVE

I sat out under the tree, thinking, unaware of the time. The rustle of leaves from behind stirred me from my contemplations. The sun was beginning to set, which shocked me when I realized how long I'd been alone.

The scent of lavender and vanilla enveloped me as Gram sat down next to me. Without a word, she took my hand in hers. We sat in silence as the sky changed from orange and pink to a star-filled black.

"It's time to come inside, love. Cole and Meg are waiting for you."

"I'm not ready for this, Gram," my voice cracked. "I can't be who they think I am...who you think I am."

"It isn't who we think you are that matters. It is who you *are*." Gram stood and held out her hand to help me up. "We have a big day tomorrow. Let's get dinner and make plans."

I took her hand, and we walked back to the house. Stopping, I grasp on her tightened. "Wait," I said. "I think we need to make more of that memory potion, tomorrow. If something happens, I want to be able to keep my promise to protect the magic."

"See, my girl, it is what is inside you already. Tomorrow morning, we'll make more, in case it is needed." She smiled at me before she gently tugged my hand. "Now, let's go eat."

When we arrived home, we found Cole and Meg playing a card game at the kitchen table.

"Cos," Meg cried out, "you cheat. You can't play that card!" Meg threw her cards onto the discard pile, and shouted, "I win! You cheated!"

"Winning isn't cheating," Cole corrected. "You're becoming a horrible poor sport."

Gram interrupted their argument. "Let's clear the table. The lasagna is ready, and the garlic toast is going to be dried out if we wait much longer."

Never wanting to miss a meal, Cole hopped up and went for the plates. "Come on, Meg, we'll play again after dinner."

Meg followed after him begrudgingly. "Why would I want to play with a cheater?"

"Because you know you love me." Cole grinned and tousled her hair.

Dinner was exactly what we all needed. The warm vegetable lasagna oozed with cheese while the garlic bread was crispy and buttery. Eating and laughing, Gram went over her mental checklist of the things we needed to finish in the morning.

With the meal finished, the dishes cleaned up, and everything put away, we settled in the living room. Meg and Gram snuggled on the overstuffed purple love seat. Cole and I chose to sit close together on the red couch.

"Everything is ready to go." Gram smoothed Meg's hair. "In the morning, we can load up the truck and head out about nine. I want everyone to bed early." Eyeing me, she repeated, "*Everyone.*"

Yawning, I agreed, "I'm exhausted already. I think I'm going to make it an early night after I take a warm bath." Resting my head on Cole's shoulder, I asked, "You won't be too mad if I head off now, will you?"

Glancing towards my grandmother and sister, who looked like they would nod off at any moment, he chuckled. "You all have had a long day. We should all hit the hay."

Agreeing, Gram stood up and kissed us both on the head. "Come on, little one," she said, tugging gently on Meg's arm. "You will be the star of the stage tomorrow."

"Can I sleep with you tonight, Gram?" Meg asked, "Mara will toss and turn, keeping me up all night."

"Of course, you can. I would miss your cold feet if you didn't." Gram laughed as she led my little sister off to bed. However, she stopped before they reached the kitchen, she gave us a stern look. "Off to bed soon, little ones."

Cole saluted. "Yes, ma'am."

"We will, Gram," I promised. "Sweet dreams."

When we were alone, Cole held out my arm to examine the healing wound. It was now a red line, not the deep cut of yesterday. "I should have known magic was infused in Gram's healing tricks. I guess you will learn her secrets, too." Kissing the inside of my wrist, he said, "Go take your bath. I'm going to get ready for bed myself."

I gave Cole one last kiss and reluctantly said, "Goodnight. I'll see you in the morning."

It seemed like days since I had been in my room when, in reality, it had only been a few hours. I looked at my dolls on the shelf. Seeing the replicas of my living guardians, I felt a warm comfort.

I turned on the water to fill the large tub and reached for Gram's special bubble bath. Vanilla and lavender filled my senses as I opened the container. I dumped in a generous amount of the white powder and swirled my hands through the warm liquid.

Stripping off my clothes, I slipped under the water, allowing the stress of the day to float away. I slowly ran my hand back and forth, gently splashing the fragrant fluid around me. I let the memories of my time with my secret friends fill my mind.

A soft knock on the door interrupted my ruminations. "Are you ok in there? You have been in there a long time," Cole called.

"I'll be out in a minute," I answered quickly.

How long had I been in here? I wondered. My prune-like fingers confirmed I had extended my soak longer than planned. I yanked the chain of the tub and watched the water flow down the drain.

Drying myself off with a fluffy pink towel, I concerned whether or not I really had the magic inside me. I lifted my right hand above me, swirled my pointer finger, and commanded, "Air, come to me."

A gust of warm air hovered above. The breeze obeyed my movements. Delighted by the elemental magic's response, I directed the air to contain me. As I moved it up and down, the moisture on my skin slowly evaporated. Circling my head, I felt my hair lift and drop as the air fell between each strand.

"Thank you, Air," I whispered.

No longer wet, I pulled my nightgown over my body. Twisting my hair into a long braid, I couldn't believe how soft and dry it felt. Before I left the bathroom, I slipped into my robe.

I found Cole waiting for me on my bed. He was dressed in flannel pajama bottoms with a tight white T-shirt. *Will my heart stop skipping like this after we were married?* I wondered, drinking in the sight of him. *I hope not.*

"I just wanted to say goodnight. I was starting to worry about you," he said. "You were in there almost an hour."

"Sorry, I was lost in my thoughts. Hey, didn't we already say our goodnights?" I teased. Then, I sat down next to him and kissed him on the cheek.

"We did, but I wanted to make sure you were ok. I can't believe everything that happened today. It seems so surreal." Cole hugged me. "We have a big day tomorrow. You should get some sleep."

When he let go of me, I wrapped my arms around his neck, kissing him long and passionately. "Can you sleep up here with me? I don't want to be alone," I murmured in his ear.

"I don't think Gram would be a fan of that, Mara." Cole slipped out of my arms.

"I meant you would sleep in Meg's bed. Gram shouldn't have a problem with that arrangement." I smirked. "I just don't want to be alone."

"She shouldn't have a problem with that arrangement," Cole agreed.

I took my robe off and slipped under the covers. Cole tucked my blankets in around me before he kissed me tenderly. "You should be warm enough now. I love you, future Mrs. Sands."

Once he had climbed through Meg's mound of stuffed toys and snuggled under her blankets, I called over to him, "Sleep sweet, future Mr. Stone."

Drifting off to sleep, I heard his soft laugh as he called back, "We'll need to discuss that later."

CHAPTER
THIRTEEN

I was woken by the gentle shake of my grandmother. "What time is it?" I asked, wiping the sleep from my eyes.

"Shh, don't wake Cole." Gram motioned at my sleeping boyfriend. I waited for her to say something about our sleeping arrangement, but instead, she handed me a long red sweater and motioned for me to follow her. "We need to be quick if we want to make the memory potions. It will be sunrise soon."

The kitchen was warm, and the smell of fresh bread and muffins filled the air. Gram had clearly been up for hours, baking. Today was the day of the Lunar Festival.

"Gram, this can wait," I said, feeling guilty. My grandmother had so much to do already. She shouldn't have to worry about this. "Let's just do this tomorrow. One more day won't change anything."

"Shush, we don't have time for you to overthink the situation. I have everything gathered." She patted a white wicker basket. "Bread is baked and everything else is loaded in the truck. Let's go."

My grandmother led me through the backyard. We walked past the large tree, where my magical picnics had been held, to the edge of the property, and into Starten Forest. Suddenly feeling scared, I grabbed Gram's hand and held it tightly.

"It's ok, love," she comforted. "Just a little way further. You're safe."

The dark green trees of our backyard ended and the crimson timber of the eastern Starten Forest began. The woods had twisted and gnarled with long, black limbs. Black flower petals and red leaves blossomed along the darkened branches. The ground was covered with the color of blood where the red leaves of summer had been shed.

An uncomfortable feeling washed over me. Something inside me warned we were being watched.

We continued to walk until we reached an open area. In the middle of the clearing, a large, gray stone table stood waist high. In the center were the words *Cosain an draíocht,* surrounded by inscriptions of ruby-colored names.

As I moved forward to inspect it, I recognized the same names that were on my grandmother's chest. When I came to Mae Silver, I stopped for a moment and traced it with my finger. The elegant shapes of the glittery red letters were scrawled in her handwriting. She had written her name here.

"Hold out your hand, Mara," Gram commanded.

Hesitating for only a second, I extended my hand. When I did, Gram pulled it into hers. In her other hand, she held up a silver dagger that twinkled with emerald-colored gems on the hilt. My eyes widened when I saw it.

With a quick movement, she sliced the tip of my finger with the blade. Gasping, I pulled my hand away and tried to stop the flow of blood. However, she grabbed my hand back and held it tightly.

"Sign your name in the stone," she calmly said. "It will heal the pain."

Listening to her words, I carefully began to sign my name with my bloody fingertip. The stone quickly absorbed my blood as a warm sensation traveled up my arm and into my neck. My autograph changed to a smooth, red-colored stone while a feeling of peace settled over me. The hesitation and doubt I had been carrying drifted away.

"You feel it don't you?" Gram asked.

Looking from my finger to my bloody signature, I felt like I was just in another one of my dreams. Wordlessly, I met my grandmothers stare with wonderment.

"The pure magic we protect has been unleashed in you. You should no longer feel incomplete. It is time for you to embrace your destiny. Trust what you feel."

Gram lined the table with different colored glass bottles, labeled in her elegant handwriting. Then, she handed me a small bowl and a grinding stick. "Place the mortar on the table. We'll do this together."

With the two bowls, side-by-side, she handed me a purple bottle, labeled *Lavender*.

"Open this bottle and begin grinding the leaves," Gram directed.

"How much do I use?" I suddenly felt unsure of myself.

"You know what to do. Just listen to your heart."

With a deep breath, I shook some of the lavender into the bowl and began to grind it. The air around me grew warm and the crushed purple leaves began to swirl around the bowl. Adding more, I heard a small hum.

The sound was my grandmother. She hummed a soft song as she ground the herbs in her bowl. Glancing over, I saw the lavender in her mortar swirling. It emitted a small smoke as she crushed it with her pestle.

"What am I doing wrong? Should I be singing, too?"

Gram held the bottle back out to me, "If your heart sings, sing. If you feel the urge to dance, dance. Just focus and listen to the magic around us."

I took the bottle of lavender from her, again. Warm magic radiated from her body and ran over my skin. It felt like someone was patting my hand.

Closing my eyes and slowly breathing, I began to focus on everything around me. The gentle swirl of my herbs softly sang to me, and I felt the need to twirl around. Embracing the feeling, I danced as I added more purple petals to the mortar. As if in response to my energy, the bowl began to emit long waves of iridescent tendrils. They lifted the crushed herbs and spun them.

I looked over at Gram. She was watching me with an approving smile. Then, my grandmother handed me a clear bottle that contained cinnamon sticks soaking in oil.

"Two sticks for this spell," Gram said. "That is, unless you feel different."

I took the cork off the bottle and the strong smell of vanilla and cinnamon engulfed me. I pulled one stick out, and something instinctively told me to break it in half. As it snapped, I heard *YES* crackle on the wind. Recorking the bottle, I gave it back to Gram, who smiled proudly.

Simultaneously, we crushed the cinnamon and lavender together until red tendrils formed. I picked up the blue bottle, labeled *Rainwater*. I let three drops slowly fall from it. The red puffs rose to meet them. As they connected, they turned into a long, beaded chain of water droplets.

"As the sun begins to rise, center your heart on this potion. Let your heart speak of the good that will be done with it. Don't dwell on what will be taken away. Instead, rejoice in what will be protected. Does it feel finished to you?" Gram asked.

I stared into the swirling bowl and felt the magic of Blaze, Breeze, and Bay. I listened longer and instantly knew what it lacked. "We are missing Earth. The magic of Daisy isn't here."

Gram laughed, and then handed me a brown bottle, labeled *Sea Salt*. "We will add a pinch as the sun rises to complete our potion."

I poured a small amount into my palm and rubbed the coarse salt between my fingers. Sparks of power shot through my hands. The magic inside and around me was intoxicating. Sharing this moment with my grandmother made it even more important.

The dark sky was lightening, and the soft orange and pink hues of the morning sky were peaking. When the sun began to rise, we added the salt, making our bowls erupt with silver, red, blue, and green vapors. A song of joy came out of them as the smoke changed into a bright, violet light.

"The Goddess?" I asked under my breath.

"Yes, isn't she wonderful," Gram said, her eyes brimming with tears of joy.

We hugged and danced around the table, soaking in the magic around us.

Squeezing me tightly, she whispered in my ear, "The power inside you is strong and pure. Just trust yourself."

As the smoke of the potion stilled and disappeared into the morning sky, we filled four small vials with the purple liquid.

"This is enough to be used on two people. After a vial is consumed, you must fill it again, but add a pinch of crushed rosemary. This is, then, put away in a safe place for when, or if, the memory should be returned."

Pausing, Gram looked as if she were deciding whether to continue or not. Then, she spoke softer, "If the memories should never be returned, the second vial shouldn't have rosemary. Instead, two pinches of dried devil's claw ought to be used. This will not harm the person who drinks it, but it will completely erase their memory and magic."

After we gathered everything, Gram held her hands to the sky and said, "Your blessings fill our hearts, and we thank you for the gifts. Bright blessings."

"Bright blessings," I repeated as we clasped hands and headed back to our home.

CHAPTER
FOURTEEN

When we returned home, Cole and Meg were dressed and waiting in the kitchen. Cole had scrambled some egg whites with fresh parmesan, asparagus, and chives for us.

"A man that cooks," Gram said. "Chester would burn water if I let near my stove."

Cole scored even more *fantastic boyfriend* points when he offered to clean up while we got ready.

"Mara, it's time to go," Gram called up to me. "We're leaving with or without you."

I had spent more time than usual getting ready. The Lunar Festival was my favorite time of year. With one last look at my dress, I felt confident in my choice. The knee-length red summer dress and my black cowboy boots would be comfortable enough for work and still dance in later if the mood struck. I had styled my long, black hair with loose curls and pulled the sides up and out of my face.

I joined my family, who was already seated inside our silver pick-up. The bed of the truck was loaded with the boxes full of items we would be selling. As I slid in next to Cole, Meg began grumbling about being squished. Cole picked her up and put her on his lap, silencing her complaints.

"Let's not be cranky, today. It's an important time for our town to join together and celebrate," Cole whispered. "Besides, it will be even more special, tonight, since you'll be in your first Lunar Dance."

Meg's frown was replaced with a bright smile. She excitedly began to chat about the upcoming dance she would perform.

By the time we arrived on Main Street, the wooden trade stands had been set up at the end of the street, and the stage was ready for the night's performances. We made our way to Gram's booth. While most of the shops were simple wood stands with a tabletop to present their goods, Gramp had designed a store for Gram, making it stand out.

Soft music welcomed visitors to my grandmother's shop. Once they entered, they were awed by the beautiful details, such as ivy vines and small flowers ornately carved into the chestnut wood. When they were finally ready to shop, there was a variety of homemade items to buy. There were shelves filled with bottles of tonics and elixirs, deep bins for the loaves of bread and pastries, and a rack for dried herbs. It always felt magical to me when I was a child. Unloading Gram's merchandise, I felt the same feeling return.

Once everything was set up, Meg said, "I have a present for you, Mara."

I carefully opened the pink tissue paper that she had used to wrap the gift. Inside, I found a yellow note with words written in Meg's child-like handwriting:

Sister for Sale – Beware
Her screams at night may give you fright.

Taking her mock price tag from me by the attached purple ribbon, she said, "Now, put this on so we can see if we have any takers."

I picked her up and tickled her. We laughed until she pleaded for me to stop.

"Now, what will you do if there are takers for your sale?" I asked.

"Hmm, we may need to rethink this," she replied thoughtfully. After a moment of consideration, she added, "We won't sell you – this time."

Laughing, I picked her up again and spun her around. Meg squealed in delight.

"I see you girls are already up to mischief," Cole said as he joined us. "It looks like Meg has put you up for sale." Turning towards my little sister, he asked earnestly, "Will you trade me Mara for two scoops of ice cream?"

"Make it three, and you have a deal!" Meg exclaimed.

"Wait," I said. "You just said that you weren't going to sell me!"

"Right, but he made a really good offer."

I couldn't help laughing as I watched Cole lead my sister towards the ice cream stand.

The rest of the morning was not only busy with customers but with attempts to keep Meg amused. By two o'clock, the crowds had died down, and most people had gone home to rest before the evening's events. We snacked on the picnic lunch Gram had brought and watched Meg practice her dance to pass the time.

Looking around the stand, I smiled. We had already sold out of many items. Before the night was over, we would have little to take home.

As the sun began to set, some of the shops started to close in anticipation of the night's activities. We boxed up the small amount we hadn't sold. While Cole loaded the truck, Gram and I prepared Meg for her performance.

When we removed the braids from Meg's hair, soft curls were left. Gram piled them high on top of my sister's head and twisted a band of baby pink roses across her head. Her costume was a long-sleeved, blue velvet dress with layers of white ruffles puffing out of the short skirt. Her knee-high socks sparkled with a soft, silvery glitter.

As I laced up her black dance shoes, she whispered to me, "What if I forget my steps, Mar? I'm so scared I won't remember and embarrass myself."

Taking her face in my hands, I whispered back, "When I went on stage for my first dance, I was scared, too. But Gram said something to me, which helped. She told me the moon was watching with an open heart and a smile. The moon would feel the love I sent her. And, you know what happened? I danced for the moon. If I missed any steps, I didn't notice. So, dance for the moon, Meg, just dance for the moon."

Wrapping her arms around me, I held her for a long time. My little sister was growing up before my eyes. All I wanted to do was to hold onto her and keep her safe.

The warm feeling I had didn't last as a sudden cold surrounded me. I turned to see where it was coming from. From the look on Gram's face, I could tell the source – a woman standing in front of her – was not a friend.

"Mae, it has been such a long time. What a nice surprise to see you still running your little stand." The woman scanned her icy eyes around our store. She wrinkled her nose, clearly unimpressed.

"You know, as well as I do, Blanche, that this isn't a surprise. I'm sure, if you are here, that you are up to no good," Gram coldly responded to her. "Why don't you crawl back up the mountain you came from?"

Blanche was tall with short silver hair that was smartly styled, and she wore dark eye makeup with deep red lipstick. She appeared to be the same age as Gram but looked as if she had never done a day's work in her life. Her black dress was long and tight with a deep slit up the right thigh. On most women her age, a dress like that would seem ridiculous. However, despite the dress having obviously been made for a much younger woman, she looked surprisingly stunning in it.

"I see time has not made you any smarter, Mae. I just came to see the lunar festivities. I was told one of my new granddaughters would be performing her first Lunar Dance. Since the girls will soon be coming to live with us, I thought it would be nice for me to show my support," she said with a smile on her face that didn't entirely hide the contempt she obviously felt towards us.

"You will have nothing to do with those girls," Gram spat back at Blanche. Small flames of fire began to spark from her hands. "I suggest you leave and take your machinations elsewhere."

Looking at my grandmother with pity in her eyes, Blanche twirled the diamond ring on her finger and said, "You never seem to learn that you cannot insult my family and get away with it. What a joy it will be to take away another of yours."

Turning on her heels, she called back to us, "Goodbye, girls. I'll see you soon."

Confused by the conversation, Meg held me tighter. "What was that lady talking about?"

"Never mind her," I said as I tried to pull Meg's attention from the retreating woman. "Just another mountain crazy coming to stir up trouble. Full moons can do that, remember? Stay here while I get some lipstick from my bag. You need a little color for the stage."

Grabbing my bag, I whispered to Gram, "Bring Meg the potion. I'm going to finish getting her ready. Would it be safe to assume that woman is Cedric Drygen's mother?"

Nodding, Gram sat down on the small stool and sighed. "I'll be over in a minute. I just need to compose myself."

I kissed Gram on the head before I left her to her thoughts. Stopping, I looked back at her and whispered, "Goddess, please protect my family."

With the final touches, my little sister looked even more beautiful than usual.

A whistle came from the entryway. "Who is this little angel before me, and what has she done with Meg? Stand up and give me a twirl," Cole said.

Twirling around, she beamed at his praise.

"Nice, nice, but something is wrong. I must say that there is one thing missing."

The smile on her face quickly turned into a worried frown. Hesitantly, she asked, "What? What's missing?"

Walking around her, as if scrutinizing her, Cole began, "Well, the outfit is perfect. Yes, very nice. Your hair is lovely – thanks to the fine talents of Gram. Yes, and Mara has done a wonderful job on your makeup, but something is just, well..." he stopped, and looked as if he was trying to think of the right word. "Something is just off."

"What!" Meg exclaimed. "What is wrong?"

Cole held out his hand, revealing a small velvet box. "Go on, open it." He winked at me.

Meg gasped as she saw her gift. Nestled inside the white satin of the box was a silver chain that held a silver heart pendant. The center of the necklace held a moon made from a blue stone.

"It is beautiful," she said softly as she stared at it.

"Well, let's see how it looks on you." Cole put the necklace on her. "Now, I can say you are the prettiest dancer at the festival."

"Isn't it beautiful, Gram?" Meg asked our grandmother as she joined us. "Cole gave it to me."

"What a nice gift." Gram smiled. "I have another present for you." She opened her hand and sitting on the palm was an even tinier version of Bay.

The petite elemental sat with a big smile on her face.

"Bay!" Meg exclaimed. "I thought you were going away."

"Now, how could I miss your first dance? I taught you everything you know." Bay giggled. "And, most importantly, I had to be here for your first drink of moon water."

Holding the small vial that I had prepared that morning, Bay held it out for Meg to take. "Drink this and let me know what you think."

"Wait," I interrupted, taking the vial before my little sister could. "Meg, this isn't exactly moon water. It is a potion that will make you forget everything you know about the magic around us and inside you."

"Mara, why would you want me to forget about the magic?" Meg turned to Gram and held out her little hand. "Gram, do you want me to forget, too?"

"Meg, when Mara was a few years younger than you, I didn't give her the choice she's giving you. Instead, I made the decision and took the magic away from her. You'll understand better when you are older, but we are responsible for protecting this gift. Sometimes, the best way to do that is by taking away the knowledge we have of it."

Meg's eyes widened in confusion. The elementals had been her friends, and now, we were going to take them away. Anger flashed on her face for the briefest moment. Slowly, her shoulders slumped, and she bowed her head. I held my breath, unsure of what to do. When Meg lifted her chin, her eyes were brimming with tears.

Gram touched her cheek. "Mara's right. It is your choice, Meg."

"Listen to your heart, Meg," I encouraged.

"Will it be gone forever?" she asked.

"No," I said. "It will not be gone forever, and I promise you that the minute Gram and I feel it will be safe for you, we'll return all of your memories. Please, trust us."

"I trust you," Meg said.

Gram pulled us both into her arms and hugged us tightly. Releasing us, she took the vial from me and handed it to Meg. "Cosain an draíocht."

As if she understood, Meg nodded and took the top off the bottle. "Protect the magic," she replied and took a small sip. Within seconds, a big grin covered her face. "Yum," she said before drinking the rest in one big gulp.

"Come, rest for a minute. You want to save your energy for the dance."

Sleepily, Meg fell into my arms. I felt tears running down my cheeks as I held her. "I'm sorry, Meg. This is the only way I know for you to be kept safe."

Gram took my sister from me. My grandmother cradled Meg as she sang softly to her, just as she had done with me. Quietly, she told me, "We'll refill the vial later. For now, just place it in the silver pouch inside my bag. There is another potion in the red pouch."

Though she said nothing further, I knew from the look she gave me what Gram thought I should do. Taking a deep breath, I prepared myself for what would come next. "Cole, let's go for a walk."

We walked by the different stands and looked at their merchandise. Anything you could think of could be found. The different smells filled the air. Ostrich burgers, popcorn, fresh fudge, and a variety of pickled items mixed with the various perfumes and craft smells.

When we reached a quiet area away from the people, we sat down on a bench.

Cole said, "I know why we're here. Hand me the vial. I'll drink the potion, too."

I started to speak, but he stopped me. "I know too much. You don't have to explain."

As he put the drink to his lips, I instantly knew this was the wrong decision.

"Wait!" I cried, ripping the vial out of this hand. "No, you can't drink this. I need you. Maybe I'm being selfish, but I would be lying to you every day of our life together if you drink this."

"I would do anything for you." Cole took the potion back. "I'll keep it with me. If I feel that you all would be safer with me not remembering, I'll gladly drink it. Just make sure I never forget you."

Wrapping my arms around him, I whispered, "I love you, Cole."

"I'm proud of you for letting Meg make the decision on her own," he said. "I understand why the Goddess has blessed your family. You are three amazing women." Cole laughed and corrected himself, "Well, two women and a girl."

Snuggling back into his arms, I sighed. I felt so lucky to be with Cole, and no dark thoughts of doubt could even sneak into our moment of peace. Gram was right; I needed to listen to my heart.

For a while, we just sat on the bench, staring at the sky, and enjoying the moment.

We cannot stay in this moment forever, I begrudgingly thought.

As if he read my mind, Cole jumped up. "We should start back to check on Meg and Gram."

Cole and I didn't discuss the reason why we had gone on the walk anymore. I felt at ease with the decision we had made. Hand-in-hand, we walked by the shops that were still open, pointing out things we thought would make a nice wedding gift.

"Honestly, Cole." I laughed as he tried on the most outrageous top hat. The black atrocity was a model of a fifty-story building, complete with glass windows. On top of the building, hung a giant monkey with a bride slung over its shoulder. "There is no way I'm marrying you if you wear that hat," I exclaimed.

Dramatically, he put it down "For you, I'll even get rid of my dreams of wearing a monkey hat on our wedding day." With a chuckle, he pulled me into his arms and softly kissed me.

Our moment of affection was interrupted by a loud shriek. "Cole! Cole Sands! Where have you been hiding yourself?"

Cole let go of me and turned to greet the loud voice. My irritation increased as I realized the owner was Jessica Harvey.

Jessica had always had a crush on Cole and never seemed to take the hint that he was not interested in her. Hugging him, she oohed and awed over how great he looked. Pouting playfully, she complained how long it had been since they'd last seen one another.

Clearing my throat, I brought Jessica's attention off Cole and onto me.

Her eyes look me up and down. With a perturbed sigh, she said, "Hi, Marina."

Dismissing me, she focused back on Cole as she twisted her long, blonde hair coyly around her finger. "You must tell me everything you've been up to since we last saw each other, Cole?"

Interrupting her desperate pleas for attention, I grabbed Cole's hand. "We have such great news, Jessica. I'm sure you will be so very happy for us." Continuing to use my overexcited voice, I pulled Cole close to me. "Cole and I are getting married. Won't it be wonderful?"

I grasped her hand. "I have the best idea. You could be in the wedding. Why you could be a bridesmaid? No, wait – I have it!" Turning to Cole, I said, "Darling, wouldn't she make the best maid of honor?"

Focusing my attention back on Jessica, I said, "It will be so much fun. You can help me plan everything, down to the tiniest detail. What do you think of pearl earrings? Too much? I agree. I think simple is better."

I continued with my ramblings about our sensational wedding until Jessica politely excused herself, claiming she had to meet some people. As the girl scurried off, I called after her, "Goodbye, Jessica. I'll be in touch soon. We have so much to discuss."

Jessica stormed away from us and didn't look back.

Laughing, Cole asked, "My, my, did I detect a hint of jealousy?" He pulled me back into his arms and held me tightly. "No need for that. You're the only girl for me. Except, I did appreciate her acknowledging how fantastic I look."

"Oh, Cole, you are just so dreamy," I said in a mock Jessica tone. I began to twirl my hair around my finger. "I am overcome by your manliness."

"Not only dreamy but manly? How kind of you to notice." Cole flexed his biceps before scooping me into his arms. "I would love to stay here talking about how great I am for the rest of the evening, but we'd better head back. Meg will be performing soon."

Cole set me down. Then, with one final kiss, we began our fast-paced walk back to Gram and Meg.

Back at the stand, Meg was practicing her dance and Gram was sipping tea.

"Did you have a nice nap, Meg? Are you ready to dance for the moon?" I asked.

Meg gave me the thumbs-up and then continued concentrating.

Kissing Gram on the cheek, I whispered, "He didn't drink it. It didn't feel right."

She squeezed my hand. I knew this was her way of telling me she understood.

"Ok, I'm ready to dance. Mrs. Ward brought us some of her famous *Stupid Chicken Soup*. There is even some left for you and Cole," Meg said cheerily.

Nothing was more comforting than Mrs. Ward's recipe. The barbecue sauce-flavored broth with pieces of chicken, pureed potatoes, red peppers, garlic, and fresh basil made the most unique tasting concoction.

Cole and I enjoyed a bowl of soup while Meg went over the upcoming events of the evening. Gram pretended to be cleaning the shop, but I could tell she was deep in thought.

As she arranged the small amount of inventory left, I overheard my grandmother softly whisper, "Goddess, please give us the strength we need to face these imminently dark days."

CHAPTER
FIFTEEN

Gram brought Meg to wait at the stage with the rest of the young dancers. A sea of girls in silver and blue dresses with bouncy curls greeted my sister. All of them were anxious for the event to begin.

Cole and I found seats several rows from the stage. We grew impatient as the time seemed to pass slower as our excitement increased before Meg's performance. Once the girls were brought up onto the stage, Gram joined us. We clapped happily, knowing the show would finally start.

As the lights flashed and the music began, the dancers came out in groups of five. When Meg's group joined the stage, Cole cheered loudly. Looking down at us, Meg gave us an exaggerated wink.

My sister's performance was vibrant. She jumped, twirled, and danced as if she had been in the spotlight her entire life. Gram looked on with a bright smile. I squeezed her hand, and she grasped mine tighter. I could see how proud she was of Meg.

As the dance ended, a bright splash of purple and silver twirled onto the stage and leaped at heights that astonished the crowd. My mind drifted back to my dance classes. The words my teacher would call out to us rang in my ear.

"Posture, ladies, posture!" the voice from my past demanded. "Sauté, Sauté, Chassé – No! No! No! Back to the barre! We must practice the basics again!"

With a seemingly endless pirouette, my old dance instructor, Ms. Lilianna, commanded the stage. When her twirling stopped, she bellowed, "Thank you, thank you! Tonight, we celebrate another year of family, friendship, and community. My little dancers have, once again, delighted me, and I hope you!"

The audience clapped and cheered in agreement.

"Each year, after the night's performance, one student is selected to perform the last dance."

Behind her, the young dancers returned to the stage in a choreographed soft tap. The girls surrounded their teacher in a half-circle. With anticipation, they waited to see if their name would be called.

"Now, to perform the solo Dance of the Moon, I ask Meg Stone to join me." Ms. Lilianna held her hand out towards my little sister.

Meg's face widened in surprise. Hesitantly, she took her teacher's hand and was led towards the bright blue spotlight in the center of the stage. The other dancers moved in a line to the back of the stage as the soft music began.

Meg extended her arms to the sky before she began her dance. Her expressive performance made me feel like she was dedicating it to the moon. I looked over to Gram, who had tears glistening in her eyes. This tiny little dancer before me was so elegant and talented. Watching my sister's graceful movements, I felt so proud and awed. With a final bow, Meg's dance ended when she dramatically collapsed to the ground as if put into a slumber. The audience roared with delight.

Walking out to take her hand, the teacher praised my sister's talent. "Ladies, come join us."

The other performers took their places, with Ms. Lilianna and Meg in the middle, and began soft tapping and clapping. Dancers from each end of the line moved forward to the front of the stage, clasped their hands together, and gave a deep bow before waving and dancing out of view. When Meg and Ms. Lilianna were the only ones left, they both gave a final low bow, and then the lights went out.

The audience was now on their feet with applause and cheers.

Suddenly, the spotlights began circling the stage. In anticipation, we watched as a soft mist covered the platform, and the light stopped in the center. This was different. Ms. Lilliana must have added a new dance to the program.

A tall man appeared abruptly out of the haze, carrying one of the dancers. As he moved forward, I recognized the child in his arms – it was

Meg. She didn't look scared, but rather, thrilled. As my eyes moved to the face of the man, I gasped. His dirty blond hair was longer than it had been when I last saw him, and his rugged face was no longer clean-shaven. Instead, he wore a short beard.

Taking my hand, Gram whispered with disbelief, "This can't be. He drowned in Sparrow Lake."

The man stopped at the center spotlight and said with a laugh, "Yes, friends and family, I have returned from the dead, just in time to see my daughter, Meg, in a dance that will be talked about for years to come. I know you'll all have many questions for me, but first, let me reunite with my dear ones."

As he exited the stage with my sister in his arms, I ran to her. When I reached Meg, she exclaimed, "Mara, he isn't dead. Our father is alive. Isn't this wonderful? Now, maybe, she will come back."

Pulling Meg to me, I spoke to the man in front of me. "If you are Elliott Stone, where have you been for the past eight years?"

Taking my hand and pulling me towards him, he whispered, "Caterpillar, I have missed you so much. Trust me, and I'll tell you everything."

CHAPTER
SIXTEEN

People didn't only surround Elliott Stone, but they flooded him with questions.

Gram sent them all away while she thanked everyone for their concern. "This is a shock to us all," she said, "but I think it would be best for us to have a family discussion, privately at home, before we share anything."

As the five of us rode in the truck together, there was a dead silence. By the time we pulled onto our property, Meg was sound asleep in Cole's lap.

"Carry her into my room, Cole," Gram directed. She turned towards me. "Mara, go grab Meg's favorite stuffed animals – the wolf and sheep. You know how upset she'll be if she wakes up and they're not with her."

I was confused why Gram would suggest the stuffed animals since they were mine, not Meg's. I nodded, anyways, and went to my room as she directed, not wanting to contradict her. My mind raced as I climbed the ladder. *What is she trying to tell me?* There must be something more she wanted me to see or do. *Does it have to do with Elliott?*

I picked up my gray wolf and propped it up by my lamp. I carefully examined it, trying to decipher the message Gram was trying to give me. I couldn't see anything out of the ordinary. There was nothing that would help me out, so I set the wolf down, again.

I picked up the small lamb. As I inspected every inch of it, I noticed the tiniest bit of red on the bottom of its white foot. Oddly, it didn't match the rest of the thread. Lightly tugging on the out of place filament, I felt a small movement. I continued to gently tug on it until it slowly began to break free. After I had pulled it a few inches, it stopped.

I tugged harder, but it would not budge. Squeezing the small foot, I felt something hard inside. Taking a small pair of scissors from my nightstand, I carefully began cutting the fabric around the small opening. With my nails, I pulled on the red string until the hidden object popped out. At the end of the string, there was a small silver cylinder that was no bigger than my thumb.

Twisting the cap off the container, I found a rolled-up piece of lavender paper. Eagerly, I spread it out and read the tiny words:

As grandmother lay in her bed, with her
big eyes and her big teeth, Red knew that it was a lie.
Removing the glamour before your eyes, Red, will not come easy.

Burn an incense made of the dried petals from the agrimony flower,
dragon's blood resin, and spiny needles of a juniper tree.

Before lighting the incense, the wolf – in disguise – must consume two
small petals of the yellow rue.
– BE WARNED –
Too much rue will reveal the truth,
But death will come to the one ingesting.

After reading the note several times and having memorized the ingredients, I carefully rolled it up and put it back into the cylinder. With the animals in hand and the container tucked safely inside my boots, I stopped at my jewelry box to look at my father's picture. Yes, the man downstairs was – in appearance – my father, but why would he return, today, of all days? I knew the answers to my questions would be revealed whether I was ready or not.

Climbing down the ladder, I could see Elliott sitting at the kitchen table, drinking from a coffee cup. When I reached the second to the last rung, Cole pulled me into his arms and greeted me with a kiss.

"Anything you need me to do, just let me know," Cole quietly whispered in my ear as he gently set me down.

Kissing him on the cheek, I whispered back, "Put on your best face. You're going to meet your future father-in-law."

Cole and I walked, hand-in-hand, towards Elliott. When he saw me, his eyes lit up. "Marina, my dear, wow, you are so grown up. Who is this?" He gestured at Cole. "Please, join me. Come tell me all that I have missed."

"This is Cole Sands. You knew his father, Thomas," I responded.

"Yes, Cole, my boy. You have grown, as well. How is your family?" he asked with a bright smile.

"I would rather know where you have been," I said, trying to control my anger. "If you have been alive, why did you wait almost eight years to return?"

Elliott slumped in his chair and slowly began to explain his absence. "The night before I drowned..." he paused and restarted. "The night before I left, I was on my way home from working in Chester's woodshop when I was met by Cedric Drygen and a few of his men. Drygen told me I had been playing house long enough with Eliza and that he was going to reclaim what was his. Of course, I put up a fight, but I was no match for the four of them. They overpowered me. Lying on the ground, I stared into Drygen's cold eyes, knowing I had failed my family. Just as Drygen was about to drive his knife into my heart, he changed his mind. Instead, he sent a warning and drove it into my shoulder blade."

Unbuttoning his shirt, Elliott pointed to the long, ragged scar.

"Laughing, he warned me that the next slash of his knife would kill me, but not before he killed both you and Meg in front of me. I begged him to spare you both. I told him I would do whatever he wanted as long as you weren't harmed. As he moved to drive his knife into my leg, Eliza appeared and told him to stop. She promised him that I would leave and never come back if he spared me. His final blow was to kick me hard enough to break a few ribs. As I writhed on the ground, Cedric and Eliza must have thought I was in too much pain to see him kiss her passionately before he left."

Stopping, as if the memories were causing him pain, he took a deep breath and continued, "When Drygen left, I asked her if she loved him. Your mother promised she was pretending in order to save us all. Slowly, she unveiled her plan. In the morning, I would go fishing on Sparrow Lake, as usual, but this time, my boat would be overturned, and my body would not be found."

"Why didn't you go for help?" I asked. "There are so many people that would have protected us."

"My thoughts were only of keeping you and Meg safe. So, I followed her plan." Continuing his story, he looked at me with tears glistening in his eyes. "The morning I left, Eliza woke me before dawn. She had already packed me a small bag. She wouldn't let me wake you and say goodbye. When I asked to, at least, take pictures of you girls, your mother refused. She said it would look suspicious if any of my things were missing. I insisted she allow me to take more food than she had packed, or I wouldn't leave. Angry that I was questioning her, Eliza stormed out of the room. I quickly grabbed the first picture I could find of the both of you – one I didn't think she'd notice was missing."

Reaching into his pocket, he pulled out a worn photo of me holding Meg when she was born. "I kept this with me as a reminder that everything I did and would need to do, was always to keep you safe."

Shaking, he stopped and took a long drink of his coffee before continuing his story, "Eliza brought me to Chester's boat. As I was pushing it into the water, she stopped me. She coldly told me that, if I failed, your death would be on me. I was to leave Starten and never return. I loved you girls so much that I left, but only until I could figure out how to save you."

Elliott's voice was tight as he said, "To make it authentic, your mother took a knife and cut my hand. She said my blood on the boat would make it seem as if I was hurt. It would help explain why I drowned. Our goodbye was cold, and I knew the woman I had fallen in love with was no longer there. Not that it mattered. I didn't leave for her, but rather, to keep you both safe."

Looking haggard, Elliott ran his hand through his shaggy hair. "It turned out Eliza was right in her plan. When the boat was found overturned with my blood smeared on it, looking like I had struggled to live, everyone believed it to be true."

"It was very convincing," I replied bitterly.

"At first, I just hid in the Starten Forest where I could watch over you all," Elliott said, his eyes shying away from me. "Eliza played the stricken widow perfectly. It was difficult to watch, but the thought of actually leaving you girls was even more painful."

"So why did you leave?" Gram asked tersely.

"A few times, I was close to being caught. It made me realize I needed to leave town, so I had a secure place to plan my return. I settled in Great Winds. It's a small town where people never settled long enough to question me, but plenty of information still comes into town about the Drygens. When rumors about your mother's remarriage and her recent return to Starten reached me, I knew it was time for me to come back."

With a look of shame, he turned towards Gram. "Mae, I wish I had told you everything. If I could have changed the way things happened, I would have." Unable to finish his apology, he wearily laid his head into the palm of his hands.

I wanted to question him more, but Gram stared hard at me. It was as if she were willing me to keep silent. I instinctively obeyed.

"We can't worry about what should have happened. You are here now. Cole, move your things out of Elliott's room. For the time being, you can sleep in Meg's bed," Gram said firmly.

With a look of surprise, Elliott responded, "No, I couldn't impose. I can get a room at Miss Adilene's boarding house."

"You are not leaving these girls again. Your clothes are still hanging in the back of the closet. You look about the same size, so they will fit." Gram stood up, signaling there would be no more discussion. "It has been a long day, Elliott. I think it's best for us all to get some rest. We can talk more in the morning."

With a relieved look on his face, he said, "Thank you, Mae." Turning from her, he reached across the table and rested his hand on mine. "Can you give me a chance to be a father to you again?"

Confused, and wanting him to be my father more than anything, I squeezed his hand and said, "I'm glad you're home. I have missed you."

"I'll make it up to you, Caterpillar," he said. "I promise."

CHAPTER
SEVENTEEN

Cole relocated his things to my room. When he disappeared to organize Meg's side of the loft for himself, my father went into his old bedroom to sleep.

Once we were alone, I softly began firing questions at my grandmother, "Do you think he's really my father, or is this just a trick? Will we be safe? What are we going to do?"

Putting both her hands on my shoulders, she just stared into my eyes. After a few minutes of silence, Gram said, "I don't know if he's Elliott, but I do know that you're safe. You found what I sent you upstairs for, I presume?"

I nodded.

She continued, "Once we're sure Elliott's asleep, we'll make a protection potion. Now, we need to gather supplies. Let me see what I sent you to get."

I pulled the cylinder out of my boot and handed it to her.

As my grandmother read it over, she said, "Yes, that's it. We can do this. We'll need to get the juniper tree needles and rue flower petals. I know of a place, not far from the binding circle, where you can find both. For tonight, it will need to wait."

Gram went into the pantry. She came back out with a small, silver book. Flipping through the lavender pages, she muttered, "Yes, this will do."

Handing me the open book, I read the page she'd left for me to see.

Rabhadh Fola was written on the top of it in a deep red ink. At least, I hoped it was ink.

The spell needed two white candles, burdock root, salt, and sage. All ingredients were items we had in the pantry. Just as I finished reading, my grandmother returned with her arms full.

"Here, let's be quick."

Gram placed the white candles on the table and lit each one. She directed me to stand on the other side of the table, across from her. Handing me a large metal utensil, she said, "Put the sage on the spoon and hold it over both flames."

She then took a knife and scraped some of the burdock root onto the piece of silverware, which was starting to get hot. "Hold out your other hand," Gram ordered.

I hesitated, knowing what was next. When she raised her eyebrows at me, I grimaced. Sighing, I submitted and held out my hand.

With a quick slice, she cut my finger before placing it over the spoon. As my red droplets dripped onto the heating mixture, Gram cut her own finger. It wasn't long before our blood mixed together.

My grandmother took a pinch of salt. I cringed at the thought. The pain the mineral caused when it came into contact with an open wound was not appealing.

"With this blood, I bind this salt to me. Once the barrier it forms is crossed, I request your warning." Gram offered me the bottle of salt. "Now, you do the same."

Pinching the tiny white crystals between my fingertips, I was surprised there wasn't a stinging sensation. Feeling confident, I repeated her words. As I finished, a spark of hot electricity ran through my arm.

Gram dropped the red-tinted salt onto the spoon and nodded for me to do the same. As soon as the mineral left my hand, the burning tingle stopped.

Next, my grandmother took the bubbling mixture from me and poured the hot contents into a vial, labeled *Waning Gibbous Moon Water*.

Calling out in a quiet voice, she said, "Goddess, your blessing is needed on this night. Please protect this home from harm. Bright blessings"

Blowing out the candles, I repeated, "Bright blessings."

"Now, take this and sprinkle it around the floor outside Elliott's door. It will dry quickly, so he shouldn't be alerted. It will warn us of anyone crossing the boundary you outline, and it will last until the next sunset." Gram began to clean up the table. When I didn't move, she said, "Go on."

"I don't understand why Blaze and the others can't be here to watch him," I argued.

"Mara, go on. The Goddess sent them to teach us to trust the magic we have inside us. They cannot interfere with our path." Gram let out a long sigh of frustration before grabbing my hand. "There are many things that can't be explained. You just have to begin to trust your instincts."

Squeezing her hand, I nodded and left to complete the task I was given. I stopped outside the bedroom door, listening. I heard soft snoring, so I began to sprinkle the liquid. Each red drop that fell was absorbed into the wood quickly. The herbal metallic smell filled my senses.

Just as I finished creating the barrier outside of my parents' room, Cole came down the stairs. "I'm officially moved into the loft. What do you need now?"

"If you could go start the kettle, we can make a cup of tea before we go to sleep." I cupped the potion bottle in my hand. Quickly kissing him, I sent him on his way smiling.

Once I knew he was gone, I continued to sprinkle the potion in front of Gram's bedroom door and went outside. The crisp night air felt pleasant on my skin. A small breeze picked up, and I inhaled the sweet scent of the various trees in bloom. It had a calming effect on me.

Renewed, I warded all the barriers to our house, beginning with the patio door and onto encircling all the downstairs windows. When I reached the bedroom my father was in, I stopped and stared at him through the part in the curtains. He was lying under a deep chocolate-colored bedspread, and his chest slowly lifted as he breathed. He looked at peace.

I hated myself because of my desire for the sleeping man to really be my father. Seeking peace of my own, I called out, "Air, blow away my fear and give me the wisdom to follow the truth." When the response I wanted didn't come, I sighed and tried again, "Breeze, I need you. Please, tell me you're still with me."

Sadly, there was no warm gust of wind to tell me the elemental was present. Instead, I heard the click of the moss beetles, and the crackle of leaves as the birds settled into their nests.

Looking towards the sky, I spoke to the crescent moon before me. "Goddess, please send them back to me." Taking a deep breath, I reminded myself to be strong and continued my task alone.

Once all the downstairs windows and doors were protected, I went back into the house. The warmth of the kitchen comforted me. Cole and Gram had already poured themselves some tea and sounded as if they were having a serious conversation. I stayed quiet and listened, not wanting to interrupt. And, truth be told, I wanted to hear what my boyfriend was thinking about everything.

"Mae, we can't just let someone stay here simply because he claims to be their father. How do we know he's telling the truth?" Cole asked heatedly.

Grabbing his wrist, she said, "This isn't the time for you to become overprotective."

I noticed the tattoo on his wrist was now just a faint silver outline. Keeping still, I remained hidden in the shadows, letting their discussion continue.

"Our family is strong enough to overcome anything that we face. I warned you when you asked my permission to marry Mara that the path before you would not be easy. Find the resolve you had inside you then and trust me...trust her."

Putting his hand over hers, he said, "I love and trust you, Mae. I just can't fathom the thought of ever losing her. I really don't know what I would do without Mara."

After a few minutes of their silence, I joined them. Nonchalantly, I grabbed myself a cup of tea and pretended that I had just returned without having heard their conversation. "It is so nice outside tonight."

I set my mug down on the table next to Gram and put my arm around her in a half hug. Gram held my arm as if hugging me back and I slipped the remaining portion into the pocket of her sweater. She patted my arm, letting me know she understood.

"You both missed a beautiful night sky. The stars are so bright, and the moon has a devious smile," I said, sounding wistful.

When I sat down at the table, I noticed how much everything was distressing Cole. His eyes were dark, and he was not full of the sunshine that I usually felt radiating from him. It worried me.

"We had a busy day. Cole, you look so tired. Why don't you go get ready for bed? Sleep will make you feel better," I suggested.

Looking haggard, Cole hesitantly agreed. As he walked past me, I grabbed his hand and kissed the inside of his wrist. He wearily smiled at me.

"I love you, Mara." Then, with a soft chuckle, he added, "Mae, I love you, too."

Gram shook her head at him but grinned, nonetheless. "Off to bed, young man. You look like you haven't slept in weeks."

Waving her off, he climbed the loft ladder. Once I knew we were alone, I updated Gram on the path I took as I sprinkled the potion. Afterward, I decided to share my fears with her.

"Why can't I feel the elements anymore? Why couldn't they stay?" I questioned, trying to hold in my frustration.

"Mara, I told you, they were sent to guide us, so we could find our inner connection. *We* are the protectors of the magic," Gram said, enunciating the *we*. "Stop blocking what you have inside you. When you were young, you could control the elements on your own. You didn't need to find your connection. You, most of all, just needed to learn to control it, which they taught you how to do. Even when you were not aware of the magic, it was still within you."

She stood up and went into the pantry. When she returned, Gram carried a four-wick candle. Placing it in the center of the table, she said firmly, "Light this candle."

I started to stand up to go get matches, but my grandmother put her hand on my shoulder and stopped me. "I want you to light the candle. Focus and look inside yourself."

As if to show me what she wanted, Gram stared at one of the candle's wicks. After a few seconds, a small flame ignited. The flicker of bright orange and yellow grew until it rose above my head. Then, as quickly as the fire began, it vanished.

"Light the candle." Gram lightly squeezed my shoulder.

Staring at the candle, I tried to focus, to remember what I once knew. Discouraged, I said, "I can't do this."

"Stop this nonsense. You can." Gram slammed her hand down onto the table in front of me. The uncharacteristic aggression scared me. "Your doubt is the only thing keeping you from connecting with the elements. It's the only thing that will keep you from succeeding. You saw what Breeze, Blaze, Bay, and Daisy could do. Now, trust yourself, Mara. This is the time to remember."

Closing my eyes, I thought about Blaze. Words from my past filled my mind. "Mara, you cannot call that much fire. You will burn down the forest. The elements will listen to your command. Kindly dance with them."

I opened my eyes, knowing what I needed to do. Once again, I focused on the wick of the candle. Each breath I slowly took made a small spark. With one deep breath, I whispered to myself, "It is inside you."

As I exhaled, a spark lit all four wicks. They burned with vibrant orange and red flames. I didn't need to look at my grandmother to know she was pleased.

"You just needed to regain your confidence." Gram grabbed my hand and patted it. "Now, off to bed, love. Tomorrow, we'll deal with the past."

Agreeing, I stared at the flames and silently released them. The fire died out, and a small thread of white smoke swirled towards me.

"Thank you, Fire," I said. Hugging Gram, I left to get some sleep.

When I entered my bedroom, I found Cole in a deep slumber. He was still dressed in the same clothes that he had worn all day, including his shoes. I untied and removed his sneakers from each foot. Then, I covered him with a blanket from the end of Meg's bed.

Cole didn't stir once.

Kissing him on his cheek, I softly whispered, "Sleep sweet, love."

Cole let out a soft moan, and then resumed snoring.

I don't think I could love him more than I do today, I thought wistfully.

Feeling no energy to change into my pajamas, I took my boots off and fell into my bed. The metal cylinder I had been hiding dropped to the floor. Picking it up, I hid it back inside my pillowcase before laying my head down on it. Unable to fight the exhaustion that was overcoming me, I drifted off into a dreamless sleep.

CHAPTER
EIGHTEEN

"Stop making that noise, Meg!" I cried.

I didn't want to wake from the sleep I had just fallen into. Still, the loud murmur and clanging bells didn't stop. Angered, I threw one of my pillows in the direction of Meg's bed.

"Please, go back to sleep," I pleaded.

"Mara, it's not Meg. Wake up." Cole climbed onto my bed, and over me, to look out the small, round window. "Those are sirens outside."

Trying to understand what was going on while I begrudgingly woke up, I stood on the bed beside him. The soft mattress and my height deficiency didn't allow me to reach. "What do you see?" I questioned.

"It's fire trucks. I see smoke and flames. I can't tell exactly where it's coming from, but it's close to my home." Hopping off the bed, he frantically put on his shoes. "I need to go there."

Following suit, I put my boots on, as well. "Are you sure it was your house?"

"No, but I'm not going to sit here and wait." Cole rushed towards the ladder.

Grabbing his hand, I stopped him. "Let me go with you." Feeling his hesitation, I said more forcefully, "I'm going with you."

Sighing, he agreed. "Ok, but we are going now."

We had just reached the front door when Gram called out to us. "Cole and Mara, where do you think you are going?"

We both turned around, shamefaced. In our haste, we had not

thought of letting anyone know our plans to leave. My chagrin passed as I took in Gram's outfit. The mismatched brash combination of a lime green sweater, gardening jeans, and red garden wellies were not something she would typically wear. This wardrobe choice confirmed she had planned on doing the same thing as us.

"Gram, I think the fire trucks are at my house." I could hear the panic in Cole's voice. "I need to go now."

Just as I was about to agree with our need to move quickly, a sharp jolt of electricity shot through my body. The intense pain it caused sucked the air from my lungs. The grimace on Gram's face told me she had felt it, too.

When I saw my father exiting his room, it registered in my brain that the spell had worked. The pain must have been our notification of the magical barriers being crossed. As I stared at Gram, she closed her eyes and slightly nodded, confirming my belief.

"What is going on, Caterpillar? Why are you all awake?" Elliott asked, looking disheveled and confused.

Interesting, I thought to myself. *Why would Elliott be in the same clothes from last night?* Looking down at my own outfit, I realized he could be thinking the same thing about me.

"There is a fire coming from the direction of Cole's house. We are going there now," I responded.

The surprised look on his face turned to concern. "I'm coming with you."

My father threw on his boots and coat. He looked me over, and then handed me a sweater from a hook. "It's cold out there. Put this on."

My heart stilled. This man before me seemed so real. He had to be my father. *Or do you just want him to be Elliott Stone so badly that you'll risk your family's safety?* I wondered. Pushing the thought away, I forced myself to focus on what was important. Cole needed me.

I opened the door and stepped outside. I felt another set of jolts as Cole and Elliott crossed the barrier behind me. Glancing towards Gram, I noticed she stopped.

She called to us, "Wait, we need to wake up Meg."

In the confusion, I had forgotten about my sleeping sister. "You go ahead with them, Gram. I'll get Meg, and then we'll join you." I kissed Cole on the cheek. "I'll be there soon." Wanting to reassure him, I added, "It'll be ok."

As Gram tried to reenter the house, I held her back. "I won't be long. Please, watch over Cole," I whispered.

She nodded and was out the door. With surprising speed, my grandmother raced down the road towards the men. It wasn't long before she caught up to them.

That child could sleep through an explosion, I thought.

Meg was buried under the covers, clearly in a deep sleep. I climbed onto the bed to wake her. In a quick movement, I ripped back the blankets, ready to pounce on her. Instead of my sleeping sister, I found pillows.

Tearing the comforter off the bed completely, I expected to find her awake and hiding. However, the bed was empty, and frustration filled me. We didn't have time for games.

"Meg, don't hide, right now. Gram and Cole need us." I forced myself to speak calmly and not to sound angry.

When my sister didn't respond, I called out a second time and stopped to listen for her giggles. Again, there was only silence. I checked under all the blankets strewn on the floor and even crawled under the bed. Meg was nowhere to be found.

Feeling panicked, I rushed into Gram's walk-in closet. I pulled out everything Meg could be concealed behind or under. Helplessly, I searched every possible hiding space. There was still no sign of her.

"This isn't funny, Meg. Please, don't do this now," I pleaded.

Giving up on the closet, I decided to inspect the rest of the room. I lifted the lid on the trunk at the end of the bed, but it only held blankets and photo albums. With a final desperate thought, I decided to look in the bathroom, but Meg wasn't in there either.

There really was no place for her to hide. Still, I continued my search. I knew my efforts were futile, yet I opened the cabinets anyway. Their emptiness filled me with disappointment.

Composing myself, I tried to remember all of Meg's favorite hiding places. I stared out of the bathroom, scanning the bedroom with my eyes. The search stopped when my gaze landed on my stuffed animals. The sheep and the wolf were propped up on the nightstand. There was something white in the arms of the wolf.

I raced to inspect it and found a white scroll with a silver ribbon tied around it. I removed the string and unrolled it. My heart sunk as I saw the embossed snake design on the paper. A sick feeling filled me as I read the dark words.

> My Darling Marina,
>
> You can stop your frantic search for Meg. I bet you felt quite a fright not finding your little sister sleeping soundly in the bed. Of course, you shouldn't worry. My sweet child is finally where she belongs – with me. She is now in the loving arms of her mother.
>
> How silly of your grandmother to forget that I know all of her little tricks. A blood alarm may work on that fool, Elliott, but anyone with half a brain would be able to counter it. She underestimates me – I'm much stronger than the weak little girl she tried to raise me to be.
>
> Now, back to the important matter at hand. I was so devastated by how you treated me at our long-awaited reunion. As hurt as I was, I couldn't blame you entirely. I understand that living with that woman has turned you against me. She always clung to her silly beliefs. I fear she will continue to do so until her dying day. Don't worry, darling. I'll do my best to try to forgive you for your coldness. We certainly haven't been apart long enough for you to forget what a wonderful mother I was to you both.
>
> Enough of the nonsense you have been spoon-fed by her. You will come to me, and you will learn what your gift can truly do. <u>Please choose wisely, Marina</u>. I may not be able to get over the deep hurt you have caused me if you make the wrong choice again. We don't want Mommy to become too angry now, do we? As you should know by now, the results can be intense – one may even dare to say fiery.
>
> When you are back in my arms, We'll build our future together. The true legacy that was always planned for our family will begin. Under my guidance, your new marriage will make such a powerful union. How lucky for you that you have chosen so well the first time. Sometimes, we are forced into situations, and our real path is blocked. Never-

theless, we can always find the way – Goddess be damned!

How exciting it will be to see what is formed from the mixing of Sarah's and my bloodlines. Such a combination will ensure my grandchildren will be even stronger than you both. Our raw magic will combine to stop even the coldest goddess. Of course, none of this will happen until you submit. All of this is better discussed face-to-face. Don't you agree?

You will come to me soon, my dear Marina. I would hate for any more little accidents to happen. Don't keep me waiting.

Mother

I read the note twice, trying to understand it. *How could I be so stupid as to not watch over Meg? Who is this monster that claims to be my mother?* Dropping the letter, I fell to my knees and began to cry. Beating my fists against my legs, I screamed as the world around me seemed to be crashing down.

CHAPTER NINETEEN

My screams were silenced when strong arms wrapped around me. I struggled against the person holding me. The more I fought to break free, the tighter the arms held me.

"Stop, child," Gram's soft voice soothed.

Realizing it was my grandmother, I stopped fighting and collapsed into her arms, sobbing.

"It will be ok, Mara. I'm here."

"She's gone, Gram. She took, Meg." I pulled myself out of her arms and handed her the note. "It's my fault. If I hadn't –"

Gram interrupted me. "We are not doing this now. You need to calm down and collect yourself. This isn't the time for self-pity."

As she read the note, Gram's eyes blazed with anger. When she finished reading, she shoved the letter into the pocket of her sweater.

"Mara, you need to focus your energy. We need to help Cole."

"No," I screamed. "My little sister has been kidnapped by a monster!"

Gram gripped me by my shoulders and spoke in a slow, tranquil voice. "We must go to Cole. Eliza will not hurt Meg. You know how charming your mother can be. Your sister will think that she is on a grand adventure."

"Ok, Gram. Let's help Cole," I relented. I was not convinced Meg was safe, but the rush of Air that she was wrapping around me allowed me to control my hysteria.

On our fast-paced walk to Cole's house, I thought about Eliza's letter. "Gram, what did she mean about Cole? He doesn't have the gift of magic, right?"

My grandmother pursed her lips.

She isn't going to silence me now, I thought. "Gram, you promised no more secrets. Why do they keep surfacing? I need to know everything if I want to keep my promise. Don't I?"

"Mara, there hasn't been enough time to tell you everything. I'll tell you the short version on the way. One day, you'll know more than you want to know. Sometimes, ignorance can be bliss, Mara."

Gram took my hand and squeezed it gently as she told me the story of how her mother received her gift. "The time my mother grew up in was much different than the one we live in now. People had forgotten about the Goddess and nature. They worried about their day-to-day lives. The old ways were considered fantasy and were stories for movies and books.

"One day, four friends were studying in the library when they met a group of strangers. Breeze, Blaze, Bay, and Daisy had come to town in search of help for the Goddess. They had a book about the magic of nature that they shared with the girls. Inspiring interest, they began to practice the craft as it was described in the guide."

"Your mother was one of the girls, right?" I asked.

"Yes, my mother, Genevieve, was one of them," she answered. "She took her oath seriously. All four girls were committed to the magic, together, and their power grew strong. As they grew older and began their lives of being wives and mothers, they still came together to honor the Goddess. At first, Genevieve Silver, Lucy Andrews, Michelle Elliott, and Camille Black were always careful not to flaunt the gift."

Her voice saddened as she continued her story. "But such a gift is tempting to misuse. My mother said Camille changed soon after she married Brandon Drygen. She started using her newly learned skills to increase her husband's influence in the community. She would stop at nothing to make sure anyone in their way was made to realize how powerful she had become. She destroyed many lives in the name of greed and money."

Gram stopped when we were less than a block away from Cole's house. The flames were consuming his home and filling the sky with black smoke. "This isn't how I wanted to tell you, but it will have to do. The three women came up with a plan and decided to bind Camille's magic. This angered her, but the Drygen family didn't need magic anymore.

"Camille never forgave the women for what they did. The betrayal she felt fueled her anger. In retaliation, she began directing her rage at her closest friend, Michelle. Camille made it impossible for her to live here. One day, Michelle and her family left town and were never heard from again."

"Is the lady that showed up at the Lunar Festival Camille's daughter?" I asked.

"Yes, Mara. Blanche grew up with a hatred for the Silver family that I could never understand. The Drygens own most of the town and have all the money they could ever need. Blanche had the gift, but it was not enough for her. She wanted what, in her mind, was stolen from her family."

"What does this have to do with Cole?" I asked impatiently. I wanted to run to him and protect him from the pain I knew he felt, not be there, listening to stories about the Drygens.

"Lucy's daughter, Olivia, never showed any interest in taking the oath. When Olivia died in childbirth, Lucy raised her granddaughter. The child was Sarah. The same Sarah, whose son is Cole Oliver Sands."

My eyes widened as I met my grandmother's eyes.

"The legacy your mother has set her mind on is the pure magic of Genevieve and Lucy combining. Your mother is naive to believe we are the only ones with access to the magic. Our family has been blessed with an understanding, a bond with all elements, and an awareness of the dark and light forces around us."

"Does that mean Cole can connect with the elements?" I asked.

"Like you, his gift was taken from him. I don't know where his potion is being kept. I don't know if Cole will be able to tap into his gift without his memories? It is up to you to help him."

Gram hugged me and swept my hair from my face. "Go to Cole, Mara. He needs you."

CHAPTER TWENTY

When I reached Cole, he was staring through tear-filled eyes at the front of his completely engulfed home. The firefighters were barely holding back the flames as they struggled to keep the fire from spreading. I didn't think they could contain the inferno for much longer.

I took my boyfriend's hand into mine. "I'm here, Cole."

"It will all be gone, and I can't stop it. There isn't a damn thing I can do to save my home." The water that had filled his eyes broke loose, and large tears flowed down his cheeks.

My chest tightened. *Cole is my rock. He is the strong one.* "We can stop this, together, if you trust me." I led him to the backside of the house where the fire had not touched it yet. "Come with me."

When we reached an isolated area, I began. "I don't have time to explain everything to you, Cole, but your family has the same connection to the Goddess as mine." "What are you talking about?" he asked angrily. "My home is burning. I'm losing everything, and you want to talk about stupid magic?"

Make him understand, Mara, the voice of Gram rang in my mind.

I held my hands up to the sky, and cried, "Air, I call to you. I plead with you to recall your power that is feeding the flames before me. Fire, I call to you. Return your flames to the soil. Earth, I call to you. Please, absorb the heat of the flames and smother them. Water, I call to you. Devour and wash away the darkness that summoned you. The anger is no longer welcome here. In the name of the Goddess, I call the Light."

When nothing happened, I turned my attention towards the distraught man beside me. "Connect with me. Connect with them."

Cole didn't respond. He just silently stared at me as if I had lost my mind.

With no response from him and my own lack of certainty in what I was doing, I tried to connect the way Gram had instructed me. I didn't have a book telling me what was right. I had to trust myself and learn to release all doubts.

Taking a cleansing breath, I tried again, "Air, Fire, Water, and Earth, release the anger that surrounds us. In the name of Sarah, protector of the magic, I ask you to save this home."

The fire still burned strong. I knew that if I could not reach him soon, it would be too late.

"Cole, trust me." Taking his hands in mine, I stared into his eyes and said, "I call to the spirits of Genevieve Silver and Lucy Andrews. Bless this union of your protectors before you. In front of the Goddess and the magic that runs through our veins, I pledge my eternal commitment to protect the magic."

These words seemed to spark a response. Small threads of white smoke danced and weaved, encircling us in a figure-eight. Cole's eyes widened in surprise as the wisps surrounding us grew stronger.

I gripped Cole's hand tighter. With confidence, I commanded the elements. "Your protection is called. Fire, return to your home. Air, rescind the life you breathe into the flames. Water, pour down on us. Earth, stand strong."

Clouds formed above us, and the boom of thunder sounded. With renewed vigor, I began repeating my pleas, "Air, Fire, Water, Earth, and Light of the Goddess...hear my pleas."

As a drop of rain fell on my cheek, I felt my strength rekindling. "It's time to show faith, Cole – in me, and in us. It's now or never."

With a small nod, Cole began chanting the words with me. "Air, Fire, Earth, Water, and Light, come to us."

As we finished the words together for the third time, the rain poured down. Cries of joy rang out from the crowd at the front of the residence as they welcomed the rain. Soon, the flames that had been consuming the house began to retreat.

Cole cupped my face between his palms. He looked at me as if he had honestly never seen me before. "How did you know this would work?"

"I didn't. I just knew I had to do something, so I listened to my heart. You've always been there for me. It was my turn to be strong for you."

Cole swept me off my feet and spun me around. "My beautiful girl, thank you for not giving up on me."

We laughed as the rain poured down on us. The smoky wisps danced away from the smoldering building. Though the fire had been completely extinguished, damage lay in its wake.

"I see you have found your connection, Cole." Gram lifted our hands to the sky, and spoke, "Water, the rain you gave served its purpose. We release you." Gram smirked as the clouds parted and the rain slowed. "We wouldn't want to flood the town, would we?"

With the emergency averted, the firemen called it safe before they departed. Now, there was nothing left for us to do, but try to salvage Cole's belongings. The only people that stayed were nearby neighbors, who came to our aid with boxes. They even helped us gather anything that wasn't ruined by the flames or water.

"I'm sorry I was so angry. As I'm looking at these *things*, I realized there's nothing in this house that I want or need," Cole whispered to us. "Anything meaningful to me is here, right now. You are my family, and your safety is all that matters to me."

Stopping and looking around, Cole had a confused look on his face, "Wait, where is Meg?"

Gram handed Eliza's message to Cole, and apologized, "I'm sorry she included you in all of this. She never could do things simply. How a child of mine ever became so cruel, I'll never understand."

I watched Cole's face as he read the note. Unsure how he'd react, I forced myself to wait patiently until he finished. When he was done, he gave the letter back to Gram with an expressionless look on his face.

"So, Eliza started this fire?" Cole gently shook his head. "Why would she bother to burn down my house?"

"Maybe a distraction? Maybe revenge? Cole, there's no use trying to understand any of the choices my daughter makes." Gram marched to the center of the clean-up crew. "Elliott, please get my truck. We are moving Cole in with us tonight."

Elliott stopped filling boxes, gave Gram the thumbs up, and headed towards our house.

Gram called out to those still sifting through the rubble. "Thank you, everyone, for helping. It's not safe to be digging around in the dark. Go home and sleep. These things can wait for another day."

Reluctantly, our neighbors finished their tasks. As they left, Cole was met with words of concern, hugs, and handshakes from our soot-covered friends. Their support was moving.

Not soon after everyone had left, Elliott returned with the truck. The bed was filled with empty boxes. "I thought these might be useful." Stopping and looking around, he faltered, "Wait, where is Meg?"

With a disgusted look on her face, Gram handed him the note. Once again, Eliza's hate-filled letter was read.

Elliott's face crumpled. "I came back too late to protect my girls. How did I fail them again?"

Gram took his hand. "You are here now, and we'll bring Meg home."

CHAPTER
TWENTY-ONE

We loaded the truck with as many boxes of the salvaged item as it could hold. I thought we would return to our home and begin planning a way to save Meg, but Gram had other ideas.

"I don't trust my daughter. We should gather your things from the cottage," Gram said.

Couldn't Eliza start a fire at our house, too? I wondered.

As if reading my mind, Gram replied, "Eliza is not strong enough to burn down our home. We'll be safe there."

"Why don't I take this load back to your place, Mae? It sounds like we'll need room in the truck," Elliot offered.

"You are right," Gram agreed.

Cole and I headed for the cottage behind the main house. As Gram gave my father instructions on where she wanted everything, we entered the small home where my boyfriend lived. The structure was warm, and it always smelled like pinecones mixed with vanilla. It was very welcoming.

The great room was an open area, defined only by the furniture. The basic kitchen consisted of a stove, refrigerator, sink, a yellow table, and large sturdy wooden chairs. The living room took up most of the space with pale blue couches, featuring white throw pillows, and accent tables.

I had been in this part of the cottage many times, but never further. I stared at the lavender door that led to a master bedroom. I imagined it to be overflowing in Sarah's favorite pastel colors.

When Gram joined us, I realized how we must have looked. My eyes fell on Cole, and I chuckled. "Before we pack anything else, we should clean up," I remarked. "We look like a bunch of wet dogs, left out in the rain to play in the mud."

I was relieved when Gram and Cole laughed. After the intensity of the evening, we all needed a light moment to ease our stress. It didn't take long before we had cleaned off most of the ash and mud that covered us. Cole brought us dry clothes from behind a secret door. It felt nice to change into them.

Renewed, we began to box the items Cole thought were important. Since it was Sarah's space, his choices were based more on it being his mother's rather than being needed. I couldn't blame him.

While Cole sorted through kitchen utensils, Gram began looking around the cottage. "Where did you keep your mother's things, Cole?" Gram asked. " I know your stepmother wouldn't have allowed any signs of Sarah to remain in the house."

"Rosalind had tried to throw out all of her stuff, but I was able to save a few things. They're here, inside my bedroom. I keep them in a wooden trunk." Cole's voice weighed heavy with sadness. He put a spatula into the box. "I think this is all I want from here."

Gram ran her aged hands along the light wood walls as if searching for something. "Cole, did Sarah spend much time here?"

"She would come over to be alone and draw, sometimes." Cole eyed my grandmother with curiosity. "Why the questions, Gram?"

Gram's brow furrowed as she went towards him. "This is important. Are there any hidden spaces that you remember playing in as a child? Do you recall spending time with your mother in this cottage?"

Cole shook his head. "No, I never really came here as a child."

Gram's eyes locked with mine. It felt like she was trying to get me to understand what she was seeking. I knew my grandmother was looking for something, but I had no idea what she wanted. *Why would she be asking about Cole being here as a child? What am I missing?* Gram was speaking more in riddles and gestures than just telling me what to do. This was something I would talk to her about later.

"Show me the chest with her belongings." Gram went towards the lavender door.

Cole opened it for her without hesitation.

Excited to see if we could solve the mystery, I followed them into the bedroom.

Cole brought Gram to Sarah's chest. Inside the room, I copied Gram's previous movements. I ran my hands against the walls while I watched Cole removing his mother's personal items from the box.

When he pulled out a lilac sweater, he stopped and held it to his face. I knew he was breathing in the scent, trying to remember his mother. I understood what he was feeling. I had done the same thing many times while I had longed for my own parents. For the briefest moment, grief flooded his face. Leaving him alone with his memories, I focused on searching the room.

When I reached the open closet door, I began my inspection. The shelves were stacked with boxes above the hung clothing. My eyes scanned every inch of the space until my gaze hit the floor. In the corner of the light tan rug, I noticed a small red spot. Upon further examination, I found it was a piece of red thread.

"Cole, Gram," I called out, "Can you come here? I may have found something."

Lifting the rug halfway towards myself, I discovered what it was hiding. A brass ring was beneath it, stuck in the wooden floorboards.

"What did you find?" Cole knelt down to take a closer look. "Hey, how did I not notice that before?"

"It looks like a trap door," Gram said from behind us. "Open it, and let's find out where it leads to."

I moved back, beside Gram, allowing Cole ample space to pull up the wooden door. As he lifted it, the silken threads of spider webs that covered the opening began to stretch.

"Mara, there are flashlights in the box that I just packed on my bed." Cole ran his hand through his hair, leaving strands of the web in his dark locks. "How did I not know this was here?" he muttered to himself.

Shaking off the urge to remove the red threads from his hair, I went to find the light we needed. It didn't take me long to complete my task. I brought back the silver flashlights that had been buried under my boyfriend's books, along with other odds and ends.

"I noticed you're bringing your doll collection with you." I teased Cole about the plastic figures I had seen.

"I keep telling you – they are collector's items, not dolls." Cole accepted the light I handed him.

Gram shined the light down the hole onto a circular staircase. "What are we waiting for? Lead the way, Cole."

We followed Cole down the steep staircase. As we walked, I counted each step in my head. *Three...seven...twelve...Big spider! Don't scream. Sixteen...twenty...twenty-six.*

At step twenty-six, our descent ended with a concrete floor. We flashed the lights around, inspecting the area. We stopped when our beams landed on a hanging light bulb with a long chain extending from the side of it.

"There's a light." Cole rushed towards it and pulled the chain. The small bulb illuminated the room.

I stared in amazement at the space around us. Under the light, there was a circular table, much like the one Gram and I had used to cast the memory spell. This table was a light gray marble with etchings of the elements on the surface. In the center, an intricate image of the Goddess, holding a quarter moon in her arms, sparkled in the light.

"She made this." Cole traced his fingers along the surface.

My heart, once again, ached for him. I wanted to remove his hurt, though I knew I never could.

Gram began searching one of the cupboards lining the wall. "Sarah fully stocked this room with supplies." She nodded her approval while sorting through the neatly arranged items on the shelves. "Very impressive. Her grandmother, Lucy, would be extremely proud if she could see how prepared Sarah was."

Gram picked up a bundle of tree branches. They had many brown needles with specks of green that hinted at the color they had once been. "This is the juniper tree needles we need. If you come across yellow rue, put it aside."

Each of us continued to look through Sarah's things.

I stopped at a cabinet with the tree of life carved on its outside. Opening the door, I was amazed by rows and rows of neatly labeled bottles. I reached inside to inspect one that shimmered from the pink liquid it held. In my haste, I knocked over several of the containers.

"No, no, no," I muttered under my breath. Attempting to catch the falling items, I bumped the back of the wardrobe. Instead of my hand hitting the side of the wood and stopping, it moved. *Oh Goddess, no. I can't break Sarah's stuff.*

I leaned in closer to see the damage I had caused. Much to my relief, it wasn't broken. It had been a false back. I tried not to knock over anything else as I slid the panel out of the way. Hidden behind it was a square, silver box. Picking it up carefully to inspect, I saw the name *Cole* inscribed on the top.

"I found something," I exclaimed.

I walked over to where Cole was leafing through a book. Gram was next to him, placing bottles and herbs into a box.

"This is for you to open." I handed the container to Cole.

Quickly, he took the lid off the box. It held a silver ring with a square, purple gem in the center. As Cole picked up the ring, I felt an odd pulsing sensation being emitted from the blue ring that I wore.

Gram pulled me away from Cole. "He needs to do this alone."

Reluctantly, I agreed, and we retreated to the opposite corner of the room. Away from Cole, my grandmother showed me the items she had found, including the yellow rue.

Still whispering, she said, "He will have to choose whether he will make the promise or not – just like you did."

Did we really have a choice? I wasn't certain of the answer. It seemed our lives were predetermined.

CHAPTER
TWENTY-TWO

While we waited for Cole, I allowed myself to take in my surroundings. The furniture in the large, round room was centered around the stone table. In each section, there was a distinct feeling of purpose and meaning. As you came down the circular staircase and entered the chamber, you were greeted by bookcases and large chests that held herbs, potions, and spells. It gave off an air of secrets and knowledge.

Following the curved design of the space, clockwise, I stopped at a small sitting area that held two red wingchairs with a small, square bronze table between them. The table held a large, white candle surrounded by four smaller candles. Behind it was a large, abstract painting filled with streaks of red, orange, yellow, white, and gray.

The art provoked odd feelings from inside me. If I stroked my fingers along the colors, I was confident I would feel the biting sting of a burn. Even with the intense sensation, it surprisingly still seemed inviting, offering warmth and comfort.

Continuing my inspection, I paused at the next area. This space contained a silver water fountain with a statue sculpted to resemble a splash of water, rising from its base. The burst of water held an elegant woman's hand that cupped a large tree, presenting it for all to see. It was not running, but I could almost hear the flow of the calming liquid. Shaking off the call that was luring me to relax and rest, I continued scanning the room.

The final section was to the right of the staircase. This space held a wooden table and a green chair. They appeared to be sized for a child. The wall above them was covered with a collection of art while the floor below had hand-painted flowers. Unable to fight off my curiosity, I stepped closer for a better look.

Most of the paintings were of trees in various stages of life. The flowers were all in their brightest bloom. The gentle strokes of detail and bold colors of green, brown, orange, and red were definitely the work of Sarah. As I absorbed each picture, a sense of change, growth, and new life surrounded me.

In the center of the works was a black and white circle of sketches. These sketches were of Cole as he had grown. They began with him as a small baby with bright eyes smiling, a toddler chasing a butterfly, a young boy with a toothy grin, proudly showing his catch – a trout that was almost as big as he was – and a young man, pushing a girl on a swing.

I ran my fingers over the image of the girl and smiled. Sarah had captured the feeling of pure happiness I had felt that day on the swing. I was filled with a sense of deep love and echoes of giggles vibrated in the air.

I was brought back to the moment by Gram's soft touch. Squeezing her hand gently, I turned my attention towards Cole. We watched quietly as he looked into the box. After a few minutes, he softly whispered something, and then closed the container. As he came over to join us, I noticed he had put the ring on his small finger.

"I was here before," Cole murmured.

Cole looked as if he had seen a ghost. Words that were probably never truer. The pain I had seen in him after Sarah's death had returned.

I took his hand and guided him to one of the red chairs. Like a small child, he collapsed into it and buried his face in his palms.

I knelt in front of him. "Cole, I know this is overwhelming, but I need you to talk to us – to me."

Cole lifted his head. Tears fell from his deep blue eyes. "It was so real. She was standing in front of me, telling me how proud of me she was and how sorry she was for not being here for me now."

Frantically, he jumped up and started pacing. "When I opened the chest, I saw four girls reading a book. This image quickly changed to a woman. I didn't know her, but she felt familiar. As she proudly promised to protect the magic, her blue eyes and soft curly blonde hair that fell down her shoulders made me think I should recognize her."

He shook his head slightly. "She stared right at me and smiled as she took the oath. It was like she was talking directly to me. As quickly as she came, she disappeared and a vision of a young mother, holding her new baby in her arms, replaced her. This lady kept saying to the infant, 'Sarah, don't be afraid of your path. Be braver than I was, my baby.' The child must have been my mother and the woman holding her, my grandmother, Olivia."

Cole stopped as if he was debating whether to continue or not. Gram and I both watched quietly while he ran his fingers through his dark hair. Finally, working out whatever was troubling him, he proceeded.

"Then, the image changed to two teen girls fighting. It was our mothers. When Eliza turned to walk away, my mother pulled on her arm, begging her to not go with him. She kept saying, 'Don't go to him. Remember your promise.' The cold look that Eliza had in her eyes told me nothing would change her mind."

Sitting back down, he spoke softly as he told the next part to us. "All of a sudden, a brilliant ray of colors shone into my eyes, and my mother stepped out of the light. Her long blonde hair sparkled with a glittery shine, and her blue eyes twinkled with bits of turquoise. My mother told me she was sorry she wasn't there to teach me everything, but she was proud of the man I had become. She said I would always be safe with the both of you by my side, and if I never forgot my promise."

He looked up, meeting my gaze. "As I began to question her, she started to leave. At the last moment, she turned around and told me my magic was safe in the hands of the Goddess. Her final words to me were, 'I'm proud of you, Cole. I know you will continue the oath our family took. I love you.' Then, she was gone again."

"Cole, I'm sorry you're finding out this way," I said, trying to comfort him. The guilt I felt over my mother's attack on his home had begun to sink in. Even though I didn't bring on any of this, I still felt responsible.

Gram interrupted me from further apologizing. "Cole, did you take the oath?"

Though I knew my grandmother was asking a valid question, she had additional motives in cutting me off. There was no way she'd let me take responsibility for what had happened. However, that didn't stop my sense of ownership for what my mother had done.

"Of course," Cole answered. "Tonight, when you called the

elements, I felt a connection...a need to protect. To protect you, the elements...well, to protect everything. I cannot explain it, but I didn't question taking the oath. It was more of a feeling as to why it took me so long to do this. Together, we'll keep the promises we made, and together we'll fight against anything and everyone that threatens our gift...even if that means facing Eliza."

Hugging him tightly, I said, "Cole, I can't ask you to get any more involved in what will happen next. It will not be safe. We don't know what she is capable of doing."

"Stop. I couldn't be any more involved than I already am. I love you, Mara. I love your family as if they were my own. Soon, they will officially be mine. Together, we'll stand against Eliza and whatever she throws at us. We'll get Meg back. You and me."

"And me." Gram took both of our hands.

"I'll be there, too, Caterpillar," a voice promised. Standing on the bottom step behind us, Elliott stood watching.

CHAPTER
TWENTY-THREE

Elliott walked towards us with a long, confident stride. "All of the boxes are unloaded. I put them in your room, Mara." He held his hand out to me.

My heart stopped when I saw what rested on his palm.

"This was on the floor under the loft ladder. I believe it's yours."

In the chaos of being woken by the fire, it must have fallen out of its hiding place. I took the small, silver cylinder from him, trying to act nonchalant. "Thank you. Did you happen to open it?" *Please, please, please, say no. Why didn't you put it somewhere safer than a pillowcase?* I scolded myself. As the words repeated in my head, I hoped he would say no, but life was never that simple.

"I did look inside, and I understand why you have it. There isn't anything I can do to change the decisions I made in the past, but I'll do whatever it takes to make it up to you. I'll not fail you, again," Elliott asserted. His words seemed so sincere, but as much as I wanted to believe him, I wasn't ready to risk trusting him, yet. "If you want, we can make the potion, right now. I'll do whatever is necessary to earn your trust."

"A conversation for later, Elliott. Let's leave Cole and Mara to finish up here," Gram said, stopping him.

I was thankful that Gram was not one to dwell on the 'should-haves' and, instead, focused on taking action. At the same time, I wanted to run to Elliott and throw my arms around him. In the end, I was comforted by the warm hug of my grandmother.

Hugging her back tightly, I breathed in the familiar scents of vanilla, cinnamon, and lavender.

She whispered in my ear, "It will be ok, love, but Cole needs you. I'll handle this. You have always been strong and now isn't the time to forget that." Releasing her hold on me, Gram turned to Cole with open arms. "A hug for an old lady?" she teased.

Cole welcomed the hug, just as I had. "I always have a hug available for an old lady. Since it's just us here, you'll have to do."

I could not make out what Gram said to Cole, but whatever it was, it made him laugh.

"We'll see you at home soon." Gram took Elliott's arm. "Come, we have plenty of things we can take care of at the house."

I watched as they began their climb up the circular staircase. Once they were out of sight, I turned to Cole and said, "She will keep him busy. Now, we can focus on you. We need to find your magic."

Cole and I decided to look through the bookcases. After a while, it felt hopeless. Obviously, we were going about this the wrong way.

"Cole, what did Sarah say about your magic?"

"She just said it was always in the Goddess's hands," he answered, not hiding his frustration.

As I wandered around the room, I played the words repeatedly in my head and a thought finally came to me. "I think I might know where to look. Come, let me show you."

Cole and I went to the water fountain. His eyes brightened as he inspected the sculpture's hand. "The tree of life – this must be where she has hidden it. This is the first thing, tonight, that has made sense."

Taking ahold of the metal tree, he jiggled it. It moved as if it was loose, but his attempts to pull it free made no impact. Not giving up, Cole decided to twist instead of a yank. This time, I could see progress.

Cole tugged harder. Several more times and one mighty pull caused the tree to pop out. Attached to it was a large, silver cylinder that looked like the one Elliott had returned to me. Opening it revealed a light-yellow note and a crystal vial, filled with blue and silver liquid.

Cole unrolled the message and held it out for both of us to read:

> My Dearest Cole,
>
> If you have found this, either you have been extraordinarily inquisitive, or I'm no longer with you. Knowing you, my child, it is the latter.
>
> I feel confident that you are not alone in your search and that you are now, ready for answers. When you were young, your connection to the magic, especially Water, was so strong. This scared me, and I didn't feel like I could keep you safe.
>
> To protect you, I bound your gifts. I took the magic from you, knowing, one day, that it would be restored. Soon, you will have everything I took from you back. Such knowledge, so quickly, will be difficult, but I know you will be able to handle it. Please rely on Mae and Mara. Mara's connection to Fire and Mae's connection to Air will be necessary for what the future holds.
>
> Mae, if you are reading this, I have always known how strong your connection to Air is. Your wisdom and extensive knowledge will be needed. Please, take care of my boy and help him understand what our families promised.
>
> If I've never told you this, Cole, I'm so glad that you and Mara found each other. I know you will continue to protect the magic, together. Please, take care, my love, and always remember the promise first made by my grandmother. I hope it is a legacy you and, one day, your children will continue.
>
> At night, when you see the moon, think of my love for you and know that I'm watching.
>
> Love Always,
> Mom

When we finished the letter, we both looked at each other with tears glistening in our eyes.

"She always told me how much she loved you, Mara," Cole said. He handed me the cylinder and the note. "I guess it really is now or never."

"You probably should take a seat before you drink it. There's no way I can carry you," I warned.

"You are right." Cole sat down in one of the red chairs. Putting the vial to his lips, he toasted, "Cheers." After a long drink, Cole handed me back the empty crystal. With a big grin, he said, "I'll see you soon, Mara. I hope I'll have all the answers we need when I return."

I noticed there was a little of the blue liquid left in the vial. As I watched Cole drift off, I wondered what would happen if I drank the rest of the potion. I justified the risk since it was such a small amount. Going against my better judgment, I decided there was nothing I could lose by trying.

I tilted the crystal vial back and let the final drop land on my tongue. The strong berry taste filled my senses, and the room began to spin. Suddenly, I felt so dizzy that I had to sit down. Unable to make it to the other red chair, I collapsed to the floor, drifting off into sleep.

CHAPTER
TWENTY-FOUR

When I woke up, it took me a moment to recall what I did, and then to figure out where I was. To my surprise, I had woken in Cole's home. The house he had grown up in, not the cottage. The same building that we had watched burn tonight.

As everything came into focus, I saw Sarah and Cole in the kitchen. They were decorating cupcakes with a bright white frosting and blue gemlike sprinkles. Cole was putting more icing into his mouth than on the treats.

"Cole, we need frost the cupcakes, too, sweetie." Sarah moved the bowl away from her greedy little boy.

"Look how good I'm decorating this. I've barely even had any to eat." Cole held up one of his creations. The sugar coating was piled unevenly and so high that the toppings teetered precariously.

"Maybe, next time, you should just not get as much on your nose." Sarah laughed as she wiped off his face and kissed him on the head. "What am I going to do with you?" she teased with her brightest smile. Clapping her hands together, she said, "I know. Let's finish up here. I have a surprise for you."

As they continued their task, I could see where Cole got his personality. They both emitted a strong feeling of warmth and love. Being around them was like drinking liquid sunshine. They both radiated joy. The bond they shared made me smile. Cole was truly loved by his mother, and it was apparent he felt it. His deep affection for her was just as evident.

With the last cupcake frosted, Sarah sang out, "Cole, it's time to share my special surprise with you. Well, actually, it is for Bay, but I wanted you to see if you think she would like it."

"What is it, Mom?" An eager grin spread across his face.

"I made her a special drink. Here, would you taste it and tell me what you think?" Sarah held out a small glass tube filled with the blue and silver liquid.

"It's so shiny." Cole eyed it curiously. "Will I like it?" Without waiting for her answer, Cole greedily took a long drink and started to smack his lips. "Well, it is good, but it's blackberry. She would like strawberry much better, so I think we're going to have to try again, Mom," Cole declared.

"Cole, you know you're the one that likes strawberry." Sarah swept Cole into her arms and tickled him.

His giggles were soon replaced by a big yawn. "Why don't we go sit down, and I'll read you a story."

"Ok." Cole sleepily rubbed his eyes. By the time they made it to the living room, Cole was already fast asleep.

Sarah held him in her arms, gently rocking him. "I'm sorry. She's out there watching. This is the only way I know to keep you safe. I hope, one day, you'll understand and forgive me."

Watching her hold him, my thoughts drifted to my little sister. *Was she safe and warm? Was she scared?* A loud knocking on the door startled me, drawing my focus back to the moment.

Sarah called out to the visitor, "Come in."

The person who entered was none other than my mother.

Eliza wore a pink and white dress with a matching headband. Her dark red hair hung loosely down her back. Her makeup was softer and more playful than the last time I'd seen her. She looked young, vibrant, and, as always, devastatingly beautiful. Looking at her, I understood why she received so much attention. She was stunning.

"I was just taking Cole up for a nap." Sarah greeted Eliza with a kiss on the cheek. "I'll be right back."

Eliza watched as Sarah climbed the stairs. When her friend was out of view, she picked things up around the house to examine them. Once in the kitchen, my mother took her finger and scraped it through the frosting bowl. After she tasted the sugar coating, giving a sound of approval, she continued her inspection. It appeared she was looking at everything, but not finding anything of importance.

When Sarah returned to the kitchen, she held out the plate of cupcakes to Eliza. "Did you want one?"

"Of course not," Eliza snapped.

My mother never would allow herself to eat sweets. She was too vain to even gain an ounce of weight and possibly lose her position as *the most beautiful woman in Starten*. The fact she even tried the sugary concoction was enlightening.

Did my mother have a secret sweet tooth? I wondered.

As quickly as Eliza angered, she composed herself. "The topping is good though. I'll need to get the recipe. Marina is always begging me to make something with her." My mother sighed dramatically and rolled her eyes. "Five began her needy year, and I hoped by six it would have passed. I can't bear another year like this one. This phase has to end."

Hearing her words gave me a sinking feeling in my heart.

"So, what brings you here, today, Eliza? It's been a long time since you've just stopped by to say hello." Sarah changed the subject. "The last time I saw you was at Cole's seventh birthday party, months ago."

"I know. I know. I have been meaning to come over more often. You just know how it is with children. Marina keeps me so busy." Eliza sat down on the kitchen stool as if even talking about me exhausted her.

Sarah sat next to my mother. "I understand. They do keep us busy. Still, she is such a darling child and definitely smart for her age."

"Oh, yes, she's very bright but so demanding." Eliza released another dramatic sigh.

I had an urge to blast her off of her seat and onto the floor.

"Lately, it's always 'Mommy, look at me. Mommy, I need you.' Honestly, this is the first moment of relief I have had from her incessant need for attention today. So, I took my opportunity for freedom, and I thought I'd come to talk with you."

Her comments stung like a slap across the face. *Was I really that needy as a child? Being away from me was freeing?*

Eliza leaned closer to her friend. "Sarah, a mutual friend of ours is in need and I hope you will help."

"Which friend?" she asked guardedly.

"Don't play dumb, Sarah. You know who I'm talking about," Eliza snapped. Again, my mother quickly composed herself, and then she sweetly began once more, "He just needs a small favor, which we both can provide. All he needs is for us to create a small, tiny spell that requires magic from Water and Fire."

"I'm not going to help him. He will just use it to hurt someone." Sarah's eyes blazed with anger.

"Don't tell me you believe all of the lies spread about him, too," Eliza said in a soft, convincing tone. "You have the wrong idea about him. He has always been persecuted here because of his family name."

Sarah firmly maintained, "Eliza, I'll not help Cedric Drygen."

Taking a new tactic, my mother put her hand on her friend's. "Sarah, it's a small favor. If you help me, just this once, I'll never ask you to help him again. Besides, it's a small spell to shield him from harm. Now, isn't that what our magic is for? Aren't we supposed to protect people?"

"He needs protection from harm? I find that hard to believe," Sarah scoffed. "What does he really need it for?"

"Well," Eliza hesitated.

I could see the wheels in her mind spinning as she tried to figure out how to convince Sarah to submit.

"It's a protection of sorts. Cedric needs to protect what is rightfully his. As I already said, all he needs is a small Fire and Water spell. Obviously, he'll compensate us greatly for our efforts. Wouldn't you like more than what you have here? He can make our lives so much easier."

"Eliza, I'm happy with my life. There's nothing I need that Cedric can get me," Sarah insisted. "Aren't you happy? You have Elliott and a beautiful, healthy daughter. What more can you want?"

Eliza sulked. "I'm sick of living in my mother's home. This town is so small, and everything here is stifling. I need so much more than what this place offers." She stood up and stormed away. "If you're not willing to help me, I guess I'll have to find another way. Don't think I won't forget that we are no longer friends, Sarah Sands."

"Stop, Eliza." Sarah grabbed her arm. "Of course, we are still friends. I just need to think about it. Can I give you my answer tomorrow?"

Instantly, changing from an angry to an appreciative friend, Eliza gushed, "I knew you would help. Thank you so much, Sarah. You are such a dear friend." My mother hugged her tightly before Releasing her and rushing towards the door. "Thanks again. I must go now, but I'll come back tomorrow to make plans. I knew I could count on you."

As I watched my mother walk out the door, my heart broke, again. Watching her leave the house, I began to question myself. *Why did I miss her when she left?* She was never really a mother. My happy childhood memories were always of something I'd done with my grandparents. *Was it just the fact she had left me?*

My grandmother had always taken care of me. When I was sad, it was Gram who comforted me. When I was hurt, it was Gram who made me feel better. What was I clinging to? After all, the idea of the perfect mother certainly wasn't Eliza.

Pushing my pity party aside, I turned my focus back onto what was happening around me. Sarah had returned to the kitchen and pulled out a small book from one of the drawers. The cover had streaks of red, silver, white, and yellow on it.

When she sat down and began to write in it, I guessed it was her journal.

Sarah didn't write for long before there was another knock on the door.

Sarah opened the door, and, to my surprise, my grandmother stood in the doorway, holding a basket of produce.

Gram was wearing her denim overalls. Her brown hair was in two long braids under a big red hat that she wore to protect her skin from the sun. She was even wearing her work boots. She called this outfit her *dirt-digging clothes.* Coming to see Sarah must have been an impromptu thought. My grandmother would never have gone to visit anyone dressed this way.

"Sarah, can I come in?" Gram held up the basket. "I brought you some vegetables and fruit that I just picked."

"Come in, Mae," Sarah welcomed her and graciously accepted the gift. "What a nice thought. Cole loves your strawberries."

When they were inside, Gram looked around and asked quietly, "Are we alone?"

"Cole is upstairs sleeping. I gave him the potion, as we discussed. Great timing, too. You just missed my surprise visitor."

"Eliza?" Gram questioned. "What does my daughter need now?"

"She wants me to help her with a spell for Cedric," Sarah said.

"What kind of spell?" Gram asked with a disgusted look on her face.

"She claims it's just a simple Water and Fire spell meant to protect Cedric from harm. When I pressed her for the real reason, she insisted it's to keep what's his from being taken away. I have no idea what the spell is really for, but I'm not going to help her with it."

"Chester told me he had heard at the club that Drygen had been fighting with Sam Heart about who owned land up north. They both had a claim to it, but the Drygens wanted all of the property," Gram said. "I wonder if that's what the spell is for."

A small voice from upstairs shouted, "Mom. Mommy."

"I'll be up in a minute, Cole," Sarah called up to him. "Mae, thank you for coming and for the gifts. How's Marina doing?"

"She is such a joy for us. My only concern is that she's becoming stronger in her magic. I have instructed her to not tell Eliza or Elliott about anything yet," Gram said with sadness in her voice. "I made a potion for her. It looks like I'll be giving it to her sooner than I had hoped. It's just getting too dangerous for her to learn more about her magic with Eliza around. I cannot fathom how a child of mine could be so selfish? I fear I'll never know the answer to that question," Gram said as she walked towards the exit.

"Does Elliott know what is going on?" Sarah stopped Gram as she opened the front door to leave.

My grandmother shook her head. "I have no idea what Elliott knows. He always seems to be snooping around, looking for something, but I'm not sure what he's seeking. I guess only time will tell. I'll see you later, Sarah." Gram kissed her on the cheek and left.

While I watched my grandmother walk away, Cole came down the stairs. Sarah immediately picked him up and held him in her arms.

"Did you have a nice sleep, my love?" she asked, and then covered his cheeks with kisses.

"Yes, Mommy." Cole's eyes lit up. "Can we eat one of those cupcakes?"

Their warm laughter rang out as she tickled him.

CHAPTER
TWENTY-FIVE

I woke to the sound of Cole calling my name as he gently shook me. "Mara. Mara."

I opened my eyes and smiled at the sight of him. "What a lovely way to be awakened." I stretched and sat up.

Cole frown as he held out the empty vial towards me. "Did you drink some of this, too?"

You didn't think this one through, I scolded myself. "I did." Pausing to find the best way to explain my actions, I decided to go with the truth. "I'm not sure what came over me. It just seemed like a good idea at the time."

The scowl on Cole's face turned to a big grin. "I'm glad you did," he said with a chuckle. "Did you see everything?"

"Do you mean, did I hear my mother wanted nothing to do with me, or that you love frosting?" Sadness washed over me.

Instead of responding, he drew me close and kissed me.

My anger subsided as I melted into his arms. Regret replaced it. "You're not mad at me? They were your memories, and I didn't ask you first. I'm sorry. I had no right to them."

"Of course, I'm not mad. Actually, I'm glad you were brave enough to follow your instincts. I just wish I had been able to the same when you drank yours."

Again, Cole kissed me. His touch was soothing, and I didn't want to leave the comfort of his arms. Holding me tighter, he ran his fingers through my hair.

Sensible as always, Cole broke away as our kisses grew more passionate. Letting out a long breath, he said, "It's getting harder and harder to be a gentleman."

"Then, don't." I slipped my hand into his.

"Soon, you will be my wife, and then all bets are off. Today is not that day." Cole affectionately squeezed my hand. "I guess it's time to go back and face another parent. We need to find out if that's Elliott and why he's really here. Do you think he is your father?"

Exhaling, I knew I couldn't hide from all of the questions – his, or mine. I needed to admit to Cole what I was feeling. "I'm not sure what I think. I want to believe he's my father, but everything is so complicated right now. Why show up now? How could he have stayed away for so long? Was he here to distract us while Eliza took Meg? Could they be working together?"

Feeling frantic, my words flew out at a rapid pace. "I'm worried the spell won't be effective. If Elliott read it, he might be able to counter it? Maybe we should use another? I wonder if your mother has one around here. Perhaps, something that will work better."

"Calm down, Mara." Cole led me to the red chair and motioned towards it. "Sit a minute so that you can regain your composure."

He went to a cabinet and pulled out several bottles. Then, he shook the contents into a small piece of cloth. Cole tied the fabric before handing me his creation. "Take this and slowly inhale. You need to calm yourself."

I took a long breath, allowing the fragrant lavender and peppermint to fill my senses. After a few minutes, I set the pouch down. "Where did you learn how to make this?" I questioned. "Did your mother teach you? I thought you were never here."

Cole picked up the herbs and held them out to me. "Mara, stop, take in the scents, and release your worries. My mother made these pouches when I was sick or scared. She had herbs in our pantry, just like Gram. Of course, nothing like what she has here."

I settled back and allowed myself to soak up the soothing treatment. Slowly, my mind stopped racing. After a few minutes, I was relaxed enough to start making sense.

"I'm not sure what that was all about, but I'm collected now," I apologized.

"Good." Cole smoothed my hair out of my face and kissed my cheek. "Now, we can try to find a new spell to use on Elliott, and all of your questions will be answered. I promise."

As we looked through the bookcases, I began to worry again. We found nothing magical. Most of the books were just stories about the Goddess or plants and herbs.

"I watched my mother write in a journal when I was little. I wonder if it's around here." Cole patted the walls of another cupboard, looking for a hiding place.

With renewed focus, we searched every cabinet and bookcase, looking for the missing notebook.

"I'm not sure we're going to find it here, Cole," I called.

That was when he motioned for me to join him in the red room. "Does this look familiar to you?"

As I drew closer, I understood what he meant. "The painting looks like the cover of the journal we saw your mother writing in."

"Let's take the picture down and see what's behind it," Cole suggested.

We took ahold of opposite sides and lifted the large portrait. It was much heavier than it looked. Setting it down gently, I turned to inspect the wall. To my dismay, there was nothing to see behind the painting, other than a square that was lighter colored than the rest of the aged wall.

Disappointed, Cole said, "Nothing there. Let's put it back up."

We started to rehang the canvas when something caught my eye. "Wait! Put it down," I said. "There's something on the back."

Once it was back on the floor, we could clearly see a small hole in the frame.

"You're right. I think there is something here." Cole carefully tore away the paper backing. He pulled out a red journal and held it in the air. "We found it. Good eyes, Mar."

We returned the painting to its spot on the wall and settled, together, on one of the chairs. Flipping through the pages of the journal, we found many spells. There was even one similar to Gram's, but none seemed exactly right.

When we turned the next page, we both looked at each other.

"This is it, Mar," Cole said in a whisper.

Labhair an Fhírinne

Prepare three small white candles as follows:
1st wick: dip in the dried petals from an agrimony flower
2nd wick: dip in dragon's blood resin
3rd wick: dip in the ground spiny needles of a juniper tree
Prepare a yellow tri-wick candle by dipping each
pith into the ground acorns of the white oak.
Grind two small petals of the yellow rue and pour into liquid.
Serve this beverage to the one whose truth is in question.
Be cautious, as too much rue will reveal the truth,
but death will come to the one ingesting it.
Light the candles
Your target will Speak the Truth.
Remember everything is not always as it seems.

"I think you're right," I agreed.

"We have most of these ingredients already," Cole said excitedly before returning to the cabinet. He held up a large clear bottle, labeled *White Oak Acorns*. "We have everything we need now. Let's get this to Gram. She'll know what is best."

Cole continued digging through the cabinets and added more items to the box Gram had packed. While he finished loading them, I continued to look through the journal. When I came to a page with *The Protectors* written on the top, I paused for a moment. Slowly turning the page, I read the name *Silver,* written in elegant calligraphy. This page held the names Genevieve Silver, Mae Silver Veracor, Eliza Veracor Stone, Marina Stone, and Meg Stone.

The page after that had *Drygen* scrawled in dark lettering. It was surrounded by the names Camille Black Drygen, Blanche Drygen, and Cedric Drygen. Oddly, Cedric had a snake drawn through his name. Underneath it, there was wording I could barely see. As I held it closer, I could vaguely make out the faint writing. It looked like *Miles*.

I turned to the next page and slowly traced my finger over the name *Andrews*. This page was a little different. Instead of just listing the names of Lucy Andrews, Olivia Andrews, Sarah Andrews Sand, and Cole Sands, there was a delicate portrait of each included. I could see Cole's eyes came from his great-grandmother. His grandmother, Olivia, looked so sad in the sketch drawn of her. When my eyes fell on Sarah, I just stared at her, studying her features. *Why did she have to die so young?*

Cole rested his chin on my shoulder. "Wasn't she so beautiful?"

"I'm sorry." I quickly handed him the book. "I should have called you over to look with me."

"I'll go through it another time." Cole handed the journal back to me. "Did you find anything else interesting?"

I flipped another page. I smiled and held it open for him to see. "You made it into the journal."

"Such a fine specimen." Cole chuckled at his joke. Then, he turned to the next page.

I was surprised it was blank.

"This book is about the original protectors of the magic, including our great-grandmothers. I wonder why there isn't anything for Michelle Elliott's family," I said.

"Another mystery." Cole took the book from me and added it to the overflowing box. "We should go home. Gram has been alone with that man for far too long already."

"We are back, Gram," Cole announced as we entered the kitchen.

The smells of the delicious food Gram was preparing engulfed the room. The aroma caused a tinge of sadness to wash over me. *Meg should be here with us*, I bitterly thought.

"Dinner will be soon. Now, tell me everything you learned today, and I might feed you," Gram called from the stove, stirring a pot.

Cole snuck up behind her. As he did, he quietly pulled a spoon from the drawer to sneak a taste. Of course, there was no fooling my grandmother. It was Cole who got the surprise when Gram slapped his hand lightly.

My grandmother put the lid on the pot and turned the temperature down. "Ok, show me what you found," she said, wiping her hands on her apron.

As Gram sifted through the boxes, I filled her in on the day's events, including my decision to try the potion.

"Only you, Mara, would be brave enough to try something like that. Did you both see the same things?" Gram questioned.

"It started with my mother letting me frost cupcakes," Cole began. "Then, she gave me the potion to drink."

"Afterward, Eliza showed up, insisting Sarah help Cedric, and then complained about how horrible it was to be my mother." I blinked back the tears I didn't plan to shed. "Then, when she'd gone, you showed up, Gram, and talked with Sarah."

"Before all of that, my mom wrote in her journal," Cole interrupted, correcting me.

"You're right." I smirked. "Then, Cole woke up and begged for a cupcake. Cole and Sarah laughing together was the last thing I saw."

"I must have woken you up too early," Cole said. "After I ate the cupcake, she gave me a plastic dolphin named Bay. I think she did that in case any memories came back. Is that correct, Mae?"

"That is exactly what she did," Gram confirmed. She looked amused as she smoothed her apron. "We did the same thing for Mara with the dolls. I didn't want to take a chance on anything. Everything had to be explainable as nothing more than a vivid imagination."

"Um, Gram, Mara and I have been thinking. We're both concerned the spell you're planning to use on Elliott might not be useful anymore since he had the cylinder." Cole handed her the journal after opening it to the truth spell. "We found this, and we both think it will work."

Gram accepted it and began to read to herself. After a few minutes, she energetically commented, "This is what we need. The other spell would have only told us if the person was not Elliott. This will not only confirm his identity but give us clues to anything he is potentially hiding. Good instincts. Both of you have made me proud."

Soaking in Gram's praise, Cole looked around and asked, "Where is Elliott?"

"He went to check on the animals. Then, I asked him to take care of some things in Chester's woodshop for me," Gram explained. "He should be gone for a while. Why don't we gather up the supplies for this spell and prepare it? We can try it after dinner."

When we had gathered up the items, Cole said, "I'll go find Elliott and try to keep him busy."

Gram stopped him, taking his hand. "Cole, we need all of us for this. You're just as important as we are." Redirecting her attention towards me, she added, "Mara, go get a mortar and pestle for each of us from the cupboard on the patio."

As I went to get the items, Cole called after me, "Don't bring one for me. I packed one of my mom's along with the bottles of herbs."

When I came back, the table was already set up with bottles and candles. Cole stood across from Gram, and I took the spot to the left of her. Handing my grandmother the mortar and pestle I had collected, she gave me a bottle, labeled *Dragon's Blood Resin*, and one white candle. Cole held the bottle of agrimony flowers and a candle.

"Let's, each of us, prepare our candles. Remember to have an open heart and listen to it for direction." Gram poured a generous amount of the juniper needles into her bowl and began to grind the brown sticks into smaller pieces.

With a look of hesitation, Cole held the bottle tightly. Then, after carefully removing the cork, he began to pour the yellow petals into the blue granite bowl that once belonged to his mother. As he ground the dried flowers, a silver thread bounced between his bowl and my grandmother's dish, stringing them together.

I poured the small, dark brown and red chunks of dragon's blood into my bowl, and a tiny spark of fire sizzled. It continued sparking as I crushed it into a red powder. When the silver thread grew from the residue, I felt static in the air along with the strong presence of the elements around me.

With a powerful voice, Gram said, "Goddess, we prepare this spell with pure hearts and a strong determination to protect the sacred magic you have granted us. We ask your blessing and guidance."

My grandmother swirled her white candle just above the greenish-brown powder. The fine dust rose and began to follow the circles she made as the tip of the wick greedily consumed the ground juniper needles. When her vessel was empty, she set the candle down on the table in front of her.

Cole and I met eyes and began to recreate the same magic that Gram had by circling our candles above our bowls. Just as hers had, our candlewicks siphoned up all of the powder we had made. When every speck of dust was absorbed, we set the candles in front of us on the table, as well.

Gram handed each of us a pale-yellow nut from the bottle, labeled *White Oak Acorn*. She then set the biggest yellow candle centered in the middle of us before pressing its three wicks down. Cole and I watched while she ground the acorn nut into a tan powder.

This time, Gram was more methodical in turning the seed to dust. She started to the right before returning to the center. Then, she ground the pestle towards herself and returned to the center. Continuing this pattern, she worked clockwise.

We followed her movements. As we turned the acorn into a powder, it changed to a silver color and rose from the bowls. The three wicks of the candle stood up as if summoning the acorn dust. The fine lines of particles arched and trailed from our containers to one of the tapers. Once again, the candle greedily siphoned all of the powder we had created.

With the candles prepared, Gram handed me the bottle of rue petals. "Only take two small petals. We want the truth, not to kill him."

Suddenly feeling scared about the possibility of killing Elliott, I handed the bottle to Cole. "You pick the petals. I'll grind them."

Carefully dumping the petals into his hand, Gram and I watched as he sorted through them, putting the larger petals back. Holding a palmful of small, yellow pieces out towards me, he said, "Mara, trust yourself like you taught me."

As I ground the smallest petals, I focused on thoughts of my father. The man I remembered from my childhood — the man who loved me. Closing my eyes, I prayed to the Goddess. When I opened them again, the yellow ash I had made was above me in the shape of a butterfly.

Gram held out a small crystal vial, and the yellow image flew into it. Corking it, she closed her eyes. "Thank you, Goddess, for your blessings."

When she reopened her eyes, Gram began clearing the table as if nothing unusual had just happened. "Cole, let's start setting the table and, Mara, why don't you prepare the salad. Elliott should be home soon."

Cole and I exchanged looks of amazement. Only my grandmother could have something so marvelous happen in front of her and then worry about getting a meal ready.

Kissing me on the forehead, Cole whispered, "She's an incredible woman."

While Cole set the table, I began to chop the vegetables. The fresh smell of cucumbers, carrots, celery, radishes, and crisp leafy lettuce permeated the air around me. It reminded me of my youth.

I recalled Gram teaching me. She'd taught me how to grow the vegetables and when to pick them from our garden. The warm breath of her voice in my ear as she guided me to properly use the knife and the best way to cut each item came back in a flood of memories.

"I think we have enough for the salad, Mara." Gram interrupted my daydream.

Before me, I had a rainbow of chopped vegetables.

Gram nodded at a bowl. "Put the extras in there. Tomorrow's breakfast will be bursting with veggies."

Smiling, I took the bowl from her and set it down. "I was thinking about how you taught me to make a salad. I was caught up in the memory." Hugging her, I whispered, "I love you, Gram. I never needed Eliza to come home and be my mother. I always had you."

CHAPTER
TWENTY-SIX

By the time Elliott returned, dinner was ready, and Cole was eager to dig in. After we enjoyed the fresh vegetable salad, drizzled with raspberry vinaigrette, Gram brought us each an individual chicken potpie. The buttery crust of the pies held a creamy gravy full of carrots, peas, potatoes, celery, and chunks of savory pieces of chicken.

"Mae, thank you for making this. I have been dreaming of the day I would come home to you all, and I would be lying if I didn't admit your cooking was sadly missed while I was gone." Elliott took a big bite and groaned his delight.

At, Cole told stories of our childhood and the mischief we had gotten into together. It felt like we really were a family, eating a typical evening meal. I was even able to push back my anger and sadness about my sister not being here, with us, and my fear of what tonight would reveal. However, a silence eventually fell over the table.

I wasn't sure what had caused the change. Maybe it was because the meal was so delicious that words would have taken from the enjoyment of eating. Or, perhaps, it was because we all knew there was a larger issue hovering. In the end, it really didn't matter.

When we had eaten every crumb, I began to clear the dishes. As I returned to my seat, Elliott was the first to speak.

"I think it's probably time we try that spell. I don't want to wait another day for you to know, in your heart, whether I'm your father or not. I failed you before, and I don't want you to doubt me anymore."

Elliott looked sad but resolute. "Of course, I don't blame you – any of you. Who would ever believe the story I told you? It sounds crazy and made up, even to me. After all, what kind of man leaves his family?"

He closed his eyes and sighed deeply before he continued. "That is what happened, and I need you to know I'm Elliott Stone. I'm your father. If there's a way I can prove that I'm the man I say I am, then let's do it now."

"I hope you are my father," I said softly.

Gram went into the pantry and returned with a bottle of her special zizzleberry wine. The drink was a mixture of blueberries, raspberries, strawberries, and blackberries. Her secret was to add zest from limes and oranges.

I had no idea she had that bottle, let alone, where she hid it. I thought the last of the wine had been used for the Winter Moon celebration months ago. I was happy to see her hidden treasure.

Cole gathered four glasses for Gram to pour us each some of the wine while I collected the tray of candles we had prepared earlier. Arranging the candles on the table, I placed one of the white candles in front of each of us and the large yellow candle in the center. Then, I patted my pocket, confirming I still had the crystal vial of rue powder.

"Mara is going to add something to your wine before we toast, Elliott," Gram said with a serious look on her face. "If you want to back out now is the time."

Elliott slid his glass towards me. "I'm ready."

I removed the cap from the vial and carefully sprinkled the powder into his drink. Listening to my instincts, I stopped when I had emptied a little over half of the yellow rue into the glass before him. A small whirlpool formed in his wine and the powder began to swirl around until it disappeared. I looked to Gram for confirmation that everything was going as planned and I saw her brown eyes faintly flicker with silver as she stared at the drink. *How many times has she done something like this without my notice?* I wondered what else I had missed.

"Before we toast, Mara, will you light the candles?" Gram asked with a devious smile. She must have realized that I had seen her stirring the powder into Elliott's drink.

I guess it was my turn to show her that I could also connect with the elements.

I nodded and closed my eyes to focus my energy on the yellow candle before us. As the wicks of the candle lit, the flames grew strong and burst high above us. Breathing slowly, I forced myself to contain my emotion and control the blaze. This tactic effectively lowered the flames. Then, I carefully lit each of the small, white candles. This time, I had more control, and the candles flickered softly.

Elliott stared at me with wide eyes full of surprise. "It looks like I have missed a lot." He flinched as if the words caused him physical pain. "I'm not going to miss any more things in your life, Caterpillar. I promise."

I held up my wine. "A toast to the truth."

With conviction, Elliott held up his drink, looked deeply into my eyes, and vowed, "To the truth."

Gram and Cole raised their glasses, and we all took long sips.

The sweetly tart flavor that I usually savored, and delighted in having, didn't taste as delicious tonight. I knew there was nothing wrong with the wine, but rather, my fear and anxiety were souring any enjoyment.

We continued to consume our drinks as we watched the candles in silence. Nothing seemed to be happening. The anticipation built as we each sat waiting in anticipation.

Just when I was beginning to feel the frustration inside me hit the boiling point, the flames blew out. Light strands replaced the burning fire.

The soft wisps of the extinguished flames rose above us. Soon, they grew thicker and covered the ceiling. Eventually, a thick mist-like haze enclosed the entire room, and I could no longer see in front of me.

I reached out to put my hands on the table to steady myself and found nothing but air. Standing up, I waved my hands frantically in front of me, hoping to find Gram, Cole, or even Elliott. My attempts were futile. I was alone.

"Where are you, Cole?" I called out. "Gram? Elliott?"

There was no response, except for the hollow echo of my words.

Panic filled me. I needed to get to the light. I walked forward through the hazy air until I smacked into a wall. Then, I slide across the cool barrier. I couldn't decide if I was more afraid of the mist or what was hiding in the darkness.

I banged my arm on a hard object. Pain never felt as sweet. I had found a doorknob and yanked. It opened, and I hesitantly walked through it.

My eyes adjusted to the bright lighting, and I found myself in the main lobby of the town library.

Great. Wrong door, I thought bitterly.

I went back to, and through, the door. Instead of returning to the mist, I was still in the library. Frustrated, I tried again. After several unsuccessful times, I gave up my attempts to return home.

"You are supposed to be here," I said aloud.

Agreeing with myself, I decided to trust that the spell would lead me to the information I was seeking.

The building was empty, except for a small light shining in the archives. When I reached the back corner of the library, I saw four girls sitting around a large book, intently reading it.

"Viv, I found it. We should definitely try this one," the redheaded girl said with excitement to the girl beside her.

The dark-haired girl had pale white skin and soft brown eyes. I couldn't shake the feeling that I knew her. She seemed so familiar to me.

"Good idea, Camille," Viv said to the redhead, and then turned towards the other two girls. "Let's meet up tomorrow night, and we'll attempt it."

"Michelle has to ask her mommy if she can come play," Camille said, mockingly turning towards the girl next to her. "Isn't that right?"

A spark of anger grew in the girl's violet eyes, and she retorted, "I don't have to ask anyone. I'll be there."

"She's just teasing you, Michelle," a quiet voice came out of the fourth girl. Nervously, she kept twirling her long, blonde hair. "I'll be there, too."

"Lucy, can you bring some candles from your mother's shop?" Viv asked the nervous girl. "I think I know the perfect spot for us behind my house in the forest. If you all sleep at my house, we'll be able to slip in and out, undetected."

"Here's the list of items we each need to get." Camille handed a slip of paper to each girl, "Let's meet early tomorrow afternoon and make a day of it."

As the girls hugged and said their goodbyes, I realized what I had seen. Viv was actually my great-grandmother, Genevieve. I had just watched the original protectors making plans to cast their first spell.

In awe, I watched as each one left the library. They all left quickly, except one – Michelle. She took her time cleaning up and returning the books to the shelves. Something inside told me to follow her. So, when Michelle exited the library, that's what I did.

Thick fog greeted me as I passed through the door. Taking a deep breath, I cautiously walked into the dense air. When it cleared, I found myself on the front porch of a large, blue house. Instead of the teenager I'd been tracking, I heard two women having a heated discussion. After a few minutes, I realized I was looking at an older Michelle. The tall redhead yelling at her was Camille Drygen.

Camille coldly hissed, "I know what you all did, Michelle. You need to reverse it." Pacing back and forth, she continued her rant, "This is my life that you're ruining. You need to give me back my magic. My life depends on this."

Michelle put her hand on Camille's arm. Her despair was apparent. "You know we can't do that. We made a promise...you made a promise. We cannot let you continue to use this gift the way you have been."

Camille twisted her wrist and dug her long, polished nails into the flesh of Michelle's arm. "You will return my power. You will give me back what is mine."

Michelle jerked herself away from Camille. "I don't have the power to do that alone."

I flinched at the sight of the blood flowing from Michelle's wound. I touched my arm, recalling the painful cut that had just healed.

"Then, you need to convince them, or I'll destroy your family," Camille snarled.

"You can't do this. You made the same promise we made to protect," Michelle argued.

Camille slapped her across the face. "You will make it happen. You will return what is mine, or I'll stop at nothing to take away everything you love. This isn't a request, Michelle. You will make it happen."

A surge of whitewashed over me, and I found myself inside a house. Michelle was sitting at a table with a man. He had sandy blond hair and a kind smile.

"We are leaving tonight. I cannot risk what Camille will do to you or our unborn child. I spoke to Viv, and she gave us some money to help us leave. You know she will not give up until she gets what she wants. She's a Drygen now."

Another wave of white washed over me. This time, it took me a moment to find Michelle because she had aged again. I saw her braiding the hair of a small girl, who I guessed to be around seven years old.

The girl began to bounce up and down as she begged, "Please, let me go. I promise I won't go far, Mommy. I'll be careful."

Michelle kissed the child on the cheek. "Don't be gone long, Eva."

As the happy child opened the door to go outside, the sun glowed intensely. I raised my hands to shield my eyes from the glare. With no relief, I closed my eyes and waited for the light to soften.

The sound of laughter told me I was no longer in the same place. I opened my eyes and saw a large group of women looking in the direction of one person – Michelle. She was a mature woman now. Her dark hair was pulled up in a delicate bun. She wore a dazzling smile on her face as she sat next to a young woman who was holding a baby boy with curly blond hair.

"He looks so much like your father." Michelle tickled the belly of the grinning baby. "Don't you, Elliott? You're going to be just as handsome as my Samuel, aren't you?"

Elliott? Is that my father? A wave of nausea rolled through me.

Overwhelmed, I needed to sit down. I turned to find somewhere to sit and ended up face-to-face with a woman and a boy. Panicked, I swung back around to see Michelle and the woman, Eva, with the baby. Instead, I found myself in front of an even older, silver-haired Michelle with a teenage boy.

I concentrated on the youth beside her. I knew without a doubt that it was my father. *Why would he keep the fact that he is the grandson of Michelle Elliott from us?*

"Elliott, our family has hidden too long. I should have stayed and fought, but I let fear guide me," Michelle confessed. She took Elliott's face into her hands. "You need to go home and protect the magic. One day, you will have a daughter, and she will be blessed with the gift."

"Ok, let's all go back, then," Elliott pleaded. "I don't want to leave you both. We can go back together."

"No, Elliott, no one will know you are my son," Eva said. "It is safe for you to return. However, we cannot. Do you understand everything we told you, tonight?" With those words, she held out a small, silver box to him.

Elliott opened the container and pulled out a silver ring with an emerald stone. After he gazed into the box, he held the ring in front of him and said with determination, "I know what I need to do now. I promise to protect the magic at all costs."

The candle in the center of the table they were seated at knocked over, and the blaze began to spread. Soon, the room was filled with fire. I could feel the heat, but the flames licking at my skin didn't burn. Reaching through the ignited wall, I felt a cool breeze.

I stepped forward into the fire, praying, "Goddess, please protect me."

Thoughts of being burned alive came to mind, but I was pleasantly surprised when I found myself sitting at Gram's kitchen table. Everyone was in the places they had been seated before the mist rolled in.

Gram stood up and gave me a long hug and released me with a kiss on my cheek. "I love you, Mar." She then turned towards Cole. "Let's make some tea, and then we can all talk."

Cole looked at me.

I felt all the questions he was asking without saying a word. Nodding, I let him know I was going to be ok.

Giving me one of his warm smiles, he winked and went with Gram.

Elliott and I stared at each other for a long time.

"So, you're the grandson of Michelle Elliott?" My tone was, once again, much colder than I had intended. "You are, also, a protector of the magic?"

Feeling the emotions of the day crashing down on me, I choked back my tears. "And, you really are my father, Elliott Stone?" As I spoke the words, my vision blurred, and then everything went black.

CHAPTER
TWENTY-SEVEN

"Maraaaaa. Maraaaaa," a soft voice whispered my name.

I opened my eyes and was greeted by a blinding light. Shielding my sight with my hands, I tried to gather my thoughts. Blinking rapidly, I struggled to see who had woken me.

"Follow me," the voice said happily.

Lowering my hands, I, once again, attempted to see who was calling me. The light softened, no longer blinding me with its brightness, and I could see Starten Forest surrounding me. Luscious green trees held heavy branches. Their trunks were covered with a dark green moss that spread down and across the ground.

Unexpectedly, a blue orb bounced around me. Giggling, the glow transformed into a young woman, who stood as tall as I did. I instantly was mesmerized by her sparkling silver eyes. Suddenly, the girl spun, around and around, whipping her long, blue hair and blue dress.

I stepped back to avoid being knocked over. My toes squished into the soft moss.

"Don't you recognize me?" The girl twirled again, and her dress sparkled like a thousand fireflies in the night sky.

"Bay?" I questioned as I continued to stare at her. "This can't be real. I have to be dreaming."

In response to my doubt, she reached out and pinched my upper arm roughly.

"Ouch!" I cried out loud, swatting at her. "That really hurt."

"Ha! It can't be a dream. You don't feel pain when you are sleeping!" Bay laughed and began to shape-shift. She transformed from the young woman back to a blue bouncing light, and then into the small dollish form that was familiar to me.

As I stared wide-eyed at her, she returned to the young woman who had just pinched me.

"Stop wasting time and come with me." Bay grabbed my hand and quickly ran through the forest, dragging me behind her.

Before I could protest, images of trees and forest creatures flashed around me as we moved at lightning speed. Abruptly, she stopped, and I crashed into her.

"You came at the best time!" Bay exclaimed before disappearing into a large oak.

Dumbfounded, I circled the tree to find an entrance.

Bay poked her head out of the solid trunk. "Tonight is the Gealach Nua. Our celebration of the coming new moon. We'll have so much fun."

Once again, she disappeared.

"Wait!" I pounded on the trunk. "I can't go through a tree. I'm human."

"You are always the doubter, Mara. Stop believing everything you see," Bay's hollow voice called to me.

I can't walk through solid objects, I thought bitterly.

I stared at the spot where the girl had vanished. A strange sensation of familiarity overcame me. I felt as though I had been here before. Pushing away my thoughts, I closed my eyes and stepped into the tree.

Bu-dum. Bu-dum. Bu-dum.

The sound of my blood pumping filled my ears. An electric pulse flowed through me and into the inky void. My head told me to panic, but a soft voice inside reminded me to connect with my feelings. Listening to my instinct, I continued forward. Abruptly, strong hands grasped my wrists, and I was jerked out of the blackness into a large cave.

Waterfalls flowed into pristine pools. The sound of the water splashing, and the smell of a summer rainstorm filled my senses.

"I told you that you could come through." Bay dragged me into the center of the room.

Now I could see small, blue lights playing in the water and sliding down the waterfalls. "Where are we?" I asked.

My voice seemed to draw the lights attention. They quickly moved towards me. Feeling apprehensive, I grabbed Bay's hand.

"It's ok." Bay squeezed my hand, reassuring me that I was safe with her. "Everyone, I want you to meet Mara. She is the human I told you about."

Bay pushed me forward. Before I knew it, lights surrounded me.

"She's not that pretty," a childlike voice whispered.

"I think she is beautiful," another said. Something lifted my hair. "Look at her long, curly locks."

"The Goddess has blessed her, so she must be special," a male voice stated.

"Enough! Everyone, step back from Mara now!" Blaze ordered as she entered the room.

Looking around, I realized I wasn't the only one in awe of her.

Blaze walked towards me. The crimson beads of her long dress sparkled brightly, and her dark red hair shimmered with streaks of gold. It was piled high on top of her head in the most magnificent up-do.

Each ball of light took their human form and bowed to her as if she was royalty.

"Mara will be with us for a while. Let's not overwhelm her," Bay said kindly to everyone.

With her words, they dispersed, returning to the waterfalls to, once again, splash and play. The calm, soothing energy emitted from the Water elementals made me feel like dancing, and I yearned to join them. The tranquility was replaced with an intensity I didn't expect as Blaze grew closer. She made me feel like I needed to be serious and determined.

"I knew this day would eventually come, and it really is the perfect time. You must have pleased, Danu, for her to allow you to visit us." Blaze clasped my hand.

"Danu?" I whispered to Bay.

With a giggle, she whispered back, "The Goddess, silly."

Was I brought here by the Goddess? My body tensed.

"Follow me. I'll give you a tour. There is plenty of time to play. Bay will join us later," Blaze said and led me away."

"Wait, won't Gram be worried about me?" I suddenly remembered where I had been before I woke in the forest. "She will think something bad happened to me."

Blaze snickered. "Mara, your body is at home and your family thinks you are sleeping from the exhausting events of the day."

"That can't be." I jerked my hand away from her. "Bay pinched me to prove I wasn't dreaming."

"Mara, your doubts tire me." Blaze sighed. "You're not dreaming. Your soul, your spirit, your being is here now. The shell that normally holds it is sleeping peacefully. Taking away your memories of the magic has set us back. I thought the confident child you were would have returned with your memories. It appears I was wrong to have had such hopes."

Blaze took my hand back and stared deeply into my eyes. The golden specks in hers flickered like flames. "Trust us. Remember the young girl inside you. She believed in the magic and knew that there was so much unknown left to learn. Listen to your heart and push back the negative thoughts clouding your mind."

"I don't know why I let fear continue to control me. I'll try to remember who I was as a child, Blaze." I forced a smile.

"I know you will find your confidence, Mara. Now, brace yourself to be amazed," she said.

Blaze led me out of the cavern of crystal pools and waterfalls into a brightly lit corridor. Gray stone glistened around us as water ran down the walls.

We continued down the corridor, along the stone wall. It slowly transitioned from gray to an orangish-red with specks of gold. The cool air around us grew warm. It felt like a hot summer night when the wind blew just enough to make the heat bearable.

At the end of the hallway, we entered another stone cavern. This room was filled with candles of many colors, and at the top of each wick, red and orange flames flickered.

"Everyone, come meet Mara," Blaze commanded.

I looked around, expecting to find colored lights, but there was nothing in the room. It was just an empty space. "There is no one here," I whispered to Blaze.

As I spoke those words, the flames left the candles and floated towards us. I moved back from the advancing fire. I stopped my retreat when I realized it had eyes. Again, the whispers started.

"The Goddess sent her here?" a loud voice asked with obvious irritation.

"Stop, you're scaring her," a booming male voice said, silencing their chatter.

Obediently, the flames stopped and took their human forms. Eyes in varying shades of gold, with flecks of dark colors, stared at me.

How many different shades are there? I wondered.

An attractive young man stepped out of the group. His chin-length hair was asymmetrically cut, showing off his strong jawline. The longer side, which slightly covered his left eye, was dark red, almost black.

"Welcome, Mara. I'm glad to meet you finally," the mysterious man said in a husky voice. Then, he picked up my hand and kissed it.

His warm mouth lingered against my skin, and the sensual act took my breath away. When he slowly pulled away from my hand, I felt somewhat dazed. As he softly wet his lips, a strong desire to kiss him washed over me.

"Kai, she is engaged to be married." Blaze poked her finger into the man's chest. "This means she isn't available."

Here icy words seemed more than just a warning. I felt a hint of jealousy in her tone.

I forced myself to snap out of the spell I had fallen under from his touch. "Thank you, Kai. I'm glad to meet you, too." Remembering the rest of the Fire elementals were staring at me, I quickly turned and said, "And I'm glad to meet each of you, as well."

Once again, Blaze cut my introduction short by taking my hand and leading me out of the room. In a stern voice, she called over her shoulder, "Everyone will be able to get to know Mara, tonight. She will be staying for the celebration."

The group buzzed with murmurs of approval.

Blaze dragged me from the warmth of the Fire elementals' room, and a cool breeze blasted me. She led me up a seemingly endless staircase with Kai in tow. As we climbed, I began to count the steps in my head, hoping to distract myself from the tempting Fire elemental beside me.

One hundred forty. Two hundred seventy-six. Why am I not tired yet? Four hundred eighteen. Oh, it looks like we're at the top. Five hundred and ninety-nine.

The last step led to the most magnificent blue sky I had ever seen in my life. Hundreds of colored birds were flying and diving around each other. My eyes fixed on a large white cloud, where a blue bird nestled in the bits of fluff.

When I made eye contact with the azure blue-eyed bird, it winked and began to fly towards me. When it reached the halfway point, it began to spin. As it turned, the cerulean bird began to transform into a young woman.

Breeze landed before me and gave me a big hug. "Mara, I'm so glad you are here!"

I held the Air elemental tighter. I wanted to soak in the love she emitted.

As we released our hug, she took my hand and called out to the sky, "Everyone, come welcome, Mara."

This welcome was much different from the other elementals I had met. The brightly colored birds formed the words, *Welcome* and *Greetings* in the air before they landed and took their human forms. All of them had blue eyes, but their hair color ranged from white, highlighted with bright colors, to a deep purple with red streaks.

"Thank you, everyone, for the warm welcome," I said with a smile.

I was instantly swept into the arms of an Air elemental and hugged. One-by-one, they wrapped me in a tender embrace before I was passed to the next individual. I was filled with not only a feeling of love and family but a sense of knowing. The tingle in the air murmured secrets. I didn't understand the meaning of the words, but I wasn't afraid or nervous.

"Enough, Mara will see everyone, tonight." Blaze rolled her eyes, obviously annoyed by the display of affection. Cutting my introductions short, she curtly said, "Breeze, meet us later." Then, she led me away from the Air elementals towards the top of a large tree.

The branches of the trees softly swayed in a zephyr. However, when we reached the edge of the platform, one of the leaves began shaking frantically.

"Pick me up," it called.

I looked to Blaze for approval. She nodded.

Carefully, I plucked the leaf from the tree. "Now what?" I whispered to it.

"Now, you jump," the childlike voice giggled.

Looking down, I could only see large white clouds.

"Go on now. I'll keep you safe," the leaf coaxed.

Sure, I'll just jump into the nowhere because a plant is telling me to.

"Always the doubter. The gift is wasted on you." Blaze glared at me.

"You're wrong." I closed my eyes and stepped off the platform.

I had expected to fall fast. Instead, I just slowly floated. The clouds felt soft and slightly damp as I drifted through them. The blue and white sky mesmerized me. Throwing my arms back, I basked in the descent.

I had just relaxed and began to trust the moment when I was brought back to reality. Before I could react, my guide slipped from my hand.

"See you later," the leaf called as she disappeared into the clouds.

Panic filled me. I was certain to plummet to my death as my slow, tranquil descent turned into a rapid freefall. The clouds around me dissipated and I could see the green grass below.

Trust us, Blaze's reminder played in my mind.

I controlled my breathing and focused on the word *trust*. As I chanted the word, I felt a feeling of peace fill the spaces within me. I embraced the sensation of falling and submitted to the fact that I would soon hit the ground. I braced for impact.

Splat! I was shocked when I set down into a large pile of mud. Standing up, I immediately slipped and fell. By the time I exited the mound of dirt, I was covered head to toe. I wiped the grunge off and found myself, face-to-face, with Daisy.

"Now, that was an entrance." Daisy's bright green eyes twinkled as she scraped some of the sludge from my cheek. "Everyone, let's clean up Mara," she called.

With those words, soft leaves swept and brushed me. Within minutes, I was tidied up and ready to greet my cleaning crew.

"Thank you." I laughed. "I think I'm clean enough now."

The leaves fell to the ground and took their humanlike forms. Elementals with light brown or blonde hair and eyes in shades of green circled me. This time, there were no insults. Instead, there were only curious stares and sincere smiles.

A gust of warm wind blew from above me. I looked up to see Blaze making her elegant entrance.

Irked at her gracious descent after my embarrassing fall, I snapped, "Thank you for your assistance, Blaze. The leaf you told me to trust dropped me."

The Fire elemental threw back her head and laughed. "You needed a reminder that I would never let you get hurt." She eyed me up and down. "I'm not sure what the fuss is. You look fine."

"I'm sorry, Mara." A brown-haired girl stood timidly in front of me. She trembled as she continued her apology, "I wouldn't have let you get hurt, either."

Recognizing her voice as my free fall guide, I looked into her teal eyes and felt such sincerity that I could not be mad anymore. I took her hand into mine. "It's ok. Next time, I'll remember to bring my own parachute."

Relieved by my response, her face lit up, and she hugged me.

"Lily," Daisy addressed the girl, "now that you have apologized, don't you think we should let Mara get ready for tonight's celebration?"

Blaze pushed through the Earth elementals and grabbed my hand. "Come with me, Mara. You have one final stop." Turning towards Daisy, she said, "Gather Bay and Breeze."

I turned and looked back at the Earth elementals. They smiled and waved at me. In the few minutes we had spent together, they already felt like family. Tears filled my eyes as I was reminded of Meg. The thought of her being scared and alone stole my breath.

Sensing my sudden mood shift, Blaze squeezed my hand. "We are almost there."

For the first time since I arrived here, I felt slightly comforted by her. I blinked away the tears forming in my eyes and took a deep breath.

CHAPTER
TWENTY-EIGHT

Blaze and I walked through the forest, deep into the serenity of the chestnut brown and green trees. If I wanted to hug the trunks, I would need arms that were ten times the length they were now. The long branches held emerald leaves that were as big as my head. The familiar sound of birds chirping and the soft clicking of the silver moss beetles comforted me.

Reaching the edge of the woods, we stood before a wall of transparent multicolored water that flowed from an unknown source. Blaze reached out, parted the liquid sheet as if moving a curtain and walked through it. Following close behind her, I felt the soft mist of the waterfall as we entered a room that stilled my heart.

The room was wide-open, packed with silver framed mirrors, much like the one in my grandmother's bedroom. Like her looking-glass, the silver frames had a nest-like design surrounding the polished metal centers. Additionally, the room smelled of lavender, cinnamon, and fresh-cut grass mixed with the hint of a summer rainstorm. The scents alternately filled my senses without overpowering them or bleeding together into one complicated fragrance.

In the center of the room, there were four silver chairs. Each seat had a unique design engraved on its high back representing an element. They were positioned around a large, granite stone. The smooth top was a lilac color with streaks of dark blue, yellow, pink, and white running through it.

Blaze walked towards the seat with the flames on it and sat down. "Mara, come sit in the center."

I was afraid to speak. Instead, I nodded and did as she directed.

Out of nowhere Daisy, Breeze, and Bay appeared. They took their corresponding places in the circle.

"Mara, you are at the seat of Danu. Close your eyes and focus your thoughts on connecting with the spirit around you." Daisy gave me a smile of encouragement.

Listening to her words, I closed my eyes and slowly began breathing in and out. My grandmother's prayers came to my mind and I softly spoke them, "Air, I ask you to clarify my thoughts. Fire, I ask you to burn away my fear and doubt. Water, wash away my anger and sorrow. Earth, I ask you to ground me in the goodness around me and strengthen me. Spirit of the Goddess, I ask you to guide me."

A gust of elemental magic spun around me. I was cocooned in strong, warm winds, swirling droplets of water, blades of grass, and embers of fire. An overwhelming sensation of being hugged by Gram washed over me. Tears of joy filled my eyes.

Then, it was all gone.

My heart ached for the feeling to return, and I pleaded, "Send the magic back."

Looking around, I gasped in surprise. The chairs were empty. I was alone.

I had little time to drown in my sorrow before the room began to glow. I searched for the source of the illumination. I found the mirrors along the outer walls were radiating light.

"Everyone likes tea," a faint voice said.

I cocked my head and listened. There was a soft hum from the center mirror, and I heard the voice again.

"Purple is my favorite color today."

"Meg," I cried. It was undeniably my sister talking. I dropped to my knees and began tapping on the mirror. "Meg, I'm here. It's Mara!"

I realized she couldn't hear me, so I sat back. I quietly watched, hoping for a clue as to where she was, and how I could save her. As I had seen hundreds of times before, Meg was preparing a tea party for the stuffed animals. Her role was the gracious hostess.

For this tea party, Meg was dressed in formal attire.

I bet she hates that outfit, I thought bitterly.

To confirm my suspicions, she tugged on the puffed sleeve of her lavender tea dress and blew out a breath of hot air. This sent one of the large curls that framed her soft face up and then back into her eye. Grumbling to herself, Meg stood beside the small, circular table occupied by stuffed animals dressed in the same attire as her.

She picked up a teddy bear and tugged on the bow around his neck. "When we have tea in my home, you won't have to wear this choky tie."

Kissing him sweetly on the head, Meg set the bear down and focused on the bouquet of white roses in the center of the table. My little sister rearranged them before she adjusted one of the cups and saucers. When everything met her satisfaction, she turned her attention towards her guests.

"One lump or two?"

As her imaginary friends silently responded, she pretended to drop sugar cubes into their cups.

"What a lovely dress you have on, Ms. Ellie." Meg complimented a pink elephant and served her several cookies.

"Mr. Ribbet, this does have the flies you requested," she said seriously to a green frog in a black suit.

I smiled as I watched my sister's interaction with her stuffed animals. I noticed how much older she looked. It seemed, just yesterday, that she was a toddler, running through the house.

Come now and read, Mara, I heard as I reminisced about the times my little sister brought me her favorite book. She would insist I read it, over and over, until my voice felt raspy.

"Miles, come here before your tea gets cold," Meg called out, interrupting my memories.

The echo of her voice told me she was in a large room. I wished the area around her would clear up. I had no clues telling me exactly where she was being kept. A small, brown table with child-sized chairs was not unique enough to help.

"Patience, Meg," a female voice purred. "He wanted to look his best for you."

Blanche Drygen entered. Her short, silver hair was perfectly coiffed.

"How lovely of you to take time out of your kidnapping to look so lovely, Blanche," I growled at the image. My eyes narrowed when I noticed a small child holding the woman's hand.

The boy had dark brown hair and large greens He looked to be about five years old. Like Meg, he was overdressed, but he looked comfortable in his black suit with a small lavender bow tie.

"Isn't your brother handsome?" Blanche asked.

As if on cue, the boy did a small turn to show off his outfit.

Your brother?

The boy stepped towards me, and I was better able to examine him. He looked so much like Meg that I had no doubts. Miles was Eliza's son.

"Are you the reason she left us?" I questioned the boy, knowing he wouldn't answer.

The boy moved out of my line of sight, and Blanche stepped back into view. "And you, also, look pretty, Meg. Isn't it nice to finally be dressed up like a reputable young lady with fine clothing?"

Meg clenched and unclenched her fists. I knew my sister, and this was taking every ounce of will she had inside her not to tell Blanche what she really thought.

"Go on, Meg. Tell her that we have better things than money," I encouraged.

Instead, in a cold, rehearsed way, she said, "Yes, Grandmother Drygen. I'm very lucky that you have taken me away to such a lovely estate and taught me how finer people live."

The small boy stood next to Meg, and pensively asked, "Did I present myself right, Grandmother?"

"Very nice job, Miles. Your manners are always impeccable. Now, enjoy your tea with Meg." Blanche patted the boy on the head before she walked away.

I kept my eyes trained on the brother I didn't know we had, but I could hear the click of the woman's shoes striking the hard floor and a door shutting.

Miles looked towards Meg for direction.

She pointed to the only empty chair. "I was saving the best seat for you."

Miles sat amidst the stuffed guests. He wore a big grin as he sipped the pretend tea. "Meg, can I ask you something and will you promise not to get mad?" The child bit his lip as he waited for her response.

Meg set her teacup down and narrowed her eyes at the small boy. "How many times do I need to tell you that, in my family, it's ok to ask questions?"

Miles blurted out, "Grandmother said you would teach me your magic. She said you have more magic than Mommy inside you. Can you tell me your secrets?"

Meg shook her head and sighed. "Miles, I keep telling you. Magic is pretend. Mommy is playing a trick on us when she makes fire appear."

Miles slumped in his chair.

Seeing his disappointment, Meg jumped up. "Ok, Miles. I will teach you how to make magic." Twirling around and knocking everything in her path over, she called, "Wind and Air, come to me."

Miles laughed as our sister threw stuffed animals so that they could fly through the air.

"Water, sprinkle your magic on us." Meg giggled, dipped her fingers into a glass of water, and flicked the moisture onto Miles.

"Enough, enough." Miles wiped the water droplets off his face. Then, he grew serious. "I like you, even if you don't have magic inside you, Meg."

"I like you, too, Miles, even if you are my bratty little brother." Meg smirked. "You are in luck. Mara taught me how to be a good big sister."

"Will she like me, too?" Miles timidly asked.

"She will *not* like you, Miles." Meg grabbed his hands. "She will *love* you as much as I do. So will Gram. She will make us yummy treats and tuck us into bed. Cole will teach you to play kickball, and he'll take us swimming. He tells the best stories about the King of the Snapping Trout."

Miles pulled away from Meg and sat down at the table. "They will never let me go with you."

Meg wrapped her arms around the younger boy. "I'll always take care of you, Miles. Gram and Mara will find us and take us both home."

With those final words, the mirror lost the image. Tapping on the reflective material, I began calling out to my sister, "Meg, I'm here, and I'll come to take you home. I promise."

Knowing she couldn't hear me, I felt the anger and frustration beginning to grow inside me. I decided to find something to smash the looking glass with, hoping I'd get to Meg. Turning around, I smacked into the elementals.

"Bring the image back! I need to find my sister!" I shouted.

"Mara, we can't bring the image back. It was a gift from Danu for you. Meg is safe, though, and she's with Miles, who you can see she loves already."

"How is a small boy being there going to comfort me? She is with those horrible people while I'm wasting time running around magic land. I need to go to her now. He can't protect her." My breath quickened, and I began to shake.

The elementals just stared at me.

"Show me how to get back home!" I barked, trying to push past them.

Bay hugged me tightly. "Mara, we still have the celebration. You can't leave, yet."

"I cannot stay here another minute." I broke out of her arms. Please, tell me how to go back. I need to find my sister."

The room lit up with a blue light. It was the mirror I had watched Meg and Miles in.

"Is this the way?" I rushed towards the looking glass.

Daisy nodded and gave me a sad smile.

The mirror crackled as if warning me to turn around.

I have to save Meg, I told myself. Not wasting another minute, I walked through the object.

Instant regret filled me as my skin felt electrified. Each second in the blue aura meant excruciating pain. With a final push, I was through the barrier. A final bolt of energy rushed through me, and I collapsed to the ground.

The blue mirror continued to zap me. I rolled away from it and tucked into the fetal position. Rocking the waves of energy away, I held myself. Slowly, the light faded, and I watched as my entrance wholly dissolved. It was now just a stone wall.

Unable to stand, I crawled to the center of the small, circular room and sat myself up. I closed my eyes. *What have you done, Mara?*

When I opened my eyes, a second mirror appeared. I crawled towards the silver light. When I reached it, I tried to go through it, but it was just a mirror. I rested my cheek on the cold glass.

I didn't know how much time had passed before I felt sturdy enough to stand again. At first, I stumbled, but soon, my legs felt strong. Circling the room, I pushed on every inch of the wall and floor, searching for an exit. To my dismay, there was no way out.

Impenetrable stone surrounded me. The ceiling was, at least, forty feet above me and appeared to be the same hard rock. Feeling defeated, I sat down in the middle of the floor and began to cry.

"I never asked for this gift. Nothing good has come from it. My mother is obsessed with power and convinced my father to fake his death. My grandmother has been stuck raising their children. Families are hiding their gift and running away to keep themselves safe. Others are kidnapping children, trying to steal more magic. What good has this *gift* been to my family?" I demanded.

"Mara, pull yourself together," a voice snapped at me.

I turned, ready to fight when I caught the image of Sarah Sands in the mirror. I gasped. "You're dead."

Sarah glared at me.

I had never heard her use a stern tone, let alone, wear such a look of disapproval. *Your future mother-in-law will think you're crazy if you don't pull yourself together,* I scolded myself. Embarrassed, I quickly regained my composure.

"If you are done with your tantrum, Mara, we can talk."

I nodded.

Sarah stepped through the looking glass and took my hand. In an unexpected move, she pulled me into her arms and held me close.

I smiled. Her familiar scent – citrus and frosting – brought me back to her kitchen where she'd always made fresh orange juice and cinnamon rolls for us. Abruptly, she released me and returned to the mirror, bringing back from my thoughts.

"I'm sorry. Come back," I cried out.

"I can't be in that world for very long. Are you calm now?" Sarah asked.

I knew this sweet, kind voice.

"You were never a burden on Mae. She loved her girls. Even if Eliza and Elliott had not disappeared, your grandmother would have been just as much a part of your lives. Our families were blessed with a gift, but it is, also, a big responsibility. You are just learning what it means, and I regret any part I had in holding that from both Cole and you. We did what we thought was best at the time. Now, it is your responsibility to unite the families and honor the gift."

Taking her words to heart, I felt guilty for my meltdown. "Sarah, I spoke out of anger. I just don't understand why everything is such a mess. My sister is scared but putting on a brave face for that little boy.

How am I supposed to feel about him? He must be the reason Eliza left us if she really is his mother."

Sarah's blue eyes filled with tears that she blinked away. "Miles is your half-brother, Mara. Eliza was always rash in her decisions when it came to Cedric. You can't blame the boy for your mother's mistakes."

"I don't blame him. I will take him away, too." I crushed my fist into my leg.

"You cannot face her full of fear and anger, Mara. You must go with strength, love, and trust of the Goddess that is inside you. Don't rush off to save Meg and lose yourself."

With those last words, her image disappeared, and I found myself staring at my own reflection. My own brown eyes seemed sad and lifeless. The dark circles surrounding them were deep and somewhat alarming. Seeing what Sarah must have seen, I felt determined to be the person that Gram raised, not this broken shell before me.

Gram would never sink into sadness and anger. She would say, "No time to worry, we have much to do," and then tackle whatever was in her way. I would become the person she believed I was. Furthermore, the Goddess saw something in me that was special. I would honor the gifts she gave me.

As I felt my determination build, my reflection changed to rippling water. The image reminded me of the choppy waves on Sparrow Lake. At first, the small swells were calm, but the speed and intensity of the water grew. I found myself being splashed as the waves slapped against the mirror.

I shouldn't feel water, I thought.

I moved away just in time to watch the mirror shatter, and the violent flood burst out towards me. The room filled with rushing water. Frantic, I searched for an exit. Behind the broken mirror, I only found solid rock. Anger built inside me as I banged on the hard walls.

"Damn! Damn! Damn it!" I cried.

Soon, it reached my knees and, what seemed like seconds later, I was wading through waist-high water. I struggled to keep my head above it. It was bad enough that the water was filling the room so rapidly, but then, it felt alive. The cold waves were like hands tossing me back and forth. I was in a game of Ping-Pong, and I was the ball.

Eventually, I found myself pulled under the icy fluid and surrounded by thousands of bubbles. I frantically kicked my feet to escape.

When I broke the surface, I focused on the times I spent with my grandfather, learning how to swim. I began to feel less scared as I recalled his calm voice and gentle words, telling me I would be safe. As I floated in the rising water, I realized it was responding to my emotions.

"Let me out!" I screamed in anger.

A massive wave crashed on top of me. I laughed at my foolishness and the water calmed. However, my brief moment of peace didn't last. Before I knew it, I had almost reached the ceiling, and with no exit, I began to panic. At this rate, I would be trapped and drowned within minutes.

Feeding off my fear, the water tossed me around again. It rose up my neck and over the top of my head. I was going to drown.

No, I scolded myself. *You are the granddaughter of Mae Veracor and the great-granddaughter of Genevieve Silver. You are the descendant of strong women. You have nothing to be afraid of.*

In response to my words, the water retreated a little bit, and I was able to tilt my head back above it.

How am I going to get out of this?

A small, silver rock shined in the ceiling. I reached my hands up and touched it. The stone was solid, but not as hard as I expected. Desperately, I began clawing at the soft rock. As I tore at it, the material crumbled in my hands. Feeling confident, I dug my short nails into it with all the power I could muster, tearing at the heavy sandy material.

I blinked away the small particles covering my face. Laughing at the irony, I mused, *If I keep this up, I'll bury myself alive, instead of drowning.*

Thoughts of giving up and just letting myself sink away crossed my mind. Then, damp soil replaced rock, and I was motivated to try harder. The black earth was like the soil in my grandmother's garden.

Finally, the small hole I had dug into the ceiling was just enough for my hands to fit through. Concentrating every bit of energy I had inside me, I continued my escape until I felt small roots. Tugging at the plant in my hand, a warm breeze blew over my scraped and bleeding fingertips. I patted the area, hoping I was touching the soft, damp moss of Starten Forest and not pursuing another trap.

My efforts of removing the soil and moss around me were not wasted. I was quickly able to reach my arms up and through the hole that I had made. Struggling, I pulled myself out of the water. I laughed as I felt the breeze on my dirt-covered face.

Digging my elbows into the ground, I was able to heave half of my body out of the hole. Panting and shaking from the effort, I rested my cheek on the ground. *Don't give up now*, I thought.

Reaching out around me, I anchored my fingers into the earth and made my final effort to claw myself out of the watery cave. Wriggling and writing, I dragged myself onto the large roots of a tree.

You freed yourself, I thought proudly before embracing my exhaustion.

CHAPTER
TWENTY-NINE

As I lay, staring at the ground, I had so many thoughts running through my head that I could not straighten them out enough to focus. *Why am I so drained if this is just my soul? Isn't my body at home, resting, right now?*

A warm breeze blew over me, and I braced myself for a scolding from Blaze.

"Are you going to just rest there all day," a deep sultry voice asked. The words ran through me like a hot wave, and I knew it was Kai.

Not moving from my resting spot, I replied, "I'm taking a rest after my near-death experience. A break seemed appropriate after digging myself out of the watery tomb I was trapped in."

"Isn't that a bit dramatic? You look alive and well, other than all the dirt covering you. Come on. Here, take my hand, and I'll help you up."

As if my mind had no control over my body, I rolled over to face him and accepted his outstretched hand. When our fingers touched, I felt the same heat run through me that I had the first time we met.

Kai yanked me hard, and I crashed into him.

Stepping back, I stood face-to-face with the handsome elemental. For the first time, I noticed the color of his eyes. They started as golden orange at the black pupil and then spread out into streaks of deep red and yellow. The urge to kiss him once again filled me. Before I knew what was happening, I found his warm lips on mine.

Kai pulled me close against his body and gently kissed me. My fingers caressed the nape of his neck. As his long hair touched the back of my hand, Cole came to my mind and I, suddenly, felt repulsed at what I was doing.

I pushed Kai away. "No, I'm in love with Cole."

Kai moved closer to me and stroked my cheek. "He isn't here, and I am." Coaxing me back into his arms, the attractive guide slowly trailed his lips along my jawline and neck.

Again, I felt myself falling under his spell.

This is just a dream. It isn't my body, I justified.

Kai kissed me again.

Just a few more seconds and I will stop him. Cole won't mind. Wait, Cole will be angry.

Fighting back my desire to let him continue, I shoved him away and slapped him across the face. "I'm engaged to Cole. You're using magic on me and trying to confuse me."

Kai traced his finger along my lips. "I used no magic on you, Mara. Fire is passion. I can feel it inside you. When you are in Danu's realm, you are free."

When Kai leaned in to kiss me again, I shoved him away. "Stop. I need to go home." I distanced myself and put my hands out to block any further approach. "Show me the way back now."

"You think you are ready to go home, Mara?" He looked at me with pity in his eyes. "Your emotions are all over the place. I bet you are like this with the mortal boy. Do you kiss your Cole passionately, and then strike him?"

"You know nothing about me. Take me home or I will..." I faltered. *What can I do?*

"Seriously, Mara, how are you going to be calm enough to face what is coming? You can't even control your urge to kiss me again."

Anger built inside me, and I realized he was right. I did want to kiss him again, which only made me feel guilty. I loved Cole. There was no doubt in my heart about my love for him, but the passion Kai awoke in me was irresistible.

"I don't want to kiss you again," I lied unconvincingly. "In fact, I need a shower to wash your disgusting handprints off of my body."

Mocking me, he said, "Oh Mara, you are right. You do need a shower, but it isn't to wash me away."

"Can you please just show me how I can get home?" I asked sweetly, trying a new tactic.

"No." Kai's voice was void of emotion.

Rage built up inside me. I screamed at him, "Show me the way! I need to get to my sister."

Again, he shook his head. "Mara, you are not ready to leave here. Your emotions are a mess. If you go back before they are under control, you will have no chance of getting your sister back."

Defeated, I flopped to the ground and blinked back my brimming tears. The soft sounds of the forest played all around me. Every emotion I had rushed through me to break open the dam holding back my tears.

Kai sat down in front of me, quietly watching me.

"I know I need to control my emotions, but I don't know how to," I admitted. Unchecked tears continued to flow down my cheeks.

The handsome elemental stood up and held his hand out to me.

In response, I moved backward, not wanting to throw myself into his arms.

"Mara, I promise I will not kiss you again unless you ask me to." Kai offered his hand out to me again. "Friends?"

The serious look on his face convinced me to believe him. As I touched his hand, I felt a warmth flow through me, but this time, it felt affectionate, not romantic.

"Friends." I released his hand. "Now, will you help me. I need to save my sister."

"Trust me, and I will help you use your emotions so they will not harm you," he promised.

Accepting the fact that I had to trust someone, I allowed Kai to lead me back through the forest. When we reached the tree where I had begun my tour of the elemental's home, excitement filled me. Kai was going to help me.

Instead of returning to the elementals, Kai led me deeper into the forest. We walked until we reached a trail lined with unique birch. Each tree had a slender white trunk covered with a thick, peeling bark that exposed its green inner bark. Crowing the trees were long branches covered with hundreds and hundreds of small, salmon-colored leaves. Even more, shed foliage canvased the path we were on.

Feeling calm, I followed without speaking. I began wondering how I was going to learn to control my anger and fear in such a peaceful place. Feeling frustrated with myself, I sighed.

As if reacting to my unspoken thoughts, the branches of the trees leaned in and blocked the path.

I whipped around to escape and found that we were surrounded. My heart began to beat fast. "Is being trapped part of the plan?" I asked with a bit more anger in my voice than I had intended.

Kai just looked at me with an emotionless face. His nonresponse infuriated me.

"You are not helping me at all," I said.

Slap. One of the tree branches struck me. The smart sting of the deep red mark angered me even more.

"Stop!" I slapped at the branch.

Instead of retreating, the tree became more aggressive and began to whip my legs. The sharp slaps continued as I fought back. I looked at Kai and saw how calm he was.

You're feeding the anger, I realized. So, instead of fighting, I accepted the pain and focused on breathing. As my frustration began to subside, the attacks lessened. When I was completely devoid of negative emotion, the trees rose and opened the path again.

"So, you can learn." Kai smirked and took my hand.

I looked at him, hopefully.

"No, you are still not ready to go home, yet."

I controlled my reaction. I chose just to simply nod before we continued our walk.

Our pace was casual, and I began to enjoy the scenery. The sky above was an azure blue with birds of many colors, soaring through the soft, white clouds. I wondered if these were real birds or Air elementals.

"Is that Breeze up in the sky?" I asked.

Kai laughed. "No, just birds."

The trail began to incline slightly, and we found ourselves at the end of the path of trees. We stood in front of a rocky road of black stone. The rocks looked sharp, so I searched for another way to go.

"Giving up already?" Kai wrinkled his brows at me.

Not wanting to give him the satisfaction of lecturing me, I stepped off the dirt path and onto the dark, jagged trail in front of us. As I expected, the ground sliced at my feet. The sandals I wore offered little protection. Every step agitated me, and I felt a slow rage building inside me, once more.

"How much farther until we are out of the rocks," I asked impatiently. "My feet are killing me."

Just as before, Kai ignored my question, which only made me angrier. Before I could tell him what I really thought of him, I felt a sting on the top of my foot.

"Ouch," I cried out in pain. Looking to see what was attacking me, I realized the rocks were smoking, and flames were starting to slap at my feet and legs. *Damn it,* I thought to myself. *"You're a slow learner. You are burning yourself.*

I pushed back the pain and continued walking. I tried not to pay attention to the fiery sparks that were still licking at my skin or the sharp edges of the rocks cutting into my feet. My focus was on the endless path ahead of us. Eventually, the fire slowly stopped burning me, and I was able to ignore the fact that the rocks were still uncomfortable to walk on.

As we continued, I began to think about how my feelings were affecting the world around me – how they were only hurting me. Proudly, I comprehended that I was capable of controlling my environment. I could prevent the fire from feeding off my anger by simply releasing it. At that moment, I realized that was what would be necessary when I faced Eliza.

I released Kai's hand and excitedly spun around to share my epiphany. However, one second of taking my eyes off the trail cost me. The ground underneath me shifted, and I was falling off the edge of a cliff that had come out of nowhere.

CHAPTER
THIRTY

I reached out to stop myself from dropping into the unknown. My hands dragged down the side of the mountain. They didn't catch, but they slowed me.

Panic filled me. *This is another test. You can stop this,* I told myself. *You can stop the fall. Just breathe and think.*

I looked around but didn't find any solutions. There were only the birds from earlier, soaring high above in the sky, and a deep blue void below me, which I guessed was water. An idea came to mind, and I focused on not stopping the fall, but rather embracing it. If it was water below me, I was going to land in it, and I might as well try to do it without hurting myself.

I remembered Gramp's stories about how his older brothers would dare him to jump out of trees into the lake. He ended up wowing them with the amazing tricks he could do. Of course, Gramp was quick to warn me that jumping into the water was exciting but could be perilous if not taken seriously. With his advice on my mind, I held my body straight with my hands to the side, and my toes pointed downward. Now, all I could do was take a deep breath and brace myself for the plunge.

I landed hard with a big splash and bulleted through the clear liquid. As my descent slowed, I was surrounded by hundreds of small bubbles. I felt my panic return. I wasn't sure what direction was up. I swam towards the surface, but soon, realized I was only going deeper.

Straining to hold my breath, the tightness in my chest became unbearable. My lungs burned, and I was sure, at any moment, they were going to explode. Waves of black washed over me, and I felt myself slipping into the darkness. Unable to fight anymore, I let the void consume me.

Suddenly, I was ripped from the serene peace the abyss offered me. Arms wrapped around my body and swam us towards a light. As we broke the surface, I gasped for air and sucked in every ounce of oxygen I could.

Kai wiped my hair out of his face. "I would give your dive only an eight for form, but definitely a ten for style."

"You save my life." I threw my arms around his neck tightly. I held on to him as if he was a life vest. I trembled as he held me close.

"You are safe, Mara. You will always be safe with me."

Once again, tears flowed down my face. I was safe in Kai's arms, and I didn't want him to let go of me. An image of my fiancé flashed in my mind. I should have let go of Kai and simply thanked him. Instead, I clung onto him tighter as I pushed away thoughts of Cole.

After I reluctantly let go of Kai, and we left the water, I realized we were on the shores of Spartan Lake. It was very close to the area where I had learned to swim. Hand-in-hand, we walked through the forest and thought I should have felt awkward, being with Kai was comfortable.

When we reached the tree line, Kai bowed to me. "After you."

He won't kiss you unless you ask, I reminded myself and stepped closer towards him. "Kai, I changed my mind. I —"

Bay burst out of the woods and spun me around. Releasing me, she jumped up and down. "You returned!" she squealed. "I'm so glad you are back. Thank you, Kai, for convincing her not to go, yet."

Kai leaned in towards Bay and whispered something into her ear. Her eyes grew large, and she blushed.

Guessing Kai was being his usual flirty self, I sighed as I found myself feeling a little bit jealous. *You are being stupid, Mara. You are going to marry Cole. Kai isn't interested in you. He is just a big flirt. Stop thinking about him.*

I brushed past Kai and linked arms with Bay. "I need help getting cleaned up if I'm staying for the celebration. I'm a mess."

"Bye Kai," Bay called as she pushed me into the tree and into the other realm.

The Water elementals were playing and splashing, just like the last time I saw them. Bay clapped her hands together to get their attention. The elementals stopped what they were doing and looked towards her.

"Everyone, we need to prepare Mara for tonight's celebration. All hands on deck." Bay leaned close to me. "I learned that command from a band of pirates."

Before I knew it, I was being tugged and pulled on. I didn't have time to feel embarrassed or shy as they removed my clothing. Soon, I was covered with bubbles and water. My hair was washed and conditioned, emitting a fragrant citrus and berry scent that invigorated me. For the first time, I was excited for the events to come.

After I was dried off and dressed, round two of *Make Mara Presentable* began. My thick hair was brushed and yanked. Finally, I was poked and prodded as makeup was being applied to my face and arms.

"Close your eyes." Bay rubbed a soft brush on, and around, my eyes. After a few minutes, she handed me a silver hand mirror. "Ok, you can open them now. What do you think?"

I stared into my hazel eyes. They were a deep brown surrounded by purple eyelashes and silver eyeshadow. The eyeliner was a combination of the two colors and ended on the outside of my eyes in the soft design of the infinity symbol.

"Wait!" Bay took the mirror from me. "I forgot the final touches. Pout out your lips for me – like this." Bay contorted her lips and made a silly fish face in demonstration.

I giggled at the absurdity. Then, I imitated her with my best guppy impersonation. I knew I must have looked just as silly because Bay's chuckles joined mine. Once we were able to control our laughter, she delicately painted my lips. When she finished, she led me to a full-length mirror.

I was shocked by the reflection staring back at me. It looked like my face, but I had never thought of myself as beautiful before. I was dressed in a lavender halter dress that fell to my ankles. It had starlike flowers throughout the chiffon material. My feet were bare, but my toenails had been painted an eggplant purple to match my fingernails. My nails looked longer and healthier than they had been when I exited the flooding water earlier. Returning to inspect my face again, I took in the way the glamorous makeup made me look, and I smiled as my dark red lips pouted.

"The final touch." Bay placed a crown of star-shaped flowers on top of my head.

For the first time, I saw my hair. They had tamed my wavy locks, making them smooth and shiny. I felt like a princess from the silly stories of my childhood.

"You look amazing," a deep sultry voice behind me said. Chills ran through my body. "I have a present for you."

I turned to face my greatest temptation. I couldn't help but beam as I saw him. Kai was dressed in a fitted, charcoal gray suit with a white shirt and a deep purple tie. His hair was smoothed back, which made his handsome facial features even more prominent. He held out a pair of silver strapped sandals for me.

"Take a seat." Kai motioned to a nearby bench. "We can see if these will fit."

I sat, and he knelt in front of me. I felt ridiculous.

Just put on your shoes, and then go. You have a boyfriend. A fiancé. But he isn't here. I hated myself for such thoughts. *No! You love Cole. You are reacting to the magic.*

"I can try them on myself," I insisted.

"Don't be silly. You are a princess, tonight, and will get the royal treatment." Kai held his hand out, waiting for my foot.

Had he read my mind? No, he probably figured it out by your childish behavior in the mirror. Go on and get this over with, I, once again, scolded myself.

I stuck my foot out for him to slip on the sandal. I warmed from the sensation of his touch, which sent a shiver through my body. When he fastened the strap on the first shoe, I pulled my foot away and held out my hand. "I think I'll be able to put the other shoe on myself." I grabbed the other shoe and slipped it on. "See, all good here."

As if on cue, Bay and the other elementals came in to gush over how wonderful I looked. Catching a glimpse of Kai watching us, I saw a sadness in his eyes. Before I could ask what was wrong, I was swept off by another group of Water elementals to begin the evening's festivities.

We took the same path as my first tour through the caves. A crowd of elementals met us, each dressed in elegant gowns or stunning suits. The excitement around me filled my heart with such joy that I was able to forget to be sad or worried about my family.

As we ascended the steps up to the Air elemental platform, a warm breeze blew over me. Kai was behind us, and I could see the sadness in his eyes was gone. He had returned to his normal self and was flirting with everyone within his range. The giggles and fake protests of *Oh Kai* from his fan club rang out. Another twinge of jealousy filled me.

I focused on the excitement around me rather than the feelings I was not allowed to have. The trail of partygoers led us to our destination. When Bay and I reached the top of the platform, we were greeted by Breeze, Daisy, and Blaze.

"You all look so amazing." I hugged my friends tightly.

The four of them always looked beautiful, but tonight, each of them was truly magnificent. They all wore their hair up in the same fashion as mine, and the dresses they wore were different colored copies of the one I was wearing, as well. Despite our similarities, I knew I must have looked like a little girl playing dress-up when compared to them. They glowed with beauty and magic. I would have been envious if I was not so enchanted.

"Off to the celebration." Blaze took my hand and stepped off the platform.

Instead of the anticipated drop, we walked on air. Well, it was not really air, but more of an invisible walkway that shimmered with soft rays of colors. Below us, I could see all of Starten, easily finding my home.

The windows were lit, and I imagined my grandmother fussing about inside. She'd be cooking and cleaning in between checking on everyone. I dismissed the thoughts of my family. I knew they were safe and together. Turning my attention towards the row of lights in the northern mountains, I tugged on Blaze's arm.

"Is that the Drygen's mansion?" I whispered.

Her response was only a quick nod.

I stared at the spot that seemed to grow larger. The Drygen's property was a fortress.

How am I going to save Meg? Is she crying and scared, right now? Are they treating her well?

Breeze stepped next to me and forced her magic around me. I smiled and tried to brush away my worry. I concentrated on the energy around me. I would figure out how to get my sister back when I was home.

The ground below us became less opaque and turned cloudlike. A mist grew, and we were encompassed by it. Ahead, the elementals began to disappear. Fear filled me.

Suddenly, I was jerked away from Blaze and greeted by an animated Bay. "This is the best part...well, almost the best part. We are just about there." Her excitement washed away my anxiety.

I was swept up by the anticipation. The closer we got to the vanishing point, the clearer it became. The elementals weren't disappearing. They were going down a steep slide. However, it was no ordinary slide – it was a colorful rainbow.

"We are next." Bay squeezed my hand and pulled me onto the slide with her.

I landed hard, and the colors around me blurred as I glided downward. The sound of Bay's laughter was contagious. After a short journey, we fell in a soft bit of white fluff. My side ached from our giggles.

Bay stood and brushed herself off. Twirling around me, she cried, "And now, the celebration begins."

The rainbow slide ended in a softly lit room filled with hundreds and hundreds of twinkling lights. Bay led me to the rows and rows of tables piled with colorful food. She handed me a plate and began to load it with bright vegetables, crackers, and cheeses.

When we reached an area of pasta and bread, I tried to stop her from adding more food on my dish. "Bay, there is no way I can eat all this."

My sister flashed to mind. Meg would have been overwhelmed by all of the choices here. She would've had a difficult time not overdoing it herself. She would have exclaimed, "It all looks so delicious, Mar. I can't choose just one thing!"

"Don't be silly," Bay interrupted my daydream and continued stacking my meal even higher. "You will need energy for all of the dancing."

I gave up the fight and allowed her to keep adding more. When we reached the drink table, I was faced with too many options. I eyed the bubbly, pink drinks and creamy, orange beverages. The Tree of Life ice sculpture was streaming a rainbow of liquid.

Bay took a large mug and held it under the trickle of color. When it was overflowing, she handed it to me. "Try this."

I took a small sip. The flavors of the drink were almost indescribable. At first, I thought it was cherry flavor, but then, I tasted an orangey citrus that was followed by a hint of banana, fresh cucumber, blueberry, and ended with vanilla lavender. Taking another sip, I found the same experience of flavors. Before I could question Bay, she whisked me off to a table for Water elementals to eat our food.

Just as I had finished one plate, I was taken to another table of elementals where I was given more to eat and drink. The conversations and the various meals made the evening exciting. I was surprised that I was able to eat so much without being full.

When I was brought to the last table, I was given a tray of desserts. It included blackberry-orange cookies like my grandmother made and a flute of what turned out to be zizzleberry wine. Before I had time to get sad, I heard the sultry voice of Kai calling for our attention.

"Tonight, we are here to honor the Goddess and the coming new moon, Gealach Nua," he shouted and pointed to the sky behind him, which I hadn't noticed before. The stars twinkled against the black tapestry of night.

Kai continued, "Tonight's celebration is even more special because we have Mara with us. Our thanks should be given to her and her family's commitment to protecting the magic. Without her great-grandmother and the original protectors, we may not have been here today."

While he spoke, a sliver of the moon peeked out from behind him and made its appearance. The tone of the audience became somber.

Blaze stepped beside Kai. "The new moon has arrived and with it, new beginnings. We appreciate all that has been given to us, and we dance in honor of our mother, Danu."

Upon her final words, the moment of reflection ended, and the music began playing. The crowd cheered and started to dance. Bay dragged me to the middle of the floor, where we twirled and spun for what seemed like hours. I think I danced with almost everyone in the room, being passed from one elemental to another.

When the fast music changed to a slow song, I found myself face-to-face with Kai.

Offering his hand, he asked, "May I have this dance...Friend?"

"I would be honored," I said sarcastically as he pulled me into his arms.

Kai held me close and twirled me around the room. I felt dizzy and closed my eyes as I gripped on tighter to him. When the music finally stopped, I looked around and found we were alone.

"Where is everyone?" I asked.

Searching for the other elementals, I realized the rows of food and tables were now gone, too. We were no longer in the celebration area, but rather, in the spot where I had clawed myself out of the flooding water.

"Why are we back here?" I said, sharper than I had intended.

Kai led me to a rock. "Mara, take a seat. I have something to tell you. It might be difficult for you to hear this, but you need to know I will be here for you."

"What is it? Did something happen to Meg? Is it Gram?" I sat down.

Kai settled next to me. Tears glistened in his eyes as he took my hand.

My heart fell.

"Mara, your family is fine, but it has been decided that you can't go back home."

Fighting back my urge to rage, kick, and fight, I closed my eyes. Calmly, I released his hand. "Why won't you let me go home?"

"It isn't safe there for you anymore," Kai informed me. "This is your new home. I promise you will be happy here."

"Who do I need to talk to, to change this decision? Who made this ridiculous choice?" I demanded. To my surprise, my emotion was more controlled than ever before.

"The decision was made. It is final. You will just have to deal with it," Kai said sharply.

My thoughts began racing. "Can I, at least, talk to Blaze about this?"

"Mara, you are here to stay. Your family is there, and they don't need you. Try to enjoy life with us and forget them. Period." Kai wrapped his arm around my shoulder.

Defiantly, I stood up and faced him. "I'll not stay here against my will. I'll go home to my family. Despite what you think, they need me, and I absolutely need them."

Proud of myself for keeping my cool. I stormed away from him and headed towards the elemental's home. No one controlled my destiny, but me.

When I reentered the tree, I discovered the Water elementals were not there. I was confused by the empty room. I went to the circle of chairs and sat on the rock in the middle.

"Danu," I appealed, "if you are listening, I need your help. It's important for me to be with my family. How can I honor my commitment to protect the magic from here? Please, I beg you. If you are listening, I must return home."

The tears forming in my eyes dried as the air around me began to swirl, and a lavender light surrounded me. The light was blindingly bright, but as it softened, I was stunned to be faced by a shimmery image. The vision before me was a stunning woman, wearing a flowing gown. Her long, silvery hair was wavy, and the sides were braided, exposing her delicate facial features. She held a small, brown cat in her arms. It purred as she carefully stroked the long fur of her content pet.

"Mara, you are home with me," the silky voice said, "but you are correct. You are needed in the human realm more than here. You were given a huge shock, but you were able to handle your anger. Instead of lashing out, you chose to seek help."

"So, this was another test?" I asked, trying to hold back my tears.

"Dear Mara, every day is a test. A test of your strength, a test of your emotions, and a test of your commitment to the promise you made. You have pleased me greatly and, my sweet child, I see great things to come for you."

With those words, she disappeared.

I found myself, again, in Kai's arms. Letting go, I tried to push him away.

However, he held me tighter and said, "I'm sorry, Mara, for deceiving you, but you were able to control your emotions and follow your instincts. Do you think you are ready to do the same when it is time to face your mother?"

Submitting to his embrace, I just breathed in his scent and thought about his question. *Will I be able to stay calm and collected when I face her?* I wasn't sure I would be able to keep my anger under control.

"Kai, I don't know if I'm ready to face her yet," I whispered sadly.

"Knowing that you might not be ready tells me that you are," Kai said, releasing his hold on me.

Taking my face between his hands, he tenderly kissed me. This time, I didn't want to push him away.

Grasping my hand, Kai said, "It's time to go back to your family, Mara."

Looking around, I realized the scenery had changed. We were back in the Starten Forest, standing where I had first woken.

"Lay down and sleep," he said, pointing to the green, mossy earth, "You will soon be back to Cole and your family."

"Will you stay with me until I fall asleep?" I boldly asked him as I obeyed his instructions.

Though he didn't answer me directly, he lay down beside me.

I rested my head on his chest and drifted off to sleep. As I slept, I dreamt of dancing with Kai and the other elementals. A warm breeze blew my hair as Kai twirled me, around and around.

When he stopped spinning me, the handsome elemental took my hands, knelt before me, and fervently said, "Mara, stay. I want you here, with me, always."

Behind Kai, Cole stood, looking at me intently with pain in his eyes. "Come home to me, Mara," he pleaded.

Looking from one young man to the other, I didn't know my answer. Kai stood up and walked over to stand beside Cole. How could I choose? I wanted them both.

"You have to choose," Kai said firmly. "You must decide which of us you want to be with. You cannot have us both. Decide."

"Wake up, Mara," Cole said softly as he began to walk away.

"Wait! Come back," I called after him. Watching him leave me, I knew my decision. There was no one I wanted to be with, except him. "Cole, it is you who I've always wanted to be with!"

Kai bowed graciously and disappeared, but Cole kept going further and further from me. Realizing I was losing the love of my life, I ran after him. "Cole, stop. Don't leave. I choose you."

I was too late. I didn't catch up with him, and he was gone. Cole had left me.

Sinking to the ground, I understood it was because of my hesitation that he was gone, and I was alone. "Cole, I'm sorry," I said as I began to cry.

CHAPTER
THIRTY-ONE

"Wake up, Mara, I'm here," I heard as I felt my body being shaken.

I opened my eyes, but everything was fuzzy. As the blurred shape took form before me, I saw the deep blue eyes of Cole, watching me with concern.

"You didn't leave me," I said with a cracked voice.

I reached out to him and stroked his face. It was rough with a light stubble that hadn't been there the last time I'd seen him. *How long have I been gone?*

"She's awake!" Cole cried out as he embraced me. He began to cover my face with kisses. "Of course, I wouldn't leave you. I've been here the whole time. I'm not going anywhere."

"Stop smothering her, Cole." Gram swatted him away.

Cole reluctantly stood up. "Ok, I'll get her water, but I'll be right back.

Gram sat beside me on the couch bed I was resting in. She hugged me and whispered, "Wasn't it wonderful?"

Surprised, I could not respond with more than a nod.

Gram patted my hand. "Rest, love. We'll talk after you are cleaned up."

"Caterpillar, I was worried." Elliott stood over me. "I thought we had lost you because of my secrets."

Sitting up, I felt a bit dizzy, but I wanted to show him that I was ok.

"I understand why you did it. You thought you were keeping us safe. Let's stop thinking about our mistakes and move forward." *Are you telling yourself this to ease your own guilt, Mara,* I wondered smugly.

"Yes, clean slate. You have missed so much while you were asleep. Mae and I have been trying to figure out what gift I was blessed with. We've determined that Earth is my element."

Gram joined us and handed Elliott a pot with a wilted flower.

"Watch this." He closed his eyes and held the container tight.

The blue petals began to quiver, and the green stem straightened. Before my eyes, I watched the small, dying flower bloom eight large petals with soft blue and yellow centers. The plant filled the area with the scent of vanilla.

"You should see the garden, Mar," Gram praised. "Elliott has been busy connecting with the Earth."

"It sounds like I've missed a lot." I twisted myself to allow my feet to touch the floor. "How long have I been asleep?"

"Six days." Cole returned with my water and sat down beside me. "Six long days. You can never be gone like that again."

"Cole, you know she didn't have a choice on how long she was gone," Gram chided. "The Goddess had much for her to learn, or she would not have kept her there as long."

"How did you know?" I asked, shocked that she knew where I was.

Instead of answering my questions, Gram laughed. "You need to go take a warm bath and come back to the land of the living before you start asking questions. You are starting to grow moss."

I tried to stand up, but my legs felt wobbly. Cole caught me before I fell. Then, he wrapped his arm around me and guided me to my grandmother's bedroom.

"I didn't think you would want to attempt the loft stairs." He smirked.

When we entered the bathroom, Cole turned to leave.

"Wait," I stopped him. "I can't do this alone."

"Gram wouldn't approve," Cole argued. "Let me get her to help you."

"No, I want you to stay. I need you to stay," I said firmly. "It's not like you've never seen me without my clothes off. I know you used to sneak a peek when we would skinny dip in the lake."

"That was a long time ago, Mara, and you were much..." Cole hesitated, trying to find the right words, and ended with, "less."

"Less?" I asked, laughing. "Less what?"

"You know." He motioned up and down me.

"Ohh, less," I repeated with more seduction in my voice than I had planned.

I poured bubbles into the bath that was running. Unsure of what I was doing, I removed my clothing. No time to be shy now. Instead of watching me undress, Cole chose to be a gentleman and turned his eyes away. Irritated by this, I splashed him.

"I don't want you to do anything, but am I so hideous that you won't even look at me?" I asked harshly.

He turned back towards me and looked deeply into my eyes. "Of course, I want to look at you. There is nothing I want more. Well, there is more, but there's time for that, Mar." Cole took my hand, not averting his eyes from mine, and guided me into the soapy water. "Sit and relax."

When I slipped under the sudsy water, he took one of the pink washcloths and gently washed my neck and back. I let the warm water and his soothing touch calm me. My cruel mind refused to give me a rest, and I began to wonder about Elliott's magic.

"Cole, what did Elliott mean about having a connection with Earth? Don't we all have that gift?"

"Gram says you're unique in being able to call all four elements. Usually, a person has a stronger connection with just one," Cole explained. "She's been teaching us how to find ours."

"So, what is your connection?" I asked, trying to absorb, yet again, more information that was foreign to me.

"My skills are not as strong as your father's because I didn't want to leave your side, but I'm still practicing my gift." Cole moved his fingers above my head as if he was playing the piano. A drop of water landed on my cheek.

Before I could protest, I was covered with a warm rain-like shower. As the water poured over me, I took the opportunity to shampoo and condition my hair. Ignoring his chivalry, I stood up, covered in suds, under the rain shower and wrapped my arms around him.

"Cole Oliver Sands," I whispered in his ear, "I love you, and there is no one in the world I would ever want to be with, except you." Then, when he kissed me, I realized the passion I felt with Kai was nothing compared to the love I had for Cole.

Cole pulled away from me and quickly looked up and down my body. "Definitely not less anymore. You are lovely."

Does Cole know I kissed Kai? I worried. *Should I tell him?*

He handed me a towel. "Come on, Mar. We better get you dried off and dressed before Gram makes me *less*."

Laughing, I took the towel and covered my body. "Cole, you could never be less to me."

All dried off, I accepted the long T-shirt Cole handed me and slipped it over my head. The scent of fresh-cut wood rushed at me. *How does Gramp's T-shirts still smell like him?* I wondered.

"We should get you off to bed," Cole suggested.

Yawning, I nodded my agreement and followed him up the ladder to my bedroom.

He went straight to Meg's bed. Seeing my sister's empty space tugged at my heart, but I pushed back the sadness. She was strong and, thankfully, not alone.

"Don't sleep there. I don't want to be alone." I climbed under the covers of my bed.

I was glad when Cole joined me, and we snuggled under the blankets. It was strange that I was so tired. *Hadn't I been sleeping for almost a week?* It didn't matter. Sleep consumed me.

Before I knew it, I was woken by the sound of Gram calling my name.

With a dreamy look on his face, Cole pulled me into his arms and hugged me tightly. "I haven't slept that well since you fainted. I wish we could just stay here all day."

"Tempting, but Gram is beckoning. Let's go down to breakfast, and I'll tell you about my…" Words failed me. I could not call it a dream. Not knowing what to name it, I settled with, "my slumber."

"Slumber?" Cole sat up with a look of interest on his handsome face. "I can't wait to hear all about it, except I need to shave, first." He stroked his chin. "I'm beginning to look like a Drygen."

"Don't be long," I called as I began my descent to my grandmother.

185

Gram greeted me with a big hug. I held her tightly and inhaled her vanilla lavender scent. I knew I was where I was supposed to be…home. As she released her hold, I tightened mine.

"Enough of the mushy stuff, Mara." Gram finally broke away. A glint of a tear had formed in her eyes, but she blinked them away. "While Elliott is out tending to the garden, tell me about your experience."

While Gram started cooking, I sat on a stool next to the kitchen island, telling her an abbreviated version of the events.

"Is there anything that happened that you might want to tell me that you won't be sharing with Cole and Elliott?" Gram asked with a devious smile. "You can tell me anything, and I'll keep it just between us." My grandmother looked more like a schoolgirl excited about some juicy gossip than the stoic person I have always known.

"There isn't anything to tell," I lied.

"You want me to believe you were in the home of the elements and there isn't anything you want to share with me?" Gram grinned at me. "From my experience, the elementals can be quite persuasive."

"They were all welcoming. One of the elementals, Kai, became my guide," I explained, trying not to reveal any of the guilt I was feeling. "When we first met, he did kiss me, but I told him right away that I was engaged, and we agreed just to be friends."

As I looked into her brown eyes, so filled with love and acceptance, I decided I had to be honest with her about everything. "Gram, when Kai first held out his hand to me, all I wanted to do was kiss him. He was so charming and exciting. When he looked at me, it felt like he could read my deepest secrets. I was so tempted to forget everything and just fall into his world. Please, don't tell anyone. Cole would never forgive me if he ever found out."

"Mara, there isn't anything to be ashamed of," Gram assured me. "I'm sure Kai was very charming, and the experience of being so close to the Goddess does encourage temptations. However, you followed your heart, and I'm glad you told me. We'll keep it just between us. I see no reason to let guilt convince you to confess. It would only upset Cole unnecessarily. Sometimes, it's better to keep your experiences in the elemental world to yourself. Of course, you can always feel free to break that rule and share your stories with me." Gram winked and patted my hand before returning to the stove.

I felt relieved after confessing to Gram. I knew she was right. Cole didn't need to know something that would never happen again.

My mind played over everything that had transpired since Eliza returned. There we so many unanswered questions.

"Gram, Sarah's letter said you had a strong connection to Air. Was she correct?" I questioned, "Is that how you always know what is going on around us?"

My grandmother smiled. "Sarah was right. I do have a stronger connection to Air than the other elements. As far as my gift allowing me to know things, I think it's more from a strong intuition. I have the same sensitivity my mother had, which I, also, see in you."

"What do you think my connection is to?" I wondered. "Do you think Fire?" As I asked my question, I thought about the times I had called Air.

Before I could change my mind, Gram said, "You and Meg are special. I think you have a connection with all four. Initially, Meg seemed to be strongest with Air, but I have been thinking Earth, lately. When you were young, yours was different every day."

"You will never believe the size of these carrots. They're going to be as big as my arm." The loud booming voice of Elliott filled the room and stopped our conversation.

Gram shook her head in disbelief. "Elliott, what are we going to do with carrots the size of your arm?"

"We can feed the town." He grinned sheepishly. "We might need to start canning the abundance. I have been tending to the apple trees."

"Mara, set the table. Elliott, go get cleaned up, and no more practicing on produce. It will be difficult to explain away the sudden overgrowth of vegetation." Gram cracked several eggs into the bowl and whisked rapidly."

As I set the table, I listened to the sounds of the house. I could hear her soft humming along with the clicking and sizzling sounds of food being prepared. The sounds of home comforted me.

Once the table was ready, Gram handed me plates of French toast, crispy bacon, cut fruit, and an egg scramble full of vegetables. We laid the meal on the table just in time for Cole and Elliott to join us.

I struggled to call Elliot my father, even with the knowledge he'd been telling the truth. It was strange to consider calling someone *Daddy* after believing he was dead for such a long time, and I had already mourned his loss. Now, faced with this new reality, I bounced between wanting to bring back my father and realizing I had to accept Elliott, the man, as a new part of my life.

"Mar, take your seat." Cole patted my chair. "I'm starving, and I want to hear about your *slumber*."

Cole's handsome face was clean-shaven. His eyes were bright and full of joy. The darkness I'd seen earlier had faded.

Rest heals everything, I thought.

"Go on, Mara. Tell us about your sleep," Gram encouraged.

In between bites, I described my experiences in the elemental world.

Cole's laughter became uncontrollable at my depiction of my drop to meet the Earth elementals. "I would've loved to see you covered with mud."

"Can I continue?" I raised my eyebrows with mock annoyance.

When Cole composed himself, my family listened quietly as I told them everything from the rainbow slide to seeing Sarah. Cole's eyes glistened with tears at the mention of his mother. When I told them about seeing Meg in the mirror, Gram's eyes narrowed at the mention of Blanche Drygen.

When my story was over, I felt it was time for me to ask some questions. "Gram, did you know about Miles?"

With a sour look, she answered, "I suspected Eliza was with child not long before she left, but no, I didn't know for sure."

"When we get Meg, we must take Miles. Meg promised him he'd be able to come live with us."

"We will." Elliott reached over and took my arm. "Cedric Drygen won't take anything else from my family. No matter what it takes, we'll bring both children home."

Tears welled up in my eyes from the intensity in his words.

The rest of our meal was finished with small talk. The avoidance of the bigger issues we faced was disturbing me. Finding out how the bacon was made to be so crunchy or talking about the flavor in the syrup was not going to help us get my sister home. Trying to control my irritation, I focused on breathing.

"I got it!" Cole jumped up. "I know how we can get them both back, safely."

Cole outlined a plan to get to the Drygen estate by going off the main roads. He described our secret path. We, then, spent the better half of the evening working out details. The four of us would be making the trip to bring Meg and Miles home before the next sunrise. Today would be a test in putting all the pieces together.

"Gram and Elliott, can you make any potions we'll need? Mara and I are going to the library to see if there is any information on the Drygen's estate. There's a section on the town's history. It might have something that can help." Cole paced back and forth.

I put my hand on his arm to stop him. "You need to calm yourself." I turned towards Gram and Elliott. "We *all* need to calm ourselves. The most important thing I learned while I was with the elementals was that my emotions feed everything around me."

My grandmother took both Cole's and my wrists and quietly whispered a prayer, "Goddess, bind both before you in love and commitment to their promises. Bless and protect them from the darkness they may face."

The air blew, and a bright lavender light glowed before us. The shimmery image of the Goddess slowly came into view. Her beauty took my breath away. It was more than her physical attractiveness that moved me. She emitted love, grace, and peace.

"My child, Mae, your request for a binding and protection for Mara and Cole is granted. Your commitment and faith to the Light have been noted over the years. Be safe, my children. The darkness can seem stronger than the light."

Danu faded away, and we all stood dumbfounded.

"Was that?" Cole stammered.

"Yes, it was Danu. Isn't she amazing?"

Gram gasped as a small spark emitted from the ring on her finger. The once dark blue stone had a silver sunburst in the center that stretched throughout the gem like a star. The silver design pulsed, and then turned white.

I examined the change in the ring. "Gram, it is beautiful. What does it mean?"

My grandmother lifted my hand up and gestured towards the band I wore. "She has blessed us."

Each of our rings had remained the same color, but all bore the same silver star.

Gram said with a delighted tone in her voice, "We are bound, and we can focus on bringing my grandchildren home."

With renewed determination, we dispersed, eager to put our plans into action.

I stopped and looked back at my grandmother. She was writing in her journal. As the pen strokes filled the paper, she cried. Teardrops fell slightly, smearing the ink.

Gram looked up and our eyes locked. I could feel her mixture of emotions. It isn't every day that the Goddess appeared to grant your request.

Cole tugged my hand. "Come on. Let's leave her to her writings."

I put my hand to my heart and mouthed, "I love you."

Gram covered her own heart, and then waved us away.

CHAPTER
THIRTY-TWO

When Cole and I arrived on Main Street, we blended into the crowd, playing the role of the happy couple. Everyone was still respecting Gram's wishes for our privacy, so our well-wishers' polite comments were limited. There was the occasional "Isn't it nice to have your father home?" and "How is your family?" We handled it politely as I tried to fight my urge to cringe at each inquiry.

When we entered the library, I felt like I could breathe again. It was a place to expect quiet, and most people would defer to the demand for silence...most people. Avoiding eye contact with the other patrons, Cole and I headed straight for the local history section, located on the shelves furthest from the door. Hidden deep in the recesses of the building, I left my fiancé to search on his own.

"Cole, I'm so so glad to see you here." The unmistakable shrill of Jessica's voice rang throughout the large room. "Why are you hiding in the back of the library, all by yourself?"

I peeked through the shelving in time to see her run her fingers up and down his arms.

I fought my urge to push the bookcase onto her. I grabbed the first book off the shelf and flipped it open. *Perfect,* I thought.

"Cole, I've found exactly what I want our *wedding* –" I faked my shock at seeing Jessica. "Oh, I didn't know you were here. What a lovely surprise."

Jessica wrinkled her nose at me, but I continued my performance.

"I'm so glad you're here. I've just been so busy that I haven't found the time to reach out to you. The hectic life of a budding bride-to-be."

I grabbed Jessica and drug her to a table. I pulled out a chair and practically shoved her into it. Before she could flee, I pushed my chair next to hers, trapping the annoying girl. "Since you are here, you can help me with the wedding plans. It is almost divine intervention that you arrived today. We can go over everything."

Jessica gave me a terse smile. "I was just..."

"I know time does get away from us, doesn't it? But you are here now." I pointed at a page inside the book with a photograph of four girls. "Don't you think it would be fabulous if the bridesmaids wore outfits like these?"

The girls in the picture had long dresses with big shoulder pads. The fabric was covered with bright colors and black geometric shapes. Each girl wore their hair slicked back into a tight bun that made their dark eyeliner and hot pink lipstick stand out. I held back my laughter as Jessica squirmed away from me.

"Won't it be fabulous?" I scooted closer, not giving her a chance to escape. "I think they'll make a perfect bridesmaid's dress. Of course, you will get first pick as the maid of honor."

I shoved the book away and positioned myself to be face-to-face with Jessica. "What do you think about food for the reception? Should it be a simple BBQ or formal dinner?"

"Stop!" Jessica jumped up, knocking the chair over. "We are not friends, Marina. I don't plan to be in your wedding or wear that horrendous dress. I absolutely don't care what you will be feeding your guests."

I gasped. "I didn't know we weren't friends, Jessica." Fluttering my eyelids, I blinked back imaginary tears and turned towards Cole. "Did you know this?"

"I thought we were friends, too." His eyes widened in surprise. "Jessica, I can't believe you would pretend to like us. That's so hurtful." Cole wrapped his arms around me. Though I shook with laughter, he pretended to soothe me. "Don't cry, Mara."

I called Water to fill my eyes before looking up at him. "I just can't believe this. She always pretended to be so nice to you."

"I guess we were both deceived, Mar." Cole shook his head sadly.

"I didn't mean you, Cole. *We* are friends." Jessica grabbed his hand.

Cole pulled away from her and jerked me up into his arms. "You should go now, Jessica. You are right. We are not friends."

Anger flooded her face. Without a reply, she turned and stomped off. "You are so bad." I laughed.

"Me?" He leaned in close and whispered in my ear, "You, my dear, were jealous."

"Jealous of her?" I replied, "Never."

Cole raised his eyebrows at me and then kissed me on the cheek. He picked up the book I had been showing Jessica and said, "Before we get back to work, let's see our fabulous wedding fashion." His face grew dark. "Did you look at this?"

"No, it was the first book I grabbed." I leaned in to examine it.

The text under the photo read: *Genevieve Silver, Lucy Andrews, Michelle Elliott, and Camille Black. New Moon Celebration.*

"Wow, it's them." Quickly, I flipped through the remaining pages, looking for anything that might be beneficial. "This is interesting, but there's nothing to help us with Meg. We should check this out to look through, later. Maybe I missed something with the Drygens' name?"

Continuing our mission, we searched the shelves without finding anything useful.

"We're going to be here all night." Resting my head against my arms, I fought back the urge to cry and stared at the books in frustration. "Please, help me," I said, barely above a whisper.

As if in response to my plea, a small, blue light appeared before me.

Your eyes are playing tricks on you, Mara, I thought, blinking several times in hopes of clearing my vision.

When I returned my gaze towards the light, I noticed it by the bookcase. I went closer to investigate, and it flashed close to a brown book with the title, *Animals of the Forest.*

Original title, I thought as I picked it up.

It was an encyclopedia of the different types of creatures that lived in Starten Forest. Disappointed, I shoved the book back into its spot. However, it wouldn't budge. A thin, black book with a silver serpent on the spine was blocking its return.

I handed the title-less journal to Cole. "I may have found something."

The book turned out to be the history of the Drygens. At the end of it, there was even a chapter detailing the construction of their Estate. Thankfully, it included plans and diagrams.

Cole slipped the journal into the waist of his pants. "We don't need to draw attention to me checking this out."

On our walk home, I informed Cole about the light, and he told me about a book he found. It was about the gypsies who frequently passed through Starten. I wasn't sure why, but fear filled me.

Am I prepared to face Eliza? I wondered. *Will I be able to save my family from her? Is my magic strong enough?*

I knew Gram and Elliott had a firm grasp of their gifts, but I wondered about Cole. "How did you know your gift was Water magic?"

"Lucky guess." He shrugged nonchalantly. "My memories of an elemental, named Bay. She was always around me and, sometimes, she would speak to me at the lake. I really don't have much control over it, yet. But I can do this." Cole summoned three balls of water and began to juggle them.

"Show me what you can do, Mara." Cole dropped the water formations on the ground, splashing me.

"I can light a candle and I, once, asked Air to blow-dry my hair. I really haven't learned my gift. Everything I did was the elemental I beckoned at work, not me. How will that help us?"

Cole stopped and placed his hands on my shoulders. "Mar, there's so much you can do. You're just not confident. When my home was burning, you called a rainstorm to put out the fire. Just concentrate on one element and see what you can do."

Taking his advice, I thought about Breeze and the air that surrounded her. I focused on summoning Air and watched as Cole's hair started to whip around. I smiled and sent a strong wind towards him. I laughed as he struggled to keep his footing.

"Now, try another element," Cole called over the howling wind between us.

I held out my hands and focused on forming a ball of fire. A flame the size of a marble appeared in my palm. I willed it to grow larger. When it reached the size of a grapefruit, Cole held his hand above mine and called a rain shower to wash over them. Steam rose as he doused the fire.

"See, you had it in you all along." Cole grinned. "Now, let's get home to Gram and show her what we found."

When we entered the house, I was overwhelmed by the conforming aroma of chicken soup and baked bread.

Elliott smiled and greeted both of us with a hug. "Did you find anything useful?" he asked. "Mae has gone to Chester's woodshop to gather some things."

"We did." Cole handed the book to him. "In the end, there is a section that describes the Drygen estate. There's even a map, just as we'd hoped."

Elliott took the journal and inspected the plans. "This looks correct."

Jumping up, he rifled through a drawer before he returned with several sheets of paper. Meticulously, he traced the plans. I watched over his shoulder with curiosity as he added notes.

"This is the most direct route up the mountain. It ends on the backside of the property." In contemplation, Elliott tapped his pen on the paper. "Cedric's room is on this side of the house. Hmmm...This is interesting. There appears to be an external entrance hidden here."

Elliott's excitement confused me. *It sounds as though he's been there before,* I realized. *I wonder when, and why.*

In response to my look of surprise, Elliott quickly explained, "I wanted to keep my eye on him to make sure you were safe."

I wondered what else he had watched during his *death. Did he watch us as we grew?* Another thing we would need to discuss, once Meg was back home.

Elliott continued to draw on the map. "The master suites are here, and the old nursery was this section. My guess is this is where Meg is being kept."

The men took over planning the routes we would take. They even made backup plans for good measure. As they worked, I glanced around, trying to decide how to distract myself. For the first time, I noticed the countertops were filled with a ridiculous number of baked items.

"Why is Gram baking so much?" I questioned, as I popped one of the fresh tea biscuits into my mouth. "There's enough here for everyone in town, and then some."

"She's been cooking since the day you slipped into your deep sleep,"

Elliott answered. "She told me it calms her." He snorted in amusement. "If you think this is a lot, you ought to check the freezer. She has it filled to the brim with meals. We have enough food to last for months."

Gram must have been really stressed, I thought as I turned towards the pantry. The shelves were stocked with rows of small bottles. *How did I miss this abundance and variety of elixirs, tonics, and potions?* I continued my inspection, even when Gram returned.

"Quick, take this," she called out. Her arms were full.

I took a box from her and almost dropped it from the immense weight. I was astounded she'd been able to carry it and the other box with seemingly little effort. The next box weighed even more than the first.

"Gram, these are way too heavy for anyone to carry. How did you carry one...let alone two?" I asked with concern. "You should have asked us to help."

"Shush," she replied, "Light as a feather. Come, let's unload these, and then finish up dinner."

Why are we preparing like this? It's as if a hard winter's coming, and we need all the stores we can get. What is she up to? "Gram, why are we stocking the pantry? Elliott said that you also filled the freezers with meals for months," I grilled her.

"While you were sleeping, I kept busy," Gram said casually. "Now, we have plenty of meals and can focus on Meg when she comes home. Don't forget that Miles will be living with us. He will need a lot of our time to adjust to his new life. We have years of love and family to make up to him. Not to mention, a wedding to plan. Haven't I always taught you to be prepared?"

I accepted her answer and continued unpacking the boxes without further inquiry. After all, Gram was a planner, and her thoughts were logical.

While I had worked on the pantry, Gram finished our meal. My stomach growled at the tempting smells. My task completed, I found that she had begun cutting vegetables for our dinner salad.

"What are you cooking?" I asked, taking the knife from her to resume cutting the vegetables. "It smells so delicious."

"I haven't made this recipe in a very long time. It was Chester's favorite." Gram added mushrooms to the caramelized onions she had simmering.

Noticing the soft smile on her face while she stirred the food, I wondered if she was thinking about my grandfather. He had been gone over ten years, but it seemed like yesterday when he was last here. I could almost smell his woodsy scent as I imagined how he'd look after a day of work. He always came in the house with a big smile, covered with bits of sawdust, and the occasional wood chip in his hair.

The first thing he would do was to sneak a taste of whatever Gram was cooking for dinner. Gram would scold him for being a mess, but he'd have a twinkle in his eyes as he whispered something into her ear while he wrapped her tightly in his arms. In response, she would touch his face and whisper something back to him that made his eyes light up. Then, he'd give her one last kiss before she sent him off with a command to 'wash up for dinner'. Gramps always stopped on his way out of the kitchen to turn back, and say, 'Olive you, Maesi'.

My memories of the past were interrupted by warm arms wrapping tightly around my waist and a soft kiss on my neck.

"When are we eating, I'm starving." Cole picked up a chunk of cucumber and popped it into his mouth.

I set the knife down and twisted around to face him. "You're always hungry. Dinner will be ready soon."

Cole laughed and kissed me again.

Sinking into his arms, I felt content just to be held by him. I looked forward to the day we'd be married, and our new life together would begin. I wanted a marriage like my grandparents had.

"Dinner is ready, lovebirds," Gram said. "Can I break you up long enough to set the table?"

Cole released me and swept Gram up in his arms. He twirled her around. "Mae, don't be jealous. You know I'll always love you best."

Gram slapped him lightly on the arm. "Put me down." When he obeyed, and finally set her back on the floor, she grinned. "Go on. Do as I asked, or you won't be eating."

"Anything for you, Mae." Cole kissed Gram on the cheek before he went off to set the table.

CHAPTER
THIRTY-THREE

While we ate our salads, Cole explained the plans that he and Elliott had devised. Getting there would be the easy part because many challenges awaited us once we were on the estate. We'd have to watch for Drygen staff that may be patrolling and any changes to the property that didn't match the maps.

Gram carried out a large casserole and herb breadsticks. As she dished out fresh pasta with chicken, caramelized onions, and mushrooms covered in a cream sauce onto our plates, her eyes misted over. "For my dear, Chester – gone, but not forgotten."

We all raised our glasses of water and toasted.

Silence filled the table as we finished the delicious meal. However, my mind wouldn't stay quiet. It kept drifting to the days ahead of us. Finally, pushing back my thoughts of worry, I tried to enjoy the feast before me.

Swallowing her last bites of food, Gram asked, "Mara, can you serve the dessert? It's in the fridge on the patio."

The enclosed room was lit by small, twinkling lights. A long, lavender bag hung on the front of the refrigerator. Interested, I went closer to inspect it. When I did, I noticed a hook with a small, white note attached to the top, that read, *For Mara*.

"Go on, open it," Gram called from behind me.

"What is it?" I whipped around to see the brightest smile she'd had on her face in a year.

"You'll see." Gram waved her hand for me to hurry up and open it.

I removed the bag from the hook and spread it out on the table. I slowly unzipped the lilac cover, stopping when white fabric showed. I knew before I finished what she was giving me.

"Gram, you shouldn't." I choked back tears. "This was your dress. You wore this when you married Gramp."

Gram removed the garment from the bag and held it up to me. "And now, I want you to have it. Try it on and see if you like it."

I slipped into the gown. The top had wide shoulder straps that connected to the ruffled bodice. Upon closer look, you could see the ruffles were actually small flowers with a pearl in their centers. The soft fabric fell from my waist to just below my knees.

"Let me help you." Gram tied a light gray ribbon around my waist. "Oh, Mara, you look even more beautiful than I imagined."

I caught my reflection in the window. I knew this was the only dress I could wear to marry Cole. It was more than just a symbol of my grandparents' love. It felt like it belonged to us.

"Are you sure? I know how special this is to you."

"Nothing is as special to me as you and Meg." Gram fussed with the shoulder of my dress, and then hugged me tightly. "I'll be proud to know you wore it to marry Cole." Shaking off the sentiment, Gram released her hug. "Now, let's wrap this up and bring the dessert out before Cole comes looking for us. I swear you are going to have a full-time job feeding him."

"*We* will be busy. You don't think Cole Sands is going to whisk me away from you, do you?" I slipped off the gown and handed it to her.

She smiled softly and rehung the dress. Unspoken words hovered in the air.

Does she expect me to move into Cole's cottage and leave her after we get married?

My grandmother handed the garment bag to me.

I set it on the table and took her hand. "Gram, please, let's not rush back. I'm scared. I know I need to focus my energy on not being afraid, but it's too much."

"You have always been your own worst enemy, Mara." Gram hugged me. This time she stroked my hair, and prayed, "Goddess, we ask for your continued spirit and guidance. With hearts of love, we will unite our family." My grandmother cupped my face between her hands.

"Marina Addisyn Stone, I promise you that we'll bring Meg home." She ended with a kiss to my cheek.

I felt the essence of the elements encircling me. It soothed me.

With our dessert in hand, we returned to Cole and Elliott.

After we ate the decadent spiced apple cake, Gram insisted we rest before our mission.

Cole and I snuggled together in my bed. We didn't speak, but neither of us slept, either. I kept reminding myself that I was not alone. The four of us would bring Meg home.

Someone gently shook my shoulders.

I looked at the clock groggily. It was a little after midnight. Yawning, I glimpsed at the person who woke me. I gasped at the inky figure lurking in the shadows. Instinctively, I jumped out of bed to find myself trapped in the corner as the stranger approached.

"Wait, it's me, Marina." A flashlight illuminated Elliott. He was dressed completely in black, including the tight-knit cap he wore on his head.

"You scared me." I swatted at him.

"I'm sorry, Caterpillar." Elliott held his hand out to me.

When I accepted it, he pulled me into a long hug. A wave of emotions flooded me. For the first time since his return, I was confident this man was truly my father.

"Mae sent up some clothes for both of you. I put them over there." My father gestured towards the dark attire laid out at the foot of Meg's bed. "I'll let you wake up sleeping beauty over there." Elliott beamed at me and left the loft.

My heart felt full of love. Thoughts of bringing Meg home made me smile. Both kids would be brought into a house of peace, love, and family. I couldn't imagine a better place to grow up. Even with the sadness of Father's *death*, my grandfather's passing, and my mother disappearing, we always felt safe and loved.

"Wake up, sleepyhead." I kissed Cole on the cheek.

"I wasn't sleeping." He rubbed the sand from his eyes. "I was just checking my eyes for cracks."

"I see." I grabbed his hands and pulled him up. "Were you just practicing your best impersonation of a sleeping giant? You could have shaken the birds out of the trees outside."

"Yes, I'm glad you appreciate my talents." Cole wrapped his arms around my waist.

I resisted the urge to push him back onto the bed, so I could snuggle into his arms. "It is time to rescue Meg. Our clothes have been laid out for us."

Not bothering with modesty, we both undressed and dressed, again, in our all-black outfits, which included black boots and caps.

Meeting my grandmother and my father in the kitchen, I felt silly. *We all look like a bunch of raccoons,* I thought to myself.

"Mara, come, let me braid your hair." Gram handed me a cup of tea. "They will see you coming for miles with that tangled mess."

Catching my reflection in the mirror, I saw what she meant. My hair was a fright. "Thanks for telling me that I looked so crazy, Cole."

"Crazy is why I love you." Cole chomped a hunk of banana bread and then held it out as if offering me a bite.

I shook my head. I was too nervous to eat anything.

Once my hair was braided, we grabbed the bags my grandmother had prepared for us and headed out.

Outside of my grandfather's woodshop, Gram pointed to a set of four-wheel bikes. "We'll take these until we get to the base of the mountain. Then, walk the rest of the way. Cole, do you feel comfortable driving?"

"Yes, ma'am." Cole clicked his heels together and saluted.

Gram chuckled. "Good, let's go." In a surprisingly agile move, she hopped onto the back of the four-wheeler that my father was already on. "Get on the back of Cole's bike, Mara. No time to dillydally."

The loud roaring noise filled the air as the bikes were started.

"Hold onto my waist," Cole shouted over the rumbling sound. "It will be a bit bumpy."

And, off we went.

The bike lurched forward, and we rode north towards the Drygens' Estate. We passed Starten Lake, and then passed the tree where I'd last seen Kai. We continued deeper into the forest until we reached the edge of the mountain. Stopping, we hid the bikes in an area of thick brush.

Thoughts of trout, snapping their warnings at us, crossed my mind.

We began our hike up the cliff on a path that seemed as if it had not been used in many years. The rocky walk was full of overgrown and slippery foliage. The forest felt eerily quiet, and a chill ran through me.

"The road will clear the higher we go," my father said. "Just follow where I'm walking, and we shouldn't run into any surprises."

Heeding his warning, I watched my grandmother as we climbed the steep slope of the mountain. *No one would know she was going to be sixty-five years old*, I thought. She was keeping the steady pace set by my father – the same pace I struggled to maintain.

We walked for almost an hour before we came to a level clearing.

"We should stop here and catch our breath." Panting, my father passed out water canteens from his black bag.

Sipping the refreshing drink, I eyed Gram as she dug in her satchel. I watched curiously as she removed items and shoved them into her jacket pockets. I could hear her quiet prayers to the Goddess.

When she saw me watching her, she smiled and said, "Everyone, join me."

We gathered in a tight circle and watched with anticipation.

"With open hearts and pure intentions, we ask for your continued blessings on this night," Gram said confidently. She placed her hands in the center of the circle. "With the aid of the Air of the east..." The breeze around us swirled, blowing leaves across the ground. "...And the Fire of the south."

I saw Gram nod at me. Listening to my intuition, I held my hand out to the center of the circle. Soft flames flickered from my fingertips, and warmth brushed my cheeks.

"And, the Water of the west," Cole said, obviously understanding what was required. Jutting his hand to the circle caused water droplets to fall onto my arms and face. Cole wore a look of pride as we were sprinkled with moisture.

"Finally, the Earth of the north." My father added his hand, and the ground shook as blades of grass broke through the hard soil.

Gram cried out, "With the blessing of Danu, we prepare our task."

The threads of Fire, Water, Earth, and Air twisted between each of us and hovered above our hands. Our rings pulsed between a soft lavender light and a bright white one. I was sure all of Starten could see us, which made me anxious.

My ring finger stung as if I was being burned. I stared in shock as the metal and stone melted into my skin. Though I could no longer see it, I felt its presence. It was as if it were reminding me of my oath.

Gram took my hand and squeezed it. Her brown eyes were bright and shone with tears of joy. "Bright Blessing, Danu. Our bind is now skin deep." Gram picked up her bag. "Ok, it's time for us to put our family back together."

We marched towards the Drygen estate.

When we reached the top of the mountain, my father whispered, "Be on the lookout for guards."

I tapped him on the shoulder and pointed towards a sleeping man propped against a tree. *I hope all of Drygen's staff are this diligent.*

Gram opened a blue pouch. We watched quietly as small tendrils of smoke slithered from the bag towards the slumbering guard. When they wrapped around his hands and feet, he shifted and opened his eyes. Looking down at his bindings, his eyes widened, and he began to cry out for help. He was silenced as strands of silver entered his open mouth and nostrils. He struggled for a few minutes before he collapsed.

"Is he ok?" I asked, nervous that we had hurt him.

"He'll be in a deep sleep for many hours and should wake with no idea as to what happened." Gram rifled through his pockets, where she found a small flask and a set of keys. She shoved the keys into her bag. Opening the bottle, she dumped the contents over the man and threw it on the ground next to him. "If he is found, they will think he had too much to drink and passed out," she said with a devious smile.

Once the first guard had been dealt with, we crept further onto the property.

My father insisted we stay behind a tree while he checked the immediate surroundings of the house.

I watched him creep away into the darkness and, suddenly, he disappeared. Panic filled me. *Has he been caught?*

"There is only one other guard stationed at the front." My father appeared from behind us.

I jumped in fright. He had made no sound upon his return. "Don't scare me like that," I hissed.

His green eyes almost sparkled. "I'm sorry." My father wrapped his arm around my shoulders and squeezed. Then, he pointed high up, indicating a set of windows. "We should be able to avoid the guard if we enter over here."

I stared in awe of the house. Realization hit me. *Eliza left our warm home to live in this cold monstrosity.*

The three-story mansion had a long staircase extending to the right from the second level patio. A stairway on the left began on the ground floor and twisted to the third story. Partially open drapes on the end of the middle level caught my attention. Something inside told me it was the room we needed.

"I feel Meg there." I glanced at the stairs leading to the top floor. "How will we get in?"

"I know a secret way. I'll get you to Meg," my father said.

"In case you need it." Gram handed me a pouch like she used on the guard "Open the sack carefully while focusing your energy on the target." Giving me a small vial with a jade green liquid that slightly bubbled, she added, "This should be sprinkled in the center of a barrier you're crossing. One drop is more than enough. It'll detect any magic or warning systems Eliza may have cast. If it turns red, leave the area. Hopefully, my daughter is as overconfident as usual and didn't protect all of the entries."

I slipped the items into my jacket pocket. "Don't worry, Gram. I'll be in and out with Meg and Miles before you know it."

My grandmother squeezed my hand.

When I looked into her soft brown eyes, I could sense her worry. I focused all of my energy into sending her all the love I had for her.

"I know you will be cautious." Gram kissed me on the cheek. "You have always been my strong girl."

Cole hugged me tightly. His voice wavered when he said, "Listen to Gram and be careful, Mar."

"I'll only be gone for a few minutes, everyone," I promised, embracing my inner Gram. "We'll be home in time for breakfast."

I clasp my father's hand with fierce determination. "Let's get Meg. One day without her was too long. It is time to take my little sister home."

CHAPTER
THIRTY-FOUR

We were careful to watch for any signs of movement as we walked down the extended patio of the first floor. Before we entered the enclosure, I placed a drop of the green liquid in the center of the dark stone. The drop sizzled, but it didn't change color. The window coverings were tightly closed, and no sounds inside could be heard. Still, I continued to check for alarms.

"This is the kitchen and staff quarters," my father cautioned. "Up ahead, there is a long metal pipe that runs up the side of the house. The pole ladder will be how we get to the third floor. Hand me the vial, and I'll place the drops along the way. Stay a bit behind me in case we need to retreat."

Climbing the pole, I could feel the sadness and anger coming from the building. *How can a house emit such feelings?* A chill ran through me at the thought of Meg having to stay here for even one night.

I was relieved when we stepped onto the landing of the second level. Thankfully, it was all closed up and dark as the first floor. Finally, we reached the third story with no signs of protection spells.

I heaved myself over the patio wall. As we passed the circular stairs, I couldn't help but think it would have been a better way to go. Keeping close to the house and watching for any signs of activity, we arrived at the desired window. This was where I felt Meg was being held.

Peeking inside, I could tell it was a child's room. It was dark, but the small twin bed was not empty.

"This is it," I whispered to him. "How can I open the window?"

"No worries, Caterpillar," my father said. "I have gathered many skills while I was gone. One of which is lock picking, among other stealthy activities."

My father pulled out a long flat screwdriver and inserted it into the top of the windowpane. Then, he slowly began to lift the window. Stopping, he placed a drop of the potion on the sill and waited to see if we would alert anyone.

"All clear," he said, handing me the vial, and then hugging me tightly. "We'll meet you at the tree where we found the guard. I'll be watching for you, in case you need me."

"Thank you," I said, pushing back my fear and climbing through the window.

When I entered the room, I realized it wasn't Meg sleeping in the bed. The small lump tucked under the dark green comforter was my brother, Miles.

I glanced around the dull room. The space was filled with heavy, dark furniture. It seemed more like an old man's room than a child's. There were no toys, pictures, or clues that a young boy lived here. Once again, a coldness filled me. I didn't feel any joy or happiness in this place.

Kneeling down beside my brother, I stared at him for a few minutes, just watching him sleep. He looked so much like Meg. I instantly felt protective of him. I found myself stroking his dark brown hair away from his eyes. I wasn't sure how to wake him without frightening him. As I sat, pondering the best approach, he slowly opened his big, green eyes and smiled.

"She promised me you would come for us, Mara." Miles threw his arms around my neck.

Surprised by his reaction, I could only hug him back. Reluctantly, I let go of him. "Miles, we'll have so much time to get to know each other," I promised, "but we need to get you to safety first. Is Meg's room close?"

"She's in a room down the hall." Miles slipped out of his covers. "I know a secret way we can go. You must be quiet, though. Grandmother Blanche is a light sleeper."

"Dress quickly, and you can show me the way. Be sure to put on warm, dark clothes."

While my little brother dressed, I arranged his bed covers to look like he was still there. *Does someone check on him in the middle of the night to make sure he's warm enough?* I wondered.

"Come this way." Miles grabbed a small box from his dresser. Then, he grabbed my hand, led me into his closet, and shut the door behind us. "Stay here."

Miles carefully rearranged items in the tiny space. When he found a small flashlight, he handed it to me. "Shine this here."

I followed his instructions and watched as my brother slowly popped off a panel of the wood that led to an opening in the wall.

"Ok, come in here, but we need to turn the light off." Miles motioned for me to follow him.

I entered the musty space and waited while he replaced the panel, hiding any evidence of our entering the passage. Then, my brother guided me through his secret maze until we stopped at a cutout in the wall.

"This is Meg's room. Wait here until I make sure the coast is clear," Miles whispered. His little face was serious.

Too serious for a child, I thought sadly.

Miles entered the walk-in closet. He quickly came back to me. "Mother is there. She's angry."

I began to enter the closet, but Miles grabbed my arm. He put his finger to his mouth, warning me to be quiet. Guilt filled me as I saw him tremble.

Would Eliza hurt him? Hurt Meg? I couldn't sit there waiting for the answer. However, when I tried, again, to enter the closet, Miles clutched my arm and shook his head violently. Relenting, I wrapped my arms around him and knelt down. I held my little brother as we listened to the conversation in the bedroom beyond.

"Meg, I'm growing tired of you and your insistence that you have absolutely no knowledge of magic," Eliza's icy voice snapped. "Stop this nonsense. You will not continue to be the brat my mother let you turn into. It is time to act like the daughter I always wanted. You could be so happy here if you would stop lying and just tell me what I need to know."

"It isn't nice to tell stories. You are trying to trick me. I don't know any magic since IT ISN'T REAL! I can't do what you keep demanding me to do," Meg shouted.

The next noise sounded like she slapped her hands on something hard. I had seen her act like this when upset. Fear filled me as I prepared for the next words that would come from Meg.

Full of anger, my sister shouted, "I'm sorry I'm not the daughter you always wanted, but you are nothing like the *mothers* I already have. I have two mothers that are much better and kinder than you will ever be."

"How can you speak so harshly to me?" Eliza cried out. Her voice sounded full of despair. "If you want to break my heart and be so cruel, I'll go. You can be alone. I promise I'll not come back."

After a few minutes of silence, Eliza must have realized her tactics wouldn't work on Meg. She said, with such venom in her voice that I felt the hair on my arms stand up, "I know you have access to the magic I need, even if you won't admit it. I have waited many years, and I can wait a few more days or weeks. Your sister will be along soon enough to try and save you. Marina has access to the magic I truly want. And, thanks to you, she will be happy to give me whatever I want in exchange for your life."

A thud sounded.

Did Meg knock something over? It was impossible being on the other side of the wall and not able to tell my little sister to behave. I needed Eliza to leave, and Meg engaging her prolonged her goodbye.

"Since you want to be alone, you will be...until she arrives," Eliza snarled. "I hope you enjoyed your dinner. It will be the last meal you have until I get what I want."

Her words shocked and angered me. It took every bit of energy I had not to burst into the room and scream at her.

Miles must have felt my anger because he snuggled back into my arms, patting my hand. He silently reminded me that I needed to control my emotions.

Wrapping my arms around him, I kissed his cheek. Knowing my sister was not going to back down, I braced myself for what was coming next.

In response to Eliza's threats, Meg launched another verbal attack. She was so unafraid and so strong in her words that my pride battled with my annoyance. "Mara will never give you anything! I won't let her! I would rather be alone forever, locked up with no food and water, than have you get your way. I'm glad you left us. You would have been a horrible mother!"

"Enough," Eliza screamed. A *Slap* rang through the air. "I'll not take such abuse from you."

My mind raced. I didn't know what happened. *Did Meg slap her? Did Eliza hit my sister?*

Relief filled me when I heard the echoing sound of Eliza's high heels hitting the granite floor as she took her leave. I relaxed further when the door slammed shut in her wake. With the *click* of the door being locked, I stood up to go to my sister. That was when Meg's cries filled the room, confirming she had been injured.

"Let me go alone and be sure it's safe." Miles stopped me from rushing to Meg.

It was clear to me that our little brother had wisdom beyond his years. I nodded and watched him enter the closet and slowly creep into the room. I trailed behind him, hiding in the shadows.

Miles climbed onto the bed and stared at our sister. Meg was lying face down on the bed with her head buried in the pillow to quiet her sobs.

"Don't cry, Meg." Miles lay beside her and hugged her. "Everything is going to be ok. Soon, we'll be with your family, and you won't be afraid anymore."

Meg popped up and angrily wiped her tears away. "I don't think they are ever going to come. If they do, she'll never let us out of here."

"Don't say that!" Miles left the bed. "You promised me they would come and take us home. You said they would love me and that we would be so happy together. You made a promise, and you always keep your promises, right?"

Miles went to her dresser and pulled out dark, warm clothes, just as I had instructed him to do earlier. "Put these on," he said with such conviction that Meg didn't argue. She just followed his directions.

While Meg dressed, Miles fixed her bed up, just as I had done in his room. Taking her hand, he pulled her into the closet. When she saw me, she stared as if she was looking at a ghost.

"Mara," she asked timidly, "Are you really here?"

Pulling her into my arms, I fought back tears. "I'm so sorry I let her take you. I should have been more careful and not let you out of my sight."

We both just held each other while our brother watched us with a big smile.

Tugging my shirt, he warned, "We really should hurry. I don't want them to find out that we left our rooms."

"Do you know a way for us to get to the back of the house without anyone knowing?" Reluctantly, I let go of my sister. "Everyone is waiting for us by one of the large trees at the far edge of the property. Can you get us there without being seen?"

"Of course," Miles said. He sounded so much like Meg that I wanted to laugh. "We just need to be careful. Follow me."

Meg bragged, "Miles can get us anywhere we need to go. He is super sneaky like that."

With a look of pride at her compliment, Miles smiled and led us into the inner walls of the house. We followed our brother as he guided us through the twists and turns of the dark passageway. When we reached another hole in the wall, he carefully opened the panel and peeked out.

"Be quiet," Miles said as he led us into a hallway inside the mansion.

Following him, we headed towards the patio doors.

"Wait." I pulled the vial of green liquid from my pocket and placed a drop in front of the exit. The green liquid sizzled as I held my breath, praying silently in my head. Slowly, the liquid turned red and spread into a large circle that slipped under the doorway.

"We can't go out through here, Miles," I said with frustration. "She's put a protection spell at this entrance. Is there another way?"

Scrunching his face as if he was deep in thought, he announced, "I got it! I think I know a way."

Once again, we climbed back into the walls of the house.,

As Miles led us through the corridors, I wasn't sure what direction we were facing. *Is he leading us closer to Eliza's room?* My heart felt like it was going to beat out of my chest.

"Let me check this way. Can I have your green stuff?" Miles asked. He looked like a little man with the serious expression he wore.

"Just put one small drop in the center of the area that we will cross." I gave him the potion.

"Don't worry, Mara," Meg whispered, "Miles will get us out of here. He is really smart for being just a kid."

I squeezed her hand. "I have no doubt he will find a way."

With those words, Miles dashed out. When he returned, a big smile was plastered on his face. "She would never think anyone would go this way. Let's go."

Our little brother brought us out of the walls and into a hallway. I felt exposed in the wide corridor, but after a quick walk, we entered a small storeroom. The space was full of cleaning supplies and other housework equipment. Miles opened a door to an empty cupboard. Peering over his shoulder, I saw it was a laundry chute. I had read about them in books, but I had never seen one before.

"Where does this lead?" I asked him while thinking, *this doesn't look safe.*

"Right to the laundry pile. It is usually full of sheets, since Grandmother Blanche has all the beds changed, every day." He wore a sad look on his face.

Why would clean sheets upset him?

"Even if no one has slept in the bed, she makes Hazel take everything off and remake it with clean sheets. She makes her do it for all fifteen of the rooms in the house! We never had those many visitors." Shaking off his gloomy thoughts, he forced a smile and pointed at the chute. "You should go first, Mara, since you're the biggest."

Miles spread his legs and arms out, and then crouched a bit. "You will need to hold your arms and legs out like this, and you want to slowly move down the tube. If you go very slowly, it isn't as scary."

"Great demonstration," I praised. I held out my hand. "Can I have my green stuff back? I'll check the area when I get to the bottom."

Reluctantly, he returned the vial to me. "Remember, go slow."

I climbed into the chute. Before I started down, I looked at Meg and Miles. Both were watching me with mischievous grins. "Come on, you two. We don't want to be found."

Heeding my own advice, I began my descent into the dark space, using the technique Miles had just shown me. The cold metal was more slippery than I had expected. Once Meg and Miles entered the tube, specks of dirt dropped on me and covered my face. Misjudging my strength, I took one hand off the wall for the briefest moment to wipe the dust from my eyes. Suddenly, I found myself slipping. Unable to stop, I began to fall.

I stifled my screams as the silver of the walls blurred past me. I must not have been very high up when I stumbled because I landed quickly in a large basket full of dirty linens, making an *oomph* sound. When Meg was in reach, I held my hands up to help her down. Before I could assist Miles, he jumped around me and into the pile of laundry.

Quickly climbing out of the basket, he held out his hand. "Green, please."

With an amused smile, I handed him the potion and let him check our exit. His grin told me the coast was clear.

As we left the stuffy laundry room, the cold air hit my face. The night sky twinkled with stars, and I felt a sense of relief. Soon, we would be far away from this wretched place and with our family.

CHAPTER
THIRTY-FIVE

As Miles led us across the property, dodging from tree to tree, it was eerily quiet. Apprehension nagged at me. I was terrified the guard had woken, and that we would bump into him.

When we arrived to find the guard still out cold, Meg stared at him with wide eyes.

"He's just sleeping," I promised, "but let's move away from him, just in case."

I glanced around, hoping to see my family. My heart fell when I couldn't find them.

A soft rustle came from the brush across from us. I pulled Meg and Miles behind a tree to hide them. "Wait here," I whispered.

Leaving the children, I crept towards the moving bush. Within the foliage, two shining blue eyes stared at me.

"Damn it, Cole," I hissed when I recognized who it was. "You scared me."

Cole crawled out from the undergrowth and grabbed me tightly. "Mar, I was starting to freak out. You were in there for a long time. Gram and Elliott went down the mountain to make sure the path was still clear when you returned." He glanced around nervously. "Where are they? Didn't you find them in the house?"

Meg and Miles left the safety of the tree. They held hands as they came to join us.

Cole's expression turned to surprise, and his smile lit up his face. "He looks just like Meg."

"Uncanny, isn't it?" I agreed.

Cole scooped them both into his arms and gave them a big bear hug. When he finally put them down, Miles stepped back. Realizing his behavior had frightened the boy, he held out his hand. "I'm sorry – that was probably too much for a first meeting. I was just so worried about all of you. When I saw you were safe, I was overwhelmed with excitement."

Miles accepted his hand and shook it. His posture was formal, but his intense gaze watched Cole wearily. "I'm pleased to meet you, Cos. Meg has told me all about you."

Cole grinned and bowed. "I'm glad to meet you, too, Miles. Now, we should be on our way. This place gives me the willies."

Miles crooked his eyebrow and studied my fiancé as if he was from another planet.

Meg took Miles by the hand and whispered to him, "You don't have to be so proper now. We aren't like the Drygens. You are in our family now, and we like to hug."

Miles beamed at his new sister. "I have a lot to learn."

"It's ok. I'll teach you. Now, come on." Tugging on their clasped hands, Meg moved to action.

Cole guided us off the property and down the path.

Turning to look at the mansion, I felt relieved to see it was still dark. No one was chasing us. "Thank you, Goddess, for your blessings and protection," I said clearly, as I looked at the bright moon.

As if in response to my gratitude, the stars seemed to twinkle.

We reached the flat area where we'd received our blessings earlier that night. There was no sign of Gram or my father. My heart, once again, felt like it had dropped. Anxiously, I searched for any signs of them. There were none.

Cole must have sensed my apprehension because he said, "They're probably down the mountain, keeping watch by the four-wheelers." He gave me a reassuring touch. "Don't worry, Mar. They will be waiting for us below."

The trek down the mountain seemed longer than the trip up had been. I wanted to run ahead to check on Gram and my father, but my somber mood appeared to have rubbed off onto my siblings. Miles and Meg were quiet, and their melancholy reminded me they were just little kids.

My realization made me feel contrite. I needed to protect them, not add to their worry. They already knew we were in danger. I didn't need to add to their concerns.

Focusing on my breathing, I tried to lighten the mood. "Miles," I said, "Did Meg tell you about Gram's delicious cooking?"

His eyes lit up as he said, "She did. She said Grandmother makes the best cookies in the entire world and that she even makes licorice ice cream with red...*sprinkles*." He hesitated before saying the word 'sprinkles' like it was a bad word.

"Yep, I told him she's a good cook," Meg confirmed. "I can't wait to have some, again. The Drygens forgot to add flavor to the meals they fed me, and the veggies were not like Gram's."

Amused, I asked, "Meg, won't it be fun to have a little brother? You'll be busy showing Miles so many new things."

Continuing our walk, I held Cole's hand and listened to Meg describe all of the things she planned to show Miles. He responded with many questions, and I could hear the excitement in his voice. It made me sad to think of the life he had before Meg was brought to him. *No child should have to endure such an empty and cold existence*, I thought.

As we approached the end of the path, I saw movement and stopped abruptly.

"What is it?" Cole whispered to me, glancing around nervously. "What did you see?"

"I'm not sure, but I thought something was down there," I whispered back.

Slowly, we resumed our descent. It wasn't long before we were met by Gram and my father. Unfortunately, they were not alone.

"How nice of you to join us," Eliza icily purred as she appeared, dragging my grandmother behind her.

My mother had a handful of Gram's silver hair twisted in her clutched hand. My grandmother wore a brave face to hide the pain, but I could see the agony she really was in. A dark bruise shadowed her eye, and her face was covered with small, bleeding cuts. Running to help her, I was stopped in my tracks by Cedric, yanking my father out of the darkness and into our view.

Cedric Drygen had a long silver knife pressed against my father's neck as he roughly shoved him forward. Blood ran down his swollen and bruised face, indicating my father had been severely beaten. Even though he was probably in great pain, his expression only showed anger. Struggling against his adversary, my father continued trying to break Cedric's tight hold. However, his efforts were fruitless.

"Careful, Elliott," Cedric taunted. "You wouldn't want to cut yourself accidentally." Then, he pressed the blade harder against my father's neck, breaking the skin and causing a small drop of blood to form.

"Stop!" I moved towards my father. "You're going to kill him."

"Oh, Marina." Eliza dragged my grandmother forward, blocking my line of sight. "Your father died a very, very long time ago. Who would really miss him if he died again?"

"You are no longer my daughter," Gram growled.

With a look of hate in her black eyes, Eliza slapped my grandmother with the back of her hand. The force of her strike sent Gram reeling to the ground.

Without hesitation, Cole ran to my grandmother, where she lay crumpled on the dirt. He put his arms tightly around her and whispered quietly into her ear.

Responding to his words, she leaned on him for support and sat herself upright.

Cole wrapped his arms tighter around her.

"I'll never understand what happened to turn you into this person. You were not raised this way." Gram's voice was filled with sadness.

Eliza stood over her defiantly. "Your mother, Genevieve, created me. She brought this pain to the Silver family. She should have left Camille Drygen alone. You think you know everything, but if you would've left my magic alone, we would not be here today, Mother."

Gram said in a defeated tone, "You are so consumed by the darkness you allowed inside of your heart that there is no hope for my daughter to return. You truly are a Drygen now."

Eliza shouted at her, "You will not talk to me like this. You will show me the respect I deserve."

Snorting at her, Gram said, "You'll never have my respect."

My mother's rage boiled. She shoved Cole away from my grandmother and pulled her up by her hair. Shaking and slapping her, she screamed at her. Her words were so full of anger and venom that they were incomprehensible. They were just hysterical ramblings about winter, snow, and all of the ways she had been wronged by my grandmother in the past, the present, and even the future.

"Stop!" I threw a ball of fire at Eliza. It grazed her face but didn't injure her. "I'll give you what you want. Just leave them alone."

I shocked myself. *How did I so easily form fire and throw it? Where did that come from – inside me? Am I capable of being just as dark as her?*

"No, Mara," Gram cautioned.

Before she could finish her warnings, Eliza struck her and sent my grandmother spinning. With a thud, she hit the hard ground.

I held up another ball of fire. "Don't make me use this."

I had Eliza's attention now. "You think your little ball of magic scares me, Marina?"

"I'll give you what you want. I'll release the binding that was put on your magic." I extinguished the flames and blew a breeze at her. "I have the power you seek."

Eliza's eyes brightened.

"I'll only do this if you stop hurting Gram. And, you must promise to leave us alone once this is done."

"Fine." Eliza's cold black eyes pierced through me. She pointed at my grandmother, who was lying motionless on the ground. "I'll agree to your demands, but only if you bind her magic, also."

Confidently, I stepped closer to Eliza. "Deal, but how do I know you will keep your promise and leave us alone forever...all of us?"

"My word is not enough?" Eliza asked with a smirk.

Don't fight her, I warned myself. I shrugged, feigning indifference. "Fine. I will take your word as an oath, but Miles is part of the deal. I want him to come to live with us – permanently."

"Whatever you want, Marina." She spun around and marched towards my grandmother. Standing over her, she said, "You are going to return everything she stripped from me."

Why didn't she protest about Miles? Come to think of it, she didn't even acknowledge him. How can a mother willingly give up her child? My mind raced with all the realities of her promises. *She's not going to keep her promise, even if I kept mine. She will never leave us alone, and she'll only keep my brother to hurt us. There's no way I'm letting her take him from us.*

Calming myself, I said, "We need to go to the forest behind my house."

Eliza raised her eyebrows.

"It's the only place with enough magic to cast this kind of spell." I looked up at the moon, trying to process my thoughts, and an idea came to me. "We must go before the sun rises, or I won't be able to break the binding."

"Cedric, put them in the back of the truck," Eliza ordered. Then, she turned and pointed her long, sharp fingernail at me. "You will ride in the front with me, my darling daughter. We have so much to catch up on."

Cedric Drygen threw my struggling father into the bed of the truck and began to tightly bind his wrists and legs with cord. He growled and punched him in the face. "You're lucky the girl is here and wants you alive. If it was up to me, I would feed your bloody carcass to the animals." He gave my father one last kick in the ribs as he hopped out of the truck and turned to glare at my grandmother. "I wouldn't try anything stupid, old lady, or I'll make you sorry."

Gram crawled into the back of the truck while Cedric watched. I stood back, expecting him to do something to make it difficult for her to get into the truck's high box herself. Instead, he just scowled at her.

Next, Cedric picked up Miles and tossed him in, next to my father. My little brother straightened up and looked at his father with sadness in his eyes. The depth displayed in his expression was haunting. Still, it didn't seem to have an effect on the cruel man.

When Cedric went for Meg, she resisted.

"I don't need your help." She kicked him in the leg, and then scrambled towards the truck.

Unfortunately, my sister hadn't been quick enough. Cackling as Cedric picked her up by the waist of her pants, he said, "You need to be taught manners."

He dangled her in the air as she struggled to break his hold. A scar under his eye glowed in the moonlight. It gave him a more notorious appearance, but it didn't deter my sister's defiance.

Kicking and clawing at the air, Meg screamed, "Let me down now! Let me down, or I'll scratch your eyes out!"

Laughing, he ignored her.

Miles tightened his fists and rushed to Meg's defense. "Put her down."

"You are threatening your father?" Cedric snarled.

Miles hesitated and looked towards me.

I shook my head slightly. The movement was almost undetectable.

Understanding, Miles unclenched his fingers and sat back down.

"Stop playing, Cedric." Eliza dragged her long, red nails along his beard and kissed him on the cheek. "She is of no use to us, anymore."

Cedric threw Meg into the back of the truck. She quickly scrambled towards my grandmother and fell into her arms, sobbing. Gram wrapped her arms around Meg and whispered into her ear. In response to the private words, Meg hugged her tightly and tried to choke back her tears.

Cole offered his hand to Miles. When he took it, he jumped into Cole's arms and held onto him tightly.

What kind of life did Miles have to make him so afraid of his father? I wondered.

My father was no longer struggling against the ropes that bound him. He'd closed his eyes, lying still. I wasn't sure if he was sleeping or just resigning himself to the situation. Either way, it alarmed me.

"I'm going to ride with them in the back. I need to make sure Elliott is ok, or I'll not be able to concentrate on breaking the binding," I said firmly.

Eliza's cold stare met mine. I gazed back while concentrating my thoughts and reached out with my mind. I needed to make sure everyone was ok.

Her black eyes bore into me as if she was searching for the truth. Finally, she nodded. "Fine, you can ride with Elliott, but your boyfriend rides with me."

Unsettled, I began to change my decision when Cole turned towards Eliza with his most flirtatious smile and said, "I would be honored to ride with you."

For half a second, I thought Cole's charisma would be a benefit to him. I was wrong. Cedric jumped into the bed of the truck and roughly knocked Miles out of his lap. Then, he reached for my fiancé, clutching him violently.

Ripping his wrist out of Cedric's bruising grip, Cole held up his hands in a gesture of surrender. "I said I would come with you," he asserted with mock indignation. "There's no need to be so rough, Mr. Drygen."

Cedric shoved him out the truck, and sneered, "Save your charm for someone else, pretty boy." Then, he jumped down and walked towards me. Standing uncomfortably close, his eyes scanned my body before they settled in a penetrating gaze on my breasts. "Do you want assistance getting into the truck? I'm sure I could help you," he leered.

Quickly hiking myself into the box, I replied, "All good here. No help needed."

Shutting the tailgate, he quipped, "Pity. Maybe another time."

Eliza glowered at him as she entered the cab, but she didn't add to the conversation.

My eyes met Cole's, and he winked. I smiled supportively at him before taking a seat near my father. Cedric started the truck and revved the engine. With a maniacal cackle, he peeled out and knocked me down onto my father, who groaned in pain.

"I'm sorry." I gently touched my father's bruised face. Turning towards Gram, I whispered, "Do you have anything to help him with the pain?"

"Untie him," Gram directed and searched the lining of her jacket. She slid a miniature glass jar with a blue gel into my hand. "Rub this on his cuts. Elliott, it will sting, but you'll feel better."

Loosening the ties on his wrists, I coated his wounds with the icy gel. My father winced, drawing back slightly from each touch, increasing my concern. *Be strong, Mara,* I reminded myself. I apologized as I continued to lightly rub the ointment on his broken skin. "I'm sorry this happened."

"It's ok, Caterpillar. It's just a few scratches." My father held out his roped hands. "Can you untie me, so Drygen won't get to throw me out of the truck when we reach our destination? He would enjoy that too much."

With my father untied, I took notice of our location. Cedric was taking every opportunity to make the ride as uncomfortable as possible for us. Hitting large bumps and erratically swerving, we were tossed around. I was knocked back into Gram, causing her to groan in pain.

"I'm sorry," I apologized.

"That maniac is going to get us killed," she growled.

Tears filled my eyes when I saw how much pain Eliza had actually inflicted upon her own mother. *No time for tears, Mara. It's time to take care of Gram.* "Here, let me fix you up a bit." I rubbed the gel over the cuts on her cheeks. I flinched when she hissed in pain.

Once I finished, she took my hand and held it. "Eliza will not honor her promise."

"I know, Gram." I hugged her gently. "Don't worry about that right now. I have a plan."

"How could I worry with you in charge?" My grandmother sighed and released some of the tension I felt in her body. "I know things will turn out as they should." Gram pulled out of my hug and held my hand.

We rode in silence for several minutes before Miles scooted out of Cole's arms and kneeled in front of us. "Grandmother Mae, are you ok?" he asked nervously.

"I'm just fine, Miles. Silvers are not weak." She held out her hand to the small boy. "Come, sit with me."

Miles hesitantly accepted her hand.

I watched as his fear and uncertainty washed away.

He nestled into Gram's lap, and she wrapped him in a big hug. When she kissed him lightly on the cheek, his body stiffened. It was as if he worried about what would happen next. Despite his reaction, our grandmother didn't release him. Instead, she held him tighter until the stiffness in his body, finally, weakened. He wrapped his arms forcefully around her neck as he melted into her embrace.

"Can you do me a favor, Miles?" Gram relinquished her hug.

"Mmhh." Miles' green eyes widened in anticipation.

"Do you think you can call me Gram? Grandmother Mae makes me sound like a little old lady."

Miles beamed at her. "Gram," he asked in a whisper, "can I live with you now?"

Tears glistened in our grandmother's eyes as she kissed him on the cheek again and held his face between her aged hands. "Miles, I would love nothing more than for you to live in our home."

"I told you they would love you. Didn't I?" Meg grinned.

Miles slid off Gram's lap and hugged Meg. She whispered something to him, and they both beamed as they looked at our grandmother affectionately.

"Miles, I'm sorry I wasn't able to be there for you, but I am now." Gram took a vial from her pocket and handed it to Meg. "I brought this for you. Drink it and tell me what you think?"

Meg inspected the vial, which I knew held the memory potion. I silently watched my sister drink the liquid. I was thankful Gram had thought to restore her memories. There was no guarantee that tonight would go as planned.

Meg returned the empty container. "We need to make some of that for Miles. It was so delicious." She let out a big yawn. "I missed you, Gram," she said, snuggling into our grandmother's arms and drifting off to sleep.

Gram smoothed my little sister's hair. "I missed you, too, my little dancer. I missed you, too."

CHAPTER
THIRTY-SIX

We continued the bumpy ride in silence as the truck drove towards our home. When we arrived, Cedric drove past the house and over to my grandfather's woodshop. Slamming on the brakes, he sent us sliding into the back of the truck cab.

"Now, the fun begins," my father whispered to himself.

Having parked, Cedric turned the engine off and hopped out of the front.

After Cole exited the black truck, he held his hand out for Eliza. "It's a long step down. Let me help you."

Eliza accepted his offered hand and allowed him to help her out. "You always had such nice manners, Cole. You should teach them to my daughter."

"I'll try." Cole smiled.

Cole and I are going to have a conversation about being too nice to the enemy, I thought bitterly.

Cedric lowered the tailgate, and roared at my father, "Stone, why aren't you tied up like I left you?"

I stood in front of my father. With hatred in my voice, I responded, "I untied him. If you want me to unbind Eliza's magic, you'll watch your tone, Cedric. My family has had enough of your threats."

Stepping forward, I glowered over him. "You might want to be very careful when you decide your next move. You haven't forgotten that

Eliza is my mother, have you? I'm afraid my temper can be just as volatile as hers."

Holding my hand out, I concentrated until I formed a small ball of fire in it. Bouncing the flame on my palm, I icily said, "Eliza isn't the only one who can play with fire."

With those words, I made the fireball grow until it was the size of a grapefruit. I threw the orb towards Cedric, aiming for his feet. The ball landed before him and sizzled in the grass.

"No need to get yourself worked up." Cedric raised his hands in submission and stepped backward. "Always having a woman fight your battles, Stone? Seems like nothing has changed."

"Don't take the bait." I grabbed my father when he began to lunge at his nemesis. Then, I threw another ball of fire. This time, it grazed Cedric's leg. "The next one will not miss." Turning to glare at Eliza, I added, "If you want me to unbind your magic, you need to put a leash on him."

"Cedric, be nice, darling," Eliza purred, dismissing my threats. "We'll be done with them soon."

Cedric snorted. "Not soon enough."

Jumping off the tailgate, I helped my family get out of the vehicle. Gram handed a sleeping Meg to my father before accepting my assistance.

Eliza stared at the exchange and tightened her grip on Cole's arm. "What's wrong with her?" she asked without a hint of concern in her voice.

"She's tired. She probably hasn't slept well with all of the threats she's been receiving recently." I locked eyes with Eliza and gave her a long, hard stare. "Lead the way, *Mother*."

I thought I saw a glimmer of sadness flash in her eyes before they turned dark, and she sneered, "Cedric, get our son."

As Eliza stormed away, I felt a pain in my heart. Reality hit that I had been praying for an idea, not a real person, to return to my life. My self-pity was halted by the gravelly voice of Cedric.

"Let's go. One trick from you and your precious family dies, starting with the old lady." Cedric grabbed Miles roughly and slung him over his shoulders.

"Please, put me down, Father," Miles begged. "I'll walk beside you. I can keep up."

Storming behind Cedric, I ripped Miles out of his grasp. My brother's shoe hit his father on the back of the head as I pulled him over the cruel man's shoulder and into my arms.

Cedric whipped around and tried to jerk Miles back by the foot. However, when he saw the cold look of anger in my eyes, he released his hold. He sneered at me before storming off towards Eliza.

Miles hugged me.

"Don't worry. I'm here. I won't let him hurt you." Carefully setting him down, I wiped the tears from his eyes and kissed him on both of his cheeks. "Take Cole's hand. You'll be safe."

Miles looked at Cedric and then to me. His eyes widened in fear.

I smiled at him. "It will be ok. Go on. Trust me."

The smell of lavender blew from the nearby bushes and comforted me. When we reached the crimson red forest, Gram took my hand. I weaved my fingers between hers and then turned to check on the rest of my family. Meg rested on my father's shoulder. Gently, he stroked her hair.

Groggily, my sister opened her eyes and smiled at me.

As we gazed at each other intensely, I knew she understood everything that had happened. I mouthed to her, "I love you."

With a sleepy grin, Meg winked and gave me the thumbs up.

Finally, we arrived at the stone table where Gram and I had made the memory spells. Out of the corner of my eye, a small flash caught my attention. When I turned to look, I saw a small, lavender light blink again. I gasped.

Gram squeezed my hand, confirming she had seen it, too.

The glow had flashed over a large nest-like opening in the ground coverings. The same nest from my dreams. A pulse emitted from my ring finger.

Gathering my confidence, I called out, "We need to go over here."

Eliza's eyes narrowed to a suspicious glare when I stepped into the center of the nest.

A cold rush of air enveloped me, and everything around me changed. I was no longer in the forest. I was standing inside a large nest of silver twigs. The ground surrounding it had a cover of soft white that shimmered with pastel colors and flecks of silver. Above me, the moon was full, and its light shined down on me.

"*Listen to your heart,*" the soft voice of the Goddess called to me.

Small bubbles of blue, red, green, orange, and silver floated around me. I held my hands up towards the sky above me. "Air, Fire, Water, and Earth, I call upon you. Your guidance and support are needed. In honor of the Goddess, I'll keep my promise, but now, I ask for your assistance."

The balls of light clung to my skin, sending a warm sensation through me. The magic intensely pulsed inside me. A blinding white light washed over me, and I was back in the circle, again.

Cole looked at me with concern on his face. I smiled reassuringly at him and stepped towards the outer ring. "Eliza, you'll need to stand in the middle of this circle."

Stepping into the nest, Eliza glided past me and into the center. "I hope you know what you are doing," she hissed.

Me, too, I thought before sending a stream of colored light towards her. Trying to contain my surprise, I took a deep breath and watched as they surrounded her. *Listen to your heart*, I reminded myself.

"Gram, Cole, and Elliott, come into the circle," I beckoned.

Elliott set Meg down and kissed her on her forehead. Miles took her hand, and my father affectionately tousled his hair.

One by one, the adults entered and joined us. When Cedric tried to follow, I held up my hands. "You need to stay out there."

Startled, he stopped, but his disbelief quickly faded to anger. "This better not be a trick," he snarled. Standing on the edge of the nest, he glowered at us.

I ignored Cedric's threat, and I addressed my siblings. "Meg and Miles, move over by the table. We'll need to focus, so you'll need to be silent. Don't move or interrupt me."

Hoping they understood that I needed them to stay away in order to remain safe, I turned back towards my family and began the unbinding. "Danu, with an open heart, I request the binding placed upon Eliza to be released." I sent a stream of magic towards Gram. "Air, may your strong winds renew the pure magic."

A powerful gust encircled my grandmother. She nodded at me, and then directed the air into the center, where it joined the colored lights twisting around Eliza.

"Fire, your gift of cleansing warmth is called upon." I formed a ball of fire in my hand. From within the ball, long threads of Fire drifted outwards to surround Eliza.

The elements slowly lifted Eliza off the ground.

Reassured that my instincts were correct, I turned towards Cole. "Water, please, wash away and renew the magic that Eliza promised to protect."

Cole held out his hands, and a stream of water droplets left his fingers. They floated above Eliza and showered down on her.

My eyes met my father's. "Earth, the blessing of your new life and growth are called upon. May the gift of new beginnings fill Eliza's heart."

The ground below us shook and began to crack. A white flower grew from the ground underneath Eliza. The stems grew tall and wrapped around her legs and body. Soon, she was elevated even higher off the ground.

"It's working!" Eliza began to laugh uncontrollably as the colors of the elements spun around her.

"With the blessing of the elements, we ask for the gift of forgiveness and renewed faith. Goddess, we call upon you and ask you to undo what was done." I lifted my arms towards the night sky.

A large crack sounded as a bolt of white lightning struck Eliza. Her body shook and convulsed before she went limp. The leaves of the flower surrounded her and formed a tight cocoon. *Did I kill her?* Unsure of what my next step should be, I faltered.

Gram stepped forward. "With the bindings I cast removed, Goddess, our request is complete. Thank you for the blessings you have bestowed upon us."

The shell shook as it cracked and slowly opened. Gently, it lowered to the ground. Eliza stepped out of the broken casing and laughed maniacally. "Cedric, it's back. It's really back. The magic is no longer bound. I'm, finally, restored."

CHAPTER
THIRTY-SEVEN

Eliza's eyes grew dark, and the tips of her fingers glowed with green fire. Turning to face my grandmother, she cried, "You took what was given to me, and it can never be repaid."

"You were bound because you were using your gift selfishly. You didn't keep your promise to protect the magic. You were taught – no, you *vowed* – harm to none, and yet, your castings for the Drygens were used to hurt people." Gram released long tendrils of Air that flew at Eliza.

The magic struck and reeled her backward. When she gained her footing, she charged at my grandmother.

"Stop," I screamed, throwing a fireball at Eliza, and redirecting her attention towards me.

Cedric's large knife glinted, alerting me that he was entering the circle. In an attempt to stop him, I threw my fireball. This one stuck his thigh.

Cedric howled in pain, but the injury didn't stop him from rushing forward. Just as he reached me, he was tackled by my father and Cole.

While I was distracted by their fighting, I was knocked down by a cold electricity that surged through my body. The dark shadow of Eliza covered me. I looked up to see hatred in her eyes.

"You always loved her more," Eliza screamed. Her cries seemed to feed the flames blazing from her fingers. She threw more of her magic at me. This time, I was knocked into the center of the circle. "I was your mother, but you always ran to her."

Eliza's body glowed as the magic forming from her hands grew larger. I scrambled to stand but stumbled. The power she emitted kept zapping me. The agony threw my balance off and sent me to my knees. I gasped for air.

Don't give up, I scolded myself.

I refocused my magic on fighting what was running through me, and a warm wave of relief washed over me. However, the comfort was momentary, and I faltered, again, from the pain. Her magic was so strong. I didn't know how to push it out of me, and I collapsed. Again, I tried to tap into the magic inside me.

"Stop! Mara, your magic will only feed hers as it runs through you." Gram sent ribbons of air in my direction. "Her magic is dark now."

Eliza screamed and cast tendrils at her mother's healing gusts of air.

Once again, I tried to stand. My attempts were stalled as I was brought to my knees, again and again, by the excruciating pain.

"What's wrong, darling?" Eliza purred. "Are you having problems standing?"

Unwilling to back down, I tried, again, only to fall.

Eliza cackled with glee at my agony. Her sinister laugh filled the air as she loomed over me. "You were so eager to save everyone else that you forgot yourself." Eliza reeled back to heave her magic at me with more force.

The bolt of electricity she flung knocked the wind out of me, and I was thrown back, hitting my head against the ground. The pain running through my body was unbearable, and I gasped for breath. Blackness rushed over me, and I fought not to slip into it.

A hard kick to the side of my leg jolted me out of the darkness. I tried to pull myself away from the sharp blows that repeatedly struck me. *Stand up, or you will die!* I scowled at my weakness and struggled to rise to my feet. I would have to fight her, or she was going to kill me.

I pulled myself upright and focused all the energy I had left inside me on blowing Air at Eliza. The wind I was able to push at her tossed her backward, but it was not far or hard enough.

"Fire and Air?" Eliza cried with delight when she landed on her feet. "Marina, you really are full of surprises." She continued to taunt me. "Too bad you won't be around to show me everything you are capable of." She sent another bolt of electricity at me.

Just in time, I dodged her attack by rolling out of the way. Frustrated that she narrowly missed, Eliza screamed and began heaving multiple flashes of her magic at me. Calling Air to me, I created a barrier to stop it from hitting its mark.

"You're no match for me." Eliza held her hands into the air. A fluorescent green blazed from her fingers, and she sent balls of her dark power at me. She wore a cruel smirk upon her bitter face.

She was right. My magic was not going to be strong enough to fight her. Every attack I repelled only seemed to feed her. When I missed blocking one of the bolts, I found myself struggling to stay standing, again, as sharp pins vibrated through me.

Eliza laughed. "Goodbye, Marina."

This time, she held the magic in her hands until she formed a large orb that sparked with green fire. When she released it, the ball grew as it sailed towards me. Realizing I was not going to be able to stop it, I braced myself for impact.

Meg's screams resonated through the air, and I realized why when my grandmother shoved me out of the way. Crashing into the wall of the nest, I regained my composure and rolled over. Moments before Eliza's magic struck, I watched Gram cast a ball of white light at her estranged daughter.

Eliza was not prepared with a counterattack and was, unexpectedly, struck in the chest. It sent her flying backward. She landed outside of the circle, on top of Cedric. She shrieked in pain and rolled off of him.

Cedric stood up with a panicked look on his face. The knife he clutched dripped with blood, staining his hands. A spot of red grew around Eliza's midsection while the white glow of Gram's magic continued to pulse through her.

"Cedric, help me," she rasped. As she tried to stop the blood that flowed from her, the blackness of her eyes melted to a soft green.

Cedric cut a strip of fabric off his shirt and drove the knife into the ground. "I can't stop the bleeding, Liza," he whispered, his voice now breaking with emotion. "We are so close to having it all, baby. Hang in there. You can't leave me. We can stop her."

Eliza touched his face tenderly. "You still can. Don't let her control your future." Her hand slipped away, leaving a bloody imprint in its wake. Her eyes closed, and her breathing slowed.

Cedric began to scream and pounded on the ground. "It's not your time. You're not meant to die."

Cole took the knife from the ground. "Let go of her, Cedric."

"She can't die!" Cedric cursed and dove at Cole.

Gram opened her blue pouch. Small tendrils of smoke slithered from the bag and blew towards Cedric. The strands wrapped themselves around his hands and feet. When he fell to the ground, the strands of silver entered his nostrils and open mouth. Soon, his cursing and cries ended. Cedric was silent.

Miles ran to Eliza and knelt down. He took her hand into his. The devastation in his youthful face was heartbreaking.

I went over and crouched down beside my little brother. I took our mother's hand from him and slipped the ring off her finger. Then, I handed it to the small boy. "This is yours now."

Unsure what to do with the ring, he slipped it into his pocket. He leaned forward and kissed our mother on her cheek. Then, he whispered something inaudible into her ear.

Her eyes opened, and she looked at us. In a faint whisper, she said, "You will never be able to defeat her. She is stronger than you."

Those were the last words she spoke. She slowly closed her eyes and as her final breath left her body, sadness washed over me. The sorrow I felt was not because she was gone, but rather, it was for Miles and Meg. My pain was, also, for my grandmother, who had lost her only daughter.

I remembered how broken I felt when my father had *died,* and when Eliza had disappeared. My father stood over my mother's body, and the grass around her grew. Soon, she was surrounded by flowers. "Goodbye, Eliza," he said, his voice slightly cracking.

"Is he dead, too?" Miles tugged at the bottom of my father's jacket as he pointed at Cedric. His green eyes filled with fear.

"No, Miles." My father picked him up. "He's just sleeping."

"He won't let me stay with you." Miles began to cry. "Grandmother Blanche won't let him."

"No, son, you are never going back there." My father hugged him tightly. "Gram, Mara, Cole, Meg, and I will never let you go." He turned to face my grandmother. "Isn't that right, Mae?"

Seeing his face turn white with fear, I looked to see what had alarmed him.

My grandmother was lying on the ground.

"No," I screamed and ran to her. I fell to the earth next to her. She was ghost-white and shivering. "Gram, tell me what to do. How can I help?"

Gram gripped my hand. I could feel Eliza's dark magic running through her. I hugged her tightly, ignoring the electricity.

"Please, Goddess, help me," I pleaded through my tears.

Cole took her from me. She looked like a small child in his arms. "You're going to be fine, Mae. Let's get you home." Turning towards my father, I stopped him from trying to pick up Cedric. "Leave him, Elliott."

"Come on, Daddy." Meg took his hand.

Flowers grew around Cedric and vines secured him to the ground. I watched as a crown of pink flowers surrounded his head. Glancing up, I caught the smirk on my little sister's face.

Noticing I was staring at her, Meg smiled and shrugged.

CHAPTER
THIRTY-EIGHT

When we arrived home, Gram insisted on being laid on the couch. I covered her with blankets and sat next to her. I held her icy hands tightly in mine.

"What can we do to stop the magic running through you?" I questioned. "Tell me which spell to cast or what potion to make."

Panic filled me. It was horrific to watch my strong grandmother in such a feeble state. There had never been a day in my life when I'd seen her sick or unable to take action. She was my rock. I needed her strength. Worse, it was my fault she was...dying.

"Mara, love, there isn't anything you can do to stop this. The only thing you need to do is to take care of them for me." Gram weakly motioned to my family, scattered around the living room. She grimaced as she saw their somber expressions. "Help me up," she insisted. "My last moments in this world will not be lying on a couch."

"No, no, no!" Meg cried out and ran over to her. "Gram, don't die. Please, please, don't die and leave me."

Our grandmother opened her arms and embraced Meg, holding her close. "My little dancer, it will be ok. Dry your tears. You need to be strong now."

Gram winced in pain as she struggled to stand. I knew what she was experiencing – the waves of cold electricity were still rolling through her body. Still, she pushed past the pain and hobbled, with my assistance, towards the kitchen.

"Put the kettle on, and let's have some tea," she said, sitting at the table.

I wasn't sure if she truly wanted the beverage or if she was too weak to go on.

"It'll take the chill out of these old bones."

I wiped away my tears. They wouldn't help her and they, certainly, wouldn't help my siblings. Instead, I pulled down the container of Gram's special herbal blend and biscuits.

"Miles and Meg, come join me." Gram patted the tabletop.

I laid out the cups and set the teapot on the table in front of my grandmother.

Meg and Miles sat one on each side of her as she told them, "When I was a little girl, my mother would make me a cup of her special tea."

I filled our cups, inhaling the familiar orange zest of the brew. As she must have known it would, it soothed me, easing away some of the darkness. Then, just as my grandmother had always done, I added a splash of milk to each drink.

Gram weakly placed a biscuit on the saucer. She picked up her teacake. "Now, take your cookie like this and give it a long dunk. Don't wait too long, though, or it'll disappear." Taking the soaked biscuit out of the tea, she popped it into her mouth.

Laughing, Meg and Miles copied her.

"Elliott and Cole, come have a cup of tea with us." Both men were standing by the sink. They looked more frightened than the children. "Mara, you haven't touched your drink, yet. You don't want it to get cold." The look on her face beseeched me to be strong.

Dipping my biscuit in the tea, I let it soak before I popped it into my mouth. "Delicious," I said with a forced smile.

"Now, Miles, there is one thing you should know about Mara," Gram said earnestly. "She needs to be reminded not to be too serious. Can you promise to remind her to have fun?"

Miles threw his arms around her neck. "I promise, Gram."

"I knew I could count on you." She hugged him tightly.

"I love you, Gram," Miles whispered.

"And I love you, little one." Our grandmother squeezed him, one last time, before letting go of him. She held him in front of her and brushed the hair out of his eyes. She kissed his cheek and said with a crack in her voice, "Miles, my angel, I'm a bit tired now, and I think I should go lie down. I want you to know that my love for you will never end. Can you remember that?"

My brother nodded, and his eyes brimmed with tears. Gently, he kissed her on the cheek. "I'll always remember, Gram."

Elliott took Miles by the hand and said, "Let me show you Chester's woodshop. You will be able to build so many things there."

Weakly, Gram grabbed my father's hand as he walked by.

He released Miles and knelt down beside her.

In a soft whisper, meant only for him, she said, "Protect them all for me. You must choose to protect them over saving yourself."

Elliott stood up and kissed Gram on the head. His voice was filled with love and gratitude. "Thank you, Mae, for everything. I'll not let you down again."

My grandmother nodded. She struggled to stand, but Cole caught her as she faltered.

"Mae, if you wanted me to sweep you off your feet, you only had to ask." Cole scooped her up before she collapsed.

Too weak to argue, Gram rested her head against his shoulder. She gave him a fragile smile as he carried her to her room. As he laid her on the bed, she put her hand on his cheek. "Cole, I need you to take care of my girls. Can you do that for me?"

"Don't talk like that, Gram," Cole said, his voice breaking with emotion. "You'll be here to keep me in line for many years to come."

She gripped his hand desperately. "Can you promise me that you will...when the time comes, then?"

Cole hugged her tightly. "I promise, Gram."

"You know you were the grandson I always wanted. Never forget how proud I have always been of you." Gram's voice was now barely above a whisper. "Now, I need to rest. Mara and Meg, come lay beside me."

We climbed into her bed like we had done many times before. Both of us rested our heads on her shoulder. Snuggled against her, I strained to hear Gram's words.

"Mara, in my journal, you will find a key to Chester's safe. He left enough money to take care of you for many years if you spend it wisely. Meg, you're still a little girl. There'll be plenty of time for you to grow up. Can you both do as you are told and remember everything I taught you?"

Crying softly, Meg nodded.

Unable to speak, I squeezed Gram's hand, confirming I would do as she asked.

"Good." Gram closed her eyes, and prayed, "Goddess, watch over my girls and guide them. I invoke the elements and pray for their guidance and strength."

I could feel her breathing begin to slow. Holding her tighter, I held back my tears. "Gram," I whispered, "I promise to remember everything you taught me."

Then, she was still. I choked on my sobs as I struggled for composure. *She can't be gone. I need her with me.*

A warmth grew from Gram's body, and I watched in awe as a violet light filled the room and surrounded us. The hand of the Goddess extended before us, beckoning the spirit of my grandmother. Lifting from the body lying next to me, she accepted the outstretched hand. Gram looked over her shoulder at us and smiled before she walked into the light.

Suddenly, the room around us glowed even brighter. The radiant white light was overpowering. Then, it was replaced with hundreds of small, colored lights, and I knew we were surrounded by the elementals.

Crying harder, Meg held onto Gram's body.

Taking her hand, I whispered, "She's gone, Meg, but she went to a better place. One full of love and light. One day, when it is our time, we'll join her." Picking up my sister, I hugged her tightly. "She will always be in our hearts."

When I set her back on her feet, she took my hand in mine, and we left the room to rejoin our grieving family.

EPILOGUE

Gram left us more than the food she prepared and basic necessities. Somehow, she managed to leave notes around the house to remind us how much she loved us. Despite those things, the house was not the same without her.

The night we went to get Meg and Miles, she knew how everything would end. Gram had foreseen the future and done her best to prepare us for life without her. The reality of that fact was both admirable and heartbreaking.

Just where she told me, I found the small key to my grandfather's safe in the lavender journal she was always writing in. As I turned the cover to read it, a small envelope fell out. On the outside of it, my name was written in Gram's handwriting. I inhaled the sweet scent of lavender and vanilla, and I began to read her letter:

> My Dear Mara,
>
> In Chester's workshop, you will find a safe behind my grandmother's armoire. Chester made sure there was enough money for us to live comfortably, and I have only added to it. The amount in there would make the Drygens look poor, but no one must know about it. Money makes people act funny. You will be safer to live your life simply, as we always have done.

When I thought I would never have any more children, my heart was saddened. However, I knew the Goddess had something better in store for me. Little did I know, it would be in the form of a dark-haired girl with more magic in her heart than I had in my whole body. And a sassy ball of fire, who reminded me to savor every bit of life. A boy with a heart of gold that showed me love could be endless. And, the boy – who I had loved even before we met...the same child who will need you now, more than ever.

You have all blessed my life and my heart. Keep your promise to protect the magic and you will never go wrong.

Love Always,

Gram

As I finished, Meg and Miles came down the loft stairs. Both had somber looks on their faces.

"Now, there will be none of that." I put the letter back into the journal. "We're going to celebrate Gram's life, so come, eat the pancakes that Cole has made for you and try not to spill on your clothes."

"You sound like her, Mara," Meg said sadly as a tear dropped from her eyes.

Hugging them both, I said, "She's still here with us. Gram is in our hearts – always. So, let's be strong and honor her memory."

Breakfast lifted our spirits, and we were ready for the celebration. The town had banded together and planned a festival to commemorate Gram's life. We would not mourn her passing, but rather, rejoice in the life she gave us.

When we arrived on Main Street, I was shocked to see the crowd. I knew my grandmother had been well-liked, but I'd never seen an event like this before for anyone. Everything had been decorated as if it was the Summer Moon Festival, and hundreds of people had come to celebrate. My father had even set up Gram's stand, and Mrs. Everstone was behind it. She handed out cookies and slices of bread with jam my grandmother had made.

"Mae once told me that life was our gift from the Goddess and what we did with it was our gift back to her," said the voice of Mrs. Ward from the stage. "In my sixty-two years, I've never met anyone as giving and kind as Mae Silver Veracor. My wish for everyone here is to remember the love she gave us. I pray we will carry it on."

As people went up on the stage to speak about their memories of my grandmother, they each told a story of how she influenced their lives. When I saw the next person in line, my heart stopped. Wearing a dark red dress and matching red lipstick, there was no mistaking the silver-haired woman about to speak was Blanche Drygen.

Miles and Meg both grabbed my hands and moved closer towards me when they recognized her. As I tried to reassure them, I searched the crowd around us, looking to see if there was any other danger around. It appeared we were surrounded only by the friendly faces of friends and family. There was no sign of Cedric or anyone else unfamiliar to me.

As Blanche tried to accept the microphone, to take her turn, my father stepped in line and took her place. Smiling at her, he said, "Excuse my interruption. Everyone, Mae would appreciate all of your kind words. Nevertheless, we all know she wouldn't want us to spend the day talking about her. Instead, let's eat, be merry, and spend the rest of our time together celebrating the woman we all loved. That really is the only way to tell her we got the message she taught us – so let the party begin."

The band began to play, and the crowd cheered. Soon, the dance floor was flooded with people moving to upbeat music. Blanche, however, stormed off the stage and smacked right into Cole.

The cold look in his eyes surprised me. It made me feel more relieved that my father had interceded, preventing her from speaking.

Cole clutched her arm and whispered something in her ear. I watched as she went white with fear and broke away from him. By the time he returned to me, the anger from his eyes had faded.

"She is gone and shouldn't be back today." He picked Miles up and took my hand. "Now, let's paint the town red for Gram."

Laughing, we joined the crowd and began to dance. Tugging on my hand, Meg whispered, "They are here, Mar. They are over there."

As I looked towards the light posts, I saw Breeze, Blaze, Bay, and Daisy twirling and dancing in merriment. When they saw us, they waved.

Smiling, I took a deep breath and said confidently, "Bright blessings, Danu, Bright blessings."

Today was not the time to worry about what we would face tomorrow. The Drygens would be our problem for another day. In this moment, all we could do was celebrate my grandmother's life – and we did.

EXIGENCY
PROTECTORS OF THE ELEMENTAL MAGIC BOOK 2

To my sister, without you I would not be able to write about such a loving sister.

To Jane for your feedback and support.

To Michelle for encouraging me to write. You will always be my red-carpet date, even if we are ready for the blue rinse.

To my readers — thank you for taking a chance on an unknown author. Your love of my imaginary world keeps me wanting to write more.

For my muse — the kitty — without you, I wonder if the story would've been written. You are my everything.

For the brilliant Dame Judi Dench — there are no words for how much inspiration I have and continue to gain from you.

And, For my Gram — always in my heart.

Acknowledgments

Thanks to L.E. Fitzpatrick for your tough critique that made a complicated web a little less layered. In addition, I would like to thank J.M. Northup for her editorial support. From our collaboration, I learned so much about not only writing but the editorial process.

In addition, my sincerest gratitude is expressed to the band of authors that I've met through this journey. Your words of wisdom encourage me to keep going no matter how hard it gets.

Exigency
Noun
A time or state of affairs requiring prompt or decisive action.

~Merriam Webster Dictionary

"We delight in the beauty of the butterfly, but rarely admit the changes it has gone through to achieve that beauty."

~Maya Angelou

"Stars, hide your fires; Let not light see my black and deep desires."

~Shakespeare

CHAPTER ONE

Light from the candles flickered and bounced off the walls, creating eerie shadows in the dimly lit room. In the center of the chamber, a man paced, back and forth, in front of a woman that appeared to be in a deep sleep. She rested on a table covered with a black cloth. Her dark red hair covered her shoulders, almost hiding the straps of her long, black nightgown. The satin material covered her body all the way to her bare feet. The man stopped, sat down, and took the woman's hand, holding it tightly.

As he stroked her hair, he whispered, "You need to come back to me. It's not your time. It's not over for us." He laid his head on her chest and cried. "I need you to come back to me. I'm nothing without you..."

The man's whispers were interrupted by the echoing click of high heels on the marble floor. "Cedric, you need to pull yourself together," a sharp voice demanded. "You've spent enough time in this icy tomb, mourning, and I would like my library back."

The tall woman loomed over the man with a scowl etched into her beautiful face. He stared into her dark eyes, but he didn't respond to her commands.

"There's nothing in this world that will bring her back. I need you here, with me. Now, stop sniveling. She would be disgusted if she could see what a mess you have become. Be respectful of the dead and let her go," said the woman.

"We can bring her back. I know we can, Mother! You're Blanche

Drygen, the most powerful woman in Starten. You have magic. We just have to figure out how to do it," Cedric begged.

Suddenly, he jumped out of his seat and shook his mother violently. "Your magic can save her. Bring her back – now! All you have to do is..."

Placing her pointer finger against his mouth, Blanche silenced him. "My magic isn't strong enough to bring her back from the dead and I won't ask *her*. Eliza's gone. You need to accept this loss and move on. We've bigger issues to worry about than a dead woman."

"She's not a dead woman!" Cedric screamed. "She is my love, my life. I can't go on without her. There's no point to a life without her in it."

"Enough!" Blanche shouted. Her face twisted in anger. Almost immediately her cold demeanor returned. She smoothed her short silver hair, confirming that not one piece had dared to move out of place by Cedric's outburst.

With a look of love, she cupped Cedric's bearded face between her hands, and her tone softened. "You're a Drygen. Letting you be with her has made you weak. Consider it a blessing that you're finally free of that curse. Now, you can be the strong man I raised. If we are going to get my grandson back from those people, you will need to pull yourself together."

Cedric slumped in defeat.

Pressing her hand on his chest, Blanche pursed her lips, and said in a low growl, "He can't live with them. He is a Drygen, and he won't be raised in that house...by those *people*."

When he didn't respond, she poked him. "He is our hope for a future legacy. Our family line depends on him. The Drygens will not end because of *that* family."

Cedric lifted his head. He now wore a faraway look on his face. "There has to be a way to bring her back. Eliza will return, and then all will be right, again. I'll ask her ..."

The sound of her slapping him across the face filled the room. Blanche narrowed her violet eyes. "Don't you think that *the girl* would have brought back Mae Veracor if there was a way? Her magic is strong, but she cannot do that. And you will never mention asking her again. You need to be realistic, Cedric. Do not make me give up on you, also."

"I just miss her so much, Mother." Cedric lowered his head onto his mother's shoulder and fell into her arms like a small child would.

Blanche held him close and stroked his cheek. Her demeanor became softer until the tender moment was encroached upon by a rattling sound in the doorway. She released Cedric and turned to face the disturbance.

"What do you need, Hazel?" Blanche snapped. "I said no interruptions. What is so important that you needed to intrude?"

A maid stood holding out a tray of tea and small sandwiches. Bowing her head, she apologized, "I'm sorry, Mrs. Drygen. I just thought Mr. Cedric might like something to eat. He hasn't eaten in several days."

Eyeing the woman, Blanche finally nodded. "Fine. Set it down and go. Go straight to Steven. Tell him to plan for a burial and tell him I want it done today."

"Yes, ma'am." Hazel fidgeted, and then she smoothed a strand of her salt-and-pepper hair. It had fallen loose from the tight bun knotted at the top of her head. "I'll tell him right away."

As Blanche watched the maid leave the room, her eyes darkened, and she turned her attention back to her son. "Say your last goodbye to Eliza, Cedric. She'll be buried today, and we'll begin our plans to return my grandson to where he belongs — with me."

CHAPTER
TWO

"She didn't make it the right way," the hiss of my little sister's voice filled my ears.

I closed my eyes and focused on the fact that Meg was only ten years old. Our family had been through so much recently. She was forced to deal with a pain that no child should be expected to handle. Just over a month ago, we buried my grandmother, Mae Veracor, and each of us was trying to find a way to fill the hole in our hearts that her passing had left.

Cole's gruff whisper responded, "No, Meg, it was not exactly like Gram's soup, but it still was really good. And the grilled cheese sandwiches were almost exactly like Gram's. Mara even cut it into the little diamond shapes you like."

"It's not like Gram's," Meg pouted.

Cole was normally able to laugh off my little sister's attitude, but even he was losing patience. Trying a softer approach, he said, "Meg, we aren't going to talk like this. How do you think Mara will feel if she hears you?"

"She'd be sad," she murmured.

"You're right. She would be really sad. Don't you think we've enough sadness right now? What would Gram say? I bet she'd say that Mara's soup was better than hers."

Meg was right. The soup is nothing like Gram's. How am I going to do this? I can't do any of this without Gram, I thought.

My internal dialogue was interrupted by warm breath on the back of my neck and strong arms wrapping around me. "Here, let me take care of this for you." Cole took the ladle out of my hand. "You have more soup on the counter than in the jar, Mar."

Staring down at the surface splattered with the tomato soup, I sighed. "She's right. The soup didn't turn out. It wasn't Gram's tomato soup – not even close. How are we going to do this, Cole?"

"The soup was different, but it was still good." He lifted my chin and looked into my eyes. "Mar, no matter how you make the soup, Gram isn't coming back. It won't bring her back. Things are going to be different. We all miss her. We just have to get used to her not—"

"I understand she's gone, and we'll never see her again in this world. I do, but of all of the people we've lost, I never thought Gram would...I never thought she'd die. I'm not ready to be without her."

Cole twisted me around and wiped the tears flowing down my cheeks. "We *will* get through this, together, Mar. None of us were ready for her to go, but she wouldn't want you to fall apart over her death. Remember the life she brought to this world."

As my fiancé hugged me tightly, I fought the urge to sob. I whispered almost inaudibly, "I'm trying, Cole, but I'll try harder."

I held him, not wanting to leave the comfort of his warm embrace. When I reluctantly released him, Cole kissed me on the forehead.

"Go connect with the elements."

I smiled at him. *How did I deserve this man? He understands me even more than I seem to understand myself.*

"Go on, Mar." Cole gently nudged with a mischievous grin. "I'll tell Blaze you have been neglecting your training."

"You would." I laughed.

Calling after me, he said in a dramatically high-pitched voice, "Come home to me, soon, Mara. I miss you already."

When I passed through the patio to leave the house, I saw the lavender bag lying on the table. The tag, labeled *For Mara*, brought tears to my eyes. The soft fabric held my wedding dress...my grandmother's dress. She had given it to me with her blessing to marry Cole.

Before Gram died, we had agreed to have the ceremony on the day after my birthday. Doubts about having a wedding so soon after a funeral overwhelmed me. Cole disagreed and had eagerly started planning the event. I should have been excited. Instead, I was riddled with guilt. It wasn't because I didn't love Cole, but because there had been too many changes, too quickly. I was scared.

Get yourself together. You're marrying, Cole. You love him. Now, no more wedding thoughts, I scolded myself.

I listened to my own advice, and I walked towards the forest. Each night, I tried to spend time outside. It was here that Gram's presence felt the strongest. The whisper of the wind through the trees calmed me. However, this time, it wasn't working. My mind was full of questions. The hardest part was trying to wrap my head around the gift and how it had impacted my family.

My grandmother, Mae Veracor, was the daughter of Genevieve Silver. Genevieve, my great-grandmother, was one of the original protectors of the elemental magic. For a reason that was still unclear to me, the goddess, Danu, had gifted four girls with the knowledge of elemental magic. The teens — Genevieve Silver, Camille Black, Michelle Elliott, and Sarah Andrews — had each taken an oath to protect the magic, and for many years, they kept their promise.

Then, Camille, the redhead with a personality as fiery as her hair, married Brandon Drygen. His family had always been the richest, most influential family in Starten. Most people, who worked outside of their own properties, found themselves working at one of their businesses. However, that wasn't enough for them, and Camille began to misuse her gift to further their success.

Having vowed never to use the magic for selfish gains, the other three women came up with a plan to stop their wayward friend. They decided to bind Camille's magic. The spell cast was so strong that it bound all her gift. The Drygen family didn't need the elementals since they had an abundance of money and power. Still, Camille never forgave the women for what they did, and the betrayal she felt fueled her anger. In retaliation, she focused her rage towards the one who had been her closest friend, Michelle.

Out of fear, Michelle and her family left town. Little did I know how deeply connected I was to these girls. Michelle Elliott turned out to be none other than the grandmother of my father, Elliott Stone.

After many years of exile from their home, my father had been sent back to Starten. As a young man, he met and fell in love with my mother,

Eliza. Their fate was tragic, and, eventually, my mother forced my father to fake his death and leave us. The whole time, she was in a secret relationship with a man, named Cedric, who happened to be the grandson of Camille, and son of Blanche Drygen.

When Gram found out about the affair and how Eliza had been misusing her magic to help the Drygen family, she became infuriated. Just as before, she cast a spell to bind all the magic my mother had. Cursing my grandmother, Eliza left our home, abandoning my little sister and me along with it.

Almost six years after her unexplained disappearance, my mother returned. Acting as though nothing had happened, she demanded Meg and I leave with her immediately. Due to this, my grandmother was forced to reveal the secret of the Silver family. In order to do so, I was given a potion to restore my memories and magic.

It wasn't enough to find out that Genevieve and Michelle were my great-grandmothers. That revelation was quickly followed by the shock of discovering I had a half-brother, whose father was a Drygen. I, also, found out my fiancé, Cole, was the great-grandson of Lucy Andrews.

How did all of these people end up connecting? Was it the plan of the goddess? I wondered. Maybe it was fate that I fell in love with Cole. Had it been fate that pulled my father to Eliza while she longed to be with Cedric? I felt my anxiety rise. Will the children pay for the mistakes of their parents?

As I walked further into the woods, the wind picked up. The cool breeze whipped my hair around, blocking my view as the dark shadows of the forest surrounded me. I didn't feel afraid. I could still hear the rustling the trees, sounds of birds chirping, and the clicking of the silver moss beetles.

As I continued walking, the air died down and the trees thickened. I quickly found myself encompassed by a dense fog. My hair was no longer blinding me, but I could barely see my hand in front of my face. A soft, internal voice told me to just keep going, and I listened until I stepped into cold water.

"Damn it," I cried out before stepping backward. Unsure which way to move, I called, "Air, please, blow away this fog and let me see where I am."

I waited while the moist vapor drifted away, showing me that I was on the rocky shore of Sparrow Lake. Frustrated, I sat down and wrapped my arms around my legs. I rocked myself gently, back and forth.

How did I get so far from home? I felt as if I was losing a connection with reality. I kept telling myself that, if I just listened to my heart, everything would be fine. Things would go as planned. Staring at the water, I questioned my recent behavior.

Crackle. I whipped my head around to see what was approaching. A shadow quickly darted through the tree line.

"Stop! Who are you? Why are you following me?" I stood, prepared to face the unknown.

The cold breeze off the lake picked up and covered my arms with goosebumps. Rubbing my arms frantically to warm up, I called out again, "Whoever is out there, show yourself."

"With all the magic you hold, you could easily climb up the mountain and give them what they deserve," said the bewitching voice of a woman. "You could start a little fire. One little ball of your magic could ignite the forest surrounding them. It would grow and grow until it burned their mansion down. Or, better yet, call a great wind and bring everything, and everyone, down into a crumbling ruin."

With more anger, the voice said, "And, there's always my favorite. Call the rain and demand it to pour down buckets of water until you finally wash everything off the mountainside. Mudslides happen all the time. Or, be lazy, and ask the ground to shake, and shake, and shake until you have created dust out of them all."

The voice taunted, "Wouldn't it be so easy? Don't you think they deserve to be punished for what they did to your grandmother?"

Fighting my thoughts of agreement, I called out, "No. I won't do any of that. Destroying them will not bring my grandmother back. Nothing will bring her back!" I clenched my fists and screamed, "Who are you? Show yourself!"

"Mara, you know as well as I do that you want to avenge your beloved Gram. You want to make them pay," she crooned in a dark, silky tone.

"I have no plans to do any of such thing. Go away or show yourself."

"Show myself?" Laughing, the voice said, "I'm right here."

A small splash came from the lake, but only my reflection shimmering in the water. The ripples stopped, and I could see an image of myself. No. This mirage was not me. The girl I saw had cold, dark eyes. She looked lost...sad...broken.

"You're not me," I said to the reflection. "You won't trick me into hurting anyone. So, show your real self."

"Why are you fighting who you really are so fervently? You know you want to pay them back. Go on. Cast a few little balls of magic or send forth a tiny bit of the elemental power inside you. No one will know it was you, but everything will be as it should be. The Drygens will be gone. The Silver line will continue. Your future children will be safe," she stated reassuringly. "Don't you want your family to be protected? After all, your family wants it, too."

An image appeared on the black water of my younger siblings. They were in the backyard of our property under the tree where I had held my elemental tea parties.

Meg put her hands on her hips and loomed over our little brother. "They're not going to take you away from us, Miles. Mara will keep us safe. Now, practice and it will grow stronger."

Hearing the confidence she had in me, my heart sunk. *How am I going to shelter them from the darkness around us?*

The water rippled, again. This time, Cole and my father appeared. They were sitting at our kitchen table. Both men looked tired and worn as they frantically wrote on the papers they had laid out before them.

"We can bring them down," Cole said. His normally bright blue eyes were dark. "If we just eliminate them now, we won't have to deal with any repercussions for taking Miles. They deserve whatever we send at them."

My father nodded in agreement and continued his writings. Under his breath, he responded, "Yes, we'll remove this threat, soon."

The dark image of the girl in the water returned. "Don't you see that they need you? You need to save them from the Drygens. It's up to you, Mara, to save them all. They will perish if they try to take on Cedric."

"Stop trying to fill my head with your nonsense. Hurting them will not help my family. You're not real. Go away!" I screamed, sending out the magic I had inside me. Fire, Water, and Air swirled around me as the ground below me shook.

Laughing, the voice said, "Exactly what I wanted to see. Now, take all that emotion and go up the mountain. Rain down your anger on the Drygens. But, this time, put a little force behind it."

Lashing out at the reflection, I screamed, "Go away! Go away! Go away!"

Covering my ears with my hands, I closed my eyes tightly and rocked myself as I pleaded for the voice to leave me. *It should have been you not, Gram. The ball of magic was meant for you, not her.*

Strong hands gripped my shoulders. I struggled to pull myself away from the danger. When I finally broke away, I landed with a splash in Sparrow Lake.

CHAPTER THREE

The icy water shocked me, and I found it hard to catch my breath. I scrambled to the shore with thoughts of running back into the forest to hide, but I wasn't fast enough. A hand roughly caught my wrist. My instinct to flee instantly changed to self-preservation. My heart beat so hard I thought it would fly out of my chest.

My mind screamed, *Fight! Fight! Save yourself!* I turned to confront the aggressor only to find myself face-to-face with Cole.

"Mar, calm down. It's me. Who were you shouting at? There's no one here." Cole wrapped his arms around me and held me tightly.

"He'll try to kill them, with or without you, and he'll fail," the voice whispered in my ear.

I jerked away from Cole and returned to the position he'd first found me in. I held my hands over my ears to block out the hiss of the voice.

Cole smoothed my hair, and I could hear his faint voice. "It's OK, Mar. I'm here. You're not alone."

His touch calmed the screaming inside me. I lowered my defenses and uncovered my ears. Realizing the voice was gone, relief flooded me. I threw myself into Cole's tall, muscular body and wrapped my arms tightly around his neck.

"Don't let me...don't let me become that person," I choked out through my tears. "I'm not — I won't. Oh, Cole, don't let them turn *you* into a person like them, either. We can't —"

"Mar, what are you talking about?" He cupped my face between his hands. His eyes burned with concern. "Oh, Mara, you're just tired. You need to relax and rest. Gram's not here, but that doesn't mean you can fall apart. Who are you afraid we're going to turn into? Last time I checked, we were just Cole and Mara."

Taking a lighter tone, he continued, "Why, we've got a wedding to plan. Our future together is just beginning, and it includes your sister, your father, and your little brother. Don't give up on yourself and lose them. Together, we'll face anything."

Cole held me for a few minutes before he kissed my cheek and released me. "Are you calm enough to tell me what happened?"

"The things she said were so horrible," I whispered. "She said —"

Something rustled behind us, interrupting me. A wicked laughter rang through the forest.

"What is that?" Cole's jaw clenched. "Is that what you're afraid of?"

I barely nodded.

With a flash of intensity, he turned towards the laughter and yelled, "Come out to face us, coward."

The laughter stopped, and a frigid wind blew crystals of ice at us. The frozen water clung to my skin before it slowly melted. Through the frigid air, a woman wearing a seductive black dress appeared. She walked towards us with long, slow strides. My breath caught as I saw her more clearly.

Her snow-white skin shimmered as if she had been dusted with frost. She was clad in a long and flowing gown with a plunging crystal-beaded neckline that fell below her belly button. The delicate crystals were faintly glowing. Long lashes surrounded the greyish-blue color of her almond-shaped eyes. When she finally reached us, she stopped in front of Cole, disregarding me.

"Well, we finally meet in person." The woman smoothed her long, black hair out of her face with lengthy silver nails. Stroking Cole's face with her fingertips, she purred, "What a pretty fiancé you have, Marina. You'll have such beautiful children." She lifted her hand from his face, and I could see faint red streaks where she had touched him.

Cole stared at the woman as if he was under a spell.

"She said you would be a challenge to my *children*. Oh, I thought I'd made the right choice when I selected Eliza. If only Mae hadn't interfered." The woman let out a long sigh before composing herself. "But, enough of those sad thoughts. I think the two of you will be perfect replacements."

Replacements? I shivered, unclear if it was from the chilly air or the menacing words.

"Aren't you tired of all the trials and tribulations that my...Danu has put you through? Wouldn't you like to be powerful and free of your silly promise?" She circled us, slowly running her fingers along my bare skin.

I flinched at her burning touch.

"All of this *protect the magic.* Protect the magic," she said in a mocking tone. "Who wants to protect it when they can *use* it?"

Stopping in front of me, she held out her hand, displaying a ring. It was a perfect diamond, surrounded by sapphires.

"If jewelry isn't something you like, what about this?" She held out her hand, again, only now it was full of golden coins. "Anything you want can be yours. All you have to do is take it."

The coins faded, and she gripped my hands. The cold sting of her magic coursed through me. I wanted to pull away from her, but I was frozen in place.

"You can have everything you always wanted, Marina." The woman swept back loose strands of my hair from my face. The burn of her touch woke something primal inside me.

Wanting to assault her, I ripped my hands from her and snarled. "You don't know anything about me or my family. We want nothing to do with what you're offering."

The stranger gave me a patronizing smile. "Oh, Marina, I do know you. I know you better than you know yourself." She swept her hand in front of me, and a sheet of ice appeared.

When my image appeared on the frosty barrier, I covered my mouth to hold back a gasp. The persona before me was in the elemental circle where my grandmother had sacrificed herself for me. I had gone to the place of her death, hoping to find peace. Instead, I found more sadness and guilt.

Sitting in the center of the circle, I had cried out to the goddess, asking her to bring back my grandmother. Tears streamed down my face. When I found no response, the vision replayed my curse on Danu for taking her from me and my vowed to destroy the Drygens with every ounce of magic I had inside me. Then, the memory ended.

Unfortunately, she hadn't shown the entire event. She'd stopped before I composed myself and acknowledged that my words had been spoken in anger. She didn't show how I, once again, vowed to protect the magic, knowing there would be sacrifice.

"You're not showing everything," I said. "I was angry, but I realized it was my sorrow speaking."

I rushed to Cole and tugged him away from her. "We're done with you…" Unsure what to call her, I paused for a moment. "Whoever you are – whatever you want – my family will not be following the path of my mother. We aren't going to trust you."

Laughing at my words, she called after me, "Oh, we'll see each other again, sweet Marina."

I trembled violently as I led Cole away from the dangerous woman. He and I walked in silence until we reached the tree line outside of our property. Guiding my still dazed fiancé to sit, I wrapped my arms around him and kissed the red marks still streaked across his face. The anger I had felt returned.

"Are you OK?" I questioned. "Are you hurt?"

Cole blinked rapidly before slowly shaking his head. A single tear fell from his eye. "I was going to follow her, Mara. I was going to break the promise I made and follow her to everything she tempted me with."

"Stop!" I demanded. "She put a spell on you, which is why you didn't move after she touched you. You would have never followed anyone for jewelry or money if you weren't under some sort of influence."

"Wait, what do you mean jewelry and money?" Cole frowned. His voice sounded puzzled.

"She held out a diamond and coins to us," I answered.

"She didn't try to give me jewels." Cole shifted away from me. "I saw us in a large mansion with children. The children kept calling us *mommy* and *daddy*. A small boy ran into the room we were in and told us how Uncle Miles had taught him a magic trick. It felt so real."

"But it wasn't real, Cole." I kissed his cheek, again, and wrapped my arms around him tighter. "We don't need a mansion and we'll have children of our own, one day. Why would you have to follow her for that?"

Cole jerked away from me. His eyes flashed with pain. "She said you wouldn't marry me unless I did."

"That's crazy." I moved closer towards Cole and took his face between my hands. "Why wouldn't I marry you?"

"Kai," he said in a low growl. "She said you were going to leave me for him."

"No, Cole." I dropped my hands from his face. "I was never going to be with Kai. He was just a guide in the elemental world."

Cole narrowed his eyes at me. "Why didn't you mention him before?"

"There was no need to tell you about him. He just helped me find my way back to you." Anger rushed through me. *How dare he not trust me.* "We've always trusted each other. This isn't a time to let someone plant a seed of doubt in your mind."

"You're right." He relented with less conviction than I hoped. "I trust you. I do."

He said the words, but I didn't feel like he genuinely believed what he was saying. There was no way I could convince him that I did love him; not at this moment. Feeling defeated, I said, "Let's go home."

We walked through the backyard, lost in our own thoughts. The night sky was filled with twinkling stars, but I was disappointed that I couldn't see the moon. *I need to find out more about the ice witch and why she wants our loyalty*, I thought with frustration.

When we entered the house, sounds of playing cards being shuffled filled the room. The warm draw of delighted giggles drew us towards the kitchen. We found Meg and Miles seated at the table with our father.

"Come play, Mara," Miles said excitedly. "Meg and I have the best game ever. Can we show you?"

"We made it up ourselves." Meg ran over to me and held out her hand, offering me a warm cookie. "I'm sorry I was mean earlier, Mara. I didn't mean to hurt your feelings. We tried to make Gram's zizzleberry cookies. They didn't turn out as good as Gram's, but they're still yummy...just like your soup."

"I'm sure they're going to be delicious." I took a large bite of the cookie. The warm buttery flavor, followed by the tartness of the blueberries, raspberries, strawberries, and blackberries, made me smile.

"You did a good job. Gram would be proud." I offered the rest of the cookie to Cole. "Try this. You'll like it."

Cole popped the treat into his mouth and slightly smiled. "Which of you made this delicious morsel?"

Meg beamed. "We made it together. Miles is really good at figuring out Gram's secret wording. We're going to try more of her recipes, OK?"

Tousling her hair, I laughed. "That will be fine as long as you have an adult there to help you."

"Great." Meg's green eyes sparkled. "Come on, Miles. Let's try the peanut butter snapdragons."

I caught Meg by the back of her shirt. "I don't want to take away your excitement, but it's getting extremely late. Why don't you both go up to your room and brush your teeth? I'll be up shortly to read you a story."

"Can Cole read to us, instead?" Meg twisted out of my grasp.

"I don't know," I responded. "Why don't you ask him nicely?"

Both Meg and Miles pleaded with Cole to read them a story. They wildly jumped, up and down, in front of him until he picked them up in his arms and let out a large growl. They both screamed in delight.

With a soft gravelly voice, he said, "I'll tell you the story of the day I ran into the king of the snapping trout and how I barely got away...*alive*." Snapping his jaw shut loudly, he set them down.

They screamed louder and ran off towards the loft ladder.

"I'll be up, soon," Cole promised. "Be sure to watch out for any of the king's followers. They might be searching for his eye that I took." Closing his right eye, he snapped his jaws again.

Both children screamed before they scrambled up the ladder, giggling the entire way.

When the shrieks of laughter quieted, my father patted the seat next to him. "What have you two been up to, tonight?"

I flopped down on the chair and half-heartedly reached for a cookie as Cole sat beside to me.

"I found Mara at the lake," he answered.

My father sat up straight. "How did you get that far?" Concern filled his voice and the etched lines on his face deepened. "It's too dangerous for you to go that far alone."

Cole stared at the plate of cookies and, finally, picked one up. Instead of eating it, he just kept breaking it into pieces.

"I was just walking, and I ended up at the lake," I said nonchalantly.

Cole muttered under his breath, "She didn't just end up at the lake."

"Yes, I didn't just end up there. I wasn't paying attention and I led myself to trouble," I snapped. "I don't know how I got there. I was walking, and then I found myself at the edge of Sparrow Lake. When I got there, I heard a voice."

"What kind of voice?" My father's eyes widened.

"It was a woman." I tried not to show the fear evoked by this unknown entity. He didn't need anything else to worry about. "She told me you've been planning to pay back the Drygens for all of the pain they've caused our family. Then, she offered us our heart's desires, if we'd stop protecting the magic and just use it."

As I continued retold her promises of riches and wealth to my father, his eyes narrowed and grew dark. "My grandmother warned me about her, but I thought it was just a story to scare me."

"Who is she?" I asked.

"If I'm right, you were speaking to Snowystra, the sister of the goddess." My father covered his mouth and chin with his hand. His nervous body signals made my heart beat faster.

"So, she is a goddess, also?" I questioned. *Please, say a good one.*

"Technically, yes." He ran his fingers through his hair, causing it to wildly stick up. "But she isn't the kind of goddess we want to get involved with. Her gifts come at a price."

Cole interjected, "She said she turned Eliza to her side and that we would be a terrific addition to her family."

My father gave my fiancé a sharp look of warning. "Why are you so shaken up, Cole? We're going to face many scary things in our lifetime. You can't fall to pieces when the first adversary shows up at our door."

Is he really going to tell Cole to be a strong man for his weak wife? Anger filled me. "He's not scared of her and I'm not a fragile flower that needs to be sheltered. She's convinced Cole that I'm going to run off with a Fire elemental."

My father held up his hand. "Who are you running off with, and why am I just hearing about this, now?"

Sighing, I put my head down on the table. *You can't hide from the truth,* I scolded myself. Reluctantly, I straightened up. I knew I had to explain this before another person stopped trusting me.

"When I was in the elemental world, there was a Fire elemental. He taught me how to control my magic," I quietly explained. "He helped me prove to Danu that I was ready to come home. There was nothing more. I was in a magical world with many temptations, but I still came home."

I took hold of my fiancé's hand and looked deeply into his eyes. "Cole, I love you, now and forever. I can't prove this to you, except for the fact I'm here and I'm never leaving you."

Cole's eyes brimmed with tears. I wiped one away as it fell. "How can you let some witch in the forest tell you I'm going to destroy what we have? Why would you believe her over me?"

Cole shook his head and squeezed my hand. "I don't believe her, Mar. I just don't understand why you didn't tell me about him before this. Finding out this way isn't right."

"I told Gram when I came back, and we both agreed there was no reason to upset you because it meant nothing. *Nothing*." I gripped his hand tightly. "It was only about learning the magic."

"If it meant nothing, you should have told me. You shouldn't keep secrets from me. You can't protect me by keeping things from me, Mar," he insisted.

"I won't. My intention was never to deceive you," I promised.

We sat in silence, just staring into each other's eyes. I wasn't sure what I should say or do to make things better.

My father halted the awkward moment by picking up the plate of cookies and carrying it away. "I'm going to put these away since Cole's just going to crumble them." My father chuckled. "These are too delicious to waste." For effect, he popped one into his mouth. "Delicious. We need to put these kids to work and have them do all the cooking. Don't you think, Caterpillar?"

Caterpillar was the name he called me as a child. He always told me that, one day, I would grow into the powerful butterfly. Back then, I would bask in his praise, but now, the thought scared me. I wasn't sure who I was anymore or what I would become. The only thing I really knew was that I needed to make my grandmother proud.

"They are pretty good. We should put those two to work," I agreed.

"Head off to bed, soon, guys. I want to go over the plans to add the extension onto the house in the morning. We're going to need more room for my grandchildren, right?"

"In time," I answered and gave a small smile.

We sat in silence for an exceptionally long time.

Finally, I stood up. "My father's right. We should go to sleep. It has been a long day for both of us."

"OK, I'll be along shortly. Go on without me." Cole's voice was overcome with sadness.

How could I so badly hurt someone I love?

Reluctantly, I left the kitchen. Stopping in the hallway, I called back to him. "I love you, Cole. I need you to know how much I do love you," I said, my voice cracking.

"I know, Mar," he said. "I love you, too. I'll be there soon after I check on Miles and Meg."

CHAPTER FOUR

I entered Gram's room and took a deep breath, inhaling her lingering scent. The sweet smell of vanilla, lavender, and cinnamon surrounded me. It almost felt like her warm, comforting hug. Once again, the reality of her death hit me. *Gram is gone.*

Closing my eyes, I softly patted my own hand the way my grandmother would. Even though it wasn't her calming me, it still gave me a sense of her presence.

After Gram's death, Miles and Meg had decided to share a room. This meant moving my things out of the loft and rearranging the space for Miles to have a room of his own while staying with his new half-sister. The two had formed a bond instantly and neither were ready to be alone quite yet.

My eviction meant Cole and I were displaced to the only space left. At night, we slept in Gram's bed, but we kept most of our personal items on the patio. I was not ready for her death to be real. If we made the room our own, it would make it final.

I half expected Gram to show up and remind us that moving too fast might lead to regret later. Her words had worked, at least for Cole, who was always a gentleman. Truthfully, he'd been the one to stop anything intimate from going too far.

With my face washed and my teeth brushed, I climbed into the king size mahogany bed and snuggled deep into the feather mattress pad. Hiding under the mauve-colored comforter, I laid on my side, hugged a pillow, and mentally went over all that had happened in the last few months. It began when my mother left us for Cedric Drygen. Then, upon her return, I was unceremoniously thrown into this new world of elemental magic, which I was supposed to guard, without warning. Finally, a new brother, Miles, was discovered.

I was feeling overwhelmed. I needed my grandmother here to talk to me about everything. I needed her to help me learn about the gift inside me. Drifting off to sleep with thoughts of Gram, the elemental world and Kai filled my dreams.

I found myself in the center of dancing elementals. A pure joy filled me as I joined in. Throwing my arms into the air, I laughed and twirled under the star-filled sky.

When the music changed to a slow song, Kai appeared. He winked and pulled me into his arms. My heart beat fast. I wanted to be in his arms. As if understanding my desires, Kai held me close and spun us around, and around, but then, my bliss changed. It was too fast, and I grew dizzy.

"Stop," I pleaded. The world around me slowed and I closed my eyes. *Will Kai kiss me?* Half hope and half fear washed over me.

When we came to a complete stop, I opened my eyes. Instead of seeing Kai's fiery eyes, Snowystra's icy stare pierced mine.

"No," I screamed. I tried to break free, but it was fruitless.

She gripped my wrist and pulled me closer. "You're losing him. Cole is going to leave you," Snowystra hissed. Her breath felt so cold that my ears tingled. "All because of your lies, he won't want you anymore."

Snowystra threw her head back and cackled. She waved her hand and Kai was standing next to me, again. "You know you really want to be with Kai. You crave excitement, not the boring boy from your childhood. Come with me, Marina. I'll give you what you long to have."

"You lie!" I screamed and tried to push her away. "You're not going to destroy us." Tearing my arm out of her clutched fingers, I felt the burn from her touch.

Laughing, she faded away.

Jolted out of sleep, I woke in the safety of my grandmother's bed. Trembling, I glanced around the room. *It was just a dream. You're safe. You aren't going to lose Cole,* I comforted myself.

"Cole," I whispered and rolled over to snuggle into his arms. I patted the spot where he should have been fast asleep. I found an empty space.

Scared my dream was right, I searched the house for him. He was nowhere to be found. My mind raced. *Where would he go?* Pacing back and forth in the kitchen, my eyes landed on the journal in the center of the table, and I had my answer.

Throwing on the first jacket and shoes I found, I stepped onto the front porch and was blasted with a burst of frigid air. Glad I had chosen to put on a coat, I wrapped my arms around myself, trying to keep in the warmth. The street was faintly lit, and distant sounds of a hoot owl seemed to warn me that danger lurking.

I picked up the pace and breathed a side of relief when I arrived on Cole's property. Ash covered the now vacant lot where Cole's childhood home had been burned down by my mother. I shuddered, knowing she had done it in retaliation for my refusal to leave with her. *Eliza left me, so why was she surprised when I wasn't excited to see her again?*

Walking through the remnants, my heart sunk. This had been a second home to me. Cole's mother, Sarah, always welcomed me with a smile, a story, and a warm hug. I remembered how devastated my fiancé had been by her loss, and how Gram comforted him through the shock of her sudden death. My grandmother became a replacement maternal figure to a young man still needing a mother. When Gram died, he felt the loss as much as Meg and I did.

I'm not the only one who's been through a lot lately, I realized.

When I reached the cottage that stood behind the missing house, there was a light on inside. Jiggling the door revealed it hadn't been locked, so I entered. The great room smelled faintly of smoke from the fire, but it was mixed with the familiar hint of pinecones and vanilla. I noticed Cole had kicked off his shoes, leaving them in the middle of the large room, and had strewn his jacket across one of the sturdy wooden chairs. I felt relieved he was there.

When I found the hatch door to the basement open, I, carefully, walked down the spiral staircase, trying to be quiet. *Why is Cole in his mother's studio?* Creeping in, I hoped to discover the reason.

As I counted the stairs in my head, I noticed the intricate web designs the spiders had created. They had multiplied since the last time I was there. Forcing back my urge to run from the green spiders with their long legs and small silver eyes, Gram's words from my childhood calmed me: *There's no reason to be afraid, Mara. The spiders won't hurt you if you leave them alone*. Taking a deep breath, I continued until I reached the last step.

Cole was sitting on a stool in front of a large canvas. Deep in thought, he dipped the brush into the paint on the palette he held. Then, he delicately covered the canvas.

Not wanting to break his concentration, I sat down at the bottom of the staircase and gawked in amazement at the moment he had created. Cole had painted a picture of our family. The image was of my grandmother at the stove with a spoon, stirring something in a pot with one hand, and a smile of delight on her face as she looked towards everyone seated at the kitchen table. Meg and Miles sat next to each other with my father across from them, scooping food onto their lifted plates. Cole and I were sitting close to one another, and I was feeding him a bit of my food.

Watching him work, tears welled up in my eyes. He had captured, in one picture, what I had hoped would have been our future. As he continued to add detail to the painting, I realized he had included his mother. Sarah stood at the butcher table, looking on proudly at her son.

Shifting myself slightly, the board I was sitting on made a small creak. Cole looked my way and our eyes met. For the longest time, we just stared at each other.

After a few minutes of silence, he finally asked, "How long have you been watching me?"

"Not very long. I just wanted to let you be in the moment," I confessed. I walked over and placed my hand on his shoulder. "It's really nice, Cole. I didn't know you wanted to paint, again. You're really talented. You shouldn't have given it up."

"I just didn't feel like painting after she died." Cole set the paintbrush down. "I didn't think it would make me feel happy, but I was wrong. Something peaceful happens when I paint."

"Have you made other paintings?"

"Just a few sketches, here and there," he admitted. "Nothing that great."

"Are you going to let me see them?"

"Maybe, one day," Cole said with a sly smile. He wrapped his arms around my waist and rested his head on my shoulder. "You know we should go home. Elliott is going to worry if he sees we are missing."

Running my fingers through his hair, I whispered, "He won't know we are gone if we stay a bit longer." Releasing myself from his tight hold on me, I sat on his lap, saying in my most seductive voice, "Cole, you can't run from me. You're stuck with me forever."

Sweeping his hair out of his eyes, I cupped his face between my hand and kissed him. Grabbing me, he pulled me closer to him and our soft kisses quickly turned stronger. Being in his arms, I felt safe, and I was able to ignore the negative voice that kept telling me I didn't deserve his love. I could not lose him.

Suddenly, Cole released me, and I caught myself from hitting the ground. When I steadied myself, I turned to face him. His eyes looked ice blue in the light of the studio.

Shock filled me. *Did he drop me on purpose?*

"Did you kiss him like that?" Cole asked through clenched teeth.

"Um...I..." My faltering for the correct words infuriated him.

"So, you did?" His eyes burned with distrust.

"Yes, he did kiss me," I blurted.

"He kissed *you*? You played no part in what happened?"

Not wanting to be evasive or withhold details anymore about Kai, I decided it was time to tell him the truth. "Yes, when I met Kai, he did kiss me. But I slapped him across the face, and he apologized. I already told you about falling off the cliff and almost drowning. When Kai saved me, I became confused and enchanted by him. When I was taken to the New Moon Celebration with the elementals, we danced and drank. I got caught up in the moment. Yes, I kissed him, but then, you appeared, and I knew what was real. I instantly regretted what I had done, and I begged you not to leave. I knew, at that moment, that losing you would be unbearable."

I tried to take his hand into mine, but he stopped me.

"What would have happened if I had not shown up?" Cole asked.

"But you did Cole, and we can't focus on *what ifs*." When I grabbed his hand, this time, he didn't fight me. "We can only worry about what is happening now and in the future. If you can't trust me, we won't be together."

The energy seemed to slip out of Cole. With his shoulder slouched forward, he said, "Mar, I can't lose you."

"Cole, you're not going to lose me. We will be together — not in a mansion and not with hundreds of children, but we'll be in our lovely home, with our children, and I repeat, not hundreds. Then, we'll grow old together with our family around us and we'll have our fairytale happily-ever-after."

Cole brightened a little before he said, "I meant it when I said no more secrets. I'm glad you told me everything you experienced in that world."

"No matter what happens or where this life takes me, I'll always come back to you, Cole." I kissed his cheek and whispered in his ear, "I promise, no more secrets, and I need you to promise not sneak away in the middle of the night, again."

Laughing, he said, "I promise. Now, let's go home."

CHAPTER
FIVE

Cole and I spoke very little before we went to sleep. There were unresolved issues in my heart, and I knew he was not satisfied with my answers. We'd quickly said all would be alright, but his hurt feelings and doubt weren't going to just go away. He needed time.

Falling into a dreamless sleep, I woke to the bright light of the day. Once again, Cole's spot beside me was empty. My heart sunk. *Am I going to lose him?*

Shaking off the words of loss and abandonment Snowystra had implanted, I left the warmth of the bed to join my family. When I entered the hallway, the chatter of Meg and Miles greeted me. *They're little kids. They need you to be cheerful,* I reminded myself.

With a smile on my face that didn't match my mood, I entered the kitchen. I was relieved to find Cole at the sink, washing dishes. He was handing them off to my siblings to be dried.

As Cole tried to hand a dish to Miles, Meg whined, "No fair! It's my turn."

Swooping in, my father seized the plate. With a big grin on his face, he said, "I think you're mistaken. It's my turn." Taking the dishtowel from her hand, he whistled as he dried the dish.

"You can dry the next one, Meg," Miles offered.

"Hate to disappoint you both, but that was the last one." Cole chuckled and handed each a wet rag from the sink. "Now, you can argue over who gets to clean the kitchen table."

Snatching the cloth from him, Meg ran off laughing with Miles following closely behind.

"They are characters," Cole said.

My father patted him on the back. "We're lucky to have Miles here with us. Best thing to come out of Eliza and Cedric's union." His face darkened with those words.

"You love her still?" Cole folded the cloth he was using and threw it down. "Why? She pushed you away from your family. You lost so much time with Meg and Mara. How could you, after all that she has done?"

The anger in his words were like a knife to my heart. I couldn't help wondering if he was questioning his feelings for me. I slipped back into the hallway and waited for his next words. Terrified as to what they might be.

"You can't just turn off love like I felt for Eliza. It was too deep...too all-consuming," My father admitted. "Anytime you open your heart, you take the chance that your love won't be reciprocated. You think too much, Cole. Don't..."

"You're awake," the cries of Meg and Miles interrupted the conversation. Both children ran to greet me and threw their arms around me.

"We saved you breakfast." Miles clasped my hand and dragged me towards the table. "Sit. We can bring it to you."

"OK, OK." I chuckled at their enthusiasm.

Cole joined me at the table and offered me a blue mug. I carefully accepted the steaming beverage and took a small sip. He had made Gram's signature coffee — a strong black brew with a generous sprinkle of cinnamon and sugar, and an even more generous splash of cream. The sweet concoction made me smile. His small act told me how much he did love me.

"Thank you, all. What a nice morning surprise," I said sincerely. "Now that I slept the best part of the morning away, what should we do today?"

"Elliott and I are going to the lumber yard, and Meg has a dance class. Why don't you spend the day with Miles?" Cole suggested as Miles appeared next to him with a look of anticipation.

"I think that's a great idea." Miles beamed at me.

"So, what do you think we should do while they're gone?" I asked Miles.

"I think we should —" Miles tapped his pointer finger on his lip. "Hmmm, I think we should have a picnic, and then we should go to the lake and swim."

An image of the previous night came to mind and a lump formed in my throat. I didn't want to run into Snowystra with Miles. Cole couldn't resist her temptations. How would a small child?

"Why don't we have a picnic and play it by ear on what to do afterward. You never know what can happen at a picnic in our backyard." My eyes glinted mischievously. "Why, we could run into a big bad wolf or three little pigs. Or, maybe, just maybe, the king of the trout will appear."

As if on cue, Cole snapped and growled.

Both children screamed in fright and ran away from him. Shrieks filled the room as they scrambled up the loft ladder.

"That should buy us a few minutes," he said with a look of satisfaction.

"What are your plans after you get lumber?" I touched his hand. "We should spend some time together, tonight."

Cole stood up and shrugged. "Maybe. It just depends on how much we get done."

Trying to hide my disappointment, I just nodded. Feeling like I had been dismissed, my mind raced with questions. The worry that was building inside me felt like it would overflow. *Are we going to be done over one mistake? One mistake that wasn't even real since my body had been lying next to him the entire time. Is he ever going to forgive me?*

Reluctantly, I returned to my breakfast. I listened silently as my father and Cole discussed their plans. When I finished eating, I quickly dropped my dish into the warm, soapy water. My mind wandered to the elemental world. It was easy with Kai. A warm feeling ran through me as I recalled his touch and the kisses we had shared. He would have forgiven me for any temptations. Fire elementals knew about passion.

"Mara," the voice of Miles called, interrupting my daydream, "can we go on our picnic?"

I glanced around and realized we were alone. "Did everyone leave already?" I asked, confused by how long I had been at the sink.

"They left a while ago." Miles' face flashed with worry. "You've just been staring out the window for a really long time. Mother used to disappear like that."

Am I becoming our mother? Looking down at the dish in my hand, I finished washing it and handed him the plate. "If you dry this and put it away, I'll go throw some clothes on and we can start planning for our picnic."

Accepting the task, Mile grinned. "This is going to be the best day ever."

CHAPTER SIX

We carried our picnic basket of treats to the tree of my childhood as we walked hand-in-hand. The sky was a robin's egg blue with wisps of clouds floating slowly. Miles questioned me about the elementals as we laid out a blanket to sit on.

"Will they come to our picnic?" Miles asked. "Meg said they like to play tricks and that they taught her how to use her magic."

"They might come. Sometimes, they like to enter with a dramatic flair and come flying in as balls of light," I said as I recalled my childhood memories.

Miles was so inquisitive that I worried how he would react if Snowystra appeared. What would she show him that would convince him to go with her? There was no way he would be able to protect himself from her. She could swoop in and take him. There was nothing I could do to stop her. Taking him on a picnic was a mistake.

My worries were interrupted by an icy wind. I stood up and pulled Miles close. "Stay right with me."

From behind a tree, the dark-haired figure appeared, bringing an even colder wind with her.

"What do you want, Snowystra?" I demanded, addressing her by name.

"You finally figured out who I'm?" Snowystra asked with a laugh of delight. Clapping her hands together, she purred. "I love your confidence. You don't shrink back from me." The Winter Goddess circled around us. "Mmm, you are dripping with my sister's magic. I hope you're smart enough not believe everything you have heard about me. Did my sister enlighten me?"

Stopping in front of us, she patted Miles on the head. Her touch left white powder on his hair. "She never tells the whole story. My sister likes to focus on how *naughty* I am. She never shares all of the wonderful things I do." Dramatically, she stuck out her bottom lip.

"Danu has never mentioned you and I'm not interested in finding out anything more about you." I pulled Miles out of her reach. "I would like for you to go, now."

Her eyes darkened, and she loomed over me. "You are not in a position to order me to do anything, dear Marina. I'll go when I feel like it and, right now, I want to talk with you."

Reaching around me, she grabbed Miles by the wrist and yanked him towards her. "Don't you think Marina should speak nicer to me, Miles?" She stroked his face with her fingertips leaving light pink marks. Pointing her sharp, silver nails at me, she warned, "I would suggest you change your tone when you're in my presence. I would hate for anything bad to happen to this sweet little boy."

Snowystra stroked Mile's hair. "Do you know who I am, Miles?"

His green eyes widened in fear, and he softly murmured, "No."

Whispering in his ear, loud enough for me to hear, she said, "I'm the reason you're here. I brought your mommy and daddy together."

"They were bad." Miles hung his head in shame.

"No, child. They were not bad." Snowystra lifted his chin, forcing him to look at her. "They were convinced to believe life was boring and that they could never use their magic. I taught them they could have anything they wanted. Do you want magic like Meg and Mara?"

Miles nodded fervently.

"You can have your heart's desire with me, Miles. Just tell me what you want, and it will all be yours."

"Leave him alone," I cried and tried to take him from her.

She knocked me on my back with her icy air and refocused on my brother. "If you stay here, Marina will never let you have anything. I, on the other hand, will teach you how to use magic. I know you have been trying ever so hard to learn on your own, but you need someone to guide you. Would you like my help? Would you like to learn how to use the magic?"

I stood to face her. A warmth came from my hand. To my surprise, each of my hands held a ball of fire. *Thank you, Danu,* I thought. Stepping forward, I shouted, "Stop it, Snowystra. He is just a child, and he isn't going anywhere with you!"

Snowystra looked at my hand and threw her head back in laughter. "What do you plan on doing with those little balls of magic? You have no idea who I really am." She let go of Miles and walked towards me. "I could turn you to dust before you could even scream for help."

"I'm not going to bow down to you, and I'll never follow you," I said. Something inside told me to stay strong and not back down. This countered my urge to flee. "Your threats do not frighten me. So, you should go. It will be over my dead body before I let you hurt my family."

"Let me? You have no power to stop me from what I want. I'll freeze you for your disrespect. You're not strong enough to challenge me."

Snowystra wrapping her long fingers around my wrist. She gripped so tightly that my hand felt numb. *What have you done?* I wondered as the sensation of ice flowed through my body.

"No!" Miles screamed. "Help! Someone help!"

I panicked as I found myself unable to move. I wanted to protect my brother and calm his fears. The fire in my hand was not strong enough to fight the ice from her grip.

"You're safe," the voice of Danu whispered in my ear.

Miles cries for help stopped. We were encircled by a strong gust of wind. The warm breeze danced around us, and we were surrounded by the four elementals.

Blaze stepped towards us. Her appearance was intimidating. Dressed in red leather pants and a tank top covered with orange, shimmery scales, her large catlike eyes burned with a glistening gold color. Her long hair was salmon orange with deep red streaks of fire.

"You may not think she is strong enough to face you, Snowystra, but we certainly are. And, if I were you, I would not doubt the gift our mother has blessed upon Mara," the strong confident voice of Blaze warned. "You have never faced anyone like her."

Blaze shocked me by removing my wrist from Snowystra's grasp and sending waves of heat through my body. My arm changed from a light blue color to a pink. It tingled as the feeling began to return.

Unsure of what I needed to do to keep my brother safe, I was relieved when Daisy appeared. Her bright emerald cat eyes glared at Snowystra. Her blonde hair glowed brilliantly and the ground under us shook. Daisy held out her hand, calling thick vines to grow before us. "It's time for you to leave, Snowystra. We're not going to let you take this family. Go now, before something unfortunate happens."

The green barrier covered with frost. With one touch, Snowystra crushed it into a fine powder. "You think a few plants are going to keep me away from what is mine?" she snarled.

"No, that won't stop you, but I didn't just call vines." Daisy gave a cold calculating smile.

The ground under us quaked and a rumbling filled the air.

I gasped as uprooted trees, with long branches and leaves of red, marched in our direction. Taking Miles by the hand, I drew him close to me.

"What is happening?" I whispered to Bay.

"We're bringing in reinforcements." The Water elemental giggled. Her silver eyes sparkled as she twirled, whipping her cobalt blue hair around.

Snowystra glared at the approaching trees. She stepped forward but stopped as if reconsidering her next move. "Fine. I'll leave you today. Marina, I do hope you come to me when you realize how silly my sister and her little minions are being," she said, sounding sincere. "I wasn't going to hurt you. I was just going to show you all that could be yours, if you just followed me."

With those lies, she disappeared in a silver ball of dust. I worried, as the dust began to clear, that Snowystra had left a little too easily.

"I'm not strong enough to face her. She could have turned me into a popsicle," I said.

Blaze's face flared with anger. "She could not freeze you if you were focused. You're stronger than you believe. You have always been stronger than you think. Start believing in yourself again. When you were young, you were confident in your magic...one might say, overconfident. But you never questioned the fact that you were able to create balls of magic and you never backed down when you felt afraid."

"You took it away from me," I protested. "I'm not the little girl that understood the magic inside her. It's been too long to become her again. I have no idea how to defend my family." My hands flamed with fireballs. Surprise filled me. *I didn't have to complete an elaborate ceremony to call magic?* I held out the orbs, and asked, "You want me to face her with these?"

Blaze took my fiery hands into hers as the others surrounded me.

"Danu did not bring you to our world to come back and doubt yourself. Did you learn nothing from your time with us?"

With softer words, Daisy said, "Remember, you create your world. You're in control of everything around you. She blessed you with a strong connection to the magic."

"Snowystra is a goddess. I'm human," I countered.

Breeze stepped closer to me. Her white hair was long and flowing with loose, colorful curls that cascaded down her back. The vibrant streaks were pulled back, showing her deep blue eyes. The long blue dress she wore had a cloud pattern on it. As she moved, the billows slowly drifted. "She is strong and dangerous, but she can't make you follow her. That is your choice."

"How will I protect everyone? She's going to use the love of my family to hurt me." I pointed at my brother. "How will I protect Miles? He's defenseless against her."

"Mile is strong. He just needs to know how to use what he has been given." Blaze looked at him with pride. "Ask him what he is keeping from you."

"What are you talking about? He's a little boy. He has no —" I began to argue before remembering I had magic as a child. Kneeling down to my brother, I asked, "Miles, what does Blaze mean? You can tell me anything, love. Whatever you're hiding, you can tell me. No matter what it's, I'll not be mad. You never need to keep any secrets from me, OK?"

He bit his lip and shifted uncomfortably.

"Tell me, Miles," I demanded, unable to be patient and wait for him to speak.

"Cole makes Water magic. Elliot and Meg both can make things grow and the ground shake." He drew in a deep breath, and continued, "You talk to all of the magic..." Stopping, he looked around with fear, as if he shouldn't tell anymore.

"What is your magic, Miles?" I wiped the tears that had begun to fall down his face. "Show me what you have been hiding."

Moving back from me, he hid his hands behind his back.

"Don't worry, Miles. Take your time and show me when you're ready," I said, trying to calm him.

Hesitantly, he held out his clenched fist. As he turned his hands palm up and slowly opened them, I could not only see the green glow of his magic, but I could feel it. The same magic my mother had thrown at me. The same magic that had pulsed through me as I watched my grandmother sacrifice herself. Miles held the dark magic that had stolen Gram from me.

I shivered as his hands sparked. Green magic dripped onto the blanket like molten lava. It sizzled and popped as it burned through to the grass. I forced myself to wear a mask of calm and understanding. This little boy was yielding dark magic, but he was not at fault. This was just a casualty of his being born to my mother.

"OK, sweetie. You can put your magic away." When I picked him up and hugged him, I flinched as the residue of his magic pricked my skin.

"My magic is bad, Mara." Miles sobbed, burying his face in my neck.

"No, Miles. Don't talk like that. We just don't understand your magic." I held my little brother tighter. I could feel all of the worries he had been holding inside. I released him and kissed his cheek. "I bet the girls can help us with this."

Breeze held her arms out to take Miles. Softly, she comforted him. "Precious child, your magic is just a little bit confused, right now. Why don't we go somewhere alone to figure out the best way for you to use your gift? You have a little bit that is dark, but the magic from Gram is really friendly. What do you think of us trying to tap into that?"

Miles hugged her tightly and nodded. Setting him down, she took his little hand. He stared up at her, his eyes shining with hope.

"Miles and I are going away for a bit," Breeze said. "We're going to find his connection to Air. Aren't we, Miles?"

"I would like that very much," Miles said with a hopeful smile.

Breeze shifted into a large blue bird and fluttered above him. Miles excitedly clapped at her. Extending her long black talons, she picked him up and flew above us. Breeze lifted him, higher and higher, until his dangling feet barely skimmed the treetops. When they finally disappeared from my view into the clouds, I returned my attention on Blaze.

"What kind of magic does he have?" I asked, wringing my hands. "It's the same magic Eliza kept throwing at me, right. Is it dark magic?"

"Yes, it's the corrupted magic of Snowystra. The Drygen's and your mother made a choice to follow the Winter Goddess, but they didn't realize how high the price would be."

"I don't understand," I said. "Why does she want us to follow her?

What makes her magic bad compared to the magic inside us? Do I have dark magic in me, too?"

"This isn't the time to talk about why Danu and Snowystra are so different. It's irrelevant. The fact is, you need to be careful and not trust her," Blaze stated. "No matter what she offers you, there will be a price. Only you can decide if the price is worth it."

"There's no decision to be made. I've made my choice," I said, not wavering. "I'm committed to protecting the magic given to Genevieve Silver. My grandmother did not sacrifice herself for me to throw it all away." I took Blaze's hand and pleaded with her, "Teach me everything I've forgotten and the things I haven't learned, yet. I'm ready to be the person Gram believed I could be."

"Our girl is back, ladies." Blaze grabbed me by my shoulder and looked into my eyes. "I'm glad you're finally realizing you're in control. If you're ready to stop feeling sorry for yourself, we can get to work. Mae taught you to be a strong woman like she was. She wanted nothing, but a wonderful life for you."

Losing my confidence, I said, "Without her, I can't be that person."

"You're strong, Mara," Daisy disagreed. "You can do it. Trust us."

Dramatically, Bay threw herself onto the blanket, moaning as if in pain. "I'm going to wither away if you don't stop being so dreary."

Blaze rolled her eyes, but even she could not keep the smile from forming on her lips.

"OK, I'll stop being boring, today." I reached out my hand to her. "I wouldn't want you to fade away due to my self-pity."

"Now, we get to work," Blaze said as the reflection of fire in her eyes grew. "Today, you decided to be the butterfly and we'll teach you how to soar."

CHAPTER SEVEN

Instead of teaching me how to use each of the elements inside me individually, the three elementals circled around me and threw their different forms of magic. As soon as I countered Bay's crashing waves with intense winds, I found a wall of fire crawling towards me. I doused the flames with oversize balls of water. The elementals were unyielding with their attacks. By the time, Blaze called off the assault, I was out of breath, soaked, and covered in mud and ash.

As I sat down to regain my energy, Bay twirled around me, cleaning off all evidence of the battle. She flitted about while sprays of salty water emitted from her long tresses. After she had fussed and prodded me into an acceptable version of cleanliness, she flopped down and dug through the picnic basket we had prepared.

She took a big bite of a peanut butter and jelly sandwich and crinkled her nose. "Ugh, this needs pickles."

"If we've had enough of a rest, let's continue." Blaze towered over us. The red streaks of her hair burned with a fire that reflected in her golden eyes.

Not wanting to ruin her pleasant mood, I quickly stood up, ready to resume my training.

One-by-one, she made me demonstrate my connection to each element. Repeatedly, I called balls of fire, waves of water, streams of air, and shook the earth. By the time we were done, I still felt confident my strongest connection was with Fire. Blaze must have agreed, because she instructed me on how to use my fingers to create long tendrils of focused flames.

"Throwing fire is useful, but there are so many other ways to command respect and protect yourself," Blaze said. Waving her fingers around, she showered the sky with small embers.

Further demonstrating her power, she created a flaming sword of fire. It was a translucent silver blade that sparked and sizzled. Her hands wrapped tightly around a red-jeweled hilt, she swung it to show me how to fight.

I held up my hands to stop her. "Blaze, throwing fire is one thing, but hand-to-hand combat seems a little too aggressive for me." I waited for her reprimand.

She lowered the sword and stared at me.

I held her gaze, not wanting to show weakness. "Maybe, next time, I'll be ready to learn this kind of defense?" I suggested.

"You might be right. We should focus on building your endurance, first." The weapon faded away into a wisp of smoke.

Blaze walked around and inspected me. "You need to work on strength — mental and physical. It is imperative we build your endurance. You have been given a special gift of all of the elements and you need to keep connecting to maintain them. Do not depend on the one that comes easiest to you."

Thinking about her words, I reflected on my connections. I still felt a strong pull to Water. I was confident in my ability to create rain and water balls, but I felt like it was Cole's special link. *Shouldn't I leave that for him?* As I continued to overthink my reasons for my focus on Fire, a strong wind blew my hair up.

Breeze appeared With Miles riding on her back. He waved frantically at us, wearing a grin that stretched from ear to ear. Breeze gently landed, and Miles hopped off. When she shifted to her human form, they walked, together, towards us. My little brother appeared so small compared to Breeze.

"My magic isn't bad," Miles shouted excitedly to us. Smiling at Breeze, he asked her something I couldn't hear.

Leaning down to him, she kissed both of his cheeks.

Running to me, Miles threw his arms around me. He smelled like the woodsy scent of the trees. He squeezed me tight, and I could feel his time with Breeze had raised his spirits.

"Mara, I can do the most amazing things, now. I no longer need to use the *dark* magic." Miles grasped my hand. "Watch, I can show you. Come with me." Dragging me away from the picnic blanket, he commanded, "Stay here and don't move a muscle. I need to concentrate."

"I'll do my best not to scream," I promised.

I waited patiently for Miles to blow a strong wind at me. I was surprised when a stream of white tendrils emitted from his fingertips and slowly wove around my ankles and legs, traveling up to my waist. The silky air tickled my skin and I shifted.

"Please, stand very still for me, OK?" Mile sighed. Closing his eyes, more lines of air encircled me.

"Can I talk?" I asked.

"No, no talking." Miles frowned at me.

I was tempted to stick out my tongue, but I didn't want to upset him. After a few seconds, the strands of air multiplied, and I was surrounded. The streams twisted and turned, encasing me, until I was being lifted off the ground. Fighting back my urge to ask him to put me down, I sucked in a deep breath of the warm air and closed my eyes. I felt myself going higher and higher, spinning around. Suddenly, I wasn't moving.

When I was finally brave enough to open my eyes, I found myself held in the sky above the tops of the trees. Below, I could see Miles' eyes were still tightly closed as if he was concentrating extremely hard. "Please, don't drop me, Miles," I called.

Slowly, he lowered me.

I was confident, if his magic failed, that I would be able to call Air on my own.

When I landed, Miles ran over to me and threw his arms around my waist. "I'm not bad. I don't only have that magic in me. I have good magic, too."

"I'm so proud of you. I never thought you were anything, but good. Your other magic isn't bad...it's simply different. You probably don't want to use it though," I suggested.

"Oh, I know. Breeze explained everything to me. We don't want to make that magic strong." Miles looked to the elemental for approval. "I should never practice using it, ever again, and I'm only allowed to use it if I need to protect my family from harm."

"That sounds very wise." Again, I felt the need to hug him. "Miles, I'm so glad you're with us and that you're my little brother."

Squeezing me back, Miles whispered, "I love you, Mara."

Pulling away from him, I suggested, "How about we clean up our picnic and go make dinner? I'm sure, by the time Elliott and Cole come home, they are going to be hungry."

Miles ran to Breeze and threw his arms around her tightly. "Good-bye, everyone."

"We will see you later, Miles," she said sweetly and kissed him on the cheek. "Remember everything I have taught you."

"Oh, I will," he promised as he quickly ran ahead.

When Miles was out of earshot, I questioned the elementals. "What are we going to do about the other magic? Is it safe to let him keep it?"

"We could take it away, but we've learned from you that that may not be the right thing." Blaze took the cloth Miles' magic had burned. She folded it into a small square, and then repeated the process until it was small enough to fit in her hand.

"Instead, he keeps his magic." Blaze looked as if she was considering her next words. "The light and the dark will stay within him. Breeze will be staying close to help him learn how to control it. As always, we are near if you really need us."

As if to emphasize her words, the cloth square erupted into a small fire. Clasping her hands together, she snuffed out the flames. When she opened them, silver embers floated into the air.

"Soon, Meg and Miles should be asked to protect the magic," Daisy insisted. "We cannot wait, again, for the time to be right."

"They are too young," Bay countered. "They are not ready —"

"You are wrong. They are ready to decide. They must know the truth of their gift and be prepared." Blaze's words trailed off and I wondered what she wasn't saying.

"You're all correct. They are young, but I don't think we can wait as long as you did to tell me," I said. "Snowystra will return, and they need to be prepared."

"I told you our girl was back," Blaze said proudly. "Now go help your brother."

As I walked away, I turned back to see the four of them standing in a circle. Small bubbles of lavender, red, blue, and green filled the center and rose above towards the sky. Then, they were gone.

CHAPTER
EIGHT

Miles decided what we were having for dinner and gave me the task of cutting vegetables. While I chopped and diced ingredients he handed me, my mind raced.

Snowystra spoke to Miles as if she's responsible for his magic. She isn't going to leave any of us alone. He wouldn't harm any of us, intentionally, but one accidental use of his dark abilities could hurt someone gravely. Meg would...I need to warn Meg.

Relief filled me as our family began to trickle into the house. All of them were sweaty and dirty from the day's activities.

"Where is Meg?" I asked.

"She's checking on the lavender bushes." Elliott stopped at the sink and scrubbed his hands. "She's been fussing about her plants every day. I tried to tell her they're fine, but once she gets something in her head..."

"She's outside alone?" I asked, feeling panicked. "Dinner is ready. We just need the table set. We'll eat when everyone returns. I'm going to get Meg."

"Is everything OK, Caterpillar?" my father questioned with a look of worry on his face.

"I'm sure everything is fine," I said, trying to hide my fear. "Miles, I want you to go with Elliott and clean up."

"OK, Mara," Miles said as he took my father's hand. Turning back to me, he whispered, "This has been the best day ever."

As the door to my father's bedroom closed, I felt the cold chill blow through the house and over me. Trying to control my emotions, I rushed out into the backyard. I glimpsed my sister, standing by the picnic tree. She was nowhere near the lavender. My heart raced as I realized Meg was talking to someone in the shadows.

When she held out her hand, as if accepting something, I shouted, "Meg, what are you doing out there?"

She continued to face the forest, talking into the air. She appeared to be in a deep conversation.

I called out to her louder, this time, "Meg, come in the house, right now!"

Turning only her head in my direction, she stared at me with a blank, emotionless expression. It was as if she didn't recognize me.

Snowystra, I realized. "Meg, step away from her," I cried out and raced towards her.

Snowystra stepped out of the shadows, confirming my fears. Not thinking, I did the first thing that came to mind – I cast a stream of fire at the goddess. My attack had no impact. Instead, it only seemed to please her. Laughing, she shifted away from my magic and continued her conversation. Holding out a small black box to Meg, she spoke in an undertone so quiet I couldn't hear what she said.

"Get away from her, Snowystra," I screamed as I formed a blade of fire in my hand.

Having no idea how I was going to use my summoned weapon, I just ran with all of my might. When I reached Meg, I slashed at Snowystra's hand. Sparks flew as I struck her, causing her to drop the container. A silver fluid began to run from the cut I'd made.

Instead of attacking me, she just chuckled.

Gripping the blade as if I was skilled enough to use it, I grabbed my sister and pulled her behind me. Backing away from Snowystra and taking a defensive stance, I forced all of the elemental magic I had inside me towards the dark goddess. The strong wind, waves of water, streams of fire, and shaking earth only made her laugh harder.

Her sinister cackle continued until she finally held up her hands. "You have delighted me, again, with your passion, Marina," she proclaimed over the high winds. "You will be a wonderful addition to my family when you stop fighting me."

Spinning around, she continued her maniacal laughter until her body dissolved into black and silver dust. The dust coated us and, as the glittery fragments of her disappeared, her taunting chortle carried on the wind.

"Mara, why are you holding a fire sword?" Meg blinked rapidly.

I dropped the sword to the ground, where it sizzled and vanished into a puff of smoke. I hugged my sister tightly, fighting back tears. "You can't go out here by yourself, Meg. You can't be alone, where we can't protect you."

Meg wriggled out of my arms.

"Why were you talking to her?" I asked, holding her face between my hands.

My sister's confusion seemed deepened.

"Didn't I warn you to run away if you saw anyone you didn't know?"

"I...I have no idea what you're talking about," Meg stammered. "I was tending the garden. The plants haven't looked sad because they don't like the cold." Pausing, she looked around and considered our location. "Wait, why am I here? I was checking Gram's lavender." Meg frowned.

She must have had a spell on Meg. I roughly put my hands on her shoulders to focus her attention on me. "You need to listen to me. You can't run off like this anymore. Do you understand? You can't run off on your own anymore."

"All I was doing was checking Gram's lavender," Meg sobbed. "Why am I not safe here? Let go, you're hurting me."

I lightened my grip as I held back my tears. I had to be the adult now. I couldn't wallow in my own sorrow and fear, but my emotions were so intense. "I need you to listen to me when I say you can't wander off on your own. I can't lose anyone else I love. I won't lose you."

Meg shoved me away and she shouted, "It's not fair to tell me I can't do something I've always done, especially without telling me why." She blew out a burst of air and scrubbed the tears from her cheeks. In a quieter voice, she said, "I'm not a baby, Mara. You can tell me the truth."

"Meg, you're a little girl who doesn't need to grow up any faster than you've already had to." I changed my tone to reflect hers. "You just need to trust me. When it's necessary, I'll tell you what you need to know. Besides, it's my job to protect you, so let me do the worrying. You just enjoy being a kid."

"I'm not a baby. I'm sick of you treating me like I'm a dumb child. You're not the only one that has magic. I have strong magic, too." Meg's eyes blazed in anger as a row of vines grew between us.

"Don't do that," I cried. *Snowystra could grab Meg and I won't be able to stop her.*

"It's time you stop treating me like I can't take care of myself...like I don't know what has happened. You're not the only one that saw them die. I was there, too!" Meg called over the barrier.

Her words hit me hard, And I knew she was right. In my grief, I hadn't considered how she'd witnessed the attack my mother launched on me or the fight that had ended both our mother's and grandmother's lives. Meg had been so strong through the burial and all of the changes that I hadn't taken the time to talk to her about her feelings, or to discuss what had happened.

"Meg, you're always going to be my little sister," I tried to explain, but stopped when I heard her harrumph of frustration as more vines were added to the barrier.

I took a moment to regroup before I shouted, "You're right, you're right."

The newly sprouted creepers retracted a little.

OK, she can be reason with, I realized. Sighing, I said, "You're always going to be my baby sister, Meg."

Green popped up from the ground again.

"Wait!" I held out my hands, considering whether or not to burn away the plants. Reconsidering, I tried to negotiate. "That doesn't mean I need to shelter you. You're right. We've gone through these past months together. Please, send the vines away. I feel stupid yelling to you."

The earth shook, and the green shoots slithered back into the ground. Meg glared at me with her hands on her hips. "I told you I am strong."

"Yes, through it all, you've been a strength, and not just for you, but for Miles, too. The time has come for me to accept that you might be able to protect yourself." My voice cracked. "I need you, Meg."

My sister's expression softened. "So, tell me what's going on. I can handle it, Mar." She stepped closer to me, but still kept her distance.

"I know," I said, taking in a deep breath.

Of course, she was correct. and, honestly, she needed to know what we were up against. Still, I didn't exactly know what we were facing myself. How was I going to explain something *I* didn't understand?

"I do need to stop keeping things from you." I dropped my hands against my sides in exasperation. "Let's get you home and warmed up. Then, I'll tell you everything I know."

"Don't you think we'll all be better off if we don't have so many secrets?" Meg asked, sounding more mature than the nine-year-old standing in front of me.

"Yes, Meg," I admitted. "The secrets have harmed us more than helped. Soon, you'll have the answers you want. I promise."

Relenting, she took my hand.

As we walked back towards the house, a small bit of white floated past my face. I turned and saw Snowystra was behind us.

She stood beside the tree in a flutter of snow. Her eyes gleamed with mischief.

I picked up the pace and Meg followed. When we were finally inside, I shut the door and frantically latched all of the locks as if it would keep the dark goddess out.

"The danger you're worried about is out there, isn't it?" Meg murmured.

"No one can get to us, right now, Meg," I lied, trying to hide my fear. *We're going to need more than solid wood and some latches to keep us safe.*

CHAPTER NINE

After dinner, Elliott suggested we settle in the living room while the kids got ready for bed. Cole and I both agreed. Before following the men, I grabbed a plate of zizzleberry cookies from Gram's reserves for dessert.

Setting the treats on the coffee table, I noticed Cole had chosen one of the chairs next to my father. The disturbing feelings I'd experienced from his dismissal that morning hit me again. *He always waited on the loveseat for me, but now...*

When I settled on *our* couch, our eyes met, and he gave me a short smile. "We need to talk about the wedding." Without waiting for my response, he continued, "At the very least, we should start working on the invitations. The day is going to come quicker than we think."

Trying to hide my surprise that he still wanted to marry me, I responded, "The cookies won't take very long to bake. The hardest part is going to be writing out the small tags to tie to the treat bags."

Many years ago, the tradition of baking heart-shaped cookies and sending them to the invited guests became the norm. The type of goody was determined by the likes of the bride and groom-to-be. Half of each heart was made from their favorite recipe. Our guests would receive sweet biscuits of zizzleberry and peanut butter snapdragon.

As we munched on cookies and discussed the wedding, my younger siblings joined us. Meg looked so sweet and young in her favorite nightgown, fluffy robe, and pink slippers. Miles wore his robe over his button up pajamas. However, having combed his hair over, he looked like a miniature old man.

Motioning for my little brother to come by me, I said, "I found out this afternoon that Miles has been keeping a secret. Did you know he has a connection to the magic, also?"

With wide eyes, my father and Cole directed their focus onto Miles while Meg bit her lip nervously. *Oh, little sister, you've been keeping your own secrets*, I discovered.

"Well, technically, Miles has a connection to two kinds of magic," I corrected myself. "The dark magic he inherited from our mother will not be used, but he's, also, been blessed with the gift of Air."

"I'm sorry I didn't tell you." Miles stepped closer and hung his head. "I didn't want you to send me back. Please, don't be mad at me."

"No one is mad at you, Miles," my father reassured him. "You're a part of our family, and you're never going back to them. OK?"

Miles nodded. The tight look on his youthful face relaxed and he yawned.

"I think your big day has worn out Miles." Cole picked up my little brother and tousled his hair. " Come on, kid. You can show us your Air magic tomorrow. Let's get you off to bed."

Unable to fight back another yawn, Miles rested his head against Cole's shoulder. Barely able to keep his eyes open, he muttered, "Will Meg come, too?"

"In a bit, honey," I answered, "but, I'm sure Cole won't mind staying with you until she comes to bed."

"I'll clean up the kitchen," my father said.

My eyes locked with my father's.

He gave me a soft smile before exiting the room.

I took Meg by the hand. "I think you and I have a few more things to talk about."

We entered Gram's room, and I directed Meg to climb up onto the bed. Removing the silver chest from under the mahogany frame and holding it in my hands, I thought of the last time I held it. Then, presenting the box to Meg, I tried to recall the exact words my grandmother had said to me.

"This box was given to Gram by her mother. Each of the women listed on this chest promised to keep the elemental magic safe from those who would misuse it."

Tracing my finger along the names, I remembered the feelings that had stirred inside me when I was presented with the box. The strong emotions I had felt the first time returned. The names Genevieve, Mae, and Eliza were still etched on the cover, but now, my name was, also, there. Touching each inscription again, all but one felt warm. Stopping at *Eliza*, I felt a tear roll down my cheek. The first time I touched it, the engraving had been ice cold. Now, it was *nothing*.

I sat on the edge of the bed and refocused my attention back onto my sister. "Before you open the box, I want to talk about the woman you were talking with tonight."

Meg pounded her clenched fists on her lap. "Why won't you believe me when I say there was no one there?"

"You asked me to treat you like an adult," I warned her and took her fist.

Slowly, Meg loosened her fingers.

"The first thing you need to understand is that I don't know the answers to everything. I'm learning myself. The woman —"

Meg's fist tightened again.

"The woman, who you don't remember, is the sister of Danu," I continued.

Interrupting, Meg cried out, "What? The goddess can't have a sister."

"Let me just tell you everything I know, and you can ask questions later. OK?" I offered Meg the chest.

Trembling, she accepted it. "I'll listen."

"Danu has a sister, named Snowystra. For some reason, she wants us to join her and no longer honor the commitment our family has made to protect our elemental gift." I touched the chest, and said, "Open it, love. It's time you learn the truth."

Inside the chest, there was a light green ring, much like my own. Meg leaned forward and gazed into the box. As I watched her, I thought back to the time, not so long ago, when I made the oath. The minutes passed slowly as I watched her expressions change. I knew how overwhelming all of the images were.

Finally, she picked up the ring and closed the chest.

I realized she was crying. "Meg, what's wrong? Do you want to tell me what you saw?" I asked.

Trembling, Meg climbed off the bed and slid under it.

"Meg, where are you going? Come talk to me?" I said with frustration. *She's too young for such responsibility. This was a mistake,* I thought.

Just as I was going to crawl under the bed to get her, Meg returned. She was holding a lavender pouch. Climbing back onto the bed, she poured out the contents of the bag — a crystal vial of dark blue liquid, a piece of white paper tied with string, and a silver heart broken into two pieces.

She unrolled the scroll and handed it to me. "Gram said this will help me tell my story."

Trasferimento Memoria
The memories are yours to share.
A drop of liquid in the eyes of the receiver.
A drop of the liquid on the tongue of the storyteller.
A heart held in the palm with a promise of love and respect.
Together, you will travel back to the first sight.
Together, you will return with new insight.

"Are you sure this is what you want?" I questioned, holding the vial. "Can't you just tell me what you saw?"

"No, please, let's use the potion," Meg replied, sounding frightened.

Fear filled me. *What's frightened my sister so much that she can't tell me?* "OK," I reluctantly agreed.

Meg handed me half of the heart. She tilted her head back and opened her mouth wide.

Following the instructions, I placed a drop of the liquid on her tongue, and then one drop into both my eyes. The liquid stung and blurred my vision as I watched my sister collapse into my arms. Soon, the haze consumed me, and I, too, lost consciousness.

I had only been out for what seemed like seconds. When I awoke, my sister was standing in front of the bed with the chest in her hands.

Meg opened the box. "The first thing I saw after the ring was Gram. Come look."

Together, we stared into the chest. As the view shifted from the contents of the box to a silver light, our grandmother stepped into the room and stood before us. The scent of fresh lavender and vanilla filled my senses. Her beauty took my breath away.

"My loves, I'm proud of how well you have worked together to keep our family strong." She kissed us each on the cheek. "Such sadness in your eyes, Mara. You have so much to be happy about. Let go of the feeling of loss. As you can see, I'm well, even though I miss you both terribly. Stay true to your promises always."

Before I could even tell her how much I missed her, she faded away. The sound of a strong wind and the light twinkling of chimes surrounded us.

Meg squeezed my hand and whispered, "Goodbye, Gram."

My sister's intuition amazed me. *Had I understood the elements this well when I was her age?* As I considered the question, another brightness flashed. As it faded, the image of our mother appeared. She was taking her oath. As she slipped the pink ring onto her finger, a red light surrounded me, and I was, soon, standing in the middle of Starten Forest.

Taking a deep breath, I glanced around for my sister. Panicked, I ran through the forest, searching for Meg. I halted when I spotted my mother, again. Eliza was a teenager now, and I gasped when I saw Blanche Drygen with her.

Blanche's hair wasn't the silver she wore today, but rather, it was as black as a raven. Her face wore a dark expression that matched her deep lipstick. When my mother tried to back away from her, she grabbed onto her and dragged her through the forest.

Eliza screamed.

Blanche stopped and hissed, "You better choose wisely. Your family has caused enough trouble for me."

Eliza stopped screaming and started crying, but her sobs had no impact on Blanche. If anything, it seemed to fuel the woman's anger. She walked faster, pulling my stumbling mother along. When they reached a tree covered with a dark red liquid, they stopped.

Shaking, Eliza pleaded, "Please. Don't make me go in there. I'll do what you want. Tell her that I'll listen. I'll do what I'm told."

"It's too late, now. I warned you." Blanche shoved Eliza through the red ooze, and then followed her.

I didn't want to walk into the bloodlike substance. However, I knew there was a reason I was seeing this. Closing my eyes, I stepped into the tree. I gagged as the warm, sticky goo covered me. Holding my breath, I forced myself to continue walking down the path. When I finally reached an opening, I climbed through it and entered a large cave.

My worst fear was around me. The cavern was covered in long strands of spider webs. I held back a scream as I saw a young man attached to the middle of the largest web. I squinted my eyes, hoping he was breathing.

"Please, let's go. I have agreed to follow Snowystra," Eliza begged. Trying to wipe the red slime off herself, she cried, "What more do you want from me?"

Blanche slapped her so hard that it sent Eliza reeling to the floor. "You promised me already, and yet, you didn't keep your word. She'll kill us all for your disrespect. One-by-one, I'll destroy everything you love... if she doesn't end us first."

The room filled with a soft light, and I looked up to see a woman floating down from above. As she came closer to the ground, I realized it was Snowystra. I almost laughed at how incredulous her attire was. She was dressed for a ball, not to punish someone. When her feet touched the floor, she glided over to Blanche and gave her a threatening glare.

Blanche shuddered and distanced herself from Eliza.

Snowystra stared down at my mother with pity in her eyes. She bent down so gently that I thought she was going to comfort her. Instead, she dug her hands into Eliza's hair and yanked her up by it, holding her off the ground.

Dangling in front of the cruel goddess, Eliza apologized. "I'm sorry I didn't listen. I'll not make the same mistakes twice. I'll do as you say."

Pleased, Snowystra carried her to the web and set her next to the young man. The trap swayed from her motion, causing him to groan in pain.

"Do you love this boy enough to save him? If you want him to live, you will have to commit your loyalty to me, and me alone. You and Cedric will never be together again...unless I give him to you." Snowystra caressed his cheek before turning back towards Eliza. Then, she warned, "If you listen to me, your life will be wonderful. I will choose a more suitable man for you to marry. And, if you are good, I will even allow you to keep the magic Danu has given you."

Tears fell from Eliza's eyes as she reluctantly nodded her agreement.

Snowystra flashed a wicked smile, and then returned her attention to the sleeping boy. "Cedric, Eliza is here to save you. Wake up, darling."

Cedric's eyes snapped open, shifting around in confusion. When he saw Eliza lying next to him on the web, he struggled to break free. "Let her go," he snarled. "She's nothing to do with any of this."

Snowystra laughed. "Quite the contrary, Cedric. She has *everything* to do with this. But she has come to her senses and has realized the error of her ways. She will not see you again unless I deem you worthy. You will stay away from Eliza. She is no longer yours."

The words infuriated him, and he bucked against the sticky trap. "Let us go. You can't make this decision for us."

Anger flashed in her eyes. She gripped Cedric by his chin, her touch silencing him, and twisted his head. Cedric was no longer cursing at her or even moving. It was as if she had paralyzed him completely.

The dark goddess stared at him with pity for a moment before she released her hold on his face. Then, in one quick movement, she dragged her long, silver nails from just beneath his eye and down his cheek. He silently screamed as his tender flesh tore open until she waved her hand across his face. With this movement, his shrieks echoed throughout the cavern.

Snowystra closed her eyes and smiled. She looked as if she was listening to a beautiful song.

Eliza paled at the sight of the blood flowing down Cedric's face. "No! Please, don't hurt him. I promise I'll do what you want. Please, stop. I'll obey you," she screamed.

In the corner of the room, Blanche stood watching as Eliza cried and Cedric, her injured son, screamed. She wore an odd smile of satisfaction on her face, which bewildered me. *Is she that cold? How can a mother watch her son being tortured in such a way with no response?*

Snowystra's cold laughed filled the cave as she swiped at the spider silk with her sharp fingernails. The web broke, dropping Eliza and Cedric to the ground with a hard thud.

Eliza started to move towards Cedric but stopped herself. I could almost feel her pain as she gazed helplessly at her love. Tears filled her eyes as she visibly struggled with her next move.

"Go now!" Snowystra screamed.

Eliza scrambled to her feet and began to run. When she reached the entrance to the red oozing tree, she stopped, and said, "I promise to always love you, Cedric. We will not be apart forever." Then, she disappeared.

Everything went dark before I found myself in our home. A younger version of myself was holding my baby sister in my arms. Our mother stood behind me, brushing my hair as I sung to Meg. When Eliza put her arm around my young version, I stepped closer to listen, and faintly heard the words she was saying to me.

"Marina, you will be the one," she said in a hushed voice.

Her words repeated, over and over, until I found myself, once again, drifting into the darkness of sleep.

"Wake up, Mara," the frightened voice pleaded.

Opening my eyes, I found myself face-to-face with Meg. Tears streaked her cheeks.

"When the woman was standing in front of me asking if I would protect the magic, I was scared, and I didn't answer her. Will she be mad?"

I sat up and blinked away the fog. *I'll never use that spell again,* I thought wryly.

Meg's breathing hard. She held the silver chest close to her, a terrified look upon her youthful face.

Reaching for her hand, I squeezed it to remind her she was safe. "No, Meg," I comforted. "When you're ready to take this commitment, you can open the chest again and make the promise."

"I'm ready to promise now, Mara. I'm not going to go with that snow lady. I love all of you and I want us to always be together."

"You don't have to accept this now," I said. "I know you love us, and you won't be tempted by the things. Think really hard before you say yes. Maybe, don't answer the question, tonight."

"No, I'm ready," Meg said firmly, "I'm ready to promise, now." She opened the box and nodded her head before slipping the ring onto her finger.

Threads of Fire, Water, Earth, and Air twisted around us.

My ring finger pulsed.

Meg's eyes widened, and she hissed as the metal and stone melted into her skin. She grabbed my hand, and I could feel the current of the magic under her skin.

"I'll promise to protect the magic, Mara."

"I know you will." I laughed and kissed her on the forehead. "Promise me you'll stay away from Snowystra. If you sense her at all, I need you to run as fast as you can until you're in my arms. Promise that to me, Meg. I can't lose you, too."

"I promise, Mara," Meg vowed. "I'll be brave, but smart."

"I know you will. Now, head up to bed," I said, giving her one last hug before we said goodnight. Then, as she entered the hallway, I called, "Meg, I know you knew about Mile's magic. Don't keep secrets like that from me again, OK?"

CHAPTER TEN

With Meg and Miles off to bed, I fixed myself a pot of tea and sat down at the kitchen table with Gram's journals. Moments ago, my spiritual body had been with her, and I longed for her to return to this world. Lost in her writing, I jumped in surprise when Cole sat down at the table and poured himself a cup of tea.

"Well, they're tucked in and fast asleep," Cole said, taking a long sip of his drink. "Meg didn't want me to leave, but she wouldn't tell me why. What happened today to shake her so much?"

My father sat down at the table and poured the last of the tea. "I never thought Miles would stop tossing and turning. Tell us what happened, Caterpillar."

I recapped everything that had happened earlier that day. I began with Snowystra interrupting our picnic and how the elementals saved us. When I told them what I'd seen while in the memory transfer, my father's eyes glistened with tears.

There are no words I can say to comfort him. I don't know how to defeat Snowystra. She's too strong.

"You said she tried to give Meg a box," my father said. "Where is it?"

"I don't know," I replied. "I guess it's outside still."

"We don't want anything she's giving. It shouldn't be opened," my father said. "I'll go find it and get rid of it."

"I'll come help," I said, standing up.

"I'll be quick. Sit down and finish your tea," he responded. "Remember that I'm skilled at my Earth magic." Kissing me on the head, he whispered in my ear, "Stay with Cole. He needs you. You're right about her messing with lives. He's one confused boy."

As my father left us, we both sat at the table in silence. The tick-tock of the grandfather clock in the living room grew louder. Unable to deal with the unwritten tension, I decided it was time to be brave.

"Cole, you need to talk to me. You can't marry someone you don't trust, and I won't marry someone who doesn't trust me."

"You're right. People who don't trust each other shouldn't get married."

His words were like a bucket of ice water being dumped over me. Twisting the ring he had given me, I slid it off my finger and set it on the table in front of him.

Wide-eyed, he said, "No, Mara. That's not what I meant. I didn't mean I don't want to marry you."

Frustrated, I asked, "What do you mean then?"

"I just meant we've got a lot to figure out together." Moving his chair closer to mine, he stared deep into my eyes. "I don't know why her words scared me so much, but I don't want to lose you over this."

"So, how are we going to get past this? How are *you* going to forgive me for what happened in the elemental world?"

"We'll work it out as long as we're together. Snowystra messed with my head a bit." Cole slid the ring back onto my finger and kissed the inside of my wrist. "I love you. I'll always love you and I want you to be my wife. Will you marry me, Mar?"

The tears that had been building inside me streamed down my face. As the wetness ran down my cheeks, I felt the coldness of a wind blowing through the house.

Snowystra.

"My father!" Jumping up, I knocked over the chair I had been sitting on. "We have to go to him."

"Mara, I need you to answer me," Cole said with a hurt expression on his face.

"I love you, but right now, we need to make sure my father is safe. You don't know what she's capable of."

He was unmoved by my reaction.

"Can't you feel the icy wind around us, Cole?"

Looking at me as if I had lost my mind, he shook his head.

"She's here," I said. "We need to find Elliott."

Not waiting for him to understand, I ran out of the house. The entire backyard was covered with a thick frost. The surrounding trees had large icicles hanging from them.

Cole caught up to me and grabbed my arm. "Wait," he said with frustration. "What are you doing out here?"

Pointing towards the icy forest in front us, I demanded, "Do you understand why we need to find my father, now?"

"How can this be?" he asked. Wearing a look of complete confusion, Cole ran his fingers through his hair as he stared at the ground. Dropping to his knees, he stroked the frozen grass like a child playing in bath water.

"Cole," I snapped. "We need to find my father – *now*. What is wrong with you?"

Ignoring me, he continued stroking the grass. I noticed his eye color had changed. His deep blue eyes were a milky white color, and his expression was frozen.

How could she have enchanted him, again? Stop, Mara, I scolded myself. You need to focus on finding your father. Think.

Channeling my Fire and Air magic on the frozen areas, I sent out a blast of warm air. The shimmery orange wind I created swirled around the trees and grass, melting everything it touched. It was, then, that I saw my father, lying in a puddle of water by the oak tree. I ran and knelt beside him. He was ice cold.

"Daddy." I patted his face, trying to wake him. "Oh, Goddess, please, don't let him be dead. Wake up, Daddy. Please."

His eyes fluttered open. He rasped, pointing towards the black box lying next to him, "Bury the box in the circle. Don't open it, Caterpillar."

"I can't leave you both, right now." I hugged him tightly. "You won't be able to defend yourselves."

"No time. Go now, before she returns." My father pushed me off him and sat up. "I'll be fine. I'll take care of Cole. Go, now."

Picking up the box, I left for Starten Forest.

Stopping at my grandfather's workshop, I decided it was time to see if I remembered how to use the four-wheeler. I had been there for the lessons, so I thought, *how hard can it be?*

After several false starts and a very choppy beginning, I was able to fly through the rest of the property and into the forest. Red and black trees blurred as I bumped along the mossy floor. When I arrived at the stone altar, I slowed, inspecting the area.

Not allowing myself a moment of grief, I stepped into the center of the stone nest. The spot where I had lost both my mother and grandmother in one evening. Inside the circle, I felt the usual rush of air, but everything around me changed. I was no longer in the forest. Though I was still standing in the center of the large nest, it was constructed from silver twigs. The ground covering was a white that shimmered with pastel colors and flecks of silver. The moon was almost full as it glowed down on me.

The soft light from above brightened and became so strong that I was forced to shield my eyes. A caress of my cheek encouraged me to open my eyes. Standing before me was Danu. Her long silvery hair swayed in the breeze. A small brown cat jumped out of her arms and rubbed against my legs. The cat purred as it circled me.

"My child, you have come here, once again, with fear in your heart," the silky voice of the goddess purred. "Release your fear. You are safe here."

Setting the box down, I said, "Danu, my family isn't safe. Snowystra…"

"I'm aware of my sister's intentions child. They are unimportant to me," Danu replied. "It's your heart and your intentions that I'm interested in."

Not understanding, I stammered, "I-I have promised to protect the magic and I'll keep this promise."

Laughing, she said, "Of course, you will, Mara. Your heart is as pure as your grandmother's. You will keep your promise, but is that what *you* genuinely want?"

"Yes," I proclaimed without thinking. "I'll protect it at all costs. I just beg you to save my family from her."

"I can't interfere with the choices each of you will make," she said. "Follow your heart and it will guide you."

With those cryptic words, she faded away and I was back in the middle of the stone circle. The box in front of me was no longer black. It glowed a neon green. Clawing at the dirt next to it, I could feel the electricity emitting from it. My father's face appeared before me.

"Bury the box in the circle. Don't open it, Caterpillar."

The shocks of the dark magic radiating from it brought me back to my mother's attack on me. An image of the cold look on Eliza's face flashed before me, reminding me how determined she was to kill me. The memory of my grandmother, falling to the ground after blocking the ball of cursed magic meant for me, ripped at my heart. My eyes burned with hot tears.

No, not now, Mara. Keep it together.

Digging harder, I stopped once the hole was large enough. Sending a gust of Air magic, I knocked the box into the hole and frantically kicked the dirt over it. The brown soil liquefied as it touched the green magic. The green and purple-colored sludge swirled, as if dancing underwater, until they froze into a solid stone. I continued my efforts to bury it completely when, suddenly, a flash of light erupted from the hole, knocking me backward. The earth under me began to shake and a crack in the ground formed.

The cat Danu had been holding appeared and ran out of the circle as the ground continued to tremble. My instinct to follow her was strong.

"Listen to your heart," the voice of Danu whispered in my ear. Without any more hesitation, I took her advice and followed the small animal out of the circle.

The cat ran to the casting stone where she laid down and purred.

"What are you trying to tell me?" I questioned, petting her gently.

Rolling onto her back and rubbing against the marble, she let out a small meow.

"You aren't going to answer me, are you?"

Again, the earth under me quaked and a crumbling sound came from behind us. Jumping into my arms, the cat meowed. Turning to see the origin of the noise, I watched as the circle and the outer twigs and leaves dropped. They sunk in towards the hole I had just dug and covered.

When the shaking stopped, I walked carefully towards the light emitting from the ground. In the circle, there was no longer dirt and leaves. It was now filled with a light purple water that sparkled with specks of red, green, yellow, and blue. Small colorful fish swam around and sporadically splashed out of the shimmery pond.

"Well, I guess the box is buried. I hope Danu's magic is strong enough to contain it," I whispered to the cat in my arms. It nuzzled me as if in agreement and I smiled. "It's time to go home. Will you be joining me?"

Rubbing against my cheek, I took that as a yes and I started for home.

CHAPTER ELEVEN

When I arrived back on the property, the house was dark, except for the light in the kitchen. The cat jumped out of my arms but followed closely behind me. Though the puddles had disappeared, the ground was still damp from the melted ice.

Cautiously, I entered the house. The hallway had an eerie glow to it. Despite being lit up, no one was in the kitchen. The crackle of the fireplace suggested they were in the living room.

My suspicions were right. I found my father and Cole on the long couch. My father was ghost white and shivering, even though he was buried under thick layers of blankets. Cole sat beside him, wrapped in a comforter. Neither looked well.

"I buried it," I said. "It's gone."

I sat on the edge of the couch beside my father and the cat jumped up beside us. As it delicately walked the length of my father's body and onto the back of the long sofa, I touched his head. He felt like ice. The cat must have agreed because it stopped and laid down, cuddling near his head.

Cole gave the cat a weird look but didn't question me. His eyes were still a whitish shade of blue. "After you left, he collapsed. I tried to warm him up."

"He still feels like ice, but thanks for trying," I said before reaching out to touch my fiancé's face. "Cole, you're like ice, too." Trying to wake my father, I beckoned, "Dad. Dad, wake up. We need you."

Slowly opening his now frosted green-colored eyes and gazed at me in confusion. "Caterpillar? Are you here?"

"I'm here, Daddy. I did what you asked," I soothed.

"The box is gone?" he questioned.

I told him a quick version of the events surrounding the burial. As I spoke, my father held my hand tighter. When I finished, his eyes were welling with tears.

"I'm fine. I made it there and back with no harm," I comforted. "And look, Danu's cat guided me home."

Struggling to lift his arm, he reached back and scratched the cat on the chin. He smiled and said in a hoarse voice, "Thank you for guiding my little girl back to me."

"What happened outside? Do you remember any of it?" I prodded.

"I found the box in the place you said Meg was. When I picked it up, Snowystra surprised me. Everything else is a blur. I know I felt confused, and I couldn't remember why I was there. The dark goddess told me that, when I first came to Starten, she was tempted to keep me for herself, but she knew the children Eliza and I would have would be more useful to her. Then, she kissed me and told me to open the container. When I hesitated, she kissed me, again. This time, her kiss felt like I was breathing in liquid ice. Unable to move, she laughed, and then she opened it herself."

He stopped as if he couldn't go on.

I squeezed his hand. "You're safe, now."

"No, the box held horrible things. It showed me everything you described, and more. I saw Snowystra forcing Eliza to leave Cedric bleeding on the floor. I even watched your mother plotting with him to get rid of me," Elliott said.

No, we don't have time to mourn over his lost love, I thought bitterly. "You knew all of that already?" I interrupted. When I realized his breathing had become shallow, I spoke kinder, "You can't let that hurt you. Let's get you warm, first, and then you can tell me the rest."

As I started to get up, he gripped my hand tightly. "No, stay. Mara, I haven't even told you what you need to know. We don't have time to waste."

I sat back down. "OK, I'm here. Continue your story."

Through ragged breath, my father said, "The worst part...the worst part." Gasping and sucking in air, he whispered, "It showed Blanche and Cedric planning to attack us. They want Miles back, and they're not going to stop until they get him. We're not safe here anymore." Closing his eyes, his breath slowed, and his eyelids grew heavy.

"What did you see them planning?" Cole understood I was trying to keep my father awake. "What aren't you telling us?"

"Cole, I need to get something to help him," I said. "Stay here. Don't let him sleep."

With his eyes closed, my father answered barely above a whisper, "No, don't go. They plan to attack on your wedding day. They're going to kill everyone in attendance before taking Meg and Miles. She showed me it all." Sobbing now, he mumbled, "It was horrible. They killed everyone. They killed you and I didn't save you."

"It wasn't real," I said. "That's just something Snowystra was showing you to scare you. She's just trying to confuse us."

My father closed his eyes and his breathing stopped. Shaking my father, I pleaded, "Don't go to sleep. Stay awake with me. Tell me what happened next." Pressing my ear close to his mouth, I willed air to come out. Five seconds passed. Then, ten.

"Cole, he's not breathing," I cried.

Cole sat emotionless.

I ran to the pantry to find something to help my father. Desperately, I dug through the shelves. Returning to my father with the first thing I found, I unwrapped him from the blankets and unbuttoned his shirt. His skin was a light blue.

Panic filled me as I smoothed the purple healing salve over his chest. "No, not now. You can't take him now," I cried. "Hang on, Daddy. This'll work. Stay with me."

Taking more of the ointment, I rubbed it on his neck and face, desperate for it to work. Cole just stared.

"Put some on his feet," I ordered, shoving the tin into his hand.

Cole watched me, and then did as instructed. He looked dazed as he rubbed the thick salve on Elliott's feet.

Closing my eyes, I focused all the magic I had inside me onto him. With a gasp, he jolted upright, only to collapse back down, again. His skin, streaked with red and blue, was fading, but his breathing was still shallow.

"This isn't going to save him!" I shouted. "We have to find a way to pull the dark magic out of him."

Holding out my hands towards the ceiling, I called Fire and Air. The response was immediate. Soon, I had filled the room with a blazing wind. The heat uncomfortably licked at my cheeks, but I continued to call more. After a few minutes, I checked to see if the heat had helped. Unfortunately, there was no improvement.

Going back to the pantry, I dug through all of Gram's books and journals, searching for anything that might help. Taking another jar of the healing salve, I brought it to Cole.

"I can't find anything else," I said, crying, now. "Let's just keep trying this."

Cole and I covered my father's body with the purple paste. As we coated him, small bursts of air would leave his mouth. It was only a temporary fix. Almost as quickly as his breathing started, it stopped. As I scraped the last bit from the jar, I closed my eyes and begged the goddess not to let him die.

My silent prayer was interrupted by a loud bang and a strong gust of wind blowing the front door open. Stepping into the house, a gray-haired woman rushed in and searched the room. Wearing a long, black jacket and a fur cap, she looked like a Drygen. Preparing to attack, I called Fire.

Loudly, she asked, "Where is my son?"

Sounds of cheering came from the loft, followed by Meg and Miles scrambling down the ladder. "Hazel," Meg and Miles shouted as they threw themselves into the open arms of the intruder.

"Hello, my loves," she said, kissing them on their heads. "I'm glad to see you, but I need to find Elliott." Fear covered her face as she realized he was lying on the couch. Going to him, she kissed his cheek. "Elliott, sweetie, don't close your eyes. Stay with us, love. Mommy is here."

"What's wrong with Daddy?" Meg cried and ran towards him. "Why are you saying, 'mommy is here', Hazel?"

"Who are you? Why are you in my house?" I caught my sister and pulled her away from the stranger. "Get away from my father."

"Mara, there's no time for proper introductions," the woman the kids called Hazel said. "We need to save my son." Standing up, she walked towards me. "Take my hand," she demanded. As I shrank back from her touch, she said, "Please, take my hand."

Miles nodded at me reassuringly. It was as if my brother was telling me I could trust her.

Cautiously, I let her take my hand.

"I need you to invoke the goddess and the elements." As I started to tell her I couldn't, she said, "Mae taught you. You must do it now, Mara or we'll lose Elliott."

Releasing her, I held my hands high above me. "Goddess, I ask for your protection and guidance on this night. I ask for the aid of the elements who guide."

Repositioning myself, I reached out and beckoned, "With my hands to the east, I call upon you, Air, and ask you to blow away any dark magic that has entered this home. I request you cleanse me of doubt and fear." A rush of Air zipped about me and swirled my hair.

I shifted again. "With my hand to the south, Fire, I call upon you, and ask you to burn away the magic that has been called to harm." Small, red embers fell from the ceiling. The sparking shower quickly died out when it landed.

"With my hand to the west," I said, reaching out towards a new direction, "Water, I call upon you, and ask you to wash away and cleanse the cursed magic." Droplets of water fell on us.

Cole tipped his head back and let the rainfall into his eyes and mouth.

"With my hands to the north, I call upon you, Earth, and ask you to strengthen us, so we can fight what has been cast upon us." The wood floor shook, and green trailing plants grew up from between the floorboards.

My father stirred as the smell of fresh grass and dirt filled the room. The long vines twisted and turned until they reached him. They slipped around his limbs, and then his center. He moaned in pain as he was carefully lifted from the couch and spun until he was wrapped in a tight cocoon of emerald green.

"Goddess, my request is complete. Your blessings and gifts are acknowledged and appreciated," I said through tears. Silently, I pleaded that my request would save my father.

Hazel squeezed my hand tightly as we watched the shell, holding my father, lower and gently set him back onto the couch. The hard vines changed into a green liquid that began a trail of droplets leading into my father's mouth. Greedily, he swallowed and tried to sit up.

By the time the last drop was gone, he was dazed, but no longer on death's door. The color of his skin had returned to a golden tan. His vibrant green eyes sparkled, again, like an emerald in the sun.

Sitting down between Cole and my father, I took each of their hands. They were both warm.

Hazel wrapped her arms around my father and cried.

With a look of shock, my father whispered, "Am I dreaming? Mom? How? Why?"

The cat jumped onto Hazel's lap and purred.

"I came to help, son," she whispered. "I'm not going to ever leave you, again."

Everyone sat in the living room with a cup of tea and cookies. No one would've known how close we'd come to losing both my father to death and Cole to insanity. They both appeared to be healthy again. Miles and Meg snuggled on each side of Hazel, telling her everything that had happened since they left the Drygen Estate.

Still doubtful she wasn't a trick, I questioned her, "You have convinced everyone that you're Elliott's mother, but I don't have a grandmother, named Hazel."

"You're so much like your great-grandmother, Michelle. She wouldn't believe me, either, without proof," Hazel chuckled. "You're correct – you don't have a grandmother, named Hazel. You do have one, named Eva, though. For the last eighteen years, I have pretended to be someone I am not. I did it to watch over my son and you girls."

Rising, she walked over and pulled me up into her arms. I stiffened, at first, but the warmth of her hug calmed me. Pressing her cheek to mine, she said, "I have watched you for many years, Mara, and I have waited for the day when I'd be able to do this."

As she held me, I felt the anger I was holding begin to release. "Why are you back, now?"

Sitting back down between Meg and Miles, she tried to explain. "My mother was friends with Lucy Andrews..." Stopping, she brightened her smile at Cole. "Camille Black and Genevieve Silver. Your great-grandmother, Michelle Elliott, was my mother," she explained.

The shock of meeting this grandmother and worry over my father filled me with such fatigue. The room spun, making me unstable.

"Steady, Caterpillar," my father said, putting his hands on my shoulders to support me. "Come sit and sip the tea you made."

Taking a seat on the couch between Cole and Elliott, I just wanted to drift off to sleep.

Hazel watched me with a look of concern as Meg and Miles clung to her. "If you feel well enough, Mara, I can explain further," she said.

Nodding, I sipped the tea and prepared myself for her story.

"When I knew it was time for Elliott to return to Starten, I followed not soon after he left," she explained.

"Why did you hide this from me?" my father questioned.

"Elliott, I needed to keep you safe. Not long after I sent you to live here, I was able to find a job as a maid at the Drygen Estate. Pretending to be one of them was worth it. All of it was worth being able to protect you."

"I saw what they have planned" My father paled again.

"Cedric's not been right since Eliza died. He refused to let her be buried and stayed with her body for almost a week. Each day, he begged Blanche to bring her back from the dead. Finally, Blanche ordered Eliza be taken away. Since she was placed in her resting spot, he's been on an angry rampage. Cedric is a madman, now. When Eliza died, she took whatever bit of humanity he had." Hazel hugged Miles to her.

"We know they're coming," I said. "But, now what? Do we prepare to fight them? If Snowystra is helping them, we've no chance."

"Snowystra?" Hazel said with a dark glare. "How do you know that name?"

"She almost killed your son, tonight. She's been trying to force us to break our vow to Danu and follow her," I explained. "She's the one that destroyed my mother."

"Oh, this isn't as I expected," Hazel said. "I thought the Drygen's were responsible. We need to take you somewhere safe."

"Where are we going to go that she won't be able to find us?" I snapped. "She is a goddess. She knows everything."

"She may know everything, but she is bound by rules. She can tempt you, threaten, and even hurt you," Hazel stated. "However, she can't kill you or imprison you. If she did, there would be repercussions."

"Then, where do we go?" I looked at Cole.

He shook his head and shrugged his shoulders.

"I know where we can go," my father said. "We will go where they won't find us." Standing up, he announced, "We'll go to Great Winds."

CHAPTER
TWELVE

"We can't just up and leave everything here," I countered as I looked around at the house. "They'll burn everything like they burned Cole's. I'll not risk losing my grandmother's home."

Wiping the tear that fell from my face, Cole said, "These are just things, Mara. Us living is all that matters."

My eyes drifted over the faces of my family. *He's right. I won't survive if I lose them.* Reluctantly, I agreed.

"Great, everyone pack yourself a bag – of essentials only – and then help Meg and Miles do the same," my father commanded. "I'll gather up some things from Mae's pantry."

"I can help the kids, Mara," Hazel said. Then, quickly added, "I mean, if that is OK with you."

"That would be great. OK, everyone, pack a small bag. Only what you want to carry and meet back here," my father continued his orders.

Meg and Miles quietly obeyed and led Hazel up to the loft.

Going towards Gram's room, I scanned everything as I stood in the doorway.

"Caterpillar, we need to hurry." My father watched me from the kitchen. "I know this is difficult."

"Do you? This is my home. This is my grandmother's home. How can you guarantee they won't destroy everything?" I asked. "You all keep saying how strong the magic within me is. Why can't I stay and fight them?"

"Mara, the Drygens have gathered men from the darkest corners of this earth." My father came to me and cupped my face between his hands. "The kind of men who don't care about anything other than the money Blanche Drygen will pay them. Your magic might be able to fight ten or twenty of them, but you're not strong enough to fight the numbers she has built."

"How do you really know what she has built?" I argued, turning away from him.

"What I saw, tonight, in the box, told me. I'm not willing to take a chance on losing you." His voice cracked. "Mae would not want you to die for any of this. I can't make you, but please, pack a bag and come with us." He kissed me on the cheek as the tears streamed down my face and left me to decide.

I wanted to argue with him. I wanted to delay what must be done. I wasn't strong enough, yet, to fight. Staring at myself in the silver nest mirror, I wiped away my smudged eye makeup. A light flashed in the mirror and my grandmother appeared.

"All will be safe here," Gram whispered. "Now, go to our family and be protected."

A crashing sound in the bedroom pulled my attention from the mirror. The lamp on the bedside table had knocked over. While I had turned away, the image of Gram disappeared. Going to inspect the lamp, I found it had broken in half. Sitting down on the floor, I picked it up.

"Mar," the sweet voice of Cole whispered in my ear, "It's OK. I'm here."

Setting the lamp down, I wrapped my arms around his neck and pressed my lips against his. At first, he resisted, but then, I felt him succumb. Soon, the power of his kiss consumed me.

Picking me up, Cole laid me on the bed. Lying beside me, he gazed deep into my eyes, and then kissed my cheek, trailing kisses to my neck. "I have missed you, Mara," he breathed into my ear.

Wanting to forget about the world around me, I let myself be consumed by his kisses. Nothing mattered at that moment. Cole was my world, and we would survive what was ahead, together.

"Oh, I'm sorry," the embarrassed voice of Hazel said, interrupting our passionate moment. "I was just checking to see if you needed any help."

Sighing, Cole sat up, wearing a grin on his face. "We were just about to finish packing. We'll be right there."

Hazel smiled, giving a small nod. When she continued on her way, I closed my eyes, trying to push back my feelings of embarrassment and shame.

"There's nothing to be ashamed of, Mara," Cole scolded. "You know that isn't the first time one of your grandmothers has found us in an awkward situation."

"Not helping," I said with a pout.

Cole laughed and slid off the bed. "Sit up and let's get our bags ready," he said, offering me his hand and helping me up.

I bent down to resume picking up the lamp. I noticed a silver edge sticking out from under one of the broken pieces. "Wait, there's something here."

Taking it from me, Cole pried off a chunk of the lamp and revealed a small journal. Trying to open it, he said, "It's stuck."

He handed it to me, and I tried to turn the cover to see what was inside. "I can't open it, either. Is there anything else in there?"

Checking again, he shook his head. "Nothing. Let's take it with us and see if we can figure it out when we're away from here."

Taking a brown leather bag from the chest at the end of the bed, he loaded things in it. After a few minutes, he handed it to me, and said, "Here, I packed a bag for you. Check to see if I got everything you wanted. I'm going to grab a few things from the patio."

Rifling through the bag, I found the clothes I would've packed and Gram's journals. Again, I was amazed by how perfect Cole was and how well he knew me. *I don't deserve him*, I thought.

Returning to the room, he lifted another bag. "I have, also, gathered us a good amount of supplies in case we need them."

Peeking inside, I saw potions, herbs, and at the very bottom, a small glass jar of blackberry tea biscuits alongside Gram's favorite loose tea leaves.

Smirking at him, I laughed. "Essentials, huh?"

Cole picked me up, and said, "Now, I have all the essentials."

As he carried me out of the room, I felt sad that this might be the last time I ever saw Gram's home.

We found everyone waiting for us in the kitchen. No one spoke. I wanted to beg my father to find another way, but I had seen what Snowystra was capable of. Maybe he was right, and we would be safer out of Starten.

"We should go, soon," my father said, picking up Miles and taking Meg's hand. "We've got a long trip ahead of us. We've done all we can do here."

As we left the house, I cried, "Wait, how are we going to get there? Meg and Miles are exhausted and none of us have slept since last night."

"We take the truck," Cole suggested.

"No," Hazel interrupted. "We can't take Mae's truck. It would be too recognizable. We'll take my vehicle. No one will notice it."

Eyeing her, I questioned, "Won't the Drygen's recognize it? You have worked for them for over twenty years."

Hazel chuckled. "Sweet girl, I have learned many things working from the Drygens. I knew there would be a day when I'd need to leave, so I made sure there was a way for me to escape hidden nearby." Placing her hand on my face, she said, "Mara, you need to release whatever fear you're holding and trust me. I'm only here to help."

The warmth of her hand and the sincerity in her voice struck a chord. The hardness I'd felt seemed to melt a little bit. When the wind around us blew, it carried the scents of my grandmother, and they engulfed me.

"Listen to your heart," the voice of Gram whispered in my ear.

Following my instinct, I put my hand onto Hazel's and softly professed, "I trust you."

A small tear ran down her cheek and she wrapped her arms around me. "The goddess has blessed me with all of you."

"When you two are through whispering, I think we should leave," my father urged.

Hazel released me, and said, "We're ready, now. Follow me, everyone." Then, she led us off our property and into an area of the forest heavily covered with shrubs.

Not seeing a vehicle anywhere, I grew nervous that I had let my family fall into a trap. *Nice old lady and you lead your family straight to the Drygens,* I scolded myself. Feeling apprehensive, I asked, "Is it much further?"

"We're here." Hazel pushed aside some of the foliage and tugged on a rope. With a mighty jerk, the grill of a vehicle appeared. Another hard yank and she pulled the front half of a dark green vehicle out of its hiding spot.

"Climb in everyone," Hazel said as she handed the keys to my father. "There's plenty of room for you to get comfortable. We've got a bit of a ride ahead of us."

With my father and his mother in the front bucket seats, Meg and Miles excitedly scrambled into the far back and snuggled in the third row. Cole and I took our spots in the middle row. With us all set to go, my father started the car. The windshield wipers went back and forth, trying to clear off the dirt coating the windows. Instead of cleaning it, it just smeared it into a muddy paste.

"Hey, Cole, can you call us a rain shower to help the wipers out?" my father called back to us.

With a smirk, my fiancé called Water, but instead of getting the windshield, he misted us all. "Oops, you meant outside, right?"

With a mischievous again, he called his element, again. Soon, a rainstorm poured down on us. The loud sound of water banging against metal slowed, and then stopped as quickly as it had started. The car was now clean and we could see out all of the windows.

My father drove forward and cheered, "And now we are off."

As we drove through the forest, I couldn't help wondering where he was taking us. Turning to look back, I could only see the roof of our house. Closing my eyes, I hoped we were making the right decision.

Cole leaned in and kissed me gently on the cheek. "I was worried when you left so quickly with Elliott lying on the ground. What was so urgent that you had to leave?"

"When we went outside to find my father, the entire property had been frozen, including him," I explained, fighting off the distraction of his touch on the back of my neck. "Your behavior frightened me, too. You just fell to the ground and stroked the grass. When I called Fire and Wind to melt the ice, my father told me to bury the box. You sat there dazed, but he told me you would be fine."

"I don't remember any of that," he said softly into my ear. "I can't imagine a life without you, Mara."

Again, he was talking as though I were leaving. *Will it be like this for the rest of our lives?* I wondered. "You don't need to worry about me not returning," I said with frustration and pulled away from him. Moving closer to the door, I needed space from him. "I have no plans of going anywhere without you."

Cole held his hand out to me. "Don't close up on me now, Mar."

I narrowed my eyes at his wrist. The peacock-colored protection tattoo my grandmother had placed on him was gone. "What happened to the mark Gram gave you?" I asked.

Cole wore a look of surprise as he held out his arming to examine it. "I...I don't know," he stammered. "It was here this morning."

Fear filled me. "Snowystra," I said. "She removed the protection spell. She isn't going to stop until she gets her way. She's declared war."

"This means nothing, Mara." Cole squeezed my hand. "We'll find the spell in Gram's books, and we can recast it, OK?"

I half-heartedly nodded. There was no spell to turn back time and return everything to what it had been before I found out about the magic. Staring out the window, I realized we were leaving everything we had known. Where this would lead, I wasn't sure.

My life had always been in Starten, and we never needed to venture out. Now, everything was changing, and I couldn't stop it. Resting my head on the cool glass as the scenery blurred by and I drifted off to sleep.

CHAPTER THIRTEEN

"Wake up, everyone," my father boomed. He was waving paper tickets in his hand. "The second part of our journey is about to begin.

Rubbing my eyes, I asked, "Second part? What's next?"

"A train!" Miles excitedly pointed at the black boxes on wheels, spotlighted by several tall lampposts. "I have always wanted to ride on a train."

Meg and Miles jumped over the seat and climbed across me to get out of the van. Both were eager for the next part of our trip. Begrudgingly, I stepped out into the night air, picked up my bag from the pile, and followed my overly excited family.

When we boarded the train, we walked in a single file past rows of seats until we reached a train car with sliding doors.

My father slid open the entry, revealing a compartment. The small space had plush benches covered with a deep red fabric that matched the framed windows. "Our own private car," he said proudly.

Hazel stuck her bag in the overhead bin. "We'll be on the train for many hours, so sit down and get comfortable."

I chose a seat by the window while I nervously waited to start the next part of our trip. The whistle of the train sounded and a man in a black uniform came into the passenger car, asking for our tickets. Miles beamed as he held the papers out to the man.

"The dining car is open all night." With a big smile, the agent punched holes in each boarding pass before returning them to Miles. With a wink, he said, "I suggest you try the banana pudding, young man."

"I will, sir." Miles rushed back to his seat beside Meg. He looked as if he would explode from all the happiness inside him.

Hazel settled between my siblings and gently said, "It's still night, little ones. Let's settle down and close our eyes." She focused her eyes on me and added, "You should try to rest, Mara." Nodding towards Cole, who was hunched over and snoring, my grandmother commented, "He already has the right idea."

My father settled into the seat between Cole and myself. "She's right, Caterpillar. We should all try and sleep."

I smiled and rested my head against his shoulder. It wasn't long before the train screeched and jerked away from the station, followed by the clickety-clack of the wheels on the rail. Elliott wrapped his arms around me.

Elliot, I thought to myself. *Even with your father here, and present, you can't really believe he's back, can you?* Gazing out at the night sky, I stared into the blackness as a single tear fell from my eyes.

Who says he won't leave, again? The dark voice inside me argued.

But he's here now, I thought. Closing my eyes, I slowly drifted off to sleep.

My dream flashed images of Snowystra in a forest. Her touch immediately froze tree bark, running up through the branches and leaves. Long icicles hung down, showing just how strong her icy touch was. Tears filled my eyes as I followed behind her. As they broke loose, the strangest thing happened.

Instinctively, I took a tear on my finger and held it out to the tree. As it dropped, an extensive line of silver stretched out and connected to me. I felt a warm tingle run throughout my body. When the globule landed, a burning sensation shot through my arm. The tendril connecting me to the tear began to freeze.

The ice of Snowystra flowed towards me. Pushing my magic against hers, I watched the line change from blue to red and back again. The colors battled as I struggled to keep her magic away. Focusing the warmth I had felt from my tears, I sent a flash of heat through the tendril.

Instead of flowing down the link, the warmth exploded outward. The blast generated a bright light with small particles of colors dancing inside it. The frozen trees began to melt and return to their lush green. The distant sound of birds chirping rang out.

Ahead of me, Snowystra turned and glared, but she didn't return to refreeze her path. Instead, she continued walking, crunching on the shards of ice she had created. Then, the dark goddess disappeared.

The sound of Meg's cries jolted me awake. I exhaled a sigh of relief when I found she was safe. Meg and Miles were playing the card game they'd invented, and Mile's was winning. Across from me, Cole and my father were quietly discussing our current situation.

Noticing I was awake, Hazel moved to sit beside me. "Mara, it's so nice to be able to talk to you. I've spent the past seventeen years watching you from a distance. My, I remember watching you in your first Lunar Dance. I was so proud of you. There were so many times I wanted to stop and talk to you, but I knew I'd risk the chance of exposing myself."

"Why did you come back to Starten, and then decide to work for *them*?" I questioned. "It must have been horrible in that place."

"It wasn't all bad." Hazel pointed towards Miles. "When your mother moved into the mansion, my job became clear. I was there to keep him safe. You don't know how relieved I was to know you were in the care of Mae.

"Why would you watch over, Miles?" I whispered, not wanting him to hear my question. "He isn't your blood relative. Wasn't it risky staying there?"

"When I thought Elliott had died, I was devastated and considered returning to my mother. But I realized my purpose when your mother arrived. Miles will always be my grandson. He was a gift from the goddess," Hazel explained. "The choices of his parents and my son were not his fault. It was such a cold place for a child to grow up."

Taking in her words, I felt a heaviness come over me. I really wasn't sure how many more secrets I could handle learning. I closed my eyes and pretended to sleep. Listening to the click-clack of the train, I thought about the home I was forced to leave and worried I'd never see it again. My mind replayed the events of the last few months. *Could I have stopped all of this? Could I have saved my mother if I had gone with her instead of sending her away?*

"We're here!" Meg cried.

The train had finally arrived at our destination. Disgusted by the view, I sighed. We had stopped in a desolate area that was nothing more than dirt and tumbleweeds. We had gone from the lush green forest of Starten to this lifeless area. *Where has my father taken us?*

Reluctantly, I stood up and stretched. My family was bustling around, making sure all of our belongings were gathered. I picked up my bag to follow them down the narrow aisle and off the train.

"Here, let me help you." Cole held out his hand towards me.

I accepted it and allowed him to assist me off the train. Stepping outside, the hot, dry air stole the breath from me. I had never felt heat like this before.

"Remember what I told you all about drinking lots of fluids," my father said as he handed us each a silver container. "While we're here, dehydration can sneak up on you. So, what are we going to do, kids?"

Miles chirped, "We're going to drink lots of water, even if we aren't thirsty."

"You're correct." My father tousled my brother's hair.

Not wanting to be outshined, Meg piped in, "And, we need to make sure we find shade every chance we can."

"We have such smart children," my father said. Both Meg and Miles basked in his praise. "Let's start heading towards town. It's just a short walk, and then we'll be there."

Squeezing my hand, Cole whispered, "This is only temporary. We'll be home, again, before you know it."

My father led us down a dusty path.

Frustration filled me. I had been too exhausted and scared to think clearly before, but now, I knew better. We should've stayed in our home, not run off to the desert. Snowystra would find us anywhere, so this was useless.

Why is my father adamant about returning here? Won't it be a sad reminder of the time we lost together?

Fatigue washed over me. It seemed like we'd gone on forever with no signs of civilization. I knew I was being dramatic, and we'd probably walked only a few miles. After all, Miles and Meg would've whined, complaining about their feet hurt, if it had truly been a long hike. But, they hadn't.

I was just about to verbalize my complaints when I saw a large wooden sign. It read – ALL TRAVELERS ARE WELCOME IN GREAT WINDS.

We entered what looked like the main street of the small town. In the center of a large, round area, there was a water fountain that sprayed blue and green water. I was tempted to dive into it and cool down, but I just kept walking.

As we continued, I took in our temporary home. The street had large, brick buildings with creative wooden signage that made it clear what each store was offering. Passing by *Jerick's Coffee Corral,* the side of my mouth quirked slightly with amusement at a picture of a man soaking in a big cup of coffee. *Sam's 'Stache Shack* had a smiling man with a curly mustache that resembled a villain I'd read about before. The imaginative storefronts seemed to help ease my tensions.

When we arrived at a building built from tan brick flecked with gold, my father stopped and stared proudly at the metallic green sign hanging above the door. The black lettering read – *Charlemagne's.*

"We made it," my father said, taking Meg and Miles by their hands. "Come on everyone. This is the best place in Great Winds."

CHAPTER
FOURTEEN

The entrance to the business was extravagant. I felt uncomfortable with how underdressed we were. We headed to the door, being watched by a man in a dark gray suit.

Under his suit, the man wore an emerald-green vest with a matching tie. His silver hair was combed back with not a strand out of place. His beard and mustache were short and well-kept. The man golden eyes looked up at us. His somber face grew into a large smile as his gaze landed on my father.

"Elliott, my boy," he said, "you have returned to us." Motioning at us, he laughed. "And you brought a clan."

"I'm glad to be back." The men clutched hands in respect. My father patted his friend on the back, and then turned towards us. "Patrick, meet my family."

After several nervous *hellos*, Patrick opened the door and shuffled us inside. "Well, come in. Come in." With a whisper directed at my father, he said, "She missed you. She'll be glad you returned."

As impressive as the outside was, it was shabby compared to the interior. Inside, we were met with a large marble floor in the same gold tones as the brick outside. The room was circular with staircases, on both sides, leading to the balcony and the four levels above. The golden banisters held lattice walls in the same color. The stairs, although covered in a dark emerald fabric, also shimmered with specks of gold. It was elegant and lavish.

I stared in awe and took in the details. Off to the right of us was a section of small mahogany tables. The people seated there were formally dressed. Waiters catered to their needs while they ate their meals. To the left of the entrance, a long metal counter stood, at least, four feet high, where people were being checked in by uniformed employees.

While my father was pretending to be dead, he hid here? I mourned my lost father and he had been living a luxurious lifestyle without us?

My father led us to the first open desk clerk, and said, "Sammy, will you tell Ms. Charlemagne that I'm here."

"There's no need to tell me you're here. I felt your presence the minute you walked into the building," a female voice called from the staircase.

A tall woman strode down the steps like a queen. My father beamed at her as she walked towards us. She wore a dark jade-colored, fitted business jacket with just enough fabric to cover her well-endowed bust.

I looked at Cole, who seemed as impressed as I was. Looking from the top of her dark auburn hair, falling loosely over her shoulders, to the slender-cut black capris hugging her body, there was no way not to be. Even her perfectly manicured toes, encased in gold-strapped sandals, were a remarkable sight.

"You have been missed, Elliott," Ms. Charlemagne said, kissing him on the cheek. Her lips lingered longer than a friendly kiss would. Her dark burgundy lipstick left a faint mark.

When she noticed my sister, she knelt down, and said, "You must be Meg. Elliott neglected to tell me what a beauty you are."

Staring at the woman open-mouthed, Meg was unusually silent.

"And who might you be?" she asked as she gently touched the side of Miles' face.

With the same look of admiration as our sister, he didn't speak, either.

Regaining her composure, Meg piped in, "He's my brother, Miles." Holding her hand up to her mouth, she directed her whisper towards the woman, "Actually, he is my half-brother because we have different dads, but I consider him my whole brother."

"That is very wise, Meg." Mr. Charlemagne stood up to face me. "Marina, I would know you anywhere from your father's description. She touched a curl that had fallen loose from my ponytail and smiled. "I'm so glad to finally meet you. I have heard so much about you."

"Sadly, I know nothing of you." My tone sounded harsher than I planned. "With him recently returning from the dead, we haven't had much time to talk about his other life."

Cutting me off, Cole stepped up and held out his hand. "I'm Cole Sands, Mara's fiancé. It's very nice to meet you, Ms., ah..." Stopping, unsure how to address her, he added, "I'm sorry. I don't know your name."

"Esmerelda Charlemagne." The woman patted Cole's hand before flourishing her arms in the air. "Welcome to my little establishment."

Stepping up, Hazel held out her hand, and said, "Ms. Charlemagne, it's nice to meet you. I must confess that I have, also, not heard anything about you, yet."

"Oh, please, don't call me Ms. Charlemagne," she said as she kissed my grandmother on each cheek. "Everyone calls me Essie."

A man in a hotel uniform came up behind Essie, interrupting our introductions and whispered in her ear.

Saying something inaudible to the man, she turned back towards us. "I'm so sorry. I have some business to take care of, but I would love to meet up, later, and get to know all of you." Then, addressing the uniformed man, Essie said, "Daniel, please, escort my guests to the penthouse and get them anything they want or need."

Daniel bowed in acknowledgment.

Kissing my father on the cheek, Essie placed a key into his hand and whispered something in his ear that made him smile. "Anything they want," she called, again, to Daniel.

"Yes, Essie," Daniel replied before he directed his attention back towards us. "Welcome back, Elliott. You're a sight for sore eyes. Would you like me to take you to the penthouse or did you want to give the grand tour yourself?"

Chuckling, my father shook his hand. "If you can handle the bags, I'll handle the tour. Can you, also, have a light lunch and some beverages sent up? We've had a long trip."

"No problem." Daniel collected our bags and loaded them onto a luggage cart. As he rolled away, he turned towards my father, and said, "She really has missed you, you know?"

CHAPTER
FIFTEEN

Before I had time to ponder what Essie's relationship had been with my father, we were moving, again. This time, it was my father who led us through the hotel, acting as the tour guide.

As we climbed the green steps, my father pointed out the work he'd done on the building. "The lattices under the banister were additions I made. Mara, come look here," he said when we reached the tenth step.

Kneeling down, he pointed to a butterfly etched into the gold with the lettering *Marina* under it. It was so discreet that a casual passerby wouldn't notice it. The wings of the butterfly were so detailed, evidence of the time and care he'd put into it.

"Every day I was away from you, Caterpillar," he said, "I thought of the little girl I left. I knew I'd return to see a magnificent butterfly. I'm sorry I missed so much of your life, but I'm here, now. Know in your heart that you were not replaced by anything, or anyone, in Great Winds."

"It's beautiful." I wondered if all of this was done to appease his own guilt for leaving us.

When we arrived on the second-floor balcony, he pointed out the engraved designs on the solid dark wood of the doors. Each entrance had a floral design with a gold number in the center. Stopping at room two hundred two, my father stopped and picked my little sister up.

"See this, Meg?" my father asked, pointing towards the flower design. "What do you see?"

She ran her finger over a violet with the name *Meg* engraved beneath it. "You did this to remind you of me?" she breathed. "I've never seen anything as pretty."

"Of course, it was for you," he said. "I missed my beautiful baby girl, Meg Violet Stone, every day I was away, as well."

Continuing our climb to the fourth floor, he led us to a large, green door. Using the key Essie had given him, our father opened the door and guided us up a set of stairs to another entrance. When he opened that one, I held back a gasp. Hanging on the wall, above the fireplace, was a painting of our house in Starten.

"I didn't know you could paint, Elliott." Cole inspected the picture. "This is really detailed."

"Essie is responsible for this work. I described it to her, and she painted it," my father said. "She's really gifted." Clapping his hands together, he added, "Let's get cleaned up before we reconvene for a bit of lunch. Follow me. Rooms are this way."

The rooms each had a large king size bed with a fluffy white comforter and green pillows. The bedside tables had brass lamps with dark green shades. Like magic, our bags were waiting for us.

I eyed the bathroom. It was as large as the bedroom. I imagined myself soaking in the round tub. If there wasn't time, I could use the glass-walled shower pressed against the tub.

"I'm going to take a bath. Did you want to use the bathroom first?" I asked.

Winking, Cole left the room, saying, "All yours. Just don't get lost in there."

Examining the fancy bottles on the ledge above the bathtub, I settled for a rose-scented bubble bath and poured a generous amount into the running water. Climbing into the tub, I slipped under the warm suds. Calling Water, I washed my hair with a citrus-smelling shampoo and conditioner. Instead of running more hot water when I felt chilled, I called Fire to reheat it.

Coming here to hide from Snowystra made no sense to me. We should have stayed in our home. I had let my father's fear drag us away from everything we knew. To do what? We couldn't hide from a goddess, and she wasn't going leave us alone. *This was a mistake. My mother hadn't been able to fight her, and she was strong.*

Longing to stop my thoughts, I sunk under the bubbles, closing my eyes. My moment of solitude was interrupted when one of the small bottles of shampoo fell into the water. As I came up, I found Cole staring at me.

"You scared me," I gasped. Covered in suds, I felt concealed enough to carry on a conversation with him.

"You have been in here for a bit. Everyone's eager to eat." Cole held out a large bath towel for me.

Stepping out of the bath, onto the padded rug, my eyes locked with his. They were ice blue, again; the same cloudy color they'd been after Snowystra put her touch on him. I reached for the towel, but Cole held it tight when I tried to take it. He had always been a gentleman and always looked away in moments like these. This time, he let his eyes scan my body. Feeling embarrassed, I tugged the towel harder, yanking it out of his hand.

"Thank you," I said, quickly wrapping the towel around me.

As I tried to walk past him, he put his arm around my waist and murmured in my ear, "You're lovely. Why hurry off?"

A chill ran through me as he kissed my shoulder. The person in front of me did not sound like, or act like, the Cole I knew. Pushing him away, I said, "Sorry. We're late. My fault."

"Don't run away," Cole called.

I turned to apologize, again, and found that Cole had stripped his clothes off. "You're welcome to stay and watch, Marina."

Without responding, I scurried out of the room and hurriedly dressed. I braided my hair to the sounds of Cole whistling. *What is happening to him? Is it my fault for always tempting him? Maybe I'm overreacting? Cole is just being flirty. Isn't he?*

There was a light knock on the door, and I opened it to find Hazel. She was wearing a colorful skirt and a flowing white gypsy shirt. Her gray hair was in a loose fishtail braid.

Still feeling shaky from my interaction with Cole, I needed to talk to someone I could trust. "Where is my father?" I stepped into the hallway and closed the door behind me.

"He's with Essie." Hazel touched my hand. "What's wrong, Mara?"

"Nothing," I started to lie. Either because of the intensity of her stare or the panic I was feeling over the change I felt in Cole, I decided to trust her. "Not here," I said, glancing at the door to my room.

"OK, come with me," she said, leading me down the hallway.

Hazel's room was on the other side of the penthouse. It was similar to the one Cole and I were sharing. However, instead of the green accent colors, this room had red pillows and lampshades. There was, also, a painting on the wall of a ranch-style house with a desert background.

Sitting down on one of the chairs, I tried to explain everything that happened. As I talked, I watched her closely, waiting for her judgment. I wasn't married, but I slept in the same bed with Cole, every night. She had even walked in on us in an intimate moment. *Will she judge me and tell me it's my fault...that Cole is only a man?*

Surprisingly, none of my fears came to light. The woman before me — my grandmother — who was so much like the one I'd lost, listened without judgment.

"We need to help Cole push out the cold that has touched him. Snowystra has been stifled before and will be again," she said with determination. "Like the magic Miles' carries within him..."

Seeing the look of surprise on my face, she chuckled. "Yes, Mara, I've seen his little sparks of magic. I've been caring for him since he was a baby. As I was saying, we'll need to find a way to contain the magic he is carrying until we can push it out."

"I have no idea what I'm doing," I whispered, not wanting to confess how frightened and inadequate I felt. "I have all of this magic running through me, and I can barely control it. I don't know the rules. I didn't know how to use it when it was needed the most."

"Listen to your heart, Mara," she instructed with a smile. "All you can do is open your heart to the goddess and listen."

"Thank you," I said. "I'm glad you're here. I'm doing my best to learn everything as quickly as possible. Still, I need advice from someone who's had their magic longer."

"Ask whenever you need help," she replied. "Just know I don't have all the answers. No one really does."

The warmth I felt with her conflicted me. I wanted to love this woman, but I felt as if it would be a betrayal to Gram.

"I know it's confusing for me to just show up. You had a grandmother already. Replacing her would be an impossible task for anyone to undertake, and I no intentions of trying." Hazel cupped my face between her hands. "Let time dictate who I'll be to you and what you'll call me. I'll never be Mae, but I'm here for you and I do love you."

"She was the best, but I don't want to close out loving anyone else. Gram would be so frustrated with me, right now." I laughed. "I hope I won't drive you as crazy as I did her."

Chuckling, Hazel said, "I'm sure you'll do your best to drive me insane. Now, let's go find everyone before there's nothing left to eat. We will figure out what to do about Cole, together."

When we entered the dining room, we found my family was already eating their lunch. Several carts behind the table held trays of meats, cheeses, vegetables, and a variety of salads. There was even one with hot teas, coffees, sparkling water, and juices. I filled a plate with food and sat down.

"Where did you disappear to?" Cole asked with a grin. Once again, his eyes had returned to the sparkling blue color I loved, but I couldn't trust him completely, not anymore. "I went to find you and you were gone already."

Staring at him in amazement, I began telling him what had happened, but the sound of Hazel clearing her throat halted my words. Handing me a cup of tea, she smiled. Understanding her concern, I gave her a slight nod.

"Oh, I just went to check on everyone," I lied.

I wanted to tell him Snowystra had put some sort of spell on him, but Hazel was watching me. I hoped her intentions were good, even if her timing seemed too perfect. She showed up to save my father just in the nick of time. Moments after Cole's odd behavior, she appeared, again, at our door. Everything felt too convenient. *Could it all be coincidental? Am I just being paranoid?*

Luckily, the focus was taken off me when Essie joining us.

"Fabulous," the cheery voice of Essie sang as she entered the room. She sat in the empty seat next to my father and took a piece of cheese off his plate. "I'm starving. Is everyone enjoying their lunch?"

My family soaked in her positive attitude. She was able to bring everyone into the conversation and make them feel like her attention was only on them. Miles and Meg struggled to stay in their seats. I knew they wanted to run over and command her complete focus.

My father wasn't discreet in hiding his feelings for her, either. Seeing the reason he'd hidden away for so long infuriated me. He could have come home and fixed everything before it was too late. Instead, he stayed because of her.

"Mara, you're so quiet," Essie said, turning her attention towards me. "I think I know what you need...a night out. Winds has a fantastic bar, with great music and lots of dancing, at the end of the main street. Grant's Tavern has not only the best nightlife, but it has the best pizza you'll ever have."

Before I could say no, she was on her feet. "I have the cutest outfit you could wear. Nothing fancy, but just a little something for a night out with a cute boy," Essie said, winking at Cole.

"That would be fun, Mar," Cole agreed. He seemed like the boy I had always loved and trusted, but I was scared to be alone with him.

"I don't think so." I shook my head.

"No, it will be what you both need," Essie insisted.

"We haven't had a night out in a really long time," Cole pleaded. His eyes flashed hope.

Once again, I felt myself wanting nothing more than to be in his arms.

"Fine," I relented, not wanting to argue. *I'll go only because I won't be alone with him.*

"Great, Marina, come with me." Essie clapped her hands together. "Elliott, love, find Cole something to wear."

I followed Essie through her extensive penthouse. I tried to change my attitude, but I struggled with how perky she was being. *She's too happy about us being here. Was this my father's plan the whole time? Did he want to return to Great Winds?*

"You have such a cute figure, Marina," Essie beamed.

I stopped at the entrance to her bedroom. "Can you call me, Mara? My mother is...was the only one who called me that name." *And Snowystra,* I thought wryly.

"Oh, I'm sorry," Essie apologized. "Elliott only called you *Caterpillar* and I thought that would be way too familiar. Your father told me what you've been through. I know you don't know me, but I can listen if you want to talk."

The corners of my mouth turned up into a forced smile. Essie's eyes flashed sadness before she clapped her hand together, again, and quickly changed her tone, "But, not tonight, Mara. Tonight, you will have fun. You're too serious. This is the time of your life to enjoy what the world has to offer."

She opened the door, revealing a room almost as big as the downstairs of the house I had grown up in. The large canopy bed had four posters with white curtains tied back onto each pole. The aqua blanket on her bed was the same as the other rooms but covered with dozens of pillows in assorted sizes, colors, and shapes.

On a nightstand, she had a picture of herself with my father. In the photo, he was laughing as she fed him a piece of cake. Both were wearing very formal attire. I picked it up and examined it. She had on a long, white dress and he was wearing a black suit with a green tie.

"This almost looks like a wedding picture," I joked. The smile on her face faded, silencing me. "It just looks like one, right? Were you at a costume party?"

Essie calmly took the picture from me and set it down. "Elliott and I, obviously, couldn't marry since he was married to your mother, but we chose to have a handfasting ceremony."

"Well, you should marry him now," I said coldly. "He is a widower."

"I'm sorry. I didn't think to put anything away," Essie apologized. "I was just so happy to see all of you. I love your father, but I know his children should come first. Mara, nothing has changed from when you walked into this room. The photo should only tell you how much I love Elliott."

With a deep sigh, I sat down on the edge of the bed.

Essie sat next to me. "He fought me every bit of the way in making a life for himself. Not a day went by that he didn't regret leaving you."

She's right, I thought. *How can I judge him for falling in love? My mother threw him away.*

"Eliza ran off with Cedric. It's not as if Elliott left us to find a new life. He was forced to leave." Tears burned my eyes. "You can't help who you love, but you can't tell Meg, yet. It'll just be confusing when we leave."

With surprising compassion, Essie nodded. "Thank you for understanding. I hope you and I can become friends, Mara."

When I didn't respond, she stood up. "Why don't we find you something to wear?"

It was strange to have my father's wife fluttering around me. Essie expertly fixed my hair and makeup, reminding me of my visit to the elemental world. Once again, thoughts of Kai flashed in my mind. It always felt more than a memory. It was as if he was with me, tempting me, again.

"Are you too warm, Mara?" Essie asked with concern. "You're so flushed suddenly."

Embarrassed, I quickly answered, "Just a bit hot. Maybe, I should drink some water?"

Essie took a glass bottle from the small fridge by her dressing table and offered it to me. "Is this cold enough or would you like some ice?"

"This is great, thanks," I said, taking a long drink. *Stop thinking about Kai. You have enough to deal with without adding him into the mix. Besides, you've already given Snowystra enough to use against you.*

"Who is this beautiful woman before me?" my father asked as he joined us. "Stand up and let me see your snazzy outfit."

I felt self-conscious in the fitted jeans and loose silver tank top I was wearing. The shirt had black beading running down the front in a series of teardrop designs. After trying on, at least, a dozen shoes that I was unable to walk in, Essie found a pair of strappy sandals with silver gems. They fulfilled her idea of how I should look on my first night out on the town while still allowing me to walk without falling over.

After pulling the sides of my hair back, Essie used a cream she said would 'enhance the natural curl of my hair'. Her finishing touch to my hairstyle was to mist glitter through my hair. As she applied dark eyeliner and dark red lipstick, I felt like a little girl who had been playing in her mother's makeup.

My father's smile grew as he took in my makeover. "Mara, you look so grown up. I would hug you, but I don't want to mess anything up."

"It's OK. Your *wife* has plenty of makeup to fix anything you smudge," I said tersely.

"Mar." My father sighed and sat down. "I didn't mean for you to find out about Essie and me this way."

"You don't have to explain anything to me," I said. I didn't want to hear about the life he'd built without me.

"No, I need to explain," he said. "When I came here, I was hoping for a place to hide. I never planned to meet a person like Essie. Before I let myself love her, I was crumbling. Leaving Eliza never meant I stopped loving her, but what I had...what I have with Essie is different. She loved me unconditionally, knowing I'd leave, one day, to return to you girls."

"I understand," I said, "but I've asked her not to tell Meg and Miles. We'll be going home, soon. It was a mistake to come here."

"It's not like that Caterpillar. I'll respect your wishes, for now, but Essie is part of my life. Can you accept her into yours?" My father's shoulders slouched.

My heart ached. I didn't want to hurt him, but I had to protect my siblings. "I'll try," I promised.

"That's all I can ask," he said, escorting me to the door. "Now, I want you to go have a good time, tonight."

"I love you, Daddy." I kissed him on the cheek. The sadness I had felt when I lost him, the first time, slightly swelled up in my heart. *Will I lose him, again?*

CHAPTER
SIXTEEN

The distance from the hotel to Grant's Tavern was far enough for Essie to insist I let her driver take me. I was surprised Cole had decided to walk ahead to see the town while I was getting ready. As I was leaving the penthouse, my grandmother stopped me.

"If you feel unsafe, at any time, with him, sprinkle this into Cole's drink or, worse case, throw it in his eyes." Hazel handed me a small white envelope. "Don't worry. It'll only subdue the dark magic if it emerges."

Clutching the packet tightly, I thanked her and left to find Cole. With luck, he'd be one hundred percent himself and not the ice touched version I had seen earlier that night. Pushing back my negative thoughts, I focused on the evening ahead. I was going to try to have a night of fun with my fiancé.

The street was crowded with people visiting all the local businesses. The tavern I entered was busier than I expected. Customers drinking brightly colored drinks sat at the bar on horse saddle stools. Behind the bar, there was a picture of a gorilla holding a slice of pizza.

Elsewhere, people were sitting at small tables, sipping their vivid concoctions, and chomping on fried foods. A crunching sound came from under my feet as I continued into the establishment. Checking to see what I was stepping on, I found the floor covered with discarded peanut shells.

Ignoring the crunchy distraction, I continued my search for Cole.

Along the wall, a large box caught my eye. The machine kept lifting records and dropping them down. Each time a record released, it started to play a new song.

I decided to check out the machine while I waited for my fiancé. On the top of it, the words *Mr. Jukebox* were flashing. As the song playing ended, a screen flashed, announcing, *Two credits available. Pick a song*.

Peering through the glass, I saw records with artists and titles that were familiar from my childhood. I recognized some of the songs Gram had loved. A couple of the songs brought an image of her singing and dancing with me. The visions were so strong. It was almost as if I was that small girl in the arms of the woman who had always cared for me.

My heart ached at the loss of my grandmother. I would give anything to bring her back...just one more chance to tell her how much she meant to me.

I pushed the button to flip through the records. I stopped when I reached the album featuring a dark-haired boy with a curled lip on the cover – Elvis Presley. He had been one of my Gram's all-time favorites. Lost in my memories, I recalled a time my grandfather had acted out a scene from one of his movies, where he danced in a jailhouse.

The sweet recollection was halted by a warm breeze from behind me. I turned to find myself, face-to-face, with my greatest temptation – Kai. I stared into fiery eyes and felt a flutter in my heart.

"You really should play this one," Kai said in a sultry voice. Leaning over me, he punched E16 into the jukebox and a record began to play a song about blue shoes.

Dumbfounded, I looked the elemental up and down. Wearing blue jeans and a black T-shirt, he dressed as if he'd been working the land. Even his boots were scuffed, creating the illusion of a real ranch hand.

Tipping the brim of his cowboy hat, he said, "Nice to make your acquaintance, ma'am. My name is Kai." When he held his hand out to me, I ignored it. "What are you doing?" I hissed at him.

"I've been sent to keep an eye on you. Where is everyone?" Kai looked around.

"Cole is meeting me here. I'm not sure they should've sent you," I said with frustration. "You're only going to make this worse."

"Mara, did you miss me?" Kai asked as he touched my arm.

A tinge of his magic ran through me, but I clenched my teeth and said, "No, Kai. I have not even thought of you."

He gave me a look that clearly said he didn't believe me. "You haven't thought of me even once?"

"No, I haven't," I insisted. "You need to go. Cole is going to be here, soon, and he won't be happy if he sees you with me."

"Why would seeing me upset him?"

"Snowystra told him about my visit to your world. She's planted a seed of doubt in his mind that I don't think he'll ever forget. Seeing you is definitely not going to help."

"Well, that is just silly, Mara. We're from two different worlds and, quite frankly, you're not even my type." Kai gestured towards a blonde with big hair and equally large breasts, who was watching us. "Now, she's my type. Tell him there is nothing to worry about."

Slightly offended by his comment, I wanted to tell him off before I realized I should be encouraging his pursuit of the blonde rather than feeling insulted. "Good. Make that very clear when Cole shows up."

As the peppy song stopped playing, I felt like I was being watched.

I was.

Cole was standing across the room. His cold stare focused on the two of us. When our eyes locked, I put on a bright smile and waved him over to join Kai and me.

"I guess it's time to get this over with," I said with trepidation.

Cole walked towards us with his eyes dark and fixed on Kai. With each step, I could see the anger building up inside him. When he reached us, I eagerly took his offered hand, and he pulled me towards him.

He shifted away and glared Kai. "Are you going to introduce me to your *friend*, Mara?" He said the word *friend* as if he had eaten something sour.

Kai ignored the cold greeting and held out his hand in welcome. "They call me Kai. I have been sent by Danu to watch over you."

Cole accepted his hand in a firm grip. As Kai gave him a hearty handshake, his jaw clenched, and he roughly yanked his hand out of the Fire elemental's. "So, you're the one I need to keep my eyes on," Cole said in a low growl.

"Keep your eyes on me?" Kai asked, playing dumb. Looking from one to the other of us, he started laughing. "You think I'm interested in Mara?"

Laughing harder, he continued, "I'm sure my intentions have been misjudged. I'm very aware that you and Mara are to be wed, and I'm incredibly happy for both of you. I'm just here to watch you guys. Anything that happened while we were in my world was just to prepare her for what she would face in this one. Everything was innocent – no harm intended. While I would love to discuss this further, today is my first day out in your world – ever. I am looking fine in this form and I'm without a chaperone, so..."

Kai punched some buttons on the jukebox, and said, "Right now, I'm going to take advantage of my freedom. I'm going to introduce myself to that sexy blonde, who has been eyeing me, and ask her to dance. Let's meet up later, guys." Kai strode away, not giving Cole a chance to respond.

"What is he really doing here, Mar?" Cole's eyes burned with hatred.

"Cole, he was sent. I didn't know anything about it. Honestly, I don't know what you want from me." Sick of his insecurities, I warned, "Trust me, or don't. I'm not going to defend myself, anymore."

As I tried to walk away, Cole grabbed my wrist. "Please, don't go, Mar. I don't know what's going on inside my head."

The record switched and a slow song played. As the singer crooned a story of distrust, his silky voice warned that their love wouldn't last if she didn't stop being suspicious. Cole held out his hand towards me and I let him lead me onto the dance floor.

He pulled me into his arms, and we danced closely. As the words in the song played, Cole held me tighter, whispering in my ear, "Mar, I trust you...I want to trust you. I don't know how to remove the images she put in my head or the feelings they evoked. I'm trying to block it out, but..."

"Cole, I chose you. Though, the truth is, there was never really a choice to be made. It was just a kiss – and in an astral plane no less. My body was with you the whole time." Even with my recent thoughts about Kai tempting me, I knew I loved Cole. *But he doesn't trust you,* I thought coldly.

Determined to get through to him, I said, "I can't live like this. Decide, here and now, if you are willing to get past this." As I said those words, my eyes drifted towards Kai, who was slow dancing with the blonde. I felt a flicker of jealousy that she was in his arms. Fear filled me.

Maybe Cole isn't wrong to be worried. This isn't the first time I considered kissing Kai since I returned. My thoughts confused me. Just because I thought about the kiss and his presence made me feel excited, it doesn't me Cole and I aren't meant to be together. Does it? My inner battle was cut short.

"Mar, I said I promise to work harder on pushing out the vision she painted in my mind," Cole repeated. "Can't you forgive me?"

"I...I..." Stammering, I tried to come up with a response. I hadn't heard all of his words.

My hesitation hurt Cole. His eyes shined with tears. "Mar, I want to be with you forever. Don't you want the same?"

Cole loosened his hold on me. I had made things worse. Once again, I had an intense feeling of not wanting to lose him. I clung to him, and said, "I love you. You're the only one I'll ever love. You don't have to ask that question." Sighing, I held him even tighter and whispered in his ear, "Cole, we can make it through this, together. We just have to trust each other."

As he held me in his arms, I rested my head on his shoulders. I needed to try harder to block out what happened and remember what I had before me.

When the song ended, Kai approached us. He stopped in front of Cole.

Unlike the first time, instead of anger and distrust, Cole welcomed him kindly and held out his hand. "I'm glad you're here, Kai," he said. "Let's talk business. Tell us what we need to know."

"Great, mate. Let's get a table in the corner," Kai replied. "We've got a lot to discuss."

Settled in a quiet corner, Kai shelled peanuts and popped them into his mouth. "Snowystra will do anything to force you to her side. Nothing is off limits. She will twist reality to make you believe your only choice is to pledge your loyalty to her. You are safest if you stay together. You cannot fight her alone."

Kai continued to describe Snowystra's typical behaviors and known ways to stop her. As he talked, Cole scratched notes on cocktail napkins. It seemed futile. A bunch of mortals against a twisted goddess? The odds of us surviving were bleak.

"How do you expect me to stop her if Danu couldn't?" I asked.

Cole scooted his chair closer to mine. "We will stop her. You just have to have faith in our gifts."

We continued to listen to Kai's stories about the Winter Goddess until Cole's stomach growled.

"Maybe we should get something to eat," I suggested. "It's going to be a long night."

"Good idea," Kai agreed. "What should we get?"

"I'm sure whatever you pick will be fine," I said, not caring. My worry had killed my appetite.

Kissing me on the head, Cole left to place our order.

I stayed at the table and reviewed the notes Cole had written. This only increased my worry. I felt an intense need to get back to my family. No longer wanting to be in the noisy tavern, I decided to tell the guys we could take the food to go. When I didn't find either at the bar, anxiety filled me.

I glanced around and found Kai at a table with the blonde draped on his arm. He was feeding her bits of the food they had ordered. The Fire elemental was whispering something into her ear that sent the blonde girl into fits of laughter.

Scanning the bar for any hidden places where Cole might be waiting for our order, I knew something wasn't right. Picking up the napkins and shoving them into my pocket, I decided to find him. Looking up, I saw a large worn sign, swaying slightly from the overhead fans, at the end of the bar. It had the word *Exit* engraved on it and a finger that pointed towards a hanging slated door, which led to the kitchen.

I walked through the sea of dancing couples. Carefully opening the swinging door, I peeked in. The walkway was filled with boxes of canned food and bottles of liquor. I noticed a door leading outside was partially open. Slowly walking through the kitchen, I didn't call the attention of the cooks and servers as they bustled about.

When I reached the entrance, I could see it led to a narrow alley. As I cautiously poked my head out, I heard Cole's voice. Slowly, I cracked the door open further and listened.

Cole's voice whispered, "You have no right to pull me out here. I'm doing what you want. I'm watching them for you. What else can I do?"

The next voice I heard both frightened and angered me. "You're spending too much time playing house and not doing what I expect of you. Time is ticking," the hiss of Snowystra rang in my ears.

"I am doing what you want. I haven't had a chance to get her alone. I know, when I do, I can convince her to come with me. You just left me, not even two hours ago. I told you I need time, Snow." Cole's seductive tone shocked me.

Why is he talking to her like this?

"She isn't one to be rushed," he continued. "Can't you trust me?"

"I want it done, soon. Do you understand me? Your power is strong, but I need both of you to ally with me for my plan to work."

"Marina will follow me," he said. "She'll be putty in my hands."

The crunching sound of gravel under their feet made it possible for me to slip out of the kitchen and further into the alley. I squatted behind the dumpster and peered around to see them. Snowystra was pressed against Cole, and she was tracing her fingernails along his lips.

"Don't you want to rule my kingdom alongside me?" the dark goddess cooed. "You will have your heart desires. How can I believe that you will be able to convince her? If she really loved you, she would be standing here, now."

"I can convince her. Then, we can be together. I promise," Cole vehemently vowed before he grabbed her roughly and kissed her.

The world around me began to spin and felt like I was going to pass out. Fighting the urge to attack them both, I helplessly crouched down and watched, instead. It became unbearable and I closed my eyes. *Please, be a horrible dream.*

My hope was interrupted when Snowystra said, "Come with me, tonight. I'll make your magic so much stronger. Marina will follow...that is, if she really loves you."

The loud sound of crunching gravel told me they were leaving. Hot tears flowed down my cheeks, leaving them raw. This couldn't be real. I wiped my face and took the same route back into the bar that I used to come out. I had to get Kai.

I slipped into the crowd unnoticed. When I found the Fire elemental, he was dancing close to Ginger. Tapping him on the shoulder, I said, "I need to talk to you – now!"

"Not a good time," he dismissed me.

"Kai, she was here," I hissed. "She left with Cole."

"What?" Finally listening to me, he released his hold on Ginger. Seeing my tear-streaked face, he took my hand. "Where did they go?" Then, as though he suddenly remembered the blonde beside him, Kai kissed her on the cheek and said goodbye. "Sorry, Ginger. Family business calls."

Once we were outside, I told Kai what I had seen. His eyes widened in shock. "Which direction did they walk?"

"I don't know. I guess that way." I pointed towards Charlemagne's. Once again, a sickening sensation filled the pit of my stomach. "She was all over him and he didn't stop her. He kissed her."

"Mara, she has used her magic on him. Cole would not do that to you."

"Why not? Don't I deserve it?" I confessed. "You have been in my thoughts since I came back. Maybe Cole knew? Maybe I deserve to lose him."

Sinking down onto the concrete sidewalk, I put my face into my hands and sobbed. The world around me was closing in. I was losing another person I loved.

Kai sat and put his arm around me. This time, the warmth that normally excited me made me feel dirty.

"No." I shoved at him. "Get away. You're the reason he's gone."

Throwing my arm into the air, I screamed, "Whhhhhhy!!!!!"

Once I started screaming, I couldn't stop. The anger, fear, sorrow, and guilt I had been holding inside me released. It was my fault Gram was dead. If I had been kinder to Eliza, maybe I could have reasoned with her. Every mistake I made was being paid for...I had lost Cole.

Kai grabbed me and refused to let go. I didn't deserve his comfort and I tried to break away. The harder I fought, the tighter he held me.

"Mara, nothing you have done could have caused this."

When I was calm enough, Kai brought me back to the hotel. The buildings blurred past us as we walked. I felt like I was moving through a dense fog. Snowystra had taken Cole. Worse yet, he hadn't fought her. He wanted to be with her.

Did I cause Cole the same horrible heartbreak when I kissed Kai? Was that why he'd been so angry? Is that he chose to go with her?

By the time we arrived at the hotel, I had composed myself. The suffocating feeling of being underwater and drowning in my sorrow was still there, but I fought my urge to sink into the pain. Somehow, I needed to fix this. I caused this, so giving up wasn't an option.

When we entered the penthouse, it was silent. We found Essie sitting in an overstuffed leather chair reading a book.

Not looking up, she asked, "Did you guys have a wonderful time?"

When I didn't respond, she stood up and came to me. "What happened, Mara? Are you OK?" She looked Kai up and down. "Who is your friend?"

"Essie, this is Kai. He's —,"

"You're one of Danu's elementals." Essie folded her arms over her chest. "Fire, I would guess from the heat you're emitting."

He lifted the copper necklace she wore around her neck. The spiral sun had a golden yellow gem in the center. It glowed as he touched it.

"And the amulet you're wearing tells me you're one of Brighid's children. Sadly, my mother has always been against educating newcomers about our world. In her defense, she has only allowed mortals into her realm less than a century ago. I'm surprised Blaze didn't know about you, though."

"I can see why you've become a concern to Cole." Essie avoided his statement and led me to the couch. "Don't you think you should hold back your allure? You know better than to entice mortals. Your presence is too much of a temptation for even the strongest girl."

"You must be confused." Kai flopped down next to me. "I'm here to protect Mara and her family."

Eyeing him cautiously, Essie sat down on my other side. "Talk to me, Mara. Tell me what happened."

Baffled by their exchange, I asked. "What are you talking about? What didn't Danu teach me?" I turned towards Kai. "What are you hiding?" Glaring at both of them, I stood to face them. "We don't have time for this. Cole's with her. She almost killed my father. Your secrets can wait!"

Suddenly a hot pain in my chest radiated throughout my body, consuming me. I gasped for air. It was as if my lungs were filling with water. I was drowning. Dark spots appeared before my eyes, veiling my vision. Reaching out for help, I fell. The last thing I felt was my head hitting the coffee table. Then, darkness came.

CHAPTER
SEVENTEEN

A soft hum of chimes sounded rousing me from my unconsciousness. The tinging sound grew louder as I opened my eyes to complete blackness. A small spark of light appeared above me and spread like spider webs. The silver strands filled the thick air. I was unable to take a full breath. I shivered as I felt something twisting around me. *Am I dead?*

Tendrils covered me and the silky threads caressed my skin. Slowly, the pain in my lungs ceased and I was able to take a long, deep breath. Thoughts of Cole and Snowystra came to mind and the ache in my heart returned.

"Child," a maternal voice called to me, "we've not much time. Listen carefully and learn."

Unable to speak, I nodded and watched as shapes appeared before my eyes. The silver formed an image of a man and a woman. A voice spoke, narrating the sights displayed before me.

Arianolwyn and Alaunius fell madly in love. Against her father, Tannus', wishes, she ran away to be with him. The young lovers were consumed only with one another.

The emotions they had for each other filled me. It felt like they were my own emotions of passion, love, and desire. The feelings grew so strong that my heart beat faster. As they joined into one, a burst of light filled the sky. The bliss they both felt ran through me but ended abruptly.

When Tannus found the young lovers, he struck Alaunius with a bolt of lightning, killing him. Arianolwyn, who was now pregnant, begged her dead mate not to leave her. As he took his last breath, Alaunius vowed their child would never be alone.

Heart-wrenching pain filled me. I wanted the story to stop, but the voice continued.

The baby inside Arianolwyn grew as she mourned the death of her lover. Her tears streaked the sky with red, blue, green, and yellows. In time, the colors drifted together to form a silver wheel. As it turned, her body changed and soon she was heavy with child.

Finally, the day for the child to be born came. Silver tendrils came from the sky and carried the infant away. Arianolwyn grabbed the many cords that held her baby, now suspended above her. Holding tightly, she struggled until she lost her grasp on all but one of the lines connected to her daughter. The released silver recovered the child and the voice of Alaunius filled the sky as he cried, "Of the one will become three."

Thunder and lightning filled the sky surrounding the baby as Arianolwyn watched helplessly. A cocoon of silver wrapped her infant before bursting into a ball of light. The orb grew larger, and then broke off into three identical balls. As each continued to grow, they changed.

One filled with the spirit of nature. The child was, named Danu, and declared the holder of the elements, the mother of Air, Fire, Water, and Earth.

The second filled with ice, sparks of electricity, and darkness. The dark-haired child was, named Snowystra, the mother of Winter and keeper of the shadows.

From the minute Snowystra was born, she had a strong hatred for her sister. The anger and struggle between the two were unyielding. When she had seen enough, Arianolwyn restrained both girls and brought down the final ball.

The third filled with a white plasma that slowly turned black. The liquid bounced back and forth between the two colors until it settled as a burning ball of orange. The red-headed child was born to be the balancing force of dark and light. She was, called Brighid.

With those words, the space I was in faded and I found myself lying in a room, staring at the blades of a fan as it swirled above me. My vision blurred and I was unable to focus. As I closed my eyes, I was pulled out of the wave of unconsciousness that I was longing to let consume me. Strong arms wrapped around me and picked me up off the ground.

"Cole," I whispered, my voice cracking. I struggled to sit up, but was stopped by strong arms, holding me down. "No, I need to go find him."

"Caterpillar, stop," my father said. As I fought against him, he held my shoulders tighter. "We will find him, but first, we need to take care of you. You fainted. Love, you have a bad gash on the side of your head."

"She took him," I cried. No matter how hard I tried to break free from my father's hold, I couldn't sit up. "You didn't see them. You don't know what she has done to him. Why are you —?"

"Sit her up, Elliott." Essie handed me a glass containing a white, milky substance. "Drink this. You will sleep again. When you awake, we'll talk about finding Cole."

As I argued with her, Hazel appeared. "You can't help him in this state, Mara. Please, drink it. I'll stay with you."

Relenting, I put the glass to my mouth. My senses were overwhelmed with the sweet smell of vanilla and lavender, followed by the spice of cinnamon. Placing her hand over mine, Hazel steadied me, and I gulped the warm mixture. My eyes grew heavy, and I felt the need to lie down.

When Hazel took the glass from me and turned to leave, I grabbed her hand. "Don't go," I pleaded.

"I'm here." She set the glass on the bedside table. As I shifted to the middle of the bed, she climbed in next to me. I snuggled into her arms and was reminded of Gram.

"Sleep, Mara," my grandmother whispered, "Just sleep."

When I woke, I found myself alone in Essie's bed. I was no longer dizzy and the pain in my head was gone. In the bathroom, I turned the silver handle of the washbasin and filled my hands with icy water. Splashing my face, I gazed at my reflection.

On the side of my head, there was a large white bandage. Slowly I peeled it off and gasped as I saw a bloody gash covered in a bluish paste. Cautiously touching it, I realized the blood was dried.

Taking one of the washcloths from the neat stack, I wet it. Carefully, I wiped my forehead. When I was done, the only thing that remained was a faint silver line, running from the corner of my eye, up past my temple, and into my scalp. I stared at the pale scar, wondering why I had fainted.

"Oh, good. You're awake." Hazel entered the bathroom. She carried a steaming mug. "I brought you some tea."

"I'm going to shower and change my clothes. Then, we need to find Cole. He's not safe."

"Mara, you had a terrible injury." Hazel put the beverage in my hands. "You need —"

I handed the mug back to her. "All I *need* is Cole. When I was unconscious, Arianolwyn showed me the triplets. Why doesn't Brighid and Danu stop Snowystra?" I shook my head, feeling frustrated. "If you're done telling me what I need, I'm going to wash the blood off of myself, and then I'm leaving."

Without waiting for a response, I took a towel off the hook and entered the shower. As I scrubbed my hair, my anger towards Snowystra grew. I was not going to let her take Cole. Whatever happened was not his fault. She had hurt too many people in my life, and I was going to stop her.

Dried off, I threw on some clothes and braided my hair. I found my father and Essie in the dining room. My father kissed Essie on the cheek and placed a plate of food in front of her. As he walked away, she pulled him down and kissed him deeply. Clearing my throat, they broke away from one another and turned towards me.

"Mara, come sit," my father said. Filling a plate with French toast and fruit, he set it down before me. I started to say no when he pointed at the chair. "Sit. You need to eat before we go."

Accepting the fact that he wasn't going to let me search for Cole yet, I picked at the meal he gave me. *Nothing like an awkward silence,* I thought bitterly. Then, suddenly I realized it was too quiet and that my siblings weren't there.

I jumped out of my seat. "Where's Meg? Miles? Who's watching them? They can't be left alone."

"I asked Patrick and Hazel to watch over them. They wanted to go swimming and I thought it would be good for them to be away while we figure everything out," Essie replied.

"I just checked on them." Kai entered the room and took my arm. "If you sit, we can calmly discuss what I found out about Cole."

"I'm not in the mood for games, Kai." I shoved him off me. "Tell me where he is and how we can bring him back."

"You need —" Kai began, but before he had a chance to lecture me further, I cut in.

"I need to find Cole. Help me or stay out of my way." I narrowed my eyes at him, and he seemed to back down. At least, for the moment. "Cole needs me. You didn't see her with him. You didn't see what she has turned him into. You didn't see —"

The sensation I felt the previous night filled me. Hot fiery pain shot through me and, once again, I felt unable to breathe.

As I stumbled, Essie held onto me and sprayed me with a citrus-scented water.

Kai told us everything he knew about Cole's location. He was careful in his words, which made me wonder what he was holding back. Fighting back the pain I was feeling, I focused on the next steps ahead of us. *If you don't calm down, he will be with that monster even longer,* I scolded myself.

"Meg and Miles will be safe here. We can stop by the pool and say goodbye before we go," Essie said as she handed me a bottle of water and a small, leather bag. "We will find him."

Essie led us through the hotel, stopping at a wall of fogged glass windows.

My father held the door open for us and we entered the pool area. The room was full of green plants with blooming flowers in bright colors of orange, pink, and yellow. The air was humid and filled with the soft chirping of birds.

We found Meg and Miles splashing and swimming under a rock waterfall as Hazel supervised. They laughed and played with no idea there was danger lurking. No idea that Cole had been taken. When they saw us, they waved and ran to me.

"Careful, you two. Didn't anyone teach you to not run by a swimming pool?" I gently scolded.

"Mar, it's so fun." Meg wrapped her wet body around me. "Are you going to sleep for another three days? You sleep so much lately."

Three days?

Before I could ask Meg what she meant, Miles chimed in. "How long will Cos be painting Mrs. Ward's house? I want him to come back."

Kissing them each on the forehead, I said, "Cole will be excited to swim here with you. He'll be back, soon. We must take care of some things, today. I want you to listen to Hazel and Patrick while I'm gone."

"We will, Mar," Miles promised. "Won't we Meg?"

Meg smiled and winked at me as they scurried back to the pool. Stopping, Meg ran back and wrapped her arms around my waist, squeezing me hard. Before I knew it, she was off, again, walking quickly towards the pool while dragging Miles with her.

"Don't worry, Miss Mara." Patrick appeared and his golden eyes twinkled as he looked at my grandmother. "The little ones will be in good hands with Ms. Hazel and me."

Hugging me, Hazel whispered, "They'll be fine. Patrick is one of Brighid's children. Now, go find Cole and bring him home to us."

Tightly squeezing her, I whispered back, "I'll bring him home. No matter what I find."

"Be safe, love." My grandmother held me tighter. "Goddess, bless and guide this girl."

When we left the hotel, I was surprised the sky was dark, but the full moon cast a glowing light on us. *I'm losing track of time and reality*, I thought. Shaking my head, I turned to address my father. "What was Meg talking about? She said I slept for three days. And why does she think Cole is in Starten?" I questioned.

"I didn't think you needed to know how long you'd been asleep," my father answered. "Meg and Miles kept asking about Cole and it was the first thing I could think of."

"Why didn't you tell them the truth?" I asked. "Tell them there's a horrible person out there that keeps trying to destroy our family."

"Caterpillar, you want me to tell a nine-year-old that a goddess stole Cole and that you fell apart from the pain and heartbreak?" my father replied.

I blanched at his words.

"Oh, Mara, I'm sorry for being short." My father hugged me to him. "I know you're upset...we all are. Kai's been doing everything he can to find out where Cole is. Just be patient and we'll find him."

"Being patient was never my strong point," I said. "It was just horrible to see him —"

"You can't think about any of that," my father advised. "We're dealing with deities dragging us into their war. We will find him, and everything will return to normal."

Normal? I thought. *When was my life ever normal?*

We continued walking past the businesses until we reached a building with a large black and red sign. It read – *Emmett's Rockin' Rides*.

Unlocking the door, Essie led us into a large cement room filled with cars and motorcycles in various states of repair. The smell of oil and tires nauseated me as she led us towards the back of the building. Then, Essie pointed at two strange-looking cars. The vehicles, constructed with heavy metal bars, were just seats set on a frame with two large tires in the back and two smaller ones in the front.

"Elliott suggested we take the dune buggies. Our search will more than likely bring us far into the desert." Essie climbed into the driver seat of the red one.

When Kai took the passenger seat of the yellow vehicle, I reluctantly climbed behind the wheel.

Essie turned over the engine and revved her buggy.

"Lead on, Caterpillar," my father commanded from beside Essie. "We've my future son-in-law to find." Under his breath, he muttered, "Men aren't going to run away anymore in this family."

I focused my attention back onto the machine. Turning the key, the engine rattled. Feeling scared, I closed my eyes and took a deep breath. "I have no idea how to drive this," I called to Essie.

"It's just like the truck," my father called back to me. "Gas, break, shift, and steer. I've seen you drive Gram's wagon. On second thought, just follow Essie out of here."

CHAPTER
EIGHTEEN

Essie slowly led us out onto the main street and stopped. "Follow the paved road out of town," she directed, and then gunned the engine.

My first attempt was an embarrassing lurch. However, once I got going, I drove at a reckless pace. My fingers gripped the steering wheel so tight my knuckles turned white.

"Relax," Kai whispered. "Remember what I taught you."

The familiar feeling of warmth ran through me. This time, my thoughts about the time we kissed did not excite or tempt me. My feelings were focused purely on Cole.

Continuing the drive, we left town just as the sun rose. The desert sky glowed a bright orangish pink. The sun blazed its golden rays as it peeked over the horizon.

A warning sign read – *Pavement Ends*. Slowing, I waited for Kai's directions.

"Turn right at the end of the pavement," Kai instructed, pointing towards a rocky dirt path.

"Really?" I questioned. "Are you sure this will make it?"

"Trust me," he laughed. "This thing was created for roads like this."

Slowing down even more, I made the sharp turn onto the path. The rocky dirt turned out to be a fine sand. We continued for less than a mile before I slammed on the brakes.

"What's wrong, Caterpillar?" my father questioned. "Did you find something?"

"Don't you see it?" I called back to him. A trail of frost shimmered on the sand.

"Follow it, Mara," Essie said. "It'll lead us to Cole."

Worried the hot sun would melt the icy trail, I pushed the gas pedal all the way down and we took off. We flew over the sand like a boat on water until the frosted earth turned to thick patches of ice. Slowing the pace, I watched for signs of Snowystra.

As I drove up and down the desert hills, I anxiously scanned the barren land for any signs of Cole. Abruptly, the ground below us turned from light cream to a black sheet of ice. I hit the brakes, sending us into a spin.

When I finally regained control of the buggy and slammed it to a stop, the air around us blew arctic cold. A darkness fell over us as black, sinister-looking clouds blocked out the sun. Shaking from the intensity of the spin, I closed my eyes.

A low growl sounded. I opened my eyes to see we were surrounded by three men in tattered black clothing. Each had skin so white it was almost translucent. Their black eyes were encircled by dark rings. With cruel smiles, they bared pointed, white teeth. Images of the snapping trout in Starten forest came to mind.

"They've come to find the boy," the tallest man said to his companions, "and they brought one of Danu's pets."

Snarling and snapping their jaws at Kai, the trio advanced on me. A clawed hand grabbed my shoulder, yanked me from the vehicle, and threw me to the ground. The men loomed over me, blocking any escape.

"She can't have him. He belongs to the Winter Goddess now," one of the followers cried out.

Kai jumped out of the buggy and blew a flame of fire at the men. "Get away from her."

"That is all you have? We will not be taking you anywhere," the leader said.

"Cerin, you never learn." Kai rapidly launched fireballs at their legs. The smell of smoke and burning flesh filled my nose. Screaming and rolling on the ground, the men attempted to smother the flames.

Cerin picked me up and used me as a shield. "Now, what will you do?" he sneered.

I kicked and clawed at him. *You can do better than this, Mara,* I scolded myself.

With an evil grin, I summoned a dagger and drove it into my captor's shoulder. He howled in pain and released his hold on me. Before he could use my weapon on me, I threw a gust of wind that swept up all three men. The wind tossed them into the air, and then sent them violently downward. Instead of hitting the soft sand, they crashed into each other as they landed. When they tried to stand, Kai restarted his barrage of fireballs.

Cerin cried out, "Enough! We'll take you to him. Stop with the flames."

Kai snarled at the leader. "You deserve more than the flames I have in store for you."

Again, the men struggled to extinguish the fire that had engulfed them.

I touched Kai's hand, silently telling him to stop. As I walked towards the men, I held my hands to the sky. "Water, I call upon you and ask you to cleanse those who wish to harm."

A heavy rain showered the men, dousing the flames. Falling to the ground, they panted and gasped for air.

Joining me, my father put his hand on the ground and quietly whispered. Under his fingers, thick, green stems sprouted and grew. Pulling hard on the ground, he freed a handful of vines. Handing half to Kai, my father said, "Bind their hands. We don't need any tricks."

"You can't do this." Cerin tried to scramble away from my father. "We will not be treated like animals."

"Until you bring me to Cole, you will be bound. My intention is to free him only, not to harm you." I glared, not hiding the fury I felt towards these men. "When he is safe, I will release you."

"I do not take orders from mortals," Cerin warned. "You're playing with fire."

Holding my hands out to the side, I created two fireballs. Tossing them in the air, I glared. "You have no clue how correct you are. Should we test out exactly how much magic I have inside me? If you're one of Snowystra's peons, I'll be happy to rid the world of all of you."

Focusing my eyes into a cold hate, I bent down to Cerin. Holding the flames close to his face, I hissed. "Mortal or not, I do hold the power inside me to remove you from my presence."

As I raised my arm to throw the ball at him, Essie clasped her fingers tightly around my wrist. "Your grief and fear will not help us," she said. Facing the leader, she commanded, "You will play nice, or I'll permit her to carry out her threats."

Hanging his head in defeat, Cerin whispered, "We can take you to him, but we can't protect you from her."

Kai and my father bound their hands in front of them, leaving a length of the vine for a leash. Cerin and his companions shuffled ahead of them with their heads hung in defeat. Essie and I drove the dune buggies behind.

We had been traveling for so long that the sun had begun to set. My father had turned over the restraints to Kai and rode in the buggy. The Fire elementals energy seemed endless.

"How much further? This better not be a trick," I warned.

The smallest of the men stopped and turned to face me. "I promise, we're bringing you to him."

"Hush, Dunn," Cerin snapped. "Don't speak unless I permit you to do so. *She'll* have to trust us or just get it over with and kill us."

The third man whispered to Dunn, "Don't upset Cerin. It does us no good to have him angry."

Dunn replied with defeat in his voice, "There's no point to any of this, Tynan. Snowystra will make an example out of us. With luck, it will be a quick and painless death for all."

A feeling of pity for the men overcame me. My mind raced. I wouldn't be the cause of anyone's death. Thoughts of how to leave them out of this consumed me.

As if Essie could read my thoughts, her soft voice filled my mind. *You can't punish Snowystra's children from the path she's led them down. At the same time, you can't save them from the choices they continue to make. Listen to your heart, not your rage, and all will be as it should.*

Glancing at her, I raised my eyebrows in response to this unsettling sensation. *You can read my thoughts?*

With a slight nod, she smirked.

For the love of the goddess, I thought. *She's been reading my thoughts this whole time.*

My contemplations were interrupted by the low growl of Cerin. We were approaching a darkened forest. I gasped as the last of the light from the sky shone on a gnarled black and red tree. It dripped with a blood-like substance. The same sticky goo from the vision of my mother and the spider web. Bile rose in my throat. *I can't go in there.*

"We need to settle until the sun rises, again," Kai insisted. "We're not being led into Snowystra's domain during the night."

"Are you afraid of the dark, child of light?" Cerin snarled. "You've bound us. We won't be able to harm you."

"You know damn well they will not be safe in there at night!" Kai shouted, sending his magic through the vines. The men shook as he shocked them. "You were hoping to lead us to one of her dorcha spiders. They're nocturnal feeders."

Essie cut in. "We'll camp away from the forest and enter after dawn."

Kai sighed. "Fine. The three of you sleep and I'll watch them." He pointed at the men. "Sit and remember, if you give me any reason, any reason at all, I'll end you."

When Cerin hesitated, Kai jerked the vine and sent him tumbling to the ground. The other men snickered as they promptly sat down.

Cerin coldly stared at Kai.

I worried what the Fire elemental would do if we left them alone.

Kai is feeding off their anger, the voice of Essie whispered in my head. *We need to calm him. Focus on the love you feel for him and let him know you care.*

I don't love him, I argued.

You do love him, Essie continued. *There are many kinds of love, Mara. Your love for him does not tarnish what you feel for Cole. Your father loved Eliza until the day she died...and still does. This doesn't lessen what he feels for me.*

Her words made sense. I did love Kai. There was definitely an attraction and a passionate desire for him that lingered in the back of my mind. However, I, also, had the kind of love you have for a faithful friend.

Slipping my hand into Kai's, I sent slow pulses of my Air magic onto his skin. "Remember what you taught me. He's baiting you," I whispered, pressing my lips close to his ear.

My touch seemed to reach him. Loosening his grip on the vines, he sighed. "Even an old elemental can forget that darkness will always try to consume light."

"We need to remind each other." I squeezed his hand. "We'll save Cole, together. Unless —"

"There's no unless," Kai insisted.

"Mara," my father called, patting the blanket he'd spread out on the sand in front of the dune buggies. "Come rest."

Hugging Kai tightly, I whispered, "Thank you for being here. It means a lot to me."

"I'll always be here for you, Mara," Kai said in a husky voice. "Always."

As I walked away, I glanced back at Kai. The look of anger was replaced with determination.

"Sleep," Kai commanded. "I'll call you if I need help. I'm sure they'll be on their best behavior."

Cerin turned away in disgust and closed his eyes.

I snuggled into my father's arm, and he kissed me on the forehead. "Sleep, my little caterpillar," he said softly. "Tomorrow, we'll reunite our family."

Again, I thought. *Will there always be someone I love who needs saving from Snowystra?* Resting my head against my father's chest, I slowly drifted off to sleep.

CHAPTER NINETEEN

Something woke me. I wasn't in the desert anymore. *How did I get to the Starten Library?* I wondered. Before I could contemplate my situation, a chill ran through me. *Run,* the voice inside my head screamed.

Without question, I obeyed, and sprinted through the building. Fearful I was being chased, I threw books and knocked over furniture. I didn't stop until I found myself in the back corner of the library. As I turned to hide behind a bookcase, my mother appeared.

"There's nowhere to hide here, Marina," Eliza warned. "You can't run from her."

"How can I trust you?" I stepped back from her.

"I have always loved you, Marina. I'll admit I was jealous of the love my mother felt for you, but I never intended to hurt you. My first love was taken away from me and I fought to reclaim it. Elliott, Meg, and you were unfortunate victims. I did end up loving you all, even as I loved Cedric. Don't hate him. He had no choice in any of this."

She held out her arms towards me. I fell into them and held her tightly. Her scent brought tears to my eyes. *My mother loved me.*

Our moment was interrupted when something tangled into my hair and pulled me away from her. I couldn't see my attacker. Holding tighter to my mother, I struggled to stay in her arms.

"Find the snake. He has the protection," my mother whispered. "It will keep you safe."

I lost my hold and, though I held my arms out towards her, I was dragged further, and further, away. "Eliza!" I screamed. "Help me, Mother!"

I woke in a cold sweat. *It was a dream.* Trying to gather my senses, I looked around the camp we'd made. Essie was on the other side of my father, who was softly snoring. Kai sat on the ground and slowly twisted the vines he was holding. Cerin and Tynan were asleep while Dunn stared nervously at Kai.

Shaking my father awake, I said, "Eliza was here."

"What? Eliza?" He patted my hand. "No, you were dreaming."

"She wasn't here – here," I said with frustration. "She was in my dream. She told me *he* had the snake for protection. We need to find the man she was talking about."

"Honey, it was just a dream. Go back to sleep," my father replied sleepily and closed his eyes, again.

"You're not listening to me," I hissed, not wanting to wake Cerin. "She came to me. She apologized and said she loved me. That she loved Meg. She even said she loved you. I wouldn't dream that! We need to find whoever has the snake."

"You're being hysterical." My father sat up. His face filled with worry. "The stress of everything is catching up with you. Sweetie, please, just put your head back on my shoulder and sleep." With his arm around me, he tried to pull me close, again.

"No, listen to me. We need to find him," I insisted, pushing him away.

Awoken by our conversation, Essie sat up. "Elliott, listen to her," she said, touching my hand. "Mara, calmly tell us what is going on."

Recalling my dream, I told them every detail I could remember. With an intense look, Essie listened. When I finished, she stood up.

"Elliott, you have the snake. Stand up," Essie demanded.

He wrinkled his brow but obeyed. As he stood, she plunged her hands into the front pocket of his blue jeans, fishing for something.

"What are you doing?" my father chuckled as he tried to squirm away. "I have nothing in my pockets, love."

"Nothing?" Essie removed her hands from his jeans and held out a silver ring. The design was a serpent's body, twisted with a curly tail on one end and a head with two small emeralds for eyes on the other. "You always carry this."

Picking up the ring, he stared at it. "This? Oh, this was just —"

Cutting him off, Essie said, "It was from Eliza, and you always have it with you. No need to conceal the truth, love." She kissed his hand. "Just tell us about it. It must mean something for her to have come to Mara's dream and tell her about it."

With his eyes fixated on the ring, he sighed. "Eliza gave me this ring when we were first married. She had a matching one. She told me it would protect me from the darkness. I would tease her when I turned the lights out. I really thought it was just a sweet gesture between newlyweds. It's just a habit to carry it that I didn't break."

"What do you think the ring is for?" I questioned, taking it to examine it closer. "Do you remember what she said when she gave it to you?"

Furrowing his brow, he said, "Mara, that was almost twenty years ago."

"Try to remember." Essie ran her fingertips up his cheek and along his forehead.

With a look of surprise, my father said, "I got it. She'd say 'eight legs of blood, darkness, and death. Fear no more. The serpent protects.'" Rubbing his forehead, he said, "How'd I remember that?"

You did that? You brought back his memory? I mentally asked.

Essie nodded but said nothing on the issue. This was one of those conversations for later, I guessed.

"Let's eat." Essie handed out a strange mash of items in a bar shape. It had nuts, seeds, and what looked like red raisins. After Kai took his, she offered the food to the men. "You must be hungry."

Dunn held out his bound hands to accept it, but Cerin slapped it onto the ground. "Don't take what she offers."

Kai gobbled his breakfast, and said, "It is time to go."

"Yes, we're ready. Get up," my father ordered the men. "With the protection of the goddesses, we'll find Cole."

"No," I said to my father. "Not all of us are going. Kai and I'll go alone. You have to go back to Meg and Miles. They need you."

"I'm not letting you –" he argued.

"Trust me, please. You need to keep them safe."

"At least, put on the clothes I've packed for you." Essie offered me a satchel.

Inside the leather bag were a cap, long black pants, black socks with flat soles, and a long sleeve shirt to match. As I ran my hands over the silky fabric, it warmed to my touch. "Thank you," I said before dressing. I tucked the hat back into the bag. When I was as mentally prepared as I could be, I said, "OK, time to say goodbye."

Relenting, my father kissed me on the cheek. "I'm sorry I can't protect you from all the darkness in the world, Caterpillar. Bring Cole home."

Watching my father and Essie leave, I wondered if this was the last time I would see either of them.

CHAPTER
TWENTY

Cerin led us back to the crimson forest. The ground was covered with a spongy moss, coated in the sticky ooze. We trudged through the woods, trusting it wasn't a trap. After a small hike, the men stopped in front of an enormous tree with a trunk, at least, twenty feet wide and over a hundred feet tall. The top of it was thin and had twisted downward. Its long branches weaved together, creating the illusion of a spider's web.

Sticking his bound hand through the tree, Cerin said, "We need to go through here."

Recalling the vision I had of Eliza being dragged through the tree, I froze. I remembered Cedric trapped on a spider web. Snowystra's cruel torture, along with the blood and terrifying screams it caused, echoed in my mind. My blood ran cold reliving the memory. Backing away, I bumped into Kai.

"What's wrong, Mara?" Kai put his hand on my shoulder. "What did you see?"

"It looks like the tree Blanche took Eliza into...where Snowystra cut Cedric's face," I said, my voice shaking. "It's horrible in there. There are spider webs covering the room and the remains of their feeding."

Glaring at Cerin, my hands burned with fire. "Do you plan to feed us to your spiders in there?" I spat the words at him. "Or do you plan to throw us on one of the webs to wait for Snowystra?"

For the first time since we met, Cerin looked meek. "N-n-no," he stammered. "That was not my intention. I have no plans to face the goddess. Once you find him, I plan on disappearing. You're bringing us to our deaths."

I lowered the flames in my hands to small sparks. "Is he telling the truth, Dunn?"

With sadness in his eyes, Dunn nodded. "Yes. This is the only way to get to your...the boy."

"His name is Cole," I said, eyeing him. "If you're lying and this is a trick, my response will not be kind."

"No trick," he said, shaking his head. "I promise you. You're correct. This is like the tree your mother was taken through, but I doubt it's the exact one. This is just one of many portals Snowystra has created. We will go through the dorcha spiders' room, but I assure you, they'll be sleeping deep underground. We will tread lightly through their area to ensure we do not wake them. I swear."

"The sooner we go through, the sooner we can prove we're not lying. And the sooner we can get away from here." Cerin held out his bound arms. "Untie us and we'll be able to move faster."

"Not you," Kai said as he removed the ties from Dunn and Tynan. "You'll stay like this until you lead us through."

"Fine," Cerin snarled. "Dunn will lead the way. I'll follow."

I dug through my bag and pulled out the cap. It was made from the same silky material as the clothes. Dreading the thought of the ooze getting stuck in my hair, I double-checked that any stray hairs were tucked away.

"When you're ready," Cerin said, looking around. "We might be noticed if we linger."

Once again, I found myself walking through a warm, sticky liquid. The pungent scent made me gag.

"What is that smell?" I covered my nose with my free hand before realizing I was covered in slime, and I had no way to wipe it off.

"It's the remains of the dorcha's feeding time. Their home is through there." Dunn pointed towards a small opening. Then, as we entered the den, he abruptly laid his finger against his lips, signaling us to be quiet.

When my eyes adjusted to the dark room, I searched the cave for the exit. Wall-to-wall, thick spider webs were everywhere. Some had small, wrapped things caught in them. I assumed these were unlucky victims. The floor was scattered with bones and the remains of animals. I even saw human shapes cocooned in the silky threads.

My inspection was interrupted by a rustling sound coming from the corner of the room. I held back a scream. We were not alone. Silver eyes glowed on a metallic green, eight-legged spider that was moving slowly towards me. At the end of its eight legs were silver spikes. *Dorcha*.

I was paralyzed by fear. My inaction was a mistake. Before I could understand what was happening, the dorcha leaped at me, knocking me down. I forced a gust of wind at the creature, pushing it back. However, it wasn't swayed and, once again, charged at me.

Before it reached me, Kai threw himself onto the beast. With a strength that surprised me, he ripped a leg off the spider and stabbed it into its own back. As he drove the improvised stake deeper, the dorcha shrieked and threw Kai across the room. Landing on a web, Kai was immobilized.

Our guides watched us but offered no assistance.

"You lied!" I screamed at them.

"Quickly, finish it off," Dunn cried out. "Others will come."

Summoning a Fire sword, I charged the spider, driving the blade into its side. Red blood gushed from the wound. I stabbed it, again. An image of Snowystra came to mind and a fury built inside me. I continued my assault in a blind rage. The blade became stuck, so I punched and kicked at the spider.

"Mara, stop." Kai pulled me off the lifeless corpse. "It's dead."

I looked at the deceased monster beneath me. My anger was not satiated. Ripping the sword out of the spider, I pointed it at the three men. "Give me a reason."

Kai touched my hand, sending his elemental power through my body. A burst of clarity rushed through me. The tranquil feeling ended when I looked down on the dead creature, and then at Snowystra's minions.

They led us into the den and watched as I killed it. I'll take care of them when we're out of here. First, I need them to find where he's being kept, I bitterly thought.

"Enough games. Take me to Cole," I insisted.

Dunn led us through the room until we reached a small boulder. Pushing the rock away, he whispered, "Through here."

The rock had been covering a dark tunnel too small to walk upright in.

Dropping the sword, it sizzled on the ground and disappeared.

We crawled through the tight space until it became necessary to slither along the ground. The clothing I was wearing seemed to be making it easier to slide. After a few minutes, the area widened and the ceiling above grew larger until we were able to crawl, again, and then walk towards the bright light at the end of the tunnel.

When we reached the exit, the light was so blindingly bright that it was difficult to keep my eyes open. Squinting to see where I had been led, my eyes adjusted, and I could see a snowy tundra. Powder white snow stretched for miles, and miles, with no end in sight.

As the men following exited the tunnel, I threw a strong wind at them, knocking them to the ground.

"We didn't know the dorcha would be awake," Cerin said, standing up to face me.

I threw several fireballs at him He screamed as he beat the fire out.

"Enough," Cerin cried. "Do you want us to take you to the boy or not?"

He's right. You need them to find Cole, I chastised myself. "Any more tricks and I'll feed you to the spiders myself," I snarled.

The men bowed their heads in submission.

I whispered to Kai. "Where are we?"

"Snowstrum," Kai answered. "*Her* realm."

The reality of our situation hit me. We would, soon, be at her mercy. *What have you gotten me into, Cole?* I thought bitterly.

Composing myself, I forced my mind to take control of my emotions. My eyes glanced over the men around me. There was so much blood coating them. Seeing my own hand, I remembered my face was streaked with the thick goo, as well.

"Clean yourselves up," I ordered before dropping to the ground.

Frantically, I rubbed my hands in the snow, turning it pink. The tinted snow horrified me. Scooping up a handful of the white powder, I called Fire to melt it. I rinsed my hat and used it to clean off the sticky blood.

With every inch of me scrubbed red, I buried the cap under the snow. I didn't want to carry around the reminder. With a final inspecting of my clothing, I noticed the only part of me that had been covered with gunk was my skin. The fabric of my outfit had repelled it.

"You missed a spot." Kai wiped my cheek. "There you go. No more signs of the dorcha on you."

"We'll want to move quickly," Dunn warned. He was cleaner, but his clothes showed signs of our fireballs.

Guilt washed over me. Shivering at the thought of what we might find, I said, "Let's go."

Crunching through the snow, we kept a quick pace. My mind wandered. *Is Cole safe? Will he still love me, or does he now love her? Will I be able to remove whatever spell she's put on him?*

A sudden awareness, of how cold my face was, came over me. My body was warm, but my exposed parts felt like ice. Holding my cupped hands over my face, I exhaled. The warm air from my body collected in my hands, and I tried using it to heat my face.

"It's so cold out here," I said to Dunn. "How do you tolerate it?"

Shrugging, he said, "Cold doesn't bother me. I find it rather pleasant."

A warmth came from behind me, and I knew Kai was close. "I forgot your human body isn't meant for such extreme temperatures," he whispered in my ear. His hot breath danced around me, taking the chill off my skin.

"Thank you," I said with a smirk.

As we continued, Kai intermittently sent heat towards me. The warm air was so strong, at times, that the snow melted, leaving puddles. Dunn and the other men seemed uncomfortable by this.

"Is the heat bothering you?" I asked.

"No, it's his magic," Dunn answered honestly. "The magic of our goddesses doesn't mix well. I'm sure if I used my mag —" Abruptly, he held his hand out. "Go behind me and play along."

"What?" I questioned.

A dark-haired woman stepped out of a concealed cave. It was too late for me to hide. She saw me.

The woman looked me up and down. Her facial features were similar to the men's. I knew she had to be another one of Snowystra's children.

Like the others, she had an animalistic appearance — sharp teeth, claw-like nails, and messy chin-length hair tangled.

"Where have you been? What's this?" the woman demanded.

Cerin stepped forward. His hands were no longer bound, and he was now pulling Kai. I started to question him when a dark look from Kai warned me to stay silent.

"Look who we found — Marina Stone and her Fire elemental snooping around outside the dorcha cave," Cerin sneered. "They are looking for Mother's new pet."

Cackling, the woman circled me. "You captured her?" she interrogated. "Wait, didn't she kill her own mother? Are you stupid? Why isn't she bound?"

Unable to control my anger, I felt the flames begin to grow on my hand and the air blew around me. "No one captured me. I have brought these fools to exchange for Cole," I snapped. "Now, take me to Cole. I have no time for games or silly girls."

Her black eyes bore into mine. "You want me to believe that Marina Stone, daughter of Eliza Drygen, is exchanging Danu's child for one man?" she scoffed.

I held my glowing hand to her face. As she shrunk away from the heat of my magic, I blew out the fire. I grabbed a fistful of her hair and leaned in close. I felt pain from the jolts of her magic pricking my skin. "Not just a child of Danu. I have brought her most devout Fire elemental. I'll do whatever it takes to take back what is mine."

When she held her head up defiantly towards me, I said, "Do you want to be my first victim, today? Snowystra may not like it if I start picking off her children, one-by-one."

Laughing, she said, "So much anger inside you. You are Eliza's child."

Throwing her to the ground and imitating the darkness I had seen in my mother, I glared and turned to Cerin. "Take me to Cole before I do something I might, later, regret."

His dark laughter startled me. "Let's find what you're looking for. Malise, join us."

Standing up and wiping herself off, Malise stared at me suspiciously, and then took Cerin's hand. Taking a deep breath, I let him lead me into the cave.

Long icicles hung from the lofty ceilings. The temperature in the tunnel was even colder than outside. Cerin guided us past several openings, where people slept on the hard floor. Everyone we saw had tattered clothes and sad faces.

Suddenly, I heard hushed voices from behind me. Stopping and turning to where the noise was coming from, I saw Tynan whispering in Malise's ear. Before I could say anything, Cerin jumped and grabbed her arm.

"What trouble are you stirring up, now?" he hissed.

"You should be answering that question," Malise snarled back at him. "Tynan told me how you submitted to her...how you didn't even fight."

Clamping his hand over her mouth, Cerin dragged her into one of the rooms. She clawed and fought against his hold. When he reached a bookshelf covered in bottles, he picked up a glass container of black liquid. Ripping the top off with his teeth, he, then, poured it into her mouth.

She sputtered and tried to spit it out. Her attempts were futile. Eventually, her eyes closed and collapsed to the ground.

Cerin shoved another bottle at Tynan. "Drink it and live. You can blame everything on me when we escape."

With a look of sorrow, Tynan accepted the vial. "I wasn't going to tell the goddess what happened." In defeat, he sat down next to Malise and drank. Moments later, he was slumped over, too.

"Dunn, do you want to join them?" Cerin glared.

"No, she'll be the one to bring change." Dunn pointed at me. His small pointy teeth glistened. "I'll take her to the boy, if you're too afraid."

Unexpectedly, Cerin punched him in the face. "Learn your place."

Dunn backed away and wiped the blood from his mouth. "Fighting each other never has worked, Cerin."

"Enough." I stepped between the men. "Are they dead?" I asked, staring at Malise and Tynan.

"No, they are sleeping," Kai said. "It's tumma uni. It helps them sleep and restore their magic."

"It's a sleeping aid?" I said. "Why would you need that?"

Looking away, Dunn said, "Sometimes, the death and sorrow that surrounds us is too much. When we sleep, we dream of more pleasant things. The Vetur go mad at very young ages unless they can carve out small bits of peace. Unlike the Ceithre, we are of death and darkness."

"Ceithre?" I asked.

Pointing towards Kai, Dunn said, "Danu's children. They are the lucky ones. I've seen their world. Quite different from here, for sure."

Shaking off the sadness that was creeping into his eyes, Dunn touched my hand. "Malise and Tynan will be fine. Now, let's find your Cole."

Continuing down the hallway, I stared at the sleeping Vetur. I no longer feared them. My thoughts were more of sympathy. I had seen the world Kai lived in. It was a world of magic, elemental enchantments, and light. Danu's children were happy and content. This world was the complete opposite.

My considerations were halted when Dunn stopped outside the entrance of a large room. Peeking from behind the solid ice door, I found my fiancé sitting on a dark throne atop a stone platform located in the back of the room. I chocked back a gasp.

Cole's hair was cut short and spiked with white tips. He was dressed in a tight black T-shirt and black pants. His dark appearance barely resembled the sweet boy from my childhood.

CHAPTER
TWENTY-ONE

An anger brewed inside me as I watched Cole drinking and laughing. Dozens of men and women hovering around him. While I was fighting to find him, he was having a party.

All the women wore skimpy black dresses. The low-cut plunging necklines and short skirts were connected on the side with solid cloth but did nothing to conceal their snow-white skin. Several of the scantily clad women pushed and pulled each other, trying to get closer to Cole. The one who made it to the spot closest to him fed him and kissed him.

Cole gave no objections to any of the attention he was receiving, infuriating me. The slow boiling rage inside me was going to flow over. I was going to stop this – now.

Before I could enter the room, Dunn stopped me. "Wait."

I slipped further back and watched. A young woman nervously approached Cole. When she reached him, she adjusted her sparse clothing and patiently waited at the bottom of a staircase.

When he finally decided to acknowledge her, he motioned for the woman to come forward.

She quickly climbed the set of stone stairs and bowed before him. In response, he waved his hand, and she offered Cole a clear goblet filled with bright red liquid.

Drinking it down in one gulp, Cole frowned. "That wasn't what I asked for."

Anger blazed in his eyes, and he threw the glass down at the woman's feet, shattering it. Then, he jumped up and slapped the woman across the face with the back of his hand. The force sent her off the platform and onto the floor.

This man could not be Cole Sands, the man I loved. Cole was kind and considerate. He would never treat anyone with such hate, and he would never strike a woman.

"All of you will do as I ask, or I'll tell *her* I'm unhappy and that you're the cause," Cole growled.

The woman limped as she returned. He smiled wickedly and snatched another cup from a nearby woman. He threw the drink on the injured woman. "Clean up this mess," he laughed.

The woman trembled but picked up the pieces of glass. She tore off a bit of her skirt to sop up the liquid. When she finished, Cole snarled. "Go, again, and get me what I asked for."

"I'm sorry," the woman said, bowing her head, and scurried away.

Seizing the opportunity, I tried to enter the room again. This time Kai stopped me.

"Come away from the door," he whispered.

"I need to go to him," I said. "I can bring him to his senses."

"Mara, you can't go in there, now. He's too angry. He won't hear you," Kai replied.

"I can calm him," I insisted, but doubt filled my mind at my own words. *It's too late. We've lost Cole to the darkness.*

Anger filled me. You're going to give up that easy? No. You can reach him. Go to him, I thought to myself. "I'll convince him that you'll submit to Snowystra. I can make him believe me," I said. *Make him believe? How am I going to make him...?*

Taking the vine from Kai, I bound his wrists. He eyed me with interest.

"I'm going to bring all of you to Cole. This will show him how strong my power was to defeat his men...and how serious I am by bringing you as an offering."

"Or, leave now and forget him," Cerin suggested.

"The love I have for Cole is stronger than any magic," I insisted. "Why do you care about me all of a sudden?"

"I have nothing left to lose. Dunn is right. You might be the answer we hoped for," Cerin admitted. "But don't say you weren't warned when your plan fails."

Returning to the hall entrance, with the men bound behind me, the woman Cole had struck rushed past me with a new drink in her hand. I grabbed her wrist, stopping her. "Take the drink and go. He no longer wants it."

Seeing the anger in my eyes, she nodded and rushed to a dark corner of the room. Pushing back my shoulders and putting on a confident, but dark smile, I walked slowly towards Cole. When his icy eyes locked with mine, a cruel smile formed on his face.

"If it isn't the great Marina Stone," Cole crowed. He scowled when he saw Kai behind me. "And, she has brought her boyfriend with her. I see you quickly found another to replace me, Marina. I guess you needed someone to be at your beck and call with me gone? How lucky for him to be the strong man, able to pick up the shattered little girl who lost her grandmother?"

I ignored his cruel words and climbed the stairs. Counting the steps to him, I tried to keep my hard demeanor. When I left the thirteenth step, I found myself standing on the platform, face-to-face with Cole.

"Cole, I have come all of this way to be with you and this is the greeting you give me?" I feigned dismay. "How disappointing. I've even brought gifts." I tugged hard on the vines, pulling Kai, Dunn, and Cerin forward, and caused them to stumble at the bottom of the stairs. "Kneel before him," I commanded.

"You brought me your Fire elemental?" Cole's eyes filled with doubt. "You think I'm naïve enough to believe this? You'd never cross Danu. No! Poor, poor Marina abandoned by Mommy and Daddy. Always so weak and fragile. You're not strong enough to do anything so bold."

The crowd around him snickered.

Taking a slow breath, not wanting to show my anger, I narrowed my eyes at him. "I brought him to you to prove I won't let anyone stand in the way of our happiness." I softly cupped his cheek. "All of it means nothing to me without you. It's you who matters...only you who ever mattered. Snowystra wants me to join her court, but it seems she'll have to pick which one of us to keep, since you don't seem to want me anymore."

Walking around the throne, I trailed my nails slowly along the cold metal. Along the way, I sent a small jolt of my magic through each of the Vetur surrounding him. Several leaned towards me, as if entranced by the touch. "Yes, they'd follow me. With her magic and mine, I'd be unstoppable."

After I made the full circle, I stopped in front of Cole, cocking my head to the side. "So, darling. It appears you have a choice to make. Will you leave willingly, before Snowystra returns, or will I have to have you removed?" I asked.

When he did not respond, I said, "Your choice. I'll have to remove you from your throne myself." Snapping my fingers, I called a ball of fire and prepared to throw it at him.

With a cold laugh, Cole grabbed my wrist and leaned in close. "Extinguish the fire. You know you don't want to use that on me."

"Are you sure about that?" I asked, calling the second orb.

Cole wrapped his arms around my waist and pulled me against him. Staring intently at me, he picked me up and kissed me hard.

The fire I was holding smoked and fizzled into nonexistence. I wanted to push him away. Instead, I bit his lip.

He didn't let go of me. Rather, he growled and trailed his mouth along my neck. The feeling of love I'd always felt when he held me was gone. This wasn't love...he was claiming me.

Releasing me, Cole laced his fingers into mine. "Aren't you bold? I knew you'd come to your senses." Directing his attention towards the Vetur, he cried, "When our goddess returns, together, we'll lead you."

Cheers from the crowd echoed in the tomblike room.

Cole set me down on the seat next to him. He placed me in the middle of women, who trembled with fear when I met their eyes. Quietly, they moved away from me. Cole leaned close and I could see the dark circles around his frost blue eyes.

"We'll reign here under the guidance of our goddess. Snow will give us our heart's desire," Cole said in a low ominous voice.

Abruptly, one of the women pushed between us and shoved me away from Cole. "I was here first. You're Ceithre. You have no right to be on this throne."

Pointing a finger blazing with fire towards her, I glared and poked her hard, burning a small hole into her dress. "You will not talk to me unless I address you. He's mine. Any grand ideas you had to be his queen were ridiculous. Now, go before I make you sorry. Playtime is over."

Moving away from me, the woman glared and looked towards the others. None of them were brave enough to try, again, to be close to Cole. Instead, they nervously watched on as the first woman regained her courage to confront me.

"Don't, Dima," one of the women whispered.

Dismissing her warning, Dima stood over me. "You don't get to choose." Pointing at Cole, she snarled, "He decides who stays or goes."

Surprisingly, her hands filled with her own magic. The green liquid she held bubbled and popped, and I could feel its electricity. Looking at her with pity, I called a large gust of air and sent her flying off the stone platform. She landed hard on the steps.

"He has chosen," I hissed. "You can choose to live by removing yourself from my sight. Or you can be stupid and try to get in my way."

Not backing down, Dima stood up to face me, again. This time, I threw another gust of strong wind at her, followed by small sparks of fire.

The wind pushed her back as the embers landed on her skin. The woman screamed in pain and frantically patted out the flames.

Feeling inspired, I called raindrops to make the floor slippery.

The woman fell hard. This time, she stayed on the ground, cowering.

Laughing at my violent outburst, Cole pulled me towards him. Turning and glaring at Kai, he said, loud enough for everyone in the room to hear, "You're right. I did choose you. Now, you need to prove you're choosing me and get rid of them."

"Excuse me, mi Shah." Dunn stepped forwards and bowed. "If you allow the binds to be removed, it would be my honor to take care of this insult to our goddess. I'll remove him from your presence, so you can focus on what is important."

Cole looked him up and down before agreeing. "Fine. Take them to the pit. The dorcha will be awakening, soon, and the fresh meat will please them."

"As you wish." Dunn motioned to a guard to remove the binds. Then, he held his free hand out to me, and said, "Mistress, you dropped this." Placing the snake ring in my hand, he added, "I'll take care of this problem immediately. I hope this will win your forgiveness for my failure."

With those words, Dunn turned to Kai and struck him in the face with his fist. When Kai fell to the ground, Dunn began to kick and punch him.

Cole watched with a sly smile on his face as the attack continued.

Cerin became tangled in the vine that still bound him to Kai and fell to the ground.

Fighting back my urge to stop the beating, I made my face appear stone cold. I thought of Blanche Drygen and the unfeeling aura she emitted. I, even, forced myself to smirk at each punch, slap, and kick as Kai cried out in pain.

The violence pleased the Vetur, and they cheered as they watched on.

I had to convince Cole I didn't care about the Fire elemental. I couldn't prevent this from happening. Instead, I laughed with the crowd, and occasionally threw small fireballs at the fighting men.

Out of the corner of my eye, I saw that Cole was pleased by my reaction. After watching the brutal beating for what was probably less than three minutes, I longed to look away. Yawning, I held my hand out in front of me. I inspected my nails as if I was extremely bored. Suddenly, an idea came to my mind. It was risky, but I decided to take a chance and push Cole to end this.

Tugging Cole's hand until he sat down, I climbed onto his lap. As he watched the violence around me, I ran my fingers through his hair and kissed his neck. As I did this, a few of the bolder women moved forward and touched him, trailing sparks of their magic. I glared at them until they shrunk away.

"This is boring," I whispered into his ear, fighting my urge to call a strong wind and send the still hovering women flying off the stone, like I had just sent Dima. "Make them *all* go away, and we can make up for lost time. If we're alone, I could show you how much I've missed you." Kissing him hard on the mouth, I dared to pull his hair.

Cole groaned in pleasure at my forcefulness. My calculated risk paid off. He stood up, knocking me off him, and cried, "Stop! Enough. Take them away. Out of my sight."

Dunn stopped his attack and forced the men to their feet. They had blood running down their swollen faces. Thankfully, my back was facing Cole, so I was able to hide my feelings of disgust and worry as I watched Kai and Cerin being led away.

"What about them?" I motioned to the women around us. "I want them gone, too."

The women fearfully stared at me, and Cole ordered, "Join your brothers and sisters below. I want you all to be here for my announcement. Bring the box to me."

Quickly running down the stairs, the women joined the surrounding Vetur. The ones who had been hiding in the shadows slowly crept out.

Cole stood on edge of the stone. He smiled as the crowd parted for three guards, surrounding one small woman.

The woman held a small box. The item she was carrying was so tiny that it seemed excessive to need three large men to guard it. She climbed the stairs alone and nervously offered Cole the box. When he took it, glaring at the bearer, she bowed deeply and returned to the guards.

Cole reached into the box and pulled out a silver band with a large red jewel on it. Inside the gem, small bubbles danced around. Holding the ring out to me, he said, "Does this please you? If not, I'll get you a larger stone or a different color. Whatever you want. Tell me your wishes."

Looking at it, I said, "It's nice, but the ring I'll wear for eternity should show the world how much you love and adore me. This ring does not."

Once again, he reached into the box and pulled out another ring. This one took my breath away. The stone was a solid red color. The diamond was beautiful, but it was the silver band that gave me joy. On each side of the square cut diamond, the infinity symbol had been etched. This small symbol was the same as the one engraved on the small ring Cole had given me when he asked me to marry him.

"You didn't think I'd give you that other tacky piece of glass, did you?" Cole slipped the ring onto my finger. "This is the ring I've always wanted to put on your finger. Marina, will you marry me and commit your life to the Vetur?"

Looking into his eyes, I searched for any sign that Cole was in there. "I'll marry, Cole Oliver Sands — the boy I grew up with, the boy I've always loved. I vow to stand by his side."

For the briefest of moments, Cole's eyes flickered from the icy blue to a bright blue, and he gently kissed me. This kiss was from my Cole. It was not demanding nor territorial.

Beaming, Cole cried out, "She's accepted my proposal. Soon, you'll all reap the benefits of our magnificent union. In the name of our Goddess, Snowystra, I present Marina to you as the future Vizier — the queen of the Vetur. Your time in the shadows will soon come to an end."

Murmurs of excitement filled the room. As I looked at the dark eyes of my future subjects, I felt their hope. Feeling guilty that I was lying to them, I stepped back into the shadows.

"Planning a wedding of this size is impossible," I said to Cole. "I don't even have a dress to wear."

"All of that will be taken care of," he said as he took my hand. "Come sit. Bask in your subjects' adoration. I don't think you understand how powerful you'll be. Soon, you'll find out."

Cole sat down and handed me a goblet of red liquid. Shaking my head, I said, "No, I'm not thirsty."

He pressed the cold glass to my lips, and insisted, "Drink."

"What is —" I started to say, but before I finished asking the question, he poured a small amount of the thick liquid into my mouth. As it slid down my throat, it seemed to solidify. It felt like I had just swallowed sticks of ice, and I'd been dunked into a tank of icy water.

Shivering, I wrapped my arms around myself, trying to warm up. In response, I felt the elemental magic inside me begin to push back. It felt like a ray of sunshine was inside me, fighting against the cold.

Again, Cole put the cup to my mouth. "Drink more. You'll feel warm very soon. When I pulled away, he said, "Just as I thought, all of this is a game to you. You're not here for me...for her. You have no intention of being loyal to Snowystra or the Vetur."

"No, that isn't true." I yanked the glass out of his hand. "If you would've asked me to drink it, I would have. Instead, you chose to force me, without telling me what it is or its significance."

Putting the glass to my lips, I slowly drank the vile liquid. My magic, once again, fought against the cold invading me and I willed it to pull back. Imagining Earth creating a shell of protection around the Water, Fire, and Air running through me, I slowly felt the magic retreat and I was consumed by the snowstorm going on inside me.

A sharp pain radiated in my chest. *Not now*, I thought. Slowly breathing, I focused my eyes on Cole. I wasn't going to allow myself to slip into the darkness. Not here...not now.

Essie, please, tell me you're all OK, I pleaded in my mind. *Tell Kai and my father that I'm sorry for what happened. I'm to marry Cole, here. If I don't come home soon, please, find a way to bind my magic. I'm worried I'm going to end up like my mother.*

Cole handed me another glass. "A few more and you'll no longer feel the cold."

"At least, tell me what this is," I said, my voice beginning to slur.

"It will strengthen you. Soon, you'll have much stronger magic inside you." Cole took the empty glass from me. "Tell me what you desire, and it'll be yours."

My eyes felt heavy. "I want to sleep." I closed my eyes and leaned back. Suddenly, the pain in my chest returned. Clutching my chest, I screamed as the world around spun.

Cole's hands tightly gripped my shoulders, and he shook me. "Did you bring me the wrong drink?" he screamed. "If she dies, you will all pay!" Whispering in my ear, he pleaded, "Don't leave me, Mara. I need you."

The words from the Cole I loved were the last thing I heard before I slipped into unconsciousness.

Once again, I woke in a pure white room. There was no one here. No sound. No smells. A complete room of isolation. There was just silence. Surveying the space, I searched for any exits.

"You're playing a dangerous game," a male voice said. "My daughter is the result of pain and sorrow. She can be contained, but not eliminated. What are you doing playing with darkness? Do you think you can really resist the temptations? Do you think you can withstand her cruelty?"

"Alaunius?" I questioned.

"Yes, child," he said. "You paid attention to my beloved's story, I see."

I noticed, for the first time since I woke, that I was dressed in a white, shapeless gown and my feet were bare. Touching my hair, I felt it was twisted into a tight bun. "Am I dead?" I asked.

He shook his head. "You'll be faced with a decision. Your choice will affect more than just you."

The room filled with a black smoke, and I found myself unable to take a breath. Hands came from the darkness, grabbing and pulling me at me.

"Help us," the voices cried.

Something slithered along my leg and up my body. I fought against it as it continued climbing. Wrapping around my neck, it tightened, choking me. The harder I struggled, the tighter it wound itself.

As I gripped harder against the constriction, it moved, allowing me to take in a gulp of air. I found myself staring into the red, glowing eyes of a snake.

Hissing, it said, "You'll not be able to save them...if you can't save yourself."

CHAPTER
TWENTY-TWO

"She's breathing," a woman said. "Send for him. Tell him she's awake."

Opening my eyes, I found myself propped up in a large bed, covered with a silver and black blanket. A long dresser, crowded with trinkets, gems, and jewels, was next to a window shaded by a heavy dark red curtain. From the ceiling, long icicles hung down, emitting a soft glow.

In the corner, a woman sat quietly reading. Another woman stood beside the bed, watching me. Both looked much different from the Vetur I had seen earlier. They wore dark, modest dresses, tight buns, and no makeup on their wrinkled skin. They looked human.

When I tried to sit up, the woman nearest to me rushed to offer her assistance. "Careful, you need to rest," she said. Her warm smile showed normal teeth, confirming she was not Vetur.

Leaning into me, she whispered in my ear, "Your envelope and ring are safe under your pillow."

"Who are you?" I whispered back to her. "You're not one of them."

"My name is Christina," she said loud enough for the other woman to hear. "Over there's Laura. We're Snowystra's mortals. Rest now, sweet girl. The Shah will be here, soon."

Laying back down, I turned onto my side and slipped my hand under the pillow. I found the envelope and ring. *Essie,* I tried, again, hoping to connect with my family.

After several minutes, there was no response.

Resting myself upright on the pillow, I said, "Christina, I want to prepare myself. Cole can't see me this way."

"I don't think it's wise for you to be up so soon," Christina argued. "The verijuoma has weakened you."

"Please," I said. "I feel strong enough."

Relenting, she drew back the covers and helped me sit up. As my feet touched the solid ice floor, I stared down in wonder. I knew it was cold, but it felt pleasant. Slowly, I walked towards the window.

"Please, open this," I said. "I want to see outside."

With the curtains open, I could see snow-capped mountains in the distance through air filled with swirling snowflakes. Brief glimpses of the roof below confused me. Realizing I was not in the underground tunnel anymore, I felt panicked.

"Where am I?" I asked, fearing the answer to my question.

"You're in one of the goddesses' homes," Christina said. Leaning in, as if she was supporting me, she whispered, "Don't worry. She isn't here at the moment."

Relief flooded me. "Please, show me where there are clothes for me to wear," I requested. "I need something more –"

"You look lovely as you are," Cole called from behind me.

Nervously turning to face him, I focused on the fact I was supposed to be the cold follower of the dark goddess, now.

"Lovely? I look like a lamb being readied for the slaughter," I sniped.

Cole strode over to me and took my hands. His demeanor was kind, and his tone was soft. "Come sit," he said, guiding me to a chair. "When you're feeling better, I can show you around your new home and we can finalize the wedding plans."

Not sure whether this was a trick or not, I decided to play it safe and maintain a cold persona. "I'm perfectly fine, except for the hideous clothing you have me in," I said with disgust. "Why are you delaying the wedding? Are you having cold feet?"

Laughing, Cole replied, "Quite the opposite. Say the word and we can marry, right now."

"Since we're only having one wedding, I probably should let you have time to plan a fabulous event. Is tomorrow too soon?"

Locking eyes with me, I felt as if he was trying to read my mind. Focusing my thoughts on the love I felt for him, I watched him soften. "Tomorrow it is," he smiled.

"Considering the clothing chosen for me, I'll want to see all you have planned for me to wear ahead of time," I demanded.

"I told you that you can have anything you want. There's a closet of clothing through there for you." Cole motioned towards a door. "If none of the choices please you, we'll bring more. Just ask and I'll get it for you."

Kissing me on the cheek, Cole said, "I promise you'll like the dress I have selected for you. Now, get yourself ready. We'll have a busy day. That is, unless you feel weak, again."

"I'll be fine," I reassured him. "Any planning that needs to be done can start now."

"Wonderful." Cole clapped his hands together. "Then, get yourself ready and you can join me for a late breakfast."

Before I had a chance to formulate a dismissive response, he left the room. His walk was full of energy, and he almost seemed like my Cole.

Oddly enough, I wanted to scream at him and hurt him like he'd hurt me. My thoughts were confused. I felt a darkness inside me that I had never felt before. *Is this anger I kept bottled inside or is it from being here?*

My thoughts halted when Laura offered me a crystal goblet. The glass was filled with the dark red verijuoma. Wrinkling my nose in disgust at the offering, I shook my head.

"The Shah has insisted you have this before joining him," Laura said. "If you don't drink it willingly, I'll need to call for assistance."

"She'll drink it, Laura." Christina took the glass from her. "Won't you?"

"Yes," I said, glaring at both women, "but I prefer to have it while I'm taking a bath." *So, I can dump it down the drain.*

"Fine," Laura snapped. "Make sure you watch her drink it. He'll know if she doesn't."

Christina nodded. "Yes, but first, let's get her ready for her big day. There's much to do." Offering her hand to me, she said, "Whenever you're ready."

Accepting her hand, I followed her into the oversized bathroom. Setting the drink down on the edge of the black, oval bathtub, she turned the water on.

Watching Christina turn the water in the coldest direction, I corrected her, "I don't like cold bath water."

Turning the water temperature up, she said, "Test the water temperature here. I think you'll find you prefer it a bit colder, now."

Holding my fingers under the water, I jerked my hand out of the stream in surprise. "You burned me." I stared at the water. There wasn't any steam.

"No, your body is changing." Christina turned the water flow back to the coldest temperature. "Trust me. I've no reason to lie to you."

Carefully dipping my fingers in to retest it, I found the icy temperature inviting. Uninhibited, I slipped off my clothes and stepped into the tub. Sinking into the water, I closed my eyes and sighed as I savored the frigid temperature.

"You'll need to drink this," Christina said, interrupting my relaxation.

Ignoring her, I kept my eyes closed, wishing I could make the water even colder.

"You can drink this, or I can call Laura in to help. Your choice," Christina said as if she was scolding a naughty child.

Opening my eyes, I glared at her.

"Drink some of it to keep the winter's chill inside you."

"If I drink this, my magic will turn dark."

"Mara, your magic is protected," she said. "You've done a very good job of guarding the gift."

"How do you know about that?" I asked. "Will Cole know? Will Snowystra?"

"Stop, child." Lowering her voice to just above a whisper, she leaned close to me. "I'm one of Arianolwyn's chosen. I can't stop you from making the choice to willingly follow Snowystra, but I can help you fight it, if that's what you wish."

Calling my magic, I found my hands covered in a green sparking liquid. "This magic?" I questioned. "Is this my magic I've protected?"

Christina took my hand into hers. She didn't flinch at the pain I must have been causing her. "You know that isn't the magic gifted to you. Now, drink this, please."

Her gentle words calmed me, and I reluctantly took the glass, drinking it all.

"Was he acting?" I asked, nervous to hear what she had to say. "In the room, Cole was kind and almost like the boy I love. Nothing like the person I saw in the tunnels."

"You think he was pretending in there?" Christina asked, holding out a light pink robe for me. "Did you not see the way he looked at you? The boy you love is in there."

Wrapping myself in the robe, I said, "You said earlier that you'd help me. I'm here for one reason only and that is to bring Cole home. Can you really help me do that?"

Nodding, she said, "In any way, I can. Now, let's get you dressed."

Sitting down on a stone chair in front of a black, gem-encrusted vanity, I felt fidgety and agitated. Trying to connect with Essie again, I received no response. My mind raced and the thoughts I had were full of dark images. No matter how hard I tried to force my mind to think of good things, it went back to pain and sorrow.

"How much longer?" I asked. "You're taking too long."

"I'm almost done," Christina said. "You're fighting the magic inside you. Stop trying so hard and they will coexist."

I snapped, "What I want you to do is finish with my hair, so I can go to Cole and..."

My words were interrupted by Christina placing her hand firmly on my shoulders. "I'm sorry," she said. When I turned to face her, I realized we weren't alone in the room. "I did not think before asking you. I'll put your hair up. Please, accept my deepest apologies."

"Next time, you should ask me what I want and not assume," I said. Glaring at Laura, I added, "Why are you lurking in the corner? Make yourself known when you're in my presence." *Becoming the evil queen might be fun if it wasn't so real,* I thought.

"My apologies." Laura stepped forward, holding another glass. "The Shah asked me to bring this to you and he would like to know how much longer you will be."

Snatching the glass from her hand, I took a long drink. This time, I enjoyed the cold as it filled my body. "Tell *the Shah* he'll need to be patient and I'll be there when I'm ready."

Giving me a look of warning, Christina said, "Tell the Shah, we're almost done. He won't have to wait much longer."

With that information, Laura turned to leave the bathroom to report back to Cole.

"Wait." I narrowed my eyes at her. "My message is the one you'll deliver. Tell him I'll be there when I get there, and he can decide then if I'm worth the wait."

Nodding, she left the room.

"We need to be cautious in our discussions," Christina warned. "She isn't a child of Arianolwyn."

"I don't want her in this room anymore," I said. "I'll inform Cole of my decision."

"You should be cautious in your demands," Christina cautioned. "While he does love you, it's the girl of his childhood that will keep his heart. This cold version of yourself won't get you what you want in the end."

"I find that I have so much anger inside me now," I said, acknowledging her advice. "Is it the drink they keep giving me that is causing such dark emotions? I want to reject the verijuoma, but it'll anger him." I didn't want to confess that I craved it and didn't really want to give it up anymore. "How much more of it can I have before I completely lose my connection to my old magic?"

"The verijuoma is only making it possible for you to live in this cold environment. It has nothing to do with the dark magic inside you." Christina pulled my hair into a high bun, smoothing the wisps. "I think you've always had this magic inside you and being here is allowing you to tap into it. Much like the way your half-brother has it."

"How do you know about him?" I asked.

"There will be more time for this conversation, but we must get you ready," she said, dismissing my question.

Taking me into another room, I was shocked by how much clothes were in such a small space. The walls were lined with hundreds, and hundreds, of kinds of outfits. Everything was coordinated and ready to be pulled off the hangers and worn. The simple task of selecting choosing what to wear was all I had to do.

Overwhelmed by all of the choices, I said, "Please, just pick something for me. When will I ever wear all of this?"

"I know the one." Christina went straight to a section of red dresses and picked up a sleeveless one. "He told me he knew it was meant for you the minute he saw it."

I gave her a look of doubt. "This is too simple and not sexy enough,"

I argued. The dress had a high neck and was young. Not sexy or tempting at all. "Find me another dress that will catch his eye."

"No, trust me," Christina insisted and handed me the dress. "If you don't like it after you put it on, you can change. This dress will remind him of the girl he fell in love with."

Accepting her advice, I got dressed. Christina zipped up the back for me, and then slipped a white ribbon with small red cherries around my waist.

"Come look at yourself," she said, leading me towards one of the large mirrors.

As I saw my reflection, I fell silent. My outfit and hairstyle made me look like a film star from black and white movies. With dark and smoky makeup like this, I could play the part of a vixen.

"Thank you," I gushed. "This will remind me of both the light and dark inside me that I need to balance."

After one long calming breath, I said, "Take me to your king."

CHAPTER
TWENTY-THREE

Christina led me out of the bedroom and down a steep, circular staircase with no railing. The confidence I had felt with my new look faded with each step. With nothing to hold onto, I ran my fingers along the dark stone walls, leaving a trail of frost behind me. *Soon, I will be just like the Winter Goddess,* I thought smugly.

When we were almost at the bottom, Christina stopped our descent to address me. "You need to remember what we talked about."

"What did you talk about?" Laura asked as she appeared beneath us.

"Why do you keep appearing where you have not been invited?" I snapped. "You're beginning to anger me." My hand blazed with a dark, green magic.

"Laura, I was teaching her how to be a lady," Christina answered smoothly. "She's young and wasn't prepared for her new role as Vizier."

Eyeing me up and down, Laura appeared to accept the explanation.

"You need to stay out of my way," I warned her. "I'll not have you lurking in corners and reporting false stories to Cole."

"My interest is to serve the goddess," Laura said. "I'll do —"

"You'll do nothing. I'm here for Cole, the Shah, and I'll be here until he deems otherwise."

Christina separated us. "Laura, she'll be the next Vizier. All of this is new to her. Remember how hard it was for you when you first came to live here. She's a young girl who is full of new magic. It is our duty to support her."

Lowering her head, Laura said, "I'll do as Snowystra wills and nothing more. Know that I'm watching."

Christina said, "It's best you leave now, before you anger her further. I'll not be able to help you if you do."

As we watched Laura scurry away, I whispered, "She's going to be trouble. Find a way to keep her away from me."

"If you push too hard to remove her, it will raise concerns," she warned.

"I can't stand by and let her poison Cole against me," I said.

"Just enjoy your time with him, today," Christina said, continuing down the stairs.

Finally, we reached a small, carpeted hallway. At the end of the corridor, I noticed solid steel doors. When we reached them, Christina tugged on a rope. A small chime sounded, and the door slowly opened. We were greeted by one of the guards from the previous night.

"She's ready to see the Shah," Christina announced.

"He's been waiting for you. Come this way." The guard pointed at Christina. "Not you. You're needed in the kitchen. Your knowledge of the Vizier is necessary to finalize the wedding."

Nodding. She silently walked by me and lightly grazed my hand. Her calming touch worked. I stood up straighter and commanded, "Take me to the Shah."

The guard led me through an enormous dining room. Its long, dark table would easily hold fifty people. Several chandeliers with burning candles hung from above, dimly lighting the room. Reaching a black door with a spider design engraved on it, the guard opened it.

I had to cover my eyes from the bright light. As I adjusted to the brightness, I could see a small glass table in the middle of the room. The guard guided me to it and pulled one of the chairs out for me. Holding back my instinctive respond of 'thank you', I nodded curtly. The manners and niceties I'd learned as a child would not be welcome here.

"Where is he?" I asked, unable to hide my irritation. "He said he would be waiting."

With a devious smirk, the guard said, "He told me to tell you he would get here when he got here, and then *you* can decide if it was worth the wait."

Not waiting for my response, the guard left. Glancing around the room, I took in the small space containing only the table, two chairs, and a tray with stemmed glasses and bottles of unusually colored liquids. When my eyes made it above, I realized the ceiling was made of ice. Snowflakes fell, and I turned to see the door open.

Cole entered the room, followed by two guards. I felt my heart skip a beat as he strode towards me. He wore a fitted black suit with a white shirt underneath and a deep red tie. His hair was cropped short with white tips, still, but he had a light beard. His appearance astounded me. Standing up, instinctively, I gave him a warm smile.

"You wore the red dress." He lightly ran his fingertip along my bare arm, sending chills through me. "You look even better in it than I imagined."

He frowned as he touched my hair. "The curls are gone. Pity, I always liked them."

I locked eyes with him and pulled the band out of my hair. Shaking my head, I released the curls.

"Much better." Cole grinned as he poured a glass of bubbling, green liquid for each of us.

Raising his glass, he toasted, "To us."

"To us," I said.

Slipping close to me, Cole whispered in my ear, "We will be so happy here. She has remarkable things in store for us."

"Good, the food has arrived," Cole said as the door opened, again.

Wearing conservative black uniforms, two women that I recognized from the night before arrived, each carrying a silver platter. Recalling one of the women was, named Dima, I glared at her.

"Don't be shy." Cole waved the women closer. Either he didn't notice, or he was ignoring my reaction to them. "Set it down."

Dima nervously set the covered platter in front of me, and then stepped back.

"Why is she still here?" I snapped, unable to control my anger. "I'll not eat any food brought by her."

Cole touched my hand. "Don't worry. She didn't make your food and I assure you, she's deeply sorry for her behavior. She's had eight days to think about her disgraceful display and has promised to be on her best behavior from now on. Isn't that right, Dima?"

What is he talking about 'eight days'? It was just yesterday. What game is he playing?

"Yes." Dima bowed her head. "I'll not make any more trouble for the Vizier."

"See, all better. Now, we can eat our breakfast." With a dark look on his face, he growled at the women, "What are you waiting for?"

Dima quickly lifted the lid off my plate. Underneath was pancakes, bacon, berries, and a small cup of zizzleberry syrup.

"Are you happy with the food I ordered?" Cole asked with a smirk.

When the other girl removed the lid from his plate, it was filled with the same food as mine, but more of everything. Immediately diving into his meal, he ate as if he hadn't in weeks. I hesitantly put a small bite in my mouth. The pancakes tasted exactly like Gram's. Savoring each taste, we ate in silence. When we finished, the women took the platters away and a third woman entered the room, carrying a glass of the verijuoma.

"Is there anything else you would like?" she asked, setting the cup before me.

"That will be all," Cole spoke for me. "We've things to discuss and need to be left alone. No disruptions."

"As you wish." She bowed and left the room.

"Earlier, you said Dima spent eight days thinking about her behavior. What did you mean by that?" I asked as I sipped my drink.

"She was sent to the Sephorian Desert to think about her actions." Cole's eye narrowed on me. "Do you think eight days was too short a punishment? I did consider sending her to one of the dorcha's dens to see how she would fair, but she is one of the prettier girls."

Ignoring his comment about her appearance, I pressed him further, "It was last night that she attacked me. Do you mean an eight-hour punishment?"

"No, Mara." Cole threw his napkin down and stood. "You've been asleep for eight days. I didn't realize you didn't know this. I thought you were going to sleep through your birthday, but you woke just in time. Do you feel older, today?"

Three months ago, I was sitting at a table with Gram and Cole, talking about my future. Never would I have thought that between then and my wedding day, I would have lost two people I loved and gained a brother.

"Do not worry, Mar," he said, taking my hands. "Today, we'll celebrate your birthday and tomorrow, we'll marry. Everything is almost as we planned."

How can I go through this? We'll miss delivering the heart-shaped cookie invitation to our guests. I won't wear my grandmother's dress. My family won't be here. But Cole's eyes are such a deep blue, and he's with me. I have to believe I can save him...save us.

"I see you're surprised. Time has flown these last few months." Cole dug into the pocket of his jacket. "I have a gift for you. I hope you like it."

Opening the black box he handed me, my eyes filled with cold tears as I pulled out a silver charm bracelet. It was nothing like any I had ever seen before. Instead of dangling charms, each was connected and laid flat.

"These represent different parts of our journey together." He pointed to the silver tire. "This is for the swing that I hung. The ice cream cone is for our first date." Cole excitedly pointed out the parts of the trinket that told our love story.

When he reached the spider, I frowned.

"This is the most important part of our journey together – a symbol of our commitment to the goddess," he said excitedly. "Snow isn't evil like she is portrayed. She's just been misunderstood."

Snow? Anger fueled in me. *Is he protecting her?* She was responsible for all of the pain in my life and ultimately Gram's death. Forcing a smile on my face, I let him hook the bracelet onto my wrist. *Just remember the good parts of it. The rest can be removed.*

"It's the most beautiful gift I've ever received," I said sweetly, trying to hide my disappointment.

When he finished twisting the hooks together, he kissed the inside of my wrist. "Are you ready to see your new home?"

"I am," I lied. *Please, be sure to show me the nearest exit,* I thought coldly.

Cole led me through the dining room and towards a small door off to the side that I hadn't noticed before. When he opened it, a cold wind blew into the room, extinguishing the candles on the chandeliers. He laced his fingers with mine, and we walked, hand-in-hand, through an icy hallway until we reached another door.

I was momentarily blinded by the brightness. I blinked away the spots and saw it was snowing outside. Fluffy white snowflakes covered us as he led me through the knee-high snow. I didn't feel cold, even though I was dressed for a summer's day, not a winter storm.

Ahead, the visibility clouded. I gripped Cole's hand tightly. Further, and further, we walked into the snowstorm with a strong wind whipping at us. Suddenly, I lost my grip on Cole's hand.

"Come to me," he called.

Blinded by the snow, with no idea which way to go, I panicked.

Out of the veil of white, a skeleton of a hand broke through, reaching for me, but I didn't move fast enough. Suddenly, the bony fingers wrapped around my waist, pulling me forward. Scratching and clawing at it, I screamed as I was thrown up into the air and into the white void.

CHAPTER
TWENTY-FOUR

My freefall ended when I landed in a snowbank with a *thump*. Sitting up, I fixed my disheveled clothing and smoothed my hair out of my face. This time, the hand before me was familiar.

Cole smirked at me. "I'm sorry. I should've warned you about the transition into this realm. I'll need to speak to Mortorcus about how he assists people in the future."

Accepting his aid, I stood up to find myself in the middle of a winter wonderland. The snow-covered ground was filled with large trees, heavily laden with snow. A small rabbit hopped through the tree line. The sky above was a deep blue with not a cloud in it.

In the distance, I could see a castle. The structure was like none I'd ever seen before. The high towers and walls looked as if they were made of ice.

"Is that where we're going?" I asked, unable to maintain the cold demeanor any longer.

"That is your new home, Marina." Cole put two fingers in his mouth and whistled.

Horses clomping sounded behind us. The skeleton man was sitting on the outside of a black and silver carriage being drawn by four skeletal horses. The driver wore a red and black uniform with a black top hat. His empty eye sockets glowed red.

The carriage slowed, coming to a complete stop beside us. When it did, a Vetur hopped off the back and opened the door for us.

"Are we riding in this?" I asked. "Isn't he the one who threw me?"

Cole wrapped his arm around my waist. "Mort will not harm you. This will be more comfortable than the long walk and it'll give us time to talk about tomorrow's events." Sensing my reluctance, he nuzzled my neck, murmuring in my ear. "Trust me."

The interior of the transport was a velvety black material with a spider web design weaved through the fabric. *Great. The arachnoid motif extends throughout the realm.* Resigning myself to the reality of my situation, I sat on the plush bench.

Cole joined me and slid open a cabinet. Billows of icy clouds escaped as he pulled out a bottle and two glasses. I accepted the cold chalice and delighted in the chilled temperature as Cole filled our glasses with verijuoma. He took a greedy swig from the bottle before returning it to its home.

When I raised my eyebrows in question, Cole said with a devious smile, "The nectar gives us our strength." Then, he added, "A toast to our future."

"Are you going to toast every time we drink?" I asked as I took a sip of the icy liquid I was beginning to crave.

"I don't think every time, but the past few days have been pretty special. You joined us. I really didn't think you would." Cole scooted closer to me. "On second thought, I might just toast every time, and every day of our new life together."

Cole's eyes lit up with excitement "I can't wait for you to see our home in person. You're going to fall in love with it. You were meant to be a queen Mara and, together, we'll have everything we've ever wanted."

He called me Mara, not Marina. So, good Cole is with me? Treading carefully with my questions, I asked, "What were we missing from our life in Starten?"

"We can make a difference here," Cole said excitedly. "We can help right the pain Snowystra was put through by Danu. We can repair the damage that was done when her magic was bound, and they forced her into isolation. Like her, our magic was stifled there. They gave us the gift but didn't let us use it. We were children with a roomful of toys told to sit, be quiet, and never play. But that is over, now. The access we have to our magic is now free of constraints. We'll be able to make a better world for the Vetur and for ourselves."

Cole honestly believed the propaganda he as spewing. He put his hands on my shoulders and leaned close to me. "They deserve a better life than the one they've had. Their suffering is because of Danu's greed for power. She took everything away from them and they've been fighting for so many years just to make a life worth living. Slowly, they've begun to rebuild."

"I don't understand. Danu did this?" I asked, doubting his words.

"She stripped Snowystra of her magic and sent her away," Cole said, frantically speaking as if he was a madman. "When she was sent away, she lost many of her children. They couldn't survive the cold without her magic. The first thing she did when she was freed was to rush back to her beloved Vetur. Every day, she fights to keep them strong and thriving."

He tilted my head up and stared deep into my eyes. "Our goddess is the goddess of darkness, Winter, and of Death. Her role in this world is hard, but necessary. She's just as important as the light from Danu, so why is Snow punished for fulfilling her responsibilities? Greed! Together, we'll restore her to her full power. She'll no longer be the black sheep of the family. She'll no longer be the outcast. Will you help me, Marina? Will you help Snowystra and the Vetur?"

His words made no sense to me. The plight of the Vetur was not his cause. I didn't know what happened to Snowystra, but she seemed quite powerful, now. If things were so horrible for the Vetur, why didn't she move them somewhere else? Why didn't she take them to this castle, instead of housing them in the tunnels? She had definitely brainwashed Cole. I wasn't sure I was going to be able to bring him back.

You must find a way to save him, I reminded myself. With a small smile, I took his hand from my face. "Cole, my love, I'll stand by you and Snowystra. I want her to regain everything she's lost and get exactly what she deserves. Together, we'll make it happen. I promise."

"I knew you'd understand. I told her we could trust you." He beamed at me.

Cole kissed me gently on the cheek and I felt an electricity run through my body. His magic was gently stroking my skin. His cold touch was tempting. I wanted more. Leaning over, I pressed my lips to his. Something inside me felt desperate. My kiss was hard and demanding, and I felt the ice in my body running faster through my veins.

Initially, Cole's response to my kiss was restrained and the magic lessened. Panic filled me. I needed to feel his magic again. I became forceful with my kisses.

With a growl, Cole wrapped his arms around me, knocking the glass onto the floor as he pulled me onto him. Kissing my neck, he ran his fingers through my hair. Slowly, his hand trailed down my back and unzipped my dress. The freezing air on my bare skin was like a slap across the face, bringing me out of the moment. *No, this isn't happening now – and certainly not here.*

Slipping off Cole, I breathed heavily. "We can't. We've only one day left before we marry. Why rush it?"

Cole pulled me back into his arms, and said, "Why wait? We've been waiting for way too long."

Fighting the urge to sink into his arms, again, I said, "No, I want our first time to be special, not in the back of a moving carriage. Soon, we'll be together, forever. One more day isn't going to change the way I feel about you."

Cole released me and moved away. His eyes clouded and his jaw clenched.

What have I done? You brought him to that level. This is your fault. Fix it!

Gently, I touched his hand. "Cole, don't be angry. This is just a momentary pause. I didn't want to stop, either, but one of us must be sensible. Now, please, zip me back up. I don't want to meet our new family half-dressed."

He nodded in agreement. "You're right. We'll have a thousand forevers, and in less than twelve hours, we'll be married. Then, Marina, you'll be mine." His words sent a chill throughout my body of both excitement and fear.

We rode the rest of the way in silence. The scenery flew by, making it impossible for me to plan my future escape. As we entered through the castle gates, I could see the building more clearly. It wasn't made of ice as I had originally thought. Instead, it was a cornflower blue brick that sparkled with a glittery frost. My heart beat louder as the carriage slowed and came to a stop at the entrance of the intimidating building.

Cole stepped out first, and then lifted me down. Taking my hand, he led me through the line of uniformed Vetur. I was pleased to see

Christina at the end of the line. As I passed by, she gave me a slight nod. Next to her, Laura glared disapprovingly at me.

The entrance to the building had a large staircase made from the same stone. At the end, I saw a large metal door with a spider crest on it. By the time we finished the climb, I was dreading what we'd find inside. A large, overbearing man guarded the door. His pale white skin and dark hair gave him the Vetur appearance, but he didn't share any other features.

Before I could cross the foyer, Cole scooped me up into his arms. "Bekan, this is your new Vizier," he said to the man. "Make sure we are not interrupted for any reason. My lovely bride-to-be needs a personal tour of her new home."

"Put me down," I hissed in his ear. "This is embarrassing."

"There's no way you're taking your first step over the threshold unless you're in my arms." Cole smirked.

"Cole, really, put me down. I feel ridiculous," I said, softly beating on his arms in protest.

Laughing, he quieted my protest with a long, sweet kiss. If circumstances were different, this moment would have been perfect. However, this wasn't really our home, and the man holding me seemed to shift in and out of the man I loved and the dark future of tomorrow. Marrying would be a risk of falling deeper into Snowystra's world and forgetting home.

Snowflakes blew into the room and circled us. Then, I heard her. "My darling, Cole, you're home and, I see, you've even brought Marina to me."

Cole set me down and bowed deeply before the goddess. "I'm so glad you're here. I was told you would not be returning until tomorrow."

"Not a delightful surprise?" Snowystra pouted.

Cole rushed to her and hugged her tightly. "It's a wonderful surprise. To my disgust, he, then, kissed her on the lips. "How I've missed you," he murmured into her ear.

My heart went cold. I wouldn't be able to compete with her.

Snowystra looked at me and her beautiful face wore a cruel smile. "Now, Cole," she scolded. "Poor Marina is being neglected."

In a lightning-fast move, she grasped my hand. "I'm so glad you've come to your senses. Tomorrow, you will show your loyalty to Cole and to *me*." Tugging me closer towards her, she stared into my eyes. "You'll find my world of magic is less constraining. Are you adjusting to your new magic?"

"You have a lovely home. Cole was just going to show me around." I shifted out of her hold. It was becoming difficult to maintain my composure and not scratch her eyes out. Every muscle in my body tightened. "I haven't had time to practice my new magic. This is my first day out and Cole has kept me terribly busy."

Snowystra stepped away from me. "Silly me. Of course, you haven't had time to really learn anything, but I promise there will be plenty of time for just that."

Squeezing my hand tightly, she smiled. Her touch felt like thousands of threads of ice were being sent through my body. Closing my eyes, I delighted in the sensation. Loosening her grip, the magic she was sending ended. Disappointed she had let go of my hand, I took her hand back, hoping it would return. My feelings of jealousy about Cole's desire for her ended. I now understood why he sought out physical contact with her. Her touch was enticing.

Whispering into her ear as if I wasn't there, Cole said, "I told you she'd come around. Everything you lost will, soon, be returned."

Sending one more stream of magic through me, Snowystra whispered into my ear, "This will have to last you, my greedy girl."

Releasing me, she clapped her hands together and walked away. She called out as she left, "Cole, give her the grand tour." Stopping, her eyes pierced mine. "And give her more than verijuoma. The poor girl is starving for more Winter before my eyes. If I would've let her, she would've drained me dry."

CHAPTER
TWENTY-FIVE

Cole led me through the foyer, past a library filled, from floor to ceiling, with books, and into the kitchen. Staff rushed around as they prepared for tomorrow. A baker laid a square cake on top of a tier of seven other layers. Each had been frosted on each side with exquisite ruffles that began as a slate gray color and faded to white. When the man saw Cole, he put down the piping tube and rushed towards us.

"Your Excellency." the man bowed to Cole. "To what do we owe this great honor? Did you come to see the cake? I hope it meets your expectations."

"Lestop, meet your Vizier." Cole eyed the cake. "You've fulfilled my wishes and more. Do you have a sample of the cake for Marina to taste?"

"Yes, yes," Lestop gushed, scurrying back to the cake, and cutting a piece off.

Seeing that he had destroyed the cake, I gasped.

"Do not worry, min Vizier." The baker waved dismissively at the cake. "It'll be as good as new tomorrow. Now, please, tell me what you think."

Taking a small bite of the cake, the flavors swirled in my mouth. My heart beat fast and my vision blurred.

"So, what do you think?" My vision cleared and my grandmother was standing before me. She held out a fork with bits of cake on it. "Do you not like it?"

"I'm not sure." I hesitated.

I glanced around the room. I was home in Starten. My grandmother was in front of me, and she was alive. Hopping out of my chair, I ran down the hallway into Gram's room. When I entered, I could see the silver mirror high above me. Jumping to see my reflection, I could not reach it.

"What are you doing, Mara?" Gram picked me up in her arms. I caught my reflection as she carried me out of the room.

What is going on? I'm a small child.

Gram sat me down on the chair and gave me a stern look. "What's gotten into you, today, little one? You're being peculiar."

My tongue was tied. I wanted to tell her everything.

Before I could muster the courage, she fed me another bite of cake. "We need to decide, soon. Your birthday is tomorrow."

Chewing carefully, I savored the delicious treat.

"So?" She grinned at me.

"I love it. This is the one I want," I exclaimed.

"I'm most pleased," my grandmother said.

Most pleased?

Gram shimmered and her appearance shifted into Lestop. I was no longer in Starten, but rather, in a kitchen three times the size of my home. There were, also, dozens of strangers milling around me.

"Wonderful, I'll finish the cake, right now." Lestop bowed and returned to his work.

"Are you alright?" Cole took my arm. "You seem off balance."

Christina gave me a glass of dark liquid. "The goddess wants her to drink this." Turning towards Cole, she said, "She'll not make it to the ceremony if she doesn't rest. Her body is fighting Winter's chill."

"She'll be fine," Cole snarled. "Your opinions should be kept to herself. Bring more of the tavi veri."

"Yes, mi Shah." Christina bowed.

I took a slow sip of the new beverage. My body stiffened as if I was frozen. Panicked filled me. I couldn't move. Cole held my hand as I stood in a statue-like state.

"It will fade, soon," he soothed.

Trying to move my fingers unsuccessfully for minutes, I felt relieved when they finally wiggled. Anger filled me when my body regained its normal state. I picked up the glass and smashed it to the ground. "Never give me that drink again. You almost killed me."

"Now, Marina, your body won't react the same way next time." Cole stroked my cheek. "Be a good girl and control your temper."

You're lucky I love you, I screamed in silent bitterness. Thoughts of freezing him and smashing him to bits passed through my mind.

Christina appeared in time to stop me. She offered a golden container to Cole. "The tavi veri you requested," she said as he accepted it. "She looks unwell, min Vizier."

"Marina is fine," he growled. "Now, step aside and we'll continue our tour." Cole took my hand, and said, "If that's fine with you, Marina?"

"Yes, please, let's continue," I replied. "I'm anxious for tomorrow to come."

"My beauty, you're always so impatient. Tomorrow will come soon enough." Cole laughed. "Now, it's time to see your home."

Cole led me up a staircase to the second level, stopping in a large, open foyer. The marble flooring was a swirl of black and silver. The high ceilings were covered with a delicate web design. The metal double doors on the right had a snowflake etched into the steel. The double doors on the left were open, showing a red carpet that extended down a long hallway leading to a closed door.

"This is our wing," Cole explained, guiding me through the open doors. "Each room has their own master bathroom. We will have plenty of space for our children, here, and this will be our room."

The chamber was decorated with exquisite furniture. The small sitting area had blue chairs with a small silver table in the center. The bed had a tufted headboard and matching footboard made of blue fabric with silver buttons evenly spaced throughout. It was framed with a dark black wood that was engraved with floral designs.

The white comforter sparkled. Running my hands along the fabric, it turned to frost. The room would be fine for the short time we'd be there. It would be like staying in a hotel, but this was not a place to raise a family. A child couldn't run free and explore. There were too many things to break or for sticky hands to dirty.

Setting the tavi veri onto one of the silver dressers, Cole poured a glass and handed it to me. "Why don't you have a seat and drink this?"

Will my child, also, have to drink tavi to be able to live in the cold temperature? Will they turn into Vetur?

"I really feel fine. Why are you trying to force it on me? I'll drink when I'm thirsty," I said, wanting to resist drinking any more of the veri. I was beginning to feel different. There was an anger inside me that I didn't want to control. I wanted to hurt Cole like he hurt me in the alley. My mind raced. *Will I, soon, be turned, like he is? Will I abandon my family like my mother? Does Cole love Snowystra? Is he only marrying me because it's her will?*

"Trust me, Mar," he said, interrupting my thoughts. There was notable sadness in his eyes. "I would never give you anything that would hurt you. So, drink this…please, drink it for me."

Relenting, I sat down on the bed and drank the entire glass of liquid. Frost formed on my eyelashes and my chest burned. It was as if my insides were ablaze with fire. Slow pulses of electricity sparked from my fingertips and the room spun.

Easing me back to lie down, Cole whispered into my ear, "Sleep, Marina, soon, your body will stop fighting it."

Unable to speak, I watched him walk away from me. Before I fell asleep, I saw Snowystra standing above me, talking to Laura.

"Make sure she drinks enough, tonight," Snowystra ordered. "I don't want any problems, tomorrow. They will marry and she'll promise her loyalty to me."

CHAPTER
TWENTY-SIX

My sleep was interrupted when I was lifted and forced, by Laura, to drink the tavi veri. Each drink gave me a different reaction — feelings of being trapped underwater, loss of feeling in my legs, and even my hair freezing. These were only some of the side effects I experienced.

Christina lifted me and tilted a drink to my mouth. "This will counter everything they've given you. Just remember, they must think you're full of darkness when you wake." Touching my forehead gently, she swiped her finger from temple to temple. "You will remember," she said. "Now, drink the rest."

Nodding, I finished the glass. Unable to keep my eyes open, I drifted off to sleep.

When I awoke, later, I found myself in a misted area. The sensation of wetness on my face revived me. I got up and walked, trying to gather my thoughts. Feeling a sense of familiarity, I wandered somewhat aimlessly, unsure where I was going. Then, I realized I was at the entrance to the elemental's home.

Stopping at the tree, I pushed my hand onto the bark and was glad to see it went through. Stepping inside it, as Bay had taught me, I entered the darkness. The comforting *bu dum bu dum* sound of the tree comforted me. When I reached the Water elementals cave, I noticed my hands weren't solid...I was translucent. I wondered if I had died and now I was going home to Danu.

Focusing my heart on finding the goddess, I walked past the Water elementals. Their joy called me, though they couldn't see me. I wanted to splash and play in the water, too. However, I resisted my urge to join them, and continued moving.

Following the stone hallway into the Fire elementals area, I strode through the sparks of fire floating through the air. Leaving the warmth of their cavern, I climbed the stairs to the Air elemental's platform. The sky held a rainbow of colorful feathers as the elementals, in their bird forms, soared above me.

When I reached the edge of the stand, I jumped. I, peacefully, floated until landing near the Earth elementals. A smile crossed my face as I watched them run their fingers through the lush grass, making flowers bloom. Even though none of the elementals were aware of me, I felt at peace here. Their knowledge, passion, joy, and love surrounded me.

Leaving the elementals, I entered the center of their world – Danu's chamber. Walking past the mirrors, I glimpsed my transparent, blue-colored reflection. *Am I dead?* I stopped in front of the mirror I'd seen my sister in when she had been taken by the Drygens. The same one I'd seen Miles through for the first time. Placing my hand on the glass, I hoped something would appear. I needed to be shown anything that would confirm my family was safe.

Holding my hands before me, I called to the elements:

With my hands to the east, I call Air to give me wisdom and insight.
With my hands to the south, I call to Fire to give me strength and passion.
With my hands to the west, I call Water to provide me with peace.
With my hands to the north, I call to Earth for protection.
With an open heart, I call to the Goddess of Life, Danu.
I beg for your assistance. Please, show me my family is safe and
that my determination to save Cole has not been in vain.

The mirror in front of me glowed before fading to an ocean blue color. As the image cleared, I could see Meg and Miles. They were playing in the waves of water. As the tide rushed towards them, they ran back onto the beach, laughing and screaming. My father and Essie were stretched out on large towels, watching my siblings play.

When Hazel joined them, she asked, "Any news?"

Essie shook her head. "I hope she's OK. I haven't been able to connect with her since the day we left. I'll keep trying."

"My Caterpillar is strong. There's nothing to worry about." My father squeezed her hand. "She's just in an area we can't reach her, but she is fierce. She'll never give up her faith in the goddess and what our families have protected for decades. The Winter will never consume her."

"What about the boy?" Hazel sighed.

"I know Cole," my father said. "The love he has for Mara is stronger than any magic or spell. She'll not give up on him. They'll both return to us, and we can go home."

Tears filled my eyes as the image faded. My family was safe. With the knowledge that they were not in harm's way, I could focus on how to save Cole. Even if I was dead, I needed to find a way.

Leaving the mirror, I went to the center stone in the middle of the room where Breeze, Blaze, Bay, and Daisy were sitting in their chairs. They didn't see or sense me.

"I have no word of where she is in there," Blaze said. Her voice was not the strong tone it normally was. "I have elementals guarding the perimeter and watching. All she has to do is give us a sign that she needs help and will be there."

"We should never have let her go alone. How do you expect her to tell us she needs us?" Bay argued.

"She does have a way to tell us, if she truly needs our help," Daisy corrected her. "There are two people in there who will help her, and Arianolwyn's blessed will do her best to protect her."

"We have already turned two of her sons. They are willing to help Mara escape in exchange for protection," Blaze said.

"Cerin helped Kai escape. He made a choice to save his life and has not been seen since," Breeze remarked. "How do we know he has not returned to her side?"

"She would never accept him back," Blaze snapped. "If he returns, she will use him as an example for the others. You have seen what Snowystra is capable of."

"There has been so much pain for this family because of the gift," Breeze said. "Danu will know what we should do."

The elementals held their hands out, sending a thread of light to the stone I was sitting on. I could feel the warm light surrounding me as the shimmery image of the goddess appeared.

"Mara, how nice to have you, once again, in my home," Danu said with a warm smile. Sitting down before me, she took my hands. Her touch was gentle, and I could feel the magic she held slipping through my fingers.

"Am I dead?" I asked, unsure I wanted to hear the answer.

Throwing back her head, she chuckled. Her laughter was like music to my ears — a warm, comforting song. "My, you are one to get right to your questions. No, Mara, you are certainly not dead," Danu answered. "You called me, and I had your spirit brought here. Much like the last time you visited, your human shell is sleeping. So, tell me why I'm here."

"I don't know what to do," I admitted. "If I marry Cole, tomorrow, and say I'm choosing to follow Snowystra, I'm afraid I'll not be able to return."

"I can't tell you what the right choice is, but I know your heart is sincere," Danu said. "Do not fall too far into the darkness, my love. There's no way out. However, know that any promise you make, tomorrow, will just be words. Your actions will be the true confirmation of whom you follow. If you choose that world, choose it openly, knowing you will always be welcome in my home."

"But I'm not choosing that world," I said, fighting back my tears. "My choice is only to save Cole."

"Like your mother, you will need to make this choice on your own," she said.

"My mother had no choice. She was a child when she was forced to follow Snowystra. Why didn't you stop her?"

She stared at me with only a look of love but offered no words.

Realizing she wasn't going to answer, I asked, "What should I do?"

"You're the only one who can decide what path you will take, Mara," Danu restated as she disappeared.

"I don't know the answer," I cried out to her. "Please, come back."

Lying down on the seat of Danu, I fought back the emotions running through me. Fear and anger were not going to solve my problems. Standing up, I noticed one of the mirrors was glowing. Thinking back to my first visit to this world, I knew what I should do. Taking a deep breath, I stepped through it.

The mirror I stepped through disappeared, but a new one formed before me. The circular room was made of a hard stone. The ceiling was, at least, forty feet above me and made of the same rock. I had been in this space before. The first time I was here, I flooded the room with my anger and almost drowned. Since then, I had learned that my emotions affect everything around me and, even though there were no exits, I was calm.

I knew I would be safe in the home of the goddess. Sitting on the floor, I waited patiently for a sign. After several minutes, when nothing happened, I found myself screaming at the top of my lungs in frustration. Against everything I'd learned, I found I was unable to silence myself. My cries echoed and bounced off the walls. The mirror before me rippled, and then shattered, sending shards of glass at me.

Wiping the broken bits away, I went to the hole in the wall that once held the mirror. On the other side, I could now see another room. As I moved closer, I could clearly see my grandfather, Chester Veracor. He sat on a chair next to my grandmother, who was rocking and staring off into an unknown place.

"She'll be OK, Maesi," my grandfather said, using the nickname he had given her. "She's just like you. Our girl is smart and she's a fighter."

"None of it was worth protecting if we lose her," she said as tears streamed down her face. "We've lost another child to the darkness."

"I'm here, Gram," I called as I tried to go to her. Instead of entering the image, I was thrown back into the room I'd started from. Shaking off the stinging sensation, I slowly approached the hole in the wall. This time, I stayed far enough back as to not touch the field that was keeping me out.

"I'm here, Gram," I said, again. "I'm not lost. Please, don't cry."

My words were not heard. It made no sense to show this to me if I was not meant to help her.

"Eliza was lost, but she has returned to us, love," my grandfather said, trying to comfort her.

"But not until after so much time was lost," Gram replied. "Our child didn't get a chance to know her daughters because I failed her. My promise was the reason we lost her, and the reason Mara is now gone. How can you say any of it was worth it, Chester? The girls lost their father for so many years, and our grandson was raised by Drygens. The price our family has paid for the gift was too high."

"So, you're giving up on what you've always protected?" he asked as he took her hand into his. "We both know that isn't going to happen. You're just tired, my love. You know in your heart it's been worth every sacrifice." Handing her a silver journal, much like the one I had found in her room, he said, "Read this and remember why your mother vowed her allegiance to the goddess."

When she dropped it, he picked it back up. Kneeling before her, he wrapped his arms around her waist, resting his head in her lap. "Read it for me, Maesi. Read it for me," he pleaded.

Sighing, she said, "Get up. You're too old to be on the cold floor. You're right, as always. You have reminded me that you're a silly old fool," she said, beginning to resemble the strong woman who had raised me.

As my grandfather returned to his seat, Gram held the journal out before her, saying, "With an open heart and mind, I read the story of my gift."

The journal slowly drifted out of her hands and hovered above her as it glowed a dark red. Spinning until the red turned to lavender, it popped open and landed on her lap. Turning the cover page, she read from it.

I sat and listened, longing to be in the room with them as my grandmother read. Trying to hear anything that would guide me in my decisions, I was confused. This was just a story about the elementals trying to save Danu. How could that help?

Gram spoke the next part louder.

"'*The four of us are strong. We were made from the fire, water, air, and earth magic inside of us. She gave each of us this power to use, not to ignore. We're more than the elements inside us. We're her children. We're her elementals. We will bring her spirit back, Blaze contended.'*"

"Bring her spirit back," I said out loud. "I need to bring Cole's spirit back. I know what to do now, Gram."

The hole in the wall closed. I turned away to see that the mirror had returned. Taking the same path back into the center room, I returned to the seat of Danu. Carefully, I took my finger, and I focused on drawing a heart made of frost on it. Feeling sleepy, I laid down and continued to slide my finger over the heart until it stood out on the dark stone. Closing my eyes, I told myself that I would keep my promise to follow my heart and I was going to bring Cole home no matter how long it took.

My peaceful thoughts were interrupted by the panicked voices calling out, "She's not breathing. You've given her too much. She's dead!"

CHAPTER
TWENTY-SEVEN

Cole stood over me, shaking me by my shoulders as I looked down on myself from above. I felt like I was breathing. I felt like I was still alive, but I could see how desperate he was. Somehow, my spirit had left my body.

Feeling confused, I looked around the room. I didn't want to return. I wanted to go back to Danu. Before I could make my decision, I found myself gasping for air and staring into Cole's blue eyes.

"Don't ever do that to me again," he said, his voice cracking. "Do not ever leave me again, Mara."

I understood the words he was saying, but for some reason, I was unable to speak.

"Talk to me. Tell me you're OK," Cole insisted.

Thousands of words ran through my mind, but nothing would come out of my mouth.

"She'll be fine," Snowystra said. "Just let her rest."

"They gave her too much," he asserted angrily. "They could have killed her."

"Come away from her," Snowystra cooed. "She's in good hands, darling. Christina and Laura will alert us if anything changes."

"No more tavi," Cole said in a low growl. "Give her nothing else, tonight."

"You're right," Snowystra said, stroking his face. "Let's try some winter's bite to balance out the tavi. Your Marina has extraordinarily strong magic inside her. I have never seen anyone fight my magic so strongly. I almost wonder if she really wants to be here."

"No," Cole said, sounding more like a frightened child than the strong leader he had become. "She wants to be here. Don't you think it's just the magic fighting? You said yourself it's strong. You told me it would be hard for her to completely changeover, but she will. Just give her time."

"And, if she doesn't accept her new life?" Snowystra asked. "If she's really just pretending, so she can take you away from me? What would you do then?"

"She wouldn't do that," Cole insisted.

"So naïve...so trusting," Snowystra said. "I'll let this continue since it's so important to you. You have shown me that you will lead my children to greatness."

"Thank you." Cole's tone softened, and he took her hand. "I promised she'll come around."

"I'll trust you," Snowystra purred. "Now, come with me. There's much to do before tomorrow if you still plan on marrying her."

Releasing her hand, Cole's eyes darkened. "Nothing has changed. The wedding will happen, tomorrow, and Marina will be mine."

"*Ours*, you mean." Snowystra stared into my eyes, and then kissed him deeply.

I snapped my eyes shut and willed them to leave. *The thought of her touching him is killing me.*

"Sweet dreams. I'll not see you until the morning." I felt Cole's cheek against mine as he whispered in my ear. "Then, you'll be mine, forever."

His words frightened me, but I couldn't fight off sleep any longer. I drifted off into a dreamless slumber. I didn't wake again until I was shaken into consciousness by Christina.

"Wake up," Christina said hurriedly. "I have things to give you before anyone else arrives."

Groggily, I replied, "I don't want to drink anything else."

"No. Nothing like that. I brought you your things. The ring and the envelope are in your dresser drawer under the false bottom." Christina showed me a jeweled tiara. "But, today, you'll wear this. When it's time, break off one of the petals. It'll turn to powder and, when it does, quickly rub it on the wound."

Interrupting her, I asked, "What are you talking about? I'm not injured."

"There's no time for questions, just listen," she said. "You'll have an injury. Rub this onto it and, if you can, onto Cole's, as well. You must convince her you've taken the Winter."

"I don't understand," I admitted, not hiding my fear.

"Today is your wedding day. What else is there to understand?" Snowystra asked, entering the room. Dressed in a long, silver dress that was way too formal for the morning, she was followed by two female Vetur. Each carried a bag. "We've much to do to get you ready. I hope you're as excited as we are. Cole's been up since first light."

Snowystra sat down on the bed next to me. "Imagine, in less than six hours you'll be Mrs. Cole Sands. Isn't that what you've always wanted?"

Forcing a smile, I said, "Yes, and you've made it possible."

"Yes, I did," she praised herself. "Now, first, you should shower. Then, Christina will fix your hair in the way I requested. When you're ready to try on your dress, they'll bring you to me."

"My wedding dress is here?" I asked too quickly.

"Oh, not that old frock." Snowystra frowned. "That rag is far too plain for the wedding of my Shah and Vizier."

"Good." I forced myself to say the next words. "I was only wearing it to please my grandmother. It was so old-fashioned."

My comments made her smile. "Yes, it was a very sad looking little dress, wasn't it? Poor Mae, she was always so simple. Don't you think it was just a pitiful gown?"

"Very," I lied.

Her eyes brightened at my agreement. "Good. Now, go shower, and then we'll get you ready for your big day."

"Follow me, Mistress, and I'll help you," Christina said.

"You need to get her some tavi if she's to make it to the ceremony," Snowystra called to us as she walked out of the room.

Alone in the bathroom, Christina handed me a glass of the red liquid. "I think you'll be fine without drinking all of it. Just drink a bit. After you shower, I'm going to fix your hair. You'll not put the tiara on until after the fitting. I'll position it so that you can pull off a petal discreetly. Remember what I told you to do with it."

Distracted by the fabulous cold sensations running through my body, I nodded. She grabbed the drink from me as I guzzled it. "You will have plenty of that, today. Try to keep your senses."

After I quickly showered, I was wrapped in a towel and led to a vanity by the Vetur women who had returned. Opening one of the bags, one of them held out white, lacy undergarments towards me.

"Do you need assistance?" the woman asked when I didn't take them from her.

I had no idea what to do with all the pieces she was offering me.

"Do I need help?" I snapped as I grabbed the panties from her and slipped them on. I knew how to put those on, but I wasn't going to admit that I didn't know exactly what the other pieces were. "No, I do not need your help, but I shouldn't be expected to dress myself. Should I? Am I not the Vizier?"

"Oh, I'm sorry," she said. "Forgive my slight."

Waving my hand like I had seen Snowystra do, I said, "Enough groveling. Just dress me."

The women wrapped a larger piece of fabric around my upper body, pushing my cleavage upward. When they finished with the snaps in the back, both stared at me, unsure what to do.

"If you have a seat, I can fix your hair and they can finish with your stockings," Christina suggested.

"Fine," I said as I sat down, mouthing *thank you* to Christina when I knew they couldn't see.

I sat on the cold, black chair, allowing Christina to rub product through my hair while the women finished dressing me. Once they were done, one stood quietly, watching, while the other brushed my face with powder.

As they fussed over me, I started to become nervous. Yesterday was my birthday, and I missed the entire day. Today, I would marry Cole. I didn't know whether I was going to marry the real Cole or the Shah. I only hoped this all wouldn't end badly. As I pondered all the negative things that could happen, a breeze filled with snowflakes blew into the chamber.

"Marina, my darling." Snowystra sashayed into the room. "I have been waiting for so long for this day."

Keeping my icy tone, I said, "Thank you for allowing me to forget about my silly promise. Finally, I'll be able to do something important with the magic, Goddess. Cole has told me everything. I wish I had only known before. I wouldn't have resisted."

"I knew my decision wasn't wrong. If only you had come around before we lost Eliza, we could've done so many things. She had so much potential, except for the guilt she always carried." Clapping her hands together, she smiled. "Enough sad thoughts. Let's focus on you. Let me see what they've done with you."

As she circled around me, the goddess commented on every strand of hair that was out of place and every line of makeup that wasn't perfect. Noticing my nails, she insisted they be done like hers. The women quickly responded to her demands and soon, I was ready to see my wedding gown.

"Here," Snowystra said, handing me a silk robe. "We'll go to my wing for your dress fitting. I think you'll be pleasantly surprised by my selection."

Snowystra stopped at the entrance to her wing, where two guards opened the heavy doors. As we were escorted down another long hallway, I heard sounds of children playing. Turning around as one of the doors opened, I caught two small, black eyes peeking at me.

"Who's in those rooms?" I questioned, stopping at one of the doors that was now cracked open.

Gazing at the door, Snowystra said, "My children, of course."

A door suddenly flung open, and we were surrounded by at least a dozen dark-haired children. Each was hopping up and down, excited by my presence.

As they shoved and scratched at each other to get closer to us, Snowystra cried, "Enough! All of you – back to your rooms."

Protests of anger echoed in the hallway.

"We want to meet her," a voice cried. One of the Vetur children shoved her way through the group and stood in front of me with her hands on her hips. "Mother, is this the new queen?"

Putting a hand on the girl's head, Snowystra addressed all the children. "Yes, darlings, this is Marina. She's come to save us from that horrible monster who treated Mommy so badly. She'll restore our magic. Won't that be nice?"

Cheers of joy were quickly followed by more fighting. The small creatures clawed and bit each other. Their behavior was ignored, as if it was normal.

When the dark goddess lifted her hand off the girl, I noticed she left a frosty handprint.

Smiling, the little girl said, "She's pretty." Then, narrowing her eyes at Snowystra, the child pouted. "I don't have nice clothes like she does." Tugging on her dress, she glared down at it. "I never get anything pretty. I'm stuck here in this horrible place."

Looking into one of the rooms that the children had come from, I saw a beautiful nursery with lots of toys and books. It didn't look scary. It looked like a magical place to grow up.

"Masha, do you really think it's true to say you live in a horrible place when you're given everything your heart desires?" Snowystra held her hand out towards the little girl.

Crinkling her brow as if she was thinking ridiculously hard, Masha said, "No, Mother, you're right. I was just being spoiled."

"Now, all of you, run along," Snowystra said in a singsong voice.

Cries of protest began again.

"Hush, there'll be none of that from you. We've many things to do before the wedding. If you listen to your metas, they'll report your good behavior to me." Snowystra smiled wickedly. "Behave and I might let you join the party."

Turning towards the women that had come to gather the children, Snowystra ordered, "Metas, remind them of how to be respectful in front of the Vizier and the Shah." Grabbing one of the women by their arm, she whispered, "Of course, they won't be going to the wedding celebrations. Keep them contained. If necessary, sedate them."

Nodding, the woman rejoined the other metas in their task of corralling the children. More fighting broke out amongst the kids as they were led away.

"Exhausting. It's so difficult being a single mother." Snowystra sighed dramatically. "Come along, no time for this today. You'll meet them all soon enough. Don't worry. They won't be at your wedding. They haven't learned how to be civilized, yet, and are so reactive. My little ones can be too naughty. I'm afraid they do take after their mother in that way."

Throwing her head back, she laughed at her own joke. *She truly is evil. I'm not sure how much more of her I can take.* A prickly sensation began on my fingertips as they dripped with dark magic. Shaking my hands and calling the magic back, I focused on pleasant thoughts.

The further we walked, the lower the temperature became. The walls even had a layer of frost on them. When we reached a silver door, more guards appeared and bowed deeply to the dark goddess. These men were dressed in black leather with spider imprints on their chests. Each man had a silver sword in a waist belt. As they opened the door, a flurry of snowflakes escaped. The cool air calmed me, and I felt myself being pulled by the need for more of it.

I was amazed at how unreal it all seemed. Scanning the room for any signs of danger, I took in the view. The space was a combination of winter and darkness. The furniture was made of ice. Snowystra's large bed looked as if it was covered with a blanket of snow. Behind the headboard, a large web extended the length of the wall. The web was covered with thousands of green dots.

"My dorcha," she said, noticing I was staring. "They are so precious. Have you had a chance to see the grown ones, yet?"

Yes, Snow, I had the opportunity to stab one to death just the other day, I thought smugly.

Walking over to the web, Snowystra held out her arm and was immediately covered with dozens of baby dorcha. Picking one up, she held it in the palm of her hands, cradling it. "They are so much more than spiders. They, like my children, are part of me. I give up a piece of myself to give them life."

One-by-one, she began returning them to their home. "Come to me, Marina. Don't be afraid." Snowystra offered one of the metallic green spiders in her hand to me.

I backed away.

"You're afraid of a small spider?" she snarled. "The magic coursing through your body, right now, is because of them. They give life to your magic."

Setting the dorcha back onto the web, she changed her demeanor. In a syrupy-sweet voice, she said, "Of course, you're afraid. You've been raised to hate anything that isn't of Danu. You'll have plenty of time to find out everything about my home, later. Now, let me show you the dress."

Snowystra led me into a circular room connected to hers. There was a black platform in the center of it. A high-backed chair and a mirror with a black web design around the glass sat atop it. Climbing the stairs,

I felt the pulse of the dark magic through my slippers. The same magic that had, once before, pricked and stung my skin, now felt like a soft massage.

Removing my robe from me, the goddess ordered, "Bring the dress."

A dozen Vetur entered the room and circled the platform. Following them, Christina and Laura entered with three more Vetur behind them.

"My Marina, darling, you have gotten so skinny. I fear we've not been feeding you enough here," Snowystra said in a concerned voice.

Christina and Laura stepped to each side of me, revealing the garment the three women were carrying. The white ball gown was covered in large diamonds on the skirt of the satin dress. Holding it out before me, Christina took my hand and guided me to step into it.

Slipping into my gown, I looked around, hoping to be able to see what I looked like in it. The mirror before me was covered in a thick black mist and I couldn't see myself.

Snowystra stood before me, analyzing the dress. As she poked and pulled on the fabric, I could see it changing before me. She made adjustments as if I was a model and she was creating her latest fashion. She tightened the fabric around my waist, lowered the neckline, changed her mind several times about the length of the dress. All of this was done with no tools, only her will.

"Much better," Snowystra said as she circled me one last time. "We really need to do something about this drastic weight loss, dear. Maybe, if you weren't sleeping for such extended periods, your body wouldn't be going into hibernation. You really must take better care of yourself in order to prepare your body for having children."

"Children?" I asked. "We don't have immediate plans for children. We always said we'd enjoy being married before we started a family."

"Things have changed, darling." Snowystra fussed with my dress. "The Shah must have an heir. How can I be expected to fulfill my promise of giving you both eternal life if he won't keep his part of the deal? Your children are essential to the success of my return."

Not wanting to incite her anger, again, I said, "You're right. Things have changed. We will honor the promises Cole made."

"You have made me so happy," Snowystra said, kissing my cheek and stepping back from me. "Let's see what you think of your wedding dress. You do look quite beautiful, almost like a china doll."

The mirror cleared as she waved her hand over it. The realization that I was going to be married to Cole and that my family wasn't with me brought tears to my eyes.

"Oh, you don't like it?" she asked, taking my hand. "What's wrong? What can we fix? You must be happy on your wedding day."

"It's lovely," I said as I soaked in the magic she was sending through me. "I'm just so happy that today has finally come and everything's so perfect."

As much as I missed my family, I was thankful they weren't here, in Snowystra's domain. Since I had to go through with this charade, I would think about the positives. And, though I wanted to hate the dress, I liked it despite my best intentions.

The white bodice was embroidered with silver thread. From a distance, you wouldn't notice the lattice design, but up close, you could clearly see the spider web. The skirt was full and layered with long pieces of fabric that were tastefully covered with diamonds. The gems sparkled as I moved.

Christina had left my hair down but accentuated my curls. It suited the overall effect. Even I had to admit it surpassed my expectations.

Snowystra made one final turn around me. "Very nice," she said. "Everything will be perfect. I must leave you, now. I'm going to go check on everything to make sure the finishing touches are as I want them. Christina, make sure she drinks more tavi and get her something to eat. We can't have the bride fainting on our wedding day."

As she walked away from us, Snowystra snapped at the Vetur standing around. "Get her out of the dress, and Marina can relax for the next few hours."

"Is there anything I need to do?" I asked, not wanting to know what she had planned.

"Oh no, darling, everything is well underway. The guests are on schedule to arrive. Everything has been taken care of." With that, she left the room.

After I removed the dress, two guards led me back to my room, where I was told to wait until I was summoned. The next few hours would be painful if I could not control my thoughts.

CHAPTER
TWENTY-EIGHT

I paced as I tried to figure out what my next move should be. I knew I was going to marry Cole, but then I'd take him away from here. No matter what I had to do, we'd be leaving here and never returning.

"You're going to miss the wedding if we don't feed you," Christina said. "Come, sit and eat something."

"I don't want anything," I said, seriously not wanting any food.

"Please, you have to eat something," Christina insisted. "Just have a few bites of one of your favorites. There's some bread with your favorite jam and a cup of coffee the way you like it."

"How would you know what I like? You don't know anything about me," I said, unable to control my anger.

Not responding to my outburst, Christina led me by my elbow to a small table that held a silver platter and a bottle of red liquid. Pushing away the platter, I poured myself a glass of the tavi veri and drank it quickly.

Taking the cup from me, she set the platter in front of me again. "Now, let's get some food inside you."

Grabbing the cup from her, I poured myself another glass of tavi. Stopping me, she took the glass and moved it out of my reach. "You can't live on tavi alone. You need to eat something. Please, try harder."

"I know if I open the lid, it'll be one of Gram's recipes. I can't eat her food today. I won't," I screamed, throwing my silverware onto the floor. "Just pour me more tavi."

With a sad look, Christina nodded and reluctantly poured glass that I quickly drank. The ice inside me responded to the beverage. The magic in me felt strong and I wondered what this new magic really could do. I closed my eyes and thought about forming a weapon much like the fire sword I had made for Blaze.

When I opened my eyes, there was a metal dagger in my hand. The hilt of the weapon, covered in green jewels, pulsed with energy. Holding it out in front of me as if I was slashing at Snowystra, a lime-colored bolt of electricity flew off the tip. The current hit one of the dressers, and then burst into flames. Immediately, two guards stormed into the room.

"Are you under attack? What's going on in here?" one of the guards demanded as the other searched the room.

"Just put the fire out and go away," I snapped.

Christina went over to the guard who was patting out the fire with his hands. Softly, she said to him, "There's nothing wrong. It was just an accident."

Giving her a knowing look, he motioned towards the other man. They picked up the dresser to carry it out of the room. Before exiting, he whispered back, "She looks a lot like her mother. Please, keep her magic under control."

"Would you like the same dresser or a different kind, min Vizier?" the other guard asked me.

"Surprise me," I answered. As the door shut, I dropped the dagger and watched as it sizzled and dissolved into the floor, leaving a black mark.

"It will take time for you to learn your new magic," Christina said.

"I need to know how to use it now," I replied. "What did he mean about my mother?"

"Your mother struggled to learn her magic, too," she said quickly.

Thinking about Eliza was never a good thing to do. Focusing back on my magic, a black fireball appeared on my palm. The small marble flickered, emitting silver and white sparks. As it grew, it turned green. *This is my mother's magic...the same that killed Gram.* I tossed it, back and forth, from hand-to-hand, trying to understand it. I realized it was a combination of my fire magic and the dark magic. Squeezing my hands together, I extinguished the flames.

If I could still call Fire, what other elements inside me could I safely use? Thinking of Air, I focused on sending a stream of wind towards Christina. Instead, a black cloud formed. Wondering how much more of the mist-like cloud I could call, I willed a gentle breeze to encircle me. Slowly, the blackness crept in until I couldn't see anything around me.

Again, the door burst open. I quickly released my hold on the magic and tried to look innocent. The thickness of the black smoke in the air dissipated and the guards stood in the doorway.

"Mistress." The head guard coughed. "We beg of you, please, stop calling your magic, today. The guards are all on high alert and we can't do our job if you keep summoning us."

Glaring at him, I said, "I'll not stop anything. You can go away and leave me alone. You were never *summoned*. If I need help, I'll cry 'help'. Until then, leave and don't come back."

With those words, I called black smoke and forced it towards the guards. They stood strong against my magic until I pushed more at them. I, finally, shoved them out of the room.

"I beg you to not call more," Christina said with fear in her voice.

"So, you think I can still use all four elements?" I asked. "What do you think will happen if I do?"

"I think, if you call your dark version of Water, you will fill the room with an acidic liquid that will burn everything around it. I'm not sure, but I think if you do call Earth, you'll generate enough strength to crumble the castle."

"Interesting," I said, considering her words. "Fine. I'll not play with my magic, anymore. Bring me the platter, again."

When she removed the lid, it held a cup of coffee. The steaming liquid smelled of cinnamon and vanilla. The way Gram liked it.

I could tell from the look on Christina's face that she was pleased with my decision to eat. Slowly, I took a small sip of the coffee, only to spit it out. The liquid burned my tongue.

"I can't drink that. It's too hot." I handed her the cup.

This time, she brought me a plate that held a raspberry lemonade and a dish of licorice ice cream. Both were Gram's recipes, but colder versions. Tears filled my eyes as I noticed the licorice was covered with red sprinkles. Meg's favorite.

Taking a small bite, I forced back my tears. Today, I would not cry. There would be no tears on my wedding day. The food would be a reminder to not get lost in the darkness. As I thought those words to myself, I felt a small stabbing pain in my heart.

When I finished, Christina cleared the used plates. "We need to fix your hair up, again, and touch up your makeup. Do you want to try to rest first?"

"No," I said, thinking I had slept enough. "I want to explore this room."

Searching the dressers, I become frustrated. They were full of clothes and jewelry. "Why is there nothing useful here. There's no paper or pens," I said. "Why is there nothing artistic if Cole has been staying here?"

"He hasn't been here much," Christina admitted. "He keeps to himself in the study downstairs."

"Can you take me there?" I asked.

"I'm afraid we won't be able to do that, today." I lowered my eyes at her, and she quickly replied, "After you're married, I'm sure he'll take you there himself."

"Could there be any worse luck than wearing a dress with a spider design and getting married in Snowystra's home?" I asked, pondering the irony of my situation.

"Yes, dear Mara, there are worse things," Christina said, not elaborating. "So, what do you want that I can get you?"

As I thought about how I'd like to distract myself for a few hours, I came up with something I hadn't done in a while. "A book would be a good distraction."

"What kind of book?" Christina directed me towards a bookcase that hadn't been there moments ago.

Is this my will or did she do that? I wondered.

Scanning the books, I was delighted to see so many of my grandparents' favorites; books that were read to me when I was young. Skimming the titles, I found it difficult to decide. *Which should I read again?* I debated between a classic, like *Little Women*, or one of the new ones I hadn't read before.

Picking up, *Kind of Like Life* by Christina McMullen, I opened it and read the first few pages. Interested in my selection, I settled on one of the overstuffed chairs, where I fell into the world the author had created.

"My life is becoming closer to a novel than reality, Christina," I said as I finished the book. "Maybe, like Dorothy, I did wake up in a strange place."

"Yes, Mara." She smirked. "But you're not in Oz."

Interrupting our conversation, the door opened, and the guard entered. "The goddess would like you to finish dressing the Vizier for the wedding," he said to Christina. "The time has come."

Christina said, "Thank you, she'll be ready in time for the ceremony."

Before he left, he looked around the room as if expecting to see more destruction. He seemed pleased that I hadn't burnt any more furniture.

By the time the dress arrived, and I was in it, I felt better. It was only an hour before I'd marry Cole. Realizing that increased my determination. I would find a way to bring him back to me.

After my hair was touched up, Christina placed a small-jeweled crown on the top of my head. "You're such a beautiful bride," she said, clasping my hand.

Hugging her, I said, "Thank you for everything. I'll remember everything you told me."

Christina put the final touches on my makeup. It was much darker than what I would normally wear. Gone were my days of eyeliner and cherry lip-gloss. Gram would've been displeased by the darkness of my appearances, especially the deep burgundy lipstick. However, she would've understood that, if I wanted to play the evil queen, I had to wear the costume.

A knock on the door announced the arrival of the guards.

"Is she ready?" the head of the detail asked Christina.

"Yes, *she* is." I stepped forward, glaring at him.

Bowing, he said, "The goddess wants you to come, now."

The guards escorted us back through Snowystra's bedroom. When we entered the platform, two more guards joined, following me up the steps. Seeing my reflection in the mirror, I realized this was the only opportunity I'd have to turn back. Looking at the guard detail that surrounded me, I knew changing my mind would mean I'd have to call all the magic I had inside.

Before I could question my decision any further, the mirror darkened. Long threads of smoke came from it and wrapped tightly around me.

Looking at Christina for help, she whispered, "Bright Blessings, Mara. I'll be there for you."

The magic lifted me off the ground and I was pulled into the mirror. Drifting through the black emptiness, I was surrounded by a pulsing, green electricity and I felt a sense of peace. With a sharp bang, the calm feeling ended, and I fell downward. Blurs of light passed me as I fell deeper into the void before I landed hard on a black throne.

The small room filled with light, and then I could see large curtains opening. The sun was shining on me through the large, curved windows that overlooked a winter garden. Going over to them, I saw hundreds of Vetur formally dressed in silver and black. They milled around as if anxiously awaiting the event.

Thousands of chairs lined the snow-covered ground, facing a circular platform that held three chairs. Standing beside one of the chairs, I could see my love talking to someone, but I couldn't see their face. Cole stood tall, looking handsome in his black and white fitted tuxedo. Whatever the person said made him laugh and he took a seat. Wearing a big grin, he was given a drink that he sipped.

A blinding snowstorm surrounded me. The flakes settled to the ground and Snowystra entered the room. "Marina, my darling, you look so beautiful. I would say almost perfect. Just one thing is needed."

Circling around me, she dangled a necklace in front of me. The silver chain held a large spider made of diamonds. The eight legs sparkled with light green gems. I shivered as she put it on me and slowly shortened the length of it.

Leaning in, so close to me that her icy breath began to freeze my ears, she said, "Your loyalty to me is appreciated."

Her magic didn't feel intoxicating. It burned.

Quickly, she yanked the chain tighter, bringing the spider into the front notch at the base of my neck. I put my hand on the charm, trying to stop it from shortening any further.

Removing my hand gently from the necklace, Snowystra whispered into my ear, again, "Cole has been such a dear to me. I genuinely want him to be happy. He believes that, once you begin your lives together here, you'll forget the silly promises you made to my sister. Those who are loyal to me are always rewarded richly."

She continued to tighten the necklace. Soon, I found it difficult to take a breath or swallow. The women near us moved away, busying themselves. Christina appeared not to be cowering in fear of the goddess, but, instead, watching her intently.

"Those who betray me quickly learn how vindictive and cruel I can really be," she said in a low hiss. Releasing the necklace, she let it drop to my collarbone. As I gasped for air, she grabbed my hands. When I tried to shift, inconspicuously, away from her, she pulled me into a hug.

Returning her voice to a louder, more maternal tone and drawing back enough to meet my gaze, Snowystra said, "I'm so glad you love your dress. You're right. Everything will be wonderful." Her grey-blue eyes narrowed as if she was sending a silent warning to me.

Releasing me from her embrace, I felt able to talk, again. With a tight smile, I said, "Thank you. You have been a gift from the Gods to my family. We'll never be able to repay you for everything you've given us."

Kissing me on the cheek, Snowystra whispered, "Careful, Marina, I might actually believe you're here for me." Then, she sent a burst of her magic through me.

I closed my eyes, hating myself for longing for even more of her winter chill.

"Get her something cold. She seems a bit weak," Snowystra snapped at Christina. "Bring her down, soon, though. I'm going to check on the *groom*. He's such a mess when he's away from me for too long."

Her comment angered me, but before I could call my magic to throw at her, she vanished into a puff of black smoke. The women circled around, staring at me with pity in their eyes. One of them, whom I recognized as Malise, stepped forward and handed me a bouquet of red flowers.

"Are you ready, min Vizier?" she asked. "You look lovely."

"Thank you," I said. "Did you enjoy your stay in the Sephorian Desert?"

Stammering, she replied with a look of fear, "Mistress? I was not sent there."

"Just an oversight. How lucky for you that you were missed. Anyone who dares to question my loyalty to the Winter Goddess was, and will, be immediately sent there," I said.

Trembling, she knelt before me, "No, min Vizier. I promise that I know your intentions are pure. Please, forgive me if I gave you the feeling I felt otherwise."

"Get up. The Vizier doesn't have time to deal with you. Consider yourself warned and your previous accusation forgiven," Christina said, looking at me for approval.

Waving her off, I said, "It's time. Take me to the Shah."

"This way." Christina promptly guided me towards a mirror, much like the one in Snowystra's room.

As I stared at my reflection, waiting for the smoke to appear, I felt an energy in the air. This time, instead of threads, the large bony hand of Mortorcus reached through the mirror and picked me up by my waist.

This time, Mortorcus didn't shake or throw me. Instead, he placed me inside a carriage through the roof. The windows were tinted, and I couldn't see where he was taking me. However, I could feel the rocking movement, making me think we were moving amazingly fast. The carriage, then, slowed and the top of it broke off, turning it into a silver sleigh. Vetur were lined up along both sides of the path, as if trying to see me.

When the sleigh stopped, I was greeted by Dunn. He was dressed in a tuxedo and his hair styled neatly. Holding his hand out to me, he said, "You have cleaned up nicely, mistress."

Shoving his hand away, I glared. "You will address me as min Vizier," I demanded loudly.

Taken aback, the smile faded from his face.

Smirking for the smallest moment, I whispered, "Or, my friends call me, Mara."

His smile returned when he realized I hadn't, yet, succumbed to the darkness. Extending his hand to me, again, I took it this time.

"The guards are all saying you were out of control and tried to burn down your wing," Dunn informed me with a tight smile.

"Not at all true," I replied. "I just had a magic mishap. All was fine in the end. They carried away the burnt dresser."

"I would've loved to have been there for that." Dunn softly chuckled.

Music sounded, indicating the start of the procession. A dozen guards in black and silver uniforms lined up, two by two, in front of me and another dozen closed in behind. Dunn took my arm as if he was walking me down the aisle.

Fear filled me when I saw the crowd stand. There was no turning back. I was going to become Snowystra's dark queen.

Taking a long, slow breath, I focused my energy on my family. Wishing they were with me, on this day, would do me no good.

Essie, I mentally projected, hoping I'd be able to connect with her. *Essie, if you can hear me, please, tell my father I love him and that above everything, I wanted him to be the one to walk me down the aisle. We lost years together, but never the love we have for one another. Take care of my little sister and brother until I can be with them, again.*

Instead of Essie, the voice of Alaunius sounded, *You're not alone, child.*

Startled, I look around to see if anyone else had heard him. The soft voice of the benevolent god whispered to me, *your family is with you, Mara. They've never left your heart.*

The voice of my father whispered in my mind, *Little caterpillar, it's time to stop hiding in the cocoon. Become the powerful butterfly I always knew you'd be. Sweetheart, come home to us, soon.*

I will, Daddy, I promised. *I'll make you proud.*

CHAPTER
TWENTY-NINE

As I fought to hide the tears that had begun to well in my eyes, Dunn called out, "Attention."

The guards in front of us stopped, took two uniformed steps towards the outside of the pathway I was intended to walk, pivoted to face their partner, and pulled out their swords.

Dunn commanded, "Present."

Each member of the saber cordon raised their weapons towards the sky and touched the tip of their partner's sword. The blades sparked and showered us with silver embers as we walked through the passage they had created.

When we reached the end of the guards, Dunn cried out, "Stand down."

The guards sheathed their weapons, and I could now see the reason for me being in this cold world.

Cole Sands, my blue-eyed love, watched me. He was beaming with pride. At that moment, I knew the choice I was making was correct. I was going to save us from the darkness or die trying.

The music changed to a dark march and Dunn slowly led me down the path between the seated guests. Vetur in fine clothing filled the back twenty or so rows. Searching the crowd for any familiar faces as we continued, I saw no one until we reached humans dressed in heavy winter clothes. Covered in fur hats, jackets, and boots, they appeared uncomfortable in the chilly weather.

My eyes locked on the emotionless violet eyes of Blanche Drygen who was seated in the front row. My blood ran cold. I could feel the hatred she had for me, and I hoped she knew the feeling was mutual.

Next to her, Cedric sat hunched over, staring off into the distance. He looked nothing like the dangerous man I had seen before. Instead, a pitiful shell of his former self sat in his place. My mother's death had affected him profoundly and he was visibly heartbroken. Cedric suddenly noticed me and watched with a look of surprise.

Jumping up, he called out, "Eliza?" His voice was desperate and full of pain. "You can't marry him. You love me."

"Sit down," Blanche hissed, tugging on his arm. "You're embarrassing yourself. It's not Eliza."

Shrugging her off, he ran towards me and knelt before me. "Eliza, you can decide. We can run away, where she won't find us. Come with me now, and we'll have the life we planned." Cedric cried uncontrollably. "I love you. Don't make this choice."

Two guards swooped in and picked him up. As they dragged Cedric away, he screamed, "Eliza! Don't do this."

"Get rid of him." Cole stepped forward and extending his hand to me. Dunn lightly squeezed my arm in support before he bowed towards the Shah.

I accepted Cole's hand and he whispered to me, "Don't let him ruin our day. He's lost his mind." He let his eyes trail over me. "Wow, Mar, you're even more beautiful than I could've imagined."

"So, I'm guessing I was worth the wait?" I asked with a sly smile. "You look quite handsome yourself."

The Drygens would not ruin my day, even if it was a dark wedding with no family present. None of it mattered. My Cole was here.

A light glowed behind us, and a woman's voice said, "We're brought here, today, to celebrate the union of Cole Oliver Sands and Marina Addisyn Stone. Not only have they chosen, this day, to show their love for each other, but they'd like to share their decision to renounce their promise to Danu, Goddess of Light. Instead, they shall pledge an oath of loyalty to Snowystra, Goddess of Darkness, Mother of Winter, and the giver of life to the Vetur."

The crowd cheered.

We stepped towards the woman. I softly gasped when I saw it was our neighbor, Mrs. Ward.

"I'm so glad you're here. It really means a lot to us," Cole said graciously.

"Your grandmother was a dear friend. I'm glad I could be here for you," she whispered before forcing a smile, and loudly saying, "The goddess has been kind in forgiving me for my lack of appreciation of her."

I could see she was afraid and that her words were forced.

With trembling hands, Mrs. Ward held three ribbons. "Please, offer your hands as an act of solidarity."

Following her directions, we held out our clasped hands towards her.

Chuckling, she said, "Well, you'll have to stop holding hands, first, for this to work."

The crowd tittered and we slowly separated ourselves. I grinned at Cole. Instead of smiling back, his eyes frosted over. *Again, I lose him*, I thought bitterly.

Instead of screaming and throwing a tantrum, I chose to offer my left hand to Mrs. Ward. She twisted a lavender ribbon around my forearm, stopping at my wrist.

"Marina, do you take this oath with free will and full desire? Do you promise to be the wife, mother of the Shah's future children, and his devout subject?"

Startled by her words, I looked into Cole's eyes. The love I could see within him stopped me from disagreeing. I would gladly be his partner in life, but not his follower. Still, without hesitation, I said, "I do."

Taking a silver ribbon, Mrs. Ward wrapped it around my intended's arm. "Cole, do you pledge your undying love to Marina? Do you promise to be her protector, the father of her children, and her king? Will you guide her through the Winter? Will you guide her through the darkness, leading her to her full destiny?"

Looking deep into my eyes, I could see his flicker and the frost faded. My heart skipped a beat. It was my blue-eyed love before me, again. "I, Cole Oliver Sands, Shah of the Vetur, pledge my life, love, and everything that is mine to Marina Addisyn Stone."

"Now, take hands," Mrs. Ward directed.

As Cole entangled his fingers with mine, she slowly twisted a black ribbon around our arms, binding us together. "These ties represent the love of Marina, the love of Cole, and the blessing of the goddess. These binds signify your forever commitment, which no one can break. Marina and Cole, I now pronounce you as man and wife. Cole, you may kiss your bride."

After he tenderly kissed me, Cole picked me up, twirled me around, and shouted, "My queen!" Then, he pressed his forehead against mine. "I'm going to make you the happiest woman in the world."

For just that moment, I believed him.

Interrupting our sweet moment, Snowystra stepped forward. Two guards gripped Mrs. Ward by the elbows and led her away. My kind neighbor's face flashed with worry. I wanted to chase after her, but the dark goddess blocked my view.

"My children," Snowystra called out. "Before you, a declaration of their endless love was made. Now. they will make their pact to me. If anyone here has reason to believe that either mortal is not loyal to the Winter, speak now and expose the falsehood."

My palms began to sweat as several minutes of silence passed. *Does she want someone to object? Will Blanche Drygen, Laura, or even one of the Vetur call me out for the fraud I am?*

Finally, my misery ended when the goddess motioned towards Dunn. "Since no one has any objections, we shall proceed."

Dunn returned with a metal bowl. When she took it in her hands, it became clear, showing two balls that bounced, back and forth, inside it. One contained a dark smoke and the other, snow. She let go of the container and it hovered in the center of us.

Snowystra untied the ribbon connecting me to Cole and moved closer to him. "Offer your hand to me."

He mechanically obeyed.

"Cole, do you promise your eternal connection to the Vetur, your loyal commitment to me, and your renouncement of Danu and those who protect her?"

"I do," he said.

A small dagger appeared in her hand, and she suddenly sliced his palm. The smoke and snow from the bowl slowly slithered onto his skin and into the open cut. I bit my lip to hold back the scream of terror demanding to be released.

"Marina, do you promise your eternal loyalty to me and my children, rejecting Danu and her gift?" she asked, waving the dagger at me.

She's going to kill me, right here, and now, I thought.

Trembling, I offered my hand to her. "I renounce all but you, my goddess."

In a quick movement, she sliced my hand. I gasped as the cold smoke forced its way inside me. With a cold glare, she cut her own hand, and then let the silver blood oozing from the wound drop into the bowl. Her blood combined with the remaining black and white threads before trailing into our bodies.

When the bowl was empty, Snowystra took our hands and presented us to the crowd. "Your Shah and Vizier. Your leaders. Your protectors. My children, welcome them as they will restore the power I once had."

My eyes connected with Blanche Drygens. She watched me with an expression that looked like sadness. I wondered if she wished it was her in my spot, right now, or if she was pitying me.

"And now, the celebration will begin." Snowystra waved her hand, calling a black cloud.

Black particles of sand surrounded us. Cole held me tightly against him as if protecting me from it. The darkness licked at my skin as it continued to wrap around us. A bright flash of light appeared. When it finally softened, I was pleased to see we were in Alaunius' sanctuary.

"Mar, where are we?" Cole asked. "Why are you dressed like that?"

Narrowing my eyes at Cole, I said, "We were just married, by our Goddess Snowystra, and we've taken an oath to follow her. We accepted the path to our destiny."

Looking around, he questioned, "We got married, here? What are you talking about? We're all alone."

Unsure if he was testing me, I decided to not take the chance. I kept my hard persona and glared at him. Even when I watched his expression change to shock, I still kept up my act.

"I'm so confused. You look so different," Cole said, sitting on the ground. "Everything's so fuzzy."

"Are you telling me you don't remember anything?" I snapped at him.

"Nothing," he said softly. "The last thing I remember is dancing with you. Then, I went to order us something to eat at the bar and..."

His expression changed to a look of fear. Though welled with tears, I realized his eyes were clear and bright blue. He wasn't pretending. The spell she had on him was lifted, for the moment, but I needed to be careful.

"Cole, she took you. She brought you to her world and I came to get you. We were just married, and we promised to follow her."

Remembering what Christina had told me to do, I broke one of the petals off the small crown on my head. It turned to a liquid that slithered into the open cut on my hand. The burning hot liquid traveled through my body. Breaking off another piece of the crown, I put it onto Cole's hand.

"What is that?" he gasped. After several seconds, he said softly, "I didn't want to follow her, Mar, but I can't just leave, now. We need to save the Vetur."

"What do you know about the Vetur?" I asked. "You said you have no memory. We probably don't have much time. We need to figure out why we've been brought here. Tell me what you meant."

"I remember it all, Mar." Shaking his head, he said, "She's horrible. She delights in the pain she causes. Most of them are kept in the tunnels, where they suffer. The few that have pleased her can stay behind the palace walls, but anything will set her off, and then she'll send them away. I'm sorry. I wasn't strong enough to fight her magic."

I wrapped my arms tightly around him. "You have nothing to be sorry about," I whispered. "It's all her."

A white fog filled the room and Alaunius walked through it with open arms. Cole and I stood up, quickly facing the bearded man.

"Mara, my child, how beautiful you look," he said. The sweet scent that emitted from him was like none I had ever smelled before. I let my anger, fear, and distrust fade away.

"Son of Sarah, you have been a pawn in my daughter's game." Alaunius took Cole by his hand. "Any shame you feel should be released. You had no power over my dark child."

Cole tensed. After a few minutes, his body relaxed, and he clasped Alaunius' hand.

The room glowed and silver wheels spun around us. Releasing the hold he had on Cole, Alaunius laughed. "My beloved has finally arrived. Arianolwyn meet Cole and Mara."

The woman's long, golden hair was streaked with silver. She had aged since the image I'd seen of her, but she still radiated youth. Her long, silver dress swished as she walked towards us.

Arianolwyn greeted up both with a kiss on the cheek. "I'm very aware of who this is, dearest. I have brought these two to me."

"May I ask why you called us at this time?" I asked.

"The loyalty you pledged is null and void," Arianolwyn said. "Your renouncement of Danu isn't accepted. Snowystra can't intimidate, force, or demand you to follow her. All agreements were made under duress. You can't make such a decision when being held prisoner."

"But I made a promise to protect the Vetur," Cole said. With a look of shame, he hung his head. "I remember everything that happened while I've been with them. They're lost and need me – need us."

"You've been misled." Arianolwyn cupped her hand under Cole's chin and lifted it. "The dark children have only been mistreated by my daughter. The life they live is because of her coldness. When I gave birth to her, I was angry and full of hatred for those that stole Alaunius from me. For the light to exist, there must be dark. I was wrong when I said Snowystra was to be of darkness. My misunderstanding is to blame. My child was of Winter. My words sent her down the wrong path and I fear Snowystra has slipped into a place of no return. In her madness, she has outstepped her role. She must not continue her reign over the Vetur. She must be stopped, again."

"How will we stop her?" I asked, not hiding my frustration. "We're mortal."

"My beloved was taken from me, and it took centuries for him to return," Arianolwyn said, taking Alaunius' hand. "She is a goddess, but she isn't invincible. It pains me to say this, but she must be stopped no matter what the cost to her life force."

Touching Cole on the cheek, she added, "You will not remember this conversation until you're free from my daughter. When this is done, I hope you will forgive yourself for everything."

Embracing me, Arianolwyn whispered, "The Vetur do need protection...but only from one, and that is Snowystra. You will save them. Mortorcus is their true leader. He must be restored."

With those words, the room filled with black clouds, once more. Afraid Snowystra had realized we'd been gone, I did the only thing I could think of – I threw myself into Cole's arms, kissing him passionately.

CHAPTER
THIRTY

Surprised by my actions, Cole stiffened under my touch. Not holding back, I kissed him harder until he relented and responded with equal passion. As the darkness spun around us, I sunk into his arms. Lost in the moment, we didn't realize the cloud concealing us had disappeared.

Loud cheers and hoots from the crowd sounded.

Instead of returning to the platform where our ceremony was held, we were in the middle of the forest. Our immediate snow-covered area had been cleared of trees and was filled with hundreds of circle tables, each decorated with centerpieces made from a silver tree dripping with icicles. The sky above was dark, except for silver stars twinkling and the full moon shining down.

Whispering in my ear, Cole said, "Let's continue this, soon. We should sneak away the first chance we get."

Snowystra interrupted his proposal with a singsong voice, "There will be time for that later, lovebirds. We don't want to keep our guests waiting."

Cole quickly kissed Snowystra on the cheek. "Very sorry for our disrespect. Forgive me?"

Touching his face with her hand, Snowystra purred, "Always." Then, she took Cole's hand and led him towards a long table positioned on risers.

Will I be sitting at my own table? I wondered bitterly as I followed.

After climbing several steps, I was on another platform. Snowystra motioned for us to sit. She took the seat to the left of Cole. Several guards followed and stood at attention behind us. Anger brewed inside me. *Who does she think she is? He's my husband.*

A waiter brought a tray of bubbling green liquid, handing one to Cole and the other to Snowystra. Again, I was disregarded. Then, another waiter poured my glass from a separate bottle, handed it to me, and bowed. When I accepted it, he quickly stepped back in line. I eyed the drink suspiciously.

Snowystra raised her glass and addressed the crowd. "With these powerful magic holders, we will take back our proper place on the Council and I'll reign in the mortal world."

The crowd cheered and raised their glasses.

Eyeing me, Snowystra took a long drink from her glass.

Cole raised his glass in respect and drank.

I reluctantly followed suit. As the liquid slid down my throat, fire trailed down my esophagus. *She is poisoning me!* I was being burned alive. Noticing that Cole didn't look uncomfortable, I fought back my urge to spit the vile liquid out. Instead, I locked eyes with Snowystra and finished the glass. *I will not die weakly and give her the satisfaction.*

After watching me for several long seconds, the dark goddess returned her attention to Cole. As she talked to him about her plans for him, I looked around. I was pleased to find Christina behind me.

"Bring me a tavi veri now," I whispered.

When the drink arrived, I gulped it down. It quenched the fiery pain in my stomach. Without pain to distract me, the slow rage began to bubble, again.

"Marina, you look uncomfortable," Snowystra called to me. "Was the polta tumma too strong for you, dear?"

"Not at all, I was just going to ask for more," I said. Pointing at the waiter who had poured my first drink, I demanded, "Fill a glass for each of us with that polta tumma."

Hesitantly, he poured the emerald champagne into the three flutes.

Raising my glass towards Snowystra, I said, "To the goddess."

As Cole started to take a drink, she said, "Wait, you'll be too tipsy if you drink without eating. Take this away and serve the food."

I tilted my glass back and drank it down. Not letting her see that I felt like I swallowed a glass of flaming shards, I forced a smile.

Christina discretely handed me a glass of the tavi veri, which I drank inconspicuously as Snowystra barked orders at the waiters. Once again, the icy liquid soothed the pain inside me. I found the tavi didn't physically affect me as it had in the beginning, but I still craved it...I needed it. *Especially, when someone is trying to kill me.*

"Bring me more tavi for my meal and don't let anyone, but you, touch my food," I ordered Christina.

Waiters carried trays of food to our guests. Everyone ate and drank, enjoying the music the orchestra played. When Christina placed my plate in front of me, I wrinkled my nose at the green meat and purple vegetables.

"What is this?" I asked, not wanting another surprise.

"Marina." Cole leaned in and kissed me. "We're so lucky. Trichank is delicious."

Stealing one of the purple cubes on my plate, he popped it into his mouth. I watched as he savored it. Cautiously, I took a bite and found he was right. It had a buttery taste, but the other flavors in it were totally unique, yet, delicious.

"What is this called?" I asked, offering a forkful to him.

"This is kanakala with rosemary. Try it. You'll love it," he said, accepting the bite. Taking the fork from me, he cut a piece from my plate and fed it to me.

As I chewed the tender meat, it was like a flavor explosion in my mouth. It tasted like wild meat, one moment, followed by an almost fishy taste, and then ended with a garlic steak flavor. I didn't know whether it was the drink or the food, but I felt a coldness building inside me. The anger I was bottling up grew. Suddenly, I felt powerful, and I wanted to show everyone here exactly what my magic could do. The urge to call all of my magic and destroy everything in my sight was unbearably strong.

Snowystra gently stroked Cole's face, and then whispered something to him. I felt the need to claim him. She wasn't going to have him. *He is mine.*

"You were right. That is good." I wrapped my arms around his neck and kissed him deeply. When I released him, I said seductively, "But, you taste better."

Seeing the exchange, Snowystra glared at me and tugged on Cole's arm. She whispered something into his ear, and he nodded.

"It's time to mingle with the guests, my beauty." Cole stood. Whispering into my ear, Cole said, "You're full of surprises, Marina. We'll continue this tempting conversation, later, but now, we need to play the happy queen and king."

"That will be easy," I lied. "I'm very happy."

I made sure to say my next words loud enough for Snowystra to hear, "I'm thrilled you're finally all *mine*."

Cole's eye burned with desire. Taking advantage of torturing our audience, I slipped my arm into his, and said, "The quicker we do our royal duties, the quicker we can be alone."

I made sure to direct my last word at Snowystra. Her eyes sparked with hatred. *Yes, Snowystra,* I thought. *The feeling is mutual.*

Cole stopped at each table and spoke to every person as if they were long-lost friends. He asked questions, telling me he really knew them and cared about them. The feeling of respect they had for him was obvious. Table-to-table, we moved, making small talk. When we reached one of the last ones, I found myself, face-to-face, with Blanche Drygen.

Cole greeted her warmly. "It's so nice you were able to be here, tonight."

"We're glad to join you on your special day," Blanche said coldly. "I'm hoping you can make time to speak. You promised my grandson would be returned to me. I was —"

"The boy can't be left in the care of an elderly woman and a deranged madman," I interrupted. "He has the magic of my mother pulsing through him. He'll, eventually, need to come live here." I leaned close to Blanche and said in my most condescending voice, "I'm sure you understand. We just have too few with *strong* magic left to risk him learning bad habits from non-magic users. Don't you agree?"

"Yes, min Vizier. You're probably correct." Blanche nodded.

Interesting. She's particularly good at hiding her emotions.

"My, what a lovely bride you are. I'm not sure your grandmother would approve of a dress as elegant as this, but what can you expect from a follower of Danu? You really have come a long way from poor little farm girl to queen of the Vetur."

Able to hide, but never able to let go, I see.

Narrowing my eyes at her, I leaned in close, again, and said, "We may follow the same goddess, but you're, by no means, my equal. You would be wise to watch your tongue in my presence. Be warned, even if I don't want that sniveling brat, you'll never have him."

Throwing my head back, laughing as if Blanche had said something funny, I addressed my husband, "Cole, isn't Blanche charming. She really should come stay with us. We could give her a tour of the Sephorian Desert. I heard it's nice this time of year."

Blanche paled at the suggestion. Thankfully, the orchestra stopped playing and we could end our conversation.

Dunn stood before the crowd. "Ladies and Gentlemen, I present the Shah and the Vizier in their first dance as bride and groom. May their marriage be long and fruitful with the blessing of the goddess."

Snowystra stopped me and ran her fingers along my sides. With her touch, my wedding dress changed. When she was finished, I was no longer wearing the long ball gown. I now looked more like I was in lingerie. The sweetheart bodice made my breasts look huge. My waist looked tiny and my hips wide. The main part of the dress was too short. It barely covered me. I felt a small bit of relief as she trailed her fingers over my hips to the lower part of my dress and layers of a chiffon material flowed from my waist.

Cole's eyes slowly trailed my body. He wore a dark smile as he drank in every inch of me. I wanted to cover myself and hide. It took all my effort not to react.

Slipping his arm into mine, Cole led me onto the dance floor. The surface underneath us was made of solid ice. Snow fell softly as he held me closer, twirling me around. When the music stopped, he held me even tighter.

"You've made me so happy. The Vetur will thrive under our reign, but tonight is about us. I know I've told you this many times, but you must know I've loved you my entire life. And I'll never stop loving you," he whispered.

A chill ran through my body.

The music changed to a peppy song. Chuckling, Cole picked me up and spun me around. His laughter was contagious and soon the crowd joined in. We danced the night away in a sea of our people, stopping only to drink glasses of tavi and chat with our guests.

The evening was magical. As the moon faded out of view and the dark sky lightened, everyone one left. Soon, we were left alone with the staff and Snowystra.

"Did you still want to honeymoon where we discussed, Cole?"

Snowystra asked. "You can change your mind and pick anywhere in the world."

"No, this will be perfect," Cole insisted. Noticing my discomfort at the secrecy, he squeezed my hand and said, "Trust me. You'll love it."

As you wish, Snowystra said, waving her hand and creating a purple cloud that surrounded us. The puff of air picked us up, spinning us. Holding Cole's hand tightly, I stared in amazement as we were carried through the sky above the winter forest.

Cole let go of my hand and floated around me as if he was swimming in the sky. Laughing, I grabbed onto him, pulling him close to me. Kissing me more passionately than I ever remembered him doing, I felt a coldness fill my body. The ice from our connection was intoxicating.

As we slowly drifted downward, I could see a log cabin in the snowy woods. The purple haze set us down at the threshold of the door. Picking me up, Cole carried me through the quaint cabin, not setting me down until we entered a bedroom.

Surprise filled me as I realized the room wasn't dark or luxurious. It was the room we would've built, together. The mahogany bed had a simple soft blue comforter and fluffy white pillows. The room was lit with flickering candles and the bed was covered in daisy petals.

Tracing his fingers over my shoulder, he asked, "Does this room please you? Is this how you dreamed our wedding night would be?"

"It's wonderful, Cole," I said breathily.

Laying me down on the bed, he stroked my hair. Removing his shirt, I could see he had red marks and bruises all over his upper body. It looked as if he'd been beaten and burned with her frost magic.

"What happened to you?" I asked as I gently touched one of the bruises.

"Nothing for you to worry about. The price of being the Shah." Cole kissed my neck and pressed his mouth to my ear. "I'll keep you safe, always, Marina. You're forever mine."

The fear I had carried with me all day melted away and I knew my decision had been the correct one. The night would not be about anything, but the love we shared.

"And you're forever mine," I said.

CHAPTER
THIRTY-ONE

The time spent in the cabin was perfect. Cole and I were free from the burden of Snowystra and worries about our future. Selfishly, I blocked out everything, but Cole. It was easy to focus on only each other with no one around. Anything we wanted and needed appeared, but the staff that catered to our needs remained unseen.

When thoughts of my family drifted to mind, I pushed them away. Here, Cole felt like the boy I had always loved. He was kind, considerate, and attentive. We were able to rekindle the feeling of our youth and freedom. Long walks in the forest around us gave us time to talk about our future together.

During one of the snowy walks, Cole sat down on a fallen log. "Come, sit. We need to talk."

"What's wrong?" I asked nervously.

"I received word this morning that we need to return." Cole squeezed my hand. "The Vetur need our leadership. We can't hide away here forever."

"I'm not ready to return," I said, kissing him. "We need more time together alone."

"No, Marina." Cole moved away from me. Standing up, he began to pace. "We don't have the luxury of hiding in the forest while we are needed at home."

"You mean, *she* needs you," I snapped. "I knew she'd never let me have you to myself. She'll always be there, fighting for your attention."

Kneeling before me, he took my hands into his. "It's not like that Marina," Cole said. "She's only thinking of our people. Without us to guide them, they'll be lost."

Even through his frosted eyes, I could see his sincerity. With a sigh, I relented, "Fine. What's so urgent?"

"We've lost three Vetur," he said. "I think Danu has taken them."

"Are they willingly leaving? Do you know for sure she's taking them?" I asked.

"I don't know for sure, which is why we need to go back to them," he said. "We leave, tonight."

"I'll support you, but the rest of the day is mine." I wrapped my arms around him. "No distractions. No thoughts of responsibility. Just you and me."

"I can live with that request." Cole smiled. "Where first? Swimming in the frozen lake, again?"

"I'm sure we can come up with something." I kissed him.

"I'm sure we can," he agreed.

Our last hours alone were haunted by the reality that was facing me. It wasn't long before Cole said it was time to leave and a carriage arrived to collect us.

As we rode across the snowy terrain, I gazed out the window. When we reached the outer walls of the castle grounds, I could see small cottages with Vetur milling about. They were dressed in simple black clothing that seemed in good condition. They watched as we passed and several waved.

When we crossed through the entrance to the castle, we saw Vetur had lined up, watching for our arrival. These Vetur were dressed in ripped and torn clothes. They looked hungry and dirty. Guards stood behind them, poking any who slipped out of line. I recognized several of them from the tunnels. As we rode by, I could see the sadness in their eyes.

"Cole, I want to visit the tunnels," I said.

"Why would you want to go there?" he asked. "It's no place for someone like you."

"If I'm going to make a difference, I need to know how our people live," I insisted. "How can I pretend to lead those I do not know?"

"Let's meet the Vetur that live in the castle and those that have cottages on the grounds," he said. "The pit is for leftovers."

"As the Vizier, I insist you fulfill my request."

Sighing, his voice lowered, "As you wish. I'll take you to the pits."

"When?" I asked, not willing to let him change his mind. "I'd like to go today, if possible."

"You won't be welcome there," he said. "You saw how they reacted to you the first time."

"I'll deal with that issue if it arises. I need to know our people," I insisted. "Now, big smiles, love. We need to look like happy newlyweds."

Sliding me across the seat of the carriage into his arms, he said, "No pretending needed, Marina. I have never been happier."

The staff lined up to greet us. I was relieved to see Dunn as we stepped out of the carriage.

"Mi Shah, min Vizier, welcome home," he said. "We've been anxiously awaiting your arrival."

"I have been informed of the situation," Cole said gruffly. "Your duties have been reassigned. I want you to, personally, ensure the safety of my queen. Until further notice, you continue to oversee the guards, but your priority will be as the Vizier's personal guard."

"Yes, mi Shah," Dunn acknowledged. "I had anticipated this action and would like to suggest that you promote Tynan to head of the guards in the interim. He has been loyal to the goddess and he's quick to act."

"Very well, Tynan will report to you. Thank you for your loyalty." Cole patted him on the shoulder. Taking my hand, he said, "Marina, I've business to take care of. I need you to make sure the household is up to your satisfaction."

Glaring at him, I said, "I'm sure I would be more of an asset to you in other ways than playing the happy homemaker. Assign a staff member to run the household."

Kissing my hand, he said, "Be a good girl and don't argue with me, right now. You're correct. You're a valuable asset to me, but the issues at hand are no concern of yours. If you would like, appoint someone to run the household."

"Do not forget your promise to me," I said. "I want to tour —"

Cutting me off, he kissed me on the mouth. When he pulled away, he said, "I always keep my promises. Dunn, assist the queen. Be sure she has anything she wants immediately."

Fuming with anger at Cole, I turned to Dunn. "Haven't you come far in the palace? Now, you're the bodyguard of the Vizier. Aren't you excited by your great responsibility?" My tone was colder than I intended. There was something about being here that brought out the worst in me.

"I'd like you to choose the head of the household. I don't want to deal with any of this, now." I waved my hand and walked away from him, towards my bedroom.

"I would suggest, Malise" he called to me.

"You can't be serious," I said, stopping and turning to scold him. "She tried to attack me."

"I make this suggestion with full knowledge of her past indiscretions. I assure you, she'll only have your best interest in mind now," Dunn said. "If she doesn't meet your expectations, we'll replace her immediately. I'll accept full responsibility."

Walking in silence, I decided to become as familiar as I could with the building. In the not-so-distant future, I'd be leaving here and taking Cole with me. It wouldn't be an easy task, but it would be necessary. When we entered the suite, I noticed the dresser I burned had been replaced. However, everything else was unchanged.

"Did you want to continue our conversation about the head housekeeper, or would you permit me to assign Malise?" Dunn asked.

"Whatever you think, Dunn," I snapped. "I'm not going to be a little housewife, worrying about silly things like meal plans."

His face fell and his brows wrinkled in concern. "I don't think anyone thinks you'll be just a housewife, but I do think Malise would be the best choice. You know I'm here to protect you, but I'm, also, here to make sure everything you need is handled. The Shah said any request you have should be fulfilled."

Checking to make sure we were alone, I moved closer to him and put my sharp pointer finger onto his chest. "The Shah just wants you to keep me out of his way, so he can take care of her needs," I said.

"Please, be careful in speaking ill of her. I'd be thrown to the dorcha if the Shah walked in on you talking to me like that."

"OK, I'll behave." I smiled. "If you really think Malise will be up for the challenge, go ahead and assign her. However, I can have nothing get in the way of what needs to be done."

"I believe I'll be able to make that happen, min Vizier. I'll send in one of the guards to rearrange the furniture immediately." Dun shifted his eyes towards the doorway.

He was telling me we weren't alone anymore. "Fine. Send them directly." Turning towards the doorway, I said, "Laura, how nice to see you."

"I brought you some tavi, min Vizier." She bowed and handed the glass to me. "Did you have anything else you needed from me?"

Trying to think how to get rid of her for an extended period, I said, "Yes, I'd like my wardrobe reorganized by type, not color."

"The outfits have already been coordinated," she objected. "They were hand selected by the Shah and the goddess for you."

"Yes, they did organize it while I wasn't here," I said, hardening my tone. "I think I should have it arranged how I like it, don't you? If it's too big a task for you, please, send someone else to me immediately."

"I'll do as you requested." Laura averted her eyes from my cold stare. "Is that all you would like me to do?"

"That'll be all," I said, dismissing her. "No, wait, please, send Christina in to assist me in getting ready for my day."

"As you wish," she said.

Laura left the room as Dunn returned with two guards. Looking around the room, one of the guards said, "What would you like moved, my queen?"

"I've changed my mind," I said. "The Shah was correct in the placement of the furniture."

Glancing at the other guard, he said, "We'll be outside if you change your mind."

When I knew everyone was out of earshot, I said to Dunn, "We need to find a way to keep Laura busy and out of my way. She's too inquisitive."

"She does seem to be everywhere," Dunn agreed.

"Please, bring Malise to me. I'd like to speak with her before I make my decision," I said.

Today, I would decide just who was safe enough to include in my plan to free Cole. There was no going back.

CHAPTER
THIRTY-TWO

While I waited, I went through the dressers. Once again, I threw everything I didn't like into a big pile on the floor. By the time Christina arrived, I had made a pretty big mess.

Raising her eyebrow at me, she asked, "What happened here? Was there an accident?"

"No, I just don't like any of these things. They look like things Snowystra would wear. When Laura is done rearranging my closet, tell her to take these to the Vetur in the tunnels."

"That isn't possible," Christina argued. "She'll not be able to go there."

"Why not?"

Christina answered, "Snowystra won't permit it."

"It's good enough for her precious children, but not her servant," I sniped.

"Do you remember how your emotions changed when you were there? You saw how Cole's behavior changed, too. It's a dangerous place. It's not for those who aren't strong. It's the breeding ground of her darkness. Didn't you see that the Vetur could barely function despite being born from it? She sends them into the pit to fight the dorcha. She uses the pain and suffering of her children to strengthen her own magic. They self-medicate. Otherwise, they wouldn't be able to survive, and, even then, many don't. If you send someone who isn't strong enough, they go mad."

Checking to be sure we were still alone, she said, "The bigger reason you can't send Laura there is because you'd anger, Snowystra. Laura is a loyal servant to her. She's been here since she was a teenager and has been the eyes and ears of the goddess ever since."

"Fine. I'll take everything to them when I go there," I relented.

"Why would you go there?" Christina's expression flashed with concern.

I need to know how the Vetur live if I'm to help them. I want to see everything."

"Do you think that's safe?" she asked.

"Why would I not be able to go there? I have sworn my allegiance to them. I'm their queen," I said, unable to hide my frustration.

Silent, as if she was thinking, Christina finally replied, "You'll need a protection of some sort." Going to the dresser, she retrieved the charm bracelet Cole had given me for my birthday. Holding it in her hands, she closed her eyes, whispering.

I couldn't make out her faint words. However, the bracelet glowed. By the time she clasped it onto my wrist, it had lost its light.

"This will help ward off the darkness, but only for a short amount of time. The longer you're in the tunnels, the more you'll be at risk of slipping into their world."

"You really are a good friend," I said, taking her hand. "I need to know you'll be safe when I take Cole away. Can you leave now before anything happens?"

"No, I'm here until you're gone. Don't worry about me. I'll be safe." Christina squeezed my hand. "I'm not alone here."

The door to my bedroom blew open and I released her hand. "And make sure that is done immediately."

"Yes, my queen." Christina bowed, and then gave me a slight wink.

"My Marina, you've become quite the harsh hand, haven't you?" Snowystra charged into the room.

With long strides, she walked towards me. Her long, silver dress dragged along the floor, making a painful high-pitched sound. When she reached me, she kissed me on both cheeks and grasped both of my hands. I soaked in her icy magic. Her lip turned up into a cruel smile as an electrical pulse rushed through me. It was like my skin was burning from the inside. Fighting back my urge to pull away, I held her hands tighter.

"Well, don't you look every bit the newlywed? Did you enjoy your honeymoon?" Snowystra asked. "Cole can be so sweet and attentive, can't he?" Her words hurt more than the dark magic she continued to send.

"Yes, Goddess. He told me how he has begun to think of you as a mother figure," I lied. "It's so nice for him. I hope our children will think of you as their grandmother."

Her eyes blazed with anger, confirming my suspicions. She wanted to be the other woman in Cole's life. She sent a final bolt of electricity through me. I swayed under the intense pain.

"Yes, won't it be wonderful. One big happy family."

Dropping my hands, Snowystra sat down on the settee at the end of the bed. "Pity you can't be all alone with Cole, again. It was greedy to keep him the entire month. He has great responsibilities here." The dark goddess glared at me. A fake smile grew on her face. "But you're now back, and we've much to do."

"Yes, we do." I leaned against the dresser, trying to recover from her attack.

"Cole has informed me of your desire to visit the Vetur and even the tunnels. May I ask why?" Snowystra asked, watching me carefully. "It seems like everything you want is, here, in my beautiful palace, not below in the dirty burrows."

"This is a magnificent place to live, but you brought us here to fulfill your plan." I walked towards her. " I need to know who your children are...all of them."

Considering my words, she sighed. "I was hoping to have a little fun before you became serious. I hate to admit it, but you're correct. Business must come first."

Picking up one of my curls, she twisted it around her finger. "I heard your words to Blanche Drygen at your reception. She was quite displeased, but you did make a good point about the boy. She's been quite useless to me, and I would hate to waste more potential on her. I'll send for the boy as soon as possible."

No! My words weren't meant to sentence Miles to this nightmare! Thinking fast while trying to hide my alarm, I said, "I thought about that." I calculated my words, tapping my finger against my lips as though considering the options. "He should be brought here, but I wonder...Don't you think the more time he spends in Danu's realm, learning her magic, would be more beneficial to us?"

"How so?" She let go of my curl, which was now pure white.

Holding out my hands, I called Air. The room filled with purple smoke. Moving my hand quickly to the right, the haze shifted, knocking everything off the dresser and tossing chairs. When I moved the air in the direction of Snowystra, the wind blew back her hair and knocked the blankets off my bed.

I willed my magic to leave, and the dark fog faded away. "As you can see, my magic is strong. I think it's because I have both inside me. If we let him develop his Air magic, he'll be even stronger than me."

She looked around the room, taking in the damage. "Interesting. I did hear about you playing with Fire. Have you tried any of your other gifts?"

"I have not," I said with a smile. "Would you like me to try Earth?"

"Not at this time," she replied. "Maybe, if I decide I'd like a new castle, we can utilize your gift to demolish this one."

"I would enjoy that," I said too quickly.

"Marina, you have become quite the surprise," Snowystra said with a laugh. "Fine, go to the tunnels and see what Danu has done to my poor Vetur. Those are my sorriest bunch. They just don't know how to be proper Vetur. They're so weak and emotional."

Snowystra ran her fingers over my comforter. "Now, is there anything you would like to make this feel more like your home?"

"You've already done everything possible to make it feel like I'm at home," I said. "It's almost perfect, except for the small mess I made, but the help will clear it."

"Yes, they will. On the matter of Laura, I know she's displeased you. She can come across as a bit gruff, but she's very loyal to me," Snowystra purred sweetly.

I knew this was a warning, not friendly banter.

"Are you sure she shouldn't be with you?" I asked, forcing a syrupy-sweet tone. "I'd hate to think any of your needs aren't being met because I've stolen someone away from you."

Laughing, she stood up and strode towards the door. "There's always someone to meet any need I have here. And, if I want..." She stopped at the door. "If I want *Laura* back, I'll take her. However, until then, dearest, just enjoy the time you have with *her*."

I knew she was not talking about Laura, but rather, about Cole. I fumed with anger. Screaming, I threw a ball of the dark fire at the closed door, not worrying that she probably could hear me. I would make sure she paid for anything she'd taken from me. Her reign as the Winter Goddess would, soon, be ending.

The next hour, or so, I spent my time creating more of a mess, throwing everything that seemed like Snowystra picked it onto the floor. Lost in my rage, I didn't hear Laura enter the room.

"Min Vizier." Laura timidly approached me. "I've finished arranging the closet, as you asked. Would you like anything else?"

"Bag all of this up," I said. "I made a bit of a mess showing the goddess my magic. All of it needs to be ready to be taken to the tunnels. Would you like to join us and help deliver everything?"

"No," Laura recoiled. "It's not safe there for…"

"Who isn't it safe for?" I prodded. "Humans?"

"The goddess insists I never go there, again," Laura said, visibly shaking, now. "It will not be allowed."

"If you'd like to join us, I'm sure she'll make an exception to her rule," I said, using a kind voice. "I'll ask her, now."

As I walked away, she grabbed my arm. "Please, don't. I beg you," Laura cried. "It'll only anger her."

"Laura, there's no reason to be afraid," I said, no longer pressing the issue. "You can stay here but prepare all of this to go. I want to leave as soon as the Shah permits. Is there anything else that you'd recommend I bring as a gift?"

"No, no, it's a terrible place. You really should not go there," she warned.

"I understand your concern. It's very dirty and dark there," I replied. "However, I need to really learn about my people. How can I lead those I don't know or understand?"

"There's nothing to learn." Laura's eyes were void of emotion. "They're lost there. Only the outcasts are sent there."

"You said *again*, like you've been there before. Can you tell me what it's like, so I'm not surprised?" I asked her. "I'd like to learn more about you, also."

"I don't know anything." Laura pursed her lips together.

"Do you like living here, Laura?" I asked, changing the subject.

"It's a wonderful place to live," she said in a robotic voice. "I've been given a great gift and I'm very grateful —"

Cutting her off, I took her hand. "No one is listening. You can be honest with me. Can you tell me the story of how you came here?"

"There's no story," Laura said, shifting her eyes. "I want to be here."

I stared intently, wanting to ask her more, but she seemed so fragile. *Will she run to Snowystra and tell her I'm asking questions?*

Tears filled her eyes "I've been given a gift to be here. The goddess has been nothing but loving and kind to me."

Realizing she'd not answer my questions at this time, I relented, "Very well, Laura. You can clean up the mess I made. If you ever change your mind, I'm here to listen."

Leaving Laura to gather everything, I entered the reorganized closet. Laughing at the rainbow of color and the absurdity of the arrangement, I walked to the wall of black clothes.

"Very interesting decision on how to arrange the closet," Christina noted as she entered. "You called for me."

"Yes, I want to meet the Vetur that live in the cottages on the outskirts of the palace, today. I don't need the Shah's approval to do that. So, can you pick me out something that isn't too regal looking?"

"You want to look like you're their queen," Christina said, holding out a knee length red dress. "This would be comfortable."

Accepting the dress, I slipped into it and fastened it. In my haste, my hair caught in the zipper.

"Here, let me help," Christina said. She released my hair from the teeth of the closure and inspected the white strands of hair from Snowystra's touch. "You really should wear your hair down. The Shah is correct. Your curly hair is beautiful." With ease, Christina pulled the sides to my hair back and quickly clipped it. "Let's put a bit of makeup on you, and then you'll be ready."

When I was finished dressing, she took a small vial and poured small granules into her hand. "Place these under your tongue."

"What is it," I asked, following her directions.

Handing the vial to me, she said, "It will help you with the cold. You can't let anyone see you're uncomfortable with it."

"I'm fine with it now," I said, handing the vial back to her. "Cole and I spent our honeymoon at a winter lodge."

"You'll need to wean yourself off the tavi. Please, just trust me." Christina, slipping the vial into my hand, again. "Better safe than sorry."

I found Malise and Dunn waiting when I returned to the room. Malise was dressed in a black and white uniform that looked too big on her small frame. Her hair had been pulled back too tightly.

"Christina, find Malise better fitting clothes," I said. "My new head of household can't look such a mess, and be quick, because the four of us are going to visit the Vetur in the cottages."

Malise's eyes sheened with moisture.

With a soft smile, I said, "Ladies, meet us at the carriage when you're done. Dunn, take me to the Shah."

Dunn led me through the castle and past the kitchen until we arrived at a solid door. Outside, two guards stood watch.

"The Vizier would like to see the Shah," Dunn said, using an authoritative voice. "Announce her arrival."

"He doesn't want to be disturbed," one of the guards responded. "Under no circumstance is he to be interrupted."

"Ridiculous," I said, pushing past them. "Dunn, open the door, now."

"We must insist," the other guard said, holding me back from the entrance. "He left strict instructions."

Holding my hands out, I called Air. This time, I focused on creating a powerful gust of wind. A small twister formed in front of me, throwing the guards out of the way.

They stood strong against my attack. Quickly recovering, they rose and charged me.

I sent a bolt of my dark magic towards them. The green electricity slithered through the air before slamming into their chests. Both men fell to the ground, writhing in pain.

"What's going on out there?" Cole asked, meeting me at the doorway.

"The guards were confused about whether or not I'm allowed to see you," I said innocently. "What's so important that you can't be disturbed?"

"Another Vetur is missing," Cole said. "I have been going through everything, trying to find out where our security is failing. We're not protected, and I can't figure out where the problem starts."

"I'm going to the cottages," I said, taking his hand. "Why don't you come with me?"

"Can't," he said, kissing my hand. "I won't be able to rest until I know they're all safe. I must figure out where the security is weak. If you hear anything that might be helpful, let me know. Now, go meet our Vetur.

CHAPTER
THIRTY-THREE

The cottages were far enough away from the palace that Dunn insisted we take the carriages and a guard detail. In addition, I was accompanied by Malise, who wore a simple black dress and elegant braids, thanks to Christina. As we approached the buildings, I could see women and men milling around. Like the others, they were dressed in dark clothing, but from a distance, they seemed clean and well cared for.

As we drew closer, more Vetur left their homes to greet us. Stepping out of the carriage, I felt uneasy. Words of doubt filled my mind. *Who are you trying to be? You're just a child pretending to be a woman.*

"Min Vizier," Dunn said. "These are your people."

A woman came forward and presented me with a bouquet of white flowers with blue centers. "We welcome you. Your visit's unexpected, but we're glad just the same."

Accepting her offering, I addressed the crowd, "A queen can't rule those she doesn't know. Today, I want to take the time to meet each of you. Your frank and honest responses to my questions are requested."

Handing the flowers to Malise, I said, "Please, take care of my lovely gift." Then, turning back towards the woman, I added, "To start, will you, please, show me where you live?" When she nodded her agreement, I instructed Dunn, "Post a few sentries around the village perimeter and send the rest of the guard to inspect the buildings. I'll be safe with only your protection."

Dunn gave me a questioning look but acquiesced when I glared at him. Giving a small bow, he backed away to deliver orders to his men.

"My home is over there." The woman pointed towards a white cottage with red trim. The outer wall of her house was covered with the white flowers she had given to me. "It's not much to see, but it's home."

Malise stepped closer to me as we headed towards the humble structure, and I whispered, "Let them know they don't need to fear me. Also, make sure I know who's safe to talk to and who I should be wary of."

"You have no need to worry here," she assured me in a quiet voice. "You'll see for yourself what I mean."

Raising an eyebrow at her, I hoped this wasn't a trap.

Entering the young woman's residence, I inhaled the light citrus smell. The cottage was tiny. Furniture inside the small space was sparse with only a table, one chair, and a twin bed against the wall. However, the walls were covered with floral tapestry designs. The room was bright and felt cheery.

"What a pretty home," I said as I wandered through the area. "Oh, I'm sorry. I didn't ask your name."

"Rose –" Having said her name, she gasped and covered her mouth. "I'm sorry. I didn't mean to...Please, don't tell her." Suddenly, she fell to her knees and was pleading at my feet. "I'm sorry. Please, forgive me. Don't send me to the tunnels."

"I'm sorry, but I don't understand. I'm not here to hurt you." I knelt beside her and wiped the tears from her face. "Please, stop crying before they send someone in to see what the fuss is."

Trembling, she tried to stifle her tears.

"Now, enough of that." I stroked her cheek. Images of Meg flashed before me, and I felt an ache in my heart for my little sister. "There's no reason to cry. I'm the queen, but I want to be your friend. Why are you suddenly afraid of me? What did I do to cause you this fear?"

Her mahogany brown eyes sheened with moisture. "The name Rose was given to me by my mother," she said in a hushed voice, "but, I'm not permitted to use it."

"Rose is a pretty name." I smiled at her. "We can keep it our little secret. Now, can you make me a cup of tea and tell me why your name isn't permitted?"

Rose took a kettle from the stove. "When I was a child, I was brought to the castle. I cried every night. I didn't understand why I'd been taken away from my mother."

She poured the beverage over ice. The smell of citrus and black tea filled the air, reminding me of my grandmother's favorite blend.

"When she first took me, the goddess told me I didn't deserve a name but now calls me Flower Girl," Rose explained, not hiding her anger. "I realize now that I was wrong. Snowystra is my mother, and I should forget the one who gave me away."

"Do you know why the children are brought to the castle?" I asked.

"I'll take you to Livia. She'll be able to tell you everything you need to know."

"Good. Let's see her last." I took a long drink of the tea and smiled at her warmly. "I want you to join me as I visit your neighbors."

Before we left the house, I hugged Rose. I felt her stiffen against my body, so I whispered into her ear, "If I'm cruel in the presence of others, remember my words. Everything I do from this point forward will be to keep you safe. Can you trust me?"

Nodding, she surprised me by wrapping her arms around me and hugging me back.

Resisting my normal impatience, I let Rose take me house-to-house, introducing me to the Vetur. Every home was small, but cozy and had been decorated with unique tapestries. The wall hangings seemed to tell a story about the person who lived in that dwelling.

I was kind, but not overly friendly on each visit. I forced myself to play the role of the ice queen. I was afraid, if anyone was watching and I didn't pretend to be the cruel Vizier, it would ruin my plans for escape. And, I didn't make the mistake of asking for names, again.

Finally, we arrived at the largest cottage, the home of Livia. We entered through the back door into the kitchen. It had all the necessities of a home, including a table large enough for a dozen people to sit and enjoy a meal.

A small woman with silver and black streaked hair, braided as if it was a crown, appeared in the entryway of the room. With a commanding voice, she said, "The child of Danu has come. Do you come on her behalf?"

She didn't wait for my response. Instead, she motioned for me to follow and walked away. Unlike the other cottages, which just had small, open spaces, she had an actual house with separate rooms. As she led me deeper inside, I found myself surrounded by looms with half-completed tapestries and shelves with hundreds of brightly colored threads.

Livia sat down in front of one of the looms and began to weave. Her hands moved quickly. Watching her was hypnotizing.

"You made all of the tapestries in the homes throughout the village?" I asked softly, not wanting to interrupt her concentration.

"That isn't the question you want to ask me." Livia set the stick down and stared at me. "You're here to learn about my people, not my art."

"Yes, tell me about them, and how I can help," I confirmed.

"Come," Livia said. "I'll give you the answers you seek."

Leading me to a corner of the room behind the looms, she knelt beside a chest. Opening it, she pulled out a tapestry. "Sit and listen," she said, lowering herself down onto the floor next to it.

Doing as she instructed, I waited anxiously while she held the cloth to her breast. For minutes, she just stared into the distance, as if she was deep in thought. When she gave the fabric to me, she whispered, "You're not the true Vizier."

"Who is?" I asked, opening the tapestry. The brown fabric held a picture of people happy and joyous. They had golden hair and skin.

"This was my people before," she said with sorrow in her voice.

"And this..." She opened a black tapestry that pictured people lying on the ground in pain. There were women holding out their babies to a long-clawed hand that reminded me of Snowystra. "This is my people, now. The lost ones."

"If I'm not the Vizier, who is?"

She laid out a red tapestry that showed a king and queen lying dead on the floor. A small girl was crying at their feet.

"Who's that?" I asked.

"My mother and father." Livia folded the cloth and put it back into the chest. "Long ago, before you were born, there was a great battle between the goddesses, and Snowystra was banished. Her sentence had her sent to an isolated place. When her banishment ended, she searched for those who would be able to renew her initial strength and replace the followers she'd lost. Time increased her anger while it lessened the strength of her magic, so she sought my kingdom, knowing my father was a powerful god."

Livia sighed. I wasn't sure she'd go on, but with a deep breath, she continued.

"We weren't called the Vetur, then. My people were called the Miezitari. One day, Snowystra arrived in our kingdom and tricked my father. He was convinced she'd make our monarchy stronger and that we would be safe from his greatest enemy. She used her time in his good graces to weaken our people."

Livia stood. Her eyes blazed with anger. "When my mother found out about her plans to grow her magic and how she was doing it, Snowystra demanded my father kill my mother and make her his wife. He refused and told her to leave. Upon exiting, she warned him he'd regret his decision and, that night, she returned to murder my parents. Anyone who objected to her claim to the kingdom was instantly killed."

"Why would she do that?" I asked, horrified.

Livia puffed up with pride. "The magic my people held was strong because we were the guardians of death. When life was lost, it was the Miezitari who escorted souls to their Afterlife." Her voice went flat. "Somehow, Snowystra found a way to use our magic to strengthen her own. When the Miezitari no longer had the responsibility of bringing peace to the dead, the magic inside them turned dark and cold. They became the people you see, today."

"So, who escorts the dead, now?" I asked, not truly understanding what she was telling me.

"There's only one, now – Mortorcus," she said. "My father."

"Mortorcus is your father?" I asked. "But I thought he was murdered?"

"When she killed my family, I called to the Gods, pleading over his dead body. I begged for my father's return. He was brought back in the form you see, today — a skeleton of a man," Livia sneered.

The gods can be cruel, I realized.

"I told Snowystra I prayed for a strong champion to continue our work and to protect her. She believes the Gods agreed with her plan. To thank me for confirming this, she spared my life." Livia sat down on the chest and stared at me.

"Why do Snowystra's children look like Vetur?" I asked, trying to make sense of everything.

"Her children? No! Snowystra has no children of her own," Livia corrected, not hiding her disgust. "She takes toddlers from the women in the tunnels and raises them as her own."

"She lied to Cole. She said her people were dying because of Danu. She's convinced him to fight her war, but everything she told him was a lie. Why would she take them?" I asked. The anger I felt towards Snowystra was boiling over. *She must be stopped.*

"The pain and sorrow the families feel from the loss of their children is food for her magic," Livia explained. "It feeds her dorcha."

"The spiders?" I asked.

"The dorcha were, once, called *silver spinners*. The small spiders would create threads used to make the finest silky material. Their intricate webs were turned into this fabric," she explained, pulling out a dark cloth.

As I held it, I noticed it was the same fabric as the clothes I'd worn into the tunnel. The outfit Essie had given me. "I have seen this before."

"It's very rare to find it, but it does still exist," Livia said. "However, sadly, the silver spinners do not."

We sat in silence for several minutes before I stood and held my hand out towards her. "Livia, I don't know where I'm going to take the Vetur, but I'm going to take you all to safety."

She clasped my hand. "I believe you'll be the one to take us home."

"I don't know where your new home will be, but I'm going to figure it out. I promise," I vowed, wanting to stop her pain.

"We must go back to our home in the Eftir Forest," Livia insisted. "We can rebuild there."

"I'm going to the tunnels, tonight. I need to see, for myself, the truth," I said.

"You'll see the pain there that I described," she replied. "You must be careful, though. You can't tell the boy any of this. He will not be loyal to you."

"I have to tell Cole," I insisted. "He's my husband and a good person. He's just confused."

"You're right in saying he's a good person," she said. "But he's lost, right now. You must do this alone. You're the one who's been chosen to save us."

"He'll need to know," I said, not wanting to admit she was right.

"You have the look of Eliza," she noted. "However, she wasn't strong like you."

"My mother? She was here?"

"Snowystra claimed and cursed the lives of Eliza and Cedric. They were to bring any children conceived in their union to her. They were children themselves and had no choice, but to promise their loyalty." Livia shook her head, a shadow of pain visible on her face.

"When Eliza was pregnant with Cedric's boy, she was brought here to give birth. I knew the minute I held him in my arms that he had strong magic inside him," she admitted. "I warned Blanche to never tell anyone, including Eliza."

Blanche knew? I couldn't believe my ears.

Livia continued, "When Snowystra came to see the baby, I told her it was a pity that such a weak child was born from the union. She blamed the Drygen bloodline. Your mother knew she'd never be free unless she grew stronger than Snowystra...Eliza never intended for you to come here."

"Why would Snowystra want our magic?" I questioned. "None of this makes any sense."

"Imprisoned and frightened, Eliza was kept in the tunnels. She was isolated from Cedric and left with Blanche and the child to die. The pain Eliza felt was strong. The more her heart broke for the men she loved and the children she lost, the stronger Snowystra grew."

"You said the dark emotions feed the dorcha?" I asked.

"Yes, they are the vessels for the pain. They hold the emotions of those around them. Go to the tunnels and see what feeds them. Of course, Snowystra never lets them live very long," she said. "When the spiders are killed, she takes their power."

"She kills them?" I questioned with disgust. "She told me they were her children, too."

"When she feels weak, she sends a Vetur to take the dark heart of the dorcha," Livia explained.

"Why doesn't she just kill them herself?" I asked.

"The ones she kills don't hold enough of the darkness to replenish her magic. The full-grown dorcha eventually become immune to the suffering in the tunnels, so they're released into the desert to feed on the pain and terror of their hunters."

My mouth dropped open as the reality struck me. "You mean...?"

She nodded sadly. "Yes, the Vetur are sent into the dangers of the Sephorian Desert to kill and take the heart of the dorcha. If she killed the spider, they wouldn't be given the extra emotions the Vetur felt during their hunt. Being alone in the desert brings emotions to the surface that you could never imagine. Consuming the raw emotion recharges her power."

"She eats the heart?" My stomach churned from the thought.

"She does, and it restores her power," Livia confirmed.

"She's supposed to be of Winter, not this monster," I said.

"She's changed her path," she replied. "Your Cole was sent out the first night he was here."

"To kill a dorcha?" I asked, my chest tightening with panic.

"He came back in one day with the heart and he promised he'd bring you to her to lead her people. He promised her that, together, you'd have strong children who would protect her."

"He really killed a dorcha by himself?" I questioned in surprise.

Livia nodded solemnly.

"She's tricked Cole into believing her stories." I sighed.

"I'm afraid the boy was tortured and threatened into believing. When she sent him to collect the heart, she promised to kill you if he didn't return," Livia said. "This fear guided him. When he returned with the heart, Snowystra was replenished with more dark magic than I'd ever seen. That night, she declared him the Shah."

"So, all of this is to feed her?" I scowled. "If Cole can stop her, why doesn't he?"

"He wants to protect you," she said. Returning to the loom, Livia began to frantically weave.

Not wanting to hear anymore, I said, "Thank you for telling me all of this. I promise I'll figure out a way to return you to your home, soon. Can I trust all of the Vetur?"

"Yes, they're all ready to leave this place," Livia answered softly.

"Why did Dunn not tell me any of this?"

"He has never been sent," she said matter-of-factly. "Only those who go to the desert truly know what happens. If they're lucky enough to return, they're sworn to secrecy."

"How do you know this?"

Standing up, she rolled up her sleeve and showed me her scarred arm. "She sent me when I was a young girl. When I brought her back the heart, she told me I was to tell no one about what I'd seen and done. My reward was eternal life with her," Livia scoffed. "Not much of a reward," she said with disgust in her voice.

"I promise you'll, soon, be free of her."

"The threads will tell us if I'm correct," Livia said, her eyes turning black. "Go now to the tunnel and see for yourself what feeds the magic of your goddess."

"She isn't my goddess and I won't fail you. You have my word."

CHAPTER THIRTY-FOUR

"How am I going to remove everyone safely?" I paced around my suite. Shivering, I put on a sweater. "She'll notice that many Vetur missing." Rubbing my arms for warmth, I said, "It's so cold in here."

Christina poured me a glass of tavi. "Patience is how it will be done," she replied. "You need to remember that you thrive in the cold. You're the dark queen of Snowstrum."

"I know what I need to remember," I said, throwing the tavi and smashing it against the wall. "I need this to be over."

"It won't be today," Malise said as she joined us. "Her magic is at full strength. Two of the men sent have returned with hearts. They've been taken to the tunnels to recover. They'll need care for a while, but they'll live. Trust me, it's not an easy thing to heal from."

"You've been there?" Christina asked and handed me another vial of granules.

Malise nodded solemnly.

"Why did she send you?" I sat down on a sofa and patted the seat next to me. Pouring the contents of the vial into my mouth, I said, "Come, sit. Tell me everything you can."

Staring off into the distance, Malise softly spoke, "I had the audacity to disagree with Snowystra. I was barely a teenager, and I was sick of practicing to kill the dorcha. I was taken to her by one of the guards when I refused."

With a forced laugh, she said, impersonating Snowystra, "'You dare to question my will? You don't want to protect me, your goddess? You're tired of practicing? It appears you are ready, then.' She ordered them to send me into the desert. As they came towards me, she said, 'Do not return empty-handed.'"

Malise shivered from the memory of her ordeal. "I begged her as two of guards dragged me away. I promised I'd learn…that I'd never disobey her, again. She told me it was too late to pretend to be loyal and now I had to earn my place in her realm. The first night in the desert, I wasn't sure where I'd find the dorcha. It was just miles, and miles, of black sand. My training at the castle hadn't prepared me. My first kill was a copper shade."

"You killed a copper shade?" Dunn asked. "Those snakes move like lightning."

"I dug a hole as night fell, thinking it would keep me safe," she explained with a laugh. "I disturbed the shade's sleep. If I hadn't been using the knife I was given to dig the hole, I don't think I would've been able to kill it. Realizing I wouldn't be able to hide in the open, I walked through the night until I found the Rocks of Praivista. Squeezing myself between two of them, I ate the cold meat of the snake, hoping I'd find the dorcha quickly and go home."

Malise laughed hysterically. Her fit ended with tears. Choking out her words between sobs, she said, "Yes, I wanted to come home to my goddess. I wanted the safety of the walls, not the fear of the unknown."

"You were a child, Malise." I patted her hand. "There's nothing wrong with wanting that."

She composed herself. "Climbing to the top of the rocks, I watched for days. Finally, I found one as the sun was setting. When light returned, I went to find it. I searched, and searched, with no luck. Returning to the rocks, I watched, again."

She licked her lips as though her mouth was dry. "The copper shade saved me from needing to find food. Water was trickier, but I spotted a vaream growing in a crack of the rocks. The green plant had a small amount of water inside it, which I rationed. My skin was red from the hot sun and my body ached."

"As the sun rose, I found it." Malise turned to look at me with a pleading expression. "I knew I couldn't wait any longer, even if I had to fight off other creatures. I didn't want to kill the dorcha, but I wanted to live."

I could see the determination return to her eyes.

"When I reached it, I threw myself on top of it and stabbed it in the eyes. The screams of pain were horrible." She closed her eyes against the memory. "When I injured it enough, it collapsed, and I rolled it onto its back. Exhausted myself, I don't know how I did it, but, thankfully, it died."

Malise rubbed her hand over her face. "Cutting out its heart, the large dorcha spider underneath me shifted and changed into a small, silver spider. I took the heart and the tiny body with me when I returned to the portal cave. Inside it, I found a young girl. When she saw me, she screamed. I imagined seeing someone covered in the green blood of the dorcha, holding a green heart, would be a nasty sight for any human to see."

"Green? Is it, also, called kan…kan – something?" I asked as I recalled the meat at our wedding dinner.

"Yes, kanakala," she replied. "How do you know that?"

"That and some purple vegetables were my wedding meal," I said, feeling sick at the thought.

"Are you OK, min Vizier?" Dunn questioned. "You look ill."

"I'm fine," I answered. "Please, continue your story. You're in the cave and you found a girl."

"The girl fainted. When I woke her up, I told her to run…to leave," Malise resumed her tale. "She wouldn't go. I begged, warning her there were scary things in the cave. I told her there were things more frightening than anything she'd seen in her world. Still, she refused."

Frustration washed over Malise's face. "She said she knew there was magic here and that I was wrong about her world. When the guards arrived to see if I had returned, they misunderstood. They thought I'd brought her for the goddess. I remember the guard laughing, saying, 'the goddess will be pleased because the last five servants haven't worked out very well.' I should've told them they were wrong. I should've helped her escape. But I was tired and scared for my own life, so I brought Laura —"

"Laura?" I asked in astonishment. "The Laura that's still here?"

"Yes, the girl I found was that Laura."

"But she's older than you?"

"Not at all. I've lived for ninety years. I think?"

"Christina, how old are you?" I asked.

Smiling, she said, "I'm sixty-five."

"But you don't look much older than my mother. You don't look sixty-five," I commented. "Dunn, how old are you?"

"I'm over a hundred twenty years. I'm incredibly lucky I was never sent to the desert in all that time," he said, taking Malise's hand. "But I always hid in the shadows, even when I was in the castle. I knew nothing of any of this. I only knew people were sent, but I thought it was just punishment. I thought it was just another of her cruel games."

"Why was Laura in the cave?" I questioned.

"Laura had run away from home. She entered one of the portals by mistake and ended up inside the cave. She was to be married to a man old enough to be her grandfather, whom she said was cruel. He had beaten her when she refused to marry him. I wonder, sometimes, if she had to make the choice again, if she would've married him rather than live here?"

"We can't go back and second-guess the decisions we made in the past," Christina said. "We've all chosen this path. The only thing we can do now is focus on today. Laura will need the most convincing to leave."

The door to the room opened. Christina stood quickly and the other servants followed suit. Cole strode into the room, looking worn.

Did he hear us talking? Snapping, I said, "I want it done – *now*! Why do I have to request these things? You should just know what I want."

"Who's displeased my beloved?" Cole asked in a cruel voice. "You were all told to promptly give her whatever she wanted. I'll not tolerate this."

"Don't worry about that, love." I kissed him on the cheek, and then pointed my sharp nail at others. "Go now and do as I ask."

Moments later, servants arrived, rolling in trays of food, and quickly set the small table. Christina and Malise had thought of everything.

Wrapping my arms on top of Cole's shoulders, I whispered, "They'll learn what I want, or I'll replace them." Nibbling his neck, I said, "I thought we could have a quiet meal together before we go to the tunnels."

Cole tilted his head to the side, welcoming my attention while giving me better access.

Cruelly, I pulled away, and said, "Come sit and see what I had sent up."

He groaned in annoyance but let me guide him towards the candlelit table.

Christina poured us each a glass of tavi. "Will that be all, min Vizier?" she asked as she placed our food in front of us.

"Yes," I barked. "Now, leave us alone."

I hated myself for acting like such a tyrant and was even more frustrated at how easily I fell into the role. My only comfort was knowing Christina knew it was an act. I watched Cole sipping the drink and realized how weak he looked. "Do you want to shower or change before we eat?"

"No." Cole shrugged off his jacket and poured himself more tavi. "This is fine."

"Did you find any answers to the issue?" I asked, trying to make chitchat.

"More guards are being sent to the outskirts of Snowstrum." Cole guzzled the rest of the drink. "I've made sure the palace and cottages are well protected, but there's more to do. The protection of the goddess needs to be my priority. Her sisters' plans to remove her magic, again, must be stopped."

"Is there anything I can do?" I questioned. "I really want to help Snowystra get everything she deserves."

Like a knife driven through her heart, I thought.

"I know you do, Marina." Cole kissed my cheek. "You've shown me, with your interest in the Vetur, that you understand. Your being here is enough." Pointing at the platter in front of us, he said, "So, what do we have here?"

"I hope you like what I chose for us to eat. I asked the chef to make one of your favorite meals," I said, taking the lid off his platter to show him.

Cole stared at the food with a look of sadness. "Gram's chicken pot pie," he whispered.

"If you'd like something else, I can have it sent up. Try it first, though. I had them chilled for us." I held a spoonful of the pastry towards him.

Accepting the bite, he said, "No, it's good. Lestop did an excellent job. It tastes almost like what she would've made. I just wish things were different. Mae would've been such a help here. Her gift wouldn't have been wasted. If she had only known the truth."

"We can't worry about that, now. She wouldn't want to hear you talking like this. So, go on and eat your food." I offered him another spoonful. "We still have plans to go to the tunnels, tonight, right?"

"I was thinking about that," he replied. "You've been there. Why the need to go again?"

"I never met them as their queen." I poured him another drink.

"I was hoping you had something a little more relaxing in mind for the evening," Cole said, taking his last bite. "You're too good to me, Marina. This was the perfect dinner with my beautiful bride."

"Why don't you rest for a bit," I suggested, trying not to be too eager. "I could fix you a bubble bath or you can just take a nap. Your choice."

His eyes were heavy, and the warm meal did nothing to reinvigorate him.

"Let's take a raincheck on the bath," I said. "You look like you're almost asleep already. Why don't you rest?"

"OK, but only for just a bit." Stripping off his shirt, I could see his chest was covered, again, with red streaks and fresh bruises. He stood, slipped out of the rest of his clothes, and climbed into the bed in his boxers. "Come lay with me and tell me about your day."

Snuggling into his arms, I rested my head on his chest while he stroked my hair. "I went to the cottages, today. They seemed really happy."

I described the tapestries and the homes, not really knowing if what I was saying was accurate. It didn't matter. He had stopped listening. His breathing became heavy before he began to softly snore.

"Cole," I whispered, "are you awake? I know the truth, Cole. I'm going to stop her, and everything will change."

"Everything will change," he murmured.

Kissing him on the cheek, I left him to rest while I prepared for my visit to the tunnels.

CHAPTER
THIRTY-FIVE

Riding in the carriage on our way to the tunnels, I was thankful I wasn't thrown through the air on this trip. I was amazed by the winter wonderland. Snow in Starten was rare and when it did fall, it melted quickly.

Cole sat next to me, silently reading a book. Peeking at it, I couldn't read the words. It was in a strange language.

"What are you engrossed in?" I asked, looking over his shoulder.

"Snowystra gave it to me to help me understand the Vetur," he said, barely stopping to address me.

"Should I read it, too?" I asked, scooting closer towards him.

"No, you'd find it boring. It's more technical information."

"I like technical."

"No, Marina," he said. "You wouldn't be able to read it, anyway."

Taking it from him, I flipped through it. "And you can read this?"

"Yes," he said, taking it back. "I'll just be a few more minutes. Look, we're almost there."

Pouting, I looked outside the window and saw a sparkling blue cave in front of us. "What is that?" I asked.

"That's our entrance to the tunnels. It's the access to the portal..." His voice trailed off.

I made a mental note to ask Dunn about this, instead of pressing Cole.

"I like the outfit you chose for tonight," he said, inspecting me.

Christina had selected a deep red dress that fell above my knees. The long sleeves and scooped neckline made me feel like a little girl playing dress up.

"You look like a queen."

"I didn't wear my crown. Will that be a problem?" I asked, laughing.

"Not at all. I'm glad you chose to wear the spider necklace Snow gave you."

"Of course, it's such a pretty necklace. It almost seems to change color, depending on what I wear."

"Well, you look magnificent, Marina," he said, kissing me on the cheek. "Red really is your color."

Entering the tunnels, this time, was quite different. There was no slime or crawling through tight spaces. Instead, we walked through a long, ice blue corridor. Along the way, there were ripples on the wall that caught my eye. Cole held my hand and kept me close, not giving me a chance to inspect it.

When we reached the end of the hallway, I saw the ripple in the wall ahead of us. "Did we go the wrong way? We're at a dead end," I said.

"Trust me," he said as he walked through the wall.

As half of his body disappeared, I realized what the ripples were throughout the hallway. They were portals. Each of them was, probably, access to the various places the dark goddess wanted to go. The one we entered led us to the great hall, where we appeared behind the thrones.

As I took my seat, the Vetur below cheered. "They are here! Hail to the Shah. Hail to the Vizier."

Cole stood at the edge of the platform. "We've come, tonight, for my new bride to learn more about you. I know many of you, but your queen would like to get to know you, too. In honor of our new reign, the Vizier has requested that we bring you gifts."

Guards entered the hall carrying four huge bags. As the contents were dumped onto the ground, the Vetur looked down hesitantly at the gifts. Once they confirmed it was real, a wave of bodies attacked the pile. I watched as they clawed, kicked, and scratched each other.

Cole laughed. "I told you we shouldn't have brought them anything."

"Stop them," I demanded. "We can't let them fight like this. Make them stop."

Ignoring me, he wore a look of satisfaction. Cole's eyes became frost white as he looked down on the violence.

Shaking his arm, I hissed, "Cole, make them stop, now. I didn't come to watch them kill each other."

His eyes returned to blue and in a deep threatening voice, he yelled, "Stop this immediately!"

Guards began tossing the Vetur off the presents.

"You're not animals. The gifts were not to be fought over. There's plenty for all. Stand up. Pick up two items and walk towards the walls. Anyone who disagrees with that, let me know. I would be happy to discuss your options," Cole said.

The Vetur stopped and stared at each other before slowly obeying his command. When they had all taken two items, the guards called, "What do we do with the leftovers?"

"Let them work it out themselves," Cole called down to them. "However, if there's any more fighting, we'll not bring the meal that was prepared for you."

Silently, the Vetur went back to the pile and took one additional item each. They repeated the process until there was nothing left. Then, they put on the clothes and jewelry, showing off their prizes. In the new clothing, they looked more like those living in the cottages.

"See how nice they look? Why do we not take care of them like those on the palace grounds?" I questioned.

"These are the lost. They'll not care for their gifts. See in an hour how they'll treat your presents," Cole growled.

"I have requested the palace chef make a feast for all of you," I said, addressing the crowd. "But I'll not tolerate any more fighting. There will be plenty for all to eat. I promise this. Now, line up nicely and take your turns."

Carts were pushed in by servants from the castle. The Vetur looked at the food with greed and desperation. I could visibly see their efforts to restrain themselves.

When they all had their plates of food and had settled to eat, I said, "I want to know each of you, and I want this to be my home as much as yours. However, there will be no more violence, tonight."

As if my words sparked a flame, a fight broke out between two men.

Cole roared, "Bring them to me."

Carried up the stairs and thrown at our feet, Cole glowered. "What is all of this? Did you not hear your queen's command?"

"I was just trying to bring her a gift and he took it from me," one man explained.

"You wanted to give my bride a gift?" Cole asked, glaring at the man.

"Yes," he said. Holding out a snake ring.

Is this my father's ring? How did it get here? I wondered to myself. "Thank you," I said, taking it. "My gifts were not supposed to start a fight."

"I'm sorry. I just thought it looked important," the man said, hanging his head.

"He didn't. You just thought you'd get in good with her," the second Vetur said.

"That isn't true," the man cried.

"The reason doesn't matter, but you both will have time to decide the truth in the desert," Cole decreed with a smile.

"No," I started to say. "The desert for fighting?"

"The desert for disobeying a command of their Vizier."

With those words, they both hung their heads.

"Take them to the jail," Cole ordered. "In the morning, they'll be sent to the Sephorian Desert. When they return in eight days, hopefully, they will have learned their lesson."

The crowd cheered.

Seeing how content the tunnels made him, I wasn't sure how much of my Cole was left inside. The chill in the air made me shiver and I could see my breath. Quickly, I opened the vial Christina had given me and dropped the granules under my tongue.

As my body warmed up, again, I said to Cole, "I'd like to see the rest of the tunnels. Can we go, now?"

"Unless you're going to borrow some of their trashy clothing for later, I can't see what would interest you here," he said with a sly smile. "Why bother? All you'll see is here already. If you want, I can have them brought to us, one-by-one."

A sudden urge came over me to punch and kick at him. I wanted to make him hurt. Controlling my temper, I said, "Never mind. I'll go by myself."

Whispering to Dunn, Cole commanded, "Escort the queen through the tunnels and keep her safe."

Forcing myself to play the obedient queen, I kissed him on the cheek. "I'll be back soon. Try not to miss me."

Malise and Dunn led me out the large doors and down a new hallway. The walls along the path were covered in dirt and spider webs. When we reached a hole with cloth hung for a door, we stopped.

"Stay here, min Vizier," the guard, called Jameson, said. "I'll make sure it's safe for you to enter." When he slipped into the room, he yelled, "Wake up. Get up and get dressed. The queen is here."

Small sounds of movement could be heard in the hallway as the guard barked orders at whoever was inside.

Returning to us, Jameson said, "They should be decent, now. Well, as civilized as possible for this trash. If you wish, I'll go ahead and make sure the others know you're coming."

"Please, do," I agreed. Catching Dunn's eye, I could tell he didn't like this. "Dunn, go with him and make sure no one is hurt."

Nodding at me, he followed Jameson. "The Vizier doesn't want anyone hurt," Dunn said in a low growl. "I'm not sure you can handle this job, Jameyboy."

Tensing at Dunn's comment, Jameson glared. "I heard her instructions, but I, also, remember where my loyalty truly lies."

"As we all do," Dunn retorted. "But, right now, you should know it lies with our queen. Why don't you go back to the hall while I check on the Vetur? Your cruelty is best served there. Go ahead. I'll make sure the others are alerted of our visit."

Jameson glared at Dunn. "As you wish," he said as he stormed past me.

When I was sure he was out of earshot, I asked, "What was that all about?"

"He's always been cruel. His presence won't help us, especially if we don't want anyone to get hurt. He's one to not trust," Dunn answered. "He's loyal to Snowystra. There are rumors that he had hopes of being the Shah before Cole arrived."

"Come with me into the first room," I said to Malise and Dunn. "I want them to know they can talk to me."

When we entered the room, there was a young woman and a man.

They both stood with hands clasped, looking extremely nervous. The nook was barely large enough for the five of us. It held a small table with two chairs and in the corner was a pile of tattered blankets.

"This is our new queen," Malise explained. "She's going to help us, so be honest with answers to her questions or you'll be taken, immediately, to the desert."

"But, but I –" the woman stammered.

Interrupting her, the man replied, "We'll be honest. Don't worry. No one is going to need to be sent to the desert. We'll tell the truth." Bowing towards me, the man added, "I'm Philip and this is my mate, Natasha."

"Were you recently married?" I asked. Both looked so young.

"We did ask the goddess for permission. She said it was OK for us to marry," Natasha said quickly.

"I asked because you both look so young. I was being curious," I explained, trying to use a soft tone. My patience felt tried. The tunnels seemed to bring out something inside me I didn't like.

Squeezing her hand, Philip said, "I apologize that we weren't able to attend your wedding. I heard it was nice."

"Thank you. It was, but I'm here to talk about you, now. Do you like living here?" I asked. I began rapidly asking questions, hoping it would throw them off guard and I'd get honest answers. "Where do you cook your food? Where do you sleep? Is there a bathroom?"

"This is just our room," Philip answered. "All of the things you asked about are in the main dorm. We're lucky to have been given a room by the goddess."

Looking around, I felt even angrier. *This is an upgrade? What else am I going to see here?* The conditions were shocking. Focusing back on the couple, I asked, "If you could have one thing you don't have, what would it be, Natasha?"

"A bed like they have in the cottages," she blurted out.

"Philip, do you have one request?"

"The goddess has blessed us with her gifts. We deserve nothing more," he replied.

"That wasn't my question. What would you want?" I asked, again.

Looking at his wife, she shook her head.

"What is it you're afraid to ask me?" I questioned, softening my tone.

"Natasha's carrying our first child and she hasn't been feeling well," he answered. "I'd like to make sure she's OK."

"I'm fine," the woman insisted. "Just normal pregnancy issues."

"You should be examined when you're pregnant." I looked at the skinny woman. She was bone thin. I would have never known she was with child. "You shouldn't have had to make this request. Isn't there a doctor here?"

Both looked at me as if I was speaking another language.

Dunn answered, "There are no doctors in Snowstrum."

"Tomorrow, you'll come to the cottages, and I'll have someone sent to examine you," I said.

"Thank you," Philip replied nervously. "But, will the goddess not be angered?"

"Your child being healthy and strong benefits our kingdom. She'll appreciate that we want to make sure Natasha is well. One day, the Vetur will rule, but only with fit children will this happen," I responded confidently. "Thank you for your honesty."

As the couple bowed towards me, I exited the dwelling. Back in the hallway, I said, "Malise, arrange for beds to be brought, tonight, for all the Vetur."

"She'll be infuriated," Malise warned.

"I'll be more enraged if it's not done," I snapped. "You're under my direction. Please, do as I say and direct any questions to me."

Continuing the tour, I visited each room, but I no longer asked for requests. I asked, instead, about their day-to-day lives. Two more women told me they were expecting children, soon, and both were not well. I insisted they come to the cottages the next day, as well.

In the last room we entered, I found a mother and her child.

"Min Vizier," the woman said, welcoming me. "May I offer you something to drink?"

On the table, she had a glass of tavi poured that she offered to me. Accepting the glass, I took a tiny sip. I restrained myself from polishing off the drink and asking for more.

The little boy, who had been sitting on the floor playing with stones, ran up and tugged on the hem of my skirt.

I picked up the small child and looked into his dark blue eyes. His dark hair and round face made me think of Miles. "What is your name, little one?"

"He doesn't have one," the woman answered.

"Why not?"

"The goddess hasn't named him, yet" she replied.

"What do you call him?"

Hesitating, she looked at Malise.

"It's OK, Anna," Malise encouraged.

"I call him, Daniel," she said. "Only so he'll know I'm speaking to him."

"That's a very nice name," I praised. "I hope the goddess will keep it."

"She mustn't ever know I call him anything," Anna insisted. Her wide eyes clearly expressed her terror.

"I'll not mention it," I promised. "When will the child be named?"

Again, Dunn answered, "When he is taken to the palace."

I watched as the woman's face turn even paler, and she choked back a sob. My heart went out to her.

"Bring this family a bed, a crib, a new table, toys for Daniel, clothes for Anna, and anything else they want or need," I ordered. Setting the boy down, I kissed him on the cheek. "Goodbye, little Daniel. I'll see you again, soon." Taking the woman's hand, I whispered, "Your son will grow to be strong and healthy. I promise he'll always be safe."

I wanted to tell her she wouldn't be without her son. That he wouldn't know what it was like to be without his mother. I wanted to tell her I was going to right all of Snowystra's wrongs. Instead, I said, "I think I've seen enough, today. Go through the rooms to see what's needed to make everyone comfortable for the time being."

They couldn't live here long, but I'd make sure they had some comfort. More so, I wanted to ensure they'd be strong enough when the time to leave came.

When I returned to the main hall, I found Cole sitting on the throne, but he wasn't alone. Two of the women had taken a seat on each side of him. They were bold in their attention as they stroked his hair. One of the women whispered something into his ear. Whatever she said made him laugh.

As I walked up the stairs, Cole and I locked eyes. "Did you enjoy your visit?" he asked.

"It was quite informative," I replied. "You might want to join me, next time."

"My time here was just what I needed," he said, smiling at the women. "I forgot how relaxing the tunnels can be."

"If you've had your fun, I'm ready to go," I said, glaring at him.

"The night has just begun. Come have a drink with us." Cole held up a glass.

Shoving the women out of the way and knocking one onto the ground, I sat on his lap. Leaning in closely and whispering into his ear, I said, "I'm ready to leave and, in case you've forgotten, we were married a month ago. Whatever's going on here won't happen in the future. Pick your excuse, but we *are* leaving – *now*."

Wrapping his arms around me tightly, he whispered back, "Maybe you don't get it, anymore, but you're not the boss of me, Marina. I'm the king here. I'm in charge."

My heart raced and my urge to attack him was strong. "I don't know if you remember, but my magic was very strong at home, and it has only increased since I've been here. Did you know I have been playing with my new magic while you've left me alone? It's quite surprising how quickly I can call all four elements. Should we test my Earth magic, today, and see if I can crumble the tunnels onto us? Perhaps you would like to see what my Water magic holds? I suspect it'll be a nice and acidic. But you're correct, your highness. It is *your* decision."

"You wouldn't do that." Cole pushed me away, meeting my gaze.

I smiled smugly before I kissed him on the cheek. "I guess you're not the only one who has changed."

Focusing on my Earth magic, I willed it to lightly shake the ground. He was right; I didn't want to hurt the Vetur. They were suffering enough. I just wanted to send him a warning.

As the ground rumbled and clumps of dirt fell from the ceiling, the Vetur screamed below.

Cole looked at me with a cold look of hate. "Guards, I'm ready to return to the palace."

The crowd booed.

"Don't worry. We'll return, again, my people." Cole grabbed me hard around the waist, pulling me against him. "We've just returned from our honeymoon, and I fear we're exhausted."

Turning towards me, he growled. "Address your people."

"The Shah is right. We'll return, again, soon, with more gifts and goodies. Please, enjoy the rest of the festivities we've planned for you. The guards will remain to ensure you're safe," I called to them.

The crowd cheered louder.

At the entrance of the hall, I could see Anna watching me. Locking eyes with her, I nodded. Seeing the hope in her eyes, I vowed change would come, and soon — even if it meant I couldn't save Cole.

When we got into the carriage, Cole was fuming. In all of my life, I had never seen him so mad. "You will never force my hand like that again. You don't make the decisions. I'm the king."

"You may be the king, but I'm your wife," I spat back, not hiding my own anger. "Is that how I should expect you to act from now on? If you want to be with other women, why did you marry me? If you want them, let me go. Send me back to Starten."

"You're being ridiculous." Cole shifted uncomfortably under my cold stare. "They were just keeping me company. It was harmless."

"And, if I'd been gone longer?" I asked. "What would I have returned to, then?"

"Nothing would've happened," Cole insisted. "They mean nothing to me. You mean everything."

"I'll never go to the tunnels, again." I slid as far as I could away from him. "It does something to us in there. You're not the man I married in there. You're not the man I love. I won't live this life with you." Staring out the window, I watched the snow become thicker.

"Mara."

Shock filled me, and my bitterness softened. *He called me Mara.*

Cole scooted closer to me and lifted my chin.

My eyes searched his, hoping the boy I loved was not gone.

"I'm sorry. I'm not sure what happens to me in the tunnels. I feel like I don't even have control over my mind, anymore."

I could see he was sincere in his apology, but I couldn't shake my fear of losing him to Snowystra. Narrowing my eyes at him, I said, "I'm the only woman in your life. The applies to Snowystra, too."

Guilt flashed on his face before Cole quickly laughed. "It's not like that, Marina. She loves me like a mother would."

I saw you kissing her! I tugged at his shirt exposing red streaks. "If that's true, where do these come from? They look like her marks."

"That's nothing. It's from training," he said, dismissing me and closing his shirt.

"We've made an oath to Winter, but I can't live in this kind of darkness," I told him. "And I don't think the Vetur should, either. Did you know their children are taken from them and raised in the castle?"

"Where did you hear that?" Cole asked with irritation in his voice.

"I wasn't told," I said. "I saw the children in the castle on our wedding day."

"Snow takes them from the tunnel to give them a chance to be strong," Cole explained. "Dunn was raised in the tunnel and so was the new maid. They've all grown to be strong and healthy because of Snow."

"Why not take them all out of the tunnels? Why not give them all a chance to be happy and healthy?" I questioned, knowing he was wrong about how Dunn and Malise were raised.

Cole grabbed my wrist and said in a low growl, "You're interfering where you shouldn't."

I yanked my arm back and glared. "I am the Vizier. These are my people, too. I've directed the pregnant women to be brought to the cottages, tomorrow, for checkups. I want you to close the tunnels. Relocate everyone to more suitable housing."

"You're speaking nonsense. We won't infect the others because you felt sorry for a few. They will stay where they belong!" he yelled. Relaxing his tone, Cole said, "But, the women will be looked at and sent back, immediately. There will be no more discussion on this subject. None. This stops now."

Running his fingers through his hair, he sunk down into his seat. "You're misunderstanding everything. You're just being suspicious. This was all to save them. Everything was to help them."

Watching the love of my life crumble before me, I decided to back down, at least, for the night. Holding him close to me, the way a mother coddles a small boy, I stroked his hair as he rested against me. "It'll be fine, Cole. I'll learn to understand."

How am I going to save him and the Vetur?

By the time we arrived at the palace, Cole was sound asleep.

Jameson opened the carriage door. "Did he drink too much? Shall I carry him up?"

"Please, do so," I said with a forced laugh. "We did have a bit too much to drink. It does seem to flow freely there."

Nodding, he agreed, "Yes, it does."

We walked through the castle in silence.

Reaching our chamber, Jameson placed Cole on the bed. "I'll send someone to undress him."

"No need," I said. "I can take care of him."

Jameson bowed in acknowledgment before taking his leave.

Finally alone, I removed his clothes, first, and then my own. I threw them on the ground. I still felt dirty from the tunnels, but I was too tired to do anything about it. Climbing into the bed next to Cole, I watched as he slept.

I'm not going to have to choose. I am going to save them all.

CHAPTER
THIRTY-SIX

In the morning, I woke to Cole whistling. "Good morning, my love," he greeted me. "Did you sleep well?"

Wiping the sand from my eyes, I replied, "I did. You're up early?"

"We've much to do," Cole said cheerily. "The palace doesn't run itself. I'm going to inspect the grounds and make sure everything's in order. Would you like to join me?"

Surprised, I said, "I would."

"Wait," he paused. "There are women coming to the cottages to see if they're healthy, right? You probably want to be there for them."

"I do." I eyed him suspiciously. *What's his motive? Last night, he told me I couldn't help them.*

Kissing me on the cheek, he said, "I've had breakfast sent up for you."

"Wait," I said. "Why are you leaving so early? Stay and eat with me."

"I'll be gone for the day." He kissed me, again. "It's tempting to stay in bed with you, but duty first."

Catching his hand as he tried to leave, I pulled him back towards me. "Just a few more minutes."

Scooping me up into his arms, Cole carried me to our dining table and set me in the chair. Kneeling beside me, he kissed the inside of my wrist. "I won't be long, my lovely temptress. I'll make it up to you, tonight. Promises of a bubble bath have, yet to be claimed and I want to cash in on them this evening. Until then, take care of our Vetur."

Nibbling on the fruit and cheese Cole had sent up, I was lost in thought when Laura entered the room.

"Excuse my interruption," Laura apologized and bowed. "Should I come back when you're done with your breakfast?"

"No, please, come sit," I answered, recalling what Malise had told me about the woman. "I need your assistance."

"But I can't sit at a table with you," she said nervously.

"Ridiculous, take a seat." I pointed at the seat. "I don't want to dine alone."

Laura sat as instructed but looked around as if someone would jump out of the shadows. Filling a plate with food, I set it in front of her. "Eat," I commanded.

"I couldn't," Laura tried to stand. "It wouldn't be proper."

"Sit," I said firmly. "I'm commanding you to eat breakfast with me. There will be no repercussions for *my* demands. So, please, eat and pretend to enjoy yourself."

As she took a bite of the apple, Laura forced a smile.

"See, it wasn't that bad," I responded. "I wasn't always a queen, you know. Quite recently, I was a seventeen-year-old girl with no idea of the magic around me. I, sometimes, wish I could go back to those days."

Instead of questioning her, I let Laura enjoy the meal. When we finished, I said, "Thank you for not making me eat alone."

"Your wish is my command, min Vizier," Laura smiled. "Is there anything else you'd like?"

"The pregnant Vetur are coming to the cottages to be examined," I said. "I understand there are no doctors here. Who helps deliver the babies?"

"They are delivered in the cottages." Laura glanced around the room, again,

"Laura, I know how you came to be here," I said softly.

Her face turned to sorrow.

"I know you're forced to stay. We're similar in more ways than you realize. If you know anything that can help these women, I beg that you tell me."

Tears fell from her eyes as Laura explained, "My mother was a midwife, and I would go with her to help deliver the babies. She taught me everything she knew. When she died, I was sent to live with my aunt."

Even though I knew how she arrived in Snowstrum, there was obviously more to her story. It was clearly difficult for her to relive what happened. I almost stopped her from telling it, but I needed to know everything.

"I was sixteen when I ran away from home." Laura cleared her throat before she continued, "My aunt had arranged for me to marry a much older man. He was an awful person. The night before the ceremony I told them I couldn't go through with it, so he beat me." She shivered though it wasn't cold in the room.

As Laura inhaled deeply before slowly exhaling, I waited patiently.

Finally, she said, "When I was able to escape, I ran as fast as I could. He was old, but quite athletic and I couldn't outrun him. I looked back to see how close he was and smacked into a tree. Instead of being hurt, I found myself inside an ice cave. When Malise showed up, she warned me, but I didn't listen." Wiping her tears, Laura confessed, "I should've listened."

"I'm sorry to make you talk about this." I reached out and touched her hand. "You said your mother taught you how to midwife. So, does that mean you helped deliver the babies?"

"Yes," Laura confirmed in a hushed voice, "but, please, tell no one." She yanked her hand from mine and stood. "She mustn't ever find out."

"I won't tell. However, I need your help," I said. "I'm going to the cottages, and I need you to accompany me. I'd like you to examine the pregnant women. Some have been feeling unwell."

"I can't," she complained. "It's too dangerous."

"I won't make you, but I hope you will reconsider," I said, not hiding my disappointment. "I need to get ready. Please, send Christina in to help me dress."

"Yes, min Vizier." Laura bowed, and then scurried away. Stopping, she said, "I truly am very sorry."

When we arrived at the cottages, Natasha and the other women greeted us.

"Thank you for coming," Natasha said. "I've been so worried."

"Let's get the women to Livia's house," Dunn ordered. "It's best to have these discussions there."

As expected, we found Livia weaving at her loom. "You've brought the women too early," she said, not looking at them. "They aren't due for months."

"They've been ill, and I need someone to make sure their pregnancies are healthy," I explained.

"There's no one here to help with this," Livia said. "We just need to wait for them to deliver."

"That's too risky," I argued. "We must find someone."

"There's no one here. In the future, there will be," Livia said, not bothering to look away from her weaving. "But, not today."

"I can examine them," a voice from behind me said. I turned to see Laura entering the room. My eyes brightened as the sight of her.

"I realized I was being weak. My mother would've helped. Now, where can I examine the women?"

Livia stopped weaving and smiled. "Follow me." She led us to a spare bedroom. It had a small bed with a yellow blanket on it and a flowered chair.

The women looked nervous.

"I'll leave you to —" I said before Natasha interrupted me.

"Can you, please, stay?" she asked. "I'm scared."

"Please, stay," the other women echoed in pleading voices.

"OK. I'll wait here while Laura examines you."

Laura asked questions about their food intake and exercise, getting a patient history to start. Then, one-by-one, she examined them. Though thorough, she was very gentle and kind. Her demeanor was nothing like the woman I'd first met.

"Each of you is really underweight," Laura said. "You need to eat more. I'll, also, bring you some heilsavi. It's a strong tonic that will help you feel better. All in all, your little ones appear healthy."

As I was leaving the room, Livia appeared. "In twelve days' time, we'll take my people from here. Will you be able to help us, or will I lead them alone?"

"OK. Twelve days and we leave," I said. "In the meantime, I'll not be back here unless needed. Run everything through Dunn. I promised I'd help you escape."

Handing me a folded tapestry, she said, "I know. It has been told."

Unfolding the cloth, I saw a dark-haired woman with an eerie resemblance to me. She was holding a fire sword in one hand and a blue orb in the other. Behind her were large, brightly colored wings.

"No longer the caterpillar...you must become the butterfly," Livia said as she walked away.

CHAPTER
THIRTY-SEVEN

Escape plans moved fast with Dunn and Malise coordinating everything. They assured me that all of the necessary steps to ensure safe and healthy travel for the Vetur were put into place. I was left in the dark as much as possible to protect the plan.

In addition to preparing, we focused on weakening Snowystra. Vetur banished to the Sephorian Desert no longer returned. Bloody clothing was left to be found while they were led to the Eftir Forest. It was up to these men to begin rebuilding for the arrival of the others. Snowystra's kanakala supply would be cut off if I could stop it.

Cole's mood was pleasant for the first week. He was loving and attentive. However, when the men continued to not return, his emotions became erratic. He would have violent outbursts that included throwing things, screaming at the staff, and storming out of the room. The only thing I could do was focus on the boy I loved still inside him. He wasn't going to be lost here.

On the eleventh night, Cole told me he was going to the Sephorian Desert to find the missing Vetur. "We've lost fifteen men in the desert this month. Either they're weak or they've been taken. I'll find out the truth."

When he began to dress, I rushed to him. "Please, don't go. It's too dangerous," I begged. "I need you here."

"I'll not be long," Cole promised, "but she needs my help." In his haste, he told the truth. He didn't care about the missing men. He was going to kill the dorcha for her.

When my husband left, I called for Dunn and Malise. My loyal servants had become my friends in this process. Now, it was time for me to act, fulfilling my promises.

"When Cole returns, he must be brought to me, first," I said. "The heart mustn't go to Snowystra."

"How will I get him to come to you before he goes to her?" Dunn questioned. He averted his eyes from mine.

"What are you not telling me?" I demanded, grabbing his wrist.

"Snowystra has isolated herself in her room. No one is allowed in, except Laura and the Shah. I'm afraid nothing will stop him from going to her, first."

"Tell him I'm ill and I've been feverish since he left," I answered. "And bring me some tumma uni. Now, go, watch the portals. I was told the last time he went, he returned within the day. He's so obsessed that I know he'll be back soon."

"Malise, everyone must be taken from the cottages to the portals. Begin moving them, now" I said. "Have Jameson moved to my door. Tell him it's imperative that I'm kept safe in my fragile state."

"Is there anything else?" Dunn asked.

"Just make sure no one is left behind. If they refuse, do *whatever* it takes to make them leave. No one will remain for her to harm," I said. Panic suddenly filled me. I had forgotten one thing. "The children...how will we take them from the castle without her noticing?"

"The metas have been planning for weeks to take the children away for snow training," Malise replied, reassuring me. "They told Snowystra that the young were eager to learn how to kill dorcha and they would, soon, be ready to do so. They've started to leave already. Everything has been planned. Now, rest."

Waiting for Cole to return, I slipped into my pajamas. I chose the simple kind I would've worn in Starten. Fixing my hair in a similar fashion, I didn't look as regal or glamorous as when Christina prepared me. Instead, I looked like the girl he'd fallen in love with, not the queen he'd turned me into.

Malise entered the room after Cole had only been gone four hours. "He's returned."

Climbing into the bed, I covered up. Malise sat beside me as if she was tending to me. "Pour two glasses, both filled with only enough tumma uni to make someone sleep for a few hours," I instructed.

Storming into the room, Cole ran towards me. "What's wrong?" he asked, sounding frightened. "Are you hurt?"

"I just have a cold," I said. "I'll be OK." Coughing and forcing my voice to sound raspy, I added, "I'm just so thirsty."

Grabbing the glass off the dresser, he handed it to me. "Here, drink this," he said, trying to help me.

"Wait," I paused. "You didn't toast us."

"There's no time for that Marina," Cole replied.

"I knew it." I pretended to cry. "He doesn't love me anymore."

Malise stepped closer to the bed. "Min Vizier, I've told you the Shah loves you more than anything in the world." Whispering to Cole, she said, "The fever has made her emotional. She's cried nonstop, insisting you no longer love her. You may want to appease her and make the toast."

"Marina, stop crying." Cole climbed into the bed next to me. "I'll make a toast to us." Taking the glass from Malise, he said, "To my beloved...my love...my everything. Without my Marina, there would be no world. Without her light, I'd be lost in the dark." Then, he took a long drink. "Now, you," he encouraged.

Sitting up, I said, "I feel much better. Thank you for those words of devotion. If only you hadn't lied to me and gone to the desert to get a heart for Snowystra, I might've believed you meant it."

Getting out of the bed, Cole replied in a slurred voice, "Nooo, you lied to meee. You have betrayed herrrr. You can't...this..."

When he fell to the floor, I went to him. "We'll be home, soon, Cole. All of this will be far behind us, and we'll be home."

I left a note for Cole and changed into one of my royal outfits. I had my hair braided into a crown. Then, I put on the spider necklace, my bracelet from Cole, my father's snake ring, and my wedding band. There was nothing else I wanted to take from the room, except for Cole, but he'd come to find me. If only to kill me.

"Did they take the heart from him?" I asked Dunn.

"Yes, Mara," he said. "I have it here." He held up a satchel.

Taking it from him, I dumped the green heart into the bathtub. Calling Fire, I watched it blacken and turn to ash. Turning on the water, I washed it down the drain.

With one last look at my husband, laying in our bed, I whispered, "I love you. Please, forgive me."

"The Vizier has requested she be taken to the tunnels," Dunn announced when Jameson questioned him on why the sick queen was leaving her room. "She needs to be with her people. She's insisted."

"The Shah approves?" he asked.

I leaned on Christina as if I really was sick.

"She looks like she should be in bed."

"Yes, we have the Shah's approval," Dunn said, handing him the note he'd written, pretending to be Cole. He even stamped it with the royal seal. "He said she must be taken there if she thinks it'll make her feel better."

"I'll stay to guard the Shah, then," Jameson said.

"No, you must protect me," I pleaded. "My husband is resting. Tynan can watch over him."

"As you wish," Jameson replied.

Riding in the carriage, I focused my attention on calling Essie as we got closer to the ice cave. *Essie, I need you to hear me. I'm releasing the Vetur far from here...far from Snowystra. I need your help. Please. I know Kai is near. Please, send help.*

"Before we get there, I'm going to cause a scene. I want Jameson restrained and taken with you through the portal," I said. "He seems strong. Will it be a problem?"

"Not at all," Dunn answered with a mischievous smile. "'The bigger they are, the harder they fall.'"

"The three of you need to listen to me on this next instruction. You'll go with them to the Eftir Forest," I said. "I left the note, telling Cole to meet me at the portals. I don't know how long the tumma uni will last. You must be gone when he arrives. I'll face them alone."

"We'll stay with you," Dunn disagreed.

"No, I mean it. You'll go," I said firmly.

Dunn shook his head and began to argue.

I placed a finger against his mouth, and reaffirmed, "No discussion. I need to know you're all safe. If you're here, I'll not be able to stay focused. Please, promise me you'll respect my wishes."

"We can't just leave you," Malise cried.

Hugging Malise and Christina, I said, "You've kept me sane while I've been here. I'll be able to face her if I know you're safe. Please, do as I say." Then, letting go of the women, I ordered, "Stop the carriage. Stop it, now!"

As we came to a standstill, I threw open the door and flung myself onto the snowy ground. The carriage following behind us slammed to a halt and everyone surrounded me. On my knees, I rocked and screamed as if I was in agony.

Christina ran towards me. "Min Vizier, what's wrong?"

"They've taken him," I cried. "They've taken the Shah. He's dying. I can feel it."

"Who?" Malise asked, playing along. "Who's done this?"

"Danu's elementals. They're going to kill him for betraying her," I sobbed. "And they'll be coming for the rest of us, too. There's no one strong enough to stop them. Go to the tunnels. Save the rest of our people. It's what my husband would've wanted."

Jameson stepped forward. "How do you know he's hurt?"

"I'm his wife. We've been bound by blood," I snarled at him. "It doesn't matter. There's no one who can save him, now."

"I'm strong enough, min Vizier. Tell me where they are and I'll save the Shah," he said.

Screaming as if injured, I cried, "No, it's too much. He's in too much pain. He'll not survive."

"We must try." Jameson knelt beside me. "Tell me which way to go."

Pointing towards the mountain in the distance, I collapsed. "Save him before it's too late."

"It's not too late," he restated. "I'll go to him, now."

"You must know..." I said barely above a whisper.

Jameson leaned in close to hear me.

"This is for your own good. I hope you'll forgive me."

"What?" Jameson asked as the strong arms of Dunn wrapped around him. As he struggled, two other guards assisted.

I stood up and held the tumma uni to his lips. "Drink this willingly, please."

Spitting at me, Jameson said, "I knew you were pretending. She'll have your head for this."

"Possibly," I said as I pushed his head back and poured the liquid into his mouth.

As he tried to spit it out, Dunn clamped his hand over his mouth, sealing it.

"Make sure he's restrained for his own safety."

Returning to the carriages, we rode at an accelerated pace. As we approached the cave, I could see the Vetur. Men, women, and children stood patiently waiting. As we approached, fear consumed me. *Have I made the right decision?*

The soft cheers as we approached filled my heart with joy. At the sight of Laura, surrounded by the children, my fears were lifted. Exiting the carriage, I stood before the crowd.

"Today, I stand before you as a friend, no longer your queen," I declared.

"You're our queen," a voice in the crowd shouted.

Followed by another. "Hail, min Vizier."

"No," I shouted. "I'm not a queen. I'm just a girl. I'm barely eighteen years old and I know very little about the world. My name is Mara Stone Sands. I was given a magical gift. I was never meant to be here or to be your queen. I came here to save the man I love."

As murmurs rumbled softly through the crowd, I added, "I don't regret coming here. The Shah is just a young man, too. Cole would've supported your freedom if he hadn't been brainwashed by Snowystra.

Now, you must go quickly. No more children will be taken from their mothers. No one will die in the desert to feed her powers. You're no longer Vetur. You're brave, strong Miezitari."

Though most of the people still looked scared and confused, there was an energy about them I hadn't experienced before. For the first time since I'd met them, the people were hopeful. "Forget the dirty tunnels where you were cold and hungry. I can't promise you won't have hardship, at first. However, know that – together – you can rebuild what was lost. Any difficulties will be short term." I scanned the crowd and my eyes landed on Livia. "My last act as your Vizier will be appointing you *the guardian of the Miezitari*. Livia take them home."

The crowd cheered as Livia approached me.

"Mara's right, we've always known that, one day, we would free ourselves from her cruel control." Livia took my hand. "My father died trying to protect us from his mistake. Today, we'll succeed."

"Time is running out. You must go, now." I kissed Livia on the cheek and motioned for them to go. "Everyone should have been collected. Go now, my friends. I'll see you, again, one day."

As they slowly walked past me, I was overwhelmed by the love expressed. Kissing and hugging me, I could feel their gratitude. One-by-one, I watched them cross the mouth of the cave.

"Mara," a child's voice called.

Seeing the little girl from the castle, I smiled. "Hello, Masha." I hugged her tightly. "Be sweet, child. You're on your way home."

"I am," she beamed, pointing at a woman and a small boy. "My mommy is here, and I have a little brother."

Laughing, I held my arms out and took baby Daniel into them. Touching my hair, he smiled. "Bufly," he said. "Pretty."

"Hello, brave boy, will you take good care of your mommy for me?" I asked as I returned him to Anna.

"Thank you for saving both of my children," Anna said, and then disappeared.

When it came time to say goodbye to my closest support, I could barely speak. "Go now," I said. "We've already said our goodbyes. Christina, take care of Malise and Dunn for me. Laura, I know you'll help the women bring healthy babies into this world."

Hugging them all, again, I insisted, "Go. Go ensure they make it to their home."

"You forgot this, Mara." Christina gave me the white envelope from Hazel. "It might be helpful."

Watching them walk away, I smiled despite the tears welling in my eyes. They would no longer be enslaved to Snowystra. They were on their way to freedom.

CHAPTER
THIRTY-EIGHT

The Vetur were free, but I wasn't confident Cole would ever be. A skeletal horse with a rider appeared in the distance. I knew it was my husband. *What will Cole do when he finds out the Vetur have escaped? Did he alert Snowystra? Is she close by or still too weak to fight?*

When Cole reached me, he pulled back the reigns. His eyes blazed with vengeance. Jumping off the back of the horse, he loomed over me. "How dare you drug me, and then summon me. Snowystra was right about you."

I could feel his hatred for me. *It's too late. He's too far gone into the darkness. She's destroyed him.*

Cole grabbed my shoulders and shook me. "You'll return everything you stole from her."

I ripped the envelope out of my sleeve and tore it open with one hand. "I'm sorry. You're right. I'll get them now."

"No tricks." Cole dug his fingers into my flesh. "Bring me to them. You've proven you're not trustworthy. If they're gone, you'll pay dearly."

Thinking quickly, I stomped on the insight of his foot and wriggled out of his grip. Before I ran, I blew the contents of the packet into his face. I ran as the purple powder landed in his eyes. I didn't look back to see if he was hurt. His screams told me that I needed to run faster.

Calling back to him, I said, "Catch me if ever want your Vetur back."

I sprinted through the snowy forest. My body felt like ice. There was no doubt in my mind that Cole would kill me if he caught me. Quickly swallowing the last of the granules from Christina, I realized I wouldn't last long in the cold weather. Blaze's words about me being weak came to mind as I sucked in the frigid air.

My lungs felt like sandpaper had been dragged over them. I wished I'd more time to become physically strong. I wasn't weak, but I was in no way prepared for this. I never anticipated I'd be forced to run and hide from my husband.

Slowing as I entered the outskirts of the forest, I felt the tears well in my eyes. *Where now?* I had no idea which direction would be safest. My plans to steal Cole away had seemed so simple. The only way out was the way I'd come in. I would have to go back to the tunnels. *Weak and lost. You should've left with the Vetur. A broken heart would be better than a broken neck.*

Creeping through the trees, I hid behind a large one with overflowing branches. In the thickness of the needles, I searched for any signs of Cole. The forest was quiet. My heart beat so loudly, I thought he'd be able to hear it.

Suddenly, the branches parted, and Cole appeared. "Running away, again? Are you running to find your Fire elemental? You'll not leave me for *him*."

Do not run. The chase will only infuriate him. Think. Think. Be the evil queen.

With a disappointed tone to my voice, I said, "No, I'm here. I was wondering how long it would take you to catch me."

As he grew closer, I tried to move around him, but he caught me by my waist. "No more games," Cole said as I tried to wiggle out of his arms. His voice was dark and foreboding, "I have been waiting for you for too many years, Marina, to lose you, now."

Giving up the fight, I relaxed my body. "Will you, at least, look at the gift I brought you?" I asked, pouting. "I've been saving it for you. Won't you even let me show it to you?"

Setting me down, he watched me carefully. "You drag me out here to give me a present?"

"Yes, the Vetur are all in the tunnels, waiting for you." The words surprised me. How easy lying had become. "I had a whole evening planned. I guess I can give you the gift now if you promise to be surprised, later."

Holding his hand in mine, I said, "Cole, I give you this ring as a sign of my love and devotion. I ask the protection of the goddess...." His eyes narrowed at me before I quickly caught myself, "Snowystra. Mother of darkness, who has given us her blessings."

I slipped the snake ring on his finger as he glared at me. *I hope you're right about this being protection, Mother,* I silently prayed.

Cole looked at his finger, and then returned his gaze to me. "Will you stop playing games, now? Does this mean you're mine, and only mine?"

"I only ever was yours, Cole," I insisted.

The green stones on the snake ring flickered and before I knew it, the silver ring came to life, slithering around his finger.

"This was a trick," Cole roared, slapping me across the face and sending me into a tree. "You'll pay for this deceit."

The snake hissed as it grew larger and larger. Soon, it was standing ten feet high, looming over us. Its silver scales glimmered as it raised up, and then struck. The serpent sunk its fangs into my husband's neck.

Cole cried out as he desperately pulled at the silver serpent, trying to escape. Writhing in pain, he fell to the ground, but continued to fight. Finally, Cole stopped struggling.

The viper slowly shrunk and fell onto the snow. Slithering, it returned to Cole's hand. Wrapping itself tightly around his finger, it changed back to the metal ring I'd given him.

Falling onto the snow beside Cole, I covered his bleeding neck with my hands. "I'm sorry," I cried. "It's the only way I could save you."

Face-to-face, he scowled at me. "You'll not win," he said, spitting in my face. "She'll have your head for this. You mean nothing to me now, Marina. As far as I'm concerned, you're dead."

"Forgive me," I said before I punched him as hard as I could, knocking him out.

He'll never forgive me.

Dragging him to his feet, I crunched through the snow towards the cave. Unable to take another step, I sat on the ground. There was no point in crying. My tears would just freeze. Shivering, I forced myself to think of warm things.

Great Winds. Hot Chocolate. Stupid Chicken Soup. Don't use your magic. You'll need all you have inside you to face her.

"Mara," a gruff voice said from behind me. "Get up or you will freeze to death."

I looked over my shoulder and found Cerin looming over me. "Why are you here?" I thought you ran away?"

"Nah, I didn't run away." He held out his hand to me. "I couldn't go too far. I have a wife and two children who need me. My little boy is quite taken with you. He can't stop talking about the butterfly."

"Daniel is your son?" I asked in surprise.

"He is." Cerin grinned. "Didn't you notice the resemblance?"

"Now that you mention it...no."

Throwing back his head, his hearty laughter filled the air. "I see the Shah has had some trouble." Cerin pointed at my unconscious husband.

"His name is Cole. There is no Shah. It was all a sick game created by Snowystra." Taking his hand, I let him help me up. "I need you to do me a favor."

"Anything," he said. "You've freed my family. What do you need?"

"Take him into the portal and through to Livia. She'll know how to help him," I said, choking back my tears.

"I'll take you both," Cerin insisted.

"I can't go, yet. If I do, she'll just follow. I need to make sure Snowystra is stopped for good."

Taking his jacket off, Cerin wrapped it around my shoulders. Slipping off his boots, he said, "Put these on, too. You will not last out here for long in the cold. Please, reconsider coming with me."

"Go to your wife and child," I insisted.

Cerin bent down to pick Cole up and I stopped him. "Wait." I gently stroked Cole's hair and kissed him. "I love you, Cole. None of this was your fault." As Cerin slung Cole over his shoulder, I said, "No matter what happens, please, make sure he knows it was never his fault."

"I will." Cerin nodded and carried Cole away.

Snowflakes fell on me. As the wind blew harder, the snow became thicker. Shivering from the cold, I wished I hadn't used the last of the granules.

CHAPTER
THIRTY-NINE

"Marina, you've been very, very naughty," Snowystra said as she stepped out of the snowstorm. "You can't steal what's mine. How will you repair everything you've broken?"

"You're a monster. You killed Faramond. You enslaved his people. Why?"

"You don't ask me questions. I'm a god...I'm *the* God! I'll repay my sisters, and you, for everything that's been done. I'll destroy you all."

"Come to me, Air," I cried. The region around us clouded with dark granules.

"You can hide, Marina, but I'll find you!" Snowystra screamed.

A strong burst of snow blew into my face and the wind I had called was pushed away by white flakes. "You are no match for me."

"Aren't you feeling weak?" I laughed. "Miss your morning meal of spider hearts?" Calling Water, I focused on growing the orb until it was larger than a beach ball, and then threw it at her.

Splashing as it landed at Snowystra's feet, spiders broke loose and crawled over her. She was still strong even in her weakened state. The spiders only served as a brief distraction while I planned my next move.

As the dark goddess blew away the small silver spinners, she growled, "I've seen that magic before, and I killed the woman who held it. I see my father has blessed you with his gift. Has he been helping you the entire time?"

"Helping me do what?"

"Turn my people against me!" Snowystra screamed. "You've taken my children from me!"

"They were never yours. They fear and despise you. They don't want to live under your control."

Her hands radiated and sparked green. "Having a sense of déjà-vu?" Snowystra asked coldly.

Her appearance changed, and I was now looking at my mother. "Marina, come to me, darling. I'm so sorry for what I've done." Snowystra held her arms out to me. "You wouldn't kill your own mother, would you? Then again..." Shapeshifting into my grandmother's image, she said, "Maybe, you would. After all, Mara, you let me die. Come to me and beg for my forgiveness." Throwing back her head, she laughed. Her maniacal cackle rang throughout the forest. Her games had distracted me, and I didn't realize what she'd been doing. The ground below was covered with green ooze. Before I couldn't move, I was knocked down. Electric sparks bounced off the slime, licking at my skin.

Not again. Not again. I struggled to get up.

The words the elementals would tell me as a child played in my head.

> *"She needs to be strong now"*
> *"And use her smart mind"*
> *"And never forget her joy"*
> *"And know she is resilient and most importantly loved."*

"Get up Mara! Don't lie there. Don't give up. Your time isn't up, yet. Be the girl I raised. Fight," the voice of my grandmother cried.

"I don't know how to stop it." The shocks continued to run through my body.

"Don't stop it," Gram said.

Forcing my body to be still, I gave myself to the pain.

Standing over me, Snowystra said, "What a difficult position you've put yourself in. Mortals have always been so fragile...so breakable. They just never seem to be able to survive my gifts."

Straddling my chest, she pinned me down, restraining my arms with her legs. The pressure of her weight on my torso made it uncomfortable to breathe. Leaning close to me, she slowly dragged her nail down my cheek.

Silencing my screams, she clamped her hand over my mouth as she continued to cut into my flesh. As the warm, sticky blood ran down my face, she grabbed me by my shoulders and pulled me to my feet. "We'll see what he thinks of his beautiful wife when I'm done with you."

"I had planned on making your death quick," Snowystra said as she wrapped her fingers around my neck. "However, I want you to feel the pain you've given me. I think I made a mistake in letting you marry Cole. Of course, now that he knows how you lied to him, he'll want to rule at my side. Don't we make the most darling couple?"

She cackled again. "I think I'll take you to replace Laura. You can serve Cole and me as we begin our life together. You know it only took a few beatings before Laura realized I'm not one to be disobeyed. Cole has been more resistant lately, but I've broken him over, and over, again. I may need more time to break you, but I'll enjoy every moment of it. And break you, I will, Marina. Do you want to pledge your loyalty to me for real this time?"

Slowly breathing, I felt the magic from her contact pooling inside me. "I'll never serve you," I vowed. "I never meant my pledge, then, and I won't, now."

Pushing all of the magic inside me outward, the ground shook. Thousands of colorful orbs surrounded us. A warmth emitted from the rainbow spinning around us.

"Is that all you have to fight? You're not making it much of a challenge." Snowystra laughed and held my throat tighter. "I almost pity you."

With one last hope for freedom, I called a fire dagger. Jerking myself out of her arms, I reared back before lunging at her. I drove the blade deep into her chest. I aimed for her heart, not sure she even had one to hit.

Screaming in pain, Snowystra fell to her knees. She twisted and turned, trying to remove the flaming weapon from her body. I turned to run, but her hand clamped on my ankle, dragging me down. The orbs encircled her.

"You were given a choice to live." Snowystra stood over me and slammed her foot into my chest. "Your chance is over."

Reaching her hand towards the sky, she pulled down a green bolt of lightning. The dark goddess positioned as if she was going to throw it at me.

Forcing the last of my magic at her, I realized I had none left inside me.

"Do you have any last words?" Snowystra taunted. "There is no one to save you, this time."

"You're wrong, Snowystra," the voice of a young girl called. The girl's light brown hair whipped in the wind as she walked towards us. "You'll not take her away from me again." The girl threw her hands out in front of her and sent out a stream of green vines.

"Or me," a young boy said, stepping forward and casting a silver stream of wind.

"And you will definitely not take her away from me, again," the voice of my father cried.

The trio joined hands, focusing their magic on Snowystra. It whipped and tossed her as it encircled her.

Crawling away from Snowystra towards them, I collapsed. The scent of ginger filled my senses, and a warm hand touched my face. Heat filled my body and I felt Snowystra's magic draining from me. I looked up and saw Essie.

"Join them," she commanded, helping me to my feet.

Taking my father's hand, I stared in amazement at my family.

The girl said, "Mara, send all of your magic. Send all of your elemental magic at her."

"It's all gone," I replied.

"It's not. Fight!" the girl demanded, her green eyes burning with anger.

"Meg? Meg? Is that you?" I asked, my voice breaking.

"Mara, it's me," she said. "Now, send your magic."

"Come on, Caterpillar. Send everything you have inside you," my father pleaded. "We won't be able to restrain her much longer."

Thinking of Cole, the Vetur, and my family, I prayed to Danu for her guidance.

Air, my breath of life.
Fire, my power.
Water, my resilience.
Earth, my strength.
Danu, my spirit.
Fill me with your blessings.
My promise is renewed.
I'll protect the magic.

The orbs swirled above me. Sending out streams of silver, they attacked Snowystra. She screamed in pain as our elemental magic drove into her. When her cries stopped, we released our power and she fell to the ground.

"Is she dead?" Miles asked.

"I don't know," I breathed. "I don't know if you can kill a goddess."

Snowystra's body convulsed and suddenly, she sat up, throwing her arms towards the sky. "You've done this to me. You created me and now you forsake me?" she cried.

Her screams called a blizzard. Through the thick snow, I couldn't see Snowystra or my family. The white void enveloped me.

"Please, don't let her hurt my family," I whispered.

A soft light glowed, and the snow flurry melted. Danu stepped out of the light, holding the hand of another woman.

"Brighid," I murmured.

"Yes, my child," the redheaded woman said as they walked past me towards Snowystra, who was lying in the snow, sobbing.

"No longer can you hurt anyone," Danu said to her sister.

"One made three, return to me," Brighid said, holding her hand out towards her triplet.

Standing up as if she had no choice, Snowystra cried, "You can't do this to me. I'm the Winter."

"Of three, no more will be." Brighid kissed the dark goddess on the lips.

Snowystra faded as her body turned to smoke. With a deep breath, Brighid inhaled the wisps that were once her sister until she was no more.

In shock, we stared until I finally dared to speak. "Is she gone?"

Brighid touched her heart. "She's here. The Winter Goddess that was born will live inside me, and through me. The good part of her will remain. The part this world was not able to see."

The forest filled with a bright white light and Alaunius appeared. "There'll be no more harm to anyone at the hands of my daughter. There's no way to fix the pain she's caused, but there will be no more. Danu, mother of the elements...Brighid, mother of the winter...Mortorcus, guardian of the dead...The balance has been restored.

Mortorcus stepped forward in his tall skeletal form and bowed deeply before Alaunius. "Thank you for saving my people. This child has succeeded where I failed. My gratitude will be eternal."

As Alaunius touched him gently on the head, Mortorcus began to glow a bright red. "Return to your people. Rebuild what was destroyed," the father god whispered.

Mortorcus' body shook and he collapsed as a bright flame grew on him. As he burned, Alaunius stood over the flames moving his hands as if he was sewing an imaginary garment. Danu and Brighid reached their hands into the fire, unfazed by the scorching heat, which I could feel from twenty feet away.

As the fire retreated, I could see they were holding the hand of a tall man with long blonde hair and golden skin. The muscular man was bare from head to toes.

Arianolwyn stepped forward carrying a cloak and wrapped it around him. "Faramond, we don't want to frighten the mortals." She chuckled. "Let's bring you to your people. They need you, now."

"It's time for you to return to your home, Mara. You've lost too much time in the Winter," Alaunius said as he walked towards me.

Before I could speak, a bright light flashed, and I slipped into the darkness.

CHAPTER
FORTY

A rustling sound woke me. I didn't recognize where I was. The young girl claiming to be my sister flopped on the edge of the bed beside me.

"You're finally awake," she said. "I thought you'd sleep the day away."

"You're not, Meg," I said, staring into the girl's green eyes. "You can't be my sister. She's just a little girl and I've not been gone that long. It's only been five months, maybe six. Why are you pretending to be her?"

"Mara, you left when I was nine. The last time I saw you, I was playing in a water pool with Miles. I'm fifteen, now. You've been gone almost six years." The girl put her hands on her hips.

"I'm dreaming," I said, closing my eyes. "I'm going back to sleep, and I'll wake up to my little sister, demanding I get up for breakfast. She'll beg for my pancakes, and she'll show me the new dance she has learned. You'll be gone."

"No, Mara! You won't wake up to the child you left," she said. "Now, open your eyes and see that I'm your sister."

Opening my eyes, I stared at her.

"I'm your sister. How can I prove it to you? See my green eyes? See my birthmark," she said, lifting her shirt and showing me the dark freckle next to her belly button. "I tried to sell you at the Lunar Festival and Cole bought you for two scoops of ice cream."

Hugging me, she said, "I'm your bratty little sister who has been dreaming of the day when she'd see you, again. So, get up!"

"Meg, I'm sorry," I said, staring at her. She was grown up and no longer the child who needed me. "I'm sorry...so sorry."

Pushing me back and looking into my eyes, she said, "You have nothing to apologize for. You did an amazing thing. You saved the Miezitari. Your being gone was sad, but it was for a great reason. I've met some of the people you freed and..."

"What are you talking about?" I asked.

"They're waiting to see if you're OK," Meg said with a smirk.

"Who's here?"

"Dunn is here," she replied, blushing. "He's really cute and so nice."

"He's way too old for you, Meg." I shook my head disapprovingly.

"He can't be more than twenty."

"Try one hundred twenty," I corrected her.

Meg shrugged. "Age is irrelevant."

"Is this what your teenage years will be like? It might've been easier to raise Vetur."

"Not all of us can find our soulmates so early, Mar," she said.

"Cole – where's Cole?"

"Cos is safe. He's being watched by Christina and Dunn. They've been taking turns babysitting him. He's a little bit confused," Meg explained softly.

"Confused?" I quickly sat up.

"He's a bit angry, right now, Mar," she said, biting her lip.

"Why is he angry, Meg?"

Looking away, she didn't answer my question.

"Tell me what he said. I command —" Stopping myself, I said, "I'm sorry. It appears I've grown quite accustomed to playing the evil queen."

"And, he has become quite accustomed to playing the evil king," Meg muttered.

"That's what I feared. Can you take me to him?" I asked, glancing around the room. The four-poster bed with a lime green blanket, small desk, and vanity mirror were unfamiliar to me.

"You're in my room," Meg said, seeing my reaction.

"Where?"

"This is our home. We built the additions Gram wanted. We've been quite busy while you've been gone."

"Gram's room?" I asked.

"Don't worry. It's the same," she said. "You'll be happy when I show you everything we've done."

"Where's Miles?"

"He's with Dad and Mom…I mean, Essie. They thought I should see you, first. We didn't want to overwhelm you, especially since you thought you'd only been gone for such a short time." Meg smirked. "You look really good for a twenty-four-year-old lady."

"Twenty-four?"

"Just kidding. You're actually twenty-three, but your twenty-fourth birthday is just around the corner. Don't worry. We'll celebrate all the years we missed.

I lost almost six years of life with my family? Trying to hide my tears, I said, "I'd like that, Meg.".

Touching my face, my sister responded, "Don't worry about the scar, either. It's light and Mom…I mean, Essie, said it'll go away."

"It's OK for you to call her mom," I said softly.

"You'll love her, Mara," Meg responded. Then, her face suddenly filled with anger. "Snowystra was really bad."

"She's gone now," I said, uncertain if my words were true. "Please, take me to Cole. I'll see everyone afterwards. I just need to go to him, first."

"I really don't think you should, yet."

"I need to, Meg." I climbed out of the bed. "I really need to see him. I know he hates me, but he needs to see me."

"Fine. Let me get you some clothes." Meg went to her closet and picked out some items.

As I stripped off my clothes, she gasped. "By the goddess, Mara, you need to eat."

Staring at my face in the mirror, I could see just how much weight I had lost. My face wasn't as round, and my sunken eyes were surrounded by dark circles. I looked horrible.

"Did they not feed you there?" she questioned.

"I guess they really didn't. Since I've been gone over five years and I only really ate a meal or two a day," I said, trying to figure out where I'd really been for five years. "We just drank tavi."

"Tavi?"

"It's a red liquid that tasted horrible, at first. I hated it. It made me feel like I was choking on ice cubes," I explained.

"Ugh, why would you drink that?" Meg asked, making a face. "The food must've been horrible."

"They made anything I asked for, which wasn't bad," I said. "However, they did serve me the green heart of a spider at our wedding reception."

"Yuck. Did you have a cake, at least?" she asked.

"Yes, there was a cake. I'll tell you everything about being in Snowstrum, later," I said. "I need to go to Cole, first."

Taking my hand, she examined my ring. "It's very pretty. I can't believe you got married without me."

"I really had no choice, Meg."

Shrugging, she said, "Well, was it, at least, a nice wedding?"

I could see the sadness in my sister's eyes. We had lost so much. Time had been stolen and it could never be returned. I needed to be with Cole, but Meg needed me, too.

"It was. I had a beautiful dress and we danced under the starlit sky after the handfasting." I skipped the part where Snowystra cut my hand and I pledged loyalty to her as her blood pulsed through me. "After the wedding, we honeymooned at a snowy lodge. It was almost perfect. But, enough talking about that, and there. I promise I'll tell you everything, but first, I need you to do something with me. Will you come with me?"

"Where?" she asked, eyeing me.

"You'll see." This time, I smirked. "Is Gram's pantry still stocked with supplies?"

"Of course, Miles insists everything be kept in order. He's an old man trapped in a boy's body." Meg frowned.

"I can't wait to find out what else I've missed," I said.

Leading me out of her room, I felt lost until we reached the familiar hallway that led to my grandmother's bedroom. Nothing had changed. We entered the kitchen, and I could've sat down and cried. It was Gram's kitchen. I went straight to the pantry, and I loaded a basket.

When I gathered everything, I said, "OK, let's go."

When we exited the house, I found the plants and trees were healthy and full of fruits. The buzzing sounds from my grandfather's workshop made me smile. "Is Dad in there?" I asked as we walked towards it.

"Probably. He's always building something."

"Let's take the four-wheeler," I said, suddenly feeling exhausted.

"OK, but I get to drive."

Meg drove us through the forest while I held on tightly. I guided us as she weaved in and out of the trees. When we reached the casting stone, I traced my finger over my name.

"Gram took me here before you were taken. We made your memory spell here," I said. My mind traveled back to images of the magic we had made that morning. Summoning a fire dagger, I said, "Give me your hand."

"Wow, when did you learn to do that?" Meg held her hand out towards me. Quickly, I sliced her finger. "Ouch, Mar."

Stopping her from instinctually putting her finger in her mouth to stop the bleeding, I said, "Sign your name in the stone."

As she wrote her name, she wore a big smile. "It feels like they're here with us, Mar."

The colored orbs of Breeze, Blaze, Bay, and Daisy bounced around, confirming her feeling, and I knew I was finally home.

Walking back from the stone, Meg and I held hands. I felt stronger. The connection with the elements and Danu restored my spirit. I was still not healthy. I felt nauseous and tired, but Meg made a good point. I hadn't been taking care of myself. However, I was home with my family now, and I'd regain my health soon.

"Oma…I mean Hazel is going to be so happy to see you," Meg said. "She's been a wreck since you left."

"Where is she? Is she here?"

"No, she's in Great Winds, helping with the hotel. I think she just wants to be with Patrick," Meg waggled her eyebrows. "He's her boyfriend. I told her she's too old for that and that they should just get married."

"You didn't!" I gasped.

"No, I didn't." Meg laughed. "But someone should tell her."

"Well, you can when we go to visit her," I said.

"Please, no. It's so hot there, right now," Meg said dramatically. "I'm way too fair-skinned for such harsh weather."

"Yes, you're rather fragile," I said with a grin. "Have you been there recently?"

"We go back and forth. Mom doesn't want to give up the hotel," she replied. "Sometimes, they talk about opening a hotel here."

As we grew closer to our residence, I could see the additions they made. It had tripled in size.

"The house is so much bigger. You have been busy," I commented. "Are you happy with all of the changes, Meg?"

"I am, Mar, and I'm even happier now that you're here," she said, squeezing my hand tightly.

"I'm glad to be home, little dancer," I replied, kissing her cheek.

As we reached the property, I stopped. "Do you remember when you took your promise, and we did the vision spell? Do you still have the pouch?"

"Of course," she said. "It's in my room. Why do you want it?"

"Can you get it for me and take me to Cole?" I asked. "I think it'll help him."

"Are you sure you should see him, right now?" Meg grimaced. "He said some really horrible things about you."

"I need to, Meg," I told her, not wanting to know what he'd said. "Let's hurry up. I know you'll have lots to show me. I still can't believe how tall you are. You're going to be taller than I am."

"I hope so."

"Do you still dance?" I asked, remembering her Lunar Festival performance fondly.

Meg twirled around me. "You know I do."

I was happy to hear she still had passion for her art. "How did clog dancing work out?"

"Disaster," Meg answered, falling into a fit of laughter.

As we walked by the picnic tree, I smiled. I was home, however, there were still things I needed to deal with. Cole was free from the dark goddess, but maybe it was too late to save him.

CHAPTER
FORTY-ONE

Meg led me to the room Cole was being kept in. Dunn was outside the door. Smiling when he saw us, he said, "You're looking very pretty, today, Meg."

Narrowing my eyes at him, I replied, "You don't want to anger your queen, do you?"

Laughing, Dunn pulled me into a hug. "No, min Vizier. Please, forgive me."

Swatting him, I said, "You've met my *baby* sister, I see. Remember, she's only fifteen and still a child."

Crossing his heart with his finger, he vowed, "You have my promise. Meg will be just like a sister to me."

"How's Cole?" I asked nervously.

His grin faded. "He's confused. I'm not sure you should see him, yet. I don't think you'll be well received."

"I need to see him, Dunn," I insisted. "Meg, please, stay out here. I need to go alone."

"OK Mara, I'll wait here for you," she said, beaming at Dunn. Raising my eyebrows at her, she quickly added, "Or I'll go see what Miles is up to?"

"Good girl," I said, smiling. "I'll see you soon."

When I entered the room, I was surprised to find it was trashed. Furniture was broken and mirrors were smashed. Christina stood next to Cole, where he was seated with his wrists and ankles tied to the chair.

"You need to drink this," Christina insisted, trying to feed him the beverage. "You're getting sicker."

"Get away from me, witch," Cole snarled. "I'm not sick at all. When I break free, I'm going to send you to the dorcha's pit and let them tear you apart, limb-by-limb, for this. Release me and I'll think about lessening your punishment."

"You know I can't do that, Cole," Christina said sweetly.

Impatiently, he began to rock in the chair, trying to break free. "Just take me back to my home," he screamed.

"You are home, Cole," I remarked, walking towards him. "We're in Gram's house in Starten."

"This isn't my home. I'm the king of the Vetur. My kingdom is Snowstorm. I'm their Shah," he growled, glaring at me. "And my people will return to me."

"No, Cole," I replied. "They won't."

"Mara," Christina said. "I don't think you should be here, right now. He's a bit —"

"What is he a bit of – angry?" Cole's asked, still trying to pull himself loose. "Why would I be upset? My wife tried to kill me with a snake and when it didn't finish me off, she punched me. Now, she has me tied to a chair."

"Cole, I had no choice," I said as I approached him. "Christina, can you leave us? We need to be alone."

"Yes, Christina, your queen has given you an order," Cole mocked. "Go. She wouldn't want witnesses to anything she does."

Christina nodded. "I'll be nearby if you need me."

"Thank you," I said, squeezing her hand.

"Cole, can we talk about this, please?" I asked, trying to keep my tone calm.

"What should we talk about? Should we talk about how you betrayed my trust? Or, how you drove my people away?"

"Yes, if you want to talk about that we can," I said. "And we can, also, talk about why someone had to stop Snowystra."

Screaming, he said, "She'll come for me. I warned you that I'd kill you for your deceit. What makes you think I won't, now?"

"You might try," I acknowledged, "but you won't kill me, and you know it."

"Why won't I?" he asked. "Besides, it doesn't matter. If I don't get the chance, she will."

"She isn't coming back for you, Cole. She's gone," I said. "You won't kill me because you love me. You love me, Cole, and you know Snowystra lied to you. She tricked you into following her and beat you into submission. I saw the wounds on your body from her punishments. I know how many times you must've come to your senses before she was able to confuse you."

"You don't know what you're talking about. You're lying. She never hurt me. She was good to us. She isn't gone. She's a goddess. They don't just disappear, especially not because of someone weak, like you. They sent her away before, but she came back. She will, again."

Opening the pouch, I dumped the contents out on a dresser. "I want you to tilt your head back and let me put these drops in your eyes. I want you to see the truth."

"I won't submit. It's another trick," Cole snarled and bucked in the chair.

"If you don't do it willingly, I'm going to force you to do it."

"Let me see you try," Cole challenged with a glared.

This is impossible. He's going to make this hard. Be his queen, I thought. *Be his queen.*

"Alright." I changed my tone and sat on his lap, facing him. I gave him no choice, but to look into my eyes. "You're too scared. Scared of your wife. Scared of the Vizier. Scared of the person that should've been the Shah. You know you weren't her first choice."

"Get off me. What would you know about her?" he snarled. "She chose me."

"Do you really think she wants you for your weak Water magic?" I threw my head back and laughed. "I control all four elements, and now her power runs through my veins. Why would she need you? I went there to save you, but all I saw was how weak you truly are."

"Fine. Go ahead. Do what you want. Don't you always? In the end, we know who she chose." Cole tilted his head back. "She'll make you pay for this, and I'll stand by, watching."

As I dropped the blue liquid into his eyes, he hissed. Placing some of it on my tongue, I closed my eyes, rested my head on his shoulder, and fell asleep.

I woke to the sound of Cole's voice. "What's going on, Mar? Are we in Starten Forest?"

Looking around, I said, "I guess so."

"Why are we here?" He clutched my hand. "I thought we were at the hotel."

"I need to show you what happened to us. How we ended up here," I explained. "I need you to remember everything."

"OK, Mar," Cole said in a cheerful voice. A voice I knew would not be as joyous after he saw the last six years of our lives. "I'm ready. Show me what I have missed." Picking me up, he spun me around and kissed me.

"You need to be serious," I chastised.

"Very serious," he said, putting on an overly solemn face. "Show me what I must learn."

The wind blew, whipping my hair, forcing me to turn my head. I knew exactly where we were now. We were by the entrance to the elementals' world.

"Come with me." I led him through the tree.

"Do you know where we're going? It's so dark in here," he whispered. "What's that thumping sound?"

"Shh," I said as we entered the Water elementals' cave.

"We're in Danu's home," he said. "Are we really here?"

"We are."

"Can they see us?"

"I don't think so."

"This is amazing," Cole cried. "I want to splash and play in the water with them. Do you feel their energy?"

"I do, but we need to keep moving."

His disappointment lifted and his excitement grew as we entered the Fire elementals' cavern. Fiery wisps danced around us. When we climbed the Air elementals' platform, he stared with wide eyes at the elementals in their bird form.

"This is one of the best parts," I told him.

"I can see why. They're magnificent colors. Are they really all Air elementals?"

"Yes, isn't it fantastic? Take my hand." I led him to the edge of the platform. "Now, what do you see?"

"Just the top of the trees. Why? What's down there?"

"We need to go see," I said. He started to turn around to leave, but I stopped him. "No, we've to go down this way. Do you trust me?"

"With all my heart, Mar."

"Take my hand and jump to find out what's below."

"Jump?" Cole asked in a panicked voice.

"Trust me. We're in the home of Danu. We're safe."

"OK, let's count it out. One. Two. Three," Cole cried, and we jumped. As we floated to the ground, he laughed and held me as if we were dancing in the air. His mirth was contagious. When we landed, he said, "That was so cool. We have to do that, again."

"It's pretty amazing. Better without the mud landing." I giggled.

"Wait, what's that?" he asked, pointing at the little green bulb growing in the ground. "Is this the Earth elementals' home?"

"Yes, this is where they live. Look in the trees for them."

"Oh, I see one there," he said. "Her hair is yellow. I almost didn't see her. We should stay and have a picnic with them."

"Maybe we can come back and do that another day," I replied.

"Oh, right, you want to show me something?" he recalled.

Leading him through the tunnels, we entered Danu's chamber, and we walked past the mirrors.

"Cole, my child," Danu said as she appeared on the stone.

Her elementals were seated in their chairs.

"Hi, Mara. Hi, Cole," Bay said in her singsong voice.

"Bay, can you just be serious?" Breeze whispered.

"Fine. I'll be serious," Bay muttered as she waggled her fingers at us.

"Come to me," Danu said. Sitting down on the stone, she stroked her purring cat. "Have a seat," she said, patting the stone beside her. We obeyed.

Clasping our hands, Danu said, "Cole, Mara brought you here to show you the truth."

"Is this about her kissing Kai?" he asked. "I'm over that...really."

"No." She laughed. "Everyone kisses Kai at some point. Do you recall the night you found Mara at Sparrow Lake?"

"I do," Cole said. "Snowystra threatened us."

"Yes, that was the night my sister began her plan to take you away," she said.

"But I'm here, so she didn't win. She didn't take me." Cole beamed.

With a gentle smile, Danu said, "I'm sorry, Cole. You're right. She didn't win, but it's time for you to remember the truth. All of it."

"OK," he agreed. "How do I see it?"

The mirror behind the seated elementals glowed. "Go there." Danu pointed towards the looking glasses. As I began to stand to go with him, Danu stopped me. "He needs to go alone."

"You want me to walk through the mirror?" Cole asked.

Blaze stood up, taking his hand. "I'll take you there," she said, using a much kinder voice than I'd ever heard come out of her.

"OK. Well, let's do it. Help me remember," he said. "I'll be back in a moment, Mara."

As they entered the reflective glass, I turned towards Danu. "When we awake, will this Cole return with me?"

"I think it will take a while, Mara. He'll need to accept what happened. He's going to see everything in there. There will be things he won't be able to share with you. You'll need to be there to help him heal."

"But will the darkness be gone from inside him?" I asked, not hiding my frustration.

"I don't know. I really don't have all the answers. There are too many factors. Gifts are given and how they are used are out of my power. Only you can decide how to use my elemental magic and the winter magic inside you. My sister has returned to us, and she'll no longer be able to harm anyone. Now, while we wait for Cole, let's think of the joy, not the sorrow."

Breeze suggested, "Let's talk about your wedding. Kai told me you were a beautiful bride."

"He was there?" I asked in disbelief.

"He said you didn't recognize him in his glamour," Breeze replied.

"I didn't."

"He was happy for you," Daisy said. "He said you were so happy despite everything."

"I was blissful with Cole for a small amount of time," I confirmed, thinking about the times that were good. "Is Kai here?"

"He's with the Miezitari. He said he'll come see you, soon, but, right now, he's helping them rebuild," Breeze answered. "He's, also, babysitting a guard who is very angry about being taken."

"Jameson?" I asked. "Will he be OK?"

"I'm sure he will," Daisy assured. "Kai is very good at helping people figure out what they really want."

"Jameson's dealing with his pain from being a small child taken from his mother and raised by Snowystra," Danu explained. "He'll need time."

"Will the children be OK?" I asked.

"They are young. They will have a chance to grow and learn. Faramond has already taken several with him to escort the dead," Bay told me.

"They'll have a purpose now," Daisy said. "It's how it should be. When you're well, you can see them for yourself and the lost kingdom they've rebuilt."

"Now, you need to focus on taking care of yourself and reconnecting with your family," Daisy remarked.

"And, having fun with your sister," Bay said. "She's the fun one."

"Fun one?" I questioned.

"We learned from you and never gave her the chance to get too serious," Bay said. "Don't worry. We keep our eye on her. She'll be fine."

"And Miles?"

"He learned his new magic much faster than I expected," Breeze replied. "He's quite the student. He's really happy with your father and Essie."

"I missed so much," I said softly.

"A brief blink of time, but you're back now, and you'll have so much to share with them," Danu soothed. "I was informed of your acting skills. Kai said it was quite a powerful performance in the snow."

Blushing, I said, "I may have overdone it."

"Possibly a tad, but you were able to restrain Jameson and lead the Miezitari home." Danu smiled.

Blaze stepped through the mirror with a serious look on her face. "Mara, please, go to him. He's a bit shaken."

As I entered the mirror, I found Cole crumpled on the floor sobbing. I had never seen him so broken before.

Going to him, I said, "It's OK, my love. I'm here. Talk to me."

"I was horrible, Mara. How can you forgive me for all of the horrible things I did?"

"Cole, I know that wasn't you," I soothed, stroking his hair. "I know that wasn't your heart."

"But all the things I did...all of it —"

"Weren't your fault," I finished.

"I sent them to die."

"No one died. They all came back. Some battered and bruised, but they lived."

"And the way I treated the women. I hit that girl and I let them fight over me, thinking I'd make them my queen."

"You can't dwell on what happened there," I said. "If you need to apologize, you can go to them and do so, but you need to move on...for us. I was there, and I wasn't kind, either."

"You were pretending." Cole sat up. "I was cruel and heartless."

"You have to think about the good parts of being there," I begged.

"The good parts? What good parts? The part where I encouraged them to beat and degrade each other? The part where I killed things to feed her magic? Or the part where I betrayed you?"

"I'm not going to listen to this," I said furiously. "I know who was there. I know what happened. I don't need a play-by-play to forgive you. I need you to just come home with me. We'll get through this, together."

"How can you forgive me for everything I've done?"

"Can you forgive me?" I asked, making him look into my eyes.

"You didn't do anything wrong." Cole's blue eyes shone with tears.

"I did. I let her take you. I knew that night that there was something wrong with you before we went to the club. We're both at fault."

Wrapping my arms around him, I hugged him tightly. "I can't make you forgive yourself, though I hope you do, but know that I do – I forgive you, and I even forgive myself. Please, my love, just come back with me. We've lost enough time already. Let's not lose more."

"I love you, Mara." Cole squeezed me tighter.

The room around us began to glow. A white light filled it, and then burst into millions of smaller white lights. As they softened, I found myself on Cole's lap in our home in Starten.

"Mar, can you untie me," Cole rasped. I could see the pain in his eyes.

Removing the binding from him, I stood up and held out my hand towards him.

"Mar, you look so —"

"I know." I led him towards the mirror. "We both look a little rough, don't we? But we're home."

"I'm sorry Mar," Cole said, kissing my cheek. "I'm so, so sorry."

"There will be no more apologies, Cole. None. We said our sorries. We've forgiven each other. No one is blaming you, so stop blaming yourself. We're home and we have a lot to celebrate, now." I tried to lighten the conversation. "I've been informed that since we've been gone long enough for me to miss five birthdays, there'll be a lot of celebrations to catch up on."

The door opened and Christina entered. "You've been quiet for a long time. Is everything OK?"

"Better than OK," I replied.

"Cole?" Christina questioned.

"Yes, it's me, Christina," he answered. "I'm sorry for the horrible things I said to you. Can you forgive me?"

"I lived with Snowystra for forty years. The things you said were pure compliments in comparison," she said with a laugh.

"How can I make it up to you?" Cole asked.

Offering him the glass he'd refused before, she replied, "Drink this. It will help to remove the years of damage from the tavi, tumma, and kanakala. It'll take you time to heal and forgive yourself. But you're with your family, now. That's what matters."

"Will you stay with us?" Cole asked.

"For a while, but I need to get to the Miezitari." Christina patted his hand. "Laura has her hands full with all of those babies. Now that the Miezitari are free, I have a feeling there'll be even more children."

"I'd like to see that. I'd like to see them incredibly happy," Cole said, taking a long drink from the glass. "This is actually good. Warm and sweet like honey."

"Yes, Arianolwyn does make a wonderful brew."

"If you're finished, I think we've had enough talk of Snowystra for the day," I remarked. "Let's go see our family. I'm sure Meg is out there with Dunn. If we aren't careful, my little sister might convince him to run off and marry her."

"She is out there with him, but I can assure you that he's always a gentleman," Christina promised.

"I'm right here and I hear you," Meg said, stepping into the room.

"Meg?" Cole asked. "You were just a little kid when we left."

Sighing, she said, "Yes, Cos, I'm almost sixteen, now. This is going to be so tiring if I have to keep convincing you it's me. If you both can get it together, dinner is ready." Meg shook her head. "Come on, Christina. Let's see what Mile's needs help with."

"We won't be long," I said. "Cole needs to get cleaned up."

When they left, I wrapped my arms around my husband's neck. "I think I owe you something," I told him.

"What could you possibly owe me?"

"I believe you had a raincheck for a bubble bath. So, let me make it for you."

His eyes widened. "Would Gram approve?"

Waggling my wedding ring at him, I replied, "I'm sure she would – completely. We've been married for five years, you know."

Kissing me, he said, "I love you, Mar."

"I love you, too."

Now that we were home, I'd have to accept everything that happened in the past and, together, we'd build our new future.

CHAPTER
FORTY-TWO

We arrived in the kitchen to find everyone sitting around the table, eating their salads. When Essie saw us, she got up and hugged us both tightly. Before we knew it, we were bombarded by our family.

"OK, guys," my father said. "Give them some breathing room. We need to get a meal into these kids. They look like they're fading away."

"Come sit by me, Mara," Miles said, setting a salad down. "I made it the way you like it."

Taking a bite of the greens with strawberries, feta cheese, glazed almonds, and raspberry vinaigrette, I smiled. "Mmm, delicious. Breeze told me how proud she is of you. She's amazed how quickly you've learned to use your Air magic."

"She's a good teacher." Miles beamed with pride.

"There's so much to catch up on," I said, sounding sadder than I planned. "We've missed so much time."

"But there's so much more for us to share together," my father encouraged.

As I looked around at the smiling faces of my family, I knew he was right. There would be many more occasions to share.

"Hey, you guys aren't eating," Miles noted. "Do you not like it?"

Cole and I locked eyes. Raising my eyebrows, telling him to answer, he responded, "No, the food is great." He took a bite. "We're just...We haven't...We are..." Cole stumbled over the words.

"We aren't used to eating very much anymore," I said, finishing for him. "We thought we were only gone for months, only to find it had been years. We weren't consistent on eating meals while we were gone."

"You didn't eat?" Meg asked. "I definitely couldn't live there."

"Well, we did eat, but it was different," Cole said.

Taking his hand, I added, "There's a lot to adjust to, I guess. It'll take us time to get used to normalcy, again."

"Now that you're back, it's important to not make you feel different or ask too many questions. But all we did tonight was make you feel out of place," Miles said with a serious expression.

"Not at all, Miles. Please, don't worry about hurting our feelings. We're a little different, right now. How lucky are you?" I asked, using my Vizier voice "One does not often get the chance to dine with the royal Shah and Vizier of Snowstrum."

"It's our lucky day," Miles said, laughing.

"It's OK to ask us questions," I reassured, kissing him on the cheek. "Really. Ask anything you want."

A child's cry sounded, momentarily interrupting any further discussion.

Hopping out of his chair, Miles said, "Charlie's waking up. I'll go get her." Then, he quickly ran out of the kitchen, shouting, "I'll be right back."

"Charlie?" I questioned.

"Caterpillar, you have a baby sister," my father announced. "Charlotte Mae Stone."

"We named her after my father and your grandmother," Essie said. "I hope you don't mind?"

"Of course, I don't," I said, feeling overwhelmed. "Gram would've loved to have had another baby in the house."

Miles returned, carrying a redheaded toddler on his hip. She clapped and smiled when she saw us.

"She's not a baby," I noted in surprise. "She has your green eyes."

"Doesn't she look like Essie?" my father asked proudly. "She just turned two."

"She is such a happy baby," I commented.

"You should hear her when she's cranky," Meg said. "Lucky for us, she's happy most of the time."

When Miles finished with Charlie's greeting, he returned to his seat. As he began to sit, Charlie whined and held her arms out towards Cole.

"It looks like you've charmed another one of my daughters," my father commented with a chuckle.

"Do you want to hold her?" Miles asked.

Cole hesitantly smiled and held out his arms. "Sure." Taking her, he said, "Hello, little Charlie. I'm your...What am I? I guess I'm your...I guess I'm your brother, Cole."

Charlie giggled, saying, "Co, Co."

"Yes, Cole and I'll be here to tell you so many stories your head will turn. When you're older, I'll tell you all about the king of the snapping trout," he said.

"Trou, trou," she tried as she bounced on his lap. Reaching out towards his plate, she grabbed a handful of his untouched mashed potatoes and shoved it into her mouth.

"She gets that from me," Meg declared with a smirk.

Yawning, I said, "I hate to be a party pooper, but can we take a rain check? I'm a little tired." The truth was that I was overwhelmed with the changes around me.

"Of course, we were being greedy. We should have realized," my father apologized.

"It's OK," I replied. "It's exactly what we needed. Being here with all of you is what I've been longing for."

"And we're so glad to have you home," Essie said, hugging me. "We haven't fixed your room, yet...."

"Can we stay in Gram's room?" I asked.

"Of course, that's perfect," Meg answered. "Now, off to bed you two. You'll be up and at it bright and early. We won't be wasting the beautiful day."

"You sound like Gram," Cole said with a sad smile.

Meg beamed at the compliment.

We said our goodnights and went straight to Gram's room. Cole was unusually silent as he sipped another glass of Arianolwyn's tonic. Christina had insisted we both drink more before bed.

"There's going to be a lot of changes to get used to, huh?" Cole asked.

"Yes, but there's a lot the same." I climbed under the covers and slipped into his arm. "Didn't you feel how much love there is in our home? Though they all continued with their lives while we were gone, we weren't forgotten. I know it's a bit overwhelming, right now, but we need to be with them. I hope Gram's able to stop worrying about me. When Danu showed her to me, she wasn't doing very well. My only consolation is that time there's different and she has my grandfather."

The nightstand rattled and we jumped out of the bed. Opening it, Cole found the silver journal. The last time I had seen it was in Great Winds.

"I wonder if it'll open this time," he said.

Sitting on the edge of the bed, we were able to open the book. Turning the pages, we found an inscription, which read:

To my Cole and Mara – May your many years of blessings, also, include the love of your family. You're loved.

Flipping to the next page, I saw *Beginnings* penned in Gram's handwriting. Below she had added:

The story of my mother, Genevieve, and her friends on their path to becoming the protectors of the magic.

The story was about how the elementals saved Danu with the help of my great-grandmother and her friends. As we finished reading, the nest mirror shined, and Gram appeared.

"It's wonderful to see you both back at home. I can be at peace now, knowing how strong you both were," she said.

Taking Cole by the hand, Gram instructed, "Forgive yourself. You're brave and strong enough to get through this. You're a good man, Cole, and my granddaughter deserves a good man. You're more than her husband. You were my first grandson."

Violently, the room shook, and the lights flickered. Suddenly, a white orb appeared in front of my grandmother. Two Miezitari children appeared with Faramond.

"Follow us, Mae. It's time," the small childlike voices stated in unison. "We're all waiting for you."

"I'm ready. You're right. It's time for me to go. No fussing. No goodbyes. Just *we'll see you again, soon*. Remember to follow your heart, my loves," Gram said.

Faramond's took my grandmother's hand and bowed towards me. "Your sacrifice has saved my people. We will meet again, Mara and Cole. You're always welcome in my home."

As they faded away, we just held each other. Knowing Gram was being escorted to the Afterlife by Faramond and the Miezitari, I knew she'd be safe.

When we were alone, Cole sat on the chest at the end of the bed. "She's wrong, Mar. I'm not a good man."

"No more of this," I said. "We can't do this forever. It wasn't your fault." I tugged him towards the bed. "You're exhausted. You just need time to heal."

Snuggled under the covers, I tried to push back the fear I felt. I had brought him home, but he was so hurt. Wrapping his arms around me, I inhaled his familiar scent and melted into his touch. As I released my hold, he held me tighter. The way he held me was like he was afraid I was going to leave.

Kissing him gently, I whispered, "You're a good man, Cole. Please, forgive yourself."

Falling asleep in his arms, I prayed that, in the morning, he would begin to find his peace.

The sounds of pots and pans in the kitchen and noisy conversation woke me. The bright sun was shining in through the curtains. Stretching, I realized Cole had already left. Leaving the comfort of the bed, I wrapped myself in Gram's robe and went to the kitchen.

"Mar, you're awake," Meg said. "You always want to sleep the day away."

"It's comfortable in Gram's bed." I kissed her cheek and accepted the coffee she handed me.

Mmm, warm food again, I thought.

"Well, come join us for breakfast." My father patted the seat next to him.

"Tell Cole I made his favorite," Miles called from the stove. "Tell him to come eat it while it's hot or before Meg gets it."

"Ha, ha, smarty." Meg tousled his hair. "Ooh, that does look good. You might want to deliver the warning."

"Cole isn't here?" Sudden fear filled me.

Essie and my father eyed each other. "He isn't in the room?" my father asked.

"No, maybe he went to his cottage," I replied, trying to be calm as I jumped from the table. I double checked the room. Cole wasn't there and he didn't leave a note saying where he had gone.

Throwing on clothes, I returned to the kitchen. "He isn't here. He must be in the studio. I'll go check."

"Do you want me to come with you?" Meg asked.

"No, I'm sure he's there," I said.

Walking down the street, I was unsure which Cole I would find. The dark magic might not have been removed and I rethought my decision to go alone. When I reached the spot where the house had burned, I saw no signs of a structure ever being there. Instead, it was a grassy area.

Entering the cottage, I went straight to the closet leading to the studio. It was closed. Opening it, I made the climb down the stairs.

"I met some of your cousins," I said to the spiders building their webs.

Cole wasn't in the studio. Searching the room, I found a sketchpad opened to a drawing of me. He must have drawn it when I wasn't looking. My hair was blowing in the wind as I gazed off into the distance.

Flipping through the book, I saw pictures of me beginning in my preteen years. He had captured some of my favorite times spent with him. However, the next sketch wasn't of me. It was Snowystra. She was stretched out on a chair, holding out her arm as if posing for him. The next several pictures were of her, also.

Ripping them out of the book, I tore them up. Calling Fire, I burned the pages. Returning to the sketch pad, I was determined to destroy any other record of the dark goddess. There was only one last picture. Cole had drawn us on our wedding day.

Closing the book, I left the table to search for any clues as to where he could've gone. There was a painting drying on the easel that looked new. He had made another painting of our family in the kitchen.

In the picture, Miles and I sat together, laughing next to Meg, who was holding Charlie. My father and Essie were at the butcher block, chopping something and grinning. Gram was at the stove facing my grandfather, who was posed as if sneaking in to steal a bite. Sarah and my mother were standing at the sink, washing, and drying dishes. He even added Patrick slipping a ring onto Hazel's finger as she beamed with pride. The picture was perfect, except it was missing someone.

Cole wasn't in it.

At the bottom of the easel, I found a rolled-up scroll. Nervously untying the ribbon and unrolling the paper, my heart sank as I read it.

> *Mara,*
>
> *Last night, I realized it was unfair of me to stay here until I'm healed...until I've learned to forgive myself...until I know I'm safe to be around. The things I did in that world are too unbearable to remember. I must repair what I broke before I can be the man you deserve.*
>
> *When I took your hand in marriage, I promised to love and take care of you. I haven't done this. I betrayed your trust and your heart. I destroyed everything and if I don't go now, I'll only hurt you more.*
>
> *I wanted to tell you my decision in person, but we both know you would've stopped me. You would've told me to stop being ridiculous...we'll figure it out. I would look into your beautiful hazel eyes and want to believe you. My love, you would've been wrong. Only I can heal myself and I can't put you through what I need to accept in order to be the man you deserve.*
>
> *Please, forgive me for leaving you without a goodbye. I promise I'll return.*
>
> *I'll love you always, Mara.*
>
> *Cole*

My tears fell onto the letter. "No, no, no," I cried. "You can't do this, Cole. You can't leave me like this."

I paced and muttered to myself. "He's wrong. He can't be far. I'll go to him."

Leaving the cottage, I ran towards the house. When I entered the room, I called out. "He's gone. He's gone."

"Who's gone – Cole?" my father asked, taking the note I held out for him.

"He just left me. He just left...me," I said, dropping onto the over-stuffed chair.

"Oh, Mara." Meg settled beside me and wrapped her arms around me. "He's not gone forever. He'll be back."

"I don't think so, Meg," I sobbed.

I was angry at myself for not listening to him, for not letting him express his concerns. I should have let him tell me all the horrible things he'd done while we were in Snowstrum. But I didn't and now, he was gone.

I didn't let him tell me because I didn't want to know. I had seen him in the alley with Snowystra. I'd seen him with the women in the tunnels. I knew there was more to his time there than what I saw. Still, I, also, knew that man wasn't Cole. It wasn't the real Cole. It wasn't my Cole.

"Here. Let me get you some tea or something to eat." Meg tried to comfort me.

"No, I just need to be alone," I said, taking the letter and walking back to Gram's room. Crawling into the bed, I hugged the pillow and cried. I wept for my lost time, for the loss of my family, and for my lost love.

My tears were uncontrollable until I finally drifted off into sleep. Waking me, Meg insisted I get up and join them for dinner. I went through the motions of getting ready, but I was numb. I felt like I wasn't really there. I didn't want to be without Cole. I might as well have stayed with Snowystra. I was dead inside.

"You need to get it together, Mara," Meg said. "If he left, it was because he knew he needed to fix himself for you. He'll be back before you know it. He'll feel worse if he sees you in this state."

"I don't care how he feels. He abandoned me. He left me and snuck away in the middle of the night like a coward," I replied. "Why would he do that?"

"He's confused, Mara."

"Do you know where he went?" I snapped at her.

"No, I don't, but I'm sure we'll find him," Meg promised.

"He didn't tell me where he was going. He just left me," I said.

"Mara, you need to take care of yourself, too. The darkness inside him was deep. He had more time there without protection."

"I know that. I know all of this, but HE LEFT ME!" I shouted. "Cole left me." Burying my head in a pillow, I began to sob, again.

"Don't cry, Mar," Meg soothed. "We'll find him."

"No, it doesn't matter," I told her.

"It does matter." Meg sat down next to me and forced me to sit up. She held my face between her hands as if I was the child. "You both have been through so much. You saw things you just don't forget because you came home." My sister sounded far older and wiser than her fifteen years. She hugged me tightly. "He'll come back when he's ready, but you have to take care of yourself, now. You're not well, either."

"It doesn't matter," I repeated.

"Mara, you need to heal, and not just for yourself. You need to worry about the life inside you," Meg scolded.

"What are you talking about?" I asked, glaring at her.

"You don't know? I thought you were waiting to tell me," Meg answered, sounding surprised. "Come with me, now."

Taking my hands, Meg dragged me to her room. Standing me in front of the mirror, she stood behind me. Wrapping her arms around me, she rested them on my stomach. "There, inside you. Don't you feel the life growing?"

Looking at the bump on my belly, I said, "What are you talking about? That's just from the food we've been eating since being here."

"You've only been here a few days. That isn't because of food," she gently corrected me. "Take off your shirt and look."

"Fine," I said, removing my shirt. "See. I just put on weight."

Turning me sideways, she put her hand on my distended abdomen. "Look again. You haven't felt well since you came back. You're pregnant, Mara. Like it or not, you're going to have a baby," she said. "Don't you feel the life inside you? You and Cole created this. This is your child."

Rubbing the small curvature of my stomach, I knew she was right. "How didn't I notice? How did you know?" I asked, my eyes welling up with tears. "How did this happen?"

"If you have to ask that, we've more to talk about than your pregnancy."

"I know how it happens, but how did you know? I'm barely showing."

"My Earth magic has grown strong. I don't know why, but I just seem to know when new life is around me."

"OK, so I'm pregnant...how am I going to raise a baby on my own?"

"On your own? You're very much not alone," she scolded. "Now, that's just insulting. You have all of us. Miles, Dad, Essie, Oma, Patrick, and the elementals. You have the blessings of Danu. What else could you ask for? And don't forget you have Dunn, Christina, and me. You know I'll be the best auntie ever."

"But my child won't have a father," I croaked, tears falling down my cheeks. "Another child without their dad because of her."

"Your baby will have a father. He's not gone forever. He just needs to make peace with his time away. Come with me," Meg insisted. "We'll tell everyone the great news. We need to celebrate this gift."

"I...I can't do this, right now, Meg. I need to be alone," I said, letting go of her hand.

"You don't need to be alone."

"Please, just give me time."

"Not before I fix your hair because, to be honest, you're a horrible mess," Meg replied, avoiding my request for solitude. Picking up the one chunk of hair that Snowystra had turned white, she said, "You think, being a queen, you would be able to get yourself together better."

"You do know I had servants who dressed me and fixed my hair, right?"

"Well, now you have me. May I braid your hair, my queen?"

Twisting my hair, I watched her in the mirror. The little girl I left was all grown up. Kissing me on the cheek when she finished, Meg said, "Such a pretty girl."

"Thank you." I forced a smile. "It's now time for you to bother Miles." Going to the bathroom, I shut the door and splashed icy water on my face. When I returned to the room, Meg was waiting.

Blatantly ignoring my request for solitude, she announced, "I put some clothes out for you."

Looking at the summer dress she picked out, I slipped it on. "I guess I'll need more clothes like this, soon."

"Oh, I have tons of clothes." She gave a dismissive way. "Are you really sure you want to be alone?" Meg asked and adjusted my dress.

"I am. I want to go into the backyard. Some sun might make me feel better."

With a nod, she turned to walk away.

I grabbed her and hugged her tightly. "Thank you, Meg. I missed you."

"I know," she said with a wink.

CHAPTER
FORTY-THREE

Walking outside, I allowed myself to feel all the emotions I had for Cole. I was so angry and hurt, but I knew the love I had for him wouldn't let me hate him. Leaning against the picnic tree, I closed my eyes and let the sun's warmth shine on me while I just breathed.

The wind blew warmly, and the scent of cinnamon filled my nose. Opening my eyes, I found Blaze. "Cole's gone," I said.

Her expression grew dark. "You forgave him, but he can't forgive himself. He'll return for both of you, but only when he is better."

I looked away from her.

"He's sick, Mara, but he is in the arms of the Goddess Brighid."

My eyes narrowed at her. "But Snowystra's inside her." I repeated what Brighid had said, "'*Of one, they became three. They are all one.*' So, how do you know she won't hurt him?"

"That part of Snowystra is gone. The part of winter that was broken, bruised, hurt, and striking out at the world has been healed. Healed in her sisters' love." Blaze sat beside me.

"He should've stayed. He's my husband. We could've figured it out together."

"Enough of this, Mara. If he stayed, he would have died. You told him yourself that he needed to forgive himself. Now, be strong and stop drowning in your self-pity." Blaze stood and offered me her hand. "Stand up and let me see you."

Sighing, I let her help me up.

Blaze circled me, and then let out a long sigh. "Still weak. Look how skinny your arms are. Did you lose all your muscle tone there?

"I was able to run pretty far from Cole when he was trying to kill me," I said defensively.

"I bet you regretted not being in better shape, then." Blaze eyed me.

"Yes, I did. I thought of you as I hid from him in the forest."

"So, together we will help you get through this," Blaze declared.

"You're staying this time?" I asked.

"We've always been here, Mara," Blaze said. "And Cole will return."

"But, when?"

"When he is ready, and then you will need to forgive him for leaving you," Blaze replied. "If you start working on that part while he is gone, then when he returns, you can move forward. Go on, Mara. Call us, again."

"What do you mean? You're already here."

"Say the prayer for your baby. Say the words Mae would say to you each night."

"That is silly. You're already here."

"Call us for your family. You need them now more than ever."

Relenting, I took a deep breath, and I threw my hands above me. "Danu, Goddess of Light, I ask for your loving guidance and your aid in invoking the elements that guide."

"With my hands to the east, I call upon you, Air, and ask you to blow away any doubt and fear that surrounds us. I ask that you clarify our thoughts." A rush of wind surrounded us as Breeze zipped around in her blue bird form.

I continued the prayer, "With my hand to the south, Fire, I call upon you and ask you to burn away any fears that fill my heart. Burn away those feelings that harm." Red embers filled the sky as Blaze appeared as a fiery dancer. Her body was entirely made of flames.

"With my hand to the west, Water, I call upon you and ask you to wash away my fears and shower me with forgiveness for those that have hurt us." Bay appeared, calling a rainstorm. The droplets of water fell hard, and then slow as the sound of chimes and laughing children surrounded us.

A tiny sensation began in my stomach and grew stronger.

Meg appeared and resumed the request, "With my hands to the north, I call upon you, Earth, and ask you to strengthen us and protect.

Your gift of life has blessed this family and we thank you." Daisy stepped forward and put her hand on my stomach, smiling. The blades of grass at my feet began to grow and we were surrounded by a field of white daisies.

I felt overwhelmed by the magic and love surrounding me.

"Goddess, our request is complete, and I ask you to keep us safe, especially the child that grows inside me. Please, watch over Cole and bring him home to us when he is healed."

The sky filled with petals that showered us as Danu stepped out of the tree. "You have all brought me immense joy. Your love as a family and your commitment to each other is the greatest gift you could give me."

Kissing me on the cheek, she said, "You once promised to protect the magic and you have fulfilled this vow a thousand times over. Now, it's time for you to embrace the magic. Heal your heart, Mara, and forgive Cole."

"Thank you, Danu," I whispered as she faded away.

As the night sky filled with stars, Meg took my hand. Standing under the night sky with both my mortal and elemental families close, I knew the future wouldn't be easy, but my child would be surrounded with love.

EPILOGUE

Nights were the hardest time for me. As my stomach grew, the baby inside me became even more active. Flipping on the lamp, I looked at the tapestry hanging on the wall that Livia had sent me. It was the beautiful girl with the butterfly wings. This time, she held a child in her arms.

"My little night owl," I said as I climbed out of Gram's bed. "If I take you there, will you let me rest?"

Kicking me, as if agreeing to my terms, I laughed. "Fine. Some fresh air will do me good, too."

Slipping on Gram's gardening boots and a long sweater to cover my nightgown, I left the warmth of our house. I felt the rush of a cool breeze when I stepped into the night air. Recalling my time in Snowstrum, I wrapped the sweater tighter around myself.

Rubbing my stomach gently, I said, "This is the yard I played in and where I first met our elemental friends. Over there is Gramp's workshop, where your grandfather has been hard at work, making you a beautiful crib."

As I grew closer to the renovated structure, I could smell wood chips mixed with the scent of furniture oil. The whirring sound of the woodworking equipment resonated in my memory. Lost in a daydream, I didn't see my unexpected guest.

"Hello, Marina," Cedric Drygen greeted me as he stepped out of the shadows.

I stopped and stared. His hair had grown longer and was peppered with gray. His face was rugged. Time had left its mark. Calling Fire, I readied myself to fight him.

Holding his hands up in front of himself, he said, "No need to call magic. I'm just here to talk."

"Why are you here?" I demanded. "You have no right to be on my property."

"I promised your mother I would make sure no harm ever came to her children. I failed before. I could've stopped her from taking you if I had been stronger."

"Snowystra? No one could have stopped her," I corrected him. "It was what had to happen, but it's over and she's gone, now. So, what do you want from me?"

"You sound just like her. You should've been my child. Eliza and I were meant to be forever before it was taken away from us."

"I have a father...no thanks to you. You can go, now."

"I've seen my son. He has grown very tall, and I'm told he's very smart."

"Have you been following him?" I asked, contemplating calling Air and sending him away.

"I just wanted to see him. I just needed to see that he was safe," Cedric replied. "He's all I have left of her."

"Did your mother send you to come take him from us?"

With a small laugh, he answered, "My mother can't take care of herself these days, let alone worry about taking care of a boy. She spends her time sitting in a chair, talking about how I've failed her, just as my father did. All the years of hate built up inside her have taken their toll. The day Snowystra left this world, I fear my mother's sanity left, too. She is too weak to come after anyone and I don't follow her orders anymore."

"Just say what you came to say, Cedric," I demanded.

"Miles was the best thing that came from me and Eliza. No matter what happened, it was all worth it just to bring *my son* into this world."

"So, you are here to take him, then. If you try, I'll have to hurt you. I'll not let you take him from us."

"There's no reason to keep my son from me anymore. He needs to know where he comes from. What it means to be a Drygen."

"Miles will never be a Drygen. You've said what you wanted to say and now you can leave."

Nodding, he said, "Fine. I'll go, for now, but this conversation isn't over. My son should be with his *real* father."

Calling a gust of wind, I warned, "Go, and do not return. If you do, I won't be kind."

The look in his eyes was cold. His hands sparked silver. "You're not the only one with magic," Cedric snarled.

Releasing the gust of air, I glared at him and called Earth. The ground underneath him shook. He struggled to stay upright. Unable to maintain the magic he was calling, it fizzled. Smoke emitted from his hands as his threat was neutralized.

"Cedric, I'm not in the mood to have a battle of magic with you. Just leave."

"I'm going, but I'll be back for my son."

Not waiting for my response, Cedric walked off. Waiting until I was sure he was far enough away, I entered the woodshop, locking the door behind me. I sat on one of the rocking chairs, contemplating. Snowystra was gone, but the damage she caused was not.

The Drygens won't rest until Miles is with them.

A hard kick in my stomach brought me out of my thoughts.

"Don't worry. No one's going to take anyone else from our family, and I'll bring your daddy home."

My child would have both of her parents in her life. Cole was going to come home to us. I just needed to be patient...and follow my heart.

MAZY
PROTECTORS OF THE ELEMENTAL MAGIC BOOK 3

This book is dedicated to those who pushed me to believe in the magic when it seemed gone. Without you, the story would not have continued:

∞

My sister *– for reminding me every day of the unbreakable sister bond*
My muse kitty, Lil *– for always bringing me back to reality*
Dame Judi Dench *– for reminding me to never give up*
Jane *– for your endless support and encouragement*
LE *– for prodding & pushing me to dig deeper*
And for Gram *– you are always*
and forever in my heart

Acknowledgments

Thanks to L.E. Fitzpatrick, with your brilliant guidance on how to make my way through the maze of a story, and to J.M. Northup for her editorial support. From our collaboration, I learned so much about not only writing but the editorial process.

Mazy
adjective, mazier, maziest.
full of confusing turns, passages, etc.; like a maze

~ dictionary.com

PART ONE

CHAPTER
ONE

"Come quick, Mommy! Mommy! Mara!"

Setting the kitchen knife down next to the vegetables I was cutting, I went to investigate. As I stepped out of the house, I could see the black hair of the child as he ran through the long blades of golden grass.

"Quick, come see what Daddy has made," the small boy said when he reached me. His deep brown eyes twinkled, and he wore a mischievous grin.

I followed him through the field and down the hill to where the grass was no longer tall. I stopped as a wall of fire appeared with the words, *WE LOVE YOU*.

"Isn't he great?" the boy yelled. He ran towards the fire creation and into the open arms of the dark-haired man that stepped out of the flames. The man's golden eyes flickered as he saw me.

"What do you think of my creation? Aidan said he wanted to make something special for you. Did we succeed?"

He set the boy down and kissed me on the cheek. "Why are you so quiet, love? Are you not happy with your surprise?"

"What are you doing, Kai?" I asked, not hiding my anger. "What game are you playing?"

"Why is Mommy mad?" the boy asked the man, his eyes welling with tears.

"She's not mad. Mommy is just having one of her sad days. She is just a bit confused," Kai said, patting the child on his head. "Why don't you go practice what I taught you. I bet Mommy will be feeling better, later, and will bake some cookies for you."

The boy looked at us both hesitantly before nodding and running off.

Kai took my hand, but I yanked it out of his grasp. "Why is he calling me, Mommy and you, Daddy?"

"Mara, I don't know how to help you remember us. You haven't had one of your spells in so long. You can't start this, again. It's too confusing. Aidan is our son. We are married. We've been married for over six years, now. Why must we do this, over and over? Why can't you remember us?"

"Lies!" I screamed and stepped away from him. "I'm married to Cole and I'm having his child."

"You're not pregnant, Mara," Kai said softly.

I touched my stomach to prove him wrong and gasped. He was right. I wasn't pregnant.

"What have you done?" I cried.

Whirling around to run back to my home, I saw a small red cottage with yellow trim. I scanned the area for anything familiar. For miles around me, there was nothing, but rolling plains of copper grass. I realized I wasn't in Starten. Falling to my knees, I sobbed.

"Mara," Kai whispered into my ear. He wrapped his arms around me. "I know you miss him, but Cole is gone. Losing the baby was too much for him. He blamed himself for it. There was nothing you could do to save him. You need to forgive yourself. Can't you stay in the present with us and release the past?"

Tears streamed down my cheeks. I felt the air inside me expel as I deflated. *Is he telling me the truth? Did I lose both Cole and our child without remembering?*

"Our son needs you to be here with us. He doesn't understand why you keep forgetting who he is. Mara, I won't keep putting Aidan through this."

Painful images flashed in my mind, telling me that Kai wasn't lying. I *had* lost everything I loved. The image of Cole lying dead in my arms consumed me. Trembling, I fell into Kai's arms. Though he held me tight, the warmth from his body couldn't remove the chilling realization of all I had lost. Pressing myself closer to him, I nestled deeper, seeking more of his heat. The fieriness of his touch cooled, and I gasped when it turned ice cold.

"Did you really think I would let a child of my blood be born to you? I told you I'd take everything you love. How nice of you to assist me with this family. You're destroying them for me."

The arms around me were no longer Kai's. I struggled to break the hold, trying to get away from the familiar body. When *she* released me, instead of running, I turned around to face her. Her cold gray-blue eyes glared at me – Snowystra.

"Did you expect me to let you live happily ever after?" she snarled. "Pity that I had to let my beautiful boy die to punish you. Although, watching you relive that pain has been worth it. But I have grown bored with finding ways to hurt you. Now, it's your turn to die, Marina."

A familiar dagger appeared in her hand. I had summoned and used it to stab Snowystra when she had tried to stop me from leaving her dark domain, Snowstrum. Her eyes gleamed with satisfaction at my surprise. Before I had time to act, she plunged the knife deep into my stomach. Her long nails dug into my shoulders, holding me close to her.

I struggled to pull away, but I could not free myself. All that I could do was scream as her cold laughter filled my ears.

CHAPTER TWO

"It's okay, Mara," Meg said, smoothing my hair. "It was just a dream. Wake up."

Opening my eyes, I touched my stomach, only to be relieved when I felt movement. My baby was still inside me and definitely alive. Trembling, I sat myself up.

"Same dream?" Meg moved closer to me.

"Yeah," I said, unable to calm the shaky feeling I had. "I don't know how to make it stop. Danu promised me that Snowystra was dead, but it feels like she's still here. I need Cole to come home. Why isn't he here if he's doing better each day?"

"I know you're worried about him, but you can't keep all of it built up inside. You should know by now that it will haunt your dreams." Meg hugged me tightly.

She was right. I was full of fears that I couldn't stop from playing, over and over, in my mind. However, I wasn't Meg's burden. She worried about me too much. I was supposed to be her protector, her big sister...not the weak patient that needed to be coddled.

Not wanting to admit what was really worrying me, I said the obvious, "I need to see Cole. I need to see him myself. I need Cole to tell me that he's ok."

When Cole was lured to Snowstrum, Snowystra made him the Shah of her Winter. As the Shah, Cole was a different man; he became cruel and abusive. I'd been naive to think returning home would fix everything. The night he left, he tried to talk to me about his fears, but I silenced him. If I had listened, Cole might not have gone.

I hated him for the way he left. Cole hadn't even said goodbye. He simply left a note that said he needed to fix himself before he could be with me. Why did he sneak away in the middle of the night like a coward? Why hadn't he forced me to listen to his concerns?

I left my unspoken words hanging. *I needed Cole to tell me he loved me and that he wasn't leaving me. I needed to know that he didn't go because he was grieving the death of Snowystra.*

"You know he'll return when he's better, Mara. Have faith that it will be soon." Leaving Gram's bed, which we had been sharing since Cole's departure, Meg opened the curtains and let the sun shine in on me. "It's going to be a beautiful day, so get out of bed. Let me finally show you the room we built for you. You can't hide forever in here, pretending nothing has changed."

Sighing, I resigned myself to the fact my little sister wasn't going to let me wallow in my sadness, today.

Cole and I were in Snowstrum for, what I thought had been, only a few months. Upon returning, we learned our absence from Starten had lasted for over six years. During that time, Meg had grown up and, many days, I felt like I was the little sister, now. The fifteen-year-old had more wisdom inside her than I remembered having at that age. Her positive outlook was so different than mine.

I reluctantly threw on a flowing summer dress. Nothing I owned did much to conceal my pregnancy. *How will I explain being pregnant with a missing husband to everyone?*

Running my fingers through my curly hair, I inspected the roots of the white streaks that had been created by Snowystra's touch. My hair had grown, but it didn't look like it would be returning to its raven color. It would serve as my reminder that, despite being freed, Snowystra had forever tainted my life. Sighing, I decided to not bother fixing my hair. Meg would redo anything I did anyway.

Images of Cole, from the last night we were together, ran through my mind as I brushed my teeth. Four months had passed, during which I thought I'd forgiven him for leaving. Now, I wasn't sure. It didn't help that I hadn't forgiven myself. The guilt I felt for not listening to his concerns and dismissing his worries grew stronger each day. If I would've just listened to him, I wouldn't be alone.

"She said you were getting ready. I think your teeth are probably clean enough," the soft voice of Essie said. My stepmother took the toothbrush from me and wiped the toothpaste from the side of my mouth as if I was a small child.

Essie had become the mother that Eliza never could be. Every day, I felt closer to her and appreciated her taking care of my family while I was gone.

"Meg told me the dreams are getting stronger. What can I do to help you?" Her green eyes filled with such warmth and love. Stroking my cheek, she took my face between her hands.

I could feel the heat from her magic.

"The baby growing inside you needs you to heal your heart, Mara. Cole will be home, soon. You need to believe in the love he has for you." Essie spoke to me using a form of ESP.

My stepmother's family had been followers of Brighid for hundreds of years before my grandmother had been blessed by Danu. The Goddess kindly referred to them as her Ateissa – her calming balance. Unlike my ability to control all four elements, Essie had been gifted with telepathy and a soothing touch.

"How do you believe in his love when I doubt it, every day? I need to see him. If we are over, I need him to tell me." My voice was as cold as my heart.

"Oh, Mara, you don't believe that," Essie said, taking my hands in hers.

"I need to see him, Essie. I'm going to go to Danu and ask her to bring me to Cole," I proclaimed. She loosened her hold on my hands, but I gripped her hands tighter. "He has been gone too long. If he's not here for the birth, he will hate himself and I don't think I will be able to forgive him, either."

Sighing, she calmly said, "I will help you go to Cole, if...."

"If what?" I narrowed my eyes at her.

"Meg has planned a day for us. She wants to take you to Main Street to pick out items for your suite," she said. "It's time to leave Gram's room. You can't hide here forever, dwelling on your sadness and anger."

Closing my eyes, I took a slow breath. "Ok. I'll give you this day. However, tomorrow, I'm going to Cole. Gram always told me to follow my heart, but it feels like my heart stopped beating the day he left."

I joined my family at the kitchen table as they were finishing breakfast.

Charlie babbled and scooped her food into her mouth. My father doted on my two-year-old half-sister, appearing amused by her. A brilliant smile graced Essie's face when she saw her husband and child.

My half-brother, Miles was at his normal station in front of the stove. He loved cooking and often experimented, using his Air magic to enhance the recipes. Carrying a plate of food towards me, he grinned.

A small smile spread across my face. I loved seeing my little brother so happy. *Miles lost both parents in the blink of the eye and was left in the care of strangers*, I thought in amazement. *Instead of sinking in his sorrow, he's accepted his new parents as his own and thrived. Why could I not be so strong?*

"So, what are you up to, today, to make you smile like that?" I questioned.

His big, green eyes twinkled with mischief. "Nothing special. Just working on how to make the pancakes fluffier. I think I've mastered the recipe."

"No secret spices?" I asked, raising my eyebrows.

"Just the usual – vanilla with a pinch of lemon zest," Miles said. When I narrowed my eyes, he laughed. "Don't use your dark queen look on me. Should I call in the royal food taster?"

Miles never missed a chance to mock my former queen status and lived for the stories I shared about my time in the dark court. I wondered if he, sometimes, missed the formality of living in the Drygen mansion.

Setting the plate before me, I admired his presentation: a stack of pancakes with butter and maple syrup next to a fruit salad of blueberries, strawberries carved into roses, and star-shaped apple slices. Waving my hand at him in a dismissive manner, I said, "This is acceptable. I will trust you, today."

He kissed me on the cheek and plopped down on the seat next to me. "I feel honored you approve. Now, eat before it gets cold."

The pancake melted in my mouth and I was unable to restrain an audible moan. My senses seemed heightened since I had returned home. It may have been from the liquid diet I was on in Snowstrum or, possibly, the pregnancy.

"I'll take that as a compliment." Miles chuckled. "What does my Neep think of it?"

Since we didn't know the sex of the baby, *Neep* had become Meg's and Miles' nickname for the child inside me.

"So far so good," I said. My period of nausea, when I had an overwhelming aversion towards food, had passed and I was thankful to be able to enjoy meals, again. "What are your plans for us, today?" I asked Meg. Reluctantly finishing my breakfast, I decided to be positive about the day.

"I thought we'd start in your room. Then, we should go to Jackson's to pick out a bedspread and some things for the new space," Meg responded excitedly. Hopping up, she stood over me. "We better get going. We have a lot to do, today, Mara." Meg offered me her hand. "First thing, let's fix your hair."

With expert skill, my little sister twisted and turned my hair, hiding the white streak and creating a long, thick braid.

When Meg finished making me presentable, I followed my father and her past Gram's room and down the hallway towards the patio. The house had been renovated while I was gone and there had been several additions made. Before my grandmother's death, she had talked to Cole about her wishes. Gram had always wanted a spot in our home where she could watch the sunrise and appreciate the morning view. My father had honored her ideas and the patio, now, wrapped around to the east. At the far end of this, there was a white door.

"This part of the house is all yours," my father said, opening the door to a wide-open space. "We didn't do anything, yet, down here. I thought you and Cole would want to talk about how to use it."

At one end of the room, there was a circular staircase. Following my father, we slowly climbed the stairs. The handrail, made from the same light wood as the rest of the space, was engraved with flowers and butterflies. When we reached the top, my eyes filled with tears.

The room had several glass pane windows looking out into Starten Forest. It was clear that my father had made all the furniture in the room, from the king-size bed with a dark wood headboard to the dressers and desks. Trailing my fingers along the smooth wooden surface of one of the armoires, I struggled to find my voice.

"Oh, you don't like it?" my father said, wringing his hands. "We can change anything you want."

Choking back my tears, I replied, "No. It's not that...it's perfect. Everything's so nice. It must've taken you forever to make it all."

"Making the furniture was my small way of keeping you close while you were gone. There's a piece missing, though. I didn't bring up the crib, yet, but I think it would be perfect over there," he said, pointing at a small section of the room. Standing in front of another door, my father added, "And, here's the bathroom. I borrowed the design from Charlemagne's, so it has a nice big bathtub and a glass shower."

Interrupting, Meg said, "And, then, when my Neep is old enough, they'll sleep in here."

She opened a third door I hadn't noticed before. It led to my old bedroom. The loft room that Meg and I had shared.

"You've thought of everything," I noted, unable to hold back my tears.

Meg wiped the wetness from my face. "Oh, Mara, don't cry. If you don't stop, I'll have to cry with you." When I cried harder, she said, "No, seriously. Enough of that."

My father laughed. "If you two don't stop, I'll be crying, too."

"We wouldn't want that, Dad." Meg smiled. "As you can see, there's a lot we still need to buy before you leave, tomorrow, Mara. We don't want Cole to come home to an unfinished room."

"How do you know about that?" I asked, not hiding the surprise in my voice.

"I didn't know, for sure." Meg laughed. "Thank you for confirming it. This time, you have to promise to not be gone so long."

Taking one last look around, I hoped Cole would soon be back at home with me. The small kick from my stomach didn't want to be left out. "Yes, Daddy will be home in time to meet you," I whispered. "Ok, Meg, I'm almost ready for the day you've planned. I'll only be a few minutes."

As we turned to leave, a strong wind blew into the room. Breeze stood in the open window. The Air elemental wore a cross look on her face.

"Not so fast, Mara," she barked. "You've been avoiding your training. How will you protect the child you carry if you're running from your responsibilities? Sorry, Meg, but Mara is mine for the next few hours."

CHAPTER

THREE

Breeze led me deep into the northern part of Starten Forest. I pursed my lips holding back the words I wanted to say to her. Several months prior, the Air elemental had requested to stay behind and be my guide while the others returned to Danu. I had been so wrapped up in my own self-pity that I didn't question why they had to leave.

If only Kai would've stayed, I thought to myself. *I would've been able to talk to him.* He would answer me honestly and without riddles.

Stopping in a clearing tucked in the middle of large red trees, Breeze sat down on one of the gnarled black trunks that had fallen over, all of its blood-red leaves piled around it. She looked dark and scary sitting in the middle of it.

"I just ate breakfast and I didn't dress for this," I pouted.

"You promised me, last week, that you would continue to practice using your gifts. Hiding and ignoring the magic you have running through your veins won't bring Cole back. If you do not know how to use your magic, how can you protect your child?" Breeze scolded.

"I'm here, now, Breeze, and I'm in no mood for a lecture," I retorted, crossing my arms.

Clenching her jaw, she commanded, "Call your magic."

Halfheartedly, I called a medium ball of fire and threw it onto the ground. When she glared at me, I cast a stream of water that doused the flames.

A burst of wind hit me. The air knocked the water out of my hands and threatened to blow me over. Breeze's attack angered me, and I flung my own Air magic at her. The tendrils of our magic pushed against each other. When hers overpowered mine, I called Earth to raise a barrier of thick vines to protect me.

From inside the cocoon I created for myself, I yelled, "I'm pregnant. Are you trying to hurt me?"

"Excuses! Blaze was right. You're letting your sadness make you weak. She wouldn't have let you slack off like this. You're not using all of your magic. Your enemies will not be gentle with you. Now, fight me!"

The violent wind she called ripped the vines, one by one, out of the ground.

Clearing my mind, I called Water to flood the soil. When it was knee high and the wind crashed strong waves into Breeze, I focused on the dark magic of my mother. I called my dark Air magic and willed it to freeze the molecules of water surrounding Breeze.

As the white crystals formed, they trailed towards Breeze. Relentless, I pushed more of the icy water towards her, freezing it. When the solid block of ice wrapped up her shoulders, I stopped summoning my power.

Smirking, she taunted, "Is that all you have?"

My hands were dripping with sparks. I threw just enough of the electricity to give her a strong jolt before squashing it in my hands. "Did you want me to create a dagger to cut you? Did you want me to call the Earth to split open, dragging you deep into the ground before burying you alive? Or, are you satisfied with what I've proven I can do?" I cried.

"I just want you to be prepared for anything, Mara," Breeze said. "You're working from anger, right now. Can you do the same when you're in a place of serenity? Do you know how to counter all of the elements and any other magic that you've not seen, yet?"

My hazel eyes locked with her silver ones. We stared at each other silently.

Calling a stream of warm wind, I melted the icy trap I had contained her in. A rumble called my attention and I could see the sky above me growing darker as thick clouds filled it. Before I could react, a funnel shot down and encircled me.

As I spun inside the small tornado, my mind raced. My attempts to push the air around me failed. Feeling dizzy and out of options to save myself, I cried into the airstream, willing it to reach Breeze, "I give up!"

The twister slowed, and I was gently set on the ground. Panting, I lay on the damp grass, unable to catch my breath. Breeze sat beside me, sending me a burst of oxygen. We sat silently, staring at the sky while I recovered.

"And, this is why we insist you train. Once you are ready, we can try, again. Never let your guard down, not even for those you trust." Breeze stood and held out her hand to help me up.

Her words had me wondering who I really could trust. *Did her warning include my family?*

When I was a small girl, I would burst out of the house to meet my special friends. These children of Danu were the physical embodiment of the elements – Breeze of Air, Blaze of Fire, Bay of Water, and Daisy of Earth. During our visits, they taught me how to call their essence, but to me, it had all been play. Throwing water balls, growing flowers, creating small flaming embers, and calling soft breezes were the extent of my education. Other than several sharp scoldings by Blaze for my ambitious balls of fire, I was ignorant.

As my gift grew stronger, Gram feared I wouldn't be safe and she bound my access to it, erasing my memories. Before my eighteenth birthday, she restored my gift and the elementals returned to help me remember. My grandmother died before she could teach me everything I needed to know. She had left me unprepared to face the dangers surrounding us. I had thought my mother was my only threat until I learned she'd been trying to protect me from Snowystra as the darkness consumed her.

Training, now, was about protecting myself from an invisible danger. There was so much I didn't understand about the unseen world around me and even more that I didn't know about my own abilities. When I questioned Breeze, she refused to answer me. She'd only tell me to focus on growing stronger. More secrets. More truths withheld.

One thing Breeze couldn't help me understand was the dark magic within me. I felt it pulsing through my veins. I was told it was Winter magic, but it was *her* magic. I feared it as much as I reveled in the strength I knew it gave me. I wondered if my mother had felt the same way. If I let myself embrace it, would I end up like her?

In the end, Breeze was right. I did have a child to protect, now, and there was a chance I could be raising my baby without a father. I would need to learn to use all the magic I had inside me. The next few hours, I spent anticipating a variety of attacks and practicing ways to defend everyone I loved without a clue as to what I was fighting against.

CHAPTER FOUR

As soon as I arrived home, Meg rushed us out the door and into Essie's car. As we entered the town's center, my heart fell. The wooden shops had been replaced by brick buildings with large storefront windows.

Stores I had considered part of my youth appeared to be gone. The sign to *Thompson's Used Book and Sauerkraut* store, now, flashed with an *Up the Hill Bakery* sign. New merchants, selling their expensive products, advertised their exclusive wares. There was even a person dressed as a candy bar, trying to lure customers into the newly opened, *Jack's Beans*. The display of colorful candy and treats was tempting.

"I guess I really was gone for six years," I said softly.

"Not all changes are bad, Mara," Meg soothed. "Simon Jackson calls *Jackson's* a department store, now. It has everything. Mrs. Croft sold her craft store to him, but she still works there. She said she's never been happier. Trust me. Change can be good."

"But, what about Mrs. Thompson? She loved her old books," I said.

"She turned it over to her son, Jack. He not only took over the bookstore, but he opened the candy store, as well. You remember him, right? He went to school with you and Cole," Meg rambled. "Mrs. Thompson was so happy to retire. She still makes her sauerkraut for her loyal customers, but the new bakery is nice. We'll go there for lunch."

Seeing all the changes, I wanted to cry. It felt like my childhood memories were slipping away. As we approached the new Jackson's

Department Store, I grimaced. The granite building was, at least, fifteen stories high, overshadowing the simple stores of Main Street.

"We are here, ladies." Essie parked the car in front of Jackson's and hopped out. Calling to us, she said, "Let the shopping begin."

People waved and smiled at us. I sank back into my seat, not wanting to get out. *They're going to judge me. They'll know that Cole has left me, pregnant and alone.*

"Come on, Mara," Meg said, unlatching the door from the seat behind me.

When I didn't budge, Essie opened the car door and held out her hand towards me. "It'll be ok, Mara. No one will bite you. People have grown up and things have changed. Just like you."

But they had time to adjust it, I thought bitterly. Sighing, I accepted her hand and was relieved when the small pricks of her magic calmed me.

Meg had been correct. Jackson's store did have everything a person could ever want. Essie guided us through the departments, picking up anything I showed even the slightest interest in. In each section of the store, she'd hand off the merchandise, asking the clerk to charge it to her account and deliver it to our home. After we finished in clothing, she insisted I pick out new things for every room in our suite.

To my surprise, I was swept up in the excitement of decorating my new rooms. I found myself drawn to a bedspread. The satin fabric was brilliant white against a black swirling pattern. Its sensual material and contrasting colors reminded me of our room in Snowstrum.

"Is this the one you like?" Essie asked. She ran her fingers over the bedding. "It is a nice fabric. What's your hesitation?"

"It might be too much of a reminder to Cole of where we were," I said, walking away from it and focusing on a pale-yellow bedspread instead.

"You can't hide from where you were and what happened. Pick the one *you* like," Essie insisted.

Across the room, a flash of color caught my eye. The rich blue and white bedspread reminded me of Cole's eyes. The white pillows had a soft floral design. It felt peaceful and calm.

"That's the one," I said, pointing towards my find.

"Simon, have that set sent to the house, please," my stepmother said to the salt-and-pepper-haired man who had been watching us.

"Will do, Essie," he replied. "You have impeccable taste. I can't wait until we're able to work, together, on our new project."

"In time, Simon. Today is about my girls." Essie smiled brightly and turned her attention back towards me. "So, we bought everything for the master bathroom, the secondary bedroom, several new dresses, and, now, we need to look at stuff for my grandchild."

My heart skipped a beat. She considered my baby her grandchild.

As we searched for bedding, I whispered to Meg. "What new project was Mr. Jackson talking about?"

"Oh, that. She wants to build a hotel here since she's not returning to Great Winds," my sister answered nonchalantly and held up a blanket with a bright animal print.

Shaking my head at her offering, I said, "But, what will she do with Charlemagne's?"

"Thomas and Hazel are running it well. I've pretty much turned it over to them." Essie handed me a soft yellow blanket. "Nothing is final. It's just something we've been talking about."

A flash of satisfaction filled me. My family wouldn't be leaving me to live in Great Winds. We would all be staying in Starten. "I don't know what color bedding to pick out," I confessed, changing the subject. "Everything seems so—"

Meg handed me an ocean blue blanket covered in colorful sea life.

"Cos would love this, Mar," Meg said, using the nickname she'd given Cole when she was a small child.

Examining the beautiful colors and the sweet underwater scene, I couldn't help but agree. "You're right. It's perfect. I think that means we are done shopping for today."

"Thank the goddess," Meg smiled. "I'm starving."

Meg insisted we go to the *Up the Hill Bakery* for lunch. As we walked down Main Street, I tried to see the good side of the changes. Despite the new exterior, many of the stores remained the same inside.

The ice cream parlor was bustling with customers. I eyed a couple who were sitting in *our* booth, sharing a sundae. Cole and I had always ended our dates in that same spot, with a banana split for him and a malt for me. The jukebox kicked on, causing a group of girls to squeal and begin an impromptu dance. Ripped from my trip down memory lane, I returned to the present.

While the outside of the storefronts had changed, the sense of community I loved was still there. The joyful mood of the people around me chipped away at the anxiety I was feeling. As we grew closer to the bakery, the smells of fresh-baked cookies and bread filled the air.

Entering the store, I noticed the familiar sight of books had been replaced with tables and a display case filled with colorful cookies, cakes, cupcakes, and other tempting treats.

"Mara," a tall blonde man called as he stepped out from behind the display. He wiped his hands on his white apron and grinned at me. "It's been a long time since I've seen you. How do you look exactly the same? You haven't aged a bit."

"Hi, Jack," I responded. "It has been a while. Look at what you've done with the store. You're a baker, now?"

"Yes, there have been many changes in my life," he said. Leading us towards a table, Jack added, "Come sit and we can get you something to eat and drink."

We sat and a willowy brunette with her hair in two braids came to take our order.

"Mara, I'd like you to meet my wife, Jill," Jack said, putting his arms around the waitress. "Mara's husband and I were good friends before he whisked her away to Great Winds. Isn't that right, Mara?"

So, Great Winds was the cover story? I wanted to shout, *No, I followed Cole to the home of the dark goddess where he was a pawn in her evil game.* Instead, I forced a smile. "Yes, we've been living in Great Winds."

"Meg told us Cole had stayed behind. Will you be returning to us or is this just a visit?"

"Cole will return, soon, and we have no plans to leave Starten, again. We are home to stay." As I said the words, I realized us being here, together, was the only thing I truly wanted. I would do all I could to make it happen.

"When Cole returns, we must get together. Well, I better get back to the kitchen." Jack waved and returned to the backroom.

"Welcome, Mara. I've heard so much about you," Jill said.

I smiled at the perky woman without replying. I wasn't in the mood to pretend my life was perfect and answer questions about my fictional time away.

Not acknowledging my coldness, Jill beamed at Meg. "Do you want your usual, Meg, or do you want to be adventurous?"

"Of course, my usual, and Mara would probably like the ginger tea," Meg answered, looking at me to confirm my approval.

"Sure, that sounds good. If you'll excuse me, I need to use the ladies' room. Anything Meg orders will be great," I said, trying to match her friendly tone.

Glad to have a reason to hide away, I locked the door and took a slow, deep breath. A sudden coldness blew over me and I turned to watch my reflection in the mirror shift into Snowystra. I gasped, and my hand fluttered to my mouth to silence my scream.

"They are all looking at poor Marina Stone. Abandoned. Pregnant. Alone," the dark goddess hissed.

"No," I cried. "You're gone."

Laughing maniacally, Snowystra said, "Far from gone, Marina. Why, I'm with him, right now. You know he loves me and that he will always."

"You're lying." I glared. I summoned a ball of fire and before I could launch it at her, the image faded, and I was staring into my own eyes. *It's just a dream. You're overtired, that's all. It wasn't real,* I told myself.

"Air, I call you, and ask for your calming aid," I murmured. The air around me grew warm, encircling me with lavender petals. The soft chime of children's laughter echoed and the life inside me moved in response.

Sighing, I decided I couldn't hide anymore and prepared myself to be the woman my grandmother had raised. Even if I wasn't sure that person existed anymore. As I left the bathroom, I trembled at the sound of her evil laughter. Only a crazy person would hear voices from the dead.

Am I losing my mind?

CHAPTER
FIVE

"Surprise!"

When I entered the room, I stepped into a small party. Miles stood, proudly holding a white frosted cake with a brightly colored butterfly on top. Essie and my father stood next to him, cuddling Charlie who clapped excitedly.

"Happy Birthday, Mara," my father shouted.

Clenching my fingers into a tight ball, I extinguished the flames I had instinctually called. I was stunned by the realization that my family wasn't the only ones in the room. I hoped no one had seen my magical reaction.

In addition to Jack and Jill, who were distracted by putting candles on the cake, there were twenty or more of my neighbors present, including Mrs. Ward. My eyes met her penetrating deep blue gaze. The intensity of her stare made me uncomfortable and I quickly directed my attention towards Meg, who had slipped in next to me.

The last time I'd seen Mrs. Ward was in Snowstrum on my wedding day. Guilt filled me. I hadn't thought about her since the guards led her away.

Everyone sang the traditional *Happy Birthday* song. While they did, I painted on the best fake smile I could muster.

"I can't believe you didn't warn me, Meg." Leaning closer towards her, I whispered, "I could've burned this place down or something worse."

"I know. I'm sorry," Meg whispered back. "I saw, but I don't think anyone else noticed. You covered it up quickly."

"Mrs. Ward did, and she gave me the strangest look," I hissed back, maintaining my surprised smile.

"Oh, her? Don't worry about her. She knows about our magic." Meg waved her hands dismissively.

"Yes, I know. She was Gram's best friend, but..." Our conversation was cut short by chants for me to blow out the candles and make a wish.

Resisting my urge to call Air, I used my own breath and blew out the tiny flames. Soon, I was swarmed with hugs and well wishes. Accepting the compliments and greetings with patience, I was relieved when Jack and Jill served the cake. As everyone flocked towards the sweet treat, I found myself, face-to-face, with Mrs. Ward.

"Mara, I am so relieved to see you. When I left you, I couldn't forgive myself for not doing something to save you," the silver-haired woman said in a hushed voice. "I should've done something more to help you. Mae would have known what to do."

"There was nothing you could've done. Not even Gram could have changed what was supposed to be. Your being there to perform the binding ceremony was more than I could have hoped for." I hugged her. "When I watched them drag you away, I feared the worst."

"I was never in harm. That nice boy, Dunn, told me he was under orders from Cole to make sure I was returned to Starten safely. He said he'd been ordered to have my memory wiped, but if I promised to keep quiet, no one would know any different. Several guards quizzed me when they released me into the forest, but I pretended I was hunting for the King of the Snapping Trout. The poor boys thought I had lost my mind," she chuckled.

Just ask her what she knows about the magic. Don't tiptoe around. Be strong and confident. Clearing my throat, I said, "Um, Mrs. Ward."

"Mara, you can ask me anything. Go on, tell me what's bothering you," she replied kindly. "What do you need to know?"

"Oh, ok..." I said, biting my lip.

"You're safe here, Mara." Mrs. Ward put her hand on my stomach.

Suddenly, a strong electric feeling built inside me. It was so disturbing that an overwhelming feeling to hide overtook me. I wasn't sure if it was coming from her or from within me. "I hate to be rude, but nature calls, again." I rubbed my extended belly.

"No apologies needed," she said. "We can talk when you return."

I hurried away from Mrs. Ward. I could feel her gaze following me. As I entered the bathroom and began to shut the door, fingers wrapped themselves around the wood, stopping my progress.

Meg pushed the door open and entered. "What's wrong? Why'd you run off like that?"

"I didn't run off, Meg," I snapped. "I just needed to get away from… from all of this."

"I was stupid." My little sister shook her head. "It's my fault. I didn't want you to miss another birthday. We could've just invited people to the house, but you were living like a hermit there." This time, Meg didn't seem confident and strong. She seemed like a sad little girl.

"It wasn't your fault. It was a pleasant surprise, Meg. I just freaked out when Mrs. Ward…I mean Mrs. Ward…touched my stomach and I felt…I felt Snowystra's magic inside me," I explained, preparing to confess my fears. "Meg, I'm afraid the child inside me holds the dark magic of Snowystra."

"Of course, you feel her magic inside you. It's in all of Eliza's children," Meg said softly. "It was in us from the minute we were born, and it has to be in your child, too."

"What are you talking about?"

"When you were gone, I found Eliza's journals hidden in Gramp's woodshop. She described the day Snowystra told Cedric and her that they could never be together, again. It was exactly like the vision we both saw. Do you remember?" she asked.

Shuddering, I nodded. There was no way the image could ever be erased from my memory.

My mother had been set on a dorcha web next to an unconscious Cedric. Waking him up, Snowystra forbid their union. When Cedric dared to defy her, the Winter Goddess took her pointer finger and drug her long, silver nails down his cheek. The horrifying sound of his screams as she cut from his eye to his chin echoed in my mind.

The horrible scene ended with my mother being freed. However, before she left, Eliza promised to always love Cedric. She vowed they'd be together, again, one day.

"The memory we witnessed didn't show us everything. Snowystra was angered after Eliza stopped and said she'd always love him. The dark goddess hurt our mother. She filled her with her magic and forced her to pledge her loyalty. Mara, Eliza agreed so she could keep everyone she loved safe, including Cedric," Meg explained. "Gram never bound the dark magic inside our mother because she didn't realize what Eliza had done."

"It makes sense that Miles has her magic since Cedric's his father, but you don't have dark magic. I didn't until I was in Snowstrum," I argued.

"You're wrong, Mara. I have the magic and I'm guessing you did before. You just didn't know how to access it. After I found the journals, I realized I could control more than Earth." Meg held out her hands and they filled with a green electricity. The same magic my mother had thrown at me and ultimately used to kill my grandmother.

"Put that away," I said, moving away from her. "You shouldn't call that."

"It's inside us. Just like the elements we control. I don't think this magic is truly bad. I think how you use it defines it." Meg blew away the sparks and shrugged. "If your child carries it, they'll learn how to use it. We'll teach them, together."

"The secrets of our family seem endless, Meg. I'm not sure how much I can handle." I closed my eyes.

Today was not the day for me to fall apart. If my younger sister could handle it, I should be able to do the same. Making her feel bad wouldn't help either of us.

I took her hand into mine. "Your strength amazes me, Meg. I need to learn from you, little sister. Let's talk about this more after the party. You went to so much trouble to make it a wonderful day. Thank you. You really have been my strength through everything."

I wasn't sure I believed her thoughts on the magic. Still, I genuinely wanted to believe she was right. I needed to trust her.

"I'm really sorry about the surprise. I was overexcited by the thought of making your day nice that I didn't think. I can tell them it's over if you want?" Meg hugged me quickly.

"Oh, Meg, the idea was wonderful. Please, don't end it early. Everyone should enjoy the party you planned. I really am thankful."

"If you're sure…" She hesitated.

"Yes, it'll be great. Give me a few minutes and I'll be back out to enjoy the party," I said, guiding her through the door.

When Meg was gone, I stared at my reflection in the mirror. "You're strong enough to deal with anything that comes. You need to pull yourself together. You're not the Vizier. You're not carrying darkness inside you."

Air whipped around me, blowing my braid up as if agreeing.

"Bright blessings, Air," I whispered.

The childlike titters of the element filled my ears.

CHAPTER SIX

After I collected myself, I returned to the bakery where Jack served us a lunch of his special vegetable pizza. The conversation was light, and I was thankful no one asked about our time away. Meg kept the conversation focused on everyone else. By the time I blew out candles and the cake was cut, my baby sister was antsy.

"Elliott, why don't you take Charlie outside for a walk? It sounds like Rick Paulson's band is starting to play," Essie suggested.

Meg and Miles decided they wanted to go and convinced Jack and Jill to join them.

"We won't break into the bakery case while you're gone," Mrs. Ward called after them.

"Feel free to clean it out," Jack chuckled. "I'll be making fresh stuff in the morning and if there's anything left, I'll have to eat it." The slender man patted his stomach.

With the store empty, I could stop worrying and finally relax. Settling at a table, I held my stomach. The creature inside me was active. I wondered what my baby was doing to make me feel like a popcorn machine.

Essie held a train of teacups. "Mrs. Ward and I plan to enjoy some of Mrs. Everstone's blackberry tea. Can we join you?"

"I'd like that," I said, accepting a cup.

I sipped the tea and closed my eyes, willing my grandmother to appear from the steam. I breathed in the earthy blackberry scent and I was immediately drawn back to Gram's mornings with Mrs. Ward. As far back as I could remember, the two women would meet almost daily. Sitting at the kitchen table, they'd enjoy their drinks and share stories. When I was young, I would play with my dolls, imitating their friendship.

"Here's a little gift for you, sweetie." Mrs. Ward slid a white box wrapped in a hot pink ribbon towards me.

I removed the tie and lifted the lid. Inside was a silver chain with an antique silver locket. It had been engraved with a floral design around a large M. As I went to open it, Mrs. Ward stopped me.

"You will want to open this in private," she warned me. "I cast a little spell on it."

"What kind of spell?" I narrowed my eyes at her. I placed the jewelry back in the box and slid it away from me. *I can't have more new magic around me. I can barely handle my own.*

"There are so many things in this world you haven't learned, yet, Mara." Mrs. Ward removed the locket from the box, she put it in my hands.

My fingers tingled this time.

"When you open this, it'll show you Cole," the woman told me. "Once you view it, the vision will be gone, and then it'll just be a nice necklace for you."

"I don't understand. Have you been blessed by Danu, too?" I asked, feeling guilty for my reaction.

"When I was a child, my mother would sneak me out to the caravans on the outskirt of town whenever they passed through," she began.

"Caravans?" I interrupted. "Do you mean the gypsies?"

"Yes, honey." She patted my hand in a way that indicated I ought to sit and just listen.

Just like Gram, I thought.

"On one of those visits, I learned my father was a gypsy and his family's gift was from a great god who had been slain. My mother told me I could never reveal this secret. Then, I met your grandmother." A tender smile crossed her lips and her eyes blurred, seeing into the past. "Together, we learned how to use our magic."

Mrs. Ward returned to the present, meeting my gaze. "I used the same spell on this locket to see you were safe in Snowystra's realm. I was so happy to find you in a wintery forest with Cole. You were walking, hand-in-hand. You looked so content and happy."

"It was our honeymoon. We were happy, then," I said softly. It had been the best part of my time away. Cole and I were lost in our love for a short period before he was summoned back by Snowystra.

"You'll have that, again, Mara," Mrs. Ward said firmly. "Cole will return, and you'll begin your life with him and your child."

Staring out the store window, I could see my father dancing with Meg to a slower song. Watching them brought back feelings of being a little girl without my father. When Cedric and my mother forced Elliott to fake his death and leave me, they stole a part of my childhood that could never be returned.

Determination filled me. My child would not be without a father. I wasn't going to let any doubts or fears I had about the dark magic my baby could be carrying keep me from bringing Cole home.

"It's been a long day," I said, feeling the weight of the day crashing down on me. "I'd like to go home."

"Of course," Essie replied. "Let me just gather up our stuff and let your father know."

"Would you mind if I went by myself to get some fresh air?" I asked. "I'm going to go out the back door and avoid the crowd. I think a walk will do me good."

"Why don't I come with you?" Mrs. Ward suggested, starting to stand.

"Oh, no, please, sit and finish your tea," I said. "It's a quick walk around the building to the car."

She looked as if she wanted to argue with me, but she sat back down. "You're so much like Mae," she noted. "Go. Enjoy the fresh air, but promise me we'll get together, again, soon."

"We will," I promised, kissing her on the cheek. "Thank you, again, for the gift."

"My pleasure, sweetie," she said. "I hope it brings you comfort."

As I walked out into the alley behind the building, I took a deep breath. My emotions were all over the place. *Did the time in Snowstrum damage me?* A twinkle above caught my attention. The night sky was full of stars and a silver crest of the moon peaked out from behind the clouds.

You are twenty-four, today, Mara, I thought to myself. *How does it feel to be an adult? Can you get your emotions under control by the time your child is born?*

Before I could answer my own question, I heard a noise behind me. Turning to see what it was, I found myself an arm's length away from Cedric Drygen.

"Hello, Marina." Cedric stepped out of the shadows. His salt-and-pepper hair glimmered from the glow of the lamppost. The silver line under his eye gleamed and I was forced to remember where it had come from. The vision of Snowystra etching the scar into his flesh reared, again, and I fought the urge to gag.

A shadow appeared behind Cedric and said, "He was weak, then and now. Why do you continue to let him live?"

She's here. Snowystra is back. How could she free herself? My heart beat faster, but I focused on my training. *Don't get distracted.*

Ignoring her taunts, I turned and glared at Cedric. "I think I made myself clear the other night when I warned you to stay away from me and my family. You weren't welcome on our property and you're not welcome to contact any of us."

"Oh, Marina," Cedric said with a cocky smile. "We didn't finish our conversation before you decided to throw around your magic."

"If I wanted to *throw* around my magic, you'd be on the ground, pleading for mercy," I replied. My voice was ice cold. I tapped into my royal persona and spoke to him as if he was one of my subjects. "I've grown tired of your threats. You're forcing me to make a decision to end this conversation...permanently."

Tossing back his head and laughing, he said, "You sound so much like my Eliza. But you won't hurt me. You're such a nice girl."

Cedric stepped closer and put his hands on my shoulders. I called a gust of wind that sent him flying across the backstreet. He hit the metal door of the ice cream parlor. He moaned in pain as he stumbled, trying to stay upright.

"You'll pay for that," he snarled. Swaying, his hands glowed with silver sparks.

As he veered back to throw the power he was holding, I sent another gust of wind, but, this time, it was infused with my dark magic. Black particles of dust surrounded him, lifting him off his feet. The violent wind and coarse magic ripped at his skin and clothing. The terror in his eyes made me feel powerful. I could rip all of the flesh from his bones and blow him away without anyone knowing the difference.

But I would know.

Slowing the twirl of the cyclone, I lowered him. "Your little sparks are nothing compared to the magic I have pulsing through my veins. This is the last warning I'm going to give you, Cedric. Our next encounter will end with you lying in the cold ground next to my mother."

His eyes narrowed. "Aren't you confident? Why don't you save all that energy for bringing your husband home?"

His words were like a slap across my face. Enraged, I hissed, "How dare you? You know nothing about Cole. My mother was a damn fool to ever trust you." I summoned a silver dagger to form in my hands. It dripped with the green acid of my mother's gift.

"Oh, Marina, what do you think you'll do with your little weapon? You can't silence the truth I speak. No amount of time or attempts to heal him will purge all the darkness from inside Cole. Do you think he's the first child of Danu's blessed that Snowystra has taken? No amount of time or love will remove the memories of her. You'll never have the boy you loved back. He's gone." The corners of his mouth turned up into a bitter grin.

"Don't speak about things you don't know, Drygen. Stay away from my family. This is your last warning."

I threw a ball of fire onto him. When he fell to the ground and patted out the flames, something dark inside me brewed. His pain amused me. Laughing, I threw the dagger at him. The blade stuck into his thigh and dissolved. The acid liquid burned and bubbled. The smell of scorched flesh disgusted me.

"Next time, I will not be as kind, Cedric." Smiling coldly at him, I walked away, ignoring the sound of his screams.

The shadow was nothing more than a wisp, now. Slowly, it slid around me, and in a voice that was undeniably Snowystra's, it said, "How weak you've become. Letting him live will be your biggest mistake."

CHAPTER SEVEN

When I reached the car, the sun was beginning to set. Cedric hadn't followed me, but Essie was waiting for my arrival. I trembled violently as I told her about my interaction with the man and my cruel behavior. Despite my protests, she insisted we gather the entire family and go.

By the time we arrived home, my father was fuming. He slammed the car door and stormed into the house. At first, I wasn't sure if he was angry with me or Cedric.

Once inside, Essie ushered the children away. They made themselves scarce as I settled into one of the comfortable chairs in the living room. I quietly watched my father pace, back and forth.

"Did he hurt you?" he asked.

"No. If anyone was hurt, it was him," I said, feeling a sense of satisfaction.

"I'm going to deal with him, once and for all," my father declared. He picked up the fire poker and jabbed at the wood in the fireplace. "He cannot interfere with my family, again. He will not intimidate and scare my kids."

I took the iron bar from him and put it down. "I took care of him, Dad. He won't be back to bother anyone. Promise me you won't do anything stupid, like go after him. That's not how our family handles problems. I can't worry about you, right now."

"The Drygen's shouldn't be your problem to deal with. This mess is my fault," he argued. "But I promise I won't do anything reckless."

I sat down on the loveseat and patted the spot next to me. "If Cedric comes back, I'll take care of him. I'm not the little girl you left behind." He sat beside me and I kissed him on the cheek before I stood up. "We both are tired. Let's go to sleep."

His shoulders slouched, and he leaned back on the couch. "Goodnight, Butterfly," he said softly.

As I walked away, I sensed my father was watching me. When I stopped and turned towards him, we stared at each other. "This isn't your fight anymore. Remember, I'm the dark queen, Daddy." I walked away to the comfort of Gram's room.

I was exhausted, and the comfort of the bed called me. I quickly changed into my pajamas and slipped under the plush comforter. I set the gift from Mrs. Ward on the nightstand. I was too frightened to open the locket and see Cole, so instead, I just stared at the box, until I drifted off into a deep sleep.

When I awoke to the soft sound of Meg breathing, the bedside clock read a quarter past five. My eye caught a silver comb, lying on the nightstand. I smiled as I recalled sitting on the counter while Gram combed my hair with it. I tried to mimic the tune she would hum.

Releasing my memories, I yawned and picked up the box. My mind raced. I couldn't bear the unknown for much longer, but would the truth be too much?

"*What should I do?*" I murmured to my unborn baby.

A flutter of kicks responded as if answering my question.

"You're right. I must face my fears. You're incredibly wise, little one."

I had been quiet enough to not wake Meg. Smiling down on my little sister, I envied how content she seemed. Reluctantly, I picked up the white box and carried it with towards the patio. Settling on one of the wicker loveseats and covering myself with a throw blanket, I tried to get comfortable.

The dark blue sky had a hint of light forming at the base of the mountains towards the east. Gram had been right in wanting the patio extended. As the illumination expanded and filled with orangey-reds and bold purples, I watched in awe. My thoughts silenced as the rising sun calmed me. I was so lost in the magnificence of the sky's colors that I didn't realize my father had joined me.

"Why are you up so early, Caterpillar?" he asked, sitting down next to me. He handed me a mug. "I brought you some of the heilsavi."

"I'm anxious about today," I admitted before taking a sip of the ginger-flavored drink. "I'm not sure if Cole…" Unable to finish my words, I turned my attention back to the rising sun. I didn't want to admit that I was worried Cedric had been right.

My father took my hand and squeezed it. "Is that your gift from Mrs. Ward?" he asked, pointing at the box on my lap. "I can go, so you can open it in private."

"No, please, stay. I don't want to be alone." I took the locket out and examined it. *Please, show me that Cole is well and healing.*

I clicked open the pendant and a stream of blue powder flew out, rapidly filling the room. The particles blocked out everything around me. I held my breath and clung to my father's hand as I closed my eyes, waiting for the air to clear.

The black dots faded, and a light shined on me. It was so bright, I could see it even with my eyelids shut. Impatient, I peeked and was relieved to find the dust gone.

No longer on the patio, I was in an unfamiliar bedroom. In the center of a large bed, Cole lay under several white blankets. His face looked gaunt. He seemed so small. As I tried to stand and go to him, I found I couldn't move.

With a rush of wind, Bay appeared. The Water elemental had not only been my guide as a child, but she had been Cole's. She was our resilient fountain of childish hopes and dreams.

"Get up. Get up. Get up!" The water elemental jumped, up and down, on the bed.

Cole groaned. "Leave me alone."

"You've slept enough," she said, bouncing higher. Her curly cobalt hair wildly rose and fell with her movement. "You need to get out of bed. You have to get the darkness out of you."

Pulling the blanket over his eyes, Cole ignored her demands.

His cold behavior didn't stop her. Ripping the blankets off, Bay jumped, back and forth, before landing on her knees beside him. She, then, started flicking water at him.

Growling, Cole said, "Go away. There's nothing to save here."

"You're being ridiculous. You need to get up and get better. Mara needs you," Bay scolded.

"She's better off without me," he said coldly.

"Cole Oliver Sands, Mara and the baby need you." As soon as the words slipped from her lips, Bay gasped and covered her mouth with both hands.

Sitting up, Cole glared at her. "Mara? Is she okay? What are you trying to tell me?"

"Mara misses you. She needs you to come home," Bay said, not answering his question.

"You said baby. What baby?" Cole demanded loudly.

"Oh no, I wasn't supposed to say anything. She said that you'd come home when you were better if you loved her," Bay said, wringing her hands. "No, it's ok. I didn't tell him anything," she murmured to herself.

Getting out of the bed, Cole struggled to keep himself upright. His long, muscular frame was pale and weak. Bay rushed to help steady him.

"Tell me what is wrong with Mara. Is she hurt?" he asked, his voice cracking. "Is she ill?"

"Breeze is going to be so mad at me and my big mouth," Bay whimpered. The Water elemental led Cole to the edge of the bed. "Sit, sit. Mara is fine, but you need to get better and go home, soon. She'll need you."

"Come on, Bay. Aren't we friends? Don't be like that." Cole sat and tugged her down beside him. "Please, tell me."

Wrapping her arm around his shoulder, she said in a voice barely above a whisper, "Mara is pregnant."

Cole's face was stone cold at the news. They sat in silence. His chest rose as he visibly took deep breaths. Balling his hands tightly, a single tear rolled down his cheek.

"So, I am going to be a father?" he asked, his voice cracking.

Bay nodded weakly.

"If you're telling me the truth, I need to get home to Mara."

"Yes, you do, so get out of bed, and let's get to work." Bay hopped onto the bed and excitedly bounced.

With a look of determination, Cole stood up. "Then, we better get busy and fix me."

Bay laughed and twirled. She filled the room with a downpour of water droplets. The rainstorm she created became so heavy I could no longer see anything.

As the spray lessened, I found myself, once again, in my home in Starten.

My father and I sat, hand-in-hand. Neither of us spoke a word. His presence was more important to me than anything he could've said. The locket in my palm had changed. Now, it held a picture of Cole and me. Tears clouded my vision of the smiling couple.

The door squeaked, and Essie entered the room. Elegantly sitting down, my stepmother sat cross-legged on a wicker chair next to us. "Good morning. You're both up early. The sunrise here is as beautiful as Galinevo. You'll see when I take you there."

Galinevo: Home of the Goddess Brighid and the healing grounds of my husband. When I'd first been told Cole was there, I begged Essie to take me. Brighid denied my request; she would allow me to come to Cole only when he was ready.

Essie was Ateissa, one of Brighid's blessed. She had the ability to communicate with her goddess anytime she wanted. Unlike me, who had not found a way to communicate with Danu. My only contact was through the elementals or when Danu summoned my spirit to her realm.

When I had asked Essie to tell me about Galinevo, she'd only say, "It was a world, which is better to experience for myself, but Cole is safe."

"Essie, will you take me, soon?" I wondered.

Essie stood and held out her hand towards me. "Last night, Brighid told me it's time for you to see Cole. If you're ready, I'll take you to him, today."

Cedric's words played in my mind. I shivered at the thought of Cole turning back into the dark king. I would lose him if he did. This time, I couldn't...I wouldn't follow him.

"It's time," my father said. "Bring him home, Butterfly."

CHAPTER
EIGHT

As we walked along the river, butterflies jumped as they swam upstream in the indigo froth. A flock of squirrels, above, dipped and dived into the water. I'd been told my entire life that the animals had been corrupted by a spill from the Drygen Cannery. As I looked at the trout scamper past before burying into the brush, I wondered if magic was the real reason.

When a tiny trout squeaked and hustled to catch up with its family, I remembered the day Cole took me to learn how to hunt. In the end, he refused to teach me how to predate them. He said it was silly for me to learn. He promised he'd always be there to take care of me. *He was wrong.*

The indescribable smell of the fresh water rushed at me and I knew we were close to the rocky shore of Sparrow Lake. I wondered how much further we'd go when Essie suddenly stopped at a large oak tree.

"Is this the portal?" I asked.

There was nothing special about the timber. Others in the grove around it had unique-looking knots or areas of peeling bark. This oak was just a plain tree.

My heart thumped harder. I was more nervous than I thought I'd be. Every visit to the realms of the goddesses had an impact on time. In Snowystra's Winter world, months were like years. And, the first time I had visited Danu, I slept for seven days while my spirit explored her world.

Essie assured me Brighid's world was a unique realm. The time that we spent there would align with Starten. Then, she led me through the tree. Inside, I could hear the familiar drumming of its heart: *bu dum bu dum*.

We'd been walking for only a few minutes when the black void of the tree ended, and we were transported to another world. Essie led me deeper into the aqua forest. The turquoise sky held salmon and purple clouds. The woods filled with twisted tree trunks, their long vine-like branches covered with pink balls. I suspected the rosy puffs were fruit. I inhaled the almost sweet lemon scent the breeze carried. *Will everyone always remind me of Gram?* I wondered.

As we reached a clearing, Essie stopped. "We're almost there. A little bit of a walk, but I know you're up for it."

Leading me through the trees, we reached a path of rippling water. I inspected the area. It seemed that we would have to turn back.

"Come on," Essie encouraged, stepping off the forest floor onto the stream. The water under her feet solidified. "You're not made of sugar, Mara. I promise you won't melt."

"How do you know I'm not made of sugar?" I asked. The corner of my mouth lifted in amusement. "There are new things I find out about myself, every day."

"That's one thing I can confidently say is not a possibility." Essie tugged on my arm. "Now, come along."

A soft wind chime sounded, and the trees swayed. The pink puffs on them were moving. Squinting to see them more clearly, I realized they were birds, not fruit.

"Oh, look, the rozkora are waking up." Essie pointed to a cluster of the blush-colored creatures.

One of the smaller ones puffed up and made a loud whistling sound. As if responding, the rest of the birds flew off the tree and encircled us.

"Hello, ladies," Essie greeted.

One bird brushed against her cheek before stopping and fluttering in front of my face.

"How sweet," I said.

Suddenly, the little bird pecked me on my head, yanking out strands of my hair and zipping off. "Ouch. It just pulled my hair out."

"I've never seen them do anything like this before," Essie said, stroking my head. "Mara, look at your reflection."

I could see my image in the floor below us. The white streak in my hair had turned a light pink at the roots. The blush color expanded, changing my frosted strands to a deep magenta.

"Did the bird do this?"

I don't know," Essie said. "Come on. Let's go find out."

We continued to follow the path through the forest. I became nervous as we passed another flock of rozkora. The small birds flew around us, but none came too close. As we moved further, the trees thinned, and we came to a mountain pass. The ground below us flickered with multicolored streaks, leading to a stacked waterfall hued in the same brilliant rainbow.

The curtain of water parted, bringing us to the edge of a flowing river. This time we wouldn't be walking across it. Instead, a long boat pulled up with a small man peddling as if he was riding a bike.

"Essie, you've returned." The man jumped out of the boat and swept her up. He flooded my stepmother's cheek with kisses before setting her down. Then, turning towards me, he grinned. "And, you've brought a friend."

Upon closer inspection, I wasn't sure the person in front of me was a man. His face was round, and it faintly looked like he had small, tan feathers coating his skin. The top of his head was covered in blue and white fluffs, falling over his open-collared shirt. Where he should've had eyebrows, there were dark blue markings, extending to his temple. The center of his eyes was black as night and surrounded by an orange sunrise.

"Giuseppe, meet my *daughter*, Mara." Essie smiled at me as she said the word *daughter*.

"Oh, you must be the lovely bride of Cole," he said enthusiastically. He extended a human hand with long black talons for fingernails. "I see from your expression that your *mother* hasn't taught you about Brighid's Curuxatyni."

"No, she didn't. I'm sorry to be so rude," I said, ashamed of my reaction "You...you just look like..." I bit my lip to stop anything offensive from slipping out.

"Is owl the word you're looking for?" He tilted his head upside down and grinned at me.

My hand quickly covered my mouth to hide my shock.

"Stop being ridiculous, Seppe," Essie scolded. "Of course, I haven't told her anything about you. You know that is against my promise to the goddess."

"You should've made an exception and prepared the former Vizier for what she'll see here. We don't want the child to join us sooner than planned." Seppe motioned at my extended stomach. "Do you forgive me, beauty?" he asked.

"Yes, I forgive you," I said, unable to resist smiling. There was something so magnetic and welcoming about this strange little man. Kicks in my stomach told me my child felt the same way. "We both forgive you."

Lifting my hair, he inspected the streak. "I see the rozi have been at play. By chance, did you bear a mark of Snowystra on your head?"

"How did you know?"

Holding out my newly pinked strands of hair, he said, "Lucky guess. Pity the pink won't stay. It's quite lovely. Now, should we take you to your Cole?" Chuckling, he held his hand out to me, again.

This time, I accepted it.

"Join me. We will get you to the Goddess straightaway. Do not be surprised if you see more *unusual beings* like me."

Before I could question him, he was guiding me into the boat with a single row of seats. Essie took the seat behind me and Seppe jumped into the front.

Madly peddling us through the water, Seppe whistled. The faster the pace of his song became, the faster we moved. The scenery blurred by at an unfathomable speed.

A queasy feeling overcame me. When I was sure I was going to lose my breakfast, we suddenly lurched to a stop. Seppe scrambled out of his seat and held out his hand to me. As he helped me out of the boat, I glanced around. He had returned us to the same place we had started.

"We'll see each other, again, soon, Mara," the birdman said, gently pecking my hand. "Blessings of the goddess on you and your child."

Before I could respond, he was back in the boat and drifting away from us.

"Wait, you haven't taken us anywhere," I called after him.

His laughter filled the air and, soon, a multitude of small colorful orbs floated in front of us. The light was so overwhelming, I was forced to close my eyes. When I dared to open them again, I was standing in a grass-covered area.

The perfectly cut emerald lawn was edged with white stones and tall trees with triangle leaves. Ahead of us, I could see a white building with an oval opening. Inside, I could see movement. Someone stepped out of the structure and into the courtyard. Like Seppe, the man was not human.

What did he call them? Curuxatyni?

The stranger walked towards me with a warm smile. Soon, others followed him. They whispered and stared at me. I was the odd-looking one in this group. I searched the wave of rainbow colors for any signs of Cole. The whispering grew louder as if a hive of bees had entered the space in front of me.

No one spoke to me directly and my mind raced. *Is Cole hurt?*

Then, it suddenly became silent. The Curuxatyni moved, clearing a path. From the building, two women emerged. One with short red feathers on top of her head. The other with a peacock plume flowing down her back. Her almond-shaped eyes were set close together, giving her a serious expression, which contradicted her bright smile.

My attention had been so focused on the women that I hadn't realized they weren't alone. There was someone between them. As my eyes locked with the man they escorted, my heart stopped.

"Cole?" I whispered.

CHAPTER NINE

Wearing khakis, rolled up to expose his calves, bare feet, and a white shirt with the top buttons undone, Cole strode quickly towards me. He looked incredible. He had always been fit, but nothing like this. His skin was a golden tan and he was muscular. He was no longer the pale shell of a man from Snowstrum.

"Mar," Cole said, his eyes glistening with moisture. "You're really here."

Falling to his knees before me, he sobbed. Through his tears, I could barely make out his words.

"Cole, I'm here," I said, leaning towards him and touching the top of his head. My touch only seemed to make him cry harder.

"You'll have to stand back up if you want to see me. I'm afraid I'm not as light on my feet as the last time you saw me."

Looking up at me with doe-like eyes, Cole wiped away his tears and stood. He hesitantly held his hand out towards my stomach. I clasped it and placed it against my belly. As if the child in me knew who he was, the movement in my stomach became intense.

"Our baby?" he whispered.

Wrapping my arms tightly around his neck, I kissed him. The minute our lips touched I felt a demanding need to become lost to the world of his arms.

A voice cleared behind Cole, breaking up our kiss, but I held onto him tightly, not wanting to let go. "Never leave me, again, Cole." I pressed my mouth to his ear.

His body stiffened, and he tugged me closer. His hands clutched me too tightly. "You thought you would get away with killing her and taking away my people without paying a price. My child, inside you, is pulsing with her blood. *My* child holds the power of Winter."

I ripped myself out of his arms. I saw the frosty glare. Cole was not inside his body. It was the dark king, the Shah.

"My dark queen is still in you, Marina," he growled. "You'll come to your senses. We will rule, again, together, or you'll join your grandmother in the Afterlife. My child will not be kept from their true destiny."

The face of one of the bird women shifted and Snowystra was standing next to Cole. She put her hand on his arm. "I told you he loved me. You will not keep us apart." She laughed cruelly before fading away.

Something inside me stirred. My maternal instinct kicked in. I slapped him hard across the face.

He smiled at me, blood trickling from his nose. "Even you can't resist the cold violence of our time there," he sneered. "Your passion, once tamed, will be quite useful."

"She's dead. Her poison will not touch my child!" I screamed. I lunged towards him, ready to attack, but was picked up and carried away.

The peacock woman pierced Cole's wrist with her sharp talons. He hissed in pain, but he didn't resist her.

"The darkness that consumes you is no longer welcome. The light of the goddesses fills you," she whispered. When she pulled her hand away, I could see a silver tendril connecting her to Cole.

Cole closed his eyes and when he opened them, they had returned to their deep blue. "Mara, I'm so sorry. I don't know how to stop it. Her darkness pulses through me," he said softly. He was stopped as he attempted to come to me.

"Let me go to her, Sarika." Cole struggled against her hold. "I need to apologize. I need to make sure she knows that isn't the real me."

The peacock-haired woman shook her head. "You're not ready. You're feeding off the power of the child," Sarika said. "There will be time, later, to be with her when it's safe. Now, you must return for treatment. I hope this hasn't set back all of our hard work."

"No," I said, pushing against the person restraining me. "He's not going to leave me, again."

"He won't be gone long," the red-feathered woman said. "Sarika and I will bring him back to you when he is stable. You don't want all of the time he has spent here to be in vain, do you?"

"It's ok, Mar." Cole hung his head in defeat. "Ruby's right. I'm dangerous to you, right now. I need to finish the work we've been doing. I'm sorry for failing you. I am fighting to be the man you deserve. The father our child deserves. Please, don't give up on me, yet," he called as they led him away.

As he left, his words haunted me. *If he can't heal here, will I have to say goodbye to him?*

"You can put me down. I won't go after him." When I turned to face the person, who had halted my attack, I found Seppe.

"The young man is in good hands," he said.

"Forgive me if I don't believe you," I said, not hiding my anger. "He's been here for four months and five minutes with me, the Shah in him comes out. If the Goddess can't take the darkness out of him, there's no point in my being here."

"You're quick to give up and throw away everything you care about, aren't you?" Seppe asked. "Give him time."

"I don't have time. I have a life growing in me that I need to protect," I said.

"You're right. You need to protect your baby," Seppe acknowledged, stroking his chin in thought. A small thread of smoke drifted off his fingertips and trailed around me. "Do you think running away from what scares you will be good for anyone?"

"I'm not running away," I disagreed weakly.

"Good. Then, it's settled. Essie will take you to rest and compose yourself."

Before I could respond, he straightened up and walked away.

The realization of what happened hit me. I knew I would have to decide. As much as I loved Cole, I would give him up. I had a child who needed me. This time, I couldn't...wouldn't follow him into the darkness.

CHAPTER TEN

Essie brought me to a row of similar rectangular homes. Each had large windows that exposed the living quarters. They reminded me of the vacation homes in the old movies we would watch.

"Welcome." A Curuxatyni woman opened a door to the center house. "Come this way and you'll find there is a variety of more festive clothing to choose from in your room."

My stepmother led me deeper into the house. I stopped at one of the floor-to-ceiling windows. My breath caught as I took in the view of the roaring waves along the beach. "Essie, you've been here before with our family, right?" I asked, recalling the images I had been shown of them while I was playing the ice queen in Snowstrum.

"Why yes," Essie said, sounding genuinely surprised. "How would you know?"

"Danu showed me that you were all safe when I first entered Snowstrum," I replied. Staring at the ocean, I remembered Meg and Miles splashing in the waves. "Seeing you here comforted me. Knowing you were safe allowed me to focus on bringing Cole home. How interesting that he'd end up here in the end?"

Essie took my hands into hers. "Oh, Mara, Meg and Miles were devastated when you didn't return. Meg cried nonstop for weeks. Nothing we could say or do could lessen her pain. She was so young, and she'd lost your grandmother, your mother, and then you in such a short amount of time," she said, her voice cracking. "Coming here restored her. The confident girl you see today was formed in this very home."

"Do you think they'll be able to remove the darkness from Cole?" I asked. "What about my darkness? I attacked him. I'm no better than he is."

Cole had been so hateful when he realized I'd betrayed him and devised the plan to free the Vetur. His cold image flashed before my eyes and the words he screamed at me on our last day in Snowstrum rang in my ears.

"You'll not win. She'll have your head for this. You mean nothing to me, now, Marina. As far as I'm concerned, you're dead."

"Essie, I need to see Brighid," I said, releasing her hands. "I can't sit here waiting to see if he will heal."

"I can't take you to the Goddess, now. You need to rest, but I will request she sees us when you are much calmer," Essie replied.

"If you won't help me, I'll find her myself. I've seen Cole. Now, I need to see Brighid." I glared and turned on my heel to walk away.

Essie's blocked my escape. "You won't be able to find her on your own. Please, calm yourself while I make arrangements."

"If you won't help me, I *will* find her myself," I repeated, my scowl deepening.

Essie trailed her finger down my arm, sending pricks on her magic. "I wish you would learn to trust me, Mara."

I took a seat in a white lounge chair, throwing the accent pillows onto the ground.

Essie sighed and left me.

I inhaled slowly. I wanted to feel calmer, but the dark look in Cole's eyes haunted me, and my own response troubled me. Essie was just trying to help, and I treated her badly. Guilt flooded me.

Abandoning the chair, I paced while I waited for my stepmother to return. Just as my patience was about to run out, the red birdwoman, who had escorted Cole away from me, appeared. The short, scarlet feathers on top of her head sparkled as though each strand had been coated with fine glitter.

"Mara, we've not been formally introduced," she said, extending her hand towards me. She had human hands, except for the talons she'd painted silver. "I'm Ruby. Essie has informed me you've requested to see the Goddess. Do you feel well enough to go now?"

Oh, good. Another person to tell me to be calm. To be patient, I thought bitterly. "Yes, please, take me to her, now," I answered, biting my tongue from the rest of the words I wanted to scream at her.

Dropping her hand, Ruby's eyes narrowed on me. She appeared to be measuring me. After consideration, she offered her hand to me, again.

As my fingers touched hers, I felt a frigid wind blow around me. The room was gone, and I found myself standing on the edge of a cliff, overlooking the ocean. Brighid stood next to me.

Her long coppery hair of flames blew wildly in the wind. She stared into the distance, deeply focused. Of the three sister goddesses, Brighid was the one I understood the least. While Danu was warm and motherly, and Snowystra was vindictive and manipulative, I could not define Brighid. When the golden-skinned goddess finally turned towards me, her green eyes locked with mine.

"I need to know if the child inside me is carrying Snowystra's darkness. I sense she's still here," I whispered.

"She's gone, Mara. It was never the magic my sister held that was corrupt," she answered.

"Then, what is causing Cole to revert to the dark king? I can't stay here and fight for a lost man. I won't be my mother and choose him over my child. Please, tell me, now, if I need to give up on him."

A flurry of snowflakes fell upon us and, soon, I was in a blinding snowstorm. When the white wall lifted, my heart dropped as I saw where I was.

"No! Please, take me back to Galinevo. I can't be here," I cried. "You can't take me here. I can't lose six more years in this world."

"Calm yourself, Mara." Brighid waved her hand out in front of us.

The space before us smeared as if it had been a freshly painted watercolor.

"This is the past. The part of your time in Snowstrum that you need to face. Your experience in my sister's world was quite different than Cole's. If you want to save him, you need to understand what created this dark man. You need to understand this part of the man you love," Brighid explained.

CHAPTER
ELEVEN

The room shifted, and we were in Snowystra's bedroom. The elegant ice furniture and accents were a contrast to the cruel goddess who had slept in this room.

My eyes flicked towards Cole. He was standing against the wall. Upon closer look, I realized he was trapped in a large web, which extended across one side of the room. The threads were covered with thousands of small, metallic green dorcha spiders.

The creatures skittered quickly. They moved across the webbing and into the hand of Snowystra.

A wave of red filled my vision. I clenched my hands, digging my nails into my skin. The anger I felt inside, from seeing her alive, almost brought me to my knees.

The dark goddess shooed the spiders away and stood in front of Cole. "Why must we do this, over and over?" Snowystra trailed her long, silver nails along Cole's bare chest.

Clenching and unclenching his jaw, he hissed, "You'll have to kill me if you want me to stop fighting you."

She smiled as if he'd told a silly joke. "I'm in no hurry to kill you, sweet boy. The pleasure you give me is worth your little outbursts. Sadly, you'll bore me, soon enough, though. They all do."

Snowystra pressed her palm against the center of Cole's chest. He screamed as her icy touch burned his skin. His cries silenced, and he hung limp.

"Let's not dwell on when I will get rid of you. Right now, let's focus on what I need from you." The cruel goddess lightly dragged her nails down his chest, leaving more red marks.

Her touch reignited his anger. Cole bucked against the sticky web. "I won't let you hurt her. Nothing you do will change how I feel about Mara," he growled.

Her eyes narrowed. "If we must play this game." She sighed and placed both palms flat against his chest. This steam rose from his sizzling skin.

Cole closed his eyes as if he was fighting off the pain. His bravado broke and he screamed.

When his screams died out and he, once again, fell limp, she cupped his face with both hands and kissed him hard on the lips. Cole tried to pull away, but she persisted. Eventually, he stopped fighting her and she pulled away.

"Has my king returned?" Snowystra asked as she smoothed his hair from his brow.

Cole lifted his chin and slowly opened his eyes. Once blue, they were now a milky white. Tendrils of black surrounded him and I knew Cole was gone. She had broken him.

"Yes, my goddess," he confirmed. "Untie me and let me show you how sorry I am for my disrespect."

Laughing, she sliced the threads, freeing him, and he landed on his feet. Cole roughly grabbed the goddess around the waist and kissed her.

"You've pleased me," Snowystra purred. "I need you to focus on bringing the girl to me. I was told Marina is close by. Together, we will convince her to give up the ridiculous promise she made to *protect the magic*. We'll use my sister's own magic against her. We'll make them *all* pay for what they've done to me."

"We don't need her," Cole growled. He brushed her hair out of her face and cupped her cheek. "Together, we will punish them for what they did."

"No." Snowystra jerked away from him and slapped him across the face. "We need the girl. Her magic is stronger than yours. First, we break her, and *then* we rule, together, but *only* if you do as I command."

Cole grabbed her wrist and wrapped his arms around her. I shut my eyes to block out the sight of them, entangled in a passionate embrace, but I couldn't block out his words.

"Forgive me. I am being greedy. I don't want to share you with her, but I'll do as you ask. As always, your will is my command," the Shah declared.

I foolishly opened my eyes to find him kissing her, again. Her cold laughter rang in my ears as he picked her up and carried her towards the bed.

"Stop, I don't want to see this," I cried, closing my eyes tightly. "I know about the beatings. I saw the man she turned him into. I saw the drawings he made of her. I knew when the Shah said she was like a mother to him, it was a lie. Please, stop this...I can't bear to see anymore."

The room flashed, and we were in the office Cole had used as the Shah. Many days, he spent hidden away in this room while I made plans to free the Miezitari from Snowystra's tyranny.

Cole sat at his desk, his eyes dark and menacing. There was no part of my sweet husband there. Sipping a crystal goblet of tavi, he wrote frantically in a notebook. When Snowystra appeared in the doorway, he quickly closed the cover and went to her.

Glaring at him, she let him lead her into the room. "I haven't had a heart in weeks. Why are you not getting me what I need?" she scowled. "It's like you're trying to hurt me."

"I sent a group of three men out this morning," he said, guiding her to a velvet chair. "I promise, you will have what you need, soon."

Snowystra flopped into the chair. "You've not met any of my needs since I allowed you to marry her. You stopped coming to my bedchambers and you haven't broken her. You spend too much time with Marina, and you know she isn't fully committed to honoring me. You vowed that you would not forget what mattered. You're making me reconsider choosing you to be the Shah."

Cole fell to his knees and rested his head in her lap. "I haven't forgotten my promise. We will make them pay for everything they did. If there is no dorcha heart by tonight, I'll go to the Sephorian Desert myself," he promised.

"And, what about my other needs?" she purred as she pushed him away. Standing up, she went to the desk.

Cole followed and grabbed her. "Your needs are all I think about."

Snowystra traced her pointed nail along his lips.

As he leaned in to kiss her, a loud knock sounded. Sighing, he moved away from the goddess. Her eyes blazed with anger.

"Come in," the Shah roared.

A Miezitari man, clutching a leather satchel to his chest, was led in by two guards.

"Forgive our interruption," one of the guards said.

"Did you get what I sent you for?" Cole wore a look of pure evil.

"Yes, mi Shah, I did as you told me." The man trembled as he offered the bag to Cole.

Cole snatched it from him and looked inside. The corner of his mouth lifted into a cruel smile. "Take him to a healer, and then bring him back to the tunnels," he ordered the guard.

"Am I forgiven for my slight, mi Shah? Will I be absolved of my crime against you?" the Miezitari pleaded.

Towering over the man, Cole growled, "You'll be released from your punishment – for now. You'll tell no one of the secrets of the desert. No one must know why you were sent. If they ask, you'll tell them your forgiving Shah had a change of heart and, out of kindness, I reconsidered the punishment. Be warned, I will know if you speak of the dorcha."

"No, I won't tell a soul," the man vowed as he was dragged away. "I promise."

When the door closed and they were alone, Snowystra looked at him eagerly. Cole reached into the bag and lifted out the bloody green dorcha heart. "My Goddess, would you like this prepared?"

Wrapping her hands around his, she drew the heart to her mouth. Like a wild animal, she took a large bite. Then, another, and another. Her eyes glowed a dark red. She moaned in pleasure and then offered it to Cole. He, too, chomped into the heart. As they ate, they laughed as if they were drunk on the magic.

"Soon, very soon, the world will be at my mercy." Snowystra smiled and wiped the blood from his mouth.

The image of them, together, faded and I was returned to my room. I felt numb like I was sinking into an abyss. I'd known she had controlled him, and I had suspicions about the intimate nature of their relationships. I had been able to differentiate between Cole and the Shah...until now. Seeing him – *my* Cole – in her arms and seeing her control over him, I felt an uncontrollable anger. I didn't care if he healed.

    He betrayed me.

CHAPTER
TWELVE

I sat by one of the glass windows and stared out at the ocean's waves. The methodic splash of the water brought back memories I had long forgotten.

"What is wrong, Mara?" Gram asked, sitting on the side of her bed. Rubbing my back, she hummed a song while she waited for me to talk.

When I had drained every last tear from my body, I turned onto my side, away from her. "He...he kissed the most disgusting person. He kissed Jessica," I whispered. The thought of his arms around her made me cry, again.

"Cole?" Gram asked. "That boy is head over heels for you. I'm sure there is a very good explanation."

Sitting up, I said, "Yes, there is. He likes her, and he's, now, going to be her boyfriend. She's been throwing herself at him forever and she finally caught him."

Throwing myself into a pillow, I sobbed.

A knock on the door sounded and Gram left me to answer it. When I heard Cole's voice, I crept into the kitchen and hid behind the wall to listen.

"Sorry to bother you, Gram," Cole said. "Is Mara here? I really need to speak to her."

"She's resting, Cole," Gram replied. "She's very upset. You wouldn't know anything about that, would you?"

"I need to explain what happened," he answered. "This is just a horrible misunderstanding."

"I don't want to see him. Go away and explain everything to your girlfriend," I yelled at him from behind the kitchen wall. "I never want to see you again, Cole Oliver Sands."

"You have to believe me, Gram," Cole pleaded. "I was waiting for Mara and Jessica came up to me and asked me about a homework assignment we were given. She was going on, and on, about it. When Mara entered the shop, Jessica practically jumped into my arms and kissed me. It was like Jessica wanted to cause trouble."

"It looked like you were enjoying her attack," I called out to him. "No need to make up any stories. You're free. Go on – enjoy your new life with Jessica. You know, she isn't even pretty. She has bug eyes and frizzy hair."

"If you wouldn't have over-reacted and run away, you would've seen me tell Jessica off. I told her she was out of line and that I have a girlfriend."

"Mara, come out here, now," Gram scolded. Her voice told me she wouldn't take no for an answer. "You're not going to shout across the house and wake up your little sister. I know I raised you better than this."

Crossing my arms over my chest, I entered the living room. "Fine, explain yourself. Just know, you can't change what I saw."

"I'm going to go fix you both a nice cup of tea. Now, go sit and talk." Gram gestured towards the couch.

Kissing my cheek, Gram whispered, "When you love someone, there may be a time when you really do need to say goodbye. You're only sixteen. In your lifetime, you'll have more heartache and anger, but you'll, also, have so much joy. Be sure that you're really ready to say goodbye to him. Are you going to give up on the love I know you feel for him? Remember some things thrown away can never be returned."

Gram always knew the words to say for every situation. I sat next to Cole on the overstuffed couch and tried to be open-minded.

"Mara, please, let me explain," Cole pleaded.

As he retold the story, I felt lost in his voice. How does he do that? I should be yelling at him and all I want to do is run my fingers through his hair.

"Did you hear me, Mara? I mean it. I love you. There's no one else that I want to be with," Cole said, taking my hand. "Please, believe me."

Cole had never said that he loved me before. Not really. He had said 'love you' or 'I love how you make cookies', but never so sincere.

"You love me?" I asked disbelievingly. What do I know about love?

"Where've you been for the past four years?" Cole asked. Picking up a *loose curl of my hair, he twisted it.* "I've loved you for so long that I can't remember what it felt like before you were my everything."

"But you never told me this," I said. "Why tell me, now?"

Silencing me, he kissed me softly. His touch was so gentle, but the electricity I felt confirmed his words were true. At that moment, I allowed myself to admit what I already knew – I loved him, too. Not holding back, I ran my fingers through his hair and returned his kiss with even more fervor. I wanted to lose myself in that moment forever. I loved him.

My memories broke, but the love I felt lingered.

"Tell me what I should do, small one," I whispered to my child. "The magic inside you has to be pure and good. You were conceived in love. How can we save your daddy from the past?

"The boy has been fighting to control the darkness inside him. I'm sorry to say this side of him has been quiet until your arrival." Brighid handed me a glass of white liquid. "Drink this. It will calm you."

"So, I'm the trigger. I'm what caused him to revert to the Shah? If I'll only hurt him by staying, please, send me home," I said, accepting the drink.

"It's not that simple. Sending you away will do more harm. You're the reason he fights it," Brighid explained. "You saw how she broke him. I only showed you a small piece of the cruelty my sister inflicted. Cole's fear has been that you will, one day, find out about the man he was while under her control. He is scared you'll see what he did to survive and that you'll never forgive him for his betrayal."

"That man wasn't Cole," I said. "I told him I forgave him for everything I knew and didn't know. How can I prove it to him? They took our memories before. Can't you do it, again?"

"No, you saw how that worked out. You will need to be patient and accepting," Brighid informed me. "Cole has to forgive himself for the harm he caused. We both know that he was not in control of his choices, but he needs to believe that himself. Mara, you will need to be honest with yourself. Did you really forgive him? Can you still after what you saw?"

"I can, Brighid. Just tell me how I can help him?" I asked, feeling angry at the riddles. "Why can there ever be a straight answer?"

"You know what you need to do in your heart, Mara," she said. "Be there for him. When he has more pain than he will be able to bear, you will help him return to us." Taking my hand, Brighid added, "Do you remember how you contained your magic while you were in Snowstrum? You imagined creating a shell of protection around the Earth, Water, Fire, and Air running through you."

"I did that because her magic was invading me. I needed to protect the Light," I said.

"Your child is of the Winter and will be an extraordinarily strong elemental. I want you to go to Cole, again. This time, when he changes, I want you to encircle your child with your magic."

A strong gust of air enclosed us. Calling to her over the wind, I shouted, "I can't do this. What if I hurt my child?"

The wind died, and I found myself in front of the building where I'd first seen Cole, once more. Brighid led me through the open door and we were immediately greeted by the colorful Curuxatyni. The Goddess greeted each with a gentle touch of her hand against their cheeks. Guiding me through the building, she stopped outside a silver door.

"Go to him," she said.

Shaking my head, I refused to enter the room. "I can't risk it. I don't want to hurt him."

"If you want to save the boy, you must remind him what he is fighting for," Brighid insisted. Kissing me on the cheek, she said, "When you're done, we'll discuss the future of your child. For now, you must go to your husband."

The door opened, and a blue light shined so brightly I was forced to close my eyes. When I opened them, I found Cole in a small room, sitting at a desk. He was focused on sketching a picture of himself, pushing me on the tree swing. He had given us both big smiles as if we were laughing.

"We haven't done that in a while," I said, placing my hand on his shoulder.

"Mara, you shouldn't be here." Cole jerked away as if my touch burned. He stood and backed away from me. "I'm sick. Go, now, before I hurt you."

Ignoring his fears, I walked towards him. "You won't hurt me."

"No, stay away," Cole insisted, trying to move farther away from me. "I haven't turned into that monster for almost a month. At least, not until...There's something about you that brings it out. Let me heal completely. Please, go."

"I'm not going anywhere. Stop trying to push me away." I continued to move towards him.

"I know the secrets you've been keeping. Brighid showed me everything, Cole. The secrets I wouldn't let you share with me. I saw the true monster – Snowystra – and how she hurt you. I'm sorry that you endured her torture to save me."

Cole tried to get away from me, but I'd trapped him in a corner. He had nowhere else to go.

Reaching out, I put my hand against his face and pressed myself closer to him. Staring into his eyes, I kissed him, but he was holding back. With more passion, I wrapped my arms around his neck and kissed him harder.

His resistance melted, and he returned my kiss with more fervor. When he broke away, he trailed his lips down my neck before pressing his mouth against my ear. "My queen will always return to me. Now that you know my secrets, you'll submit. With Snowystra out of the way, I'll have all the power I desire," Cole murmured.

I felt a chill run through me. Jerking away from him, I could see his eyes were frosted blue. His expression was cold.

"I'll break you, Marina," he said, venom dripping from his words. He grabbed me by my throat and pinned me against the wall. "What is your plan, now, Marina?" he sneered. "What – no powder to blow into my eyes?"

I struggled to break his hold.

He leaned in closer to me. "If you would've just followed her like you promised, it wouldn't have come to this. We could've overtaken her and ruled, together. You squandered away our chance. If it wasn't for my child – her child – inside you, I'd end your pitiful life."

His hand tightened around my neck and I realized he was right. I couldn't run away, this time.

"You carry my chance to reclaim what you destroyed. You'll learn to obey me."

I hope you're right, Brighid, I thought to myself. Focusing my magic on the child inside me, I called the elements. I felt a warmth grow in my stomach and, soon, the sensation built.

"What are you doing? I feel your magic pulsing through you," Cole said, glaring at me. "Another of your tricks?"

He tightened his grip, strangling me. I forced myself to focus on the magic, creating a shell around my womb. As my stomach walls tightened, the movement inside me became stronger. A burst of energy flowed from me, knocking Cole backwards.

"Mara...oh, no. What did I do?" Cole asked. "I'm sorry. I told you to go. I'm so sorry. Why didn't you listen to me?"

He caught me as I crumpled to the ground. Then, picking me up, he carried me to the bed.

"I'm so sorry, Mara. I didn't – that wasn't me. I don't know what's inside me or why it comes out when I'm around you," Cole said, stroking my hair. "I'm sorry I hurt you. Let me call for help."

I shook my head and held his hand. I tried to tell him not to leave, that I was fine, but my voice was gone.

"How did you stop me? Mara, I almost killed you." Cole's eyes glistened with tears. "Please, let me go get help for you."

Still shaking my head, I tugged on his arm. Relenting, Cole climbed into bed beside me. Resting my head on his chest, I tried to comfort him. I had pushed him too far.

"How do you know I won't change back into that monster? Mara, I need to get help. What if I change, again?" he asked.

I was unable to speak. Even though it was extremely painful to move, I didn't want it to have all been for nothing. Kissing him, I tried to bring out the Shah. I had to be sure I could control the darkness.

"No, Mar," he pleaded.

Before he had the chance to argue with me further, I kissed him, again. He gently pressed his lips against mine. Suddenly, there was an urgency to his kiss, and he wrapped his arms around me. His response filled me with fear. *Was the Shah back?*

"What's wrong, Mara?" Cole let go of me and took my hand. "Did I hurt you?"

When I knew it was Cole, I shook my head and rested on the pillow.

Cole rested his hand on my stomach. He smiled when he felt a sharp kick. "I never wanted to hurt you. I can't bear to think what I could've done if you hadn't found a way to stop me. Please, let me call for Ruby. I won't be able to live with myself if I hurt you, again."

Touching my finger to my lips, I kissed them, and then placed them against his before closing my eyes. As I drifted off to sleep, I felt him move away from me. I wanted to stop him and make him stay, but I was unable to fight the fog that I was slipping into.

CHAPTER
THIRTEEN

I awoke on the mossy floor of Starten Forest, outside the entrance to Danu's world. A lavender ball of light floated above me and entered the tree. The Goddess must have summoned my spirit, leaving my physical body resting in Galinevo. There was no one to guide me, this time, but I knew my way well. I entered through the heart of the tree and into the Water elementals' room. The blue balls were splashing and playing.

The light appeared again. Instead of the usual walk through the homes of Fire, Air, and Earth, it was leading me directly towards the hallway of the Goddess' chamber. The orb led me down a silver corridor ending in the large room of silver-framed mirrors.

The scents of lavender, cinnamon, and fresh-cut grass along with the smell of a summer rainstorm rushed at me. The familiar fragrances calmed me. Walking to the center of the room, I sat on the seat of Danu. The area around me filled with multicolored orbs, and I felt the presence of the elements.

Danu materialized in a silvery veil. I was always taken aback by her beauty. She had the most delicate facial features. Smiling serenely, she stood before me with her long, lavender hair gently blowing.

"Why am I here, Goddess?" I asked.

"I brought you here to warn you. Cole will be called to answer for his attack on you. Our attempts to heal him have failed. He will be forced to take responsibility for his part in all of this."

"Why? It's not his fault. I was able to stop him," I cried out. "Who will he answer to?"

"He will face the Council. The truth will be revealed then. We cannot have Snowystra's incarnate in our realm. I'm sad to say, only time will tell the fate of the boy." Danu shook her head slightly.

"You know it's not his fault. She took him. Snowystra tortured him and poisoned his mind." Fury rose in me like none I'd ever felt before. "You knew, but you didn't stop her. That means you're as much to blame. Will you face the Council?"

"My only mistake was gifting mortals and I'll never apologize for that," Danu said calmly.

Changing my tone, I pleaded, "I need Cole with me, now. I can't do this. How can I raise my child alone?"

"You're far from alone," she chided. "No matter what is decided, he'll need time. Isn't it wiser to give him a chance to heal, so he can become the man you love? If you force the recovery to have instant peace, you may end up with what you fear most."

"You said she was gone," I retorted. "I don't understand. How does her darkness live? And, what is the Council?"

A loud gong sounded.

"It's time. Go to Cole. They'll be taking him, soon." Danu faded away.

"Where are they taking him? Why can't you ever just answer my questions?" I threw my hands up in frustration. "Please, tell me what I need to do to save him," I shouted into the empty chamber.

Following the path through the elemental world, I exited the tree and returned to the spot that would return me to my body.

"Gram, I need you, now," I whispered as I lay on the mossy ground. "I cannot give up on Cole. Please, tell me what to do. I can't do this without you."

A warm wind gently caressed my hand and the scent of vanilla with lavender surrounded me.

"Please, Gram," I whispered. "I don't know what to do."

CHAPTER
FOURTEEN

I woke to the smell of sweet flowers and the soft feeling of salve being spread on my chest and neck. My eyes fluttered, trying to open. My need to awaken couldn't compete with my body's desire to sleep. Through cracked eyelids, I could see Cole being taken away.

"No," I struggled to say. My voice was like sandpaper. I fought harder against the black abyss I was floating back into. "Cole," I rasped. "Cole."

Guilt filled me. I couldn't believe I was going to have to turn my back on him and hide away in Starten.

"I'm here, Mara," Essie's tranquil voice soothed. "Please, don't speak."

"Don't let him go," I said. My words were barely above a tarnished whisper.

"Rest." She slid her fingertip along my brow, but her attempt to use her calming magic didn't work.

I tried to push myself up, but Essie stopped me. Wobbly, I struggled against her. I needed to go to Cole.

In the mirror across from me, I could see my reflection. My hair was pulled back, exposing a neck and chin covered with blood-red bruises. Touching my skin, I flinched in pain.

"Don't speak. Cole has been removed, so you can be treated. We couldn't risk him reverting again and, this time, killing you. You need to let the salve absorb." Essie handed me a small vial. "Sip this if you can. You're lucky to be alive, Mara."

Pressing the vial to my lips, I tried a small sip. The drop of orange liquid burned as it slid down my throat like thousands of small needles stabbing me. The red marks in the mirror turned to dark purple bruises. I drank the rest of the liquid and my eyes filled with tears from the excruciating pain.

"Now, drink this," Essie instructed, handing me a purple liquid. It fizzled and popped.

The thought of drinking the bubbly concoction reminded me of tavi and the sensation of choking on ice it had given me. I fought back my urge to knock it out of her hands.

"Drink, Mara. This will help the healing," Essie soothed.

Taking a hesitant sip, I found the smooth drink coated my throat. Greedily, I took another large gulp. My neck changed colors, again. Pins were replaced with the sensation of a thousand earthworms wriggling under my skin. A grotesque greenish-yellow replaced the dark bruising, making it no longer tender to touch.

Daring to speak, I said, "Essie, please, take me to Cole. I don't understand why they're taking him away. He didn't mean to hurt me."

Hugging me tightly, she choked back tears. "He's been taken to the Council to answer for his crimes against you and the child."

"It wasn't Cole who did this. Take me to them and I can explain."

"I can't, Mara," she said.

I could see the pain in her eyes.

The door opened behind me and Sarika entered. With a somber look on her face, she inspected me. Touching my neck, she let out the smallest sigh that sounded like relief to me.

"Has the child been checked for injury?" She spoke directly to Essie as though I wasn't even there.

"I called the elements to contain my baby's magic by protecting it in a cocoon," I explained. The quick movements inside me told me there had been no injury. "It's my fault this happened, but the baby wasn't hurt."

"Release the magic, so I can assess the child myself," she demanded.

With a silent prayer, I said goodbye to the elements. The hardness of my womb softened.

Sarika rubbed her hands along my stomach and uncomfortably

prodded. "Good. All seems in order," she determined. "Come with me, and do not worry. Cole won't be able to hurt you."

I wasn't worried about my husband harming me. I wanted to make her understand that I had caused my own pain. But I didn't have time, as she quickly left the room.

I followed Sarika down a hallway with hundreds of doors. She selected one and opened it. Inside the bare white room, silver robes hung on the wall.

"Put one of these on and I will take you to answer the questions we have about the attack. Your words regarding what happened will be important for how Cole's punishment will be decided," Sarika said. "Essie, you'll be allowed to attend to support Mara, but you must watch in silence. Even your telepathy will not be permitted."

"I understand," Essie said, bowing her head.

Slipping the flowing silver robe on, I felt ridiculous. The long sleeves were wide, and the fabric was heavy. Sarika opened a door that hadn't been there a moment before and motioned for us to follow.

Sitting in the middle of the room, Cole was cuffed to a chair. His head hung low and his slumped form made me fear he was injured. My shoes squeaked on the marble floor and he lifted his head. When he saw me, he shuddered. The bruising on my neck was still visible, but it had changed for the better.

"Cole Sands," a booming voice called. "Are you ready to hear our decision?"

"No," I cried out. "You've not heard from me, yet."

CHAPTER
FIFTEEN

A light flashed. I was standing in front of a wide stone platform. I could make out the silhouettes of people – at least, I thought they were people – sitting in high back chairs. There was a haze around them and, no matter what I did, my eyes wouldn't focus enough to allow me to see clearly.

"What do you have to share that will change the decision I have made?" a loud voice demanded.

The air cleared, and I could, now, see a man with a white, curly beard. Sitting in the center on a massive gilded and jeweled throne, his muscles glistened.

"If you have nothing to share to save this boy, then why are you interrupting?" His golden eyes gleamed with fury, shaking me out of the trance I'd been in.

"Cole's being judged for hurting me. As you can see, I'm perfectly healthy," I said, trying to appear confident. "Who are you to decide my husband's future?"

The light brightened on the people sitting around the imposing man.

"Aren't you a brave girl? I am Tannus. You're in my realm, now, and in Asceraunia, I make the laws. It is irrelevant. The boy has confessed to his crimes."

My heart fell as I realized who he was. Tannus, the father of Arianolwyn. A God so self-righteous, he would strike down his pregnant daughter's mate. His actions caused the pain and suffering that created the darkness in Winter. Now, his judgment would determine the fate of my husband?

"So, you are the almighty Tannus, who can decide on a whim to take away a pregnant woman's mate," I said bitterly.

Surprise washed over his face. Composing himself, he narrowed his gaze at me. "While I am quite powerful, the Council will decide his fate."

The light grew brighter on the woman next to him. "You've met the Goddess Sarika," he said, gesturing towards her.

I looked at the rest of the people and my eyes landed on Arianolwyn. She spoke, but her voice became muffled.

Why would she be sitting next to the man who had killed her love? He destroyed their – wait! Alaunius was killed, yet he helped save Cole? Did I misunderstand? He's sitting on the throne, helping this...this...monster judge my husband even now.

"Mara, did you hear me?" Arianolwyn asked, frowning at me. "You seem unwell. Maybe you should be taken back to Galinevo to be examined?"

Shaking my head, I responded, "I'm sorry. I'm not sick. I was just surprised to see everyone. Please, continue."

"As I was saying, you know the rest of the Council – Sarika, Alaunius, Danu, and Brighid. Oh, and Seppe." The quirky man tipped his head at me. "We must decide how to deal with this terrible situation," Arianolwyn said.

"You insisted on speaking...so speak," Tannus boomed impatiently.

His words infuriated me. Who's he to make decisions that impact our lives?

"There's nothing for you to decide. We're in this situation because of you and your decisions." I boldly met the eyes of each Council member. "The Elementals were allowed to trick my great-grandmother and her friends into believing they had magic to save Danu. Evening knowing Snowystra would attack everyone who Danu gifted, you did nothing."

My voice grew stronger. "You allowed Snowystra to enslave the Miezitari and destroy countless lives, like my mother. Cole is broken, but that isn't his fault."

My sense of injustice fueled my fearless confrontation. "My husband was taken by Snowystra to be tortured, brainwashed, and used in her game for power. Where was your council then? Where were you when we needed your help? You left it up to a mortal girl to stop her. Release Cole to me and we'll return to Starten to finish his healing."

"You're bold to speak to us in that way. As you said, you're just a mortal. You know nothing about our world. We don't control the decisions of all gods and goddesses. We are not their guardians. Nonetheless, Cole is a danger to the future of the balance. We cannot risk the loss of your child. She is the Winter," Tannus replied.

"I *can* protect my child."

Ignoring me, Tannus turned towards the other Council members without masking his rage. "I advised against allowing the mortals to meddle in the world of gods." The room tremored, filling with sparks of electricity. "Snowystra was dark and corrupted, but she was Winter. With the hasty actions of all of you, the balance has been disturbed. A balance that must be restored. You've given the Mrak the opening they needed to rise to power."

Arianolwyn glared at him. "*Your hasty* decision to kill the father of your granddaughters is why we are here, today. *You're* the reason for my daughter's darkness. It's because of you that my daughter is gone."

Tannus roared. "I brought Alaunius back. What more would you like me to do, Aria? I gave you what you wanted. I let you deal with Snowystra as you saw fit."

"Fighting amongst ourselves will not change what was done. The past is the past," Alaunius interjected, putting his hand on Arianolwyn's. "Bring the boy forward."

Cole appeared next to me, restrained by two large guards. His eyes blinked and frosted in color. "Pity that my plan to tame you didn't work. In time, you will submit to me, Marina."

"You say such sweet things to me, darling," I replied.

Lunging at me, he said, "Next time, you won't have a chance to call your magic."

I sent a gust of wind that threw Cole and the guards across the chamber, slamming them against the stone wall. When my husband rose to his feet, he charged at me. Calling Water, I made the ground slick and he fell to the floor. Before he could get up, again, I sent a rush of my icy magic, freezing him in place. With balls of Fire blazing in my hands, I loomed over him.

My stomach fluttered, and I stopped. *What am I doing?* I encircled my child with the elements and watched as the Shah faded from Cole. Slowly, the man I loved returned.

"Mara, I thought I'd killed you." His face filled with pain and defeat.

"As long as the Winter in our child is contained, that side of you will be gone. I can control it." I tried to offer my hand to him, but one of the guards blocked me. "Stop," I snapped. "He won't hurt me, now."

"The risk is too great, Mara," Cole disagreed.

"The boy is right. You're carrying Winter, Mara. Your daughter will be born to restore the rift that was caused by the loss of Snowystra. She will be the Winter Guardian," Tannus declared.

"Wait," I said, touching my stomach. "What do you mean my child will be the Winter? I won't let that happen. Don't you see what it did to us?"

"Unless a suitable replacement is found, the child will be brought to us and she will be raised amongst the gods," Tannus commanded.

"No, you can't take my child. Take the Winter or make me the Winter. I ruled as the Vizier and I have dark magic running through me." My hands blazed with green fire. "I won't let you take my child!" I screamed and threw my magic at Tannus.

A guard blocked the ball from hitting him. The large man patted the flames out and glared at me.

"Mara, please, calm yourself," Danu pleaded.

The Fire in my hands extinguished.

She gave a small nod of approval. "The gift you were given by me has grown too strong. You cannot be Winter."

"What about me?" Cole asked. "I only have a small bit of water magic inside me."

"And, the corrupted magic of Snowystra running through you. You carry none of the pure Winter," Tannus answered. "Enough of this nonsense. My decision is made. The child will be brought to me on the eve of her first birthday. She will be raised in my home. And, the Shah will die, tonight."

"No," I screamed, pushing at the guards dragging Cole away. "You can't do this. You created the Shah."

"Silence!" Tannus yelled.

The room quaked. Tears streamed down my face. They were taking Cole away from me and I was helpless.

"Collect yourself, child," Tannus said. Despite his obvious annoyance, his voice softened. "Cole will only be stripped of his magic, making him entirely mortal, again. This is the only way. The boy will live, but his gift will die along with the dark king."

"Don't cry, Mar," Cole called. His piercing blue eyes begged me to compose myself. "I loved the gift Danu gave me, but I love you and our child more. I can be the man you fell in love with, again."

The guards removed the cuffs from Cole and Danu went to him. She gently stroked his cheek before embracing him. As the goddess held him, she whispered something privately to him. My husband's body shook with tears. When she broke the hug, he nodded and kissed her on the cheek. Their eyes locked and he knelt before her.

"Cole Oliver Sands, I perform this task with a heavy heart. Water, essence of life, your presence in this boy is rescinded. The gift bestowed upon you is removed, but the love I have for you is endless. Your commitment to protecting the magic will not be forgotten."

A blue bubble surrounded Cole. The soft sound of children crying echoed in the hall. The sphere exploded, sending droplets of water everywhere. Cole stood up. His eyes were wide, and his face was contorted, frightening me. He screamed and clutched his head as if he was going to rip all of his hair out.

Danu wrapped her arms around Cole, restraining him. An orange glow emitted from her, twisting around him. After several minutes, she released him, and he fell to the ground. Black particles covered his body and he writhed on the floor.

Essie held me back when I tried to go to him.

When his screams quieted, strands of black and silver ripped from his body, soaking into the marble. As the last thread left him, he lay completely still. Before I knew what was happening, Alaunius picked Cole up and carried him away.

"Where is he taking him?" I asked. My heart was beating so fast and I found it hard to breathe.

"Back to Galinevo, to the Waters of Zdravi," Essie whispered. "Cole will need you."

"Let me escort you to him, Mara," Arianolwyn said, squeezing my wrist.

Words floated from my mind. There was a dark room. My clothes were taken. A door. Blinding light. So, white. Snow. *Snowstrum?* Tears welled in my eyes. I felt Arianolwyn's arms around me.

"The destiny of your child will be in your hands, Mara. It's a great responsibility to be the mother of Winter...especially, now," Arianolwyn said, hugging me tightly.

The fog my brain was in lifted. She released me. The night sky above me filled with blues, pinks, and greens. When the ground under me moved, a circle of steaming blue water appeared. From the haze, I could see something floating.

"Go to him, Mara," Arianolwyn whispered. "He will need your strength."

Then, blackness.

As my mind cleared, I realized I was no longer on dry land. I was standing in water up to my neck. I had been dressed in a two-piece swimsuit. My head finally began to form thoughts, but only one word meant anything at this moment: Cole.

CHAPTER
SIXTEEN

Floating on his back, Cole drifted in the small ripples of the water. His face was emotionless. His eyes were different. The blue I had always loved was, now, a golden brown.

Slipping closer to him, I caught his hand. "Cole, I'm here," I said softly.

He entwined his fingers with mine and held my hand tightly.

It was odd to see him so helpless. With my free hand, I traced the infinity symbol on his cheek with my fingertip.

He didn't move.

Sarika sat on the edge of the water, watching us. I tried to release my hold on Cole's hand to go to her, but he gripped it tighter.

"I promise, we're going to laugh about this, one day, Cole," I said. I dragged my husband through the water towards Sarika. It was as if I was escorting a small boat to shore. When I reached the bird goddess, I took a calming breath. "Can I expect to see Cole improve soon? Other than gripping my hand, he isn't responding at all."

"Call your Water magic," she said firmly.

"That's cruel," I scolded in a hushed voice. "You took it from him and, now, you want me to throw it in his face that I still control Water?"

"Do as I tell you and you can apologize to me later," Sarika replied.

I stared at Cole's lifeless body, hoping for any response. He wasn't there.

Sarika gazed down at him. Her face was no longer cold; instead, it expressed concern.

She cares about him, too? I realized. Well, I guess a few drops of rain couldn't hurt him.

I brought Cole to the center of the water. Smoothing his hair, I pressed my lips close to his ear. "I know you're in there, Cole." Throwing my available hand into the sky, I said, "With an open heart and mind, I call Water."

Clouds drifted above us. I could feel the element surrounding us. Yet, Cole was unresponsive to his gift.

"Water, I beg for your help," I cried.

The billows above grew dark and released fat drops of rain.

Cole still didn't move as the warm water covered him.

Cupping his face between my hands, I kissed him. "I cannot lose another person, my love. I need you. Our child needs you. We've been through too much for it to end like this."

My plea didn't move him.

"How dare you leave me," I cried. "Gram would tell you to—"

Then, I realized exactly what Gram would say. The emotions of the elements are the same as those pulsing through my body. I couldn't help Cole with my anger. I needed to connect with *his* feelings.

"Water, I call your joy, your tears, your fear, and your anger to me. Bless us with your raw emotions. Purify us. Restore the spirit which has been removed," I raised my voice to the sky.

The air rumbled with thunder. Crackling blue lights surrounded us. I held Cole close to me as the rain poured down. A strong wind rocked the water and Cole wrapped his arms around me.

The electricity between us was so intense, I felt the need to release him, but he held me tighter. His skin flushed bright red. The heat emitting from him felt fiery hot against my skin. I could feel the anger inside him as if it was being channeled towards me. I called Air and its calming touch.

White licorice-scented petals drifted by us.

Cole's skin rapidly cooled. He shivered. His breaths became short and quick.

I held my face close to his. "You're safe, Cole," I said. "Release your fear."

Cole stood. Tears rolled down his face as he looked into the sky and screamed. When I wrapped my arms around him, he held me back. His body shook with a gut-wrenching sob. This was more than just losing his magic. These were the same tears he shed when his mother had died and, again, when we lost Gram.

I couldn't stop his pain. I knew he needed to release this emotion and free it when he was ready. When I thought I could bear no more of the sorrow, his cries softened. And, then, a small flutter inside me began kicking. The movement felt like our child was drumming a song.

Love will heal him, I thought. I placed his hands on my stomach. "Feel your child, Cole." During the pregnancy, I had felt movement and kicks, but these were different. "If nothing else makes you smile, our baby should."

For the longest time, he just stared at his hands. I counted the seconds until the corner of his mouth lifted and his eyes lit up. "Our child," he whispered.

Hugging me tightly, Cole rasped, "We're not giving up our child, Mara. I promise you. I will find a way to stop them."

I needed to believe him. For the briefest of moments, I almost did.

CHAPTER SEVENTEEN

Essie returned to Starten, but Cole and I weren't permitted to leave Galinevo. Sarika insisted we remain until *she* was confident Cole was well enough to be home. Instead, we were immediately brought to a cottage by the ocean, where we were told to rest and calm our minds.

Every day, Cole was taken away for treatment and I was left alone. They had expected us to act as if we were on a romantic getaway. I was told, "Why don't you spend a day on the beach?"

Why should I? I wondered bitterly.

The sun and sand wouldn't save my child. I declined invitations to explore Galinevo and, instead, found myself staring at the ocean, watching the waves crash against the shore.

How can I connect with the elements knowing my husband's connection has been ripped from him?

Alone with my thoughts, my anger grew. Once again, we were prisoners. Trapped by gods with their own agenda under the guise of helping us.

Days turned into weeks. When Cole didn't come home before dark, I knew I couldn't stay here much longer. I was alone in more often than not. My solitary time allowed me to imagine every horrible scenario possible. Not only were my emotions out of control but we were wasting time.

There was nowhere we could run where they wouldn't find us. The only option was to stop Tannus, but my magic wasn't enough to kill a God. Even if my family helped, I doubted it would be sufficient. And, there were the others to think about, too. *Would Danu and Brighid help us?* I couldn't be certain.

Cole's warm breath touched my ear as he kissed me softly. "Why are you sitting in the dark, Mar?" he asked. Flicking on the light, he held up a tureen. "Dinner is served."

My husband sat at the kitchen table and scooped the warm stew into a bowl. "You requested more kreas patata? Aren't you sick of this, yet?"

"Nope. It's a mystery every time, and the baby likes it."

I took a big bite, contemplating the strange dish. With each chew, the flavor changed. It was sweet, then salty before being extremely spicy, and then cooling. The texture changed, too – creamy, then crunchy.

Tossing my spoon onto the table, I pushed the bowl away. "I hate it here, Cole. I want to leave."

"You'll never figure out the secret of the mystery stew if we leave." Cole grinned at me.

I scowled at him and cleared the table. I wasn't in the mood for his cheerfulness.

"Don't be mad." Cole slipped his arms around my waist and rested them on the bump. "They say I'm doing better. The Shah is no longer inside me, Mara. I promise, we'll go, soon."

"How soon? I've been thinking. Gram's journals must have a way to remove the magic from—"

He interrupted me with a long kiss. As he broke away, in the softest of whispers, he said, "Not here. We'll talk about our child's future at home."

He was right. If I was going to plan an attack against the Gods, I shouldn't – couldn't – do it here.

The next morning, before Cole left for therapy, we received a request for our presence from Sarika. The goddess met us outside the entrance of the great hall.

"It's nice to see you both so healthy," Sarika said. "The last time we spoke, you were so angry, Mara. You seem to have collected yourself."

"I shouldn't have taken my worry and frustration out on you," I apologized. "You were only trying to help."

"All is forgiven," she said, taking my hand. "It's time for you to return to Starten."

Sarika opened the door. Inside, the room was filled with the colorful Curuxatyni. At the end of the room, Brighid sat on a throne. Her red hair was fanned out around her and emitted a golden glow. Sarika guided us towards her.

"The Miezitari have been restored to their rightful place in Eftir Forest. As our guardian of the Afterlife, Faramond has rebuilt the connection that was lost. This has come at a great cost. The division of three was created to balance the dark and the light of the world. We do not have this equality, now. Our world is unstable and the Mrak grow stronger, each day," Brighid spoke.

Terrified whispers came from the crowd.

Brighid raised her hand. "Enough, my children!" Her voice was commanding, and silence fell on the room.

I feared her next words.

"A solution has been found. The mortals before us have the key to restoring Winter."

Cole rested his hand on my back and rubbed it gently. His touch reminded me to slowly breathe and not react.

"Tannus has decreed that the child within Mara is the Winter. Mara and Cole will make the ultimate sacrifice to restore the balance by delivering their daughter to us."

"My daughter?" I whispered.

"The child of Winter will complete the divine circle. As we bid them goodbye, know that they will return with the greatest gift one could offer."

With these words, the room exploded with bright light and colorful orbs. Cole held onto me. As the room spun, I wrapped my arms around his neck.

"They said our daughter. Cole, they can't take her from us. This can't be. I won't let them."

The color around us blurred. I felt dizzy. Releasing the hold I had on my husband, I felt faint. His strong arms held me tighter, pulling me back to him.

A lavender hue filled the air around us. The spinning slowed and the blur took shape. Danu appeared briefly.

As she faded, she softly called, "Do not submit to your fear and sorrow, my children. The threads of fate are fickle and can turn quickly."

With her last word, we moved faster, and I felt myself slipping from Cole's arms.

"Hang on, Mara," Cole said. "I need your strength. Together, Mar. Together, we will find a way. Stay with me, love."

Seizing his arm with every ounce of fight I had left in me, the sinking feeling stopped, and the blur of light faded. We were no longer in Galinevo. We were standing in Starten Forest, outside the former circle of stone.

"We're home, Mara. Everything will be ok, now." Cole declared, inspecting the area.

I knew we were pawns in the Gods' games, but his eyes pleaded for me to believe.

Cole turned towards me. His face was, now, Snowystra's. "Enjoy your happiness, Marina. Soon, it will be gone."

As quickly as she had appeared, the cruel goddess was gone.

She's dead. Your hallucinating, I scolded myself. I took and deep breath and forced thoughts of Snowystra from my mind. "You're right, Cole. We are home."

As we walked through the forest towards our family, I focused my energy on my surroundings. The moss beetles began their recognizable clicks as the sky paled. The crisp, cold air pushed the familiar smells of Starten through me. With everything changing, the constant in my life had always been the calm feeling I'd gotten when I was in the outdoors.

By the time we reached my grandfather's workshop, the sky was dark and bursting with twinkling stars. The moon peaked out in a crescent sliver. Abruptly, Cole stopped me. A look of pain flashed on his face.

I waited for the dark goddess to appear, again.

"I'm scared, Mara," Cole admitted. "I hurt everyone with the way I left. Essie saw how badly I injured you. They are never going to forgive me. I can't imagine what Elliott is going to say to me?"

"He's going to say you're family, Cole," I replied. Pressing my hand against his chest, I called Air. "Breathe slowly. You are important to each one of them. We were all sad when you left, but they were always your champions. Over and over, I was reminded by them that you had to leave to get better. So, trust in the fact that this is your family and they love you, even when you think you don't deserve it."

"How can you forgive me for what I've done?" he asked. "I wish I could go back and change everything that happened. I wish more than anything, I could take away the pain I've caused you."

"Stop. I know that man was not you, Cole," I said. "I forgive you, or, at least, I'm trying really hard to. Please, stop beating yourself up or everything we've gone through will be for nothing."

"I'll try, Mar," he promised. "I understand why you don't trust me. I hurt you."

"Cole," I started to scold him for not forgiving himself, but I was interrupted.

"She's right, you know? No matter what dumb mistakes you make, you're family and we'll always love you." My father, exiting the woodshop, came towards us with a warm smile. He offered his hand to Cole. As they clasped hands, I saw the respect and love they had for each other. Their bond of being forced to leave their families connected them.

"Thanks, Elliott," Cole finally said, breaking the silence. "I promise, I'll never hurt Mara, again."

Patting him on the back, my father replied, "I know you won't. Now, come on. It's getting late and we have much to do if we intend to find a way of stopping them from taking my grandchild."

"Granddaughter," I whispered. "They're taking our daughter."

CHAPTER
EIGHTEEN

By the time we entered the house, the lights were dim, and everyone had gone to bed. Two steaming cups of tea with biscuits had been left on the table beside a note. Scrawled in Essie's handwriting, it read: *Welcome Home.*

"I'll say goodnight and leave you. We can talk in the morning." My father kissed me on the forehead, and then he tousled Cole's hair as if we were small children.

Seated at the familiar table, Cole and I sipped our tea. I breathed in the cinnamon-vanilla scent. We were home.

"I want to find the journals and start going through them," I said, finishing the last of my drink.

"Not tonight, Mara. I'm tired." Cole stood and offered me his hand.

Reluctantly, I accepted it. "Tomorrow, then."

When we reached Gram's room, Cole stopped in the doorway.

I pulled him away from it. "Not here. *Our* room."

Cole frowned at me but followed as I led him through the patio to the section of the house built for us. He stared in silence at all of the changes. His hand trailed along the banister as we climbed the staircase.

When we reached the landing, Cole said, "Stop."

"What?" I looked around prepared to call my magic.

Picking me up, he replied, "If this is our home, I'm supposed to carry you over the threshold."

"You're ridiculous," I said with mock irritation. "Put me down before you hurt yourself."

Nuzzling my neck, he whispered, "I want to carry my new bride across the threshold properly."

"Cole, I'm almost eight months pregnant and I'm far from a new bride. The years we've been married couldn't have blown by that fast, dear," I said sarcastically.

"You'll always be my new bride," he murmured.

My husband set me down by a new piece of furniture – a rocking chair. My father had added to the room while we were gone. I looked around, taking in the changes. Everything I had picked out during our shopping trip had been delivered to the room and set up.

"They did all of this for us," I said, noticing the crib. Running my fingers along the detailed woodworking, I sighed. "All of this effort and she'll never sleep here."

This was the room I had always envisioned we'd have. A life of our own, but in my dream, my family would still be together. Our home should be filled with warmth and laughter. I needed my grandmother. She always knew how to fix everything. What would she say if she saw how everything was falling apart?

Lying in our bed, together, for the first time, I rested my head on Cole's shoulder. We were in our home, where we shouldn't have to fight to raise our child.

"A daughter." Cole shifted from under me and laid his head on my womb. "It's my fault they even knew she carries the Winter. If I'd just left and went back to Snowstrum—"

"No, they did this to us," I sat up. "I would've gone after you no matter where you went."

Cole tangled his fingers in my hair. He stared at the pink strand and then sighed. "If you hadn't come after me in the first place..."

"We wouldn't have a child. You would've died in the desert, fighting her spiders, and I would've died from a broken heart, here, alone," I argued. "As much as I hate what she did to us, we're together and..." I couldn't finish the words. *We were together, but for how long?*

A shadow stood in the entrance. "You will never keep him. Prepare to lose more people you love, Marina." Snowystra smiled wickedly and left the room.

I tossed and turned, afraid the minute my eyes were closed that Snowystra would return. Finally, my body forced my mind to shut down. I woke to the morning sun, streaming into the room. Sleepily, I felt for Cole. The bed was cold, and he was gone. I sat up quickly to search for him.

Not again. My sudden movement made me feel dizzy. I forced myself to lie back down. As I slowly inhaled and exhaled, I could hear it, the sound of the shower running. Cole hadn't left me. I hadn't been abandoned, again.

"Knock, knock." My father appeared, carrying a tray in one hand and a box in the other. "I come bearing gifts."

"Good morning," I said, forcing a smile. "Where is everyone? I'd expected to be bombarded this morning."

"Nope. We have the house to ourselves." He put everything down on a small table.

This time, getting up slowly, I joined him. I picked up a scone and took a bite. *Gram's recipe.*

My father took a seat at the table across from me. "I thought we could go through the journals, together. Take me through everything I've missed, step by step, and don't leave anything out."

I replayed the events from the bird pulling my hair to our return to Starten. My father frantically wrote in a notebook as he listened. When I stopped speaking, he was still writing.

"Tell me, again, what Danu said to you. Try to remember the exact words. Leave nothing out," my father instructed.

"Do not submit to your fear and sorrow. The threads of fate can turn," I said, considering the goddess's words.

"That's all she said?" my father asked.

"Yes, except...I think she said the threads are fickle?" I frowned. "Why is this important?"

"I think she wants to help you," my father said, tapping the pen. "I don't think she wants your child to be taken from you. We just need to figure out what she was trying to tell you."

My father sorted through the journals. He took a silver one out of the middle and put it on his pile. Quickly, he sorted through the remaining books.

"We'll find something in here to stop them. You're having a girl, huh?" My father beamed at the idea.

"Yes, Brighid said our daughter."

"Imagine that," my father said wistfully.

Leafing through one of my grandmother's journals, I stopped. "Can I ask you something?" I checked to ensure we were still alone. "Do you think if magic is combined, it could be strong enough to kill a god?"

"I understand why you're feeling this way, but don't let the darkness inside your heart. We'll find a way to stop them," he said, resting his hand on mine.

"You're probably right. Thank you for breakfast. I need to get ready for the day." I stood up.

"Mara," he called.

I turned and could see the concern on his face. "I was just asking a question. Don't worry, Daddy. I won't kill anyone."

Unless they try to take my child.

CHAPTER NINETEEN

Cole and I spent the day reading every one of my mother's journals. If I had found them years ago, I would've understood better why she left us.

The books would've told me how my mother had fallen madly in love with Cedric Drygen and how different their life would've been if Snowystra hadn't kept them apart. The cruel goddess manipulated my mother, just as she controlled Cole. She forced Eliza into my father's arms. No matter how hard she tried to be a good wife and mother, she lived with the torment of being apart from the man she really loved.

Will this be my future, too?

Picking up another journal, the first page was about me.

> *Mara asked me, today, why, when I put Meg to sleep, I didn't say a prayer to the Goddess. How could I possibly tell an eleven-year-old that I had pledged loyalty to the Winter to save the man I loved...a man that was not her father? One day, we will be free from her. The gypsy told me the answer was the Golden King of the forest. The old bat only talks in riddles. She never just answers the questions.*

I almost laughed at the irony. Eliza hated how no one gave her a straight answer to her questions as much as I do. A trait we clearly shared.

A warm breeze blew over me. Blaze appeared. Dressed in crimson leather pants and a tank top covered with black shimmery scales, her large cat-like eyes burned with golden fire. She looked ready for a battle. The dragon of my childhood had come to scare off any *creatures* in the night. She was the one who taught me to summon weapons for the times when magic wasn't enough.

Blaze wasn't the one to dry away tears. She was the one who taught me to fight back. I knew her words would only make me stronger – so strong I could do anything...like save my daughter. *Could she help me kill Tannus?*

"Isn't it time you put the books down and got back to training?" Blaze put her hands on her hips and loomed over me.

I threw my arms around the elemental and whispered in her ear, "I'm so glad to see you."

Blaze stiffened at my touch. Detaching herself, her eyes inspected me. "I see we have a lot of work to strengthen you. I knew Breeze would be horrible at forcing you to take your training seriously. Trust me, I will have a long talk with her about her failures. But, enough about my incompetent sister. I am back."

"Blaze, I'm really, really glad you came," I gushed and took her hand.

The Fire Elemental's mouth pursed into a hard line. Blaze wasn't one to let sentiment get in the way of business. Gently, she released my hold on her.

"We are running out of time, Mara. Let's see how strong you can be."

Blaze led me past the picnic tree where I would meet the elementals as a child and, instead, took me deeper into Starten Forest. I thought about asking her, but then, decided against it. It was always better to keep the elemental in a good mood rather than wasting her time with a bunch of questions. She would tell me whatever I needed to know when I needed to know it.

"Now that we are away from the house, I want you to call a winter storm," she commanded.

"What? I can't call snow," I reminded her.

"If you're carrying Winter, you can. Channel her energy," Blaze insisted.

Closing my eyes, I tried to find the words to summon Winter. I thought of Snowstrum. "Winter, daughter of Arianolwyn, I call your cold power," I said, throwing my hands into the air.

Nothing happened.

"I can't call something I don't have inside me."

"*I don't know how,*" she mocked. "All of the flowery words don't invoke the power. We used those to convince silly mortal girls they had magic." Blaze's eyes burned with actual flames. "Now, focus! When will you trust yourself? Listen to what is inside you and you will *know* what to do."

My instinct told me to call all of the elements at the same time. Closing my eyes, I spoke from my heart. I know she said the words weren't necessary, but I needed them. *You are, in fact, just a silly mortal girl,* I thought bitterly.

Taking a deep cleansing breath, I held my hands out. "Air, I call your intuition. Fire, please, send your courage. Water, I need your calming spirit. Earth, your strength is needed. Danu, spirit, mother of the elements, through your children, please, bestow your blessing."

A sudden burst of the elemental magic surrounded me. The air was alive with sparks of fire, droplets of water, and petals of lavender, enclosing me in a strong, warm wind.

"Now, call the Winter," Blaze shouted.

Resting my hand on my stomach, I said, "Winter of Snowystra, no longer corrupted and dark, I call you to me."

Small flakes of white joined the swirling elements and the movement inside me became intense. "Winter of my child, show yourself, I call you to me."

A sharp pain in my stomach sent me to my knees. When I looked up, large snowflakes fell on us, covering the trees. Within seconds, the limbs drooped with the white powder.

"Thank you, Winter. You're released," I gasped.

The movement inside me calmed. The ache lifted as the snow whirled and blew away.

"Here, you look like you need help, Mara." With unusual kindness, Blaze offered her hand to me.

I accepted it and sighed at the warmth of her touch. With a mighty pull, I was on my feet and standing in the puddles of melted snow.

"I am so sorry. I did not believe you were carrying the Winter," she said. "I thought they were wrong."

"What am I going to do, Blaze? I can't give her away to them." I grabbed her hand. "We have to stop them. There has to be a way."

The golden king, I remembered. "My mother was told the golden king would help her. Could he help me?"

As if she was considering my question, Blaze bit her lip and her orange eyes glowed. "Faramond!" she exclaimed. "He was, once, called the Golden King, but he'd been killed by the time your mother was born."

"That's it," I exclaimed. "The journal said the Golden King of the forest. Faramond had lived in Eftir forest. Maybe the woman knew he would be restored?"

Blaze nodded slowly as if considering the possibilities.

"I know you're right," I said emphatically. "We need to go to Faramond. Can you take me there?"

As I made the request, I realized I knew nothing about Eftir Forest. "Wait...is time different there?"

"Time is fluid," Blaze replied. "Snowystra was the only god to manipulate it. Another cruel way to control the mortals she took. By the time she released them, they had no one to go home to."

"Can you take me to him, then?"

"Essie knows the way."

"Do you believe he can help me? Help my baby?"

A sour look washed over her face. Finally, Blaze shrugged. "I guess if anyone can stop Tannus, it's Faramond. Let him know Danu and the elements support you. Now, let's get you home."

The storm I had called blanketed Starten in thick snow. When we returned to the property, Meg and Miles were throwing snowballs at Cole and laughing. The three of them were like school children on the first day of summer vacation.

"Should I call Fire to melt all of this?" I asked. Starten rarely had snow and this would shut down everything.

"No, let everyone enjoy it, tonight. I will be sure to warm up everything before morning," Blaze smirked.

"Mara, have you ever seen so much snow? Come help us," Miles called. "Cole has a wicked arm."

"I'm sure you can handle him. I'm really tired." I smiled and waved them off.

"All right, I'll come in soon," Cole called to me. "I have to show these two who's the king of the snow."

"Go on, quit already. We're going to embarrass you if you stay, Cos!" Meg yelled.

Cole scooped up the white powder and packed it tightly. Pleased with his creation, he wound up and pelted Meg with a flurry of snowballs. "Victory will be mine, Meg!"

Watching from the doorway, I saw how much love Cole had for our family. I pictured him sweeping our daughter into his arms and saving her from the barrage of snow. She would cling to his neck and tell him he was the best daddy in the world.

Or, she'll be scared and alone, without a father, if I don't save her, I thought bitterly.

CHAPTER
TWENTY

Staring out our bedroom window at the snow-covered forest, I knew I had to stop Tannus from taking my child. If Faramond wouldn't help, I would have no choice, but to try to stop him alone. I had defeated Snowystra with the help of my family. I would make them understand how much I needed their help, now.

Cole's strong hands were suddenly on me, his fingers massaging my shoulders. "Mar, you're so tense," he said. "What happened out there? Did you have anything to do with the frosting of the forest?"

"Your daughter did." I sighed, leaning back against him. "Blaze had me call the Winter and you can see how well it worked. It felt like our daughter was going to rip out of my stomach. She has powerful magic already."

"Did Blaze tell you how we can stop them from taking her?" he asked.

Twisting around to face him, I shook my head. "I read something in Eliza's journal. Faramond might be the answer."

"Did Blaze agree?" Cole's eyes shined amber in the light and my anger towards the Gods grew.

"She did. She said Essie could take us and told me to tell Faramond that Danu and her elementals support us. Why didn't she support us before they took your gift away? Why didn't she stand up to the Council? Why should I believe she'll help us, now?"

"You know she had no choice." Cole smoothed my hair out of my face.

"Every time I look into your eyes, I'm reminded of what they took from you. Why don't they take the gift from me, too? Take it from our baby? They could take back their curse and let us live normal lives." My voice filled with venom.

"Mara, it was never a curse to have the magic. It was a blessing, but I don't feel anger towards them for taking it away. Don't wish for yours to be gone because of me." Cole kissed my neck. "I don't believe they'll take our daughter away. The last time you challenged a goddess, you freed her people and spared the world from her darkness. If anyone can save our child, it'll be you."

My eyes narrowed as I regarded him. "We can't sit back and wait for —"

Cole lifted my chin and gazed lovingly into my eyes. "*We* will figure this out. Our daughter will grow up here. One day, we'll watch her from this very window as she has her own picnics with the elementals."

"You're wrong, Cole. I can't stop them. I can't save our child." I drew in a breath.

"Maybe not, but we can – together. You faced Snowystra alone. Now, I'm strong and healthy. Our child will be raised by us," Cole insisted.

Our child...our daughter. How cold we sound. We need to give you a name, little one. I may not be able to raise you, but I need you to know that you were loved from the minute I knew you were inside me. I want you to hear your name and hear my voice calling you no matter where you are, I thought.

"What about Maesi? It's what Chester used to call Gram," Cole said.

"What do you mean?" I asked, surprised by his statement.

"We should call our daughter Maesi," Cole restated. "If there was anyone that could face a battle, it was Gram."

"Was I talking out loud?" I asked.

"Well, I heard you, so you must have been. You might want to rest before we go back downstairs," Cole suggested, his face lined with concern.

I was tired of everyone telling me to relax and rest. There wasn't time.

Maesi? How appropriate, my child will be named after the twists and turns in the puzzle of our world. But, not spelled like Gramp's special name for Gram. How about M A Z Y? It's the same name, but your own? If you were a boy, I would've named you Jareth after the goblin king who controlled the labyrinth.

"Or, we could name him Toby after the baby stolen by the goblin king." Cole laughed.

Or Finnegan, I thought. *Gramp's middle name.*

"Finn for a boy?" he asked with a look of consideration. "I like it."

I looked at him in surprise, Certain he had heard my thoughts. Testing my suspicion, I deliberately thought, *I need a glass of water.* A soft chime rang, and I knew I wasn't imagining things.

"I'll get you one, and then you need to promise you'll take a nap."

As he walked away, I grabbed the back of his shirt. When he turned around, I watched him carefully. *Cole, I'm not talking. Look at my mouth. How can you hear my thoughts?*

"I can?" Cole asked, his eyes widened in surprise. "How in the heck? Wait – I can hear your thoughts!"

A small blue light appeared and hovered over us. The sphere grew larger before a beautiful young woman formed from it. Her long, slender frame was clothed in a simple dress. Her tangled hair was a greyish-blue. Her large, cat-like eyes, which were once a piercing silver color, were, now, a shade of dull charcoal gray. The once vibrant elemental looked different as if her spirit was gone.

"Bay, are you ok?" Cole asked, reaching out to her. "Are you injured?"

Sniffling, she wiped her nose with the back of her hand. "I failed you," she said through her tears. "I should've protected you. It was my job to keep you safe."

"You did everything for me. I wouldn't be here, right now, if you hadn't helped me heal." Cole wiped the tears from Bay's cheek and hugged her tightly. "I don't have Water magic inside me anymore, but it'll always be in my heart. I need you, now, more than ever. *We* need you. Who else will conjure a ball of water to throw at Mara for me?"

"But, you're an Ateissa, now. You're one of Brighid's gifted," she said, barely choking out the words through her sniffles. "You won't need my help anymore learning your gift. You'll need the Curuxatyni." Crying harder, she held onto him tighter.

I'd always known she had a strong affection for him, but I hadn't considered how she would take this loss. Gently rubbing her back, I said, "Bay, we can't have you sad. You're our joy. We need your strong spirit more than ever before. Who else is going to tell us the truth and teach us about their world?"

Throwing herself into my arms, she uncontrollably sobbed. I could feel her elemental energy surging from her body into mine.

"Water of the West, I call you. Your cleansing magic is needed. I ask you to wash away the fears of Danu's chosen. Provide her with the clarity and strength she'll need to guide us."

Water droplets filled the air and sprinkled down. Bay tilted her head back.

"Thank you, Mara," she said. "I will do anything I can to stop them from taking Mazy away from you."

Shaking my head, I rubbed my belly and smiled. "I guess it's been decided that we'll call you Mazy. We'll have to convince Auntie Meg and Uncle Miles not to call you Neep anymore. Don't worry. I think they'll like your new name."

"You're wrong to say you aren't strong enough." Bay gently rubbed her hand over my belly. "You've got the power of the elements inside you. If there is a way to stop Tannus, Faramond will know how. He has done it before."

Then, she faded into a blue ball of light and floated away.

CHAPTER
TWENTY-ONE

The next afternoon, our entire family was off on another adventure. Essie was leading us through the woods where I'd spent my childhood exploring.

Earlier in the morning, Cole and I had told her about the telepathic experience. After a few minutes of silent reflection, she confirmed Brighid had blessed Cole. His Water magic had been taken from him, but another gift had been bestowed. He was Ateissa, like her, which couldn't have been more fitting.

Under the guidance of Essie, Cole would learn about his new powers. I felt envious of this. While I had elementals to teach me, I didn't have a mortal who could help me work through my emotions.

"I can't believe we'll soon be in the home of the Miezitari," Meg said excitedly as we walked deep into Starten Forest. "I've missed everyone."

The people she missed had once been under my rule. My last act as Vizier of Snowstrum had been to free the Vetur and allow them to reclaim their true identity as the Miezitari. Even while they were held captive by Snowystra, they never gave up hope of, one day, returning to their home in Eftir Forest.

"Everyone or someone in particular?" Miles asked with a mischievous grin. "Maybe a certain guard of the Snowstrum court?"

"No, smarty. I mean…yes, I'm excited to see Dunn, but Laura and Christina, too," Meg replied and stuck her tongue out at him.

I couldn't help, but smile. She looked like the ten-year-old I had left and thought I'd never see again. Shaking off my bittersweet memories, I glanced at the area around us. The trees were in various shades of transition.

"Is this the one?" Cole asked. The trunk he was standing by was nothing special.

"What do you think?" Essie wondered. Her tone made it clear that she was teaching him how to use his gift.

"My instinct is telling me this is the portal," Cole said.

Essie swept her hand, telling him it was his turn. "Well, lead us through."

Dark pine trees filled Eftir Forest, bursting with saffron pinecones. We crunched through the dried fallen needles lying on the forest floor until we arrived at a stone path.

Essie stopped us. "See over there?" She pointed ahead of us. "This is where Faramond lives, now."

The home of the *Guardian of the Afterlife* was a hunting lodge. No, it was so much more than a cabin in the woods. It was stunning.

The three-story building, built with golden logs, showcased many stained-glass windows. Each pane was a replica of Livia's tapestries. His daughter's art gave her glimpses into the possibilities of the future. I gasped when I saw the window on the ground floor; it was me with bright butterfly wings. The child I held was gripping a snowflake in one arm, the other extended beyond the frame, the hand cut out of the picture.

My heart flipped when I saw Christina standing at the front entrance. She was a vibrant blonde in colorful clothing, now. She had abandoned her black apparel and tight bun. Her skin was no longer wrinkled. She wasn't the invisible help anymore.

"Mara," Christina greeted. Holding my hands in hers, she kissed them. "I'm so glad I stayed to see you. I can't believe how well you look, my dear. How much I have missed you."

"You look so wonderful," I gushed.

"The darkness was lifted from us." Christina hugged me tightly. "Thanks to you, we are home."

"And, home is where we will remain," Faramond powerfully crowed. "Mara, you've come to see the success of your great plan to free my people? You'll be surprised at how well my children are doing. All thanks to you." Stepping onto the porch, he motioned towards my stomach. "May I?"

Faramond was no longer the skeleton with burning red eyes. He had become a muscular man with golden skin and locks. His gaze was penetrating. Unable to speak, all I could muster was a nod. When he placed his fingers on my pregnant belly, his magic flowed through me. It was a warm, comforting sensation.

"She's strong," he said.

"Mazy," I announced, finally able to speak. "We have decided her name will be Mazy."

"Mae will be pleased. Such a strong name for a strong child," Faramond praised. "Now that you're all here, I want you to make yourselves at home. Livia has planned an evening of dinner and dance." Turning towards the radiant woman, he asked, "Christina, will you give them a tour of our home and show them the way to their rooms?"

"But I need—"

The Golden King stopped me. "There'll be time for serious business later, Mara. I know you're anxious to talk, but I promise you, we have time." He placed his hands on my shoulders and looked deeply into my eyes. "Now is the time to witness your gift to the Miezitari. You're not the queen here, but you are a most celebrated guest. Go to your former subjects and revel in their joy."

Will there be time to discuss the future? I hoped he was right, but I had no choice. I had to believe he would help us. There was nothing else I could do. I couldn't fight, yet, another God.

CHAPTER
TWENTY-TWO

Christina led us. We passed a large room filled with comfortable couches, chairs, and an impressive stone fireplace. The atmosphere held a strong feeling of family and love.

"Most nights, we meet here to tell stories about our day and for Faramond to share happy stories of the past," Christina explained.

"Has everyone adjusted to the new world?" Cole questioned.

"Jameson has been hesitant to embrace the return, but he is old enough to remember Snowystra killing everyone that stood against her. He'll come around. Kai has been wonderful with him," Christina answered.

The way she said Kai's name gave me a twinge of jealousy, though I shook it off immediately. Kai was a friend. We shared a memorable kiss...well, several, but nothing would hold a candle to Cole.

"Did someone mention wonderful?" Kai appeared. His black cherry hair was shorter, giving him a boyish look. Stepping out of one of the rooms, he went to Cole. Shaking hands, they had a pleasant exchange, like two old friends. "Being an Ateissa suits you."

"It really does," Cole said, and I felt he meant it. "I miss my Water magic, but there's something peaceful inside me, now."

"Mara, you look fantastic. I love the pink streak." His eyes blazed gold. He took my hand and a warmth filled me. I instantly felt a fervent desire to kiss him.

You're married, Mara and carrying Cole's baby. What are you thinking? You're just feeling his magic. If Cole senses your ridiculous reaction to his touch...I checked for telltale signs of Cole tapping into my thoughts.

Nothing.

"Kai, I'm so glad you've been here to help the Miezitari rebuild." I quickly squeezed his hand and released it.

Our eyes locked for the briefest moment. I thought I saw a look of regret and longing. I had seen this, once, before in his eyes. However, he quickly recovered to his confident, cocky self.

"Well, why don't I take over the tour and get you all to your rooms? After, I'll take you to the cottages. Everyone has been eager to see you both." Patting Cole on the back, Kai said, "It's good to see you looking so well."

"Wouldn't you rather go with your Fire Boy?" Snowystra whispered. "Careful, Marina, you don't want to bring out the strong champion I know is deep inside of poor, pitiful Cole."

I whipped around to see where she was and stumbled. Cole caught me before I fell.

"Are you alright?" he asked.

"I just moved too fast," I said dismissively. Rubbing my extended stomach, I forced a laugh. "Your daughter throws me a bit off balance."

Cole frowned but took my hand as we continued with our tour.

When we reached our rooms, Kai left us to settle in. I asked Essie to join Cole and me.

"I wanted to tap into the thoughts of the Miezitari and see if there's anything useful to be learned," I said in a hushed voice.

I considered telling them about Snowystra, but something inside warned me not to bring it up. It wasn't real. It had to be my mind playing tricks or an overactive imagination.

"Here," Essie said, taking off her spiral sunburst necklace and placing it into my hands. "This will help you create a connection."

Essie and Cole locked eyes. The air around us felt electric. When their gaze broke, Essie nodded at me and left with a quick goodbye.

Cole inspected the necklace and twirled it around.

As it spun and spun, I stared intently. The yellow center stone seemed to be changing. When it stopped, I took it out of Cole's hands.

Shock filled me. The gem was no longer the sun symbol. It was, now, an opalescent white with a half-moon on each side.

Smirking, Cole spun it again. This time, it ended in its original form.

I gave it a spin and watched in wonder as the necklace transformed back into the triple moons.

Cole touched my hand and stopped me from continuing the hypnotic game I was playing. "This can be used to join my empathic channel. It's a way for you to borrow a part of my gift." My husband touched my cheek. "When you're ready, put it on. I should warn you that it can be overwhelming. There'll be many voices inside your head at the same time. Essie said it won't work on Faramond or Livia though."

"What can it hurt?" I asked. "We should, at least, try."

"Will it hurt your feelings to see how much you're hated by my children, poor, pitiful, Marina?" Snowystra appeared as a reflection in the window.

My breath caught and I closed my eyes, forcing her away. When I opened them, again, she was gone. I trembled in fear. *Either she was here or I'm losing my mind.*

"You seem anxious, Mar." Cole caught my hand and lightly tugged. "What's up?" His eyes penetrated me as if he was trying to figure out why I was so quiet. "You've gone white. Tell me what's going on."

"I just got a little dizzy," I lied.

"Do you want to rest before we go to the cottages?" Cole frowned.

"No, I'll be ok after a few minutes. Let me splash some water on my face."

Once I was locked in the bathroom, I set the necklace down and stared at myself in the mirror. I looked like the girl I had been before the magic was returned – before I knew about the Gods and Goddesses. *But you aren't that girl anymore.*

Kai's face flashed in my mind. The way he looked at me as if he could see much more than what was on the surface. *What if I had stayed in Danu's realm with him?*

My reflection in the mirror changed. My curly hair grew long and straight, the white streak disappearing. My hazel eyes frosted, and the dark goddess appeared. The corner of her mouth curled upward, forming a mocking grin.

"It's not too late to go after your desires, Marina. Always keeping your silly promises and never taking the pleasures you could have. Cole will fail you. You're an incubator for the Gods. The child inside you is not yours," Snowystra hissed.

"No," I snarled, slamming my hand against the mirror. "You're wrong. Leave us alone."

"Mar, are you ok?" Cole asked, frantically knocking on the door.

The corner of Snowystra mouth turned and she wore a sly smirk. "Bring him in. See how happy he will be to see me."

"I'm ok, Cole. I'll just be a minute," I called. Then, turning back towards the mirror, I hissed, "You're not real."

The door latch unlocked and opened. Snowystra threw her head back, cackling, and faded away. My own image reflected back at me.

"I said I'd be out in a minute," I snapped.

Cole's face fell. "I heard yelling. It sounded like you were talking to someone. You sounded like you needed help."

What can I tell him? Don't worry, I was arguing with my reflection?

"I was talking to our baby," I lied. Quickly, I splashed some freezing water on my face, and said, "Ok, I'm ready to go to the cottages, now."

Cole picked up the triple moon necklace I had set on the counter and fastened it around my neck. Tenderly, he centered the moon on my chest, and then took my hand. When his fingers touched mine, electricity shot through my arm, over my heart, and back into him. The necklace grew hot, as if it was a conduit of his power.

"I call you, Brighid, Goddess of Balance, gifter of the calming touch. I request to share your gift. Our intention is for the knowledge required to save our child from a dark life without her parents. Your blessing of love and light will guide us," Cole prayed.

The necklace on my chest glowed. I could feel a pulsing beat traveling through my body and, once again, connecting me to Cole. As the charm cooled, I felt a twinge of pain in my temple.

My blessing has been granted. May this hold the key to save your child, the voice of Brighid declared.

Mar, can you hear me? Cole asked telepathically.

I can, I mentally responded.

Good, then you'll be able to hear the thoughts of others, my husband projected. *Are you ready?*

Taking a cleansing breath, I thought. *I'm as ready as I'll ever be.*

"I'm here for you, Mar. No matter what feelings surface from either of us. I know you're mine and I am yours," Cole whispered in my ear.

I realized at that moment that he'd noticed my reaction to Kai and that he may have a similar reaction to the women from the tunnels. Suddenly, I was aware of what might really happen. Seeing our former subjects could bring up more painful memories and I regretted my request.

"It'll be ok, Mar. Just breathe," Cole said.

CHAPTER
TWENTY-THREE

Kai led us through the lodge, out of two giant glass doors, and to a wonderland in the back of Faramond's home. Two-story cottages had been built around a courtyard of green grass. We walked through the pastel-colored houses.

The Miezitari were cheerfully carrying on with life's responsibilities. Laundry was being hung. Flowers were being planted. Children were playing. Laughter filled the air.

When they saw us, their voices quieted. They stopped and watched.

I forced myself to put on a bright smile, even when it wasn't reciprocated. Although we were no longer the Shah and Vizier, I understood why our appearance might bring back dark memories. They no longer lived under the cruel rule of Snowystra, but they'd only been free for a few months.

In the center of the houses, a large fountain sprayed water around a statue of Faramond beside a majestic queen. In his stone arms, he held a child. A group of women standing by it considered us as we walked towards them. Bursting out of the group, a small girl with strawberry blonde hair ran to me, dragging an even smaller boy behind her. I knew instantly it was Cerin's children.

"You're here. Oh, and you're having a baby!" Masha cried.

The girl had been one of the children taken from her parents by Snowystra to be trained in the castle. Masha was the most rebellious of the stolen children; never afraid to tell the Winter Goddess what she really thought. Her father was the one who had carried Cole to safety when I stayed to fight the dark goddess.

"Butterfly," her little brother, Daniel, screamed and threw himself around my leg.

"He has been practicing how to say butterfly since we left the snow. Leave her be, Danny. She has lots of people to see." Masha pulled the small child from me, and then took my hand. "Come with me."

Masha proudly led us to the group of people as Daniel followed behind, chirping "Butterfly." The small child's affectionate nickname for me was drowned out as I was instantly hit with their internal thoughts.

He is even more handsome, one woman noted. Pity he isn't free.

I can't believe they came back to visit us. I thought they would never want to see us, again, came a voice that sounded pleasantly surprised.

Another filled me with pain as they mused, how sad – she saved our children, but they are taking hers away.

Isn't she all high and mighty? The Queen has returned to have us grovel at her feet. Someone should put her in her place, a male thought bitterly, preferably a shallow grave.

Goddess, I silently called, focusing on the angry man's voice. *Please, lead me to this man.*

A small chime sounded in my head and as I walked, it picked up tempo. When the speed of the sound slowed, I knew I had gone in the wrong direction. My mind was playing a game of *Hot and Cold.*

When the tone remained strong and steady, I found myself standing in front of one of Snowystra's loyal guards: Jameson. The last time I saw him, I had him drugged and taken to Eftir Forest with the rest of the Vetur, who were making their escape. I couldn't risk him stopping them.

"Hello, Jameson." I offered my hand to him as the chime stopped. "I know the last time we saw each other I hadn't been very kind. I hope you understand the choices I made."

"Of course, min Vizier. I understand you were doing what you thought was best to save us," he said, accepting my hand.

Your game of being sweet and phony will end soon, Vizier. You'll give back what you've stolen. Jameson's internal dialogue played in my mind.

"Jameson, I'm no longer the Vizier. Please, call me, Mara," I said, trying to push back his dark thoughts. "I really would like to clear the air with you. I feel you may be holding onto anger towards me."

"I can promise, I have no anger towards you," he said with a frosty tone.

Again, his dark thoughts ran through my mind. *Your time is almost up. You'll know soon enough what it feels to lose, again.*

"Good, then I'll have the chance to get to know you better in the future," I said. As I walked away from him, I turned to see him glaring at me.

Brighid, I request you break my connection. There's nothing more I need to learn, I silently prayed.

The necklace grew ice cold. A soft feeling ran across my forehead and I knew the connection was gone.

By the time I reached Cole, I was ready to find a quiet place, but I was, also, eager to find out if he'd heard anything useful.

"I don't know how you can handle all of this," I said, kissing my husband on the cheek. "It's draining to hear so many voices."

"You get used to it. I'm much better at closing connections than I was, at first," Cole replied.

"Jameson was the only one I sensed any bad feelings from. How about you?" I asked.

"No one else," Cole answered. "A few of the women were a bit flirty, but it was all very innocent."

"Yes, it's a pity you're no longer free," I said mockingly, trailing my fingers down his chest.

Pulling me into his arms, he kissed me lovingly. "No pity needed. I'm with my childhood sweetheart and the future mother of my little girl. Don't be jealous of a few charmed women when you have your own fan club, my love." Cole nodded at Kai, who was walking towards us.

"How sweet," Kai commented.

Cole let go of me and grinned sheepishly.

"Everyone is so glad to see you," the Fire elemental noted. "Livia asked that you come to her cottage when you're free."

"Oh, why is she not staying in the lodge with Faramond?" I asked.

Livia loved her father so much that I was surprised she wouldn't want to live near him. When he'd been slain by Snowystra, she had pleaded for him to be restored, which the dark goddess ultimately allowed. However, he was brought back as a shadow of his former self and while they lived in Snowstrum together, she'd been unable to acknowledge him as her father.

"She claims she is old and too set in her ways." Kai chuckled. "Honestly, she needs her own space for her looms and her stained-glass projects. She has been quite busy with the restorations, as you can see."

"Well, I guess we're done here." I glanced around at my former subjects, who had returned to their daily lives. "Lead the way."

"Yes, min Vizier." Kai deeply bowed as he chortled with amusement.

CHAPTER
TWENTY-FOUR

Livia's cottage was nestled behind the circle of homes. The view from her front porch faced the backside of the Lodge. The windows of her home were made from the same colorful stained-glass designs as her father's home.

As a young girl, Livia's life had been spared by Snowystra, but she'd suffered greatly as a result. While she was captive, she was forced to silently witness the abuse of her people. Her tapestries recorded their stories. I didn't understand the magic inside her, but I knew the threads of knowledge flowed through her. They told her the future. This led her to predict that a Butterfly would be their savior.

"Come, let me look at you," Livia cried, opening her arms wide to welcome us. She looked half the age she did when I'd seen her last. Her once silver hair was, now, a golden blonde.

When we reached her, Livia placed her hands on my stomach. She smiled as Mazy swirled around.

"My father was right. Your daughter is strong with the Winter." She furrowed her brows. "However, I feel something else."

The colored glass behind Livia swirled with dark black and gray. Snowystra appeared. "She feels me, Marina. I will always be within you."

"Is she ok?" I asked. A panic rose in me. "What do you feel?" *Is the dark goddess living inside me?*

Tilting her head, Livia pursed her lips. "The child is fine. I just feel more than Winter inside you. Maybe, she is like you with many gifts or, maybe, I'm just feeling your strong magic?"

Does Livia know I was cursed? That my child is born from Snowystra's blood?

Livia smiled warmly at me and then turned her attention towards Cole.

"Hello, Livia." He kissed her cheek in greeting. "I'm happy to see you. Why, you're sparkling."

"And, you look well, too, my boy." She laughed. "The last time I saw the Shah, he was a bit undone."

"Yes, he was, but that vile creature is gone. Our Mara saved me, too." Cole smiled proudly.

"The Shah will rise, again," Snowystra taunted.

"Stop," I yelled, instantly regretting my outburst.

Snowystra laughed maniacally. "Poor Marina. They will think you're going crazy. Can't you control yourself?"

"What's going on, Mar?" Cole asked, wrapping his arm around my waist.

Livia stared intently at me, and then followed my eyes towards the window. She looked back at me. Her eyes were lined with concern. "She needs more rest. I can feel your internal conflict, Mara."

She doesn't see her? I am losing my mind. They're going to lock me away somewhere!

"Is Livia right?" Cole asked.

Agree, Mara, I warned myself. "Yes, yes, " I answered too quickly before forcing a bright smile. "You're right. I've not been sleeping very well, and the baby is kicking like crazy. I'm sure our stay here will be just what I need."

Livia nodded, but the concern didn't leave her face. "I insist you rest. Please. Come in, come in. Laura has been waiting to see you."

The look of worry Cole wore faded and he let go of me as we entered the home.

The minute she saw us, Laura leapt out of her chair and threw her arms around me. I was amazed at how her new home had changed her. She was vibrant and full of life. The love I felt from all the women, today, overwhelmed me. Out of the darkness of Snowstrum, my family had grown.

Gram had always said that even when there was no hope for light, love could still grow the strongest flowers. Now, I had a new understanding as to what that meant.

"Have you been drinking the heilsavi I sent?" Laura questioned.

"Of course. Meg has me following your instructions to the T." I smirked.

"Sit, sit," Livia insisted. "I want you to tell us about your time in Galinevo."

There was no need to hold back. We were with family and I felt free to tell them everything. They had been by my side in Snowstrum and they would understand. Cole paled as I described the vision I had of his time under Snowystra's control and his attacks on me. When I finished the story, we all sat in silence for what seemed like an eternity.

"More victims of Snowystra," Livia finally said, breaking the silence. "Cole, I'm enormously proud of you. You both were very brave and will grow from the pain you were forced to endure. Now, enough of the past. We focus on the future. I want you both to stay here until the child is born. This will ensure you're safe while you plan to stop Tannus from taking Mazy. Laura will, also, be able to keep an eye on you, Mara. A child with such strong magic should be carefully monitored."

"Do I need to worry about losing the baby?" I drew in a breath and waited for the bad news.

"No, child. I'm more concerned what the toll of carrying her will have on *your* body." Livia squeezed my hand. "Laura is wonderful at taking care of pregnant women. So, you will be in her care."

"So, I have a healthy baby growing inside me. How will we stop Tannus?" I asked.

"I do not know, Mara. I really don't know, yet," Livia answered honestly. Her eyes blazed as she said the next words. "But you have the protection of the Miezitari as long as I'm still breathing."

CHAPTER
TWENTY-FIVE

Eftir Forest was like a land of lost time, where anything could happen. Even after nine days, I found myself amazed by how many different trees were in one place. When we had entered Eftir, large pine trees filled the woods. But, as we further explored, there were the green, leafy trees of Starten and even the twisted turquoise trees of Galinevo.

One afternoon, Meg and I decided our walk would end with a picnic beside the lake. Along the way, my little sister picked flowers and decided we both needed colorful crowns. As we joked and laughed, my heart filled with happiness. The day couldn't have started better and, that night, my sister would know the secret I'd been keeping from her.

Meg had turned sixteen the week before. I knew my sister was too smart to not catch on to a party being planned for her. To keep the big event secret, we decided having it later was the best.

On the day of her birthday, we had a small family dinner to celebrate. Being in a new place made it easy to explain just having a meal. While we dined on Mile's famous veggie pizza, it had been a challenge to not blurt out all of the exciting details between each delicious, cheesy bite.

Today, it was my job to keep her busy while the preparations for the evening were finalized. Too many birthdays had passed with us apart. I wanted this one to be something she would never forget.

"I never want to leave this place, Mar." Meg threw her hands into the air and spun around.

"It's pretty fantastic," I agreed as we sat down at one of the several picnic tables lining the edge of the lake.

Since our arrival, Meg had embraced the culture and became part of it. Shadowing Laura as she cared for the pregnant women, Meg had become quite knowledgeable about childbirth. But this wasn't the only thing endearing Meg to Eftir. My sister was head over heels in love and the object of her affection appeared to reciprocate the same feelings.

As much as I was happy for her, I was concerned about the time Meg was spending with Dunn. She was growing up and I didn't want her to end up disappointed because I didn't stop her from making a mistake. He was immortal and a hundred years older than she was. There was no way around the inevitable. She would end up with a broken heart in the end.

"Gram once told me I had to be careful about the choices I made when following what I desired. She was right. Once you make a decision, you can't always take it back," I warned.

"Are you giving me *the birds and bees* talk?" Meg laughed. "Mara, Dunn isn't like that and neither am I for that matter. Mara, I found my Cole."

"I know what it's like to be your age. I really was there not so long ago," I said. "Please, don't rush into something that will be impossible to keep alive. I wish you'd spend less time with him and really think about the emotions running through you. I'm here for you if you want to talk, ok?" I reached out and rested my hand on hers.

"Don't worry. We don't have any plans to run away and get married." Meg pulled her hands out from under mine. Her eyes shone with moisture. "We're going to enjoy the time we have together. Can't you just trust me? I'm not a child anymore."

"I never said you were a child, Meg. I just don't want you to rush into anything and regret it later."

"You of all people should know that time with our loved ones is precious and shouldn't be wasted. Mara, I'm not you. I can't block people out to keep my heart safe."

"I...I don't do that," I stammered.

"Mara, you've *always* done exactly that. You have a wall up." Meg threw her hands into the air in frustration.

"You're so young and—"

Meg jumped up from the table and glared at me. "And, impulsive? Foolish? I don't know if you noticed, but I've grown up while you were gone. I would say recently I've acted more like an adult than you."

I gasped. Her words were like a bucket of icy water being dumped onto me. "Meg, I'm an adult. You've no idea what I went through...what I'm going through."

"Can I join you, ladies?" Faramond called.

We both turned towards him.

Faramond may be a god, but he acted as if he was human. There was no superiority in his attitude. He worked as hard as any of the Miezitari in any of the daily tasks, rarely using his magic. "Did I interrupt something?"

"No." My eyes locked with my Meg's. "We're just talking."

"I'm sure Mara won't mind sharing our lunch. Right, Mar?" Meg handed him one of the ham and cheese sandwiches and took the seat next to me.

"Oh, of course not. You have perfect timing. We were just starting to each lunch. Help yourself to any of the other treats." I motioned towards the picnic basket.

"Lucky for me." Faramond chuckled as he dug through the hamper. "I see Miles has been at work."

I leaned close to my sister and whispered, "We can continue this conversation later, Meg."

"No need, Mara. I think you've said what you wanted to say," Meg hissed. Her emerald eyes turned grey and her delicate features grew dark. The young girl sitting next to me transformed into the dark goddess.

"Doesn't she sound just like your mother? I should've waited for her to grow up, and then lured her to Snowstrum. She would not have failed me," Snowystra mocked.

"I'm glad you're both here. I wanted to talk to you." Faramond took the seat across from us.

My eyes returned to where Snowystra had been. She was gone. In her place, Meg stared at me wide-eyed.

"About my...my child?" I stammered. *Why am I seeing her everywhere?*

"Yes, Mara. In a way," the Golden King answered. "We have offered you protection through your pregnancy. Once the child is born, it will be up to *you*."

Frustration filled me. "I can't stop Tannus from taking my child. I don't have the magic he has. He's a God and I'm a—"

"You're more than a girl. You're a woman who carries the four elementals *and* the magic of the Winter. By now, you know your mother was gifted with Fire and Winter magic. Even though she used it for darker purposes, her power was pure. Not many can say they have a gift from two goddesses. Not to mention, you are bound for life to one of Brighid's blessed. What would make you think you are any less powerful than Tannus?"

"He's older, stronger, and immortal. Also, he has the backing of the Council." I exhaled a shaky breath.

"Yes, the Council," he said with a slight chuckle. "They do always appear to support whatever my brother wants. Pity, it is all just nodding and agreement."

"Your brother?" Meg interrupted.

"Yes, Tannus is my brother." Faramond nodded.

"I didn't know. Are there any other relatives we should be aware of?" I asked

"Sarika is my sister. There are many things you do not know about our world, Mara."

"So, if the Council doesn't have real power, who is strong enough to stop Tannus?" I asked.

"Tannus isn't in charge of anyone. His ability to convince others that he is the most powerful of the Gods is his truest talent." Faramond's eyes blazing with anger. "Do not misunderstand my words. Tannus does have great magic, but he is fallible. As he has demonstrated with Alaunius, he is quick to react, and this impulsivity has come back to bite him later."

"Why does Arianolwyn stand by him if he killed her lover? Is it only because he restored Alaunius to life?" I questioned. *More half answers... more riddles.*

"I can't speak for my niece, but I believe she is wise in playing the good daughter and keeping in Tannus' good graces. As they say, 'keep your friends close and your enemies closer,'" Faramond said with a sly smile.

"If you can't stop him and the Council won't, who can I ask for help?"

"I believe the Council will do what is best for this domain. What this means, I'm not sure? If your child holds the absolute key to keeping the balance, I cannot stop it. However, there must be a way for you to raise your child and allow her to fulfill her destiny." Faramond's handsome face lined with concern.

"So, you know how to make this happen?" I asked.

"I find it best to not interfere. I know you're strong enough to find a solution that will be a win-win for all," he said.

"Livia said you, once, defeated Tannus. How did you do it?" Meg prodded.

"Yes, there was a time," he said, looking off into the distance. "My daughter does love to tell stories of her father's great power. Livia has been terribly busy with her loom and, like Arianolwyn, the threads do speak to her."

"What exactly are the threads?" I asked. Being patient and not demanding he tell me how to save my child was becoming impossible.

"All the possibilities and 'what ifs' of the world. The strings of decision and action are bound to us and connect each other. One slight decision can change the path for many."

"If there was a time when you defeated Tannus, how did you do it?" I blurted out.

Faramond's face fell.

I've caused him pain. Now, he'll never tell me, I thought bitterly.

The seconds ticked by before he finally spoke. His face had changed from hurt to anger. "My battle with my brother will do little to help you. You will know what is right when the time comes, Mara. There is nothing more you can do until then. You must learn, there is no sorrow for yesterdays and tomorrows. We have only our todays to live for."

I felt frustrated by his inability to answer me. *What am I going to say to him to make him help me? Until you save my child? No promises were made by him to stop it, only to support me.*

"Can you, at least, tell me how you stopped him? Even if it won't help my child?" I pleaded.

"If you give me one of the beet deviled eggs, I will share my story. And, maybe, some of the raspberry iced tea would loosen my lips," Faramond said with a wry grin.

"You may be pushing it," I teased, smirking back.

With a loud laugh, he said, "There is no doubt you are Mae's grandchild."

Accepting one of the purple eggs with a star-shaped center, he popped it into his mouth. After taking a long, slow drink of the iced tea, he set the glass down and, once again, stared off into the distance. "Now, I will share my story."

CHAPTER
TWENTY-SIX

Clouds covered the sky and blocked out the sun. Meg took my hand and squeezed it tightly as everything quickly went black. Out of the darkness, a luminous orb appeared. Suddenly, the bright light exploded.

I held my sister tighter as threads of gold rushed around us. It brushed my skin, leaving pinpricks of electricity. It was so intense that I closed my eyes, hoping to stop the bile from rising in my throat. After several seconds of cleansing breaths, I opened my eyes and we had transported to the middle of a forest.

Faramond stood before me. A gold glow emitted from him as he spoke. "Tannus and I were born with the responsibility of being the Guardians of the Afterlife. In the beginning, we reveled in our duties. Escorting souls to the next realm was satisfying for the first four hundred years, but it, then, became mundane."

I squinted my eyes, trying to find my sister. She was gone. *Am I in another realm?*

"On one of our soul deliveries, we came across a group of people like none we had encountered before. Tannus and I had spent little time getting to know the mortals until we found them." Faramond's voice grew louder, pulling me back to him.

Sounds of people laughing and music rang through the air. Faramond pointed across the way towards the noise. "You know where my children were held and where they are now. But, now, you need to know where they came from."

With those words, he faded away and Meg was by my side. She was wearing a flowing white blouse with an aqua and purple skirt. A matching scarf wrapped around her head, letting loose brown curls flow. My brow wrinkled in confusion at her appearance.

"What are you wearing, Meg," I gasped.

"What are *we* wearing?" My sister laughed, lifting my arm and shaking it. The row of bracelets, now, adorning my wrist softly clinked.

Before I could understand what was going on, we were swept up into a crowd of young girls dressed in similar clothing. One of the women grabbed our hands and pulled us into their circle of dancers. With the dark eye makeup and deep burgundy lips, Meg blended in with the exotic women.

The men around us were more reserved in their dress, wearing dark pants, a white shirt, and vests. However, their appearance didn't match their robust behavior. They were loud and passionate. One man jumped into the middle of the circle and began to kick his feet high. As the crowd clapped and cheered, another man would take his place.

My eyes widened as Faramond jumped from the sea of people and landed in front of one of the dancers. He delighted the group with his exuberance. He flipped, jumped, and clapped to the music. The group cheered and demanded more, to which he eagerly obliged.

Suddenly, a big smile crossed over his face and he stopped. He narrowed his eyes at something and walked away from the dance.

My eyes flicked towards the target of Faramond's interest. He was approaching a woman who emitted a glow of joy and happiness. I could see why he was attracted to her. She was a beauty with caramel hair flowing down her back and violet eyes that twinkled with both compassion and mischief.

"That's Theodosia," Meg whispered.

I frowned at her, not knowing what she meant.

"From the statue," my sister clarified. "Faramond's wife."

"Oh," I said, suddenly wanting to look away. It felt like an intrusion to witness what was clearly their *love at first sight*.

A light flashed, and we were transported, again. Meg stood at a butcher table with a pestle in her hand.

"The herbs won't grind themselves, ladies," an old woman said to us. She took the pestle from Meg and ground purple petals into a fine powder. "Like this. Come along, chav. We cannot sell our magic if we do not make it, can we?"

Intrigued, I asked, "What will we be making today?"

"Have you gone, prost?" The woman laughed. "What we always make."

Meg's face grew a sly smile, and she said, "Please, tell us, again, about how we learned our great magic."

The old woman beamed and squeezed Meg's cheek. "You'll go far with this inquisitive mind. Sit, the tonics can wait. Gather, I'll tell you the story of the bird woman and why she granted her blessings upon us – her iubit."

As she settled on a chair, the girls began to circle around her. Meg and I sat close together.

"On one stormy eve, our caravans stopped to rest and replenish our energy," the old woman began. "As our people slept, my mother, Penelope, heard what she described as 'the painful chatter of a small bird'. Leaving the comfort of her warm bed, she searched the forest until she found the small brown bird."

The old woman had a fond expression as she recalled, "Mother, once, told me it was the most pitiful thing she had seen in her whole life. Scooping up the bird, she checked it carefully for injury, though she could see nothing wrong. Penelope carried the seemingly injured creature to the campfire, where she fed it a bit of bread before wrapping it gently in the layers of her skirt. As the bird nestled in her lap, Penelope told the stories of our people that had been passed on from generation to generation."

I glanced at Meg, briefly meeting her eyes before the old woman's voice drew us back to her story.

"As the morning light filled the sky, my mother realized the small bird was not breathing. Tears streamed down her face as she pleaded with the creature to move. Sadly, it did not live through the night." The old woman frowned. "Penelope ran as fast as she could to her mother and begged her to perform the ceremonial *Passing of the Spirit* ritual. Seeing the pain in her child's eyes, my grandmother agreed and called for everyone to join her. All came willingly to honor the lost spirit."

I wasn't sure if I was more emotional because of my pregnancy, but I was struck with an intense sadness. I glanced at Meg long enough to catch her wipe her eye. *She's touched by the loss, too*, I realized.

"As the blessing ended," the old woman said, "the strangest thing happened. The lifeless bird began to glow and change as it rose into the air above Penelope. The transformation continued until finally a glorious blue-chested bird expanded its wings, displaying a fan of feathers. The plumes were silver with the blue and green eyelike circles. Slowly lowering to the ground, the once dead bird changed into a breathtaking woman with bird features."

There was a collective gasp from the group of listeners.

"Kneeling before my mother, the strange woman asked, 'Why did you stay with an injured bird of no relevance to you?' Penelope's eyes welled with tears as she answered, 'I was taught that all life deserves to be treasured. We were put on this earth to share our love and help each other.'"

The girls around me murmured in agreement as Meg turned to regard me. With glossy eyes, she smiled warmly and nodded her understanding.

Silence fell as the old woman resumed her tale. "The bird woman stood and faced the amazed crowd. 'I am Sarika, the immortal daughter of Kinema, Mother Earth,' she announced."

A young girl's breath caught. Holding her hand against her chest, she asked, "She's a goddess?"

The old woman nodded, and said, "The crowd fell to their knees before her, but Sarika responded, 'Rise my friends. The teachings of your people and the selfless love of Penelope have touched me.'"

More murmurs circulated through the audience.

"Hesitantly, they stood, one by one, as the goddess decreed, 'From this day forward, you will bear the gift of sight and illusion.'" The old woman raised her arms and spread out her hands as they imagined Sarika might have done. "'Your vision of the Afterlife will bring peace to the living. My gift of illusion will aid you in your travels. This should be used for protection and never to cause harm.'"

The gathered listeners bobbed their heads while a few vocalized their concurrence.

Smiling with approval, the old woman added, "Each of the travelers began to emit a lavender light from the hands as the immortal, Sarika, disappeared."

The door opened, interrupting the story and Theodosia stepped into the room. Again, I noticed there was something special about her. "They always love your stories, Bunica," she said to the old woman, kissing her on the cheek.

"What makes you smile so brightly, today?" Meg asked with a cunning smile.

Theodosia shrugged. "Faramond has asked me to marry him."

"And?" one of the girls asked, her voice booming with excitement.

Her smile grew even brighter as Theodosia exclaimed, "I said yes."

Soon, she was surrounded by giggly girls shouting questions and hugging her. The exciting moment was halted by a thunderous crashing sound from outside the makeshift home. Theodosia rushed to the window.

"Oh no. Stay here," the woman warned as she fled the building.

Interested to see what was going on, everyone ran to the window to investigate what made such a sound.

Outside, I watched in horror as Tannus threw a punch, sending Faramond flying through the air. He crashed into the building and it collapsed around us. Thankfully, the temporary structure was made of such light materials that no one was hurt.

Bunica led us out of the rubble and away from the violence. From a safe distance, we observed the two gods as they punched and slapped each other. The power of their fight was momentous. Mountains and a dry lake were formed from their thrown bodies.

"Tannus, you're being unreasonable," Faramond said, holding his hands out in front of him in a halting gesture.

"You cannot marry a mortal," Tannus said, removing his mortal glamour. The god stood over six feet tall with rippling muscles over golden skin. His jet-black hair glistened, and his golden eyes burned with anger.

"I love Theodosia and I will be true to her. She *will* be my wife, brother," Faramond replied, losing his glamour and revealing a golden hair version of his sibling.

Battered and bleeding, Faramond begged his brother to come to his senses. "I don't want it to end this way, Tan. We are guardians. We are brothers."

Raising his hand into the sky, Tannus pulled down a claymore. The sword was filled with the power of the atmosphere and crackled with the electricity of lightning. Swinging wildly, he struck. With one hit, he knocked Faramond down. I grabbed Meg's arm to stop her from running towards the god.

"You can't interfere. This is a memory," I whispered.

With a darkness in his eyes, Tannus loomed over Faramond's fallen body. "You will regret your choice, brother." Once again, he reached into the sky. "Lightning!" he cried and returned with a sparking bolt.

"No," Theodosia screamed.

Tannus' eyes glanced at the woman for the briefest moment and Faramond was able to pick up the weapon. With one deadly swing, he struck Tannus, knocking him down. Faramond lifted the weapon as if planning to drive it through his brother's heart, but Theodosia threw herself over the fallen god.

"Do not do this, Faramond. I cannot let you make a decision that will haunt you for the rest of my life," she pleaded.

Faramond dropped the blade and held out his hand to her. "You're right, my love." Facing the crowd, he said, "Friends, I ask your forgiveness for our deceit. The time I have lived with you has been the best of my life. I ask for your permission to stay amongst you, even though I am an immortal."

The crowd was silent as Bunica hobbled towards him. "We've welcomed the brothers into our home. Through the years, you've shown us love and respect. Tannus, though you've been a respected friend, these actions are not of our ways. We ask you to leave our home. We will follow you, Faramond...our new kingdom of Eftir Forest."

"This is not over, brother," Tannus snarled, then faded away.

The air went black, again, and we were transported to the inside of the Eftir Forest lodge. It was filled with the villagers we had first met, but many looked much older. Bunica sat hunched over on a chair, telling a story to girls who listened attentively.

"And, the eight sons and four daughters of our beloved Theodosia have, themselves, married and had children of their own. The gift from our great goddess has been passed on, generation to generation, while being strengthened by the Guardian god. Yes, my little Miezitari, Faramond has named you well. In honor of our Goddess Sarika and at the side of our beloved Golden King, we will lead the passed souls onto the Afterlife forevermore."

Meg nudged me as she saw Theodosia enter. Her hair was wild, and she looked panicked. When Faramond pulled her out of the room, Meg and I slipped away from the group and followed the direction they went.

"She has lied. Tannus is not planning to attack you. She is doing it from inside our home," Theodosia hissed.

"Slow down, love," Faramond said. "What about the Miezitari – who have gone missing? I can find no trace as to where they went. Are you sure you are not mistaken?"

"She lied. She's not here to strengthen our magic, but rather, she's stolen our people to feed her own. We were naïve to trust your great niece. We have invited her into our home and blindly allowed her to convince us that Tannus became cruel and heartless, not just jealous. Snowystra is the true threat."

"How do you know this?"

"I followed her, tonight. She entered a portal that leads to a winter land. See?" Theodosia handed him a ball of packed snow. "She has monstrous spiders, which she's sacrificing to consume their hearts. Our people are being kept in tunnels underground. She's starving and beating them, Faramond."

Faramond's eyes blazed. He stormed back into the main room. "Where is my niece?" he demanded.

"Are you looking for me?" Snowystra purred as she stepped into view.

"What have you done?" he bellowed.

"I have done as I promised. I am strengthening your magic. Now, you can fulfill your part of the deal. Make me your queen. Theodosia has served her purpose by giving you many children. Kill her and I will serve by your side." Snowystra's eyes glowed madly from her dark magic.

"You're insane," Faramond growled and pointed towards the door. "Leave, now, and I will spare you."

Snowystra threw her head back and laughed. "Oh, I will leave, Uncle, but you are a fool. You will regret how you have treated me."

Meg and I waited anxiously, knowing what was to come would be horrible. I wanted this vision to end, but there seemed no way out of it. Silently, we waited in one of the small rooms outside the main hall. The sound of screams told us our wait would, soon, be over.

"Nooooo!" the pain-filled cry of Faramond echoed through the Lodge.

Instinctually, we ran towards the sound of screams and cries for help.

"Wait! Meg, this is horrible. We know what happens. We can't go in there," I said, stopping my sister.

"We'll hide over there," she whispered.

Slipping inside, Meg guided me to a dark corner of the dimly lit room. Bodies were scattered, confirming the dark goddess's savage attack had begun. In the center of the room, Snowystra jumped onto one of the tables clutching a bloody dagger.

"You see the power I hold. Your god lays dead alongside those who were foolish enough to question me. I am your queen. Your only god!" Like a wild animal, she leapt onto the floor and grabbed one of the nearby women. Her voice was filled with madness as she held the blade against the crying women's neck. "Will come with me willingly, or do you want to face the same fate as them?"

The woman trembled. "Yes, Goddess, I will follow you."

Snowystra released the woman and turned towards the crowd. With a wicked grin, she said, "Dead guardians cannot deliver souls to the Afterlife, can they?" When no one answered, she screamed, "Can they?"

The crowd shook their heads. Murmurs of "No, Goddess" rumbled through the room.

Smoothing her hair, she sweetly smiled. "Good...good...now, come along. I will show you what a true god can do."

Reluctantly, the Miezitari followed her.

Snowystra was too distracted by herding the frightened people out of the building to see who she had left behind. Surrounded by death, Livia fell to her knees and pleaded for her father to be returned. For her people to be saved.

After many painful minutes, Sarika appeared. "I cannot undo what has been done, Niece, but of his death, a champion will return."

Faramond's body began to writhe and turn as it transformed. With a blinding light, he was lifted, and a skeleton man stood before Livia.

"She must never know who I am, daughter," the corpse rasped.

"What is this?" Snowystra snarled. Standing in the doorway, she glared at Livia.

"I prayed for a strong champion to protect you, Winter Goddess," Livia said, kneeling before her. Faramond followed suit.

"The gods have spoken. They have acknowledged that I am the most powerful," Snowystra cried with delight. Walking towards the newly formed Faramond, she ordered, "Rise, Mortorcus. You will stand by my side as I reclaim everything I lost."

My heart broke watching him accept her hand. He was forced to pretend that the creature who had killed his family would have his protection.

The images of the Miezitari faded and we were returned to the picnic table. We sat in silence, the tragedy of the situation sinking in. We shared a common pain — one inflicted by a mad goddess.

Faramond finally broke the reticence. "My powers were weakened. I was a shell of the god I had been. I served in the shadows, unable to comfort my people. As time went by, my strength grew, but my small attempts to stop her failed." Faramond's voice cracked. "When Cole was brought to Snowstrum, a message was sent by Sarika that the curse would, soon, be lifted and that the Butterfly held the answer to our freedom. And, then you came, Mara."

"Thank you for sharing your story with us, Faramond," I said, wiping away the tears that slowly leaked from my eyes. "I'm only sorry that I couldn't have done something earlier."

"There was nothing more you could do. There is no sorrow for yesterdays. We have our todays and tomorrows to live for."

CHAPTER
TWENTY-SEVEN

F aramond stood and clapped his hands together. "Enough sadness for the past, tonight is the Fiore Valle. We will eat, drink, dance, and be merry."

"Dance?" Meg asked. "I didn't know anything about a dance."

Looking towards the sky, Faramond frowned. "The event is probably underway without us. Gather your things and come right away. I will go ahead and speak to someone about this oversight."

I noticed, for the first time, that the sky had taken on a brilliant lavender color as the apricot sun began its descent. The warm breeze was filled with the sweet fragrance of the blooming trees. Meg's surprise party should be prepared, and everyone should be waiting anxiously for her.

"We should start back," I obeyed, gathering our picnic basket.

"I can't believe we didn't know anything about a dance. I'm a mess," Meg said, not hiding her irritation.

"We'll go back to our room and get ready," I soothed. "Don't worry. You always look picture perfect."

Brushing off her sour mood, Meg linked her arm through mine. "This has been a nice day, Mar. I'm sorry I was testy. We'll need to spend many more days like this together."

"We will," I agreed.

As we walked towards the cottages, I had an uneasy feeling. My mind raced. Faramond wouldn't help me. I'd be on my own in finding a way to stop Tannus. A tightening in my stomach caused me to stop and gasp.

"Are you ok?" Meg asked, worry lining her emerald eyes.

"Just a cramp," I said, rubbing my stomach. "All good. It has already passed."

Meg's eyes widened. "If you've anymore, let me know immediately."

"We just sat too long. You're always telling me to keep moving because it's good for my pregnancy," I said, dismissing her.

I didn't need to appease her concerns for long before Christina met us. "Faramond told me you weren't aware of the event, tonight. I will speak to Dunn about his oversight," she said. "Come with me and we'll get you ready."

CHAPTER
TWENTY-EIGHT

Christina led us through an area of the woods I hadn't explored, yet. The trees around us had long silver vines hanging from them. After a short walk, we came to a house. It was a grander version of the homes in the main area and it emitted an iridescent glow. I wondered how we hadn't seen it for miles away.

"Where are we?" I asked.

"This is Faramond's private cottage. He told me to take you here," Christina explained. "It's the last of the Kingdom's original structures."

Inside the house, I was surprised to find a quite modest home with cozy furniture. Clearly, a family had once lived here. Christina led us down a long hallway into a master bedroom. The room was lavished with gold accents and a large sitting area. One of the walls held a picture of Faramond and Theodosia.

I met the penetrating gaze of the queen's violet eyes and was convinced she was watching me. The intensity of her stare made me uncomfortable and I quickly directed my attention towards Meg, who had slipped in next to me.

"Theodosia was so beautiful," Meg said in a hushed voice.

"Yes, she was an exceptional woman," Christina answered. "Follow me, we can pick out something for you to wear."

The large walk-in closet had so much clothing to choose from, but I was confident there'd be nothing in my expanded size. I'd seen the slender physique of Faramond's wife.

"Let's pick out a dress for you both," Christina suggested.

Meg excitedly searched through the dresses, oohing and ahhing.

"I'm not sure any of these will fit me, right now." I frowned.

"The queen was pregnant many times, Mara. Of course, there'll be something for you in here. See, this would be perfect." Christina held out a silver chiffon gown. The fitted bodice ended just below the bust before transforming into a flowing skirt. It reminded me of something a Grecian goddess would wear.

"Thank you for thinking of clothes for the evening. In my excitement, I hadn't considered what she would wear," I said softly. "Are you sure it's ok for us to be here? Will Faramond mind if we wear these?" I asked, realizing we were raiding the closet of the God's deceased beloved.

"He told me to bring you here." Christina chuckled. "He insisted that Theodosia would be sad if her lovely garments weren't enjoyed. She loved to bring the women back here to prepare for events."

As Christina helped me dress, I felt more confident, like I was a young woman, again. She smiled as she twisted my hair up.

"You don't have to do this for me anymore, Christina," I said. "You're not my servant."

"No, I'm not, but I am your friend," she replied, squeezing my shoulders. "And, we both know, if you try and fix your hair, I'll just have to redo the mess you create to make you look presentable."

"Have you been speaking to my sister?" I laughed.

"How does this look?" Meg asked, appearing in the closet doorway.

My heart stopped. The little girl who used to play dress up had grown and was no longer a child. She wore a ball gown with a wide skirt and small purple flowers on the hem. The bodice, covered in bright crystals, sparkled and changed to the same iridescent color as the house. The waist had a green belt that, upon closer inspection, I could see was a vine. The creeper was fresh and looked as if it had just been pulled off a plant.

"Meg, this is perfect for you," I gushed. "You look so grown up."

"I know. It was like it was left here for just me," she said in a hushed voice.

"Come, sit and I will fix your hair, too." Christina patted the chair.

Meg beamed as our friend easily manipulated her fine hair.

Her excitement pleased me. "You'll be the most beautiful girls at the dance, tonight," I praised.

When she finished putting a bit of makeup on us both, Christina said, "You're both ready. Let's go."

"Wait, what about you?" Meg asked. "You need to get dressed, too."

Selecting a crimson gown, I handed it to her. "Here, put this on, and then Meg'll fix your hair and makeup. Unless you want me to try?"

Christina wore a look of surprise. I was certain the time she'd spent in Snowstrum as a servant would take many years for her to forget. It pained me to realize her life had been filled with such cruelty that kindness surprised her.

Meg said, "Come on. We don't want to be late for my first ball."

When we were all dressed, Christina led us through the forest on a paved path. We arrived at the cottages, seeing the center of the communal area lit up with fairy lights. A bandstand had been set up and the musicians were playing soft music. When they saw us, the band played a song that sounded like a royal announcement was about to be made.

"The lady of honor has arrived," one of the musicians called to the crowd. "Don't be shy, Meg. Come forward."

My sister stared in amazement at the smiling crowd.

"Happy Birthday, Meg," I said, kissing her on the cheek. "Go on. Tonight is your night."

CHAPTER
TWENTY-NINE

Meg had disappeared from the party with Dunn. Just as I became worried enough to go find her, she returned alone with a wistful look on her face.

"I need to go check on Meg," I said to Cole.

"No, leave her be, Mar. She'll talk to you if she wants to. She has a good head on her shoulders. Trust her," Cole replied.

"I know, I know. I just don't want her to get hurt."

"I don't think you need to worry about that. I spoke to Dunn, today, and asked him to step back. She's young. If they're meant to be together, they will be," Cole said.

"You're practicing being the protective father already?" I asked.

"I waited many years for the girl I love to admit she loved me, too," he said, kissing me.

"You're not being fair. I told you I loved you many times," I insisted.

"Come on, Mar. You were always pushing me away. Anytime it became too real, you would retreat," he said, taking my hand.

He was right. I did keep my guard up with him. My magic had been taken and I didn't know why I had such an empty feeling. My father was thought to be dead and my mother disappeared. I was always waiting for the next person to leave me. I'd done my best to keep him at a distance, even though my heart wanted nothing more than to be with him forever.

"Don't be mad, Mara. Let's enjoy the party you worked so hard to plan." Cole batted his puppy dog eyes at me. "Come dance with me."

Relenting, I let Cole lead me to the dance floor. A soft love song was playing.

The party went on for many hours with Meg dancing and laughing with the Miezitari. Dunn joined the group, but he kept his distance from her. Still, he watched her every move. Even though Cole had already talked to him, I needed to speak with him myself.

"Dunn, can I steal you away for a minute?" I asked.

"Always," he answered.

"Not here," I said. "Let's find a place away from the crowd."

I led him away from any listening ears. "Meg's only sixteen years old. She isn't ready to be in a committed relationship...let alone, one with an immortal."

Dunn flinched. "I know that, Mara. I've spoken to her already."

"You did?" I watched his eyes to see if he was telling me the truth.

"I did. I told her that, for now, all we can be is friends. When she is older, if her feelings are still as strong, we can talk about being more. Until then, I have pledged to protect her. As I guarded you in Snowstrum, I have, now, promised my loyalty to Meg."

"She is so young and you're—"

"Very old? Yes, I guess I am, but in many ways, I'm as young as she is. I knew very little about the horror of the Sephorian Desert and I was lucky to be sent to the cottages instead of the tunnels until shortly before you arrived. The Goddess paid no attention to me, for which I am grateful," Dunn explained. "I promise you, my intentions are pure, Mara. Your sister is a remarkable girl and will, one day, be an extraordinary woman. Until then, I vow, there will be only friendship between us."

"Thank you for understanding," I said.

"You're very different than your sister...you're more cautious," Dunn said. "Meg told me losing so many people had reminded her that life needed to be lived and that waiting for the perfect moment to happen could be throwing away happiness."

While I was pushing people away from my sadness and guarding my heart, Meg was embracing the world. All the passion and spirit she had inside her amazed me. "She is quite wise, isn't she?"

Nodding, he agreed, "She is. But I always keep my word."

"If that were to change, I hope the two of you would come speak with me," I said.

A cold wind blew from behind me and I felt Snowystra's icy breath on my neck, "The boy will lie to you. You're just jealous of the love he has for her. Love like Cole has for me."

"Are you ok, Mara?" Dunn wrapped his arms around me as if I was falling. "You've gone white."

The warmth of his embrace lifted the chill that had filled me. "Yes, just a long day. Let's return to the party."

CHAPTER THIRTY

"Wake up, Mara," a rich male voice whispered in my ear.

Groggily, I opened my eyes to see Kai was inches from my face. When I went to speak, he cupped his hand over my mouth and shook his head. I nodded, understanding he wanted me to remain silent.

Then, he uncovered my mouth and crooked his finger, motioning for me to follow him.

Cole slept soundly as I left the bed to follow Kai. I smiled down at my sleeping husband. *How much I love you.* I thought.

When we were in the hallway, I asked, "What's going on Kai?"

"Not here," he whispered, taking my hand.

A warmth filled me as our fingers touched and I shivered in surprise.

Kai smiled at me and led me through the corridor. When we stepped out into the courtyard, it was still twinkling with the party lights.

"Why are we here?"

Kai pulled me into his arms and pressed his lips against mine.

"No," I said, pushing him away. "What do you think you're doing?"

"I can't pretend anymore, Mara. You're the only one I think about. Thoughts of you consume me. I know you feel the same way, but you're being loyal to the promises you've made."

"You're wrong. I love Cole and that's why I'm with him. I want to be with him and to raise our baby together," I said, rubbing my extended belly.

Resting his hand on top of mine, his eyes flickered with burning embers of gold. "He'll only hurt you, again. His healing is an act. Mara, I will care for you and your baby. Come away with me, tonight. I can protect her. I know how to keep your daughter safe."

"Kai, I..." my words were halted by his soft lips touching mine.

The tingling sensation rushed through me, again. I found myself unable to deny how I felt and returned his kiss. *I can't. I love Cole and I'm carrying his child.*

Kai's arms wrapped around me, pulling me closer to him. He broke away as our embrace deepened, and I sighed in displeasure as his mouth left mine. I wanted it to never end. His lips returned for a moment to tease me and gently trailed down my neck.

He'll love and care for me. Cole isn't safe for my daughter or me. Don't lie to yourself. You've always wanted him. You love Kai. My jumbled mind played with the idea of being his.

"I'll go with you," I rasped.

Our eyes locked. I could see the relief and joy my words gave him.

"I'll make you so happy, Mara."

Our lips met, again, and I let myself accept the love I felt for Kai. The love I'd always felt. With him, I would never want for anything and my daughter would be safe. He trailed his warm tongue slowly down my neck.

"Isn't our Fire Boy delicious," Snowystra's words whispered in my ears.

His fingers unbuttoned my nightgown, exposing my breasts. His hands were no longer tender, but rough, and his lips burned my skin. This was the cold sting of ice, not the warm pleasure of Fire. I tried to push him away from me, but his grip became tighter.

"You weren't foolish enough to think I could keep you safe on my own, were you? This time, you'll rule Snowstrum with me by your side. We'll raise the Winter, together, under the guidance of the Goddess."

Kai released me and cruelly smiled as I covered myself. His eyes were milky white. He wrinkled his nose at me as if I disgusted him. "I promised you I'd bring *her*. She will fix everything she destroyed."

Holding out his hand, *she* stepped out from behind a statue of Livia. *Snowystra.*

Had she been there all this time? She stroked his cheek with her long, silver nails. "You've proven yourself worthy to be the Shah."

"We don't need her," Kai said, roughly grabbing and kissing her deeply.

The dark goddess laughed and pushed him away. "Don't be a fool. You will make powerful children, together." Snowystra turned her attention towards me.

I was exposed.

She was before me in the same form as the first time I'd seen her. Her snow-white skin shimmered as if she'd been dusted with frost. She wore the same dress, long and flowing, with the plunging crystal-beaded neckline falling below her belly button.

I tried to escape, but Kai grabbed my wrist and forced me into his arms. "She'll submit, this time. Won't you, darling?"

"No!" I screamed, thrashing against him. "She's dead. This isn't real."

Laughing, he held me tighter.

I screamed.

"Stop, Mara!" Kai demanded, squeezing me tighter. "Mara, stop."

I beat my fists against him, struggling against his hold.

"Mara. Mara. Stop, Mara." His lips were moving, but it was Cole's voice.

"Stop, Mar."

Blinking, everything around me changed. Kai was gone. Snowystra was gone. I found the arms tightly wrapped around me were Cole's, not the Fire elemental's.

"Is this what you've been dealing with because of me? Have I done this to you?" Releasing his hold on me, Cole cupped my face between his hands. "Mara, you need to be honest. No more secrets. Tell me what's really going on."

"I think Snowystra is back."

"She can't be." Cole's eyes blazed with anger. "She's gone. Why are you saying this?"

"I hear her...see her – everywhere. She comes to my dreams. I think she puts Kai in them, too," I confessed.

"Why would she bring Kai into your dreams, Mara?"

"She wants to hurt us. She wants me to be confused. Why would I want to leave you for anyone? Cole, you're sweet and loving."

"Predictable and boring," Snowystra taunted.

"You were my strength all of my life."

"Until you showed how weak you are," the dark goddess hissed.

"I want to spend my forever with you, Cole."

"Boring. Familiar. Safe. Not the passionate life Kai would offer." Snowystra's face appeared on Cole's body.

"Tell me what you dreamed, Mar," my husband's voice was shaky.

"She's around me, right now, Cole," I admitted.

As I described it, my husband's face paled. He sat down, dropping his head into his hands.

I had hurt him. I didn't have to tell him about Kai. I could've lied to protect him. He was sweet and safe, but I always wanted the security he represents. *Oh, Goddess, am I like my mother? Do I only want what I can't have?*

No! It was Snowystra messing with my mind. Her magic ran through me. She was forcing me to destroy everything and everyone I loved. Now, Cole would never trust me.

The silence was killing me. I sat down beside him, touching him gently.

"Are you afraid to be with me?" Cole's amber eyes glistened.

"Oh no. It was a bad dream. I don't want to be with Kai! She's planting feelings I don't have. I love you, Cole, and only you."

"How long has this been happening?" he asked.

I didn't want to tell him. I didn't want him to feel any more pain.

"It's ok, Mar. Tell me the truth."

"Since you left," I blurted out. "Either she has returned or I'm losing my mind. You must believe me. I want to be with you, and only you."

Cole's shoulders slumped, and he sighed deeply. "I trust you. She's gone, Mar. This isn't your fault. Livia was right. The stress of everything...everything I caused...it's too much for anyone to bear."

"We're being ridiculous. She is gone. I'm not in love with Kai. Cole, no more blaming yourself. This is finished – tonight. We're going to see Liv," I said sharply.

CHAPTER
THIRTY-ONE

Livia decided I was hallucinating. She insisted rest would prove to be the best cure. The next few days were uneventful as I followed her advice, and sleep did seem to help.

Livia had been right. The voice of Snowystra was gone. I didn't know if it had been her words or mine running through my head, but I was grateful for their retreat.

One morning, after Livia had agreed I was well enough to leave my bed, Cole and I settled into Faramond's den. We were snuggled by a fire when my sister came bursting into the room.

"Anna had a baby girl," Meg exclaimed. She was red-faced and breathless. "Masha is so excited to have a baby sister, now. I can't wait until Zee is born."

"Zee? We've given her a nickname already?" I smiled.

"Well, it was just one of the ideas I've been playing with. I'm just so excited to see her. There are so many things to show her in this world. I can't wait," Meg said, rapidly firing all of her thoughts at me.

"I'm ready to meet my daughter, too," I admitted, rubbing my belly. "It'll be nice to see who's been beating me up."

"Oh, I almost forgot," my sister announced, handing me a silver scroll. Then, in a hushed voice, she added, "This is from Livia." She plopped onto the couch and wiggled between us. "Go on, then."

When I didn't move fast enough, Meg took the scroll and unrolled it. She held it out, reading out loud:

Kinema Delli
Mother of Tannus and Faramond
Holds the answer you seek
Send her your prayers

As she read the words, they disappeared from the scroll.

I could feel the heat emitting from it and when I grabbed it from her, the metal burned my fingertips. Dropping it, I cried out, "It's gone, and I don't know what it means."

"Kinema?" Cole asked.

"Did Livia say anything else?" I blew on my fingers to cool them.

Shaking her head, my sister frowned. "She just asked me to deliver it. Was there anything on it that might help? I can go ask Livia to write the message, again."

"No, Meg. Let's not disturb her. She's been told to not interfere. She has done enough for us," I replied.

"But we don't know anything," Meg complained.

"We do. We know we need to find Faramond's mother. I have no idea where she is, or how she can help, but we need to find out," I said.

"Let's go to the library. We've had luck finding what we needed in archives in the past," Cole suggested.

He was right. Libraries were magic for my family. The first meeting of the elementals and my great-grandmother was in one. When Meg had been kidnapped, we were able to find the building plans of the Drygen Mansion with help from the same elementals in the exact library. *Will the key to saving my child be in a book?*

The bibliotheca was in the back of the lodge, near Faramond's bedroom. The hallway leading us there had more of Livia's tapestries. These told the story of the building and destruction of Eftir Forest. I wondered if she would add more to show their return.

We found the door open. The room, lined with thousands of leather-bound books reaching up to the vaulted ceiling, was overwhelming. Looking around, I felt exhausted already. There was too much to go through.

"Where do we even start?" I asked. "We should just go and ask him."

"You know the Gods only speak in riddles. Stay here," Cole said, pointing towards a chair. "I have an idea."

Sitting down at a round table, I watched Cole saunter through the stacks. Trailing his fingers along the spines, he would occasionally stop and pick one up, leaf through his find, and then deliver it to me. Most of the books he brought had the names of gods and goddesses and their powers. There were so many different deities listed that I had never heard of. Vesiatura, Goddess of Water. Besk, Messenger of the Afterlife. Sabedora, Goddess of Wisdom.

Cole returned, carrying a large burgundy book covered in odd etched symbols. He set it down on the table. A warmth emitted from it, drawing me forward.

"What is this?" I asked, my voice barely above a whisper.

"It feels like the one." Cole slid it closer to me. "See if you can open it."

Resting my hands on it, it started to hum. Quickly, I pulled away. "No, you do it."

Cole carefully opened the cover and the pages rapidly turned before slamming shut. He blinked at me in surprise and slid the publication towards me. When I tried, it reacted the same way.

"You need to tell it what you want to see." Faramond's deep voice surprised me.

"How long have you been standing there?" I questioned.

"A few minutes. You need to tell the book what you seek." Faramond pulled it towards himself. "Faramond."

The book opened to an embossed picture of the golden god. Words filled the page, telling the story of Faramond's and Tannus' birth. The next page held a proclamation by Kinema Delli. Her sons had been born to guide the dead to the next world and their sister, Sarika, would be their logic.

As it fluttered by, I saw the story Bunica had told about how the mortals became blessed by Sarika and how the brothers had stumbled into their world. It even described the brothers' tight bond and their eventual falling out. The story stopped at Faramond's death in Eftir Forest. There was no mention of his time in Snowstrum as Mortorcus.

Suddenly, the pages madly flipped, landing on the word *Uusfarah*. Under the name, there was a picture of Mortorcus. The image hovered over the pages, transforming into a butterfly before changing to the God I knew now. The words told the story of his rebirth by fire and the rebuilding of his kingdom.

"Is there something specific you are looking for?" Faramond inquired.

I closed the book. "Kinema Delli"

Instead of showing me, the book went flying off the table. Faramond watched silently as Cole picked it up.

"Show me, Tannus," Cole commanded.

The pages came to life, again, showing us Tannus' story.

"Why would we not be able to see Kinema Delli? Are we saying her name wrong?" I questioned.

"No, I don't think that would be the problem." Cole opened the book, and said, "Delli Kinema." The book shook, but it stayed on the table.

Cole rested his hand on the top of the cover and closed his eyes. Suddenly, he shouted. "Wait! I got it. The scroll said to *send* her your prayers."

Turning towards Faramond, I asked, "Why didn't you just tell us this?"

"I cannot interfere, but I can tell you the clearing in the forest is a wonderful place to pray," the Golden King said with a wink.

CHAPTER
THIRTY-TWO

By the time we left the library, the sun had started to set. The night creatures were awakening, and their noises echoed in the air. Cole led me through the forest until we came to a clearing in the middle of the pine trees.

"Call the elements, Mar," Cole said.

Nodding my head, I held my arms out. "Air, I beseech you to join me."

The wind blew hard. Instead of the silver tendrils I'd become accustomed to, small, winged creatures encircled me. One floated in front of me and I could see its catlike face on a tiny human body. It closed its eyes in a slow blink and, instinctually, I did the same. Delighted, the creature started spinning around me. Soon, the others were following it.

"Fire, your presence would be a blessing," I said, encouraged.

The circle grew warmer and winged lizards filled the air. Their forked tongues poked out of their mouths. As Cole imitated them, their wings turned fiery red and they surrounded him.

"Water," I said, trying to hold back my laughter. "Come to me."

I had called a rainstorm and we were covered with large drops of water. As they splashed onto the ground, winged seahorses appeared and rushed towards Cole.

"And, finally, I call you Earth."

The ground trembled before winged creatures burst from the soil. These had child-like faces attached to long wispy bodies.

"Now, call her, Mar," Cole whispered.

"Kinema Delli, we request—"

"It took you long enough to call me," a silky voice chided.

The air around us began to glow in kaleidoscopic color. The winged elements left us, swarming around the light. From it, a petite woman appeared. The deep sage color of her wavy locks fell over her shoulders, browning at the tips. She was breathtaking. One of the Earth beings sat on her hand.

"How interesting that my children appeared so easily for you. You must be deserving. My little Ledli would have sent them all away if you were not trusted." Kinema held her companion up and whispered something inaudible to her. Ledli quickly flew away.

"We've never seen anything like them before," Cole said.

"Your world tells stories of them. Of course, the accounts are never quite accurate. What imaginations mortals have," she replied, approaching Cole.

"I've heard the tales, but I thought they were made up," Cole admitted. When she reached him, he brashly asked, "Do you know why we called you?"

Laughing, she stroked his cheek. "Of course, I know why I'm here. You've called me because of my son." Kinema let out a long sigh. "Sadly, my sons and their descendants have been neglectful in educating their gifted. They give you the magic, but not the knowledge."

"We are ready to learn," I interrupted. "Please, tell us what we need to know."

Turning, Kinema eyed me with pity. "Oh, there is much more than I can tell you in one day. I cannot give you a lifetime of education, now. What you want to know is how to stop Tannus, but I will not interfere. There is no need for me to. You *can* stop him, Mara."

"I have no power to stop him," I argued. Tears burned my eyes.

"Oh, but you do." The corner of Kinema's mouth twitched as if she was going to smile.

"Tell me how to do it, then. Please," I pleaded.

Reaching into the air above her, Kinema Delli cupped her hand as if she was holding something fragile. Extending the palms of her hands towards us, she held a droplet of water.

"Your world is so small. You look down on the ants and think they are your tiny guests. Have you ever wondered who was looking down on you?" she asked. "Worlds inside worlds. Even the ants can do remarkable things when they work together."

"But, I'm not a god," I insisted. I was at my boiling point. The gods and goddesses seemed incapable of giving a direct answer.

"You've been given great gifts. The both of you have." Taking Cole's hand, she spoke softly, "Sweet boy, even though your gift was taken from you, you'll always bear the mark and Water will respond to you."

Putting her hand against his heart, Kinema said, "The empty void you have will, one day, be filled. The pain you still feel from the loss will be released."

Cole choked back a sob. Hanging his head, he whispered, "Thank you."

"As for you Mara, the child does bear the Winter. This does not mean she cannot live with you...if you choose wisely. There is always a way to stop a battle. My son is impulsive and scared – understandably. But even he can be reasoned with."

"And, if I can't find a way to reason with him?"

Her beautiful face became stern. "Then, you're going about it the wrong way."

My patience had ended. There was no point in hearing her out if she wasn't going to tell me what I needed to know. "Why can no one just give a straight answer to my questions?"

"You seek for others to do your work...to tell you how to live your life path. I cannot make the decisions that will control your destiny. You might need to sacrifice something to save what you want. But, the child within you is not your greatest worry. While you hide in the forest, the world around didn't stop. There are outside forces plotting against you. You should be more cautious. Worries you thought you left behind in Starten are closer than you think."

Her radiant glow was fading. "You're strong like Eliza, Mae, and Genevieve. If only you would really embrace it."

"But, I have," I insisted.

"You did stand against Snowystra, but how long did it take you to get there because of your doubts? You are your own worst enemy, Mara. The force you have inside you should be enough. You should not need to be reminded of your strength. You were raised with it. The only thing you were missing was knowledge, which I have, now, given you. Go to your family. The time for your child to be born is coming soon...but you already know this."

With those words, she faded away entirely. The air filled with specks of light and the tightness in my stomach returned.

"Mara, are you ok?" Cole asked.

"Let's go back to the cottages. I think she's right, and I should see Laura," I said.

"Is the baby coming now?" Cole asked.

"I'm not sure." I had an unsettling feeling.

"Soon. Marina, you will give birth to the child of my blood and you will restore the Shah to his power," Snowystra whispered in my ear.

Are the dark forces that Kinema talked about Snowystra? Has she somehow returned? My thoughts were halted by another sharp pain. It was so intense that it almost sent me to my knees.

CHAPTER
THIRTY-THREE

Cole and I walked back to the lodge in silence. Another contraction began and the gripping pain in my stomach halted me. Stopping to catch my breath, I closed my eyes and tried to force the feeling away. The baby wasn't supposed to come, yet. I wasn't ready for my child to be born.

"Mar, you can't tell me that you're fine. Talk to me." Cole wrapped his arm around my waist to support me.

"I think it's time," I said. Tears filled my eyes, threatening to spill over.

"Time?" Cole asked, turning ghost white. "The baby really is coming?"

As another cramp struck me, I nodded. "I think, soon."

It felt like a giant had wrapped his hands around my waist and wouldn't stop squeezing. I called the calming presence of Air and warm tendrils encircled me. After several painful seconds, the pressure lessened, and I could continue. Livia's cottage appeared in the distance and I saw my sister, standing on the porch.

Meg met us at the steps. "When was your last contraction? Has your water broke?"

I felt another strong contraction. "Right now," I gasped. "But my water hasn't broken."

"They're close together. Minutes maybe. She's been in a lot of pain," Cole said quickly. He sounded terrified.

You're not the one about to push this child out, I thought.

"Let's get you inside and comfortable," Laura called from the doorway.

They led me into the section of the house used for childbirth. The center room had a small kitchen and couches for the family of the mother to wait. Six birthing rooms around it. The cream walls of my room were adorned with Livia's tapestries, depicting women with their babies.

I was hit, again, with an intense pain. This time, a warm liquid ran down my legs. If there was ever a time I needed my grandmother, it was right now.

"I'm not ready for this," I cried. "We don't even have a plan to stop them from taking her."

"We can't worry about that, now, Mar," Cole said, hugging me.

"Stop sniveling. The Vizier would never behave like a weak Vetur." Snowystra's image replaced my husband's.

"Cole, promise me, if you have any feelings of the Shah, you'll tell me right away," I demanded.

"Mara, he's gone."

"Promise me," I insisted.

"I promise, Mar," he said. "Please, stop worrying. I won't become the Shah, again, and they're not going to take our child."

Another pain consumed me. "Air, please, stop this. I'm not ready," I whispered before I raised my voice. "We have to stop this. I can't have her, now. Give me something to delay it. Please, I need more time."

The pain inside me grew stronger and I could no longer focus. The time had come. Soon, I would have to face the truth.

"Here's another kipia stick," Malise said, offering me the brown twig.

The small amount of relief chewing the stick gave was not enough. The pain was so intense, I felt like I was going to lose consciousness and drift away.

Not now, I pleaded. Since my magic had returned, I had slipped into unconsciousness on numerous occasions only to awaken in the presence of Gods. I needed to be alert and able to protect my daughter when she was born. I didn't need to be off listening to enigmas.

Cole stopped pacing and sat beside me. Taking my hand, he said, "I'm here, Mara. I won't leave you."

As another strong contraction eased, I cried, "Where's my sister? Meg should be here."

I could hear Laura talking to me, but the words weren't making sense. I felt myself slipping away. A pungent flower held under my nose jerked me back. I felt fuzzy, but I forced myself to focus on my friend.

"On your next contraction, you're going to push," Laura instructed.

"I can't. I'm not ready." My body ignored my mind and responded to her directions. This time, I felt a forceful pressure, but it was no longer painful.

Cole held my hand and counted with Laura.

I tried to fight it, but it was inevitable. I couldn't keep my child safe inside me. A stinging sensation sent tingles through my body. *Don't let go. Don't let go.* Then, it was too late, and Laura held up my daughter before me.

"It's a boy," Laura said. "A beautiful baby boy, Mara"

"It can't be," I murmured. "I'm carrying the Winter." My mind was stunned. *A boy? My child wasn't the Winter? They were wrong. He would be safe.*

Laura set the baby with a headful of bright red hair into my arms.

"My son," I murmured, examining the small being in my arms. His skin felt so hot against mine.

The wrinkled child yowled. "It's ok. Mommy's here." I laughed through my tears. Gently, I kissed the small child on his cheek. "Was Tannus wrong? I wasn't carrying the Winter, right? A male—"

A strong contraction filled me. I gasped in surprise. A wrenching pain silenced me from asking any more questions. "Something's not right," I rasped.

Another intense pressure to push built inside me.

"Cole take the baby," Laura commanded. She poked and prodded me. As she inspected me, the corners of her mouth went down.

"What? What's wrong?" Cole asked.

"Mara, I don't know how we missed this, but you aren't done. There's another baby coming."

"Mara, you need to push, again," Laura said.

"No, you're wrong. There's only one," I cried. "Please, no. Not a girl."

This time, I was aware and present for the delivery. I wanted to fight and stop the baby from being born, but again, my body was working against me. I gave into the building pressure. With one last push, I collapsed back, closing my eyes.

Please, don't let them be right, I prayed.

I heard the cry and opened my eyes. Laura was holding a baby girl. Her hair was snow white and her pale skin sparkled.

"She is of the Winter," I whispered.

"Yes, my power has been returned." Snowystra's cackle echoed in the room.

"No, she can't be," I sobbed. "She's here to take our child."

Cole wrapped his arms around me and held me as I cried.

The birth of our children shouldn't feel like mourning a loss. I didn't want to lose another person I loved.

Releasing his hold on me, Cole swiped his pointer finger across my forehead.

When my sobs stifled, Laura gently returned the baby boy to my arms. This time, he was clean, and I could see his hair was a deep red, like my mother's.

"These are our children, Mar." Cole took the baby girl from Laura and placed her in the crook of my other arm. "And, this is our daughter. No matter what, Mara. She's ours and we'll fight like hell not to lose her."

CHAPTER
THIRTY-FOUR

Laura encouraged me to hold both babies against my skin. I wanted to resist. I wasn't ready to be a mother, but they were so tiny and helpless as they wriggled against me.

"I'm going to clean up this little one, and then she'll be back to nurse," Laura said, taking Mazy from my arms.

"Cole, will go with you?" I asked firmly.

Kissing my cheek, he whispered, "I'll watch over her, Mar."

I'm not prepared for this, I thought, staring down at my son. *How am I going to feed one baby, let alone two? If I was still the queen, I wouldn't have to take care of them. I could order Laura to look after them.*

"You're going to have to help me out," I whispered to my baby boy. "I'm afraid I'm going to be pretty bad at being a mother." Smoothing his fiery locks, I guided him.

He immediately understood what I wanted from him and quickly latched and nursed. His little body felt so warm. Guilt overcame me for my selfish thoughts of giving my babies to someone else to be cared for. I was relieved when Livia entered the room.

"Is he ok? He seems like he has a fever," I said, stroking his hair from his face.

Livia shrugged. "Can't you feel his magic pulsing through you as he feeds? Your son has strong Fire magic, Mara."

I ran my fingers gently down his back. I did feel it. His strong magic *was* pulsing throughout his body. As I looked down at my child, emotions of intense love and protection filled me. Focusing my mind on his suckling, I felt the sensation of magical threads being drawn from me.

"I do feel his magic, but it, also, feels like he's taking mine," I said softly.

"It's not surprising he would have strong Fire magic. He shared a womb with Winter," Livia rested her hand on his back. "He is only taking a small bit of yours. Don't worry, your magic will replenish and his will grow stronger. Just relax."

Mazy's wails filled the room, announcing her return. She looked even lighter being held against Laura's blue dress. Guilt filled me. The sight of my daughter should not make me feel so wary.

"He's not done, yet," I said. Shamefully, I hoped Livia would send Laura away.

Livia took Mazy from Laura and rested her in my other arm. "I know this was a surprise, but you must get used to taking care of two children at the same time, Mara. It's time to feed your daughter."

"Are you going to let the servants talk to you like that, Marina? How soon they have forgotten your power," Snowystra's cold breath whispered in my ear.

She's right. These are my magical children. I created them.

"Mazy. Remember, her name is Mazy. I will feed my daughter when I think the time is right." I glared at Livia.

Livia picked up Mazy and held her tight. Our eyes locked and her focus became intense as if she was searching my mind.

Embarrassment washed over me. *You're being rude to a friend at the advice of a dead goddess.* My face flushed with heat. "I can take her, now," I said weakly. This time, I didn't refuse Mazy when Livia placed her in my arms.

"Have you named the boy?" Livia questioned.

I shook my head and averted my eyes away from her. There'd only been one child to consider during my pregnancy. We'd talked about naming him after my grandfather, but what would you name a child whose other half would be taken from him? How could I name him after the other half of Gram? It would be wrong to separate twins. *When they take my daughter, will I have to let them take both?*

"Well...then," Livia said, "we'll leave you to bond with your babies. Call if you need me. I will be at my loom."

Her sudden departure made me wonder if she was seeing the path my children would travel. Mazy whimpered, forcing me back to the present.

"Now, now, Mazy," I said, preventing her from slipping out of my arms. "Can't you be sweet like your brother? You know I'm new at this. Can't you be patient with me?"

Where is Cole? He should be back by now. Why did he let Mazy out of his sight? Is he going to run off, again, and leave me with them? My frustration built, and I knew I needed to calm myself. My temper was not helping.

"Air, I welcome you and ask for your blessings on my children. Please, send your calming touch," I pleaded.

A wave of warm wind blew over us. The element quieted Mazy's crying. Comforted, I tried to encourage her to feed. Unlike her brother, Mazy resisted nursing. Not being able to console her was frustrating. Every time I moved her into position, she pulled away from me. After a few attempts, I realized what was wrong. Mazy *needed* to be closer to her twin.

"I hope this works," I said as I crossed their bodies.

It was only when her twin grasped her hand that she truly calmed, and I could coax her into feeding. In contrast to his heat, she was ice cold. There was a sharp stinging feeling as she began to suckle and, again, I felt like I was being drained. This time, it was different. It felt as if every ounce of my gift was being sucked out.

"I need someone's help. She's pulling too much of my magic," I called out. Gently, I held her away from my breast.

Taking away her food source upset her, and she yowled.

"Livia, please, come back. I need you," I called, again.

"I'm here. I can take her," Cole said from the doorway. Cole gently picked up Mazy. Rocking her, he kissed her cheek. "Don't worry, little one. You'll eat."

Once she was quieted, Cole tried to put her back into my arms, but I moved away.

"No, Cole," I said. "I can't feed her like this. She's hurting me. She's stripping me of my magic."

Cole paced as he rocked Mazy. Stopping, he exclaimed, "I got it. Remember how you protected your magic when you were in Snowstrum? Why don't you try and see if that helps?"

Slowly breathing, I called to my elements and asked them to conceal themselves in a shell-like barrier. I felt my power retreating. My son whimpered, and I knew he felt it leave. "Ok, I will try, again," I said, not hiding my worry. "Just stay close."

Mazy greedily latched onto me and fed. She grunted in frustration. Silently, I willed Air to nourish her. The small amount I released satisfied her. I continued to send her little tastes of the elements. When I called Fire, her feeding slowed, and she slowly drifted to sleep. Now, both children slept peacefully in my arms.

"You're beautiful, Mar," Cole said, taking our sleeping son from me. "We need to name this little guy. Do we still want to use Chester's middle name? What do you think if we name him Finn?"

"No!" I said, harsher than I had planned. "We're not naming anyone without Meg. She already missed the birth. She needs to be a part of this in some way." Bile rose in my throat as I realized she hadn't been there for the labor and delivery. "Wait. Where is Meg?"

"Your sister is insignificant," Snowystra hissed.

A queasiness overcame me and, soon, there was nothing, but darkness consuming me.

PART TWO
MEG

CHAPTER
THIRTY-FIVE

Miles had been so reckless by running off to look for Mara and Cole. Despite knowing the forest better than all of us, my foolish brother had gotten himself lost. While I marched through the forest looking for him, I realized we were going to miss our niece being born.

We had only been here a little over two months and, even though I missed Starten, I had grown to love Eftir. It was like my second home. Although I would've preferred to not be wandering around in the dark while Mara needed me.

I followed a familiar trail. I lost myself in thought, recalling the last time I had walked this way. Back then, I was still new to the forest.

"Why so quiet, Meg?" Dunn had wondered, peeling back the bark of a tree and giving it to me.

"What is that?" I asked and reluctantly accepted it. Purple beads lined the back of the husk.

Dunn tore off another piece and licked the contents. "Try it. It's sweet."

Suspiciously, I tasted the weird paste. "You aren't feeding me bugs, are you?"

Dunn threw his head back and laughed. His laughter made my heart smile. "No, I wouldn't give you insects to eat." He reached up into the tree and returned with an emerald green apple. "Are you going to tell me why you've been so quiet, today?"

When I first met Dunn, I instantly had a crush on him. His dark, brooding eyes made me want to learn more about him. Books had filled my mind with dark strangers riding into town on white horses, ready to whisk me away. I felt like mine had arrived.

Dunn was no longer a captive of Snowystra. He had changed in appearance to match his sun-filled personality. His dark hair was, now, golden brown and if the sun hit it right, it would sparkle. His sharp teeth were replaced by a brilliant white smile.

He offered me the shiny fruit. I tried to take it, but it ended up slipping out of my hands and falling to the ground. We both went for it at the same time, ending up nose to nose. For one breathless moment, I moved awkwardly close to him. I didn't want to move away, but I forced myself to do so.

"I was thinking about how happy I am here," I answered softly.

This time, Dunn gently placed the apple in my hand. When his fingers touched mine, I felt a spark of magic between us.

"Sorry," he said, stepping back.

I took a bite of the tart apple and beamed at him. "Can you tell me more about what it was like to live in Snowstrum? Not the bad parts. I want to know about the good times."

Crunching into an apple of his own, he laughed. "You're always full of questions."

"I'm sorry," I said and averted my eyes. *You're embarrassing yourself, Meg. Stop acting like a silly schoolgirl.*

"No, I like how you're so interested in the world around you, Meg." Dunn grinned. "You're a ray a'sunshine. Walk with me and I'll tell you about the world I came from."

As Dunn told me about his experience living under Snowystra's rule, my affection grew stronger for him. He was a kind man. Despite living in such a dark environment, the Winter hadn't killed the light inside him.

Not even my magic makes me feel as complete as Dunn does, I thought.

Collecting myself, I stopped. Miles was missing, and I'd been caught up in my silly daydream. Suddenly, an idea came to mind. My strong connection to Earth would help me find him. My gift was more than being able to make flowers grow. I felt connected to something larger, something mystical when I called it.

"Earth, I ask for your guidance in my search." I pressed my hand to the ground. A soft light glowed on the dark soil. I let it guide me deeper into Eftir Forest. *Miles should have used his Air magic to fly above and figure out where he was,* I thought bitterly.

"Let me go!" a voice cried out.

Twigs broke. Rustling echoed around me. I kept moving towards the noise until I saw my brother. I hid inside the skirt of a gigantic pine tree, where I could see Miles. He was struggling against a dark figure.

"Let me go, now. I don't want to live with you anymore!" Miles screamed.

"Quiet him," a deep man's voice commanded.

"Stop this nonsense, Miles. You're my son. You're a Drygen."

My blood ran cold. I knew who the voice belonged to. *Cedric Drygen.*

"Please, I don't want to live with you anymore," Miles said, slumping in defeat.

"That isn't your decision. The blood that runs through you is mine. When you're home, you'll remember what it means to be a Drygen," Cedric snarled.

"I am NOT a Drygen!" Miles screamed. "Why won't you let me be free? I'm happy where I am."

"Happiness is a luxury. You have a responsibility," Cedric said coldly.

"I will never be what you want me to be." Miles sobbed.

Cedric gripped his shoulders and violently shook his son. "You're my last connection to Eliza. You will return home with me."

"My mother would want me to live with Elliott. Do you plan to take me back to your big house to leave me alone, again? It's not like we're a family." Miles wriggled under Cedric's tight hold.

I was about to step out to protect my brother when I heard another man speak. "Do not talk to your father this way." The gruff voice sounded disgusted. "If you wouldn't have been weak, we could've taken him back years ago. Look what a spoiled brat those people made. The boy needs to be reminded who his real family is."

Cedric set Miles down and turned towards the shadow. "I'll handle this, Father."

When the unknown man stepped into view, I couldn't believe it was Jameson. *He's Cedric's father?*

Shoving a length of rope into Cedric's hand, Jameson growled. "Bind him. That is if you think you can handle such a menial task."

Miles cried out as Cedric obeyed.

"If you can't quiet him, I will. It won't be long before they'll start looking for him." Jameson snarled and glared hatefully at Miles. "If you make one sound, I'll go back and kill every one of your precious kidnappers, beginning with her royal highness."

Miles started to speak when Cedric clamped his mouth shut. The actions almost seemed protective.

Is it possible Cedric loves his son? Dismissing my curiosity, I called my Earth magic.

The ground under the men began to shake and Cedric released his hold on the boy. "We need to get out of here." Cedric hurriedly tied Miles up, ignoring his whimpers of pain.

No time to appear sweet and kind. I need to save my brother. Stepping out from my hiding place, I said, "I wouldn't do that, Cedric." My hands blazed with dark magic.

"You're always meddling where you don't belong. I promised your mother that I would protect you, but I'll break that promise if you interfere with me taking my son home," Cedric warned.

Miles and I exchanged glances. I gave my head the slightest tilt, hoping he'd understand that I needed him to step away.

He did. Slowly, Miles inched away from Cedric and I moved closer.

With my stepfather distracted by the sizzling balls of green in my hands, I summoned vines to grow. Breaking from the ground, they slithered around his legs. I willed the element to be patient and twist gently.

I narrowed my eyes at Cedric. "My brother isn't a trophy for your family. Miles is with a family who wants him and needs him. We love Miles. I was in your cold mansion. I know that there was no love there. If you leave, now, I'll let you walk away."

He laughed. "Oh, you'll let me, will you? Turn around, Meg, and tell Stone to have a son of his own."

By now, the creepers had trailed high up to his waist and Miles was far enough away to not get hurt. I commanded Earth to me, making Cedric topple over. He crashed to the ground, cursing and screaming at me.

Miles cried, "Look out, Meg!"

Before I could see why my world went black.

CHAPTER
THIRTY-SIX

I could hear my brother's pleas for me to answer. *Doesn't he know I'm safe?* Soon, more voices were calling my name, but the light before me was so powerful, so enticing.

"Stay with me, Meg," Dunn's sweet voice pleaded.

I could feel his strong arms wrap around me. Arms I had longed for. But I had to choose – the light or him.

The light called me. It didn't tell me I was too young. Wait until I was older. Instead, it wanted me. The glow slowly turned lavender. It was so peaceful, and I wanted to rest.

I would just close my eyes for a few minutes. A quick nap would refresh me. Dunn would understand.

The purple hues abruptly shifted to white, and then it all stopped. No sound. No light. *No me?*

"Go back to sleep," Gram whispered.

"But, I'm not tired," I said, trying to open my heavy lids.

Out of the corner of my cracked eyes, a flicker of light caught my attention and I heard childlike laughter. I sat up, feeling groggy. My body weighed down. I struggled hard to get up, but hands were pushing on my shoulders.

"Lie back down," the voice insisted.

As my mind started to clear, I knew this wasn't Gram, but it did sound like a sweet little old lady.

"All will be well. You must rest, child," the voice soothed.

I nodded sleepily. She sounded like she just wanted to help me. *What could it hurt to close my eyes and rest for a bit longer?*

The light returned, emitting a twinkling sound. I opened my eyes to see it charging at me. When it reached me, it began to tug on my hair. The sharp pains awakened me, and the room came into focus.

"I'm tired. Come again, later," I said to a small, winged creature.

Shaking its head violently, it zipped around me on the bed I lay on. The reflection from the light shined on the cracked ceiling and walls, exposing the peeling paint. I could hear a slow *drip, drip, drip* that explained the musty smell. My drowsiness lifted enough for me to make out a sweet-looking old woman bending over me.

"Ignore that pest and rest, child."

Blinking, I tried to focus my eyes. The stranger looked so much like Gram. She wore a flowered dress and her gray hair was pulled back into a soft bun. The same as Gram. But she wasn't my grandmother. She had dark eyes, not soft brown. She didn't smell like Gram with sweet vanilla, hints of lavender, and fiery cinnamon. Instead, she smelled like moldy cheese.

I didn't have much time to ponder the differences before the hovering being bit me hard on the hand. The woman tried to swat it away, but it was too late. Her bite jolted me wide awake. Something told me that whatever it was trying to tell me was important. I needed to listen. With all the energy I could muster, I sat up.

"What are you?" I asked.

Holding out its tiny fingers, it threw flowers at me.

"Do not rush yourself, Meg. I will chase away this pest," the old woman cooed.

I turned back towards the flying creature. "Are you an Earth elemental?"

Throwing more flowers, it nodded and excitedly spun around. She reminded me of Daisy, the Earth elemental who had taught me how to control my gift. Although she was far smaller and winged, I could sense her Earth magic.

"What are you? You don't look like Daisy," I said, standing up.

It shook its head.

"So, you're different? I wish you could talk to me."

It pulled on my hand with all its might and I let it guide me. Excitedly nodding, it dropped my hand and flew ahead of me. Then, it stopped and turned to make sure I was following.

"You don't want to follow that. Her kind eat small children," the old woman said, rushing after me.

When I stopped to ask why, the Earth creature flew in front of my face, and then away.

The old woman stepped closer to me. She wore thick eyeliner and creepy blue eyeshadow. Gram never wore makeup, except on a special holiday. "You don't want to go with her. You're safe here with me. Let's get you back to my home. I will make you fresh cookies and a big glass of chocolate milk. Wouldn't that be nice?"

Earth zipped around me. She came close to my ear. "Run!"

"You're not real," I said to the old woman and slowly backed away.

"Of course, I am," she purred.

The little creature tugged on me harder.

"Where are you going?" she snapped. I moved further away from her. Her appearance flickered, and I could see something dark...something unnatural. I recoiled in fear.

The little creature flew fast around me. *Run. Run. Run. Run. Run. Run. Run. Run. Run.*

Slowly backing away, I shuddered. The monster in disguise was growing closer. I could see its eyes glowing a ghoulish green. It bared its sharp, discolored teeth. It wasn't a sweet old lady. It wasn't even human.

"I didn't say you could leave. Come back, now, Meg," it screeched. The air filled with the smell of rot and decay.

"No, I can't," I said, backing away.

I bumped into something sharp.

When the creature drew closer, it threw out a hand towards me. Grey flesh hung from long spindly fingers and arms. Underneath, thick black liquid flowed and slithered up its body. The dark tendrils flowed from its fingertips for me.

I ran.

In response, it shrieked. The high-pitched wails pierced my ears.

I ran further, and further, away, desperate to save myself. When I could no longer hear the screeching noise, I slowed my pace. My heart felt like it would, soon, beat out of my chest.

Stopping to catch my breath, I realized I had run into a forest – one I'd never seen before.

CHAPTER
THIRTY-SEVEN

Giant multicolored trees with furry trunks surrounded me. I was tempted to stroke the texture, but I restrained myself. Gram had taught me from an early age to not touch or taste things I found in the forest. Rules to life like this would help me survive anything.

Above me, leaves twice my size rustled. It was as if dozens of large almond-shaped blankets had been hung out to dry. Below, brightly colored flowers covered the cobalt blue forest floor. When a gust of warm air blew against my face, I was reminded of the tropical garden at Charlemagne's Hotel.

No, this isn't a forest, I thought. *What is this place?*

A woman called to me. "Please, sit."

One of the gigantic leaves lowered towards me, creating a seat.

I hesitated.

The little creature appeared. She bounced her head, up and down, as if telling me it was safe.

"If, you're sure." I nervously settled upon the green frond and my new friend twirled in the air with a big grin on her face.

I waited anxiously, wondering who had spoken to me. Suddenly, my chair rose. *What have I done?* I scooted myself forward, preparing to jump before it got too high.

"Do not be afraid," the silky voice soothed.

The greenery wrapped itself around me. It was too late to escape. I was lifted, higher and higher. When it stopped, I was surrounded by the thick leaves, swishing as if there was a strong breeze. But I felt no wind. The bark of the tree moved, and I noticed the unusual pattern on it. *How odd it looks like a face.*

Unexpectedly, two giant green eyes were looking at me.

After what seemed liked minutes of awkward silence, I finally gave a hesitant smile. *Introduce yourself*, I chided. "Hi. My name is Meg Stone and I'm—"

"I know who you are, child," the tree said. Her breath smelled of cedar chips.

"Well, you know me...so, who are you?" I asked, feeling brave.

"I am Princess Kinema Delli and you have entered my realm," she said.

"Princess—"

"You may call me Kinema," she proclaimed, and her wooden lips lifted into an almost smile.

"Kinema." I nodded. "I'm sorry to be rude. I didn't mean to...I was just running from..."

"The Ladarsha." Her mouth twisted as if disgusted. "You're very lucky that Ledli found you and helped you escape. If not, you would have been just another lost soul to add to her collection."

"Lost soul?" I asked.

"You're not very perceptive, are you?"

"What do you mean?"

"Hold out your hands, child."

Doing as I was told, I gasped. They were translucent. "Am I dead?" my voice trembled.

A sharp pain in my right side stole the air from me and I fell. My screams were silenced as I landed softly on the ground. Moaning in pain, I opened my eyes.

Across from me, Cedric was lying on the ground. The vines I had called continued to wrap tightly around him.

Miles knelt over me. Tears ran down his blood-streaked face.

"Don't die, Meg," Miles pleaded. "I'm sorry. It's all my fault." He pressed his hands against my side.

I wanted to comfort my brother, but I couldn't speak. When he lifted his blood-covered hands, I realized it was me who was bleeding. In a blink, I was no longer with Miles. I had returned to Kinema.

"So, I'm dead," I said, holding back my tears. "Why have the Miezitari not arrived to take me to the Afterlife?"

"They cannot take you, child. Your soul has left the mortal world," Kinema explained.

"Why? If I'm dead, I want to be with my grandmother," I insisted.

"But you're not dead," she said. "Your body is spiritless. The shell that once held you is working as if you were there. You appear to the mortals as if you're in a deep sleep."

"I need to go back. My family will be worried. My sister—"

"You need to worry about yourself, young one. They will be fine without you. The living always learns to adapt."

"That isn't true. I'm not fine without Gram," I argued.

"Look how strong you've become since her death. You've been instrumental in helping those around you heal. Mae would be immensely proud of the woman you've become. Your strength is what makes you special, Meg," Kinema praised. Her green eyes locked with mine. "You will need your fighting spirit more than ever, now. You cannot go back in the form that you once held. However, your next steps are in your own hands. I'm giving you a gift – one rarely given. You will decide your future."

"What? You said I wasn't dead." My fingers clenched as I fought back my urge to scream.

Pink petals from above covered me. "Listen carefully, Meg. You have a choice to make. Take the Winter from the unborn child and become the guardian of it. Free the child from the curse of her gift. Or...if you are unwilling to make this sacrifice, join your family in the Afterlife."

"I don't want any more of Eliza's cursed Winter magic. My gift is Earth. It's who I am. Please, just let me go home," I pleaded.

"Hushhhh," she said, expelling a burst of wind over me, sending the petals flying. A sweet citrus scent engulfed me. "You may not want the Winter, but it was not only your mother who carried it. Your father has passed it on to you. Your Winter is much stronger than the small speck coursing through him. But you know that already, don't you?"

"My father has Earth magic, like me," I said defiantly.

"No, Meg. You know of what I speak. You can't hide from the truth. Not all paths we are given are what we desire. You must deal with what is before you. You have got a decision to make. The time is now."

Anger filled me. She knew nothing about my father. The man who loved me and cared for me. The man who gave up his life to save mine.

She had no right to speak about my family. Glaring at her, I said, "Time for what?"

An overwhelming urge to dig back into my childhood and throw a tantrum overwhelmed me. I would yell and cry until she returned me to my home. She would turn back time as if Cedric never took Miles... Jameson never—

"You're much smarter than this, child." Kinema pulled the frond out from under me and dropped me.

"You must choose for yourself. Nothing you do will change the fact that a choice will be made," her voice called after me. "Accept your destiny, Meg."

CHAPTER
THIRTY-EIGHT

I fell through a lightless void. I screamed for help, but there was no answer as I floated into the unknown. My descent ended with my submersion into a gooey substance. *No, not sticky. Wet? No, not wet, either.* Dragging my hands around me, I determined I was in a pool of small green balls. Picking one up, I squeezed it.

"Squeak," it cried out in protest.

"Oh, I'm sorry," I apologized and quickly put it down. "Can you tell me where I am? I don't know where to go."

The balls circled around me, creating a whirlpool. I dropped, again. This time, I didn't scream. The orbs had combined to make a chute for me to slide down. The soft ride ended in a green meadow and I laughed uncontrollably.

I shouldn't be laughing. I'd been chased by a soul eater, saved by a pixie, dropped by a talking tree, and shot through a tunnel of living balls to end up on a mound of grass. Still, I felt intense joy and peace. It was a feeling I hadn't felt for a very long time.

"Dunn would like it here," I told the balls hovering above me.

I stood up and the orbs gathered, rising high into the sky.

"Where am I? Please, don't leave me," I called to them as they moved further away from me. "I don't know what to do. I don't want to give up my magic."

Searching for anyone, I saw nothing, except miles and miles of lush green grass. Accepting my isolation, I sat down. Gasping, I realized I wasn't only transparent but rather, I had no clothes on. Touching my arms and legs, my hands felt tingly.

"I hope my decision means I can put clothes back on," I said. "I'm not solid, but I wonder if..."

Resting my hand on the ground, I called Earth. The blades of grass grew long. As the sprouts poked out of the rich soil, I carefully broke them off. When I had a large pile, I wove them together. Then, I called flowers to fill in the spaces. When I had enough to cover me, I slipped into my creation.

I probably looked ridiculous but being covered in my element made me feel more comfortable. The connection made me even more confident that I wouldn't give up my Earth magic. I would find a way to hide from Kinema.

In the distance, the air grew thick with a dark haze. *You're not safe,* my internal voice screamed. I was exposed. There was nowhere to hide. I needed to disappear. *If* they couldn't find me, then they couldn't take away my magic.

Next, I summoned trees, bushes, and flowers. I needed my element to help hide me. Vines grew, weaving themselves into a wall of green until all spots the darkness could peek in were closed. Inspecting my work, I worried it wasn't enough to block them out.

Again, I rested my hand on the ground. It shook and split open as a large piece of stone rose. If I called more rock with the trees and vines hiding me, I would never be found.

"You've created such a peaceful world." A young woman stepped out from behind a tree. "I wish I had your talent."

My heart stopped. I had already been found.

The blonde girl put on a brilliant smile as she walked towards me. I eyed her suspiciously. I considered my recent experiences.

The hag had chosen a glamour of someone I loved. She didn't look familiar, but...*Is this another trick? Or,* I wondered, *could she be someone waiting for death to take her, also?* Focusing on every inch of her, I didn't see any changes to her appearance.

Still, something inside me screamed, 'No, don't trust her'.

"Go away," I yelled. When she didn't move, I bared my teeth and wildly shook my fist.

"Oh." She jerked back, and her eyes filled with tears. "I just wanted to welcome you," she murmured.

"You've welcomed me. Now, go."

The girl choked back a sob. Her body hunched over, and she slunk away. A twinge of guilt hit me. *You were so mean. Maybe she knows how to help you.*

"Wait, come back," I sighed.

"Not if you are going to be rude," she said, sniffling.

Oh, Meg, you made her cry. Gram would be so ashamed of you. She taught you to look for light, not darkness. Feeling chagrin, I said sweetly, "Come back. We can start over."

Carefully, she returned to me. After flicking her eyes over me, she touched my dress. "How creative. I never thought to make clothing to cover myself when I first arrived here. My name's Rebecca. What's yours?"

"I'm Meg. Have you been here long?" I questioned. "How did you hide from them?"

"I have my ways." Rebecca touched the flower in my hair. "You'll be so pretty when you regain your form."

"Do you know how I can get my body back?" I asked.

"Of course, didn't they tell you?" she asked, touching my arm.

"No, they told me I had to make a decision." I stepped away from her. I still wasn't confident she was friend, not foe.

"What kind of decision?"

I shrugged. Being nice didn't mean I had to tell her anything. "Doesn't matter. I refuse to make any decisions, today or ever." I said, crossing my arms over my chest.

"Good idea. Ignore their demands." Rebecca nodded her agreement. "Since you are going to be here awhile, can you make me a dress like yours? I'm tired of this old thing." She lifted the hem of the simple frock with a faded flower pattern and then dropped it with a look of disgust. Even in her plain clothing, Rebecca looked beautiful.

"I can, but why would you want a silly plant dress? The one you have on is much nicer than what I'll make you," I said.

"Please," she begged.

"Fine," I moaned and dropped to the ground.

Rebecca sat across from me and carefully watched as I used my element to gather the materials. With her no longer asking questions or touching me, I let my magic calm me. No matter what worries I had, growing life always released my fears. I embraced the warm tingle of my gift and let myself connect with the Earth.

When I finished the dress made from vines and flowers, she exclaimed, "I love it. You should make these for my friends."

"You didn't say there was anyone else here." My mouth gaped in a look of surprise.

"Oh no, I am definitely not the only one here." Rebecca twirled around and grinned at me.

"It doesn't matter. I'm going home, eventually."

"Why do you want to go back to the world you came from?" she asked.

"I have a family I love there. My older sister's having a baby, right now. I was supposed to be there to help." I closed my eyes to will away the tears that were brewing. "I don't think that my father would survive losing someone else he loves."

"Why is that?"

"My father died when I was a baby and my mother disappeared—"

"How did he die?" Rebecca interrupted.

I raised my eyebrows and she held her hands up in submission. "I lived with my sister and my grandmother. Even with my parents gone, I never missed out on love. Gram taught me to dance when I was little, and it became my passion. When I was nine, I performed my first solo at the Lunar Dance. It was, also, the night I found out my father was alive."

At first, her nose wrinkled in disgust, but it was quickly replaced with a nodding smile. Her response seemed odd.

Continuing my tale, I said, "Later in the night, my mother stole me from my bed as I lay sleeping. She brought me to her mansion on the hill. She had married a horrible man. I was so scared and alone until my sister saved me. I was so happy to see her."

"I bet," Rebecca chimed in.

Despite her interruption, I couldn't help smiling. "My sister really is the best. She threw a surprise party for my sixteenth birthday. The courtyard had been decorated with strands of twinkling lights and the food was amazing. I danced and danced until I thought my feet would fall off."

Rebecca yawned. She looked bored. "You've had such a sad life. Everyone seems to leave you, Meg."

"No, my life's been really good. Gram always took great care of me. There've just been a few moments of sadness," I argued.

"But you were devastated when your grandmother died. She was your world," Rebecca said, taking my hand.

"How did you know my grandmother died?" I asked, jerking my hand from hers.

"You told me, of course," she said dismissively. She picked one of the flowers. "These are such a pretty color."

"I didn't. I'm positive I didn't tell you she died." My mind was screaming that there was something wrong with this situation.

"Of course, you did. How else could I possibly know that?" she asked sweetly. "This place can confuse your mind. Tell me more about the day your grandmother died."

"I don't want to talk about that. I'll tell you about the day my little sister was born," I said, narrowing my eyes at her.

"No, don't skip ahead," Rebecca pouted.

"When my sister was born, she had a full head of red hair. We were so happy to—"

"Don't skip ahead! You were telling me about your horrible mother killing your grandmother. We have time to hear about babies later." Rebecca wrinkled her nose in disgust.

My mind raced. I hadn't told her any of those things. She wanted to hear sad stories. *Why does she want me to cry?*

"Would you rather I only tell you my tragic stories, Ladarsha? You seem to already know everything. Why don't you tell me about the day my sister died?" Standing up, I backed away from her.

"What are you talking about, Meg? Your sister is alive." Her face filled with hurt. "Why did you call me that name? You know my name is Rebecca."

"Well, you're one of them if you're not her," I growled.

"One of who?" she questioned. Her eyes fill with pity for me.

"Your lies won't work. You're not going to trap my soul here with you," I shouted.

Ominously, the clouds covered the sun and a shadow fell over us. The vines I'd called to create my sanctuary parted and black tendrils slithered through the opening.

"Don't be cruel, Meg. I just want a little bit of your soul." Rebecca licked her lips. Her beautiful face became lined and aged. "I know you have more sorrow to share. Just a little bit more to ease my pain. We haven't even got to the part about your sister leaving you. How did that make you feel?" As she spoke, a darkness pooled under her, oozing outwards.

"Earth, I need you more than ever," I murmured to my element.

The vines of her dress roughly twisted around her wrists and ankles. More creepers grew from deep in the earth, pulling her to the ground. When she was pinned, I stood over her.

"You won't feed on any of my sadness, now or ever," I threatened.

She struggled against the Earth magic, but I had trapped her. The darkness of her magic turned to long, smoke-like hands as they fought against my bindings. She wailed, and the intruding tendrils entered her gaping mouth. Flesh melted and dripped from her exposed skin, turning into black ooze. I jumped back in disgust. Suddenly, one arm broke free and she grabbed my leg.

"You can't hide from us!" she shrieked.

In defense, Earth quickly bound her arm, again, and held her tightly to the ground.

I knew it wouldn't hold her for long. The ooze had pooled under me, licking at my skin. I ran. I didn't look back as I moved as fast as I could to get away from her.

Eventually, I reached the edge of the barrier I had created. The vines easily parted, and I stepped out of the sanctuary I'd been cocooned in. *I could hide from her, but for how long?* I thought wearily as the creepers closed me out and Rebecca in.

CHAPTER
THIRTY-NINE

Glancing around, I took in the area I had fled into. Instead of a lush grove, my new location was an icy landscape. Looking down at the snow, I gazed at the blue sparkles within the white powder. I couldn't decide if it was safe to cross over.

Out of the corner of my eye, something caught my attention. In the distance, there was a frosted pink willow, swaying next to a fence with a black iron gate. There was something about it that called me. Crunching through the snow, I hoped I wasn't falling into a tempting trap.

When I reached the tree closest to me, I placed my hand on the trunk. Still worried about the ground's stability, I whispered, "Please, tell me which way to go."

Kinema's green eyes appeared and slowly a face developed. My hand rested on her cheek. This time, her features weren't gnarled bark, but smooth skin. Quickly, I dropped my hand and stepped back. *I wouldn't be able to hide from her,* I realized woefully.

"Have you made your decision?" Kinema questioned.

"No, please, just let me go. I can't pick either of the choices you gave me. I just want to find my way home," I pleaded.

"There is no way for you to go back. You can only move forward. Which direction you choose is up to you."

"If you're forcing me to decide, how will I know which is the right one?" I rebuked, putting my hands on my hips and glaring.

"Search yourself for the answers."

Kinema blew out a mighty breath, sending the scent of lavender and vanilla over me. The fragrance was intoxicating. I swayed as the gate blurred, in and out, of view. When my vision cleared, I felt a desperate desire to go through it.

"May I pass?" I asked. "I think I need to go this way."

"Do you think, or do you know?" Kinema questioned, her mouth turning into a tight line.

The fence glowed a dazzling blue and white. Whatever was behind it, I needed to see for myself.

"I know," I said confidently. "Please, may I pass?"

The gates opened, and a silver path shimmered, guiding me onward. Hesitantly, I passed through. When I turned back to ask Kinema if I'd be safe from Ladarsha, she was gone. Closing my eyes, I took a deep, cleansing breath before beginning down the trail.

Wandering down the path, a strange calmness surged through me. I didn't know where I was going, but I wasn't afraid.

Suddenly, an aura enclosed me. Its pulsing touch brushed my skin. This harsh magic felt like my mother's, but with the soft persistence of my grandmother's touch. The further I walked, the stronger the magic became.

A gust of cold air almost knocked me over, but I kept moving. The chill of the wind licked at my skin and I shivered. Soon, I felt unbearably cold – a bone-chilling cold that seeped deep into my core. The icy feeling grew stronger as if my body was freezing.

Is this what Winter feels like? I definitely don't want this.

Trying to distract myself, I forced my mind to think about Kinema's offer. My thoughts played with what accepting each choice would mean. How could I take the Winter? My gift of Earth held life and connection. I didn't want to be eternally cold and cause things to wither and die. It was cruel.

Unexpectedly, my feet became difficult to move. It was as if I had cement shoes on. Looking down, I gasped. They were frozen solid.

Checking the rest of my body, I gulped down a scream. My fingers were like long icicles and my hair crystalized strings.

Desperate to find warmth, I continued along the path, which became steeper. Above me, silver sparks lit up the sky. When the trail was too slick for my ice feet, I found myself needing to dig my nails into the icy ground to keep from sliding backwards.

Slowly, hand-over-hand, I struggled to climb the hill. After counting off thirty desperate minutes, I finally reached the top. I was completely out of breath, and my muscles burned under their icy wrap. Collapsing, I fought for air.

How does my body ache if I'm just a soul? I wondered.

Lying on my side, I watched the puffs of frozen air leave my mouth. When I heard a soft childlike voice behind me, I dragged myself into a sitting position. Twenty feet away, I could see a little girl building a wall of snow bricks. The child looked to be around five years old. She was bundled up for the wintry climate – puffer jacket, thick black pants, and snow boots.

At least, someone was smart enough to dress her for such weather, I thought bitterly.

The small girl hummed as she scooped up snow, formed a brick, stacked it, and repeated the process. The face held a bright smile the entire time.

She set another brick onto her wall and turned towards me. "Are you here to help me?"

"What do you need help with?" I asked, standing up.

"I'm going home as soon as I open the portal. Can you help me?" she asked, again.

Her blue eyes were wide and innocent, surrounded by thick black lashes, just like my brother. When she looked at me, I could see Miles in her face, helpless and full of hope. This couldn't be a trick. There could be no evil in her.

"If you show me how, I can try," I answered.

"It's easy. Watch me." Taking a mound of snow, she carefully patted each side until she held a perfect brick. "All you have to do is push it really hard together and it makes this." Pointing at the snow, she commanded, "Now, you try."

My first attempt was a misshapen triangle, which sent her into a fit of giggles.

"No, like this," she said, demonstrating again.

The bricks I made were not like hers, at first, but soon, I could make my own with equal skill.

She continued to hum and softly giggled while we continued to add to her wall. It was so comforting being with this small child after my escape from the darkness. She didn't question me, and I didn't feel the need to talk. There was nothing she wanted from me, except my help with her construction.

After she placed the last brick, she said, "Now, I just need one last thing."

Taking a mound of snow, she formed a ball and stuck it on top of one of the middle bricks. A rumble came from under us and the earth quaked and cracked. I took her hand to protect her just as a house burst from the ground, destroying her creation.

Her eyes widen in surprise and anticipation.

A lavender-painted house towered over us both. From one of the white-trimmed windows, a heavy light glowed. The shape of the building reminded me of somewhere I had been. I just couldn't quite place it.

Letting go of my hand, she beamed at me. "It's time for me to go, now. Thank you."

I pulled off one of the purple flowers from my dress. "Here, for you," I said, gently placing it into her hand.

"It's so pretty," the girl squeaked, and then she hugged me tightly. Breaking away, she whispered, "I better go. They're calling me."

"I don't hear anything," I said.

"You don't? She's so scared. I need to go and tell her everything will be fine," she said, furrowing her brows.

"Who's scared?" I called as she reached out to turn the doorknob.

"Goodbye," she replied without looking at me.

When the little girl opened the door, I was blinded by the light emitting from it. As it softened, I could see her inside the building, twirling around as thousands of colorful bubbles covered her.

"It tickles. Can you hear them calling my name, now?" she giggled.

"No, I can't. What is your name?" I asked, stepping closer.

She curled into a tight ball, mimicking the orbs surrounding her. "They are calling me—"

I could no longer see her.

"Wait," I cried. *It was a trap for her, not me. I let a little girl walk into their lair!*

It wasn't safe for a small child. She could get hurt. I entered the room to stop her, but the orbs and the girl disappeared. Everything faded.

My vision blurred and panic set in. I turned, only to discover the door was gone. In desperation, I felt for the wall, pounding on the wood. It had all been a trick. I had trusted my instinct and it led me into a trap.

CHAPTER
FORTY

I closed my eyes tightly and counted.

"Be brave, focus your energy, breathe slowly, and remember I love you." My grandmother's words filled my mind. I would be ready for whatever was before me if I just remembered everything she had taught me.

On ten, I opened my eyes. I was no longer in a snow-covered area. I was standing in front of a lake. The blue water lapped against the shore, creating white foam. A trail formed before me in the shape of stepping-stones, stretching across the lake.

I stared into the distance. Relief flooded me. At least, I wasn't trapped in a room filled with soul stealers. But I wasn't sure that my new path was safe, either.

"Why are you waiting?" A young boy appeared. Nodding at the lake, he said, "The water won't bite."

"Are you a soul stealer?" I asked.

"Ewww, one of those? No way," he said, puffing out his chest. "I chase them away from my lake."

As I considered his bright blue eyes, I recognized the boy. There was no doubt in my mind that I was standing before Cole Sands. It was a younger version of my brother-in-law, but it was definitely him. It didn't make sense for him to be here. He needed to be with Mara.

"Cole? Why are you out here?" I asked.

"I'm watching over my water. I have to protect it," he said nonchalantly. Flicking his eyes over me, he cried out, "Hey, you're dripping all over the place. Did you already go swimming?"

Examining my body, I was surprised. I was no longer a frozen piece of ice. Running to the edge of the water, I knelt and stared at my reflection. My skin was peachy, my body solid, again. My brown hair was lighter, but the rest of me had returned.

"Are you sick or something," Cole called after me.

"No, I'm great! My body is back," I squealed and jumped up and down. *I'm back. Kinema changed her mind. She'll send me home!*

Cole raised his eyebrows as if he was questioning my sanity.

"Really, I'm fine. Now, tell me why you're here," I said, composing myself.

Cole sat down on the edge of the lake and splashed the water with his feet. Sitting next to him, I decided to let him tell me why at his own pace. We sat in silence while he gazed into the waves. Suddenly, his face paled and he shivered.

"They took our magic away from us," he said, his voice barely above a whisper. "When it left our body, I followed it."

"You need to go back to him…to you. You're not whole like this," I replied.

"No! He should've fought harder. He was too sad and weak. I had to leave him to protect my water. We made a promise and he just gave up." His eyes welled with tears that he quickly rubbed away.

"You need to—"

"I live here, now. You need to go on your way," he growled.

The darkness in his tone scared me. Such a small boy with such anger inside him. He needed to return to his body, but I couldn't help him now…maybe never.

"I need to follow that path. Is it safe to cross the water here?" I asked.

"Of course. His demeanor changed and, once again, the bubbly boy was in front of me. "You need to step very carefully, or you will get wetter," he smirked.

"Can you take me?" I asked.

Shrugging, he said, "Why not? Ok, follow me."

Cole jumped to the first stone before he turned back towards me. "Hop to me," he ordered. When I landed, he laughed as we wobbled. "See easy."

We leapt, stone to stone, until we were in the middle of the lake. A large fish with pink scales and blue polka dots jumped out of the water, splashing me.

"Don't scare her," Cole scolded the fish. "She's afraid of the water."

A silver-whiskered nose peeked out of the lake. A second fish flew into the air, before splashing down. It trilled. The first fish poked its head out of the water, again, chiming in with its own set of whistles and clicks.

"Ok. Ok," the boy said, placing each foot on the backs of the fish. "Sorry, I need to go. You don't have much further before you reach land."

"Wait. Where are you going?" Anxiety washed over me.

"Don't worry. I'll be back, soon, but right now, I need to protect my water. You just keep going forward."

Cole stood tall, balancing himself as he rode away on the backs of the fish. I watched until he became a small dot in the distance before I continued.

You are a dancer, I reminded myself. *Yes! And, this is my stage.*

Stone to stone, I leapt as if it was the performance of my life. When I could see I had only six more rocks until I reached land, I stopped and stared. I couldn't make out what was ahead of me. My heartbeat drowned out the sound of the water.

Go! Stop standing in the middle of the lake and get to land. I jumped to the next stone. Just ahead, I could finally make out the faint outline of a house.

Splash! Something jumped out of the water and back in before I could see what it was.

Without thinking, I performed a series of leaps and ended with a grand jeté. With my arms high in fifth position, I soared through the air in the highest split jump I'd ever accomplished. When I landed on the rocky beach, I couldn't help but do another twirl.

Standing on the shoreline, I could, now, see the house clearly. Lights inside the wooden home illuminated the glass pane windows. Loud footsteps sounded and a tall man stepped through the door onto the extended front porch.

As he stepped under the light, I could make out his familiar features. I had seen pictures of this man since the day I was born. For the first time in my life, I would meet my grandfather, Chester Finnegan Veracor.

Gramp's hair wasn't the silver color it was in the later pictures I'd seen of him. Instead, it was a chestnut brown. In this realm, he was a young man in his forties.

His blue eyes twinkled as he called out, "Are you going to come say hello to me, Meg?"

"Um...um..." I stammered.

"Don't let the cat get your tongue. Come on up here and give your grandpa a hug. I have been waiting for you."

"How do I know you're not a soul stealer?" I asked nervously.

"Those fools won't come around me. I have no sad stories to share with them," he claimed.

"Tell me something only you would know," I said, eyeing him suspiciously.

"Only something I should know...hmm. That's a tricky one. Would it be that your favorite food my Mae made you was her famous chicken pot pie? Or, could it be that you once snuck into my woodshop and carved your name on a wall? You tried to carve a little flower, but it looked more like a swirl." The man chuckled as if the memory delighted him.

Dashing up the steps, I threw myself into his arms. "Gramp, I'm sorry. I just had to be careful. I'm so glad you came."

"My pretty girl, you're so grown up. Come in. Come in. I made you something to eat while I was waiting. It's not like what my Maesi would make, but I tried to remember the recipe." He motioned for me to sit.

"It's a sandwich," I said, looking at the plate on the table.

"If I had cooked a meal for you, you'd know that it was one of those soul stealers. Making this sandwich took every ounce of my cooking skills," he scoffed. "Now, sit and tell me how I did."

Taking my seat, I picked up the overstuffed sandwich and tried to not drop any on myself. It was piled high with turkey, cheese, salami, lettuce, tomatoes, and peppercinis. Squishing it together, I took a big bite as my grandfather watched me.

"This is so good. I didn't realize how hungry I was," I gushed, not considering my mouth was full.

"I'm glad you like it." He beamed at me.

After a few more delicious bites, I set my sandwich down. "How come you're here? I thought you were in the Afterlife?"

"I asked to be sent. Your Gram is raising hell back there. I wouldn't want to be any of those Gods, right now. So, I'm here to help you with your decision," he said, taking my hand.

"I don't know what to do. I don't like any of the choices," I muttered, staring at my food.

"Well, sometimes, we don't always get everything we like. The longer I've been gone from the mortal world, the more I've realized some things just don't matter. But..." He squeezed my hand and looked into my eyes. "Some things matter more than I thought they would. Do you know what counts, Meg?"

"Family?" I asked.

Gramp frowned. "Yes, family is important and you're always one to do what is best for ours. You worry about Mara. You worry about Miles. You worry about Gram. You even worry about your parents. But, it's time to stop worrying about your family. This decision must be for you."

My grandfather's words took me by surprise.

Gramp bobbed is head as though he'd solved a troublesome puzzle. "You should make the choice for you alone, not how it will help anyone else. The best thing you can do for your family is to live a happy life. You can only worry about what is best for Meg Violet Stone."

"What do you think I should do?" I asked.

"Honey, I can't decide that for you," he answered. He paused a moment, looking thoughtful. "Perhaps you should decide what scares you the most and if it's worth the price you'll pay for it. What will you be able to give up?"

"If I take the Winter, Mara and Cole won't have to worry about their baby being taken from them."

"But?"

"I lose my Earth magic and I don't know what else I might lose," I answered.

"And, your other choice?"

"To say goodbye to the mortal world and join you and Gram in the Afterlife. I'll have to say goodbye to my magic, my friends, my home, and...Dunn."

"It's not so bad in the Afterlife. It's harder when you can't – or won't – break ties with the mortal realm. I'm afraid you'd be like Mae and refuse to release your connection. I know she'll never give up that world as long as she's worried about her grandchildren. Don't get me wrong. My Maesi did an excellent job raising you girls. She only lost you one or two times." His eyes sparkled with those words.

"Gram was the best," I sighed. "I still don't know what to do, Gramp."

"I know one thing. You need to finish up your sandwich. It's never smart to make a major decision on an empty stomach."

Smirking, I picked up the sandwich and took another big bite.

Gramp smiled at me and picked up his own. "Mae, once, told me her mother, Genevieve's, gift had been passed down through the generations with not only elemental magic but with the curse of short lifespans. When Mae had turned sixty-seven, she thought her luck had changed. As you know, it hadn't."

I considered his words. *Is it the gift or because of dark gods and goddesses, like Snowystra?*

"Your Gram had a tough time when she first heard of your injury," Gramp said, interrupting my thoughts. "For a minute, I was worried that I'd lost her to the darkness."

"What do you mean?" my words croaked out. *My grandmother would never fall into the darkness.*

"The day you were hurt, I found your grandmother. She was frantically gathering supplies in the kitchen. When I asked her what she was doing, she refused to answer my questions," Gramp explained. "Instead, Maesi told me to help her or go away. So, I gathered up her things and laid them on the table in a circle, just as she'd taught me."

Gramp looked heartbroken as he continued, "Mae was going to call black magic. I tried to convince her it was a mistake, but she felt the gods wouldn't help her save you. She felt she had to contact *them*."

Them? I wondered to myself.

"I wasn't going to let her throw away everything to bring darkness into our lives," Gramp said firmly. "I threw the mortar from the table and wrapped my large hands around hers. I'd never seen her so angry. She screamed at me. Then, you know what she did?"

I couldn't help myself. I shook my head from side-to-side in response.

Gramp scowled as he recalled her actions. "She fell to the ground and pushed the potion off the floor and back into the mortar. Her hands turned red and blistered as it burned her. I wrapped my arms under her and dragged her away from it." He cast his eyes towards the floor. "You know Gram is strong. She broke free and tried to save her spell, again. By the time she reached the potion, it was too late. The magic was gone from it."

A sense of relief flooded over me. *I'm glad she couldn't conjure the darkness. What was she thinking?*

"Eliza appeared and begged her to not call them. You would've been proud of her," Gramps praised. "Your mother said, 'You're right. I wasn't a good mother, but I can't undo any of my past mistakes. Mother, you need to remember the light. In your life, you kept your promise and you raised my girls to do the same. Please, don't give up on everything you believed. Everything you tried to teach me. Call out to the Light, Mother. Don't seek the dark.'"

"Wow," I said in a near whisper, surprised by my mother's reaction.

"Then, you won't believe who showed up?" Gramp asked. "Kinema Delli." He bobbed his head in affirmation. "Your Gram pleaded with her to save you. Well, you know the rest. Now, it's up to you to decide your destiny."

"Was she really going to summon the darkness to save me?" Gram was so strong in her commitment to Danu that I was amazed she'd even consider such a thing.

"Meg, you mean more than anything in the world to your Gram. She felt so desperate that I don't know what she would've done."

"Eliza was right. She'd always taught us to focus on the light and not seek dark...no matter what." I shook my head sadly.

A chime sounded and Gramp sighed. "Well, that went by too quick. My time is up, sweet girl." Kissing me on the forehead, he said, "Like your Gram always told you, 'follow your heart and you can't go wrong.' No matter what you decide, I'm proud of you. And, one day, I'll see you, again. Next time we meet, we should have Miles cook for us. I hear my grandson has a way with a spatula."

"He does." I laughed and hugged my grandfather tightly. I whispered, "Thank you. I'm so happy we finally met."

Gramp kissed me on top of the head. "Me, too, little dancer. Me, too."

Gradually, his body grew softer, and, soon, my grandfather faded away. After a few minutes of reflection, I left the house and went back to the beach. I sat with my feet near the water's edge, letting the waves beat against me.

An image of the little girl flashed in front of my eyes. She was so happy building her snow structure.

Don't be afraid of the Winter, Meg. Fear will just make you cold and hard.

I thought of Cole, who believed he was nothing without his magic.

And, then there was Gramp. He'd told me to follow my own heart and to make the best decision for me. I knew what I wanted, but I didn't know if my family would understand.

Throwing my head back, I called to the night sky. "I know what I want. I've made my decision."

The lake lit up a magnificent silver color and the silhouette of a woman appeared.

CHAPTER
FORTY-ONE

As the woman moved towards me, her body took shape. The unfamiliar goddess locked eyes with me and I knew I was staring at Kinema Delli. "Are you sure you're ready to make this decision, Meg?" she asked.

In her human form, she was petite. Her sage-colored, wavy locks fell over her shoulders, browning at the tips. She was breathtaking.

"I think I'm ready to make my choice, Kinema," I replied.

"You're not ready."

"I am. I want—"

Placing her pointer finger against my lips, she said, "When you're truly ready to decide, come to me."

When she removed her finger, I responded, "I know what I want. I'm sorry I sounded as if I doubted my choice. Please, I'm ready."

"No, Meg," she said. "You're not ready. Come to me when you've collected your thoughts."

"Why? I can tell you know. I promise, I'm ready," I insisted, hoping I didn't sound as frantic as I felt.

"You will need to come to me," Kinema repeated.

"You're here. Why are you not letting me choose? I don't understand," I said, clenching and unclenching my fists. My hands trembled, and my heart felt like it would beat out of my chest. I was livid.

"Your temper tells me that you are not ready." Kinema smiled softly at me.

This was not the first time my mood had got me into trouble. Gram had taught me how to calm myself as a child. Now, I needed to prove I could make an adult decision. I inhaled and slowly exhaled.

As I felt the anger inside me fading, I said, "You're standing before me and I'm listening. See, I'm calm."

"You are very persistent, Meg Stone," Kinema remarked with amusement. "Do as I say and come to me in the grove. I will be waiting there for you to accept your decision."

"The grove? But, Ladarsha is there," I gasped. "You said I was lucky to get away from them."

"She can only take from you what you offer. If you offer your sadness and pain, she will feed. Only you can choose what you will give to her. She has no great gift other than glamour, a convincing tone, and a soft touch to comfort you. Otherwise, she is quite powerless here."

"She didn't feel powerless. Who is she really? Was it just another test?" I asked.

"In your present journey, Ladarsha is of little consequence. The darkness is always around us. With the light, there will be dark, balance. I promise you that I have not brought Ladarsha to test you. However, your reaction, right now, is telling me you are not ready to make such an important decision. One which will be irrevocable," she said.

"Wait, there is no more darkness. Snowystra's gone." The words became too real. "There's no more darkness. If I choose the Winter, will I fill that role?"

"The darkness is within all beings. Can you not see that you are not ready to give me your decision? You still have many questions you need to answer within yourself."

"Fine. I will ask you questions," I argued.

I had been confident moments ago, but now, doubt filled me. She was correct. I wasn't ready. I wasn't sure I'd ever know the right answer.

"Snowystra took children to feed her magic. If I take the Winter, will I have to fuel my power? Will I have...followers?"

"If you choose Winter, you will have more power than you could ever imagine. I promise you will not need to resort to the cruel ways of Snowystra. Nor will you be alone, Meg. There is much more to being the Winter than what Snowystra offered the world. She did not understand her role. She isolated herself."

I would be a Goddess? The responsibility was unfathomable. *I would be alive, or sort of alive, and I could see my sister and Cole...and Gram? But I'd lose my Earth magic and the ability to create new life. Wouldn't I?* It was as if I finally understood what I would be choosing, and it scared me as much as it excited me.

"My Earth magic feels like it's part of the Winter. I could be wrong, but I think all life and growth needs time to rest and heal." As I said the words, I felt they were true. Confident, I continued, "When the ground begins to be covered by the Winter, it rejoices in its time to recover and relax. Am I wrong to think this? You would know better than anyone."

"Yes, Meg. We do need the time to rejuvenate. Winter is often thought of as death and loss, but as you said, it is a time to renew. It is nature's way to clean the slate. You already have a strong insight, Meg. Otherwise, you would not have been chosen. Danu's Ciethre were wise when they chose your family. Now, come to me, child, but know that, along the way, you will have temptations. You will reconsider your choice many times. By the time you return to me, you *must* be ready. You will need to make the absolute and final decision."

"But I understand now. I can choose," I said.

"Then, the temptations will be no trial for you. Come to me and I will hear your decision." She vanished.

I was, once again, standing on the edge of the lake. The sun had set, and the night sky was full of dazzling stars. I looked back at the house I had come from and saw my grandfather in the glow of the porch light.

"Don't go with them. Make the choice to come to live with Gram and me," Gramp called.

"I love you both, Gramp, but I have to make this decision on my own. Tell Gram I'm following my heart," I called back to him.

Glimpsing at my grandfather, one last time, I could see his mischievous smile.

Not a particularly good test, Gramp.

CHAPTER
FORTY-TWO

Hopping back across the stones, I felt focused and prepared for what was ahead of me. It seemed like there were many more steps than the first time I crossed. Each stone was blocking me from finding Kinema and beginning my new life.

When I finally arrived on the other shore, I found Cole. He sat with his head buried in his arms. He was crying.

"What's wrong, Cole?" I sat beside him and rested my arm on his back to comfort him.

"They took my magic…all of it. Why did they do it?" he sobbed. "I'm nothing without it."

"That's not true. You're strong and brave. One day, you'll be an amazing husband and father."

"But I feel empty inside. *He* feels hollow. Don't let them take your magic. You'll feel horrible for the rest of your life," he trembled, grabbing my hand tightly.

I kissed him on the forehead. "Don't worry about me, Cole. Everything will be ok. I promise. One day, we will meet, again, and you'll know I'm telling the truth. Can you do me a favor?"

"Maybe." He sniffed and wiped the tears from his face. "What do you need?"

"I need you to return to your body. You're needed at home. I know Cos needs you."

He pursed his lips together and stared at me.

"I'll see you, again, Cole. Please, go home."

Leaving him beside the water, I hoped he'd listen to me. If he didn't, I would find a way to return and convince him. *But what if you can't return to him?* a nagging voice in the back of my mind asked.

I stopped and called back to him, "Wait, I need you to come with me, Cole."

"Where?" he questioned.

"I need to return to Kinema," I answered. I couldn't leave him by the lake feeling horrible. I needed to find a way to repair Cole's fractured spirit.

"Fine, I'll go with you," he said. "But I'm not promising to go back. I'm just helping you."

"Thank you, Cole. I'll feel much braver with your help," I complimented.

A rumble came from above us and the earth violently shook. The skies filled with ominous pink-gray clouds and I shuddered as it illuminated with streaks of light. Before I could suggest we head for cover, a large boom sounded, followed by a bolt of lightning.

It struck the ground between us. The electric shock sent us flying through the air in opposite directions. My landing ended with a thud as my head cracked against the trunk of a tree, my skin stinging from the electricity. Dazed, I wrapped my arms around the rough bark. Water rushed around me, forcing me to hold tighter. Cole shrieked in terror. I struggled to shift myself around to see him.

"Meg, help!"

The current slowed and I forced myself to stand. A wave of nausea rolled over me and I swayed as I steadied myself in the knee-high water. Blinking away the fuzziness from my vision, I scanned the area. I couldn't find Cole.

What had once been a pebbled island was no longer visible. It was as if everything before me had dropped off the earth.

"I can't see you," I called out.

I wiped away the wetness dripping from my forehead and cringed in pain. My hand was covered in blood. I didn't have time to consider my injury before Cole's scream rang in the air.

"Please, I'm slipping," Cole pleaded.

My eyes darted around my new surroundings trying to find the little boy. I could hear him, but I couldn't see him. *What would Gram do?* Finally, it came to me – she would tell me to quiet my mind and listen. I tried to slow my breaths, hoping I would find him. Instead of hearing him, his head popped out of the water, only to quickly vanish from my sight.

My heart sank. The water I was standing in was rushing over the edge in the same place Cole had just been. The lake was falling. There was no time to think. I needed to act. Running to him as fast as I could, I prayed I wasn't too late.

When Cole appeared, peaking just over the brim, I could see him struggling to climb back up.

"Hold on, Cole. I'm coming," I said.

When I was a few feet away from him, the ground shook, again, and I was knocked down. Cole screamed as he lost his grip and fell out of view. *Please, no...please, no!*

An odd sense of relief filled me when I heard Cole's cries. "Please, help! I can't hold on much longer."

Choking back a sob of relief, I called out to him. "I'm coming, Cole. Just try to hang on."

The ground was still vibrating. I was afraid any move I made would trigger another quake. Instead of trying to stand, I scooted towards him, letting the waist-high water drive me forward.

When I finally reached him, I froze. Cole was holding onto the side of the newly formed waterfall. The cascade flowed down a staircase of small ledges. The drop would send him onto boulders in the thrashing waves below.

"I'm here, Cole," I reassured him. Then, I dangled my legs over the first edge. "Can you reach me?"

He leaned and immediately shook his head. The water rushing over him was pushing him. He would soon fall, and I wouldn't be able to stop it. Drops of rain fell on my cheeks. I looked up at the thick black and grey clouds that had formed overhead.

"Come on, it's starting to rain."

My words invited the skies to release. It poured down on us.

"Cole Oliver Sands, you *will* jump to me, now," I commanded. "It's no different than climbing trees at home and swinging branch to branch."

"I can't—" he started.

"There's no time to be a baby. Jump now!"

Cole closed his eyes and leapt.

When I felt his arms wrapping around my calves, I gave a sigh of relief. The rain poured harder and he started to slide. My hands grazed his skin, but he slipped off me.

Cole's blue eyes grew wide and his face filled with terror. I watched in horror as he fell, and I was unable to do anything to help. Another bolt of lightning struck nearby, and the ledge crumbled underneath me.

Grabbing for anything to stop my fall, my fingers dug into the wall. The soil and rocks were too wet. I couldn't maintain a connection for more than a few seconds. With nothing else to hold onto, I let myself fall, too.

Splash.

The water knocked the air out of me. I flailed and kicked my arms, trying to stop my body from being propelled deeper into the watery abyss.

Mara grabbed me. Pulling me into her arms, she said, "You can do it, little dancer. Just kick, kick, kick."

"I can't, Mara. It's not working." I sunk deeper and deeper.

The light dimmed. Voices surrounded me, blocking out my own thoughts and memories.

Give up. No one will miss you. You're not strong enough to be the Winter.

The whispers were right. I was weak and should just let go. My body went limp with defeat. I closed my eyes and submitted to the inevitable. Suddenly, something grabbed my ankle and dragged me, pulling me further into the darkness.

Suddenly, I saw a small light. A tiny flicker of hope. *No, I'm not giving up.*

Kicking my legs, I tried to free myself. It gripped me tighter. My lungs burned with the pain. I needed air, but I forced myself to resist the urge to breathe. When I thought it was too late, something gripped my hand and pulled me to the surface. I broke above the water, gasping for air.

"I've got you, Meg," Cole said. He hooked his arms under mine and swam with me. "Don't struggle or we'll both drown."

I let Cole drag me through the water. He was such a small boy in this form – no more than eight or nine, but he felt much stronger. "You should be able to stand, now." He released the hold he had on me.

He was right. The water was shallow enough, but my legs felt like jelly.

"Come on, we're almost there," he insisted.

Cole held my hand and led me towards a grassy bank. When we reached land, I collapsed. Digging my fingers into the blades, I called my magic, letting it restore me.

"I thought you were gone," I said as I sat up.

"I'm a good swimmer. Water is – was – my element." Cole sat next to me. "You scared me. I thought I lost you. Why didn't you try to swim?"

"It felt easier to give up," I admitted.

"It was them." Cole scowled.

"Ladarsha?"

"No, not her, but one of her kind. The others are scarier. She pretends to be someone nice, at least."

"There are more of them?" I asked.

"A lot more." Cole shivered.

I felt confused. "How do you know all of this?"

"They used to talk to us when he was inside us. They tried to convince us to follow them," he said.

"Who?" I wanted to understand, but I couldn't.

"The Shah – when he was inside of us," Cole explained. "They wanted us to come to them."

"You're wrong. It was Snowystra," I argued.

"No," he corrected me, "she feared them. She brought us there for them."

She brought them...? I shook my head. "How do you know this?"

"She told us." Cole frowned.

I searched his face for understanding. "Wait, so the Shah was never Cole...um, never you, I mean?"

"No, it was alive inside us, like a monster." A shudder wracked the boy's body. "I don't want it to come back. It scares me."

"He can't come back. Your magic has been removed. There's nothing left for the Shah to come through," I said, hoping it comforted him. "Can you tell me more about them?"

"You don't want to know more. It might let them get into your mind, too," he whispered.

"I need to know who we're fighting against," I insisted. "What all of this means."

Looking around, he said, "The Mrak. It's the darkness."

There were so many things I didn't understand. *What's the Mrak?* I needed to know more. I needed to protect my family. "Come on," I said, standing up. "We need to go to Kinema."

Cole threw his arms around me tightly. "I really thought I lost you, Meg." Releasing his hold, I saw his blue eyes were filled with tears.

"But, you didn't," I reassured him with a smile. "Oh, you're bleeding," I said, wiping the blood off his cheek.

"No, I'm not. It's your blood. You're a mess," he said, pointing at my head.

"Oh, that's just a little scratch," I replied, remembering my injury.

Cole shook his head. "No, we need to get something to clean you up and heal the cuts."

"I'm fine. It's just my soul," I said dismissively.

"It doesn't hurt like just a soul, does it?" he asked, narrowing his eyes at me.

I couldn't lie to him and say I wasn't in pain. "No, it does hurt like it's my body injured. But we need to keep moving forward and we need to figure out how to get over the falls. There must be a way down. So, let me think."

There were so many things running through my mind. Kinema sent me back to Cole. She wanted me to save him. I had to find a way to convince him to return to his body. That on top of making the most important decision of my life without my grandmother or my sister to talk to about it.

"We need to go over there," Cole insisted. "That's where we can find stuff to clean you up."

"No, that's going in the wrong direction." I shook my head.

"We need to focus on the important things, first, and that is to fix you." Cole frowned at me. "You don't want to be in pain. It'll call them."

Raising my eyebrows, I relented. "Ok, but we need to be quick."

We sloshed through the water until we reached the shoreline of soft grass.

"Look over there!" Cole exclaimed. "I told you. Just what we need."

Dragging me quickly through trees, he stopped at a pink and lavender bush. Picking the petals, he instructed, "Chew these, and then rub the paste on your wounds."

When I hesitated, he said, "Trust me. You'll be healed in no time."

The sweetly flavored petals warmed in my mouth. Spitting it into my hand, I rubbed the tincture on my feet. The warm sensation continued and then burned. "It stings."

"Yeah, but only for a minute," he smirked. "Who's the baby, now?"

"How do you know about this kind of stuff?" I asked.

"Someone taught me how to do this. She was nice," he said, looking away.

"Who taught you, Cole?" I asked, touching his hand.

"It was Gram...I mean Mae," he answered. "I don't have a grandmother of my own, but she was like one. I couldn't help her though."

"Cole, is that why you're hiding here?" I asked softly.

"I'm not hiding," he pouted. "He gives up too easy and loses everything. He didn't save Mommy. He didn't save Gram. He followed her into the Winter and made Mara cry. Why would I want to go back there? He's too weak to save anyone."

"You're wrong, Cole. *He* needs you. You're mad about things that neither of you had no control over. Sarah and Gram died and it was sad. But what would they say to you?" I gave him a minute to process what I'd said. Giving him a knowing look, I continued, "They would say you did your best. Snowystra was bad and there was no way to stop her. Horrible things happened, but it's time for you to forgive yourself and go home."

"No!" he screamed. "He gave up our Water. He didn't even fight. I would have slapped that old man hard and told him that it was *my* water. He cried like a baby and let them take it."

"You know that's not what happened," I chided, rubbing more of the mashed flowers on my forehead.

He grew silent. There was no point in arguing with him. Cole had to come to grips with the pain he felt on his own.

After I was cleaned up, Cole and I walked until we reached the edge of the forest. On the other side, we found the entrance to a winter wonderland. Snowbanks extended for miles and miles.

"We can't go there," Cole cautioned. "We'll freeze to death."

"No, we won't. We'll think warm thoughts," I said. "But, if by chance we do freeze, we'll to it together."

"Not helpful," he said, scowling.

The thought of being frozen, again, worried me. This time, I was flesh and bone, not ethereal. I didn't think it would be a good thing for my skin to solidify into ice. Earth had no power to control the snow. *But, water does,* I thought.

"Hey, Snow is just frozen water. Can't you tell the snow to part for us?" I asked.

"Maybe." Cole's eyebrows lifted in consideration.

"Well, then bend down and talk to it," I suggested.

Obeying, he called, "Water, please, clear a path for us."

The frosty powder in front of us melted, forming a blue path.

"It worked," he cheered.

Continuing the method, we walked deeper into the wintery area. Around us, snow-covered trees appeared. Rabbits hopped past us and birds flew above.

I was surprised to discover that even in the cold, life surrounded me. It was so peaceful here. The Earth was resting and when the Winter finally thawed, there would be new life all around.

"Have you thought any more about going back?" I asked Cole.

"No. I told you, I'm never going back. He doesn't need me," he snapped.

"You're wrong. He does need you. Without you, there isn't a Cole. This is so weird, talking to a piece of someone's soul. Don't you think? You're just as much Cole as he is. You need to return to complete yourself," I theorized.

His expression grew sour. "Not anymore."

"Ok, I won't mention it, again." I sighed.

"Good," he said gruffly.

"Even though you're wrong," I muttered under my breath.

Cole glared at me.

After we walked in silence for a few minutes, I said, "It's nice being older than you."

The boy scoffed. "You're not older than me."

I tousled his hair. "Yeah, I am. The Cole at home is an adult. You've decided you're separate, so you're still a child. One who is clearly younger than me."

Wrinkling his brow, he said, "I just look younger."

"Oh, Cole." I giggled. "You're younger."

His eyes blazed and as he began to counter my statement, something appeared in the snow. It was a young woman. When she stepped onto the path in front of us, we stopped.

"Mara?" I whispered.

"Hello, sister."

CHAPTER
FORTY-THREE

I couldn't believe it. Mara stood in front of us, but she looked different. She wasn't the vibrant pregnant woman I'd last seen. The person before me resembled my sister when she'd returned from Snowstrum. She was shockingly thin and pale.

"Mara, what are you doing here?" I asked. "You look—"

"What do I look like, Meg?" she asked coolly. "Are you not happy with my appearance?"

"No, it's just you look different."

Different was an understatement. With her tight black leather pants and burgundy halter top, she looked like the cold woman my mother had turned into. Her upper arm had a snake cuff and the silver chain around her neck held a large spider made of diamonds. The eight legs sparkled with light green gems.

"I'm just surprised to see you here," I admitted. "Is everything ok?"

"No, Meg. Everything is not ok," she spat the words at me. "You're trying to take the Winter away from my child. You're trying to take it away from me."

"But, I-I-I'm not taking anything. I promise. I just…I…"

"I know your plans to steal the Winter. I am the only Vizier. I am the Winter!" she screeched. Her hazel eyes narrowed, and I could feel the hatred she had for me. "My kingdom will be restored."

"But everyone is gone from your Snowstrum," I said softly.

"I will rebuild. Not with leftover children of Faramond, with no power. I'll collect my own, and then I'll raise my own family. A strong family."

My brow furrowed with concern. "What about Cole, Mara?"

"What about Cole?" she asked. "He'll rule by my side."

Cole stepped out from behind me.

Mara glared at the boy. "What is this? Picking up more helpless strays, Meg?" She threw her head back and laughed. "Isn't that what you do? How predictable. You always have to help the weak and broken."

"Yes, I found this strange boy, who I've never seen before," I lied.

She looked Cole up and down, again, before dismissing him.

"Yeah, you wouldn't have seen him before, would you, Ladarsha?" I challenged.

"What did you call me?"

"You heard me. You're not my sister. If you were, we wouldn't be having this stupid conversation. I know you're not my sister and *you* have no power here," I warned.

Mara scowled. "I have no power, little sister?" She motioned to the forest.

A green dot moved quickly towards us. As it grew closer, I lost my confidence. Silver eyes glowed as a metallic green spider charged at us. Its silver spiked legs smashed into the snow.

I recalled Mara's stories of the spiders used to fuel Snowystra's power. *Dorcha.*

Cole hid behind me, again.

'If you don't hurt it, it won't hurt you, Meg,' Gram's words played in my mind.

The spider stopped in front of me, baring its fangs. I held my hand out to it. "What a pretty spider you are."

I held my breath as it considered my offering. Like a cat, the dorcha rubbed against me. Examining the metallic fur of the creature, I decided the back was the safest place to pet.

"You're such a nice spider," I cooed.

When Cole peeked around me, I said, "Don't be afraid. Come pet the dorcha spider. It's very friendly."

The spider brushed against Cole, knocking him over. This sent Cole into a fit of joyous giggles.

"No!" Fake Mara screamed. "I commanded you to attack."

"You're really trying too hard to convince me you're someone you're not." I laughed. "By the way, it looks like you're leaking oil."

There was a black pool of liquid underneath her and the glamour she had created of Mara shimmered.

I waved my hand in a shooing motion. "Go now, Ladarsha. I don't want to do something unkind," I said patronizingly. "Thank you for calling a new friend for me. You know, you can never have enough allies."

Throwing her head back, she let out a piercing scream and melted. The black oil-like residue absorbed into the ground.

"That wasn't Mara, right?" Cole whispered.

"No way. If that had been her, you would've known."

"How'd you know it wasn't her?" Cole asked.

I shrugged and said, "Mara would've known who you were in an instant. She's loved you since she was a child. You grew up together. No matter how angry or crazy she was being, she'd always know you, Cole. She'll always be connected to you."

Cole opened his mouth to speak but then clamped it shut tight.

"Now that that nonsense is over, let's continue on. I have a decision to make," I said. "And, you're going to help me get there, right?"

"Yeah, I'll help you," he said, fidgeting.

A smile formed in the corner of my mouth. Talking about Mara had stirred something in him. I hoped this meant he was closer to being ready to go home.

Turning towards the dorcha spider, I patted it. "Goodbye. We have to go, now."

We resumed our travels down the path. My determination to find Kinema became intense. When we first started, the trees around us were heavy with snow. Some even had long icicles hanging from them. However, the forest in the distance and around us had less snow.

I wondered, *Will there still be snow?*

Click click click.

I turned around to see what was making the noise. It was coming from the dorcha that was closely following us. I sighed.

"No, you can't come with us. Go back to the snow," I chastised.

We started, again, and the clicks of the spider continued. The spider was almost touching me, now.

I turned to scold it and it rubbed against me. I couldn't help smiling at the gentle monster. "You're not going to give up, are you? You win.

You win. Come with us, but we're leaving the Winter, soon." I patted it gently.

The spider brushed against me and I gave it one final pat. As we journeyed, I talked about Mara. Cole laughed as I reminded him of stories about the card games, ice cream, and family times we shared.

"We're almost out of snow to melt," Cole said, stopping.

He was right. We had reached the end of the frozen landscape. On the other side, there was just the lush forest. Hesitantly, I looked around. It looked safe enough, but I had trusted too quickly already in this realm. I didn't want to repeat that same mistake.

"What are you waiting for," Cole asked.

A chime sounded and I could see Ledli zipping around the trees.

"We need to go that way," I said, pointing in the direction of the Earth elemental.

The spider stopped, refusing to follow further.

"It's ok," I said soothingly.

It reared back towards the snow.

"Oh, right, you're part of the Winter." I stroked its fur and a strange sadness filled me. "Well, we have to keep going. I hope we will meet, again."

Cole hugged the dorcha tightly. "Goodbye, Spidey"

When we crossed into the green forest, the dorcha skittered off into the snow.

I was suddenly hit with the overwhelming smell of lavender. Following the familiar sent, we eventually ended up in a mossy area. Something rustled, and I prepared myself for an attack.

From behind the tree, a familiar woman stepped out. It was Mara, again.

CHAPTER
FORTY-FOUR

"Meg, Cole!" Mara exclaimed. "They said you'd come if I just waited here." My sister hugged me tightly before kissing my cheek, over and over. "You don't know how good it is to see you. There's so much for me to tell you. Why aren't you home, yet?"

Sitting down on a mossy area, she patted it, and said, "Sit. Come sit. Why are you being so quiet?"

I stared into her hazel eyes, searching for signs of my sister. Her pregnant belly had returned, and her hair was wild and unruly. I couldn't see anything to tell me she wasn't my Mara, but it was too convenient for her to show up here.

"Aren't you going to sit?" she asked.

When I didn't respond, she raised her eyebrows and smirked at me. She called it her *signature eyebrow lift*.

"Even in this world, your hair's a mess," I teased.

"Well, you haven't been there to help me fix it," Mara said with a sheepish grin.

I knelt by her and ran my fingers through her hair. Twisting it and braiding it, I inhaled her vanilla scent.

"So, what is keeping you from coming home, Meg?" she questioned.

"Um..." I said, struggling to find the right words. "Well, I've been given a choice, Mara. I must make a decision. A pretty big one."

"Do you want to talk about it?" she asked.

"No, I know what I want. I know what the best choice for everyone is, especially me." I was excited to share my experiences with my sister. "Mara, you won't believe it. I met Gramp."

"Our Gramp? Chester?" Mara asked. Her eyes widened in surprise.

"Yeah, he's so great. He even made me the most delicious sandwich," I gushed.

"That's impressive because he's a horrible cook. He tried to make me a grilled cheese one time and was banished from Gram's kitchen for a week."

"He was not." I laughed.

"No, she didn't banish him, but she was mad that he ruined one of her best pans. Gram could never be angry with him for long, though. Why did he appear?" she wondered.

"He said I needed to make choices for me. That I had to live for me, not for everyone else," I admitted and averted my eyes from hers.

Mara took my hand down from her hair and squeezed it. "He was right, Meg."

"But you guys need me," I protested.

"We do need you," she agreed. "We will always need you. That will never be the question, but…"

"I need to live for myself?" I conceded.

"Exactly," she said. "Now that you've made your decision, come back to us, Meg." Mara yawned. "And, ask Cole why he's hiding?" Realization filled her eyes. "Hey, wait. Why is Cole here?" Yawning again, Mara lay down in the moss. "I'm so tired all of a sudden. Are you coming home, Meg? If so, come with me. Let's lay down and close our eyes. Then, we'll be home before you know it."

"I can't come home, right now," I told her. "I must finish what has started. I have a decision to make. Please know that the decision I'm making is not just for you. It's for me, too."

"Tell me you're coming back home, soon, Meg," she murmured. "You have to come because I have babies who need you," Mara said, unable to keep her eyes open. "They need their Aunt."

Before I could ask her any questions, she was sleeping, and her body faded into wisps of smoke.

Cole poked his head out from behind a tree. "Is she gone?"

"Yeah, why did you hide from her?" I asked.

"I didn't hide. I just didn't want to upset her."

I smiled. "See, I told you that you'd know the real Mara."

"I...I did. You're right, Meg. I need to go home. I need them as much as they need me," he said.

I took his hand. "Let's find out how to get you home."

"Oh, I know how to go back," he said, pointing. "Can you see that?"

"It's beautiful," I said as I stared at the lavender field ahead of us.

Cole let go of my hand and ran. Stopping in the purple bushes, he turned and waved. And, then the world around me went black.

CHAPTER
FORTY-FIVE

"If you're still confident in your decision, come to me," the voice of Kinema called.

Behind me, the tree of Danu glowed. Placing my hand on the bark, it slipped through. I closed my eyes and stepped inside. As I walked through the complete darkness, I felt a tingling sensation throughout my body. The sound of my heartbeat filled my ears and the *bu dum, bu dum* around me led me onward. I found the isolation comforting, even though I was uncertain where I was being led.

"Breathe," Gram whispered.

Obeying, I inhaled the woodsy fragrance of the tree.

The black void ended, and I found myself in a large room filled with silver-framed mirrors, much like the one in my grandmother's bedroom. A rush of the scents – lavender, cinnamon, fresh-cut grass, and summer rainstorms – engulfed me. The fragrances alternated without overpowering each other or bleeding into one.

In the center of the room, there were four high-backed silver chairs. Each had a distinctive design representing the elements running up the back. In the middle of the circle of chairs sat a large granite stone with a smooth top.

Daisy sat in her Earth chair with a somber look on her face. Puzzled by her behavior, I started towards her. I stopped when the room suddenly grew warm and a lavender light surrounded me.

"Hello, Meg."

I whipped around to find Danu sitting cross-legged on the granite stone. She was petting the small brown cat she held. I felt drawn to her. I was in awe of the beautiful goddess. She had given my family this amazing gift, and yet, I knew nothing about her.

She smiled lovingly at me.

Intense emotions ran through me. I felt something strong from her. *Love?* I couldn't put a name to it, but it was powerful and unspoken. It was like the connection I had with Gram and Mara.

"Why have you come here, Meg?"

Yes, I'm feeling the safe comfort of a motherly love, I realized before blurting out, "I'm scared. How do I know I'm doing the right thing, Goddess?"

"Enter the mirror and confront your fears," Danu suggested. "The choice at hand is yours to make and yours alone."

The silver around one of the mirrors glowed, and Daisy stood, offering her hand to me.

I nervously accepted.

In silence, she led me towards the silver-framed glass.

When I saw my reflection, I gasped. I was in a silver dress, much like the one I'd, once, seen Danu wear and my hair had been piled on top of my head in intricate curls. I couldn't remember when the change took place, or how I hadn't noticed it. I couldn't stop staring at myself. I looked grown...I looked like her. I looked like a Goddess.

Hugging me, Daisy whispered, "I will always be here for you. No matter what you choose. Now, go on. Step through the mirror." With a final squeeze, she released me.

The mirror led me to an empty stone room before it vanished before my eyes. Spinning around, I hoped to find an exit. In its place, I found Dunn, sitting against a wall sleeping.

Softly touching his cheek, I smiled as he woke. I expected his warm smile. Instead, his eyes burned with hatred and fear, not love.

"No matter what you do to me, I won't follow you. I will never pledge my life to you," Dunn growled. "Send me to the desert if that is your plan, but do it, now. I won't ever be a slave to the Winter, again. You should have died."

"No, Dunn," I cried. "It won't be like that. I'll be nothing like

Snowystra. Why are you saying such cruel things to me? The Winter will be a time for healing and celebration. A time for new life to be born."

"You say that you're not her? Can you not even see what you've become?" he screamed at me.

Dunn jumped up and roughly took me by my shoulders, pushing me against a wall. A mirror appeared. "Tell me that you've not accepted the darkness. You can't lie to me, Meg."

The reflection in the mirror was not me. It was Eliza...It was my mother. She wasn't the lovely woman she'd, once, been. The image was the tainted mother who left me. Her auburn hair was streaked with white and her cold black eyes glared at me.

"You've always been a Drygen," Eliza sneered. "Don't hide behind the fear and the cowardice instilled in you by my mother. Accept your destiny."

She disappeared and the image staring back at me from the mirror was a person I didn't recognize. The girl had black hair and dark eyes. It was me, but I looked like Mara had after her return from Snowstrum. I gasped at the sickly sight of myself. My nose wrinkled as I realized my mouth was covered in a green paste.

"This isn't me," I argued.

I turned around to convince Dunn that he was wrong, but he was gone. Lying in the center of the floor, there was a dead dorcha. I screamed in horror as I realized its heart was in my hands. The same spider that I had befriended.

"No," I cried, throwing the heart down. "I don't want to be like her. It will be different."

The mirror vibrated and an image of my grandparents appeared.

"She's not coming, Maesi." Gramp wrapped his arms around my grandmother.

Gram wept. "We lost another child to the Winter, Chester."

"No, Gram!" I cried. "I'm not lost. Please, believe in me. I promise you that you'll never lose me."

Falling to my knees, I sobbed. Seeing my grandmother in so much pain was unbearable. The mirror rippled and the sounds of Gram faded. The mirror held an image of Mara, holding a baby in her arms.

She rocked the child. "I'm sorry, my sweet baby boy, that I couldn't save her. I'm sorry that you'll never meet your aunt."

Cole appeared. He was, also, holding a child. "She will never meet her Neeps."

"It's my fault," Miles said, stepping out of the shadows. "I'm the reason for your pain. I must go back to my father. I am a Drygen."

"No, Miles!" I screamed and pounded on the mirror. "You're not a Drygen. Don't believe that. You're a Silver. You're my brother. It's not your fault."

"Your right," Mara softly agreed. "You should be with *your* family, Miles. We understand why you've made this decision."

"You will always be welcome in our home," Cole said, shaking Miles' hand.

"Thank you for understanding. Will you tell Elliott and Essie for me?" Miles asked.

"Of course," Cole agreed.

"What is wrong with you all? No, he can't go. Why is no one stopping him?"

Miles walked away and I pounded my fists on the mirror, trying to get his attention. My efforts were useless. Crumpling to the floor, the mirror vanished.

The room became ice cold and I could see my breath. I scrambled to the center of the room, I looked at the ceiling. Snow had begun to fall.

"If I choose the Winter, I'll be alone," I cried.

The light in the room faded and I was in the dark, truly alone with only my own heartbeat and my own thoughts. Everything I had seen replayed in my mind. Everything I feared most.

Lying down, I stared into the void. My mind felt like a maze of twists and turns leading me to dead ends. There were no answers to my questions.

Then, a tiny dot appeared in the absolute darkness. It was so small that I shouldn't have been able to see it. It shouldn't have reassured me, but it did. Sitting up, I placed my hands on the cold stone and called for Earth's strength.

Bu dum Bu dum Bu dum

I could hear a strong heartbeat and I knew I was in the center of Danu's tree. My own heartbeat fell in time with the tree's as I walked. After several minutes, I finally exited the darkness. Slowly, my eyes adjusted to the light change and I found myself in the center of a grove of large pink trees.

"I told you that you were not ready to make the decision. You are not ready to become the Winter. Return to your body," Kinema said, stepping out from within one of the trees.

"But—"

"No, child. It was wrong of me to give you such a choice. Your fears are too strong. You are too young for such responsibility. How can I turn over the Winter to you?" Kinema's eyes filled with so much pity for me.

"You're wrong. I understand the Winter, now," I appealed.

"But, what about your family?" she asked. "You won't be able to help them."

"I won't be able to in the Afterlife, either," I argued.

"They will grieve your death, but they will not feel abandoned," Kinema countered.

I straightened my back and raised my chin slightly, gathering my strength. "They'll be grieving either way. If I don't take the Winter, they will take my niece from her parents."

"Possibly, but is that enough to give up your life?" Kinema shrugged. Her nonchalant tone infuriated me.

Wiping my tears away with the back of my hand, I took a deep breath. "I've made my decision and I insist you hear me. I am not a child."

"Fine, Meg. Speak. I will accept your decision, but remember, there is no turning back." Kinema offered me her hand.

PART THREE
MARA

CHAPTER
FORTY-SIX

I woke up from my sleep in a cold sweat. My dreams were blurred images that I couldn't make sense of. Sitting up, I groaned. My body ached, and my stomach was sore.

I touched my belly. It felt different. Now, the hard roundness was deflated and jiggly. An image of Laura holding a baby boy up for me and other memories slowly returned.

Cole and I had twins. We named them Mazy and Finnegan after my grandparents. My daughter was the Winter.

"Cole," I cried.

"What's wrong, Mara? Do you need some pain medication?" Laura asked.

"Where are my babies?" I demanded. "Who's watching them?"

"They are right here, Mara." Laura pointed to a bassinet at the end of the bed. "The babies are sound asleep. You fainted about an hour ago. Why don't you lie back down until they wake?"

I have a decision to make, Mara, Meg's words filled my mind.

"Where is Meg?" My panic seemed to be increasing.

Laura's face paled. I could see her hesitation. Finally, she said, "Cole is with her. There has been an accident, Mara. Meg was hurt."

I looked at my sleeping children and I felt torn. My sister needed me, but I couldn't leave them alone, unprotected.

"They are in the first birthing room. I can send someone to get you when the babies wake. I promise, I won't leave their side," Laura said, squeezing my hand.

"You're right. I need to go to her." I hesitated as I looked down on my sleeping babies. Their hands were clutched together.

"Go to Meg, Mara," Laura encouraged.

My heart was racing so fast, I felt like it would jump out of my chest as I went to find Meg. I had seen my sister in Danu's grove. She was trying to tell me something important. *Why had I fallen asleep? Why did I not stay and make her tell me the choice she had to make?*

When I reached her room, I found Cole weeping over Meg. She was turned onto her side and I could see her back was covered with a heavy patch of blood-soaked gauze. My panic turned to anger. My sister was hurting, and no one told me.

"What happened? Why didn't you come get me immediately?" I cried as I rushed to her side. "We could have called the elements to heal her."

Kneeling down, I touched Meg's face. She was ice cold.

"You were having a baby, Mara. Then, you passed out. I'm sorry I left you, but I had an overwhelming feeling that she needed me. She was so frightened. It was like she was calling me."

The torment in Cole's face made me pause. I sat down beside him. "Is she better, now?"

"She's not as scared, but I can't break away from her. You must think I'm crazy, but I had to be with her. It was like she was pulling me to her," Cole explained. "As I sat with her, holding her hand, she suddenly squeezed mine. I felt my Water magic surge through me. It was wonderful. The feeling of emptiness I've been carrying filled and I had the most incredible dream. I was with Meg, though I was just a boy. And Meg was wearing the most ridiculous outfit."

It hadn't been a dream. He was describing my sister as I had seen her. "She was wearing a plant dress," I offered.

Cole's eyes widened in surprise.

"I saw you both there. I wasn't sleeping. I had been brought to Danu's realm. I think it was to see Meg." I took a deep breath and steeled myself for the news I dreaded. "Now, tell me what happened to my sister."

Cole looked deep into my eyes. "Dunn found Meg in the forest. Cedric and Jameson had tried to take Miles. Meg found them and attempted to stop them. Jameson snuck up on her and stabbed her with one of Snowystra's daggers. There was so much damage to her internal organ. The injuries were from the dark magic running through the weapon."

I choked back a sob. "Go on," I whispered.

"By the time Dunn arrived, Cedric was bound by Meg's Earth magic and Jameson was dead." Cole's voice was flat with emotion.

"What about Miles?" I asked. "Is he ok? My father?"

"When Miles tried to stop Jameson's attack, he cast his Air magic. The force of the wind sent the old guard crashing into a tree, killing him instantly. When your father arrived, he went crazy, beating Cedric until Faramond intervened. Elliott and Miles are, now, resting under Essie's supervision."

"I don't know what to do to help any of them," I cried.

"Mar, I know this is a lot to digest. You know what you can do? Go to our babies. They need you," he said, "and I'll stay with Meg."

When I returned to our room, Laura was rocking and patting Mazy. "You're just in time. This little one is ready for you."

Laura was so comfortable with my daughter and Mazy was so content in her arms. I wasn't confident my child would be as serene in mine.

"Where is Finn?" I asked. I felt surprised by my sudden worry about where he was and if he was safe. It was ridiculous since Laura had been caring for babies for years.

She nodded towards the bassinet. "He is sleeping. Why don't you start with Mazy, and then I will bring you the boy?"

"She won't feed without him," I said. It would be so much easier if she'd let me feed her alone, but I had the feeling she didn't quite trust me. *Does she know about the darkness inside me?*

"See you're already getting used to having twins. Have a seat over there." She pointed towards a cushioned rocking chair. "And, we need to get you something to eat and drink."

"I'm not hungry," I argued.

"Mara, at least, let me bring you a tonic," Laura coaxed. "You'll need the energy for your children."

"Ok," I relented and took Mazy from her.

Laura had been right. Mazy was hungry, but she was, also, resistant. She wailed as I tried to help her latch on.

In a low whisper intended only for my daughter's ears, I said, "You're not from her blood. You're my daughter. I know that you were created by love. Your brother will be here, soon. So, please, trust me."

I stroked her cheek and half expected my hand to be covered by fine frost from her skin. My touch ignited her natural instinct and the newborn could no longer hold onto her protest. She fed, but she made sure to remind me of her discontent with the situation by expelling small grunts.

When Laura finally set Finn into my arms, the babies wriggled together. Once again, they clasped hands as they fed. It was as if a magnetic force pulled them towards one another. Finn's touch calmed Mazy and she no longer whimpered.

"He has such red hair. Such a contrast to your pure white. My fire and ice," I professed.

As Mazy feel asleep, Laura took her from me. Gently rubbing her back, she lay her in the bassinet while Finn continued to feed. My little boy seemed more content than his sister. When he finally fell asleep, Laura took him and handed me a glass of thick purple liquid.

"Drink this, Mara. After, I want you to rest and restore yourself," she said.

When the babies were fed and sleeping, again, I left them in Laura's care. Against her wishes, I returned to Meg instead of my bed. To my surprise, Cole hadn't left her side.

I played our conversation, over and over, in my mind. Cole was a child when I saw him in Danu's world. *How is that possible?*

"Cole, how do you think you were with Meg? You've never left us?"

"I have no clue. I have these odd memories, now. Things I could never have done. I remember riding on a fish and falling off a cliff. I remember —"

A small bird flew into the room and spun around Cole. It hovered, fluttering its wings. The bird glowed and changed, rising into the air above us. The transformation continued until finally a glorious blue-chested bird expanded its wings, displaying a breathtaking woman with bird features: Sarika.

"It was a piece of his fractured soul who had those experiences. When your magic was taken, a small part of your soul left your body. It has been restored," she explained.

Sarika had no reason to be here. Cole was healed and, it wasn't the twin's first birthday. *The babies*, I thought before understanding struck. *Oh no! Is she coming for Mazy, now?*

"Sarika, why are you here?" Cole asked, quickly standing up.

"Don't worry. I came to see if you were ok," she said and placed her hand on his chest. Sarika smiled. "I was worried that the returning piece of you would be carrying the darkness. But I can feel that is not true."

His eyes lit up with her words. "Do I have my Water magic back?"

The goddess frowned. "No, Cole. Your magic will, now, just be a memory. You'll never lose your connection to the element, but you won't be able to call the magic at your will."

Silently, they stared into each other's eyes for the longest time. I didn't understand her motives. She acted like she was concerned about Cole and he trusted her. There had to be something else she was after. She had to have something planned.

"I don't mind that the magic is gone. Don't misunderstand me. I did love my gift, but I just want to know that my children and my wife will not have to worry about the dark side of me showing up. I'll never hurt Mara, again. Nothing matters more to me," Cole vowed.

"May I?" Sarika took his hand.

Cole nodded and when he turned his wrist over, she stabbed her nails into his forearm. Cole grimaced but didn't pull away.

I watched in shock as his arm glowed with silver streaks.

Removing her nails, she rubbed her fingertips over his skin, sealing the gouges in his forearm.

"Is it gone?" Cole probed.

"I still do not sense the darkness inside you. You can release your fears." Unhanding his arm, Sarika turned her attention towards me. "I am told your sister will be making her decision soon. With your permission, I would like to be here when she wakes."

I shrugged noncommittedly.

Sarika's eyes narrowed, but before she could speak, Faramond strode into the room. I felt relieved. He wouldn't let her do anything to harm Meg or my children.

"Sister," Faramond greeted, bowing his head. "The girl does not have much time left. Her body will, soon, release her spirit. Do not give them false hope. They do not need any more promises and pain."

Shock flooded me. *Meg is dying?*

"Always so quick to deliver the dead." Sarika clucked her tongue. Her blue eyes flashed a warning. "Some things are beyond your control, Faramond."

"She told me she has a decision to make. All I know is that she told me she'd made up her mind," I interrupted, hoping to stop their conversation from escalating.

Faramond weakly smiled at me. "I did not come to quarrel. I came to check on you and your children. I have seen the twins. They are sleeping peacefully. But it is you that I am worried about, Mara. You just gave birth and I am told you have not rested at all." Faramond's eyes shone with concern.

"I'll sleep when my sister returns," I corrected. "While you are here, you can tell me about my father. How is he doing?"

"Elliott is resting," Faramond assured.

"And, Cedric? What will be done with him?"

"Cedric is, also, resting. He was not a healthy man before this, and he is not taking the death of his father very well." Faramond shook his head sadly. "He will be taken to the Council when he awakens."

"How didn't you know that Jameson was dark?" Cole asked. His tone was harsh.

"I had known of Jameson's relationship with Blanche Drygen. There was nothing I could do to stop it as Mortorcus since I was bound to Snowystra. It had not mattered because it was over before it began. I was told their dalliance ended because she had a child with another man." Faramond met my eyes. "There was no reason for me to ask any more questions."

When I glanced away, he added, "As far as Jameson's connection to Snowystra, he was desperate for power. He always had dreams of being the Shah until that was taken away from him."

Cole became the Shah, I realized. *He replaced Jameson.*

As much as I wanted Cedric to be out of our lives, forever, I knew how cruel Snowystra had been. He was a victim as much as anyone else and Miles would feel the pain of losing both of his parents...no matter how selfish they had been.

"I don't want Cedric hurt," I insisted.

"The Council will be fair," Sarika said.

Faramond let out a small laugh.

"They will not make a decision without me there and I promise you that the judgment will be fair." Sarika glared at her brother.

"I hope you're telling me the truth. I haven't seen the fair side of the Council, yet," I said.

"Right now, Tannus' focus must be on restoring the balance. There have been warnings of a rising from the Mrak. The need for your child to be named the Winter – and soon – has become crucial. I know we promised a year, but I must ask you to consider bringing her forward earlier."

"You say evil is rising and you want me to hand off my child to you. I can't bring my daughter to you, now. We don't want to give her to you at all," I shouted.

Cole squeezed my hand, trying to calm me. "It's cruel for you to ask us to give her up," he said weakly.

"I understand this, Mara, but won't it be easier to say goodbye to her, now, rather than later?" Sarika asked.

"No, it will never be easy." Cole's voice filled with anger.

"I will give you time to think while I continue to do everything I can to stifle the Mrak. However, each day, they grow stronger and, soon, I will not be able to stop them."

"We don't know who the Mrak are or why it has anything to do with our child."

"The Mrak are a dark force that we have controlled for centuries," she explained. "Not even Snowystra was naive enough to go against them."

"My child needs to be taken away to go fight? How can you expect me to separate my children?" My ability to control my emotions was wavering.

"I cannot ask you to do that. We could take both and raise them, together," Sarika said.

"How convenient. Both of my children in one swoop. No, won't give you our daughter. Go. You can't have them. I will find a way to stop you!"

As if on cue, a young Miezitari girl rushed into the room. "Laura asked me to come get you, Mara. Oh, Goddess." The girl came to an abrupt stop and bowed deeply before Sarika.

Waving her hand as if to tell her the formality was unnecessary, Sarika asked, "What were you sent for, child?"

"The boy is ready for his feeding." The girl lifted her head long enough to answer before bowing it quickly, again.

Sarika raised the girl's head up by placing her finger under her chin. "Your respect is appreciated, but you will find with me that there is no need for such formalities, child." Turning towards me, Sarika said, "Mara, go to your babies."

"I want you to stay here," I said to the young girl. "I want you to watch my sister. If she moves at all, please, come get me right away."

"Mara, you are so convinced I have ill intentions?" Sarika asked. "I hope, one day, you will realize that I always have had your best interest at heart. You will understand what a guardian I have been to you. Now, go feed your child."

CHAPTER
FORTY-SEVEN

By the time we reached the room, I realized my mistake. Leaving Meg with only the young Miezitari wouldn't guarantee my wishes would be followed. If Faramond decided to escort her soul, she would be helpless. As far as Sarika, the girl would be no match. I sent the one person I knew loved Meg as much as I did — Laura.

Alone with my little family, my anxiety kicked in.

"We're not going to let them have either of our children," I declared.

Finn whimpered.

"Shh, it's ok. It's ok, Finn," I said, gently rocking him. Pacing back and forth, my anger grew. "I'm tempted to contact the Mrak myself and make a deal."

"Don't talk like that, Mara," Cole scolded and took Finn from me. "Never say anything so foolish, again."

"Either way, we lose, Cole. How do we know the Mrak are bad? Because they told us? They demanded our daughter. Now, they have the audacity to say they want our son, too!"

"I trust Sarika, Mar," Cole said, laying our sleeping child in the bassinet next to Mazy.

"Why? She didn't heal you. They took your magic, instead. Everything's changed. We won't give away our daughter and how do you separate twins? How did these all-knowing Gods not know I was pregnant with them? They examined me enough. And, Sarika – so high and mighty – claiming to be my guardian. How has she been guarding me,

Cole? I lost my mother, my father, my grandmother, and I almost lost you."

"But you didn't lose me, Mar." Cole sighed, taking my arm. "Let's let them take the children, today. We'll go with them and insist to be set up in a house with our babies. As long as we're together, we can make anywhere our home."

"You heard Tannus. He won't allow this. He plans on raising our daughter," I ranted and shook off his grip.

"He'll accept our terms, or we won't go," Cole promised and pulled me into his arms. "I'm not your enemy. Stop fighting me. We're a team."

In his arms, the fight left me...or, at least, for a moment.

"He's such a fool," Snowystra hissed. "None of you can stop the Mrak. It looks like you picked the wrong side." Her maniacal laughter rang in my ears.

When I tried to pull away, Cole held me closer. *He didn't hear the dark goddess. Maybe, in the end, my children would be safer with someone else*, I considered.

"She's awake," Laura cried as she ran into the room, interrupting my self-deprecation. "Meg is awake."

I ran faster than I ever thought I could. My sister was awake. I had to get to her. When I entered the room, Meg was sitting up in the bed. She was smiling as if she had just awoken from a restful night's sleep.

"Meg!" I rushed to her and sat beside her. I was afraid to hug her because she'd been so injured. How could she be sitting here as if nothing happened? "Oh, Meg, you scared me."

"I'm sorry I missed everything," she said, touching my stomach. "I can't believe I wasn't there for the birth."

"You're here, now, and that's all that matters." I kissed her cheek and looked deep into her eyes. "Are you sure you're really ok?"

"I feel great. Now, can I see my niece?" Meg nodded. Looking towards the doorway, she saw Cole and beamed. "Is that her? Quick, bring her to me."

"Meg...um," I started to explain when Laura followed Cole, carrying Mazy.

"Wait, two?" Meg's eyes flicked back and forth between the babies. "Oh, my gosh! You had two babies?"

"Yeah, twins. Surprise." I laughed and held my son out to her. "Finn, say hello to your Aunt Meg."

"He's so beautiful, Mara. I can't believe I missed the birth." Meg's eyes welled with tears as she stared down at her nephew. "Was it amazing? You have to tell me everything."

"I think you would've had more enjoyment out of your part in the process than I did with mine. But the end product was worth it," I admitted.

"Hey, Meg, you're looking much better since you lost your plant dress," Cole said, taking Mazy from Laura.

"I needed some clothing and I had to work with what I could find. If you would've been dropped into that world like I was, you would've been stuck running around naked." She giggled.

"Only you would come up with a crazy idea like that." Cole kissed Meg on the top of her head and held out Mazy to her. "Let me take my son and you can hold your niece."

"Mazy, you're so pretty," Meg cooed lovingly, examining her. "Hey, you, what are you holding?" Meg opened Mazy's tightly clenched fingers. "How did you get this? Why are you guys giving your child flowers? Isn't this a choking hazard?" she scolded.

"What?" I looked at Mazy's hand as she closed her palm. Squished in her fist, petals poked out between her fingers. "I didn't give her that." I gently forced her finger open and saw a bright purple flower.

She quickly clamped her hand closed.

"I didn't give her it, either," Cole said, looking over my shoulder.

"I can't believe this, but I gave it to her. I mean, I met her in the other realm. Didn't I, Mazy? If I only had known who you were," Meg said softly.

Mazy wailed when Meg took the flower from her.

"Here, let me take her from you," I said. "You probably should get some rest before your visitors start arriving." I turned towards Cole. "Has anyone let my father know that Meg's awake?"

"Is Dad ok?" Meg asked, standing up.

"He's resting. You need to sit back down. I'll send for Livia. She needs to examine you," I gently chided.

"I feel great. Look," Meg replied as she spun around. "I don't hurt at all. Don't call for Livia. Instead, can someone get my satchel from my room?"

"I can," Cole quickly offered. Before I knew it, he left, taking Finn with him.

"Meg, I was so worried," I said. "I really don't know what I would've done if you..."

Meg took Mazy from my arms. "I'm here, now. Aren't I Mazy? Do you know who I am?"

Mazy stared at Meg with a look of wonder.

Does she know her? I wondered to myself.

Meg's eyes welled with tears. "She's so beautiful. I'm sorry I missed the birth."

Mazy started to cry and Meg rocked her, trying to calm her.

I held out my arms to take her. "Let me feed her and we can talk about the decision you have to make." I sat in one of the chairs and started to feed Mazy.

Meg's eyes widened as she watched me. "You're a mom," she murmured.

"Yes, and you're an aunt. Now, come sit by me and tell me everything." I patted the chair next to me.

Meg let out a long sigh. "I was given the choice between my death and my life. No, it was more than that." Meg bit her lip as if contemplating her next words. "If I accepted my death, I would be escorted to the Afterlife to be with Gram and Gramp. Or, I could become the Winter."

"What? You've no Winter magic, so how can you become it? Your gift is Earth magic. Are you sure I shouldn't call Livia?" I wondered if Snowystra's magic from the dagger was still poisoning my sister.

"I'm not crazy, Mara." Meg frowned at me. "I can prove it."

Cole returned with the satchel. "Here you go."

"Can you take Mazy? She needs a change I think." I smiled, handing her to Cole.

"Diaper duty?" Meg laughed.

"Yes, just until you're well enough. Then, I'll turn it over to you." Cole snorted and left us alone.

"You should see him with them. It's like he's been a father his whole life," I praised.

With a grave expression, my sister stared at me for the longest time. Finally, I took Meg's hand. "Are you ok? What's wrong?" I asked.

Meg was so quiet that it suddenly scared me. My sister wasn't one to hide her feelings.

"Tell me what you mean by choosing the Winter or the Afterlife."

Meg reached into her bag and pulled out a silver journal. "I, once, told you that Eliza's children carried the dark magic. While this is true, I didn't tell you everything. Even though it shouldn't change anything, I was worried you'd feel different about me."

"You're scaring me, Meg." I trembled.

"Well, you know you're my sister and you'll *always* be my sister," she said.

"I got that already, Meg," I replied, not hiding my frustration. "Just spit it out. I can't handle any more riddles. Say what you need to say."

"Cedric's my father," she blurted out.

"What did you say?" My eyes narrowed at her. *She's mad!*

Meg was Elliott Stone's daughter. They had the same green eyes. The same happy personality. Her injury must have done something to her memory.

"Cedric Drygen is my real father," Meg insisted.

My body felt tight and my breath felt short. A wave of nausea rolled over me. Eliza had green eyes.

"Mara." Meg grabbed my hand. "I'm telling you the truth."

"What? You're wrong, Meg," I argued, blinking the tears from my eyes.

Meg opened the journal to a page marked with a dried piece of peppermint-scented lavender.

"I tried to make it all go away," she said, offering me the journal, "but I couldn't."

I took the book from her and stared at the open page. It was Eliza's handwriting, but it was hurried, not meticulous.

> *Today, she lured Marina into the red forest, following a baby deer. If the owl woman hadn't appeared, I think Snowystra would have taken her this time. I DO NOT KNOW HOW TO PROTECT MY DAUGHTER! I need Cedric!!!!*

A faint memory came to me of chasing a baby deer. As soon as I got close enough to touch it, the fawn would rear back and run. It was playing a game with me. A fuzzy image of piercing eyes and talons came to mind.

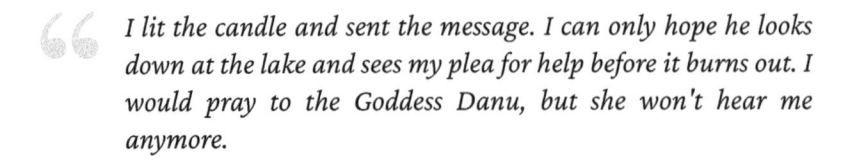

> *I lit the candle and sent the message. I can only hope he looks down at the lake and sees my plea for help before it burns out. I would pray to the Goddess Danu, but she won't hear me anymore.*

Eliza could have talked to Gram. She would've helped her. She would have told her the Goddess loved her and would never give up on her.

> *I saw Sarah this morning. Her son has grown up so much. I look at her family and I am saddened. Cedric and I were supposed to have this life. Don't get me wrong, I love Elliott despite myself. I want to be in love with only him, but I LOVE CEDRIC. I have loved him since I was fourteen years old, but she took him away from me. She put me in the horrible position of loving two men – but the one I want...the one I need... he's the one I can never have.*
>
> *Sarah has agreed Cedric can meet me, one last time, at her cottage and she will not tell my secret. My loyal friend...my alibi. I'll continue to play the self-absorbed princess who needs to have everything perfect. I'll claim my hair...my nails...my body needs to be improved and Sarah will help me. My mother will believe it. She thinks I am a selfish, vain, horrible mother. But I will keep up the act. I'll be that person if it will protect my daughter.*

Snowystra took my mother away before I even met her. The woman raising me was not the real Eliza. I knew the perfect woman she described. I wanted to be like her. She was beautiful and confident. Would I have to lose myself to save my daughter? My son?

> *How could I make such a mistake? My fears should have never led me into his arms. I've never betrayed Elliott. Throughout this marriage, I have kept our marriage bed sacred. One stupid mistake and I have ruined it all!*

Reading of her betrayal surprised me, even though I knew about it. She had forced my father to leave us, so she could be with Cedric.

> *Elliott watches me like he knows what I did. He knows I deceived him. Does he see my scarlet letter or am I just being paranoid?*
>
> *I can't use the excuse of being tired of being a wife and a mother as the reason for keeping my distance anymore. I should forget what happened no matter how much I want to be with Cedric. In his arms for just that one night, again, has fueled my desire for him and my hatred for her. Her Winter. Her need for power. I'll find a way to save my daughter from her. Even if I must sacrifice my own heart.*

Skimming through the next pages, Eliza detailed my father's kindness and his loving gestures, but her entries were sprinkled with her pain of losing Cedric. I stopped at the next entry. My tears fell onto her words.

> *I'm pregnant and there's no way the child can be Elliott's. I must hide this pregnancy for another month and proclaim the birth came early. I have to hope my mother doesn't see through my deception. I can NEVER let Cedric know I'm carrying his child. His mother would use it for her benefit.*

She was lying to everyone to cover up her affair. There had to be another journal — one where Eliza would say she was wrong. She would say she'd made a mistake about the dates.

> *I cannot write in this journal anymore. It holds my lies. I will hide it and, one day, you may find it, my beautiful baby girl. Dear sweet Meg Violet Stone. Yes, Stone.*
>
> *Can you ever forgive me? I hope I have told you my secrets and you're not reading them for yourself. Please, forgive me for not telling you Cedric Drygen is your father, but you've not missed anything with Elliott as your dad. Elliott's the kindest and sweetest man in the world. If only I could convince myself that your green eyes were like his, not mine.*
>
> *Look in the mirror, my daughter. You're a Drygen. No*

matter how much I don't want you to be – You are! I hope you will forgive me and, one day, you'll meet Cedric and see the kind, loving man that I know and love. I pray that the darkness will not have consumed and tainted him by the time this day comes.

I pray for you, my baby. I pray that you don't carry the magic and that you'll be kept safe.

I shut the journal and, once again, wiped away tears. Meg was a Drygen.

"You can't tell anyone," I said, my voice barely above a whisper. "You can't tell our fa – you can't tell Elliott." I choked back my tears.

"Oh, Mara, he knows. Please, please, don't cry. I told him many years ago. I found the journal and I was devastated. I didn't know what to do. Essie found me and I confessed everything. Do you know what our silly father said?"

I shook my head, unable to speak.

Meg smiled sadly. "He said that no matter what genetic makeup brought me to him, I was always going to be his daughter." My sister began to weep. "He said from the first kick, he knew I had his heart and I'd always be his. So, I do carry the Winter, Mara," she said, grabbing my hand and hugging me. "We will *always* be sisters."

"She's glad to not be one of Elliott's sniveling children," Snowystra hissed. "Don't believe her lies. She's glad you aren't really sisters."

Meg pulled away and looked into my eyes.

A coldness filled me. She had lied to me. "You should've told me. Why would you hide this from me? Are you relieved you aren't my sister? You have your new family, now."

"Of course, not." Meg picked up the journal and shook it at me. "This doesn't change how much I love you. You mean more to me than anything. I'm sorry you had to find out this way. I couldn't find the right time to tell you. You had just come back. Cole left. You were already so broken."

Her bravado cracked and she could no longer maintain her role as the strong sister. "How could I take one more thing away from you, even if it was just words? Do you hear me? It changes nothing. How could you doubt this, Mara?" Meg asked, throwing the journal.

As the tears fell down her cheeks, we glared at each other. *Snowystra was right. I will destroy everyone and everything that means anything to me.*

I grabbed Meg's hand and forced her to look at me. "I'm sorry. You were so strong when I returned. You were there when I couldn't take care of myself. Promise me I won't lose you. I just...I can't lose you."

"There's nothing that can ever separate us. When you were gone, I felt incomplete. You were gone. My sister was gone. My world was gone. Please, don't let this destroy us." Meg fell into my arms.

Stroking her hair, I held her tight against me. "I'd been incomplete without you, too," I whispered.

We silently clung to each other as the hateful words and anger melted away. A sweet smell wafted into the room and we reluctantly released our hold on one another. The room was hazy, filled with lavender smoke.

The image of Kinema Delli formed. Her green gown waved in the breeze of her elemental air. "Meg, you made your choice. It's time for you to accept your responsibilities."

"What choice?" I asked, stepping in between the Goddess and my sister.

"Your sister has made her decision, one which cannot be undone. Step aside," Kinema commanded.

"Not until you tell me what choice she made," I said defiantly.

Kinema waved her hands and Meg groaned. I turned around to watch her collapse to the floor.

"No," I cried, falling to my knees next to her. I wrapped my arms around my sister. "You can't have her."

The room illuminated and Sarika appeared.

"Daughter, pick up the girl," Kinema ordered.

"Don't touch her," I screamed and held her tighter. "What are you doing with her?"

"Release her, Mara," Sarika said.

When I resisted, she lifted her hand and blew an amber dust into my face. The powder immobilized me, and I felt Meg's body slip from my arms. She'd taken my sister from me.

As the powder cleared, I saw Kinema encircle Sarika, Meg, and herself in a cloud of silver particles. I dived at them to stop her, but I was too late. The room flashed with a brilliant light for the briefest moment, and then they were gone.

My sister's gone because she's the Winter? What does this mean for my daughter?

I ran through the hallways and into the birthing area. It was eerily quiet. *Where is everyone?* I swung the door to our room open and found Cole changing Finn.

"What's wrong, Mara?" Cole picked our son up and rocked him.

"Where's Mazy?" I asked, not answering his question.

"She's in the bassinet, Mar. She just fell asleep. Calm down or you'll wake her."

I scooped my daughter into my arms and held her tight. "They took Meg."

"Who?"

"Kinema. Sarika. They took her. We must hide, Mazy. They'll take her, too."

Cole caught me with his free hand and pulled us close. "Stop, Mara. Slow down and tell me what happened."

Silver particles permeated the air. Before I could warn him, a light flashed.

CHAPTER
FORTY-EIGHT

Once again, Cole and I stood in the Council's chamber in Asceraunia. Tannus looked down on us with an expression of satisfaction on his face. I held onto Mazy tighter, as Cole held Finn.

"Good, I see my sister has convinced you to accept the change in our agreement. Bring the child to me," Tannus ordered.

Suddenly, Kinema and Sarika stepped through a doorway, escorted by two guards. Sarika still held Meg's lifeless body in her arms. I had to stop them from whatever they had planned. They couldn't take my sister.

"Not so fast, Tannus," Kinema ordered. Even with her petite frame, she commanded the respect of everyone in the room.

"Mother, what are you doing? You cannot interfere with this. I am doing what is best for our realm." Tannus sounded more like a petulant child than an almighty god.

"You will have your Winter, but it will not be the baby," she announced, flicking her wrist.

Tannus was transported from his throne to his mother's side. Stroking the back of her hand along his cheek, she soothed, "You must trust that I know what is best." She smiled at him lovingly. "Sarika is holding your Winter, my son. Meg has offered to fulfill the role."

"She does not hold the Winter," Tannus scoffed.

"Are you questioning me, Son?" Kinema's eyes flared.

"The child Mara is holding is clearly the Winter. Have you ever seen a child born with skin and hair so white?"

Kinema waved her hand, again. Two prismatic tubes, like jar specimens from a science class, appeared out of the air.

Instead of opening the jar, Sarika pushed Meg's body into it. What initially seemed like glass, welcomed Meg inside and coated her body. She moaned as though in pain.

"No, you are hurting her!" I cried.

Kinema turned towards me. "She is in no pain, Mara. Bring me your daughter."

"No!" I cried. "I didn't agree to this."

Turning to Cole, I hissed. "Stop this."

Cole stepped forward. "You can't have her. They promised us a year."

"Mara, bring me the child. I am offering you a solution. No harm will come to the baby," Kinema promised.

I wouldn't give them my child. This was not an option. We had all lost too much because of their cruel games. I could not lose another person I loved. I wouldn't sacrifice my daughter.

"Give the child to me or to Tannus. You must decide, now."

I was frozen. I couldn't make this decision. I didn't want to turn my baby over to either.

"Give her to me," Cole said softly. He took her from my arms and handed me Finn.

We would stand against them, together. We wouldn't let them take our babies.

Finn wailed as Cole carried Mazy away.

I reached out and grabbed his arm. "What are you doing?"

He gave me a pleading look. "She promised Mazy would be safe."

"Why would you believe them? Give me my daughter," I demanded.

Cole removed my hand. "Trust me, Mar."

Stunned, I watched Cole walk away with Mazy. *Just like that, he gave her away. As if she meant nothing.* I screamed as Cole offered our daughter to Kinema.

Before he released his hold, he said, "You promise me our daughter won't be hurt?"

"You have my solemn vow," the goddess promised.

Kinema held Mazy tightly, whispering soothing words to her.

Tenderly, she placed my daughter into the cylinder of liquid next to Meg. Suspended in the fluid, threads of silver left both Meg and Mazy's skin, traveling through the glass containers. The threads twisted and combined, changing through the colors of the elements – red, green, silver, blue – and then it repeated.

When they turned black, I gasped. "No, please, not the darkness."

Cole wrapped his arms around me.

I tensed. I could've killed him for his betrayal.

The binds changed, again. Yellow. Orange. Mazy's skin lost its white frost and became rosy. Her snowy locks turned raven, like mine, and she emitted a healthy glow.

The transfer stopped.

Kinema lifted Mazy out of the tube and offered her to me.

Mazy's flesh, now, was warm as she wriggled and squirmed towards Finn. Only when I held them close to each other did she settle down.

I sighed with relief. *She's safe. It worked.*

Sarika reached through the container towards Meg's lifeless body and checked her pulse.

Please, don't be dead. Please, not Meg. My heart pounded violently in my chest. "Is she alive?" I choked out.

"Her body will not last more than a few days," Sarika answered solemnly.

Both babies cried, and I wanted to join them. My sweet little sister, who had done nothing to harm anyone, had sacrificed herself for my child.

"You need to go and take care of your children," Sarika said.

"No, I won't leave my sister," I refused.

Kinema waved her hands in the air above us and the room faded black.

Mazy and I were transported to my bedroom in Starten. Finn was no longer in my arms. Panicked, I look around and couldn't find Cole either. I had no idea where they might be. Thinking of Meg alone in the cold chamber of the Council, I hoped they were still with her.

My pulse raced. I searched the bathroom, closet, and even out the window for my family. Mazy started to wail and I paced frantically, trying to calm both of us. Finally, Sarika appeared with Cole and Finn beside her.

"Where's my sister?" I demanded, forcing myself to remain calm. "I told you I wouldn't leave without her."

"Your sister is healing, and we will need to be patient. I believe the transformation will happen, soon," Sarika replied.

"Send me back to her, then. She isn't going to go through this without me," I insisted.

"Mara, you're being unreasonable. She is being cared for—"

"I said I wouldn't leave my sister and I meant it. Bring her here or send me there. She's not going to be alone during the most important decision of her life." As I said the words, the tube holding Meg materialized by the window.

My beautiful sister lay motionless. I pressed my hands against the tube, but it didn't bend for me. *I'm sorry, Meg. It should be me in there, not you.*

"There is nothing you can do for her, Mara. She must remain where she is until her body has accepted the transfer."

"And, if her body rejects it?" I didn't want to think about that possibility, but I had to know.

Despite my unnerved state, Sarika's patience was as endless as her kindness. "If it does, we will deal with it then."

"If Meg rejects the change, could Mazy, too?" I asked. *I could lose them both. There's no way to avoid losing the ones I love.*

"Enough focusing on the negative things, Mara," Cole said harshly. He took Mazy away from me.

I was about to object when I realized what he was doing.

He laid Mazy on the changing table, cooing at her and calming her. I hadn't even noticed she needed a new diaper. This was all so easy for Cole. Being a father came so naturally to him.

I knew I shouldn't be so hard on myself. I hadn't had time to bond with my babies, not with everything going on.

"You're going to make yourself crazy. Focus on our healthy babies, not the gloom lurking around every corner, Mar," Cole chastised.

His words felt like a bucket of ice water had been splashed in my face. My initial anger softened, and I realized he was right. One day, I would have to let go of my fear about the terrible things I thought were always waiting in the shadows.

As Cole walked towards me with our freshly changed daughter, he said, "Here's Mommy, Mazy. I bet she's ready to feed you."

I had no words for Cole. Instead, I forced myself to smile at my daughter. Sitting in the rocking chair, I held out my arms for Mazy and she cried. *Of course, she doesn't want me.*

My child grunted and turned her head away, refusing to feed.

"Just try to relax. You're doing great, Mar," Cole encouraged.

As I rocked and stared into my baby's eyes, the anger I had for myself consumed me. Cole was doing my job taking care of our children. Since their birth, I hadn't changed one diaper. I hadn't worried about putting lotion on their new skin or even changed a onesie.

"Tell me what you want, Mazy," I whispered. "How can I make you happy?" I took a deep breath and stroked her cheek.

Mazy grunted and resisted.

I patiently rocked her. Then, eventually, she latched on and nursed. My eyes caught Cole's. He was smiling at me with eyes so full of love.

"Did you need to contain your magic, Mar?" Cole questioned.

While I was lost in my self-hate, I neglected to control my magic. Even though I could feel she was hungry, I didn't have the painful experience like the first time. Instead, I only felt a small amount of magic pulling from me. There was no need to stop her from taking it. She had lost her powerful magic.

"No, I forgot." Cole laid Finn in my arms. "I'm sorry about my tantrum. Thank you for taking such loving care of our children, Cole. I'll try to become better at this."

"You're doing great, Mara. If you could've just delivered the babies and had time to care for them, it would've been different. Don't beat yourself up," he said, kissing me on the cheek.

He was right; our world had been turned upside down. I'd been a good sister to Meg when she was a baby. Maybe, I'd have been a better mother if things had been different.

When Finn suckled, I felt an odd sensation ripple through me. He was pushing his magic through me to Mazy.

"Finn is trying to protect his sister." Sarika stepped closer to me. "You have very powerful children. The girl still carries a small grain of the Winter magic and I wonder if the boy might, also. You both will have a great responsibility with raising such dominant children."

"Can I ask you a question, Sarika?" I inquired nervously.

"Of course."

"I read Eliza's journals. Were you the one saving me from Snowystra when I was a child? Is that why you said you were my guardian?"

"Yes, Mara," she confirmed. "There was something about you, calling me to protect you. I didn't know you would be the one to save Faramond, but from the minute you were born, I knew you were special."

"Why didn't you stop her from taking Cole?" I asked.

"The moment she found you by the lake and opened the door to the Shah, I could no longer save him. I had to let you both fulfill your destiny. Your sacrifices freed the Miezitari." Sarika waved her hand and a set of silver platters appeared on the table. "Later, we can discuss this. For now, I will leave you. I insist you both rest and care for yourselves."

"What about Meg?" Cole asked. His eyes shifted towards her body, floating in the thick liquid.

"I will return as soon as there are any changes to her condition. Now, eat the dinner I had prepared for you," Sarika smirked. With those words, she vanished.

With the babies tucked into their bassinet, Cole and I sat down to eat. He lifted the lid on the platter, revealing a bowl of the kreas patata. We picked at our meal and even though we should've talked about what had happened, neither of us spoke. The lack of sleep had caught up.

"I'm too tired to eat," Cole said, standing up. "You look like you're finished yourself. Come, let's get some sleep while we can."

On my night table, there was a glass of purple liquid. Next to it, a note read: *Take care of yourself. I am nearby if you need me. Love, Laura.*

Taking a few sips of the drink, I climbed into our bed and closed my eyes. I had just fallen asleep when a warm gust of wind roused me. The cylinder Meg floated in flashed. The curtains blew as if there was a breeze, but the window was shut.

Cautiously, I went to the tube. I gasped. My sister was gone.

Silver threads twisted from the container to the window. Looking out, I could see them traveling towards the big tree in the backyard. There was something out there. Squinting hard, I forced myself to make out the image. It *was* Meg.

I glanced around. Cole and the twins were still sleeping soundly. I knew I didn't have time to ask for help. I had to get to my sister.

When I stepped into the backyard, I was surrounded by the silver essence. I could feel the energy of the elements pulsing through it. It was like they were guiding me towards my sister.

As soon as I thought I'd reached her, she darted off. Meg was always just out of reach. From the picnic tree to Gramp's shed and into Starten forest, I followed until she disappeared. She was nowhere to be found.

Stopping, I scanned the tree line. *Where did you lead me, Meg?*

CHAPTER
FORTY-NINE

My heart raced. I was in an area of Starten Forest I had never been before. This wasn't completely accurate. I had been there many times, but this time, I was awake. I'd never been here in my human form.

I looked around, expecting to see Meg or one of the elementals. Instead, I was alone, standing outside of Danu's tree. Resting my hand on the trunk, I felt for the entrance. I had no idea how to get in. It was solid, but I was convinced there had to be a way inside.

Slowly, I circled the tree. The rough bark scraping against my skin confirmed I wasn't dreaming. My search for an entrance seemed useless. I'd never realized how big the tree was. Every time I had arrived in this world, I just walked through it.

It has never been this much work. Focus, I thought.

Suddenly, my hand slipped through. I jerked back. Maybe this was a trick – a way to lure me into danger.

"Poor Marina. Always chasing after the dead. Are you sure you should trust them? Look what they did to me," Snowystra appeared. A dagger stuck out of her chest and her skeletal frame reached out to me. Cackling, she faded away.

I shut out her words. Pressing my ear against the solid part of the tree, I listened.

Bu dum bu dum.

The heart of the tree soothed my apprehension. Taking a deep breath, I put my hand through the portal, again. This time, I followed it.

It felt different. The hair on my arms stood up as the pure magic of Danu brushed against my skin. Abruptly, the soothing beat of the tree stopped. I was left in a dark silence. Picking up my pace, I felt the need to leave. Danger and darkness filled me.

When I stepped out into the Water elementals' pool, my apprehension was not calmed. There was no joyous greeting or roomful of happy elementals at play. No giggles or teasing splashes. Not a single elemental in the room or even the feeling they had ever been there.

Running out of the room and through the stone hallways, I found the same emptiness in the Fire cavern. Instead of the warm heat, I found an ice-cold tomb. They had to be here somewhere. I followed the trail to the Air platform.

The walk was much steeper than I remembered, and my lungs were burning by the time I reached the top. I had hoped to see the brightly colored elementals in their bird forms, waiting to greet me. Sadly, the sky above was empty.

Reluctantly, I peered over the edge of the platform. No Earth elementals below. But I did see something...someone lying in the grass.

My sister.

I'd jumped off the edge many times, knowing it was just my spirit. This was different. I didn't know if my Air magic would work, but I had to try. I needed to get to Meg before she ran off, again. She required my help. Otherwise, why would she lead me here?

I didn't understand what was happening. Why there wasn't anyone here for her? She shouldn't be alone, now.

I coached myself to jump. "Just go for it, Mara." Stepping off the ledge, I fell way too fast. "Air, I need you!" I cried.

My body jerked back as if a parachute had opened. Air stopped my freefall and I floated to the ground.

"What are you doing here, Meg?" I asked as I landed.

Sitting up, Meg shrugged. She was disheveled. Her hair was wild, and her clothes were muddy with grass stains. "I don't know. I was just thinking." My sister rubbed her hand along the ground, growing purple and yellow flowers.

"You know you don't have to take the Winter, Meg. Everyone will understand if you've changed your mind." My words felt like I would choke on them. She had to accept the Winter. If not, who would? They might try to take Mazy, again.

"Accept my death?" she questioned.

"Yeah," I said. "But you'll be with Gram and Gramp. I'm sure Eliza will be there, too. So, you won't be alone."

"But, what about Mazy? She'll be taken from you," Meg countered.

"She no longer carries the Winter."

"My body holds it. If I die, there will be no balance," Meg replied softly. "They'd probably take Miles to replace me."

Miles was just a boy and the only magic he had was dark. He couldn't be the Winter. Our little brother wasn't strong enough.

"Why would you think Miles?" I asked.

"Just a guess. We have the same magic." She sighed.

"I carry that magic, too and they said I couldn't take the Winter," I argued.

"We have different fathers."

Her words felt like a slap across my face. My sister would never intentionally be cruel. I couldn't let her words hurt me. "You're right. Our magic might be different. Whatever you decide, I'll support you."

"I made my decision. I chose the Winter," Meg pouted.

Relief and sadness filled me. It would be over. I wouldn't have to worry about my daughter's safety anymore, but what would happen to Meg? She was just an innocent girl, too.

"It's a big responsibility, Mara. I'm not sure I understand it. I'll be immortal. I'll be a goddess." Meg narrowed her eyes at me. "I barely had my first kiss and, now, I'll be the Winter."

"Then, don't accept it, Meg." I had been the ruler of the Winter Goddess' dark kingdom. I understood how conflicted she felt.

"I wish I could just stay here," she said. Her eyes welled with tears.

"Where are the elementals? Have you seen any?" I asked. "It's empty. Where've they all gone?"

Gazing into the distance, she said, "They're scared...and they should be." Meg wrapped her arms around herself. In a voice barely above a whisper, she added, "The Mrak are strong. Too strong."

My eyes widened. "How do you know this, Meg?"

"Can't you feel it? They're growing stronger, even as we speak. I won't be able to stop them," she whispered, curling back into herself.

Glancing around, I saw nothing. I didn't understand why my sister had changed from so confident in her choice to a frightened child. Meg was falling apart in front of me. The Gods were all afraid of the Mrak. Could she be seeing something I didn't?

"It's so cold, Mara." Meg shivered. "I feel them. They're everywhere. They're coming for me."

An eerie feeling overtook me, and I suddenly knew what she meant. Black tendrils of smoke oozed from the ground, twisting around my ankle. The mist covered Meg's legs and slithered up her waist.

"This area feels wrong. We need to go." I jerked her up out of the smoke. "Now, Meg."

Danu. Take her to Danu, said a whisper on the wind.

"We need to go to Danu's chamber," I cried, tugging harder on her. "Come on, Meg."

As we left the grove, the smoke followed us. It was slow, taunting us.

When we reached the end of the forest, I dragged Meg through the wall of transparent multi-colored water. Blaze wasn't here this time to turn the falls into a cool mist. Instead, we were doused by the water.

"Meg, you have to make your choice, soon. Sarika said your body won't last long," I insisted, dragging her into the tunnel leading to Danu.

CHAPTER
FIFTY

When we reached the chamber, each of the silver-framed mirrors played a scene from Meg's life. We stood in front of one showing an image of our mother holding baby Meg in her arms and offering her to me.

"I will always protect you, Meg. I'm your big sister. You and me forever," my young image said.

"Oh, Mara, I'm so sorry for what I said to you about our having different fathers. Cedric will never be my dad. He was just the mistake our mother made," Meg apologized, squeezing my hand.

Squeezing it back, I replied, "Nothing will change the fact that I love you."

This time, Meg dragged me to the next mirror.

> It displayed Gram dressing Meg for her first lunar dance. The little girl in the mirror bounced eagerly as each ruffle was put into place. When Cole appeared and presented her with a moon necklace, she threw her arms around his neck, hugging him tightly. I watched as my sister danced her solo and I relived the experience of her first performance, again.

Leaving the joyous scene, we found the third image.

> Meg and Miles shared the journal, which revealed Cedric was her father. Unshaken, my father said, "No matter what nonsense any piece of paper says, I'm your father. I am both of your father and I always will be."

The fourth mirror was an image of Meg's birthday party.

The crowd started singing.

Sixteen years you've sung your tune.
Sixteen years around the sun.
Sixteen years blessed by the moon.
Your journey has just begun.
Your path will soon be chosen and soon you will be grown.
But never forget your heart is forever young.
Sixteen years blessed by the moon.
Sixteen years around the sun.
Thank you for the blessings given to this treasured one.

Meg's attention was drawn away from the crowd as the song continued and even after Faramond's speech. Dunn was coming towards her. Their eyes were locked.
"Meg, I have a gift for you," he called.
Her cheeks flushed.
I watched Dunn take Meg's hand. He looked at her with such affection. Placing a small silver box into her palm, he smiled.
Meg was trembling. I could see the love in her eyes for him.
"There isn't a spider in there," he said with a chuckle. "What are you waiting for? Go on open it."
"What is it?" she asked.
"You will have to open it to find out, won't you?" Dunn smirked.
Carefully opening the box, Meg held up a small glass sphere on a silver chain necklace. The globe contained a purple flower nestled on top of a white substance.
"Snow? Where would you find snow around here?" she questioned.
"You said you wanted to see where I had lived," he said. "Instead, I brought Snowstrum to you. When I went to gather it from my favorite

spot, I saw this small flower peeking out from the deep snow. It reminded me of you." Dunn had gone to Snowstrum for her.

"Dunn, that's so sweet," Meg gushed. Her hands were shaking, and she couldn't unhook the clasp.

"Here, let me help you," he said. As Dunn put the necklace on her, she smiled softly. The necklace fell on her décolletage and he leaned in closer to her. "I hope this is the best birthday you ever had."

"It's already so much more than I could've ever expected," she responded.

Kissing her softly on the cheek, he whispered, "And, you will have many more just like this, sweet Meg."

A throat cleared behind us. *I* was the one ruining their special moment.

"We're being watched." Meg sighed.

"Min Vizier," Cole said, bowing towards me.

"Stop that nonsense," I had chided. "Meg, come see all we have planned for you. I'm sure Dunn understands that you have other guests that would like to see you."

With reluctance, Meg left Dunn and we walked away towards the buffet. But, when she turned to see him, he was still watching her. She placed her hand on her cheek where he had kissed her and smiled.

The mirror rippled. Now, Meg was leading Dunn away from the crowd and into the forest.

When they were out of earshot of everyone, he stopped her. "What is going on?" Dunn asked. The light from the party reflected in his eyes.

Taking a deep breath, she blurted out. "Dunn, I know you think I'm too young for you, and I might be, but despite everything, I have fallen in love with you. I have no doubt it's love I feel, and the thought of being kept from you is breaking my heart. Let's leave and go to Snowstrum. We can live there for a few months and when we come back, I'll be old enough in their eyes."

He didn't respond, at first. He just looked at her with a pained expression on his face. Finally, he said, "I can't mislead you, Meg. You're special to me, but we can't run off. You'd miss so much here. We can't—"

"We can't what? Have a life together because you're immortal? Because my sister thinks it's a bad idea? Tell me you don't love me, and I'll let it go," Meg demanded.

"Meg, our timing isn't right. I'll always be here for you, but you need to listen to your family. They're right. I am too old for you and you still have many years to fall in love," he said.

"Your age is irrelevant. Look me in my eyes and tell me that you don't feel the same way I do. Do that and I'll walk away, right now."

Gently stroking her cheek, I could see his hesitation. Staring into her eyes, he used his thumb to wipe away a tear that had broken loose. "There is no doubt in my mind that, one day, we'll be together, Meg. I'm sorry, but today is not that day. Please, don't cry. I will be here for you until then."

Impulsively, she wrapped her arms around his neck and kissed him firmly on the lips.

He hesitated before kissing her back. When Dunn pulled Meg closer, the ground trembled as if she called her Earth magic. Releasing his hold on her, his lips lingered. Shamefaced, he backed away from Meg.

"No matter what you say, my feelings won't change, and I know you feel the same." She didn't give him a chance to say anything. She just walked away and didn't look back.

"I know you love me, Dunn," she said to herself. "We will be together, one day."

Guilt filled me. I'd tried to stop their relationship. She was so confident in her love. I envied how free she was to share it.

The final mirror rippled, but no image was there to be shared. Yet, Meg scrutinized it intently. After several minutes, tears slowly fell down her face.

"I'm scared," Meg confessed. "I'm strong enough to face the Mrak, but I'm still afraid. My fear won't stop me, though. I'm ready." Without another thought, but with great resolve, my sister announced, "I accept the Winter."

"You don't have to do this, Meg. You don't have to take the Winter," I said.

"Oh, Mara. I know what I'm doing, now. I love you," Meg said, hugging me. "No matter what happens. We're going to be sisters forever, right?"

"Nothing is going to change that – ever. Even when I'm old and gray, I'll be your big sister. I don't know what this means for us, but we'll figure it out." I smiled at her reassuringly. "You are Meg Stone. There's no one in the world stronger than you."

We both looked at each other and laughed, saying, "Except Gram."

"You have her fighting spirit, Meg. There's no way you won't succeed at this. You'll be the most incredible Winter ever," I praised.

From the hallway, a hissing noise sounded.

"Go, make your choice, Meg," I insisted, releasing our hug.

"But, what about you?" she asked.

"I know the way out. Remember, I've done this before," I said with a wink.

As I watched my little sister step through the mirror, my breath caught. The image of Meg slowly changed in front of me. Before I knew it, the teenager had begun to transform into a young woman.

CHAPTER
FIFTY-ONE

A strange noise came from behind me, but I didn't want to take my eyes off Meg. I'd missed my little sister growing and changing for six years of her life. We wouldn't finish the awkward teenage years, where her mature body and her feelings would be so intense. The late-night talks about boys she liked or how unfair our father was being. Our relationship would be different.

"She will be a beautiful goddess." A woman I'd never seen before stood beside me. With her red hair and brightly colored dress, she had to be one of Danu's Fire elementals.

I glanced around to see if she was alone. It was just us. I ignored her, hoping she might go away. She had no right to interrupt this moment.

With each passing second, Meg changed. Her arms thinned and lengthened. Her face lost its roundness and her cheekbones became more prominent. It was as if her next six years were speeding along before my eyes.

"How sad it must be for you to lose another of your family members," the woman considered.

"Do I know you?" I glared and shifted away from her.

"I know of you, Mara. You were once the dark queen. It must have been difficult for you to have your husband love a powerful Goddess like Snowystra. How could you compete?" She looked at me with deep pity for me.

I sucked in a breath. I wanted to argue, but I couldn't. I wasn't as beautiful or strong as Snowystra. She was evil, but she went after what she wanted. I was so weak I had to be taken care of by my little sister when things became too hard.

I hadn't even redeemed myself by being a proper mother. I'd let Cole take care of our babies. Eventually, he'd grow tired of having to pick up the pieces and, this time, he'd leave me for good.

The woman stepped closer to me. Her voice was full of sympathy. "You've had so much pain in your life. Your mother left you. Your father left you. Everyone leaves you, Marina. I can't imagine how hard it is for you to be a mother to those poor children. You're so torn apart inside. What can you offer them?"

What can I offer the twins? How can I be their mother? All I knew was loss. I was to blame for all the bad things that happened. It was all my fault. I could have stopped most of it.

"You're not ready to be a mother. Come with me. You can stay with us until you are. They won't miss you. They barely know you." She slid her fingers along my skin, sending an electric current through me. "With us, you can stop blaming yourself for letting your grandmother die."

But it was my fault! Eliza had forced me to restore the magic Gram had bound. With it returned, she became mad from the sudden burst of power. She attacked me, and I responded.

My mother had been smarter with her magic, casting enough to make me fall to my knees and writhe in pain. When Eliza had thrown her remaining magic at me, intending for me to die, Gram threw herself in front of me while directing her own magic towards Eliza. Gram accepted my death sentence and took her own daughter's life to save me.

I should've died instead. It might've stopped the cycle. Cole wouldn't have been taken. My sister would still have Gram to care for her. There'd be no children to hurt. *My sweet babies are poor and defenseless. I won't be strong enough to protect them. They'd be better off with me gone – everyone would be.*

Tears streamed down my face.

"There, there. You will continue to lose more of those you love, but we won't ever leave you. Your sister will forget about you. After all, you're just a mortal and she'll have her new life as a Goddess." She tsked. "The babies are too young to even know you and your husband would be better off with a human. How painful it must be for him to see you use your gift, now that his was taken away," the woman continued speaking the truth. "He'd have no problem replacing you."

"I...I..." I couldn't disagree with her. She was only saying what I thought, anyway. If I had been smarter with Eliza, my grandmother wouldn't be dead. Strangers wouldn't have raised my sister. She'd barely known our father and Essie when I left her to chase Cole. *I left her when she was a child. It's my fault*, I admitted to myself. *All of this is my fault.*

The woman touched my arm and a chill ran through me. I looked at her hand resting on my shoulder. Tendrils of darkness slithered off her, wrapping around me. The threads licked at my skin. I hesitated for a second too long and the blackness surrounded me. I wasn't sure where to go.

"We've been waiting for you, Marina. We hoped you'd come to us. You will follow us, now, and we'll protect your family from you. Tell me you want to come with me," the woman's voice changed, becoming gravelly and demanding.

"I don't know..." I whispered.

"We have seen the darkness inside you. I can feel it pulsing, aching to come out. It's time for you to embrace it and take your place alongside Amaro. You were never meant for the mortal world, Marina. You'll only hurt those around you if you stay. Your children will feel the poison inside you. Wouldn't you like for it all to stop? Let me take your pain away."

I did want it all to stop. I could go with her. I would go with her. I'd agree.

A frigid air blew over me and Meg stepped out of the mirror. "No, she isn't going with you. Step away from her, Ladarsha."

I stared in shock. *How can this confident goddess be my sister?* The person in front of me was a strong, powerful force, not my baby sister.

Meg walked towards us, her, now, platinum white hair blew wildly, showing the bright lavender tips. She was magnificent. Beyond her great beauty, she commanded my attention. Her movement was one of a dancer taking the stage. She wore a warm smile, but her frosted eyes gave a warning to not test her.

"She's right, Meg. I've hurt too many people. I'm sorry," I wept.

"Do not submit to this, Mara," Meg said, slowly enunciating each word. "The Mrak feed on your sorrow. She's trying to bring out everything that scares you or makes you sad."

"You're too late. She accepted my proposal," Ladarsha said, snarling at Meg.

"She didn't accept. You can't take her against her free will." Meg blasted a stream of cold at the Mrak.

Ladarsha screamed as the icy air coated her.

Meg caught one of the tendrils wrapped around me and held it tightly. "Release my sister," she growled between clenched teeth.

Ladarsha looked different. Her appearance was gruesome. Underneath her, now, transparent flesh, I could see a skeleton dripping black ooze. I shuddered and held back a scream.

"We do not release those who accept our offers. Tell her you want to come with me, Marina," she demanded.

"You are too weak to fight her, Marina." Snowystra appeared in one of the mirrors. "Accept your fate."

I didn't know what I wanted. Ladarsha scared me, but she was right. I'd continue to hurt everyone I loved. Meg tugged on the tendrils binding me, pulsing her magic through the threads of darkness.

"I won't let you take her," Meg warned.

"How will you stop us? Your power isn't strong enough to defeat the Mrak. You're just a small child playing Goddess." Ladarsha laughed.

The tendrils squeezed harder against me and I felt the sharp sting of darkness's anger along with the icy burn of Winter.

"You're wrong," Meg growled, pushing even more of her power through.

"How will you fight us all alone? Your sister is fragile. I could break the great Marina Stone with one word. There is no one here to save you. They have all fled in fear. They know our strength."

"Amaro was smart to send you. You're a master manipulator, Ladarsha." Danu stepped through the mirror and stood beside Meg. "Using the voice of my sister against her was quite ingenious, but you must have realized she could not be broken so easily. Snowystra would never have played with her victim for so long. Go now. Tell Amaro you failed. You are not strong enough to fight the two of us."

Danu placed her hand over Meg's. The tendrils pulsed a rainbow of colors. The magic inside me fluttered as if cheering for the Goddess.

"Ah, ah, ah. She hasn't refused my offer, Danu. You know the rules. Release my prize and I will leave."

"Tell her, Mara. Tell her you don't want to leave with her," Meg encouraged.

Snowystra's gone? I'm not losing my mind? It had all been a trick? I felt frozen. The voice inside my head screamed, *No, I don't want to go with her,* but the words would not form.

"You will not take this child." Brighid appeared from the large mirror to my left. She stepped into the room with her authoritative presence.

The Elements, the Winter, and the Balance stood before me. Each held tendrils that bound me. Three goddesses had come to save *me.* I wasn't broken.

"You cannot speak for her," Ladarsha hissed. "Tell them you want to come with me, Marina. You know you will only hurt those you love if you stay."

Meg's emerald eyes locked with my hazel. All the love and hope we shared reflected in them.

"N-n...NO! I don't want to go with you, but I don't want to hurt anyone else," I shouted, finally finding my voice. "I don't want to lose my sister."

Brighid shined and pushed her magic through the tendrils. Ladarsha shrieked as the power of the trio drove through the threads and she exploded into thousands of small black particles. The air became thick and it became hard to breathe. I began to cough uncontrollably as I felt myself slipping into the darkness.

Suddenly, someone grabbed my hand and pulled me close to them. Fear filled me. Had the Ladarsha survived? Slowly, the space around us cleared and I found myself in Meg's arms.

Smiling, my sister blew the final bits of dust away with her frigid air and kissed my cheek. "You're ok, Mara," she soothed and wrapped her arms around me tightly.

I collapsed against her and wept. "I thought Snowystra was inside me, Meg. I thought I was tainted."

"You're safe. She really is gone, Mara. I will never let anyone hurt you," she whispered, smoothing my hair. Letting go of me, she kissed me on the cheek. "Now, it's time for you to let go of the pain you carry."

The air around us swirled with snow and we were transported outside of Danu's tree. Meg led me to a mossy spot. The same place where I had begun and ended my visit to this realm many times.

"Come sit." Meg sat down and patted the ground.

I bowed my head in awe of the Goddess before me.

"Oh, Mara, nothing has changed. Well, nothing that matters. I'm still your little sister. Never bow to me," Meg insisted.

Her voice was enchanting, and I found it hard to remember the little girl she'd been. "You're so different," I murmured. "I can feel it with your touch."

"But, I'm the same inside. I need you to remember me as I was," my sister pleaded, taking my hand and placing it on her heart. "Promise me, Mara."

My eyes locked with hers. Within her irises, images of the old Meg flashed before me. The little girl who'd convince me to share my breakfast, the little dancer practicing until she collapsed into sleep, and the strong young adult who had helped me heal when all was lost. They were all still inside her.

"It's time to go home, Mara." Meg coaxed me to lie down beside her.

"I won't forget, Meg. I promise." I snuggled close to her and allowed myself to drift off to sleep.

CHAPTER
FIFTY-TWO

"It's ok, Mar. Wake up." Cole gently shook me.

I opened my eyes. "She's gone, Cole. Meg took the Winter."

"I know. I saw her fade away," he said, wiping the tears from my face. "But, I'm still here. Our children are here and need you."

"How am I going to be a mother? I'm not prepared for any of this?" I blurted out.

"Stop! You're going to be a great mother. Remember, you had the best example – Gram. You know what it takes to be a loving caregiver. You saw it first-hand. Now, is there anything else dark you need me to chase away?"

Sniffling, I said, "I think you covered it all, for now."

Cole kissed me on the forehead. "Well, let's go back to sleep. You've not slept enough to recharge yourself and the babies will be awake soon enough. Lay your head down and listen to my heart. It beats for you, Mar. As you sleep, I'll be here to protect you and I'll scare away anything else that frightens you."

Cole kissed me gently and laid down. Resting my head on his chest, I closed my eyes. Listening to the beat of his heart, I fell asleep.

The sun had risen and was shining into the room. I awoke to the sound of Cole talking sweetly to Mazy. It seemed like I'd just fallen asleep for the third time. Our night had been interrupted with feedings and changings.

"Is it already time, again?" I asked. Mazy had surprised me with how willing she was to nurse, now.

"Yes, Mommy," Cole said, in a singsong voice. "I'm very hungry, again, and Daddy has already changed me."

I stretched and sleepily got out of bed.

Cole gently placed Mazy in my arms. His whiskers tickled my skin as he leaned in to kiss my cheek.

I reached up and stroked the light stubble.

"Do you like?" Cole grinned.

"I do." I ran my fingers along his face, again. Then, looking down at Mazy, I purred, "Do you like Daddy's facial hair? Doesn't he look all grown up?"

For the first time, I noticed my daughter's eye color. They were Violet. I laughed at the irony. It was as if a piece of Meg Violet Stone lived within her.

"Gram, once, told me her mother had beautiful purple eyes like yours," I told the tiny baby girl. "Will you be strong and brave, too?"

Mazy grunted and threw out her legs before curling them, again.

"Of course, you will be. What a silly question." I laughed.

"See, Mar, you are already a brilliant mom. Look how quickly you mastered feeding not one, but two babies." My husband grinned lovingly at me when he set Finn into my free arm.

"I couldn't do this without you," I said with a sheen of moisture on my eyes.

"And, you'll never have to." Cole kissed me softly. "It looks like this one is ready for her daddy."

Cole picked up Mazy. He placed her on his shoulder and rubbed her back. I watched as he walked our daughter around the room, speaking so sweetly to her. He was having the moments with our children that I'd feared would never happen. When she finally dozed off, he tucked Mazy into the crib.

Before, I always used to worry that I loved Cole too much. It was nothing compared to the love I felt for him, now, but for once, I wasn't scared. I could do this. We could do this — together.

I smoothed Finn's hair and searched his features for a hint of who he might resemble when he grew up. My little boy was so content. His fiery gift didn't match his personality. I wondered if this would change as he matured.

When Finn was done feeding, Cole insisted I take the opportunity to have a shower. The warm water was welcoming, but I couldn't relax. I couldn't stop thinking about my wonderful little family. Cole had been so good with the babies. He deserved a nice shower, too.

As I hurriedly dried my hair, I heard a strange sound from the other side of the wall. Pressing my ear to it, I could hear muffled crying. It was coming from the loft.

I threw on some clothes and exited the bathroom. In our suite, I found Cole sound asleep in our bed and the babies in their crib. Quietly, I turned the door latch that led to my old bedroom.

I found my father lying in my sister's bed, staring at the ceiling. "Is Meg okay?" he asked, quickly getting up. His eyes were red and swollen. They locked with mine and I could almost feel the pain inside him.

Anyone describing Elliott Stone would tell you he was the happiest, most jovial man you could ever meet. This man was neither. As my father stood before me, he looked beat down and defeated.

"Why have the gods taken so much of us?" he questioned. He drove his clenched fists into his thighs.

"Meg's not gone. Meg's not gone, Dad, she's just...she's just, um..."

"What is she, Mara? Another of my children taken away from me?" he asked harshly.

"It's not like that. Meg's the Winter," I informed him. "She is beautiful and marvelous. You'd be so proud of her. And, she saved me."

"Are they going to tell Cedric he's her father?" He sniffled, his words almost inaudible.

I smiled reassuringly. "No, that would be a lie. He may have planted the seed, but you're the only father she knows and wants. Do you think of Miles as Cedric's child?"

"Never! Miles is *my* son," my father insisted.

"So, what's changed? You've known about Meg for some time and, now, you aren't her father? What's happened to you?" I admonished.

My father, Elliott Stone, wouldn't act like this. He always found the solution to every problem and the positive side. *Who has he become, and why?*

"Nothing, Mara. I'm just feeling sorry for myself. Your father's a crazy old man," he said with a half laugh and ran his fingers through his hair.

"Why don't you come spend some time with your grandchildren?" I suggested. "You know you'll have a big role to fill as their Gramp."

"Gramp, huh? I think I'm more of a Papa," my father said, wrapping his arms around me. "I love you, Mara."

"I love you, Daddy." I held him back, inhaling his familiar scent of earth and lemon.

Whatever might come, I knew we'd get through it together, as a family.

CHAPTER
FIFTY-THREE

After Meg left us, the months blurred by. I was so busy being a new mother that I had no time to worry about my little sister. I'd seen how strong she had become, and I knew she was in safe hands.

When the twins turned two months old, I learned how strong their gifts were and how my own magic was connected. Finn's had been the first to appear.

I had just laid Finn down and he began to coo at the mobile above his crib. As I tended to Mazy, I had a strong sensation run through me. I felt as if I was calling Fire. I turned to find my baby boy was showering our suite with his embers.

The very next day, Mazy's power revealed itself, only more subtly. As we had a picnic under the oak tree, purple flowers grew around us. Once again, I was warned and able to control the element.

I knew I'd have to be on high alert until my children were able to control their own gifts. Thoughts of binding their magic did flash through my mind, but I knew I'd never be able to really take it from them.

One morning, after my daily training with Blaze, I returned to our room to find Cole telling a story to our children.

"Isn't that a lovely picture," I said, drinking in the sight of my family.

Cole grinned and held out a freshly changed baby to me.

"Hi, sweetie," I said, kissing Mazy on the cheek. "Has Daddy been taking good care of you?"

An overwhelming smell of sugar cookies, fresh pinecones, and a hint of cinnamon wafted into the room. Searching for the origin of the wonderful fragrance, I found Meg by the window. She stood motionless, looking like an ice sculpture from her crystal gown to the twisted icicles of hair on the top of her head. When she finally moved, her skin shimmered with snowflakes.

Meg's green eyes sparkled. "And, what about Auntie Meg? Will she get to see her little ones?"

The voice of Miles echoed in the loft bedroom. "I'm telling you. They're baking something in there."

Opening the door, I beamed at my family. "Miles is right. We have been baking. How would you like a Winter Goddess?" I stepped out of the way, so they could see Meg.

Wide-eyed my family stared at my sister.

"Like you've never seen a goddess before." Meg laughed.

Miles beamed and ran straight into her open arms. "You're magnificent," he said, hugging her tightly.

"You've grown so much since I last saw you," Meg said, tousling his hair.

"How long are you here?" my father asked.

"Not very long, Daddy. I need to return. The Mrak have been stifled, but we're far from safe from them. I've made sure you'll be guarded always. The Elementals will be close by to protect you all."

It felt like yesterday when she was asking for my extra pancakes and performing her first dance. Sadness filled me. My little sister was, now, all grown up.

"Don't worry, Mara. I won't be far." Meg took my hand. "One day, I want to show you my new home."

"Snowstrum?" Miles gulped. His eyes widened with fear. "The next time I see you I'll be an adult."

"No, it'll be a different place," Meg promised. Cupping his face, she stared into his eyes. "I'll bring you all there to visit, but, for now, my time here is brief. So, why don't you make me one of your famous meals and we can talk? If you don't mind, I mean."

"I know the perfect dish," Miles exclaimed.

"First, I need to change. I feel a bit overdressed," Meg said, examining her gown.

"Come with me," I laughed. "I have a closet full of new clothes. The person who picked it all out had impeccable taste."

Meg changed out of her elegant gown and into one of my summer dresses before we joined Miles in the kitchen. As we all took our places around the table, the banter of my siblings warmed my heart. My sister wouldn't let this change her.

"Fried chicken and macaroni?" Cole laughed, piling his plate. "This doesn't seem a meal befitting a Goddess."

Meg took a large bite of her food and beamed. "This goddess doesn't need fancy food. She just needs her family."

"And, we're here for you always," I said, bouncing Mazy on my knee. "Aren't we?"

Mazy cooed and held out her hand to Meg. Eagerly, Meg scooped the little girl into her arms and showered her with kisses.

My daughter giggled in response.

"Your magic is strong, little one." Meg opened her tiny hand. Once again, Mazy held a small purple flower. "Has Finn shown any signs of using his magic, yet?" she asked.

"There were a few small incidents, but not much since. He seems to be the cautious one," I answered. "When nursing, he still sends magic to Mazy. Blaze said Fire elementals are by nature more restrained with their gift."

Stroking his fiery red hair, Meg's eyes glowed a brilliant green. "He's very aware of the power of his magic already. Aren't you sweet boy?"

After we finished our meal, Meg and Miles decided we'd play one of their favorite card games. Anyone walking by our house could hear the laughter. When Finn's little eyes could no longer stay open, we reluctantly said goodnight to everyone and left for our room.

"She'll be here all the time, Mara. You need to stop worrying," Cole said as if reading my mind.

"I know," I sighed. "I'm worried about her going to Snowstrum. Will it change her?"

"You heard your sister. It'll be different with her in charge," Cole said, setting Finn in the bassinet.

"He's right," Meg called from the doorway. "Starting with a new name. Snowstrum. Wasn't she full of herself? For now, we will call it *Winterland*. Yes, not very original, but maybe, I'll be more creative after I've spent some time there."

Leaning down over the bassinet, Meg gently stroked the cheeks of the sleeping babies. "Sweet dreams, my Neeps. Auntie will be watching you."

"Oh, are you leaving already?" I asked. A feeling of panic rose inside me.

"I am, but I would like you to come with me somewhere," Meg said.

"Where?" I asked with surprise.

"Trust me." Meg smiled. "We won't be gone long. Cole seems a capable enough father to watch the babies for an hour or two."

Kissing me on the cheek, Cole agreed, "We'll be fine. Go, enjoy time with your sister."

Taking Meg's hand, I asked, again, "Where are we going?"

Instead of answering, a silver glow surrounded us, and my bedroom faded away.

CHAPTER
FIFTY-FOUR

Meg transported us to a bright room with a rainbow on the farthest wall. We walked amongst people I recognized as the Miezitari. The guardians were each holding the hand of a person that I'd never seen before.

"Where are you taking me?" I whispered.

"We're going to see Gram," Meg replied nonchalantly.

Ahead of us, people walked into the spectral wall and disappeared. When it was our turn in line, we stepped through the multicolored veil. My body felt tingly. All my fears and worries dissolved instantly. I felt a complete sense of peace run through me as the soft sound of children singing surrounded us.

At a leisurely pace, we walked down a long corridor. Finally, Meg opened a silver door and we stepped into a home much like my own in Starten. It wasn't our home, but it was almost an exact replica from the colorful couches to the loft bedroom. I could hear the soft clinking of dishes being washed. Quietly, we tiptoed towards the area I knew the kitchen would be.

"Go to her, Mar," Meg urged.

Just as I expected, I found my grandmother standing at the sink, humming softly. I cleared my throat and she turned around to see who was making the noise. Our eyes met, and she dropped the plate she was holding.

"Mara?" she whispered. Her light brown eyes glistened with tears.

Without thinking, I ran and threw my arms around her. "Gram. Oh, Gram, I've missed you so much. I'm sorry I couldn't stop her. I couldn't save you." I cried as she held me tight.

"There will be none of that, my sweet girl. You were so brave. Let me look at you." She squeezed me before breaking away. "Mara, my love, you're so grown up. You're a woman, now – and a mother."

"You would love them so much, Gram," I said, grasping her hand. "Mazy's so strong and Finn is such a guardian to his sister. You would be proud of what a great father Cole has been to them."

"I never doubted that he'd be a great dad." She smiled, But, slowly, her grin faded. "Wait, how are you here, Mara? You need to leave – now. You can't be here."

"Hi, Gram," Meg said softly as she stepped into the room. "I've brought her to see you."

My grandmother's eyes widened as she stared at Meg. "You can't be my little Meg?"

"Yes, Gram, I'm your little dancer, all grown up." Meg grinned. To confirm her claim, she did a little twirl and Meg's signature bow.

Sweeping both of us into her arms, Gram hugged us tightly. "My girls." When our grandmother finally released her hold, she led us towards the kitchen table where she poured us both a cup of tea. "Wait, I have your favorite tea biscuits."

"Please, sit, Gram. We need to talk," Meg said, stopping our grandmother in her tracks.

"You sound serious. Is this the time you tell me why you're really here?" she asked with concern lining her face.

"You've been here for over six years," Meg stated.

"Yes, but I never left you, girls," my grandmother insisted.

"Which is the problem, Gram," Meg replied gently.

"Problem?" She shook her head in confusion.

"You can't continue to hold onto the mortal world and really live in this realm. Don't you find it odd how Gramp looks like he is forty while you've held onto sixty-seven?" Meg's mouth turned into a deep line.

"No, he's a vain old fool. I'm comfortable in this skin. I earned every wrinkle and every gray hair," Gram insisted.

"Your attempt to live in both domains is a strain on your tether to this one. You can't protect us from here. It's futile to keep trying. You must embrace the Afterlife," Meg explained, touching her cheek tenderly.

"She's right, Gram. We need to know you're happy here. One day, we'll be with you, again." I sniffed, holding back the tears I felt brewing.

"I can't leave you," Gram wept. "You're my heart. You girls were the greatest gift I could've ever received."

Meg held out a snowball and set it on the table in front of her. "I thought you would say this. Go ahead, pick it up and look inside it."

Gram carefully picked up the white powder and it sparkled. Images filled the sphere of Miles and Charlie frolicking in the backyard. When she twisted it, she could see Essie and Elliott playing with the twins. Another turn found Cole washing dishes and doing a silly dance as if no one was watching.

"What is this?" Gram asked, setting it down.

"This is, now, your only connection to the mortal world. No more living through us, Gram. For your protection, I've blocked your sight out of this realm. You'll be able to see the happy moments we share in this globe, but I won't allow any more to be shared until I know you've committed to truly living here," Meg warned.

"You can't..." Gram frowned.

"The girls are right, Maesi." My grandfather stood in the doorway. "Remember me?"

"I've never forgotten you, Chester." Gram glared at my grinning grandfather.

"You've been so focused on fixing their world. You're no longer there and yet, you still haven't enjoyed one minute of this magnificent realm we live in. The home you fashioned is even the same as what you left. Isn't it time to start fresh?" Gramp asked.

"I can't leave them," Gram protested.

"Gram, you aren't leaving us," I said, squeezing her hand. "You've been there for me my entire life. You're still with me, every step I take. Nothing will ever replace the love you gave us."

"Marina's right, Mother. Nothing can ever replace the love you gave my daughters." Eliza appeared beside my grandfather.

Gram's eyes filled with tears. "How can I protect you from the darkness lurking?"

"You can't. But Mara and I are both strong enough to take care of ourselves." Meg answered firmly. "The snowball will be here as long as you begin to live in this world. Will you promise to try?"

"I can't argue with a Goddess, can I?" Gram wiped the tears from her eyes.

"I'll make sure she lives up to her promise. There's so much to show her here," Gramp said, sitting down next to Gram and taking her hand. "Come join us, Eliza. I heard promises of biscuits."

"Old fool," Gram said, leaving the table.

When she returned with the treats, I took them from her and placed them on the table. Wrapping my arms around her, I hugged her tightly, inhaling the familiar scents of vanilla, lavender, and cinnamon.

"You're in every word I speak, every step I take. My babies are being loved the way you loved us. Please, let go of Starten, Gram. I need you to be here when it's my time to join you."

I could feel the tension in her body release. "I'll be here for you, my sweet girl. Do you know how proud I am of all of you? Your strength amazes me. You've become the butterfly Elliott always said you would be."

"I love you, Gram," I said, squeezing her tighter.

Meg touched me on the shoulder and whispered in my ear. "It's time, Mara."

Before another word could be spoken, the warmth of Gram's hug left me, and I was standing under the picnic tree behind my home in Starten. Sitting on the ground, I sighed.

"She needed to move on, Mara, and you do, too. Forget the pain, the things you lost. The darkness feeds off sorrow Find joy in your new little family and let them be the light that fills you."

"I will, Meg. I'll do my best to be a strong mother. I want to be the woman Gram raised me to be," I said.

The sky around us filled with the colors of the elementals surrounding us.

CHAPTER
FIFTY-FIVE
MEG'S WINTER

Standing on the snow of my new home, I considered the distance. Danu and Brighid stood on each side of me. Before us, a forest of trees in various stages of change and thick mountain ranges extended. I could see the faint outline of Snowystra's ice castle in the distance.

"I can't believe I'm going to be the Winter. Are you sure I'm up for this?" I questioned, biting my lip.

"Meg, you *are* the Winter. There is no question about it. You've shown us that you are ready by the way you handled Ladarsha. I have no doubt, Meg," Danu said. "You will be confronted many times by the Mrak, but you will continue to use your strong instinct. A constitution which will only grow stronger," she assured me.

I still felt some apprehension. "What if I mess up?"

"Oh, you will not be infallible. As you know, we all make mistakes, but over time, you will learn when it's right to interfere...especially with mortal lives," Danu said, squeezing my hand.

"And, you may have regrets for not interfering sooner," Brighid added, taking my other hand.

"We will leave you to explore your realm. Remember, every change you make, no matter how minor, creates a ripple in the universe. Some will have little or no effect, while others can create momentous rifts."

"How will I know the effect I make?" I asked. "I want to align time in this world with the other realms. I want it to be fluid for my guests. I want my family and your children to be welcome. The Elementals and the Curuxatyni are, also, important parts of my life."

"A very wise decision," Danu praised.

"How do I...?" I started to ask, but then stopped myself. I knew the answer already.

Holding my hand out in front of me, I waved it. "Frozen Time, I release you. Join the continuum of time around you."

The air rippled in front of me and the change was made.

"Are there any other changes you would like to make but are afraid to?" Danu questioned.

"No, I feel confident in what needs to happen. Thank you both so much. I know I'll need your guidance and support to do this," I said gratefully.

"And, we will be nearby," Danu said, kissing me on both cheeks.

"Enjoy your realm. Soon, we will need you to return to the Council to discuss the future dealings with the Mrak. But I think a few weeks to become familiar with your home is more than fair. And, I see you have your first visitor." Brighid winked. Her smile was bright and mischievous.

"Is it ok for him to be here?" I asked nervously. The sun was shining, and his hair glowed a golden color.

"Meg, you are the Goddess of Winter. You answer to no one," Danu reminded me.

"If you are making decisions from your heart, I can't believe you will go wrong," Brighid said. With those words, the Goddesses faded away and I was left alone with Dunn.

"Meg," Dunn said softly. "Is it ok I came? I felt like you needed me."

"I'm glad you're here," I said warmly. "The first thing I'd like to do is tour this area. Can you guide me?"

He nodded. "I can."

"Should we walk, or should I transport us there?" I wondered.

"I would like to walk with you. That is if you don't mind."

I smiled at him. "I was hoping you would say just that."

Taking my hand into his, he said, "Meg, I am sorry I told you we couldn't be together. I just..."

"I know why you did it and you were right. I was too young to fall in love and be in a serious relationship," I said, squeezing his hand.

"Oh, ok." Dunn's face fell.

"I *was* too young, Dunn," I repeated, stepping closer to him.

"But you aren't anymore?" he asked, closing the distance between us.

"No, I'm quite ready for love, now." I smiled and touched his face.

Before anything else could be said, Dunn kissed me.

The electricity from our kiss stole my breath away. No matter what I would face as the Winter, I knew I'd never be alone with Dunn by my side.

EPILOGUE

"You failed, again, Cedric. You've given me no choice."

The glow of the candlelight flickered on a man's blue-black hair as he loomed over Cedric Drygen, raising fists adorned with gold rings. Bands for pain, not adornment. The cracking sound of flesh hitting bone echoed as his fists struck Cedric again.

"No, please. Give me another chance. Please, tell him I deserve another chance, Mother," Cedric begged. His broken and bruised face dripped with blood.

The silver-haired woman stepped out of the shadows and glared at her son. "My son has always been a fool, Amaro," Blanche said coldly. She traced her long nails along the side of the attacker's ruggedly handsome face. "But my impulsive offspring's mistakes have resulted in a delightful surprise. You want Marina Stone? You think her power is the answer? Well, circumstances have changed. I am told sweet Eliza has been keeping a secret from Cedric all these years."

Cedric's eyes widened in anger. "You lie. How dare you speak about Eliza. You don't know her. You've always been jealous of her," he raged.

Ignoring him, Blanche continued, "Eliza lied. The girl is not Stone's daughter. Meg Stone is a Drygen. *My* granddaughter is the Winter."

Amaro's expression grew dark. A cruel smile spread across his face. "This information might be especially useful. Yes," he said, rubbing his chin thoughtfully, "this may be the key to bringing Marina to me. How I have grown to love my fiery beauty."

"There is nothing special about Marina," Blanche said dismissively.

"Don't be jealous, my treasure. Remember, you rejected *me* for love."

"She will never follow you," Blanche hissed.

"Oh, you are wrong," Amaro said. A cold smile washed over his face. "She responds to me. The Shah always ignited her passion. A small taste of her desire is what I need. I could feel how much she craves the strength and power I have when I occupied her pitiful husband. Marina will be mine, again, and we will use her sister to bring her to me. Through your granddaughter, you will deliver her to me. She holds the key to my rising."

The End

The story continues in ENVY

About the Author

Marnie Cate is a writer of coming-of-age and urban fantasy novels. Born in an Irish mining town in Montana, she always had a flair for the dramatic and a vivid imagination, and spent her childhood lost in the elaborate worlds she created with the help of her dolls.

One day, Marnie Cate was struck by a powerful image in her mind. This seed created the world of Starten and the complicated world of goddesses and their touch on the mortal world.

Inspired by the actress Dame Judi Dench, she pursued her dream of sharing the stories that were brewing in her mind. With the urging of friends and family, she wrote in every spare moment she had.

After countless weekends spent at the local coffee shop, typing away and people-watching, Marnie finished her first novel, Remember: Protectors of the Elemental Magic. With the world of elemental magic and the humans they lived in released, the stories have just begun.

Her book, *Chasing Caitlyn*, has inspired Marnie to expand her writing genre to include Adult Fiction. When not writing, Marnie is drinking coffee while spending time with her family and her beloved kitty. She lives in Arizona.

To learn more about Marnie Cate and discover more Next Chapter authors, visit our website at www.nextchapter.pub.

Protectors of the Elemental Magic - Books 1-3
ISBN: 978-4-82418-693-5
Paperback Edition

Published by
Next Chapter
2-5-6 SANNO
SANNO BRIDGE
143-0023 Ota-Ku, Tokyo
+818035793528

8th September 2023

Milton Keynes UK
Ingram Content Group UK Ltd.
UKHW041029260124
436746UK00003B/112

9 784824 186935